Africa Par Adventure

Over 100 Tales, Insights and Observations of the Inconceivable…

Written and Compiled by

Peter Ward

ISBN: 1-4033-4963-0 (e-book)
ISBN: 1-4033-4964-9 (Paperback)

This book is printed on acid free paper.

All proceeds of the book will be donated to Raleigh International
(http://www.raleigh.org.uk), an international charity which develops young
people through challenging and worthwhile community and environmental
projects on expeditions around the world.

1stBooks – rev. 08/26/02

acknowledgments

I'm not sure what kind of people read the acknowledgments page in a book. If you're looking for your name, the authors' bios are at the end of each story. Perhaps you're the kind who reads the advertising supplements in the Sunday New York Times. There's no intro, no plot, no conclusion—so what's the deal?

There are many acknowledgments that immediately come to mind. First, there is a special "thank-you" to all the professional writers, journalists, Africans and travelers who have contributed or allowed me to use their work, given me contacts, and offered advice and encouragement. At the end of each story there is a short biography of the author. Without the effort and commitment of these people, this book would be a lot smaller than that which you are holding. They have not only written about their African experiences, but have also expressed a passion for that place, its people and its future. That should truly be acknowledged.

Extra special thanks to Ronald Prybylowski, who has edited many of the stories and has been the book's chief critic. He's now more than qualified to put his experiences to paper and write an _Amsterdam Par Adventure_. And kudos to Mike Matera (http://www.michaeljmatera.com), Jessica Powers, Paul Fucetola and Timothy Shea, whose sharp eyes and linguistic senses have helped numerous parts of this volume move along seamlessly.

Many thanks must also go to America's CIA, which had a few spare moments from hunting down terrorists and briefing the President (as well as other senior US Government policy makers) to provide the maps for this book (that was a small favor to ask, given their budget of over $26 billion). The maps appear to be accurate and up-to-date, with no reference to any Chinese Embassies. Source: http://www.cia.org.

A big thank you to Pat Lamb (1 973 566 9281), who is an editorial cartoonist and brilliant stand up comedian. He's presently working on a pop-up book of aggressive panhandlers and plans to follow that with a scratch and sniff history of New Jersey. He drew the political satire cartoons and the book cover.

Thanks to Sean The Builder and Chris Ashworth. Those two travel companions were arguably the best hitchhikers in Africa, if not the Galaxy. Their thumbs were instrumental in obtaining instant lifts from people. In some cases car drivers were fighting over themselves to provide a means of transport. 'Incredible' is a word that comes to mind. If anything, Sean and

Chris should get their thumbs examined by a doctor, as those digits were like magnets.

Finally, to all those who must remain anonymous (for their sake as much as mine), my sincere thanks. They include the border guards in Mozambique and several policemen who wandered across my path while on the African continent.

table of contents

introduction

We live in a time when the opinions of column writers, newsreaders, commentators and celebrities shape our own. Whatever is written in the newspaper, broadcast on the radio, or shown on television is presented as the only truth. That can be inaccurate and wholly misleading.

What an amazing world we live in. A sixty-second interview, a five hundred word article, or a two minute segment of camera footage can be beamed into our living rooms and completely fill us in on any place or situation on the globe. Complex and perhaps boring issues are grossly oversimplified. We all realize that the earth is not flat, but how many of us truly have both sides of the story—so that an educated opinion can be made?

Since returning from a stint in Zimbabwe, I've been to many dinner parties and social gatherings at which people have said at the end of one of my anecdotes:

"I never knew that."

"CNN never mentioned this."

"That's an amazing story—no way can that be true!"

Such remarks are usually followed by the comment: "Have you considered doing a book?"

Well, that is exactly what I have done. I've compiled and edited a book on Africa that presupposes that people from all walks of life have interesting stories, viewpoints and experiences to share that will touch, inform, move and inspire the reader, as well as offer insight to that part of the world.

The contents of this book are only individuals' opinions, which are their experiences through their eyes. In places, this book is not politically correct and describes nightmarish hellholes and appalling situations that people have to live through—sometimes just to feed themselves or get to a hotel. Of course dwelling on tragedy is always easy to write about, to be just another foreigner presenting the continent as a lost cause. What follows is a range of stories, from the tragic and provocative to those in which the writer's tongue is planted a little less firmly in cheek.

These stories are from travelers and locals who've provided detailed firsthand accounts of their experiences and observations on the African continent, focusing on the challenges and triumphs of personal experience, or events in modern African history. They include the person who brought Sesame Street to Africa, photographers who witnessed civil wars, and backpackers who took a year off to wander along the hot and dusty roads.

It does not cover half the countries on this continent and most of the statistics and facts are probably out of date. The ones that are quoted are guesstimates and should be used as an indicator. That is typical of Africa. To my knowledge only a few names have been disguised.

The book is not intended to be a definitive guide to Africa, but a collection of over one hundred tales, insights and typically unreported observations. It has adventure, mystery, political intrigue and the pathos of any good thriller story - WHILE REMAINING ENTIRELY TRUE. It also captures the moods, prejudices, opinions and frustrations of ordinary people who at some stage in their lives have been in the boiling pot of 20th Century Africa. Stories have been contributed by anthropologists, drag queens, retired teachers, TV reporters, politicians, war correspondents, academics and that modern day explorer: the businessman. Each story is the opinion of the individual writer and not that of the other contributing authors.

Contributors have submitted stories and articles both in British English and American English. That has not been edited or changed, so as to preserve the writing style.

In compiling this book, I've also discovered that people love learning about others' travels or adventures in far-flung places—locales few people have visited or even heard about. There's a longing for adventure not just from fictional "Indiana Jones" characters, but also from ordinary people, someone who has accidentally or deliberately stepped outside of his comfort zone; been confronted, confused, misunderstood (and perhaps let down); but at the end has a short tale to tell that makes the reader think twice about Africa.

Too often, information on Africa is presented in a sterile and academic format, such that it never reaches the masses. This book presents—in an entertaining format—the history and current affairs that would not normally make the seven o' clock news, along with the bizarre and culturally shocking situations that can only happen in Africa. The intent of the book is to give the reader a grounding in Africa, as well as a good laugh- something which my history teachers rarely did!

I also believe that most of these stories would make Sunday Travel Section editors choke on their morning toast. There are other travel and history books covering such topics. The distinction here, however, is that the source of the material is from **"Africa BA-BY!"**

Warm regards and enjoy the read,

Peter Ward

culture shock

At times I like to think of myself as a man of adventure, wandering off the trail, not bothering with the guidebook and getting away from it all.

Sometimes I go away not to escape reality but to engage in it, to see for myself what it's all about. To be presented with culture shock situations is not always pleasant or comforting. Yet I, like many, love to do it. A fragile nature reserve, a remote village, an area of poverty in a large city, each could be the place where our wanderlust, learning and understanding go beyond the photographs, as each event or feeling is ingrained in the mind.

This chapter has such stories, ones that a traveler will roll off his tongue at the first possible moment.

The rewards of traveling with your eyes open and a conscience awakened are very deep indeed, even years after the event.

language lessons in west africa	ethan zuckerman ghana 1993

The international language schools

I was living in an apartment in Accra, Ghana, allegedly studying traditional African music. Primarily, I drank an awful lot of beer.

I shared my apartment with an unhappily married couple, Stephanie (a sculptor) and Raul (a photographer), both American expatriates, or, as my friend Francis likes to say, "migrant workers."(Francis runs a bar in Accra called "Nuku," the clientele of which is at least half expatriates. He points out that "expatriate" implies "exiled from one's homeland," while most Northerners in Africa are here voluntarily because they like it and because the work pays well. I agree with his reasoning and have started referring to friends and colleagues overseas as "migrants.") I blame Steph and Raul's unhappiness, in part, for my alcohol consumption, but then again, that Club Beer is good stuff.

Stephanie and I were both leeching off the US government, beneficiaries of the Fulbright program. The Fulbright program is the generous legacy of Senator William Fulbright, who believed the world would be a better place if scholars from the US and other lands traded places occasionally and built long-lasting cultural ties. He was undoubtedly correct, though I suspect his global vision included very little thought on the specifics of what a 20 year-old philosophy major would do, day to day, on an all-expenses paid vacation funded by the US government. When I pay my taxes, I think fondly back to 1993 and wonder which irresponsible twenty-year-olds my contributions are sponsoring this year.

Many Fulbrighters are PhD students, spending a government-funded year overseas completing their research before writing their dissertations. These folks are generally obsessed, driven, focused, busy and rarely much fun. These were not the folks I generally hung out with. Significantly more mellow were the professorial Fulbrighters. Overseas on sabbatical, they'd research books with less intensity than the PhD candidates (likely because they'd already achieved tenure) or teach classes at one of the universities. In 1993, the University of Ghana at Legon was on strike, and many of the professorial Fulbrights were mellow indeed. And then there were the undergrad Fulbrights.

Graduates of liberal arts colleges, unless they are independently wealthy, generally face two choices after finishing their Bachelor's degrees, both onerous. You can go to graduate school – going further into debt and remaining mired in the world of classrooms, exams and papers – or you can go to work – painful for reasons too numerous to detail here.

With a bit of imagination, a third path is available: fellowships. The Rhodes, while handy if you're planning on a later career in politics, sends you to Britain, which has good beer but lousy weather. The Fulbright, on the other hand, is available for a wide variety of nations, and the difficulty of obtaining the grant is directly proportional to the popularity of the destination. In other words, if you're reasonably clever and take care not to pick a destination like France, there's a decent chance to receive an undergraduate Fulbright.

The Fulbright was extremely popular with fellow Philosophy majors at Williams, for the obvious reason that career prospects as working philosophers are extremely slim. My classmate Brian wrote a truly creative Fulbright proposal for Argentina. Following in the steps of literary philosopher Jose Luis Borges, he had obtained an internship at the Buenos Aires newspaper, El Sol, where Borges had published numerous influential essays. Presenting letters from the Editorial board of El Sol inviting him to join the staff, Brian requested the fellowship to pay his internship expenses. What Brian knew, and the Fulbright review board evidently didn't, was that "El Sol" was an entirely ficticious newspaper invented by Borges as an appropriate venue for his musings and that Brian, in the spirit of a Borgesian prank, had invented the internship.

Lacking Brian's postmodern panache, I was forced to seek other options. My philosophical studies were a dead end, grantwise. I had focused on "philosophy of mind" – rooted in Britain, land of good beer and bad weather – and existentialism, rooted in Denmark and France. All of the above are "popular" countries and it was clear to me that they were poor hunting grounds for funding.

So, like a high school student with lousy SATs, I focused on my extracurricular activities. Coming to Williams in 1989, I thought myself an excellent musician and a strong tenor. This notion was quickly dispelled as I auditioned for, and was rejected by, every singing group on campus. (As I've got a high tenor, I applied to all the all-women's singing groups as well, so I was rejected by literally every vocal group on campus.) My stoner roommate Dave concluded that the new African Music and Dance ensemble being formed on campus would be "just like those drum circles at Dead shows, dude." So I became one of the founding members of Kusika, and, over four years, became a reasonably competent percussionist.

My Fulbright proposal addressed the relationship between traditional Ghanaian percussion and contemporary Afropop music. It took me about three days in Ghana to discover that: a) the traditional musicians and Afropop musicians didn't speak to each other, never mind acknowledge musical influence on one another and b) all the successful Ghanaian Afropop musicians were living in Germany, where the recording studios were better. Without a research project, and with all possible professorial mentors on strike, I spent my time bumming around the National Theatre of Ghana, taking lessons from master drummers and xylophonists on their lunch breaks, and drinking a lot of beer.

Stephanie had an entirely different and utterly similar undergraduate Fulbright experience. After an undergraduate degree in visual arts, she'd written a proposal that allowed her to study traditional mask-making in northern Nigeria. Evacuated by the US government in response to political violence in Nigeria, Stephanie found herself in Ghana, sans master teacher, but with woodcarving tools and husband. Steph and Raul had discovered another clever truth about the Fulbright – the amount of your award doubled if you traveled with your spouse. (I proposed marriage to several female friends on discovering this and had approximately as much luck as I'd had with joining a campus singing group.)

Despite living thousands of miles from American college towns, we recreated for ourselves the slacker artist lifestyle we'd likely have pursued in the States. Stephanie sat on our porch, desultorily carving surrealist masks. Raul would periodically shoulder fifty pounds of camera bodies, lenses, filters and other gear and wander around Accra shooting pictures of billboards. And I'd sit on the roof of the National Theatre of Ghana and hope one of my teachers would keep an appointment.

Periodically, to remind ourselves that we were alienated artists in Africa instead of in New York, we'd take excursions to other towns, usually trying to visit a market rumored to have a wide selection of antique trade beads or hand-woven kente cloth. These attempts were thwarted by a pair of Ghanaian traits – the modular calendar and the Ghanaian "I don't know."

In the allegedly developed world, we are used to events happening on a day of the week: "My book group meets every Thursday evening." This method of scheduling is not universal. In Ghana, market days are every four days in certain towns, every fifth day in others, every sixth in still others, and so on. Knowing that there was a market in Koforidua this past Thursday isn't useful unless you know how frequently the market occurs, so you know whether to return on Monday, Tuesday or Wednesday.

As no one has printed a table of market days – or a bus schedule for that matter – finding a market is a matter of going to the local lorry park and

4

asking drivers when the next market day in Koforidua will occur. This is when you encounter the Ghanaian word for "I don't know," which is pronounced "Tuesday," or in some cases "Monday" or "yesterday."

It's very impolite not to answer a direct question, so Ghanaians will rarely tell you that they don't know something. This leads to difficult situations. Ask a person for directions and they'll smile, take your arm and start walking you through the streets. Sometimes they know where they're going and will lead you to your destination. In other cases, they're hoping your destination happens to be a few blocks ahead and that they, by the grace of God, will be able to help you.

So, when Jessica invited us to a yam festival in the town of Dzolo-Gbogame, I had visions of the various different ways in which we could be thwarted. "The Yam festival? Oh, that only happens every third year and only on years when the rains are good."

Jessica, on the other hand, inspired a certain amount of confidence. She was also a Fulbrighter, but this was not her first time in Africa. Indeed, she'd spent three years in Zaire as a Peace Corps Volunteer, and I considered her an Old Africa Hand. Furthermore, Jessica had been made aware of the festival by Fortune, the savviest Ghanaian I'd met thus far. Fortune was a market trader who, for years, had traveled on buses from Nigeria to Mali trading fabrics, beads, foodstuffs and any other commodities. I discovered that shopping with Fortune generally reduced my expenses by a factor of two, even after paying for her lunch. If Fortune thought we'd have a good time in Dzolo, I was willing to give it a shot.

Our host for the trip was Ben, a lab technician in a small medical clinic in Accra. Born in Dzolo, he was returning home for the festival and was happy to escort American guests. Consulting with Fortune and her husband, Patrick, we learned that Ben was hoping to become an elder of his village and thought that by bringing "honored guests" with him, he'd have a better shot in the elder election. We all agreed that, whether or not Ben's plan was sound, this would be a unique experience and one we should embrace.

The trip from Accra to Dzolo is roughly 100 miles. In the US, we'd have hopped in the car and reached our destination in two hours. Things take a little longer in Ghana. First, we packed the necessities for a trip to the bush – water bottles and filters, iodine tablets, anti-malarial medication, gift bottles of schnapps for our hosts and boots for hiking in the rainforest. Then, after the predictable two-hour delay to rouse Raul and wait for him to sort through, test and pack his camera equipment, we walked to the local tro-tro stop with Ben.

We took the tro-tro – the universal motorized transportation of developing nations: a Volkswagen minibus converted to carry 18 passengers with a maximum of economy and a minimum of safety and comfort – to the downtown bus station, where we boarded a bus to Ho, the capital of the Volta region. Jessica and I squeezed into seats near the front of the bus, arguing all the way whether we were less likely to die in a crash in the front or the back of the bus. Raul, Stephanie and Ben squeezed into seats further back, hedging their bets.

We bought our lunches from young girls carrying hardboiled eggs, meat pies, biscuits and oranges on their heads, transacting business through the bus window as the bus filled with passengers. Like most transportation in Ghana, the bus left not on any particular schedule, but when it was full. Early on in my travels, I'd resorted to buying empty seats in shared taxis to make them leave earlier, but my strict Western sense of time had disappeared months ago, and I placidly stared out the window as the middle seats of the bus were folded down and the fifth and sixth passengers in each row took their seats.

(An apocryphal, popular story amongst the migrants in Ghana: American guy takes a cab to Kotoka Airport in Accra, to check in about two hours before his flight. He gets to the counter and presents his bags and ticket, when the gate agent announces, "Oh, your plane already left." The guy protests, explaining that he's got a ticket and that the flight isn't supposed to leave for two more hours. The ticket agent says, "It was full, so we left" and charges the guy a $100 ticket change fee to fly out later in the week. Live in Ghana for more than a few weeks and you'll conclude that the story is likely true.)

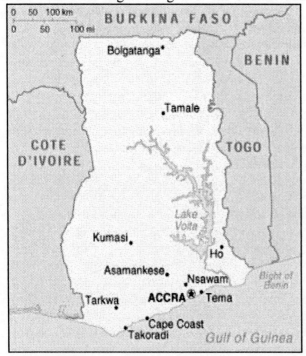

The last guys to get on the bus were the "bus sellers," itinerant merchants who took advantage of the captive audience on board to pitch their products, usually patent medicines or evangelical Christianity. Since the trip to Ho was a long voyage, we had a double-feature, a cough syrup salesman followed by a charismatic preacher. I was enjoying the cadence of his sermon, but missed most of the content, as he was switching languages rapidly, speaking mostly Twi (the language of the Akan people, the most common tribal language in Ghana) and Ga (widely spoken in Accra), throwing in some Ewe (the language spoken in Ho) and some English. He caught my attention when he raised his arms to the roof of the bus and asked the powers on high to "bathe this bus in the blood of Jesus!"

Jessica and I agreed that being in a packed bus racing down a potholed highway in West Africa was not a time when one wanted to think about being bathed in blood, even if it was just a theological metaphor. But I slipped a few hundred cedis to the preacher, figuring that Ghanaian roads were a good place to avoid divine retribution. The preacher and snake oil salesman got off at the northern outskirts of the city, and hopped a tro-tro downtown for their next gig. Climbing north out of Accra, the scenery suddenly turns lush, deep green tangles of vegetation contrasting with rich red earth. Every few hundred meters, the earth would rise into a two-meter cone, a termite mound, looking geometric and alien. I knew from my environmentalist friends that this landscape was sometimes referred to as "a green desert," that the natural rain forest had been cut down and replaced with small cassava, banana and pineapple farms, but my naïve eyes had a difficult time distinguishing cultivated and uncultivated land, the natural forest from farmers' fields.

In early afternoon we lurched into Ho, an unremarkable but pleasantly green city and set about finding transportation for the next leg of our trip. While Ben quizzed tro-tro drivers in Twi, the rest of us set out to relieve ourselves, or as Ghanaians say, "to pay our water bills."

Imagine the platonic ideal of "bathroom" – a gleaming, white, porcelain space, smelling faintly of disinfectant. Folded cloth towels, distant classical music, brass fixtures, fine milled soap. Make that a "ten" on your mental scale of bathroom cleanliness. Place the men's room at Port Authority Bus Terminal in New York City at "five." The restrooms at the Ho bus station are a "one." You smell them first, the unmistakable scent of human feces drying in the sun. Then you hear them – the low, Beelzebubian buzz of thousands of well-fed flies. Visually, I found myself thinking of MX missile silos filled with shit: six holes in the ground, surrounded by whitewashed concrete, each capped with an irregular brown dome – the leavings of those who came before me.

The question seems obvious: "If the bathroom was that gross, why didn't you wait until you got to the village?" This question reveals

7

ignorance of a basic fact of my life in Ghana – perpetual gastric distress. The first couple of times I had serious diarrhea in Accra, I was foolish enough to go to a clinic. I'd bring a stool sample, answer a series of questions, and be diagnosed with "white man's stomach," a vague condition that wasn't quite dysentery, but sure did keep me near the bathrooms. (The upside of this condition was that I lost forty pounds in nine months, a remarkable feat given my rate of beer consumption, which would have made a rugby player blush.) Two months into my stay, I invented the expatriate cocktail – a shot of Pepto-Bismol over boiled-water ice cubes.

Immodium? Don't make me laugh. I ran through my stash three weeks into my stay.

Necessity being the mother of invention, I did a complex center of gravity calculation, tightened the straps on my backpack, and perched birdlike above the Stygian hole. Silently I prayed to the patron saint of restrooms, whoever he or she may be, that my knees would hold out and that my encounter with the Ho bathroom would not be a close encounter. And indeed, I was delivered from the Ho restroom and found myself at the "Drop In Clinic," the bus station bar next door, where I celebrated with a beer the fact that I had not, in fact, dropped in.

I rejoined our group, which was anchoring the back seat of a northbound tro-tro. This one filled up quickly, and by the time we were underway, we were several passengers over the rated capacity of our van. This surprised me, as I'd never realized that tro-tros had a rated capacity – I always assumed that the "mate" kept loading in passengers until only the driver was capable of drawing a breath. But as we neared the first police roadblock on the outskirts of town, three athletic young men jumped out of the van and began running along side it. As we slowed for inspection, the men ran on ahead, and we caught up with them a few hundred yards up the road. We passed through the checkpoint with a legal number of passengers, let the runners back in, and sped to the next barrier. We repeated this four or five times in the span of ten miles, reducing our overall average speed to that of a fast jog.

I was annoyed that the driver was slowing everyone's trip in order to make a few more cedis, but Ben pointed out that the driver's intentions were probably more charitable. Very few vans traveled the potholed route, and there was a decent chance that our fleet-footed friends would have otherwise been stranded in Ho. Raul helpfully pointed out that, had I been seated in the front row of seats, I too might have been jogging my way through the Volta region. So I shut up and counted termite mounds.

We arrived in Dzolo in the cool of early evening. A few concrete buildings with tin roofs and several cane and mud structures with thatch roofs surrounded a petite Spanish-styled church, whitewash contrasting with rusted metal roof. As we walked down the road to Ben's family house, we passed the three-stall market, and I thought about life in a town where a cold soda would represent a minor miracle. Jessica noticed that the road was lined with neither power nor telephone wires, and Ben confirmed that electric power in the village came only from diesel-powered generators. The elementary school had one, so the children could study for a few hours by electric light after working in the fields. Ben's family house also had one.

We unpacked and were ready to sit down to an evening meal of yam when Ben announced that we were to be presented to the village elders. As we took turns smearing off road dirt with a trickle of warm tapwater, I wondered what our encounter with the elders would entail. A few weeks earlier, I'd traveled to a Durbar in the Ashanti region, a gathering of regional chiefs replete with gold, kente cloth and lots of pomp and circumstance. Paramount chiefs were carried through town in sedan chairs, and those doing business with the chiefs spoke only through their linguists, graying men carrying golden staffs to convey their status. Was I ready to confront royalty in my dirt-stained khakis and Tevas? Was our two-dollar schnapps an adequate gift? Did it matter that we didn't speak Ewe?

Unsurprisingly, an audience with the elders of Dzolo was a low-key affair. Ben led us back through town, now lit by kerosene lamps propped in windows, to a palm-thatch lean-to. We sat on a low bench facing a row of middle-aged Ghanaian men, dressed not in traditional kente, but in middle-American leisurewear. Ben, in acid-washed jeans and a tank top, introduced the four Americans individually, presenting our occupations and our missions in Ghana. As the elders, loosening up, began to smile and nod, Ben formally requested permission for the four of us to stay in the village and to attend the next day's yam festival. Sensing an opening, I reached for the bottle of schnapps I'd been carrying and presented it to the eldest of the elders, thanking him and the village as a whole for their hospitality.

This was evidently the right thing to do. Reaching behind his bench, one of the elders produced a two-gallon jerry can and a set of calabashes, dried gourds used as bowls or cups. He splashed a small amount of milky liquid into the calabash, said a blessing in Ewe and poured it on the ground: libation, an offering to the ancestors. Then he poured a pint or so of liquid into each of four calabashes and handed them to each of us. As I wrinkled my nose at the sour-smelling fluid, Jessica leaned over and whispered, "Palm wine. The alcohol should be strong enough to kill off most of the germs."

I thought briefly about dropping a few iodine tablets into the palm wine before knocking it back, and then concluded that I needed to address the more immediate problem: the fly noisily drowning in my calabash. In a fit of cross-cultural inspiration, I took the calabash in two hands and, emulating my host, poured a small amount of liquid on the ground, freeing the fly and generating a hearty round of laughter. And, unfortunately, another half-pint or so was poured into my cup "as compensation."

The palm wine tasted better than it looked – like a slightly sour, flat beer, almost like a Lambic – and as I tackled my calabash, Ben explained that palm wine was a strictly rural delicacy. The palm sap – sometimes removed by tapping, more often by felling, the palm tree – fermented naturally and a day or two out of the tree was delicious. A day more and it spoiled.

Interpreting our politeness as thirst, our hosts produced a bottle filled with a clear fluid and a number of water glasses. One of the elders poured me several ounces of the fluid, while another protested, "Oh, my friend, you do not know his capacity." Poking me in my belly (I am a large person by American standards, and Ghanaian men are significantly smaller than American men), my host assured us that my capacity was vast, and topped off my glass.

My memory becomes a little fuzzy here.

Stephanie asked what we were drinking, and Ben explained that the beverage was "local gin": Akpeteshie. Distilled from sugarcane or palm wine, Akpeteshie has the taste of tequila and the impact of absinthe. My friend Patrick had introduced me to it, mixed with sugar and lime, while we played chess. Three glasses and I'd find myself staring at the board for minutes at a time, trying to make the pieces stop moving so I could decide which one to pick up.

Halfway through this glass, my hosts had invited me to study Ewe drumming in Dzolo. Three quarters of the way through, I seem to have joined one of the elders in a drum duet, played with our hands on the bench. Sometime later, I was being led away by Stephanie and Raul, and found myself on the front steps of Ben's house, wondering at the number of stars in a sky unspoiled by light pollution.

It took a few hours and several boiled yams before I was fully functional. As we choked down the starchy tubers, Jessica revealed that our trip was a bit more complicated than she'd originally explained. Later that evening, she was slated to become the Queen Mother of Dzolo Gbogame. While this was evidently supposed to be a surprise to all of us, our friends Patrick and Fortune had wisely decided that Jessica be warned what was ahead.

Evidently, the women of the town would appear at our house around midnight, lift Jessica out of her bed and onto their shoulders, and parade her around town, singing her praises, which is exactly what happened a few hours later. I'd fallen asleep after methodically killing the flies, mosquitoes, cockroaches and spiders that resided in my borrowed bedroom. I woke to the sound of distant rain, which as I woke resolved itself into the sound of dozens of gourd rattles. I threw on a t-shirt and grabbed my camera in time to see Jessica, in a pink t-shirt, lofted onto the shoulders of a dozen ululating women. And as suddenly as they came, they left, and we went back to sleep.

I know now that the phenomenon of "development chiefs" is fairly common throughout West Africa. Villages invite foreigners to a ceremony where they are named to positions of power in the village. They are expected to donate and raise money for the village. At the time, though, no one had explained this to any of the four of us. We learned that Dzolo had chosen Jessica over Stephanie because they had an easier time pronouncing her name – a village a few miles up the road was called "Jesikan." I still don't know why men were ineligible for development chieftancy in Dzolo – I think they were afraid Raul and I would drink all their palm wine.

After breakfast – yams – several of the rattle women arrived at Ben's house with kente, beads and gold earrings. As we were draped in rich, heavy cloths, Ben explained our roles. Stephanie was to be Jessica's linguist – she would speak for the Queen Mother and interpret her regal thoughts for general consumption. This seemed to ignore some obvious difficulties – Stephanie didn't speak Ewe, and Jessica, an outspoken lawyer, was unlikely to let anyone speak for her, under any circumstances, ever. Then again, I was a lousy choice for court musician, as my studies of Ghanaian music had centered on xylophone music from the North, not drum music of the East.

Raul, at least, was well chosen as court photographer. Raul quickly realized that this was his opportunity to be an observer, rather than a participant, in the ceremony. Shrugging off his kente, he explained that to photograph the ceremonies, he would need to be very mobile, and therefore should keep wearing his t-shirt and shorts. He then disappeared to the perimeter and did incomprehensible things with filters and lens tissue.

As an American college student, I had encountered my fair share of rituals staged for public consumption, the culturally relevant pieces carefully explained for the audience. This was not one of those rituals. Told to walk, we walked. Told to sit, we sat. Odd things happened all around us, and we groped for the occasional words in English that punctuated the staccato of Ewe. We whispered to one another, trying to determine protocol, only to be pulled apart by attendants who fanned us, danced, snapped photos and sang. I have never dreamed of being famous, but I suspect that it must feel something like this – all eyes are on you, continually, and you can't quite figure out why.

Wrapped in a toga of heavy color-flecked black kente, trying to walk without dropping the precious cloth in the dust, I saw little of the procession that led us into the town square. We were seated on benches under a makeshift tin roof, surrounded by attendants, and hushed into silence as we asked questions. Eventually we reached a state of regal dignity and silence, which basically masked incomprehension, anticipation and boredom. Putting aside the color, smell and sound, the overwhelming otherness of being the featured attraction in a village festival thousands of miles from home, the whole gathering resembled nothing so much as a Memorial Day celebration in small-town America. Children from the village marched in formation and sang. The church choir sang hymns. Long speeches in Ewe praised the success of farms and local businesses', the achievements of local sons and daughters who had made good in Ho, Kumasi, or far-off Accra. Hoes were awarded to the yam farmer who'd grown the most yams, the best yams, and the largest yam – a 50 pound monster that looked more like a small child than a vegetable.

Three hours into the ceremony, we had our moment in the spotlight.

Jessica's Fulbright had been granted for research on Ghana's role in international drug smuggling. Her research had convinced her that the reason Ghanaians were so often arrested at JFK airport with balloons of heroin in their intestines was that the US held smugglers in America rather than extraditing them. This allowed families to finesse questions about why Kwame had disappeared for his five-year sentence: "Oh, he's in America at university," turning a family humiliation into a source of pride.

Jessica, while lobbying the Ghanaian and American governments to research extradition of drug smugglers, realized that most of the people arrested became mules out of ignorance and economic necessity. So she spent much of her time in Ghana giving speeches, explaining the legal and health dangers of smuggling. Never one to pass up an opportunity, Jessica decided that our newfound celebrity status was a chance to spread the message to the people of Dzolo.

So that's how I ended up playing a drug baron, to an audience of rapt Ghanaians, convincing Stephanie that if she'd just swallow these balloons, I'd give her a plane ticket to America, a visa and five hundred dollars. Jessica explained, "He may tell you that you are swallowing gold nuggets, but you are swallowing heroin, and if the balloon bursts in your stomach, you will die." Ben provided simultaneous translation, so our laugh lines got a polite chuckle when we delivered them and boisterous applause fifteen seconds later.

The festival reached its climax soon after, as the Elders began a fundraising campaign to electrify the village. An almost unimaginable amount of money - $5000 – needed to be raised, and the Elders took turns challenging townspeople to give what they could. As local businessmen presented gifts of thousands of cedis – twenty, fifty, seventy dollars – the Elders announced each amount donated and sang the praises of the individual's generosity.

There was much I didn't understand in Dzolo, but I understood immediately that, as honored guests, we needed to make a donation to our friends in Dzolo. One problem – none of us carried much cash in Ghana. The largest widely available note was the 500 cedi bill, worth approximately 70 US cents – carrying $20 required a roll of bills worthy of a 70's pimp. Did any of us have any cash? How much were we each willing to contribute? What amount was appropriate?

How do you converse when everyone in the town square is watching you? You'd whisper…but we were separated by numerous bodies and voices were drowned out by cheering. Stephanie had the idea first, yelling, "Francais?" Jessica shook her head – "Non." We were five miles from the Togolese border, and most of the villagers spoke better French than English. "Deutsche?" she offered in response. "Lo siento, no comprendo," I offered – my German is limited to a number of nouns that describe existential angst, while my Spanish is ugly, but more flexible.

So, en espanol, we negotiated a joint gift of $100, to be given by Jessica, in the form of a bill Stephanie was carrying. The amount seems embarrassingly small now, but felt like a lot at the time, as it represented more than a month's rent for my Accra apartment. And, as with the schnapps, it appeared that we had done the right thing. The bill was lifted into the air by one of the elders and was delicately passed around through the crowd, so that everyone had the opportunity to touch the bill.

The bill had an iconic force beyond its value. Several of the local businesspeople had given larger sums – stacks of cedis in plastic bags – but the bill captured the imagination of the crowd. I remembered that taxicabs in Accra often had stickers on their rear windshields depicting $100 bills, often with the slogan, "God will Provide." We'd turned symbol into reality, and were rewarded with smiles and cheers.

The rest of my stay in Dzolo was wonderful – a celebratory meal of yam, chicken and akpeteshie; walks in the rainforest; palm wine served directly from the tree; services in a tiny community church. I returned later for a long weekend, and was received kindly, though not with the celebrity I forfeited when I handed my loaned kente back to its rightful owner.

Dzolo's choice of Jessica was a deeply wise one. She returned some months later to teach English, for a month, at the local school. Now an officer with the Food and Agricultural Organization of the UN, she travels around the world and returns to Dzolo at least once a year to visit with friends, mediate disputes, and raise funds. There is now electricity in the village, and a kindergarden named in her honor.

My most lasting legacy from the trip was the discovery of private language. Perpetually frustrated when Ghanaians would shift into Twi, cutting me out of the conversation, I began conversing in Spanish with American friends when I wanted to keep discussions confidential. This habit caused me to receive my next language lesson in Ghana.

Ghanaians, despite intense poverty, don't beg for money. Pride, dignity and self-respect make such behavior unthinkable for able-bodied Ghanaians. People with visible disabilities will ask for money, and I give, realizing that there's a thin social safety net to support people who cannot work for a living. Children will occasionally ask for a "dash," but they're usually joking, looking for a chance to start a conversation, and would usually rather get your address and have you as a pen pal than get a few coins from you.

That said, as a white person, you will often be surrounded by beggars in the streets of Accra. The beggars are children from Arab nations to the north – their skin and hair is visibly different from Ghanaians, and they are treated with extreme contempt by most Ghanaians I know. I asked my friend Bernard why Ghanaians were happy to give to the disabled and so hostile towards these refugee children. He pointed out that, carefully watching a team of child beggars, was an apparently able-bodied man resting under a nearby tree. Bernard explained, "The children aren't begging for themselves – they beg for their parents, to support the family. But that man is whole! He can work! Why doesn't he support his children instead of making them support him!"

I'd like to say that I carefully evaluated Bernard's logic and decided to stop supporting Sudanese child beggars. I didn't. Instead, I simply got sick of feeling like a walking dollar bill, shaking children off my arms when I walked through certain parts of town.

Once, on a very hot, very long day, when I was in a very bad mood, I decided to try a new technique. I'd just gotten into a taxi and three child beggars crawled halfway through the window, hands outstretched. Instead of ignoring them, I protested in Spanish: "What do you want? I don't understand what you want! Leave me alone."

As the cab pulled away from the intersection and the children scattered, the taxi driver looked at me over his shoulder and, in flawless Cuban Spanish, began to explain the Sudanese civil war and the resulting refugee situation. He went on to express his concern that I would have a difficult time navigating Accra without speaking English. Bright red, I admitted my deception – which amused him – and wondered how he'd learned to speak Spanish so beautifully.

Ghana, he explained, did a skillful job of navigating Cold War geopolitics. When NATO countries were funding African nations, Ghanaians were good capitalists; when Warsaw pact nations had the money, Ghanaians were working towards a socialist revolution. As a result, many Ghanaians had been educated in Moscow in the 1950s and spoke Russian. Ghanaians educated in the 1970s and early 1980s, like my cabbie, often had studied in Cuba and spoke Spanish.

Languages are a weakness for many Americans, perhaps because most Americans feel such little need to reach out to the rest of the world. Unlike my European friends, who seem to speak half a dozen languages fluently, I speak one tolerably, and one badly. Perhaps this is because I can drive ten hours from my home without crossing national borders while a European driving the same duration would cross dozens.

Or perhaps it's a product of the arrogance that comes from exporting our culture around the globe, an assumption that because other people are wearing Nikes, eating McDonalds and watching MTV, they should speak our language as well.

My work takes me to Ghana frequently these days, and I often ask Ghanaian colleagues how many languages they speak. "Three," they'll say. "French, Spanish and Italian." I'll point out that they're speaking English, and they say, "Oh, but everyone speaks English in Ghana. That and Twi." I'll say, "I know you speak Twi, but I just heard you speaking Ga. Is that because you're Ga?" "No, I'm Ewe, but I live in Accra, so I learned to speak Ga. When I went to school in Cape Coast, I had to learn Fanti." I leave these conversations feeling parochial and poorly educated.

My final language lesson, almost a decade ago, came a week before the end of my Fulbright. I was waiting at Sankara Circle for a tro-tro to take me to Legon, the university town to the north, so I could say goodbye to my sponsor. Very few people were at the stop, and when a clean, airconditioned (!) minivan stopped, and the driver said, "Legon?" I got in, not noticing that no one else entered the van. As I sat down, reveling in the cool air, the driver turned to me and introduced himself. In German. Not knowing what to do, I introduced myself. In Ga.

This sent the driver – a representative of the German-Ghanaian friendship society – into hysterical laughter, as he had assumed that I was a lost German tourist. We laughed all the way to Legon, in air conditioned luxury, and I felt, for a fleeting instant, that my ineptitude with languages might just be a good thing.

Ethan Zuckerman's love for African travel helped lead him to found Geekcorps, a non-profit technology volunteer corps. Geekcorps pairs skilled volunteers from US and European high tech companies with businesses in emerging nations for four month volunteer tours. Volunteers are currently serving in Ghana and in locations throughout Eastern Europe, and Geekcorps is developing new programs in East Africa and Central Asia. Prior to Geekcorps, Ethan was a full-time geek, serving as VP of Research and Development for Tripod.com. When not meeting telecommunication ministers in Kampala or debugging printer drivers in Yerevan, he lives in the Berkshire Mountains of Western Massachusetts, USA, with his wife Rachel. Since he's a big geek, he spends most of his free time building medieval siege engines, designing board games and playing the accordion.

| kazbahs and culture in mysterious morocco | carey goodman
morocco
1985 |

No time like the present to travel

The time: October 1985. The place: Tangier, Morocco. It was the height of the American hostage situation in Lebanon: The perfect time for my family and me to take a day trip from Gibraltar to Tangier, a very Arab city in a very Arab North African country. The fact that Tangier is predominately Arab did not disturb me in the least. I have always believed that in general people are quite similar regardless of their ethnic label. There are good and bad Arabs just as there are good and bad Europeans, Asians, Americans, and members of every other cultural group. But as a life-long news-aholic, I could not ignore or entirely obliterate the stereotype many Americans have of Arabs. And given the rather tense relations the US had with many predominately Arab countries then, the mere act of having a US passport entailed certain risks.

The transition from very developed Gibraltar to rather undeveloped Tangier was quite apparent. I only needed to glance over the ferry railing to see the pollution that floated in the harbor. Tangier was definitely no candidate to receive the Good Housekeeping stamp of approval for waste disposal. The filth was not confined to the harbor. It littered the streets, the outlying areas, and the markets. It made the small villages along the narrow and winding dirt roads of the Spanish countryside

17

we had traversed the previous day seem as modern as the trendy districts of any Western metropolis. My thoughts varied from "When does this ferry leave for Gibraltar?" to "Hey, this will definitely be some sort of adventure. Exactly what sort of adventure, I don't know, so let's get on with it so we can be finished with it."

Sharif first took us to some typical tourist traps. We visited a place that allows tourists to ride camels. Just my luck, the camel I was assigned to ride was in an extremely un-co-operative mood that day. What exactly can you do when the camel you are supposed to ride simply sits there and refuses to budge? Simple. You inhale a few breaths of the foul stench surrounding the beast, and you sigh with relief. Well, at least I can say I had a camel experience T.E. Lawrence probably never had. At least it is an experience he never mentioned in his detailed history of his Camel Corps expeditions.

After the camel non-ride, Sharif and the driver took us to the kazbah, a winding maze of narrow streets where the main markets and housing areas are located. Sanitation was obviously an unknown concept in Tangier: Flies covered the hanging meat; trash littered the streets. When he realized we were speaking English, a boy of about eight or nine years old ran up to us and proudly declared: "I speak English: Hot dog, hamburger, Coca-Cola, Chevy Chase!" Chevy Chase had just finished filming a movie in Morocco. That was how he knew those words. At some point a woman approached Sharif and asked him to come to her house. She led us down the maze of dusty streets and vendor stalls and into her home. Unsure of what would happen there, we simply looked around the living room area while Sharif and our unintended hostess conversed in Arabic. The dwelling consisted of four or five rooms; the floor was tile, and the furnishings were sparse, but there was a television prominently located in the living room. Nothing amazing or shocking happened during or after our visit to her home, but for a few seconds the thought crossed my mind that I really didn't want to become the latest "missing American," and I knew it would be virtually impossible to find the way out of the kazbah.

After the kazbah, Sharif took us to some touristy stores to buy leather, rugs, and other allegedly locally made items. After earning his four months of salary in one day, Sharif vigorously tried to convince us to buy these products at prices that would have got him the rest of his year's salary that day. He was quite annoyed that we didn't buy anything. Deduct a point for the Suckers Division.

At last it was time to return to the dock to board the ferry to Gibraltar and to bid farewell to Sharif. We were among the first passengers to arrive at the dock. The organized tour must have followed a very precise schedule. On the way back to Gibraltar, some other tourists asked us how we had spent the day. When we told them, most of them gave us the you-did-what? look, then they offered some casual comment such as "Gee, we're glad it wasn't any more exciting than that!" I am, too, but reflecting on it all these years later, I am rather glad we weren't on that organized tour. Thanks to the confusion at the ticket counter, I have an experience in a place during a time I will never forget. It is those adventures on the road less traveled that can, as Robert Frost wrote, "make all the difference."

Carey Goodman among other things is a freelance writer of sorts who lives near Key West, Florida. She's traveled to approximately fifty countries and territories-approximately because some of them (like Czechoslovakia and Yugoslavia) don't exist now and have fragmented. It is no stretch of reality to say that she's learned more than half of what she knows of the world from hours of sitting around the beer kegs and having long conversations with people from eclectic backgrounds. Most recently she visited Thailand and took an elephant safari. The ride lasted only two hours, but it was more than enough of the jungle and encounters with indigenous groups whose villages resembled something straight from the National Geographic to give her renewed respect for the rigors of expedition life. In addition to such travel adventures, she earned a degree in international relations from Florida International University. She has also earned a law degree, but wants absolutely nothing to do with the legal "profession."

	**the day sesame street came to town**	rebeka ndosi south africa present day

Children's shows are harder than you may think

"Wow, Becky. Your dad tells me you're working with Sesame Street in South Africa. That must be amazing! Were you a communications major in college?"

I was supposed to be in medical school.

Instead, I was on a plane to Johannesburg. International medical internship? Nope. Post-undergraduate Peace Corps? Nuh-uh. Graduation travel gift? Not even.

I was on my way to South Africa to help grow a crop of indigenous and imported furry monsters in every color of the rainbow. I was going to South Africa to introduce them to Sesame Street.

After five years of planning, Sesame Street had finally made its way to South Africa, which, one-and-a-half years later, would join Mexico, China, Russia, Israel/Palestine and others as a country that produced its own version of Sesame Street.

Children's Television Workshop, now known as Sesame Workshop, had hired a Radio Producer. The uncanny thing was that it was me.

October 3rd, 1998 was my first day of work. It wasn't a typical first day. Seeing my office for the first time would have to wait. There was work to do and my new colleagues were awaiting my arrival. I boarded the plane not knowing what to expect, never having flown longer than 8 hours in a row (the flight was 17 hours non-stop), and without yet having acquired a place to live when I returned to New York City. Yikes.

Remarkable. This was Sesame Street, after all – the most successful and beloved children's program in U.S. history. A program and a company that had the world beating down its door to learn how to do the same thing for their children. And South Africa was hot. Apartheid may have ended, but it was fresh in the minds and hearts of the country and the world. Equal opportunity, reconciliation, and moving ahead carefully so as not to let it happen again – the atmosphere was electric. A good time for change. A good time for Sesame Street.

"Sesame Street is on the radio? I've never heard it. What station is it on?"

During a fact-finding mission that some of my colleagues at the Workshop conducted years before my time, one thing was made very clear to them by South Africans: If you go to South Africa, you have to have radio. Radio was, and continues to be (at the time I am writing this), the primary medium for information, news, and entertainment. TV was certainly catching up, but in the areas that had the neediest kids, mainly rural areas, radio existed and television did not.

The South Africa Sesame Street Project was special because it was a multimedia effort – with radio, television, and outreach components – and because it was the first time Sesame Street would EVER be produced for radio. We would follow suit domestically after South Africa's first season was successfully produced.

"So how does it work? The South Africans just dub the US character voices into, er, whatever the South African language is?"

Eleven. There are 11 official languages in South Africa. I freaked out.

How, exactly, do we produce ONE show that can be understood in 11 languages? We don't. But I'll get to that later. The biggest, incorrect assumption that people make when they hear about Sesame Street in South Africa, is to assume that it is a dubbed version of the US show. Not so. Not only were we bringing the show to South Africa, we were also bringing skills. I trained a radio production team—and my television counterpart did the same with a TV production team—how to produce Sesame Street on the radio – and, for that matter, how to produce children's radio. The ultimate goal is to make the productions self-sufficient so that we can let go and let them run it. There was no way that we could know, ultimately, what South African children need or what their experience is. What we knew was how to produce the Street, and in doing so, incorporate a curriculum specific to the needs of the children of a particular country. Well, ok – THEY knew how to produce Sesame Street for television. I knew how to watch Sesame Street on television. I'd grown up with the show—it was older than I was. I was, sort of, winging it. Don't get me wrong (I'm sure that the entire radio team from Season 1 are reading this right now, disgusted). I was winging it from a base of experience producing children's radio, and from training I'd received along the way at the Workshop (watching it religiously as a kid didn't hurt either). It was all pretty amazing and incredible – even from a personal level.

"Wha?"

Hold on, I'll explain. When I arrived at the hotel I proceeded to the desk to check in.

"Name?"

"Rebeka Ndosi. N, as in Nancy, D, as in David, O-"

"I know how to spell Ndosi."

She knew how to spell Ndosi! Spelling it out for people was a habit – no one in the States ever knew how to spell it (and after learning, some still refused to write it without an apostrophe after the N) – especially where I grew up in the Midwest. The check-in woman continued.

"Ndosi is a Zulu name. You're Zulu! Do you know anything about your family? My sister's husband is Ndosi."

I was too polite to stop her from telling me about my family history – the history of the Zulu Ndosis of South Africa. I got that everywhere I went. South Africans who saw my name and then heard me speak were baffled at first, but then ecstatic to take me aside and tell me about my history.

The only thing was – I'm not South African. My name comes from the Ndosis of Tanzania. My father is Tanzanian and moved to the U.S. in 1960 to go to college.

But even after explaining that, I was treated more as family than as an American foreigner. I was special because I wasn't one of the thousands of African Americans spending time in sub-Saharan Africa to "discover my roots" – a trend, which, I discovered, was somewhat bothersome to many black Africans. I didn't have to "discover" anything because my siblings and I were first-generation Ndosi in the U.S.. The link was direct. The family was there and my last name spoke volumes. It was something I'd never experienced before, outside my family in Tanzania. Your last name links you deeply to a vast number of people. If you wear the name, you're family. It's as simple as that.

In a broader sense, I was finally able to put my finger on one of the major differences I have experienced while spending time in many foreign countries. There is a connection to the land that is palpable. Connection to the land itself is very different from pride in one's country, like we have in the U.S. What the U.S. lacks, aside, perhaps, from Native American peoples, is the opportunity to find answers about our origins that begin on American soil. Instead, we ultimately have to look back to the rest of the world to find our beginnings.

And perhaps that is one reason why the black South Africans, from the ones I worked with to the ones I met only briefly, were some of the happiest, most hopeful and determined people I've met in my life. Forget about small talk – there's work to be done, issues to be ironed out and serious fun to catch up on. So who are you, what drives you, and how are you working to make things better?

"Well, how did it work out? Did Sesame Street work on radio?"

Remember those 11 official languages? In the end we had to choose three and produce the show 3 times in those languages to be aired on three

22

regional stations of the South African Broadcasting Corporation (each language had its own station). Each show's language was mixed with English – another first for the regional stations, and one we had to fight tooth and nail for. It sounds like American imperialist crap, right? Well it wasn't. It had become clear that parents wanted their kids to learn English, and put them in schools often specifically because they taught English, because English was seen as the language of power and empowerment. So our shows were Zulu/English, Sepedi/English and Xhosa/English.

On the creative front, Sesame Street ran beautifully in pure audio form. With expressive character voices of Moshe, Zuzu, Zik and Neno – 3 of the 4 created originally by both the South African TV and Radio production teams – and the dedication and creative talent of my production team, we ended up with a series of programs that entertained and delighted kids and adults. But what stood out most was the music. The television version of Takalani Sesame was brilliant. The depth and variety of South Africa's musical culture gave rise to 39 original songs that blew everyone away when Takalani (be happy) Sesame Radio premiered.

After all the "work" was done, it seemed inconceivable that I had to just let it go. Takalani Sesame was on three times a week in three languages – and I can't even hear it, except on the CDs I have in my office back in New York. But it's not the same as turning on the radio and hearing it live and breathe amongst the rest of the programming. I can only hope it brings joy and encourages curiosity and imagination of kids and parents like it did for me when I was growing up. Knowing that we may have succeeded in doing that, even on the smallest scale, in sub-Saharan Africa fills me with a pride that is much more personal than anyone may have known. Next stop, Tanzania…

Rebeka Ndosi: From Minneapolis to the Big Apple, Rebeka Ndosi has produced numerous children's radio programs - international and domestic. During her tenure at Aahs World Radio, the nation's first kid's radio network, she functioned as news director, producer and reporter as well as working on-air. For the popular Aahs science show SFX, aired nationally and broadcast weekly, Rebeka not only co-hosted, but also co-wrote and co-produced, creating programming from Aahs bureaus in Minneapolis and New Jersey. Arriving at Sesame Workshop in 1998, she began producing Takalani Sesame, a South African Sesame Street Radio series in four languages. Sesame Sounds, a unique collaboration between Sesame Workshop and XM Satellite Radio will be airing starting this fall on XM. Currently the Director of Audio Production, she's involved in all aspects of music, production, cd compilations and radio projects for Sesame Workshop. Rebeka is a graduate of Swarthmore College.

	**she kept dancing**	tanya shaffer ghana 1999

An invitation to stay with a woman's family in West Africa opens the door to more than her home

I hadn't noticed Brigitte until we pulled up to the curb in downtown Ouagadougou and she leaned over and tapped me on the shoulder. "If you don't have a place to stay during your visit," she said with breathless timidity, "you are welcome in my house."

I was used to sudden changes in plans and to West Africans' amazing, nearly overwhelming, hospitality. I'd just finished a six-month stint as a volunteer in Ghana and was on my way to Mali to visit a friend. I hadn't planned to stop in Burkina Faso's sprawling capital, but after two days and nights in a packed minivan, I needed a rest. My cream-colored t-shirt and olive skirt had turned road-dust gray, and my shorn hair—the only part of my body retaining any natural oils—was plastered to my scalp. Something odd was going on in my body, which for days had produced the sensation of sweating, though no actual moisture appeared. I felt like a kettle that rattles and shakes, but never quite manages to sing.

I stood guard over Brigitte's cloth-tied bundles while she used the phone box outside the upscale *Hôtel de l'Indépendance* to call her husband. Oceans of *motos* swerved around me; the air was thick with dust and exhaust. Brigitte was in her mid-twenties and had a plump figure and a perky, impish face with round, shiny cheeks and eyebrows that leapt and danced when she spoke. She had managed to stay astoundingly clean on the journey from Bobo, where she'd gone to visit her cousin. Her bright orange and green print dress still looked freshly pressed. A matching cloth wrapped her head.

"I'm bringing a friend home," I heard her say. She paused for emphasis, then added, "a *white* friend," her voice simmering with excitement.

An expensive taxi ride took us to the outskirts of town, to a neighborhood where solid cinderblock houses with clean-swept dirt yards alternated with vacant lots filled with rubble. She lived in one of the cinderblock rectangles with her husband—a mid-level customs official, their three children and two servant girls. In the open-air bathroom, a mud wall separated the neatly swept section where a board covered a hole in the

25

ground from the area where you carried your bucket of water to bathe. With a television, boom box, and telephone inside the house, it was a solid middle-class home.

It was love at first sight for me and little Rod, who stood shyly at the gate with her three middle fingers in her mouth, twisting her upper body back and forth as the taxi pulled up. As I swung my bulky pack out of the overhead rack, she was already at my side, and I swerved off-balance to avoid hitting her. When I flopped onto the couch in the tiny living room, she came and sat silently on my lap.

Rod was five years old and had silky skin, the color of fresh coffee grounds, kept creamy by her mother's daily applications of shea butter. Her small face was a perfect oval with grave, wideset eyes so dark you couldn't separate iris from pupil. She seldom spoke, but always stayed within a few steps of me, often slipping a hand into mine as I sat writing or talking in the yard.

"This one's too quiet," Brigitte said, holding Rod at arm's length and brushing dust off her pink skirt with a brusque hand. "Here comes the smart one." Her face lit up with a smile as a chubby two-year-old careened through the doorway while a stocky teenager followed a step behind. The older girl's clothes were oversized and shapeless, her feet bare.

"Lidia already speaks French, don't you?" Brigitte said to the little one. *"Tu parles français?"*

"Oui!" the baby shouted, and Brigitte laughed with delight. She barked a command at the teenager, who rushed out into the yard. "I've told her to get water for your bath," Brigitte told me. Brigitte and I spoke French, while she usually spoke to the children and servants in her native Mossi. She turned back to the crowing Lidia.

"This one," she said, smiling, "this is my girl."

Her son Constantin came home a few hours later, dragging a book bag behind him, his school uniform covered with mud.

"Tintin—Did you greet our guest?"

He slid to a halt in front of me, a nine-year-old bundle of kinetic energy; hands, knees, feet trembling to go.

"Pleased to meet you," he murmured, sneaking a glance from lowered eyes.

My pleasure," I said.

He flashed me a smile, dropped his bag in front of the couch, and took off running out the door and through the gate.

"Change your clothes," Brigitte called as he tore around the corner. "Did you see him? That one is bad," she said to me. "Bad."

26

I never met Brigitte's husband, who arrived home that night after we went to bed, and left early the next morning on a business trip. When I asked her about him, she simply shrugged her shoulders.

"He's not mean," she said.

That day Brigitte and I wandered together through le Grande Marché, an enormous market housed in a blocky cement building. "It used to be outside, the African way," Brigitte said, with disdain.

Brigitte wouldn't let me pay for anything, insisting on playing the perfect hostess. She bargained fiercely to get the price of a woven bracelet I wanted down from 65 cents to 40. When she began buying vegetables for lunch, I stopped her.

"Why don't we go to a restaurant?" I said. "I'll treat."

"Restaurant?" She looked hesitant.

"Come on," I said. "We passed one yesterday when we got off the bus."

Still skeptical, she followed me to *La Grotte,* a restaurant in the international section of town, close to the chichi *Hôtel de l'Indépendance.* Its white plastic tables were set up in a leafy garden, shaded by large umbrellas. Rotating fans provided a light breeze. The clientele was mostly white.

From the moment we entered, Brigitte grew quiet, looking around her with widened eyes. She sat with her hands in her lap, not picking up the menu the waiter placed in front of her.

"Don't you want to order?" I asked her.

She shook her head. "I'm not hungry," she said, her eyes flicking back and forth.

"Are you sure?" She nodded. "At least have a drink, okay?" She nodded again. "You can share my food," I added.

I ordered a chicken dish with *tô,* the staple of the area, a firm porridge made of cornmeal and water. When the waiter asked Brigitte her order, she mouthed, "Coca Cola."

"Excuse me?"

She cleared her throat, "Coca Cola."

"Why do you order this dish?" she asked me, when the waiter had gone.

"What do you mean?"

"This isn't your food."

"I'm in Africa. I want to eat African food."

She shook her head with incredulity. "This food is too plain. I wouldn't serve you this food."

She continued to shake her head as I paid the $5 bill.

"A bit of a splurge," I said. She was silent all the way home.

But sitting in the yard the next morning, Brigitte was full of plans.

"You will find me a job in your country," she said. "I can do anything. I can cook, I can clean. All kinds of African dishes. I worked for a German family; they were very content with my work." She paused, then continued. "You'll find me a family. They can send the plane ticket, then when I work, they don't pay me until it's paid for. They can get a visa for me."

"What about your children?" I asked.

"They'll stay with my mother," she said. "It's only two, three years. I'll make a lot of money, then I come back. I'll open a restaurant, my own, like the one yesterday. Cook African food; white people will come."

"And your husband?"

"He doesn't mind." She flipped her hand. "He's not mean. You will find me a job?"

"I don't think—"

"I know it's not sure."

"It's really not—"

"You will try?"

I shrugged helplessly. "I'll try."

"How did she get the name Rod?" I asked that evening over a dinner of savory chicken soup. Rod had pulled her chair as close to me as possible, so that our knees touched as we ate. Lidia, sat at a small table by herself, her face covered with food. Constantin had eaten quickly, and dashed off to play with his friends.

"A white man," said Rod, in perfect French.

I looked at her in surprise. Brigitte started to giggle.

"What white man?" I asked the little girl.

"Mama's boyfriend," she said, and went back to eating her soup.

"An American, named Rod," said Brigitte. "Peace corps. He wanted to marry me, but my mother said no. I was only seventeen, and I was scared. If it was now, I would go with him. I would go like that." She made a whisking motion with her hand.

"So you gave her his name? Your husband doesn't mind?"

She shrugged again, a bored expression crossing her face. "I told you..."

My voice joined hers, "He's not mean."

When I accepted Brigitte's invitation, I'd planned to stay two or three days. A week had gone by, and I was expecting my visa from the Malian embassy any day. As the time for my departure approached, my conversations with Brigitte developed an urgency, as though there weren't time for her to say everything she wanted to say before I left. I too had begun confiding in her, discussing my ambivalence about Michael, the boyfriend I'd left behind.

"You say you love him?" she inquired.

"Yes, yes I do. Very much."

"Then what again is the problem?"

"Well, it's like we're brother and sister. I thought my lover, my soul-mate, well, I thought it would feel different."

"How should it feel?" she asked.

"Oh, I don't know, exciting. Passionate," I paused for an instant. "Like travel. When I travel, I feel so *alive.* Every moment is charged. I guess I thought love would be more like that. You know, constant discovery."

Brigitte raised an eyebrow at me. "You are like a man," she said. "Always wanting something fresh."

"No, it's not that, it's just…" my voice trailed off.

"Just what?" she asked.

I shrugged helplessly.

She shook her head. "Just like a man."

Rod became more affectionate than ever, clinging to my hand, sitting on my lap, hanging onto my legs. I sat with her sometimes from afternoon through evening, stroking her hair, singing. Her presence brought up my own latent mothering instincts. I loved children, always had, the touch and feel and smell of them. They opened my heart in a way that nothing else could. There was a part of me that wanted children of my own, yearned for them with an ache so fierce it stopped my breath. Michael had wanted children too, had even tried to persuade me, on occasion, to play a little Russian roulette between the sheets.

"I can't do it, Michael," I'd said.

"Why not? You're great with children. Look at my nieces and nephews. They adore you."

"I know that."

"Well, then?"

"Because. I'm not ready. You know that. I have things to do. If I got pregnant now, I'd never forgive myself. Or the child."

Michael shuddered. "Don't say that," he said.

Now, with Rod on my lap, I was hard pressed to remember what it was I had to do that was so important. I wanted to squeeze her little body close to me, to bury my nose in her neatly braided hair. Perhaps what I'd said to Michael was wrong. Perhaps having children was exactly what I needed, the catalyst that would drag me, kicking and screaming, to the pool of my own happiness. But what a heavy expectation to place on a child.

One evening, I sat next to Brigitte on her bed while she worked the sleeping Lidia's hair into tight little braids. Rod had already been put down for the night.

"Lidia never lets me do this when she's awake," Brigitte explained.

I watched her fingers fly, dipping into oil, then sectioning, braiding, sectioning again.

"I don't love my husband," she said to me. "I used to love him, but now I don't. He goes with other women."

"How do you know?" I asked.

"I've seen the woman. My friend has pointed her out to me." She made a disgusted face. "It makes me sick. And he doesn't give me money."

I looked around. "How do you buy things?"

"Oh, he pays for food, you know. School things. But anything for me, my clothes, my hair, I have to get it for myself. He's giving it all to her. But he won't let me get a job. And he wants me to have more children." She pulled another face.

I watched her fingers, now layering the braids into overlapping arches.

"When I find someone else, I'm going to divorce him. I just have to find someone first. I don't want to go around, going on dates. A woman isn't safe that way. But I must hurry, before another baby comes. Can you find an American husband for me?"

"I can't even find one for myself," I joked.

"I want an old man," she said. "Young men are too complicated. I want one who'll appreciate me. I'll give you a picture of me to give him and he can send a picture, and if we like each other, then he'll send me the plane ticket and I'll come."

I pointed out that the visa might still be a problem.

"He'll get it for me," she said. "If he's hot, he'll do it." She took her hands from Lidia's hair, and ran her palms up and down the sides of her body, across her breasts, her arms, her thighs. She closed her eyes. "An old man, who'll treat me well."

I said nothing. After a moment, she opened her eyes, and went back to her hair sculpture. Lidia startled for a moment, opened her eyes and whimpered. Then, seeing her mother, she closed them again, drifted back to sleep.

"What about Lidia and Rod?" I asked. "What will they do if you go to the U.S. and marry some old fart?"

She shrugged impatiently. "Their father will take them. I'll send money. It will be better for them."

I looked down at the sleeping baby. "If I...If I had children like yours," I said, "I could never leave them."

Anger crossed Brigitte's face, and I was immediately alert to my own hypocrisy. Who was I to scold her? I had no children, and I was hardly a poster-child for stability.

"They'll be okay," she said.

We sat in silence. Her hands, on Lidia's head, lay still.

"In your city, will you show me around?" she asked me later that night, as we lay side by side on her white-sheeted bed, under the gauzy canopy of the mosquito net.

"Of course," I said, eager to reestablish our intimacy. "We'll go dancing together, go shopping, to the movies."

"Oh yes," she said, "yes, that's it. I'll be in the movies. That's the way to make money."

I laughed, and she turned her head sharply toward me.

"That's not so easy," I said.

"Oh, but I can do it!" she said, and in the dark, I could feel the motion as her hands stroked the sides of her body, her head thrown back. "I can do the movies like that, the love scenes…I know how to do it." She stopped abruptly. "Of course, if I had a husband, he wouldn't let me. On my own, I could make some money."

"Your husband probably wouldn't stop you. In the U.S., it's normal for women to work. Most women work."

"Oh yes?" she said. "Good."

When I got back from the Malian embassy the next afternoon, passport and visa in hand, I found Brigitte in the smoke-filled kitchen, waving a large stick at the teenage servant girl, who cowered in fear.

"She's *bête!*" she shrieked, when she saw me, using the French word that means both "stupid" and "beast."

"What? What happened?"

"*Bête!* I had some mayonnaise, did you see the mayonnaise? I bought it—it was supposed to last until Easter—and yesterday, they served it *all* to the people that were here. *All* of it. *Il faut economiser.* I don't earn the money here, it's my husband who earns the money. What's he going to say? Stupid beast!" She held the stick above her head, her face livid. The girl, huddled in the corner, began sobbing. My eyes teared in the heavy smoke.

Behind Brigitte, Constantin appeared in the doorway, a guilty smile on his face. Afraid his presence would further escalate things, I gestured with my head, and he scampered off. I approached Brigitte slowly, holding out my hand for the stick.

"Everyone makes mistakes," I said.

31

"The same stupid mistakes, again and again."

"We all make mistakes," I said again. "I'll buy you some more mayonnaise."

The look Brigitte gave me was unreadable. In the corner, the girl wailed. Out in the courtyard, I heard Constantin laughing. Slowly, Brigitte lowered the stick.

At eleven o'clock that night, Brigitte and I sat on the couch in the living room, drinking beer. It was my goodbye party. Brigitte got up, went to the tape recorder, and put in a tape, a funky, bluesy groove. She pulled me up off the couch, and we started to dance. After about twenty minutes, I collapsed back onto the couch, my head swimming from the heat. Brigitte kept dancing, her eyes closed. I stared at her, mesmerized by the extreme grace of her bulky frame. Her hips seemed to move independently of her upper body, which hovered above them, regal and still. Her behind taunted the beat, tantalized it, waiting till the last possible instant, till I thought she wouldn't make it, couldn't, then it snapped into place, twitching and popping like corn in hot oil.

Over the rhythmic thump of the music, I heard Rod's voice coming from the bedroom, soft and plaintive. "Mama. Mama. Mama. Mama."

I longed to go to her, ached for it, in fact, but what good would that do either of us? Tomorrow I'd be gone, and besides, she wasn't mine. I don't know whether Brigitte heard her or not. She just kept dancing.

Tanya Shaffer is a San Francisco-based writer, actress, solo performer and travel-head, who combines all her favorite things by creating performances based on her travels. She has toured over forty cities in the U.S. and Canada with her solo show "Miss America's Daughters" and her play "Brigadista." Her most recent solo show, "Let My Enemy Live Long!" based on her journey up the Niger River to Timbuktu, won a Bay Area Theatre Critics Circle Award for Solo Performance and is now touring the regional theatre Circuit. She was a frequent contributor to the sadly extinct Wanderlust section of Salon.com, and her stories have appeared in numerous travel anthologies. She has just completed her first book, Somebody's Heart is Burning: Tales of a Woman Wanderer in Africa. Visit her online at http://www.TanyaShaffer.com.

|  | **anyone for goat?** | kate waddecar
namibia
2000 |

Food for thought

Thirty kilometers south of the border with Angola lies the small Namibian village of Otjorute. Comprised of little more than a cluster of wooden huts, a single dirt track and a football pitch, Otjorute is home to some of the traditional Himba tribe, whose pastoral people live in the far northwestern regions of the country. It was here that I found myself after a long and dusty journey in an open sided truck, about to embark on the second phase of a school building project.

I had spent the previous month in southern Namibia on a black rhino game reserve near the Hardap Dam, where I had endured several uncomfortable nights in freezing temperatures, my sleeping bag proving to be not quite the cosy snooze it had promised. Much to my delight (and relief) the warmer climate of the north allowed us the opportunity to sleep under the stars with just our mosquito nets providing protection from unwelcome scorpion intrusions.

33

Half a dozen skilled local villagers had joined our not entirely able, amateur bricklayer team as part of the 'Food for Work' scheme. Following a brief lesson on the basics of mortar mixing and block laying from the civil engineer who was the guiding force behind the project, we set to work constructing the walls of the new village school. We had a constant crowd of observers who spent most of their time engaged in hysterical laughter at our building efforts.

With temperatures nearing 40 degrees C at midday, we began our work early each morning and continued until sunset, spending the hottest two hours of the day lazing in the shade. These two hours were important for recharging our batteries to ensure we had the required reserves of energy needed for the daily cow chases (lunch time being the preferred slot for passing cows to steal various items of clothing hung from nearby trees) and for the weekly soccer match against the local squad.

The 'Otjorute Eleven' were a selection of the finest athletes from the village. They waited on the pitch (a string of drink cans between two posts marking the goals) for the arrival of our team who, despite being covered in cement from a busy day's bricklaying, were eager to play the big match. Team talks beforehand from our captain had suggested that we go easy on the tackles as we were equipped with footwear, compared to our opposition who were barefoot. Five minutes into the game and sporting heavily bruised and battered shins, the cry came from our captain to ignore all pre-match tactics and give as good as we got. Shoes or no shoes, these boys were good.

The weekly football matches were enjoyed by the whole village and together with some other amusing incidents during the three weeks, ensured friendships were formed and knowing smiles exchanged. One such incident occurred just after lunch in the second week of building. Balanced on an 'A' frame high up the far wall, my spirit level and I were engrossed in some serious brick straightening, when screams and shouts from the gathered crowd below grabbed my attention. Peering over the wall, I saw several villagers leaping around in alarm, hurtling rocks at a pile of rubble. Climbing down from my platform, I soon caught sight of the cause of the excitement; a large brown snake was weaving frantically between the bricks, trying desperately to dodge the cascade of heavy objects being thrown in his direction. His attempts to escape, however, proved futile as a large block, accurately dropped from a great height, squashed him flat. Somewhat distressed by this over-the-top display of snake killing, I sought an explanation from our English speaking Namibian builder. He told me that this was not an unusual reaction by people who were living in such a remote part of the country. Their chances of ever reaching a hospital in time to treat snakebite were so remote that killing any potentially poisonous snake was preferable to the risk of getting bitten. Until then, I hadn't fully appreciated the back-up support option I had to be airlifted to the nearest hospital should anything similar occur whilst I was working there. The villagers' rock throwing, however elaborate it had first appeared, suddenly made a whole lot more sense.

That same evening saw the highlight of the week for many of us: a barbecue with some of our fellow builders and their families. The get-together had been organized last minute (which posed no problem for our social calendars, what with night life being fairly quiet after sunset) following the news earlier in the day that the village chief was to present us with a gift as a 'thank you' for their new school.

The gift took the form of a goat and we were asked to select our preferred beast from the local herd. Once chosen, it was decided that the poor creature be tethered to a tree in our camp so as not to escape whilst we carried on working. His bleats and whimpers during lunch made me slightly uncomfortable about his imminent slaughter, but, determined to stick to my belief that eating a goat was morally the same as eating a beef burger back home, I did my best to ignore his cries. I did, however, air my feelings later in the day when the time came to kill the goat and the debate arose over who should perform the act. A few of the lads in our group had taken the whole slaughter idea a bit too far and their bloodthirsty desires to take a machete to the goat's neck and delight in his death was too much. Instead, it was decided that two of the more experienced local men should carry out the killing and the boys would have to be content with a ringside seat. Me? I headed for the village cattle trough for my weekly wash.

It wasn't so much the actual eating of the goat (which, incidentally would not be my first choice on the menu) that made for the great evening I experienced. It was more the spirit in which it had been given to us and the way it had brought us all together. Granted, had this been your average barbecue, I may have heard shouts of "Chuck us another shrimp on the Barbie, mate." But, as the last month and a half in this country had taught me, there ain't nothing average about Africa.

Kate Waddecar was born in Lancashire in 1976 and grew up in Leyland. After graduating in 1997 with a degree in Social Ethics from Lancaster University, she moved to London to study at Brunel University and start a career in Youth and Community Work. She had her first taste of Africa in the summer of 2000 when she spent three months in Namibia on a Raleigh International expedition. Currently working for a leading HIV prevention charity in London, she plans to return to Africa to clock up some more adventures and hopefully write a little along the way.

	**us dollar is king**	peter ward mauritius 1997

The island of Mauritius is in the middle of nowhere, on the way to nowhere. Not many people have heard about the place. So when a good friend of mine who lives in London, works in London, and has even been known to take his vacation in parts of London, said he was going to get married on this island, I was surprised. I was even more surprised that he wanted me to be his best man; after all he does have other friends!

Mauritius is a small island in the Indian Ocean, off the southeast shoreline of Africa and has the typical history of most of Africa. It was first occupied by the Portuguese, then the French, who lost it to the British who gave it independence in the 1960's. Since independence its similarity with the rest of Africa stopped, as things remained pretty peaceful. In fact Mauritius is often cited as an example of racial harmony.

My friend, his wife to be, his father, and a few friends were staying in one of those exclusive hotels on the beach with an army of security guards patrolling the grounds to keep out any local nuisances - or even the locals themselves. Even though I was not staying in this hotel, I could walk in and out freely because of my dress code. The whiter than white look, which after 20 minutes in the sun turns to traffic light red, after a week looked touristy bronze. If this tried and tested passport into any hotel complex ever happens not to work, then a backup approach is to attempt to speak the local language (French), or order American champagne (Pepsi) at the bar. Then they know you are a tourist.

I was traveling my usual way, not booking a hotel, not knowing exactly which city I would be staying in or even bothering to exchange US dollars into the local currency. The only preparation I did was to buy a Lonely Planet book on the way to the airport back in New York. This is my idea of travel: adventure, surprise and a good story at the end of the trip.

When traveling abroad, I am a firm believer in staying in a town where the locals live and do their day-to-day activity, someplace where the culture can be absorbed, as opposed to a tourist resort that is an imitation of reality. I can stay in America and go to Disney for that!

After arriving at the airport, I got a taxi to the Capital - Port Louis - and decided to check in at the cheapest hotel in the Lonely Planet book. At the hotel, there were the mandatory negotiations at the check in desk.

Confusion ensued, as the owner claimed he spoke no English, just French and tried to price the rooms to me by the hour (not by the day) and had one of the most adverse exchange rates to the US dollar I've ever come across. I was amazed, I had made an impression with the owner on our first interaction and was even more amazed that he knew the names of most of the Yankee baseball players. He must have been reading or listening to English somewhere on the island, even if he claimed not to understand what I am saying to him. Maybe this was his negotiating tactic.

On walking up the stairs to my room, I did wonder why he was trying to charge me for the room by the hour. I felt this was the confusing French mentality, which I could never quite understand and felt that anyone who claims they are able to, doesn't really know what they are talking about. On opening the door to my room, I could see why it was an hourly rate. The hotel was a knocking shop and most of the people staying in the hotel were prostitutes.

The room was very bare, clean sheets, naked light bulb, working showers, cold water of course and a view of the sea if you stood on tiptoe. I was happy because of the price I paid. There are a lot of hours in a week, so that equates to a good bulk discount, coupled off with US dollars over local currency purchasing.

That evening I had dinner with my friends in the hotel and I was telling them of the day's little adventures. They were completely astonished that I paid for my taxi and dinner in US dollars.

They had guidebooks, learned a few local words, and exchanged their British pounds into wheelbarrows of local currency. I am originally from London and had been living in New York for nine months and they felt I had become very Americanized in my attitude. I explained to them that, after spending a considerable amount of time in Southern Africa, Central Africa and Central America, I had learned that typically, the locals prefer payment in a hard currency, like dollars. That is because this form of monetary payment holds its value over time. I explained this belief of mine to them and they dismissed it as being too American for this developed country. 'This is Mauritius, not Mexico,' one of them said.

For the next couple of days we all enjoyed the sights of the National Park, the beaches and the hotel poolside with quantities of large tropical drinks with plenty of tiny umbrellas. As I wasn't staying in the hotel complex, I explored the local area, attempting to have conversations with restaurant owners and people you repeatedly meet within your stay at a place.

On one of the evenings before the wedding, it was decided that the men would have a 'guys night out,' so I suggested we all meet at a dubious night club next to my hotel, called 'No. Ones.' The reason why I thought this place was dubious was that it had no windows, unheard of for a bar next to the beach. There were 4 bouncers outside screening people as they went into the club. This is Mauritius, not Manhattan! I had made previous plans to meet a French guy who was staying at my hotel, so it made things convenient for me.

On entering the club, you could feel the thumping of the garage style music. I quickly found the French guy, who did seem quite interesting, but it was difficult to hear a word he was saying, as the music was so loud we mutually decided to wait until breakfast at the hotel to continue our conversation, and just people watch for the time being.

I soon noticed my friends entering the club and they joined me at the bar.

No. One's attracts an eclectic mix of clubbers, ranging from brave trendy tourists venturing away from the hotel bar, house diva wannabes, local muscle-boys kitted up in jewelry from finger to tooth and the token white guys like myself, glaring at the scene. The girl groupies seemed to be serious as cancer about good music and the DJs who spin it. The candle-lit, torn leather-lined booths definitely gave this place a sense of intimacy, but the abundant pools of darkness gave it an eeriness as well.

After 45 minutes of people watching, it became clear that the house diva wannabes were prostitutes and the local muscle-boys were their pimps. I recognized them from the hotel. I was trying to avoid eye contact with them, as they knew where I was staying. I pointed this local tit- bit of information out to one of my friends from London who I knew was prone to using these ladies of the night. He was delighted to have discovered this local hot spot and immediately engaged in conversation with some of them. He soon left the premises. Not alone.

Some time later, the French guy and I decided to call it a night and return to our hotel rooms. I then got a sharp tap on the shoulder, turned around and to my surprise it was my friend who had left some time ago.

He wanted to know if I had any US dollars, as he would get a better exchange rate on the service than using the local currency!

See back cover for **Peter Ward's** biography.

 **sao tome**	miles bredin sao tome 1992

The African paradise

There can be few better places to which to evacuate than Sao Tome. We landed on a Hong Kong-style runway in the sea and stepped from the industrial bowels of the aircraft into bright sunshine.

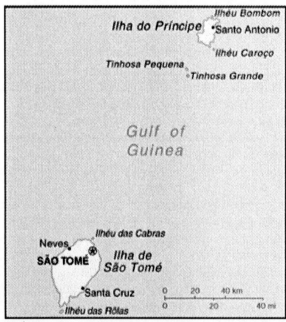

Insects and birds chirruped and squawked against a background of total quiet which you seldom experience in the west -no buzzing of electric wires, no motorway noise -just stillness. It was the first time we had heard it since we had arrived in Africa two months earlier, and it had an immediate therapeutic effect. Unconcerned by the absence of a car to take us from the airport, we slipped straight into the rhythm of the island and sat.

From the airport's empty car park you could see the high peaks of the island dressed in ruffs of cloud, a pristine beach that lines a deserted bay and the brazenly picturesque town of Sao Tome. In an overgrown field by the airport stood the rotting remains of some CanadAid Constellations that had been used to transport food to the starving of Biafra thirty years earlier.

Perched on the headland is the perfectly preserved fort that used to house the Portuguese governor. Sao Tome is littered with the remains of ancient civilizations, which betray its past as a pivotal economy. It is now slowly and peacefully returning to bush.

In the sixteenth century, it was the world's biggest sugar producer and a vital sorting point for slaves. The mainland slaving capital Ouidah (of Viceroy fame) was an enclave of (and used to be administered) from Sao Tome until 1961. The islands faded into obscurity when the West Indies took over sugar production and then in the nineteenth century returned to the world stage as an important coffee producer. Now its 120,000 citizens are among the world's poorest people and produce virtually nothing. High up in the mountains, clapboard plantation houses crumble. They look down on disorderly ranks of coffee bushes that are being pushed back by the counterattacking rainforest.

The volcanic islands of Sao Tome and neighboring Principe, which together form a country, were founded in the 1470's but were not exploited immediately. The mountains are uncommonly tall for the small area of land, which they crown. This gives the islands a mad but pleasant climate, where one bay will be bathed in sunshine while the next one is being soaked with fresh warm rain. They can be humid and wet yet they can also be blisteringly hot. Subject to extreme microclimates, none of the weather lasts for very long.

Sao Tome is so tiny that it was once fined by FIFA for not sending a team to a World Cup qualifying match. The government refused to pay the fine since no one had told them they were meant to and, anyway, they had neither a football team nor a pitch. Ambassadors ride mopeds in Sao Tome, and their accessibility meant that getting visas for Gabon (the only access point to mainland Africa) was not a problem. Leaving paradise, however, was.

Printed with permission: Blood on the Tracks: A Rail Journey from Angola to Mozambique (1992). By Miles Bredin.

Miles Bredin was born in London in 1965. Before becoming a journalist he was an antique lace restorer and a mini cab driver. He has written for most British nationals and spent two years at the Evening Standard, where he was briefly shopping editor of ES Magazine. From 1990 to 1992 he was the fast failing United Press International's last East Africa bureau chief. He wrote the book Blood on the Tracks: A Rail Journey from Angola to Mozambique. His latest book is The Pale Abyssinian: A life of James Bruce (HarperCollins) and is currently writing a novel at his home in East Africa.

	**the day electricity comes to gatsi**	peter ward zimbabwe 1996

The people now have the power, right?

The Honde Valley in Zimbabwe is relatively unknown for anything other than bird watching and its tea factory, but tucked away is the sleepy village Gatsi. Not much happens here; there's a cult where people worship a flag and when you enter their premises you are asked to remove your shoes. Recommended that you hold onto the Reeboks.

I'd spent some time in the village and had built up a relationship with Nathaniel, the owner of a local store. This store was in a prime location as it was on the main road through the village and Nathaniel was very proud of his achievements as a businessman. He had the biggest store in the village, which stocked more items than any other store. He had his fingers in almost every activity in the village whether this was sugar cane farming, selling chickens or buying second hand clothes', if there was money to be made, he'd be interested in having a conversation.

The village had no running water, or electricity; however, intuitive souls were known to be watching television with the use of a car battery.

Nathaniel was his usual upbeat self and explained that in 2 years, electricity would be piped into the village on a grid system, so everyone could have this modern feature if they wanted. He also pondered its potential impact to the community. He went on to say that when people started watching TV, particularly the soaps, they believed there was some reality to them, and when young girls left school, they left the village and headed to the capital Harare, for the bright lights and modern life style.

This would explain why, when I was working in the local school, I was asked by so many of the girls the details of city life; "do you have a car? Where do you shop and live?"

This new way of being had its implications in the village. There was a growing imbalance in the sexes of young people and for a guy to meet a girl was becoming difficult. As children grow up they normally look after their parents while they enjoy retirement, but this was going to be difficult with the children living in a different part of the country. In the village the main

42

form of employment was working on the farms or tea plantations, not the glamour jobs of retail, tourism, or media.

Nathaniel seemed to think it'd be great when electricity arrived, as people would stay up later and watch more TV. Currently by 8:00pm the main road in the village is empty, as most people are in bed. The upside to this is that people get up when the sun rises at 5:30am, and by 6:00am there's a constant milling of people around the village doing their daily business or going to work, so there is plenty of time in the day for activities.

This is in contrast to the West, where most city centers are beginning to get busy by 8:00pm, and people go around their business until late at night, and need electric alarm clocks to wake then up in the morning.

I wasn't sure if Nathaniel had been watching too much TV himself, as he'd soon realize that people just go to bed later and get up later (and pay for this privilege!) I'm not saying there aren't benefits to having electricity, but just because the big cities or a modern country have a lifestyle that appears to be great on television doesn't mean it's going to be great in a different part of the world.

The 'rural to urban' migration is not unique to Africa. I've been living in New York for the past 5 years and see this all the time. Almost a third of NY residents are from foreign descent and in the last 10 years over a million Non-Americans have arrived in the city, all wanting to make a new life and to better themselves. This figure includes me. New York City attracts 100,000 new immigrants a year from outside America and I'm one of them.

The figure stated above doesn't include US citizens who are moving to New York, attracted by the bright lights to a perceived life style. Of course New York being a truly *International city, 'rural to urban' migration affect is somewhat on a larger scale.

The new arrivals are still attracted to NY by what they see on television, and believe the life style portrayed is realistic. How it's possible to live a few blocks from Central Park and be a massage therapist called Phoebe, I'm not quite sure, and having such a cohesive group of friends who frequently gather at each other's apartments and share sofa space at the Central Perk Coffeehouse is also rare.

The 'rural to urban' from the America's suburbia may seem a world away from Gatsi, but the unfulfilled expectations of the young people in city life is very similar.

New York, the city known as America's socialite cutting edge is of course a modern city, but there's a price to pay- the workdays are long, it's difficult to make friends so there's a sense of isolation, the cost of living is expensive with people living from paycheck to paycheck (or more likely credit card to credit card). Divorce is high, with over 50% of marriages ending this way. To top it all off, the media portrays a completely different lifestyle to add to the sense of failure!

Gatsi may appear primitive from the outside, but it's not too advanced for its own good. I wonder how life turns out.

*International City: In my opinion and this is my opinion, there are only two truly international cities in the world, New York and London. When I say international, I mean they do have ethic minorities from around the world, creating their own restaurants and sub cultures within these cities. They also have characteristics that are internationally recognized:

New York: Empire State Building, Time Square, Brooklyn Bridge, yellow taxicabs.

London: Big Ben, Buckingham Palace, fish and chips, black taxicabs, red double decker buses.

LA, Paris, Tokyo, San Francisco and Hong Kong, do not have these perceptions. Try to name five buildings in Tokyo that people in another continent have heard of, show me a view in LA that is used for global advertising of products that is recognized as LA.

Since living in NY, I sometimes think that you don't need to travel to see the world, as the whole world comes to New York.

See back cover for **Peter Ward's** biography.

	gabon	miles bredin gabon 1992

Not cheap

Arriving in Libreville brought us down to earth with a sickening jolt. X-ray and baggage-weighing machines adorned the hi-tech airport, which could have been a satellite of Paris's Charles de Gaulle. In the bank at the airport they had a swipe machine, which refused my credit card, leaving us penniless in the third most expensive city in the world. The *Sunday Times Magazine* had not paid back our expenses, which caused us problems for the rest of the trip. Instead of having thousands of dollars in cash with which to oil our way round Africa, we were left with a bouncing credit card and a British cheque book.

We checked into a sordid hotel on the beach -the cheapest we could find at $150 a night -and set off to find some cash. Gabon -a former French colony -has an economy based on oil. It is peaceful and allows foreign companies to exploit its resources with little government interference in return for a share of the cake. This has led to a situation in which shops in Gabon look the same as French supermarkets -except for the prices, which are astronomical. You can get foie gras, smoked salmon and vintage champagne with ease, but it's best to organize a mortgage beforehand. I could not afford to eat in the doubtless excellent restaurants so I decided to have a meagre picnic -it cost $70. During the four days in Gabon I spent the majority of my time drinking bottled water at $8 a go on the beach. Having bought Zairean visas on our first day, it was the cheapest place to sit and wait for the plane.

Printed with permission: Blood on the Tracks: A Rail Journey from Angola to Mozambique (1992). By Miles Bredin

See page 41, for biography of **Miles Bredin**.

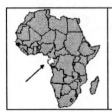	**water**	rachel schneller mali 1996

When a woman carries water on her head, you see her neck bend outward behind her like a crossbow. Ten liters of water weighs twenty-two pounds, a fifth of a woman's body weight, and I've seen women carry at least twenty liters in aluminum pots large enough to hold a television set.

To get the water from the cement floor surrounding the outdoor hand pump to the top of your head, you need help from the other women. You and another woman grab the pot's edges and lift it straight up between you. When you get it to the head height, you duck underneath the pot and place it on the wad of rolled-up cloth you always wear when fetching water. This is the cushion between your skull and the metal pot full of water. Then your friend lets go. You spend a few seconds finding your balance. Then with one hand steadying the load, turn around and start your way home. It might be a twenty-minute walk through mud huts and donkey manure. All of this, without words.

It is an action repeated so many times during the day that even though I have never carried water on my head, I know exactly how it is done.

Do not worry that no one will be at the pump to help you. The pump is the only source of clean drinking water for the village of three thousand people. Your family, your husband and children rely on the water on your head; maybe ten people will drink the water you carry. Pump water, everyone knows, is clean. Drinking well water will make you sick. Every month, people here die from diarrhea and dehydration. The pump is also where you hear gossip from the women who live on the other side of the village. Your trip to the pump may be your only excuse for going outside of your family's Muslim home alone.

When a woman finds her balance under forty pounds of water, I see her eyes roll to the corners in concentration. Her head makes the small movements of the hands of someone driving a car: constant correction. The biggest challenge is to turn all the way around from the pump to go home again. It is a small portion of the ocean, and it swirls and lurches on her head with long movements.

It looks painful and complicated and horrible for the posture and unhealthy for the vertebrae, but I wish I could do it. I have lived in this West African village for two years, but cannot even balance something solid, like a mango on my head, let alone a pot filled with liquid. When I lug my ten liter plastic jug of water to my house by hand, it is only a hundred meters, but the container is heavy and unwieldy. Changing the jug from one hand to the other helps, but it is a change necessary every twenty meters. Handles do not balance. On your head, the water is symmetrical like the star on top of a Christmas tree. Because my life has never depended on it, I have never learned to balance.

A native Montanan and graduate of the University of Montana creative writing program, **Rachel Schneller** served as a Peace Corps Volunteer in Mali from 1996 to 1998.

misadventure

This can be known as getting carried away with an idea, or perhaps when the gods are not on your side. That is normally accompanied by alcohol, over ambitious plans and the misunderstanding of local customs.

This is nothing new in the world of misadventures. It happens to the best of us:

- Hannibal, of Carthage on the north shore of Africa. He was the chap who crossed the Alps with elephants and gave the Romans trouble for a while (The second Punic War 218-201 BC). He ended up suffering a crushing defeat and having to accept humiliating peace terms including ceding all of his Spanish possessions to Rome. Unfortunately most people are only aware of his early success and not of his final failure.
- In May 1999, the Libyan peacekeeping forces arrived in Uganda with the intent keeping the peace between the Ugandan forces and forces loyal to DRC President Laurent Kabila. The problem was that no one asked them to do this!
- The Scottish missionary and explorer, Dr. David Livingstone, who was missing in East Africa for years, without realizing it! He was found by Stanley in 1871.
- The United Nations and USA deciding that it was going to run Somalia, even though Hussein Mohammed Aidid (an ex-U.S. Marine) had been elected by the Somali Congress with 66 percent of the vote. Naturally, he declared war on the United Nations and the United States. United Nations and US troops killed between 8,000 and 10,000 Somalis while in the country - That's peace keeping! Source: The World's Most Dangerous Places.

The list is endless.

	**a night in beira**	chris ashworth mozambique 1996

Welcome to the Hotel California

Our journey to Beira proved rather swift—after we were checked out by the local police officers to see if our papers were in order. It was the first time I'd ever had my passport checked one hundred miles from the nearest border! The language problem came close to causing an incident as the officer was looking at a transit visa in our passports from the month prior. We were not too far from being expelled. That is, until she turned the page of the passport.

Feeling that she'd unnecessarily given us a hard time, she started waving down cars to get us a lift, which proved extremely successful. The chaps we got a lift from were racing down to the airport so we had a very speedy journey indeed.

Considering my journey into Zimbabwe, I had expectations for this country. In Zimbabwe, my ready-formed expectations had proved wholly wrong, based as they were on press reports and nature programs—not the greatest sources of influence. For Mozambique I expected a place similar to Zambia. The ravages of twenty years of civil war made it a rather different country. The poverty was greater, quite visibly so in the center of Beira. There was also a certain sense of lost majesty, with the ruined shells of once great buildings, stylish hotels, and the poignantly-holed and rusting ships at port.

We arrived at an area on the outskirts of the city. Referring to an ever-useful guidebook, we found a campsite—one that felt like a junkyard as we entered. A couple of workers were doing some metal work in a ramshackle shed. Not wholly convinced we had made the best choice, we checked in—my friends in one of the buildings, which was single-floored with four rooms, and I in an African-style hut, that, only after the mandatory negotiation and deal-making.

There was one other traveler staying the night. Originally from the Netherlands, he had been teaching in Mozambique for some time. There had been a lot of fighting in the area where he taught. Some of the children were staying at the school overnight. A friend from the government army was visiting him one evening, when gunfire pierced the background. After a panicked conversation regarding the children's safety, the kids fled the school to hide. The officer didn't know what was going on in that area and was about to make some calls when more shooting erupted. The gunfire went on for quite some time. It finally transpired that this wasn't the anti government forces coming to take the city, but the returning government forces, jubilant after a victory over rebel extremists, firing their weapons in the air.

The next morning, the Netherlands chap left, leaving my friends and me as the only guests. That day, a major topic of conversation was that there seemed to be a lot of coming and going in the other rooms of the building. Also, we were struck by some of the pretty girls working at the site, with their makeup and attractive clothes. That seemed a little odd, considering the location. Nonetheless, our thinking shifted to other matters, and we left to explore Biera.

Perhaps the building that struck me most in the city was an old, grand hotel. It would have been the best in the area, as it was only a short walk from the beach. We went in to investigate. The building seemed almost Victorian with its ancient wallpaper, seats, brass fittings and browned windows. The electricity had obviously been lost either by choice to cut costs, or more likely, as the country's infrastructure had collapsed. This old hotel particularly represented the decline of the country and it evoked a very odd feeling of nostalgia. It was unusual to watch people at work in this powerless relic from another age.

I was astounded by the generosity of the people I met. In the evening, we found a seafood hut by the beach where a couple of locals bought dinner for us. The reason for this commendation is that it is too easy to misread the "bought" as "brought", implying that they were our waiters, rather than our benefactors. I couldn't imagine a random encounter of that kind in Britain, in spite of all its wealth. But this had certainly not been the first time I'd experienced this in the poorest areas of Africa.

After a few days, it was time to move on, and after a few evenings of curious comings and goings in the other rooms, the explanation for the pretty girls was finally revealed. A shift system was displayed on a notice board: "Guests by the Hour."

We'd been staying in a knocking shop for the last three days!

Chris Ashworth currently lives Reading, the unfashionable part of South West London's urban sprawl. His passport boasts stamps from many countries and he has an adventure to match each stamp. Having traveled large areas of the warm climates of the world throughout the Mediterranean, Africa and Asia, it's starting to look like he'll soon have to bite the bullet and visit Siberia for variety.

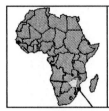	**african iron age**	mark igoe zimbabwe 1993

All in a day's work

I wonder what odds Ladbrooks - the - betting shop would give against being accused of setting light to a golf course, of making pornographic movies and of trying to blow up the Queen all in one week? All false, by the way, and if this story sounds as though it should have happened to the fictional character Flashman, rather than to me, I can only say that I wish that it had. And it was not Flashman's infamous lust, but lure of the little screen that was to blame.

I once found myself helping in the production of a TV series on Zimbabwe in my capacity of Old Africa Hand, student of the African Iron Age and writer of travel guides. Off we went in a Toyota truck painted like a giraffe. The director was from London, not too familiar with Africa but with enough self-confidence to make up for it. We had two white cameramen; two black soundmen; and an irrepressible driver-cum-Mr. Fixit called Aaron. We filmed rhino dehorning, leopards drinking, giraffe capturing, scouts patrolling and all the things you would expect of a good conservation series. I acted as continuity person and consultant on history, geography, flora, fauna, bars, booze and local hangover cures, one of which consists of putting you on a drip.

Eventually we came to the beautiful eastern mountains, which are full of great tourist spots and Iron Age sites, and were my specialty. We started at the famous Troutbeck Inn, which lies in a pine covered valley at seven thousand feet. This gracious demi-centenarian mainstay of the Nyanga district is fronted by a trout lake and surrounded by a golf course; it is more like Scotland than Africa, with weather often as wet, but thankfully warmer. We filmed golfers grinding teeth as they knocked balls into the lake and I subconsciously registered a sound-man flicking a cigarette into the long grass, the significance of which didn't strike me until we met a fire engine on our way back to the hotel. We denied the accusations of a skeptical hotel management but it was a harbinger of things to come.

We had worked together for some months and that night, the strain began to tell. Everybody had a complaint, the most delicate being that of the soundmen. Could the director be persuaded not to break wind so much in public? He did so to establish his plebeian credentials with them and Africa in general, being ignorant of the opprobrium in which most African society holds the practice. Delicate also was the problem of selecting actors for our Iron Age reconstruction. What sort of clothes would they have worn, the director had asked me. Very little, I replied, the Nyanga Culture being materially poor. So we got some leather kilts. "We'll get some women," announced the director. I doubted that the local ladies would be prepared for that sort of frolic. "But this is Africa!" he objected. It soon became clear that the only ladies who were going to help were those of the night.

Now he said, "Let's go down to the village and get some whores."

"You go," said I. And he did. He paid a retainer to eight girls, and with breathtaking and Machiavellian logistics, ensured that I was the one who had to be there at daybreak to make the final selection. I chose two and scuttled back to the ruined fort where the cameramen did an excellent job of creating topless phantoms grinding millet.

Scene two, take one: Nyanga Police Station. The director is groveling to the large Inspector. The inspector's problem is that last week the Harare Herald carried a story about foreigners making bestiality film with local actors, the wicked, degenerate West corrupting innocent Zimbabwean womanhood. And the innocent Zimbabwean womanhood whom I had not employed that morning had gone straight round to the cop shop to complain. The Inspector was not into the African Iron Age and the director calling him "Sir" only made him more suspicious.

As expensive time passed, I took a gamble and asked him to ring a government minister with whom I had shared quite a lot of beer. It took the best part of the day to track him down but eventually he came on the telephone, and the Inspector explained the situation. "This is all a huge misunderstanding," I whined, "We were just asking the women to grind…no, no, like they do traditionally; what's so funny?" When he had stopped laughing, he asked to speak to the policeman and we were released on the understanding that we left the district next day. And we did.

Which was not what I had envisaged. I dearly wanted to record the secrets of these ancient hills for an international audience. We went to Mutare, the provincial capital to the south, and probably the most attractive city in Africa, only to find it covered in unseasonable cloud. We took a few disappointing shots and moved on south again to the spectacular Chimanimani Mountains. In my fantasizing I had visualized filming this border range from the air. Its lakes, gorges, forests and waterfalls would make stunning aerial photography. There was no time, let alone a budget for such things and anyway, the cloud was down here too. We set off for the

World Heritage Site of Great Zimbabwe, pivotal point of the production, sustaining a puncture on the way.

Big Zed is the largest of about a hundred similar ruins scattered over Zimbabwe and its neighboring territories. It was occupied between the thirteenth and sixteenth centuries and although the work of Zimbabweans, still poses some questions. Its huge walls have attracted absurd and romantic theories over the years; its creepy ambiance, especially at dawn, explains why. I was looking forward to trying to capture something of that. We checked into the site hotel only to be told that our booking were canceled because the Queen was visiting next day.

"The Queen of…Sheba?" somebody suggested facetiously.

"Of Britain."

"Of The United Kingdom of Great Britain and Northern Ireland?"

"That is the one."

We had one night, again we would have to move on. How we hadn't heard of this event, or why the hotel had accepted the reservation in the first place, remained a mystery. We drowned our sorrows.

Next day we loaded up the truck, only to find another tire punctured. The spare was now also flat. Aaron took both wheels into the neighboring town of Masvingo and we sat round the disabled giraffe as the other guests left. The forecourt began to empty of cars and fill with large numbers of policemen. Time passed. In Masvingo, the shops were shut and a crowd began to collect in the main street to welcome the Queen, as Aaron searched desperately for an open garage. In Harare, the royal party began its journey to the airport. At Great Zimbabwe, camouflage clad Para-militaries and troops were joining the police. And a film crew stood around a three-wheeled Toyota Land cruiser.

"If you don't move it," said an officer of the Zimbabwean Special Branch, "we'll have to blow it up." We didn't know if he was being serious or not. It isn't that easy to move a fully laden land cruiser, which is on a jack. Somebody with a walkie-talkie said that HM was airborne. An increasingly hostile crowd of officials, soldiers and police now surrounded us. We almost wished we were back in the Nyanga nick. People began to look nervously at the sky to the north and strain their ears for aircraft noises. Some obviously English security men appeared and listened to our woes. One said I had an Irish accent. This could have been true but the implications, coming on top of a week of disaster would make you weep.

"We'll carry it!" announced a beefy policeman employing the African philosophy that numbers and brute force can solve anything. Fifty men grabbed the giraffe and began to inch it the hundred yard to the back of the kitchen. "Heave! *Donza!*" they chanted. But it seemed to me that there wouldn't be time to get it clear and the royal party would find a giraffe painted vehicle obstructing their way into tea. Just then Aaron arrived in the back-up car with the two repaired wheels. Monza pits weren't in it. That wheel was changed, the giraffe reloaded and we were on our way before you could say Zimbabwean Iron Age.

"Just get off the main road!" they shouted after us as we drove off. Not so easy. The only way back to Harare, without doing a few hundred miles detour, was through Masvingo, along a road now flanked by thousands of flag waving people. Clearly, the police didn't want us to meet HM head on, but we had had enough of waiting too. Also the crowd was cheering us which was such a nice change. So we drove back to Masvingo, and up the main street, waving regally as the people roared. As we passed the main hotel, the royal jet was seen making its approach, and we knew we would clear town in time. Flashman would have loved it.

I am happy to say that the video guide was not bad at all. There was some great game footage in it and even if I didn't get my more exotic pieces, the sponsors should have been quite happy with the result. Neither the minister nor anybody else tormented me with the adventures in the Nyanga police station because Zimbabwe was soon to have other things to think about. Writing this at troubled time, you forget what an intriguing place it usually is. That is…if you haven't got some ancient curse on you.

Mark Igoe wrote the first guide to Zimbabwe and is that country's most prolific travel writer. He has worked extensively in Africa and Europe. His historical novel The Rivers of Good Portent is electronically published by http://www.onlineoriginals.com and he runs a net based guide series at http://www.cyber-guides.net; he divides his time between Harare and the UK, is married with three kids, and has a number of small animals.

|  | **nightmare of egyptian banking** | cam mcgrath
egypt
2000 |

Franz Kafka would have loved Egyptian banks, where even routine transactions require multiple visits to different windows.

The neurotic Czech writer would have marveled at the extent of bureaucratic inefficiency that Egypt's overstaffed state banks demonstrate. Forms require duplicates, triplicates and even - as it requires its own word- octoplicates.

I recently decided to open a bank account in Egypt. The handful of foreign banks that have branches in Cairo are fairly efficient, but charge exorbitant fees for their services. Not Misr Bank, I was told. One of four state banks, Misr Bank is actively seeking foreign depositors and bending over backwards to facilitate them. Again, this is what I was told. The reality is that the only contortions at this bank are those expected of its customers.

My Thursday morning visit to the bank's special new 'overseas' office, i.e. the branch specially equipped to deal with foreigners, proved that state banking in Egypt remains in the Dark Ages. While the marble foyer, complete with a working fountain and cascading chandelier, was beyond any luxury I'd seen at other banks, there seemed to be a peculiar lack of computers. In fact, there weren't many adding machines, calculators or even abacuses.

English is widely spoken and written in Cairo where even bathroom graffiti is often bilingual. So I found it peculiar that nothing at the 'overseas' branch, which handles foreigners' transactions, was in English. Not even the 'accounts for non-Egyptians' window sign. While my Arabic is passable, I was extremely fortunate to have a native-speaker to guide me.

I'd like to open a dollar account, my friend said on my behalf. The man at the window seemed unsure whether this was possible, and after considerable dialogue, we were referred to his superior. Sharing a desk in the uninhabitable corridor behind the teller window, the account manager was helpful in explaining the procedure for opening an account. But I began to nod off as the briefing dragged on, and might have fallen asleep if there had been a place to sit.

On the manager's advice, before opening the account, we took the elevator to the second floor to visit the office where foreign checks are cashed. It was staffed by a man and two ladies, each having desks that appeared to be repositories for the bank's octoplicate forms. Again, no computers or abacuses- accounting was done longhand.

I had brought two small foreign checks that I wished to deposit into my would-be account. After a perfunctory examination, one of the ladies explained that each foreign check would cost LE25 ($7) to cash, plus unnamed foreign transaction fees. On top of this, a non-refundable security fee the equivalent of LE50 would be tacked onto each check by the corresponding bank in case it didn't clear. Whatever was left would be deposited into my account after a minimum of 45 days...insha'Allah (God willing).

My primary concern was to obtain a written fee schedule. This, I was told in a mechanical response, was unavailable. Fees are whimsical and apparently based on staff consensus. I was, however, offered a 'special bank client' exemption from the corresponding bank's security fee. Once I opened an account, they would gladly consider cashing my checks, they assured me.

Returning downstairs to the new accounts window, the teller gave me a foreign currency account application form to fill out. Indeed, the form was very foreign- it was entirely in Arabic. An appeal for an application form in English earned a shoulder shrug from the teller, who gazed off into space. My friend filled in the form for me and I signed my name at the bottom in English, smiling at this tiny linguistic transgression.

The teller needed a copy of my passport to go with the application, and instructed us to use the photocopier rumored to reside in the office at the front of the bank. Staff in this area seemed genuinely unaware of the alleged copy machine in their midst and insistently directed us to the back of the bank. Staff at the back of the bank, however, were convinced that the staff at the front of the bank were pulling our leg. They tried to send us to the front again. We soon discovered that the bank had no photocopier (I'd seen one on the second floor, but by this point I was certain it must be out-of-order) and we would have to go outside and find a stationary store to get copies.

Returning fifteen minutes later, it was time to pay up. Foreign dollar accounts have a one-time LE50 fee. This must be paid at a kiosk on the opposite side of the lobby. A trip to this booth proved fruitless, as the cashier was absent and the young man sitting in his place didn't know how to operate the register. He just smiled and suggested the cashier was using the bathroom.   Over time I began to grow concerned about the missing cashier.   When he finally arrived, he rung up the application fee.

"Thirty-one pounds," he said.

The teller had said fifty.   The cashier explained that we would pay LE31 to him, and another LE19 when we returned to the teller.   Only the former amount required a receipt.   This was the system, he assured us.   Bizarre, but we went along with it.   If we waited long enough, there would be a new-potentially more expensive- system.   This, I realized, was why there were no written fee schedules or pamphlets.   Banking in Egypt is like shopping blue light sales at K-Mart. customers try to hang out at the bank long enough to increase their odds that a bargain will appear.

Returning to our familiar teller once again, we finalized our paperwork and submitted it.   That I had written my name in English caused a controversy, but with my friend's assurances, and a translation of it into Arabic, it was allowed to remain on foreign currency account form.   With my account seemingly open, we were ready to deposit the two checks.   The process began with a trip to a different cashier's kiosk, this time to pay a LE50 check-cashing fee.

With my receipt in hand, we returned to the second floor.   The three employees at the foreign checks office, still behind piles of paperwork, seemed surprised to see us so soon.   It had only been two hours.   If all went well, my checks would clear in 45 days, they reiterated.

"How will I know my checks have cleared?" I asked.

One of the ladies explained that Misr Bank, having embraced the computer age, now had an automated phone service in English and Arabic. The teller downstairs would give me a pamphlet on the exciting new service. I was impressed, naively.

A senior bank employee downstairs handed me a glossy pamphlet on the bank's phone service, dismissing the presumptuous idea that the service was bilingual.

The pamphlet's author, however, had tried his best, typing the English words 'phone bank' in red text amid a sea of black Arabic text.   I struggled to find logic for the anomalous inclusion.

"Select a PIN number and the bank will choose a PIN number for you," my friend translated to me.   This made little sense, but was yet another strange 'system' to be reckoned with.   I chose a four-digit PIN number and was given a five-digit PIN number by the bank official.   I don't know what either of them is for.   It was definitely time to leave- I just nodded in approval and headed for the door.

I now have a bank account in Cairo. At least I've been told I do.

Cam McGrath is a Canadian journalist who has traveled widely across Europe, Asia, Africa and the Middle East. His background in anthropology and ancient history have sent him to Africa in pursuit of the nomadic tribes, lost tombs and the Ark of the Covenant. Cam now lives in Cairo, where he works as an editor for a local newspaper and a correspondent for various news agencies.

| ship wrecked sailors | mark davies
senegal
1998 |

You can see why African battles are on land and not the sea

I arrived at France's De Gaulle airport at 9:36 AM for a 9:35 AM Swiss chocolate flight to Zurich, after which I'd be on to Africa. A cosmic swing in my direction, with the Swiss running ten minutes late, enabled my connection. Grazing over dusty fields and into Dakar (the capital of Senegal), I smelled the sweet heavy air as we piled into the arrivals' lounge to fight for baggage. Pretending to be totally in control, I fended off all offers for taxis, friendship, or other services, and got a hotel shuttle. My school-taught French didn't help.

Dakar freaked me out. Little did I know that I'd arrived in the few days before Tabasci—"La Fete De La Moutons." Purportedly a religious sacrifice of sheep on Sunday, it was in fact a deft social custom of working out publicly who had the cash to buy one. Cash-poor after two currency devaluations, the street hustlers were now in rare form. I was clearly to be sacrificed as well.

I've wandered through Hillbrow in downtown Joburg, lived fourteen years in Manhattan, and wandered Rio at night. But Dakar was different. That first evening, I lost two hundred francs to a fellow who bought me drinks at Bar de la Poste, and the following day I was threatened as another demanded one hundred fifty quid for his mouton wine. It was the first time I'd ever truly been scared. The isolation of Dakar's fancy Sofitel hotel, which I had rejected after the first night, now made much more sense to me. Alone, with my very blank and sputtering nonsensical French, I made for quite a target.

Dakar was a choking hot sprawl of concrete, without much of the fantasy-bright colonial-era architecture I had hoped for. You can discover some embassy neighborhoods that are serene, but it can also be an unrelenting cacophony of tooting horns, incessant begging, aggressive selling, and dust.

It took me a while to relax. You can defuse the street life (well, there was that one guy who continued to spit at me) by smiling and indulging the locals a little. I had resorted to babbling in English, and that helped. But generally, if you throw an arm around them and take them out for a beer they revert to their natural, hospitable Senegalese selves. You've also got to pay cab fares and buy lunches—but why not?

Those tactics apply to the ones who are chasing you. If you have reason to approach the Senegalese, however, they all turn out to be interested and charming. I had some advice in Paris before I left: "Don't trust anyone who approaches you, but you can trust anyone you approach"—and it was absolutely right. I met a couple of folks who helped me sort out the Dakar online guide, including a particularly nice French guy and his sister.

I guess you get used to the reality of the desperate poverty there—a recent phenomenon, it's said. Everyone is trying to sell something indiscriminately—from peanuts, to flowers, to fluorescent lamps, to cutting shears. Sellers swarm over the streets or wait on the roadside. Beggars are everywhere, including kids starting at about six years old. I had seen this before, but had never been the object of such desperation. Taking time, talking with them, and indulging in their elaborate rituals of making tea brought Dakar into focus.

The following day I arrived on Goree, an island three kilometers from Dakar, which is the capital of Senegal. A peaceful place, it was perfect for a little wonder without the hassle of the mainland. Or so I thought.

There were two navy gunboats moored at the dock, staffed with about a hundred officers-in-training who had come to the island for a day trip. One of the gunboats had gone a little too close to the beach and was stuck. Three hours of chaos and excitement ensued as the trainees stood helpless and somewhat embarrassed on the pier.

First, they tied a rope between the two gunboats and tried to pull it off. Smoke billowed out of both boats as their engines strained. Everyone seemed to be shouting orders and instructions and waving their arms. No one could hear anyone.

Then the locals got into the act and started heaving on the rope to help. It didn't take long for the rope to snap and recoil along the pier, sending everyone scrambling for safety.

Then there was more trouble as one of the broken ropes got caught around the propeller of the beached boat. A diver went down (one of the locals). At this stage, I thought it couldn't get any worse.

While this was going on, the ferry to the mainland couldn't dock, so the pier was backlogged with stranded visitors and villagers, each elbowing the other for the best view.

One of the local restaurateurs tried to reason with the general. But no one really seemed to be in charge. The general lifted his arms in despair and disappeared inside the cabin for some peace and quiet.

Suddenly, cheers erupted as a young man in scuba gear appeared at beach's end. Apparently the best local diver, he'd come to save the day. Now, the village had someone to root for—and the sense of competition warmed up. The jubilant crowd screamed its support as he jumped in.

Everyone was frustrated. The navy had no clue what to do. Smoke continued to billow from engine rooms as the futile effort to free the boat continued. The diver was not able to disentangle the rope from the prop.

Finally, about four hours later—with a new rope brought over from the mainland—the ship was back at the pier. The entire village cheered. Sheepishly, the officers climbed aboard their boat. Apparently, nothing so exciting had happened in Goree in ages!

Mark Davies' first real taste of Africa was a 1981 journey overland from Nairobi to London through the magnificent Sudan. After studying anthropology at University, he migrated to the jungle of New York where he worked in theater, TV, and publishing for ten years. In 1995 he switched to Internet publishing, founding the award-winning city guide Metrobeat (now Citysearch). After helping seed Citysearch across North America, he moved back to London (he was born in Cardiff, Wales), co-founding the internet network FirstTuesday. In '98, he toured West Africa, and has now returned to Ghana to launch BusyInternet, a series of technology centers that will create a network of digital entrepreneurship across Africa. Mark lives in Bahia, London and Accra.

	**rule number 1, no number 2**	peter ward zimbabwe 1996

Just drop in

You know you have experienced a country when you have a good toilet story. The best ones usually end with the reader or listener squealing, "That's disgusting!" So, it's best not to tell such stories at the dinner table.

A good, rip-roaring toilet tale is on the same par as a good frat party hangover story. People find such stories fascinating and often trade observations, frustrations and humor about their experiences with a country's sanitation—or lack of it.

This is one of those stories.

I was in Zimbabwe, working for the charity Raleigh International, on a three-month expedition with a diverse population of one hundred twenty other volunteers. To an American, Raleigh International is very similar to the Peace Corps, and to my knowledge none of these Peace Corps people had bowel movement problems.

The volunteers ranged from students taking a gap year (a year off to travel or do something other than studying and taking exams) to people like me who had graduated and were trying to delay the rat race as much as possible. To add to the mixed grill of people, there were also volunteers who were either socially or mentally handicapped. One could say they were 'a few French fries short of a Happy Meal', 'a few steps from the top landing,' or 'a can short of a 6 pack.' You get the picture.

There was one individual who was a great guy. Let's call him Tony (name changed). At this stage of the story, I would like to acknowledge my admiration for Tony, as he'd come to Africa to put himself in challenging situations.

When it came to doing his business, however, there was always an incident. Here's a recap of just a few.

Incident 1:

Twelve of us were spending a week kayaking across Lake Kariba, which is in a National Park in Zimbabwe. The Kariba dam was completed in 1960, and it was the largest man-made dam ever built. Two hundred and twenty kilometers long—and in places up to forty kilometers wide—it provides a fair bit of the electric power for both Zambia and Zimbabwe. The dam also supports the commercial fishing industry.

Like most things done while Africa was a white-run country, the building of the Kariba Dam was surrounded by controversy—both environmentally and socially. Nonetheless, the dam is an impressive monument to man's engineering expertise. Of course, it's easier to build that sort of infrastructure when $12,642,000.00 has been handed over from both the World Bank and the Development Bank of Southern Africa (DBSA).

The massive valley which now forms Lake Kariba has survived (with most plant and animal species forced to relocate or adapt to the altered real estate). Today the lake is a gold mine for both Zambia's and Zimbabwe's tourist trade. The lake's vastness creates spectacular panoramas as the sun casts its glow across the shimmering waters, catching the distinctive half-submerged trees and islands.

Given the importance of the lake to the local economy—and the delicate microclimate of the vegetation around it—it's difficult to get permission to kayak there. You usually have to bribe a local official or convince the government that what you are doing on the lake has something to do with conservation. The latter was our method of access.

Our group had just finished lunch on one of the many islands. We started loading our kayaks with the remaining food and cooking equipment. Once that was complete, we began to launch the kayaks to continue making our way across the lake. But before Tony could get inside his canoe, he had to make a "restroom" stop.

When performing "number two" in remote areas—usually behind a rock or tree—the toilet paper should be burned so as not to attract mosquitoes or beetles. Tony had complied with those guidelines and was now kayaking with the group.

One minute into the afternoon's kayaking, however, someone from the group looked back at the island. Much to our horror, we saw a mini inferno. Apparently, Tony had thought the lit toilet paper would burn itself out, so he left it burning.

Picture the scene. Zimbabwe is in the middle of a drought for 10 years, there has not been any rain in this area for weeks, it's the height of summer in the midday sun, and twelve people are trying to stamp out a fire wearing sandals. Oh, and the fire contains "number two."

Well, at least a doctor was with us to deal with the heat stroke, sunburn, mild burns and short tempers.

Incident 2:

It was the middle of the night and the group was asleep on an island somewhere on the lake. Tony woke up feeling the need to go to the toilet. It was dark, everyone was asleep—and this guy woke up. An incident waiting to happen.

Tony did not have a flashlight, so he borrowed one. It was the kind that miners wear on their heads. Unfortunately, it did not fit his head properly and yes—it fell off. Right where was Tony looking when he was doing his "number one."

Incident 3:

On the final night of the three-month expedition—in keeping with custom—there was a huge party for all one hundred twenty volunteers at the base camp, which was in a suburb of Harare. Given Zimbabwe's scant rain situation, flushing toilets with running water would be wasteful. So, in the typical fashion of such hot, arid countries, a "Long Drop" was built. This is a six-by-two foot hole, with two planks of wood three inches apart strategically placed over it. The planks were to prevent people or objects from falling down the hole. No seat, no running water—just planks and three months of accumulated output from one hundred twenty people. To most who used it, the Long Drop was fittingly known as "S**t Creek."

After three months, there was a six-inch layer of black oozing slime coming out of the hole. The stench frequently made your eyes come out on their stalks. It could make your nostril hairs drop off. I recall being taken aback by the smell and having to reenter after taking some very deep breaths outside.

At the party, there was plenty of drinking, partying and celebration, which can be expected at an end-of-expedition bash. During the festivities, Tony needed to go to the restroom, ala' S**t Creek.

What happened next is a bit speculation, a bit fact—and one of life's less enjoyable moments.

Tony entered the Long Drop, noticed the lizards and dragonflies engaged in violent combat, and peeked between the planks of wood to acknowledge the millions of white maggots happily swimming in the muck.

After mustering his courage, he closed the door, rolled down his jeans, and tried to straddle the hole. Unfortunately, the efforts of previous occupants had made the floor into a skating rink, and he quickly found his ill-clad feet sliding towards the hole. With nothing solid to grab onto, he was whooshed down. Trapped, Tony had his head jammed between the planks.

He supported himself with his arms while an army of maggots advanced up his neck.

Unable to get out, Tony could do little but wait until someone else needed to use the facility. Shortly thereafter that happened, but the person initially thought Tony was a giant mole trying to get out of the ground. Nonetheless, Tony was finally pulled out of the Long Drop. Covered in unspeakable filth, he stumbled onto the dance floor.

Now you know that when a really bad song is played after a series of good ones, people leave the floor very quickly. This scene was like that, although more as if an authority figure had shouted "FIRE!" at the top of his lungs. People leapt over tables to scramble out of the way

To this day, I wonder who sat next to him on the flight home.

See back cover for **Peter Ward's** biography.

	**let's do egypt- mission impossible: a race across egypt in 5 1/2 days**	paul israel egypt 1992

True great adventures stay fresh in one's mind, even if they last for hours and days rather than weeks

11 AM August 19th 1992: Jerusalem.

In 1992, I spent five and a half days speeding across Egypt in a highly challenging trip, which demanded resourcefulness, guile, and lack of sleep—to their full natural boundaries.

Six days before I was due to fly home to the UK after a long stay in Israel, I sat chatting with my new friend David from Sydney. En route to a bakery tour, we remarked that it was a pity we had no chance to travel to Egypt.

A few careless words later, we left the tour and parked in a Ben Yehuda Street coffee shop. An overambitious "Napkin plan" was scribbled. We were going to Egypt!

Weds 19 Aug - Leave Jerusalem - collect passports in Bat Yam - arrive Eilat (Egyptian border)

Thus 20 Aug - In Eilat get visas - arrive Cairo

Fri 21 Aug - See Pyramids and climb them- arrive Luxor

Sat 22 Aug - Luxor, sail on the Nile in a Felucca ride, see temples of Luxor and Karnac

Sun 23 - See the Valley of the Kings at sunrise - return to Cairo

Mon 24 - Return to Tel Aviv

Tue 25 - Fly home

Americans are well known for trying to see the whole of Europe in eight days; were we getting a bit carried away? Did we really know what we were doing? Armed with a crisp new "Lonely Planet" guide, we established that our project might just be possible, but it would require a fair amount of luck.

Our first objective, Bat-Yam, was a sleepy working class town south of Tel Aviv, where we would dump dirty laundry and pick up my passport from a friend's house, then board the bus south across our first desert.

The Granny and the Ghetto Blaster

By the skin of our teeth, we boarded the midnight bus to Eilat. A passport was briefly left behind. Sleep was our desire, but some of the passengers had other ideas. A large group of Israeli teenagers were in a party mood, accompanied by the music of a ghetto blaster. As we settled down to sleep, the music began to scream. For thirty minutes or so this was tolerated, with some people joining in and singing, but there were complaints. So the music stopped.

Soon the music started again. Tempers rose. Heated discussions ensued between an old Israeli woman, who represented the largely "silent majority," and the young Israeli custodian of the ghetto blaster, which was belting out Hebrew-style Iron Maiden. Soon, a physical struggle occurred for its possession. Briefly, the outcome seemed in doubt and threatened to involve everyone on the bus in a giant wrestling match. Finally, youth overcame experience, and the old woman returned to her seat, temporarily defeated.

Rescue came from the driver. Initially he made no difference, so he changed tack by turning the radio on the bus loud enough to drown out the ghetto blaster. But that didn't help the noise. Then, for a moment, there was golden silence. The ghetto blaster soon started up again. Then in an orchestrated movement, the radio of the bus flared up.

Finally, there was golden silence. Real peace, with sleep upon me, a few hours maybe—alas! I was jolted awake. The lights of the town in the pitch-black were not those of Beersheba halfway, but Eilat. It was 5:30 AM and, considering how much farther we had to go, we felt incapable of going another five minutes anywhere.

Our planned hitchhike to meet friends in the nearby Kibbutz was shelved when we fell asleep while waiting for a lift. We moved instead a few hundred meters to the golden sands of Eilat's beach, and collapsed for a few precious hours of sleep before the Egyptian Consulate opened and we could apply for a visa.

Thursday August 20th - Psychological Warfare in the Sun

Like many embassies around the world, the Egyptian consulate in Eilat is the gathering place for adventurers and travelers. It's where the hardiest and greatest tales are traded as currency in a kind of pecking order; who is the more worthy adventurer? A New Zealander proudly shows his deportation stamp from the UK, a hardy Australian girl describes being stranded in the desert by some Egyptians. David and I establish some credibility for our plans, but it is generally suggested that our plan is not quite possible. A few questions about our itinerary make me feel that we are embarking on a true challenge.

The consulate reopened between 1:00 and 1:30 PM to issue visas. We hitchhiked the five miles down the coast road to the border, thanks to a young immigrant mother from South Africa. We rode along the edge of the brightest blue water of the Red Sea, with the rising sand-colored rocks of the Negev Mountains on our right.

It took an hour to clear Egyptian customs, what with the copious paperwork. The police on the Israeli side were invariably attractive girls, perhaps deliberately in contrast to the bored Egyptian soldiers opposite, who stared longingly over the border. There were impressive buildings on the Israeli side and in between was the towering Taba Hilton, where everyone goes to change money. Past this hotel was a shabby little town of fifteen or so houses, which resembled something from a Clint Eastwood "spaghetti Western." After paying our border tax, we passed through the gate to Africa, a gate to another country, and it seemed almost another time and another world! The buildings were totally different. The few people in the cafe seemed more laid back, and even the sun felt hotter.

We missed the only bus to Cairo at 2:00 PM. As we discussed our route, taxi rates to Dhahab doubled from (Egyptian pounds) E£14 to E£24 when the last bus to Dhabab departed. The fifteen travelers bound for Cairo embarked on psychological warfare with the waiting hordes of taxi drivers. For an hour, despite our finest barter skills, we were unable to agree upon a price, and wondered who in the one hundred and ten degree sun would drop first. As we approached 4:00 PM local time, the whole plan seemed to be off, and the only option would be a few days in Dhabab. Meanwhile, a black South African girl sought our help, as she was receiving too much attention from one of the locals.

Finally, in a master compromise, one of the drivers agreed to lower our fare, but not to Cairo—to Suez. Having asked for E£350, and not dropping below E£280, he accepted E£240 (UK£40) on the deal.

We had unwanted company. The driver introduced us to another man, who waved both a piece of paper with Arabic writing and a handgun! He said that he was a policeman, and asked for a free lift. David and I conferred. Of course he could come for free; the thought that we may never come out of the desert alive didn't even enter my mind!

The most epic taxi ride of my life began. The bright sand and enchanting blue beauty of the Red Sea disappeared, replaced by the barren, rocky, mountainous, and completely unwelcoming Sinai desert. One can almost imagine Moses appearing on the road with thousands of Hebrews trying to hitch a lift out of there. The only things we saw in this enormous space were the occasional goat and some Bedouin women, dressed in distinct black, tending the goats. By sunset the terrain was less mountainous, with forbidding flat, rocky sand and hills in the distance.

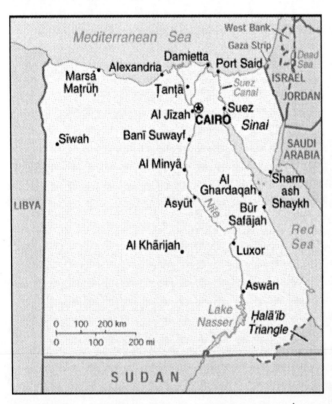

We passed several burnt-out vehicles, reminders of more recent conflict in the Sinai. Our driver stopped twice for prayers and again at a café. He tried hard to make us buy something; we suspected a cozy arrangement with the owner. The only conversation that we could make with the two Egyptians was in very halting Hebrew (Sinai was Israeli-controlled in the recent past). We were lulled into a state of half-sleep after glimpsing the impressive sunset. My mind lingered on the gun, which the policeman kept fingering in the front passenger seat. If we were not killed or robbed, would we be abandoned in the desert?

At 10:00 PM, the driver announced that we were approaching Suez. With a magnificent maneuver, he managed to get a small bus to stop for us. For a mere E£10, the bus would take us the final two hours to Cairo.

At midnight we arrived in Cairo. Nothing in the world can prepare one for Africa's largest city; it strikes every sense and defies superlatives. With its fifteen million inhabitants living in a third world urban sprawl, Cairo is a world of endless beeping horns, countless rows of houses, and roads built for three lanes (but with cars using six). Traffic lights, if they're working, seem to indicate that green means "go" and red means "go just a bit slower whilst hooting." Traffic police, of which there are many, seem to have the job of waving cars but are generally ignored.

We found the Oxford Hotel (described as a five-roach hotel in our guide-book,) on the fifth floor of one of the unpleasant crumbling buildings which exuded the spirit of Cairo and which reminded me of the film Casablanca (for some unaccountable reason, especially as that was filmed in Hollywood). For £E6 (£1UK), we had no complaints. George, the receptionist, was from Sudan. Apart from describing African style rugby (which sounded like some of the more gory scenes from the movie Gladiator), he gave us advice on our ambitious travel plans. George even offered to guide us on a night out in Cairo, but time did not allow for the fleshpots.

We found a tasty falafel (for a princely £E25 pence; 4UK pence) a few doors down at the Café Redina, and relaxed with a game of backgammon amidst hubbly-bubbly smokers. Next to the office of the Oxford was a movie company where Westerners could earn money as extras; in the café I was offered £E28 for a day's work. I informed the man who offered that it would make my year, but my movie career would have to wait.

Our room in the Oxford was a rather intimidating experience, as the two Algerians there had probably not met Westerners before. Everything we did was watched hypnotically; their eyes did not leave us even for a second. Finally, we managed some sleep. But it was also snack time. Not for me, but of me, as the many insect inhabitants in our room made my back resemble Dresden in 1944; by the morning, it was thoroughly in ruins.

Friday 21 August. Up, Up and Away. The Climb.

At 8:00 AM we were up; we had one day to see Cairo and to arrange our trip south. Armed with addresses from George the receptionist, we discovered that an airplane at £E215 would be beyond our budget, as the principle of the whole trip was to avoid luxury. As we sped around travel agents, a man in the busy crowd tapped us on the shoulders and handed David his passport. A bit freaky, but lucky.

We dashed through the crowded and busy Cairo streets; each one looked and smelled different We arrived at the chaos of Ramses station. We were served by a woman straight from an Agatha Christie novel, a woman with inordinately long fingernails. After we struggled to find the right queue for our destination, we discovered that all the tickets were gone. Had we failed?

We met a couple who paid £E 35 extra baksheesh (this is Egyptian for 'bribe,' in very common usage), apparently for the last two available seats. After prolonged negotiations, we clinched the E£17 "student" price (very important in Egypt), thanks to a Brazilian girl, who bought our tickets under the system in which men queue up and women go straight to the front (who says women here are oppressed?). The train would depart at 1:00 AM, giving us time to arrange a coach from the Sheraton Cairo to Tel Aviv for a reasonable E£77. Of course, we had to return by 5:30 AM on Monday—and the train was fully booked. How we would return we didn't yet know; we would solve this problem later.

It was now midday, so we had thirteen hours in Cairo. Where should one go with a day in Cairo, but to Giza and the Pyramids? We took a thirty-minute taxi ride, and the giant tombs appeared through the sprawl.

Now, everyone has an opinion. Some are disappointed and view the Pyramids as just huge rocks. Some are overawed.

We, on the other hand, decided to climb them.

Our guidebook described the climb as taking twenty minutes. We understood from this description that the writer had not achieved it without bright red underwear, a blue cape and an embroidered "S" on his chest.

The climb, albeit not strictly legal, was a serious challenge. David had a rush of vertigo halfway up, and we remained stationary for fifteen minutes.

The big one takes one and a half hours to ascend—depending on one's courage/stupidity factor. It takes slightly less time to come down. That is, unless you fall off. The steps are four to five-foot slabs, which have suffered four thousand years of weathering—but the view and the satisfaction are awesome.

At the top, there were various names inscribed in the rock. Many dated from Napoleon's army—as well as Australia's shortly before Gallipoli. I wondered how many of them came here and did not return? The names are a poignant reminder of different eras of history.

The views and the wind were astonishing. On two sides, we saw raw barren sandy desert; on the other two sides the views went from the creeping metropolis of Giza almost to the base of the Pyramids.

The Pyramid experience is amazing. As in an Indiana Jones film, there are people hawking everything. Precious stones, camel rides, horses, and donkeys mill everywhere. Inside the pyramid, David got revenge as I suffered from the low ceilings. The heat inside with the weight above became apparent as we went deep underground to the nearly empty burial chamber.

After the obligatory walk around the Sphinx, we headed back to Cairo and rushed to board our train. Too tired to be expectant, we met our Brazilian friend and her companions on the packed south platform. In moments, every seat was full; the general cleanliness, like most of Egypt, leaves something to be desired. But this one night, we were too tired to complain.

Saturday 22 August - Step Back in Time

I awakened to daylight to find the carriage nearly empty, as people had either moved in the train or gotten off. The view from the window was almost biblical; the fertile belt of the Nile where life has barely changed in thousands of years, palm trees and lush green fields, muddy brick and earthen houses, the dirty brown water of the Nile tributaries, donkeys and oxen, and the busy Egyptians wearing the long clothes that have not changed styles in centuries. Although only a few hours away from the more modern city of Cairo, the train ride seemed like a journey back in time.

After marveling at the scenery for several hours, we arrived in Luxor at 1:00 PM. On the train, we met a young Egyptian man who told us about his new hotel. I told him about our quest; he promised to arrange our felucca trip and a trip to the Valley of the Kings the following morning. Most importantly of all, he would arrange our connection back to Cairo on Sunday. As soon as we arrived in Luxor, we realized that we might just fulfill our travel plans.

We were taken through the intense dry heat to our hotel by horse and carriage. Luxor has a distinctly Egyptian Oasis town feel, despite its location as a tourist Mecca. Half of the Egyptians seem oblivious to travelers, the other half are interested in making (or taking) a living from them. As the girls we met in Cairo retired to sleep, David and I had no time for a break. Instead, we hired bicycles and rode down the banks of the Nile to the famed temples of Karnak and Luxor.

The view of the Nile from Luxor was as I'd imagined, packed with the white sailboats (feluccas). The other side of the river featured palm trees, along with green-turning into-brown mountains and desert that led to the famed Valley of the Kings, which we would visit the following morning.

The Temples of the past Egyptian civilization which adorn the banks of the Nile may cause an art critic to bemoan the similarity of the sites, but the sheer scale of the countless columns and statues is astonishing. Even at the edges of the sites there are huge piles of pottery, which the archaeologists seem to have abandoned.

At Karnak (named after the French ancient site in Brittany,) one of the Egyptian guides actually pulled out a hammer and chisel, offering to sell us one of the small four-thousand-year-old wall carvings we admired. We were not sure, however, that this was fully in the spirit of conserving his heritage.

By 5:00 PM, we returned to our hotel to get ready for our sunset felucca ride down to Banana Island (where, ironically, I saw no bananas). Later we were informed over a hearty dinner that our early morning donkey ride was arranged. For E£25, we ate our way through the menu.

We were awakened by the Brazilian girl and her friends—who appeared to have spent all their money—and were in considerable trouble with our host. We were commissioned to sort it out. Marginally annoyed, we retired with the problem temporarily solved; the girls' finances meant that they would not be joining us on the journey to the Valley of the Kings.

Sunday 23 August - Mr. No Problem and the race home begins

Grumpy and half-asleep, we met our guide at 4:30 AM. The very likeable, self-described "Mr. No Problem," who told us in broken English; "You have problem and you tell me, it is no problem." He showed us his very entertaining visitors' book before we left to join his eight-year-old son and his donkeys, all of whom seemed to be named "Casanova".

Our donkey derby, won by er...Casanova, was greeted by sunrise, as we journeyed through the fertile strip next to the Nile and past villages, fields and ruined temples on which modern western civilization has left not a mark. It's where, even considering the early hour, the fields are busy with workers, including the awesome two ruined monolith statues that spawned the poem loved by English public school boys, "My name is Oximandies, King of Kings."

The final ascent up the sandy rocky cliffs to the top of the mountains added to the excitement. We awaited the first view of the valley, although we were no longer alone. A few other travelers arrived, also on donkeys, along with a few Egyptians who tried to hawk drinks and merchandise. One Egyptian could not understand why I didn't want to buy his little piece of pottery, despite his dropping the price from E£160 to E£12 over half a mile of banter, and with the biggest price drop occurring when I uttered the magic word "student." I asked him whether he would buy it from me, and was answered with a puzzled affirmative. He told me that he he'd sold pieces for large amounts to Americans and Japanese, with the price geared to how much one can afford to pay; did we in the West have anything to learn from this way to do business? However, I did not buy.

We passed the Queen of Hapeshut's tomb, which would soon be a modern scene of tragedy from terrorists. Our first view of the Valley of the Kings was highly emotional, as we were both sleep-deprived and travel-weary. We approached the resting place of the Pharaohs. The tombs, despite the early 8:30 AM hour, were like the entrance to a furnace. Even a few tourists made an unpleasant difference to the tombs, which were relatively empty of artifacts, though not of wall paintings. But the heat and the journey added to the experience.

David and I spotted an opening that was not a sealed tomb, and we passed an accumulation of used water-bottles, hidden by a Pharaoh's tomb. Armed with flashlight and a little courage, we proceeded over the wall and through the opening. A few feet inside, our feeling of adventure grew.

We reached a forked passage and tiptoed past some rubble. No daylight was visible. I walked on strange and somehow soft ground. There was movement and something passed over my head, David shone the torch upward, and we discovered that we were not the only living creatures in the tomb. Above us roosted hundreds of bats. Suddenly, I realized what I walking in; if bats are above, underneath our feet must be…In seconds, our exploration was suspended, and our shoes were in need of a good clean.

I don't remember that happening to Indiana Jones.

Soon, we were on our way back to the Nile, via Mr. "No Problem's" house, which had a cow-dung coating on the walls, giving it distinctive brown color. We tucked into bread and goat's cheese and, despite having overeaten the previous evening, we were hungry and found this Egyptian culinary experience remarkable—both in texture and taste (not a hint of cow-dung). Mr. No Problem was thrilled that we liked it, and told us a little of his (at times) happy and yet tragic life as a donkey guide.

The human perspective of honest and uncomplicated friendship, built in only a few hours of travel over the mountains, was very rewarding. It's part of the magic of travel, and seems impossible in the West. Mr. No Problem had recently lost his wife, his young son, and his elderly mother all lived in almost absolute poverty, yet that simple life seemed contented—though we can barely understand it any more than they can comprehend our lifestyle.

By 3:00 PM, we returned to Luxor for a final browse through the market. It was Sunday, and strange things were afoot. No other tourists were around, and the traders were in a funny mood. We witnessed two of them arguing, an altercation which came to blows and which descended into a full blown fight. Soon, others got involved, and a stool flew in an almost Wild

West punch up. As a soldier bearing a rifle arrived, we discretely slipped away.

At 4:30 PM, we caught the bus back to Cairo, courtesy of our reliable hotelier. The bus was as colorful and full of life as those in Egypt, but we were exhausted. Due at the Sheraton in Cairo at 5:30 PM, we were advised to drop the driver some "Baksheesh" to ensure that we would be on time.

Monday 24 August - The Vagrants

Sure enough—at 5:20 AM—with David having bribed the driver (with an eternally appreciated E£10, which was nearly £2UK), we hurtled through the Cairo suburbs to the Sheraton. Remarkably, this was with all the bus passengers' approval (despite their being diverted), because they were aware that we were in a hurry. Despite a thirteen-hour bus journey, we arrived at 5:28 AM at the hotel, to cheers from our fellow Egyptian passengers as we dashed off. We were then advised that the bus would leave ten minutes late, so we had a little time to relax.

It had not occurred to us before, but after five days of hard travel on the road, bereft of sleep, our appearance was not what one would expect in a Sheraton hotel, and we were refused entry. We waited for the doorman to be distracted, and made a run inside, both to clean ourselves up and to eat a quick breakfast. Fortunately, we were unrecognizable when we returned— somewhat cleaner—past the doorman a few minutes later.

It took an additional twelve hours of drifting in and out of sleep before we returned to Tel Aviv, where we arrived at sunset. We dashed to the beach, dumped our bags on the sand, and jumped into the Mediterranean Sea. It was a very long five-and-a-half days, but it was the race of a lifetime…

Paul Israel was born and lives in North London. Periodically he sets off from the world of finance, armed with his trusted connect-four game and a battered Nikon on new adventures. His travels have included working on a ranch in Uruguay, discovering Africa on a Raleigh International expedition to Zimbabwe and a year in Israel and the Middle East. In a forthcoming attempt at curing his ridiculous obsession with the Football World Cup, Paul is shortly to do an overland trip from London to Seoul for charity. Paul also fears his greatest tales can never be told, and although having survived several of nature's various attempts to hurt and kill him, hopes nature will be nicer to him from now on.

	**a night to forget**	mark davies senegal 1998

Not all is good when the local hot spot turns too hot

In the early evening, I spent three hours in the heat of Senegal, crammed into the preferred mode of transport: a Peugeot 504. Our destination was the old French colonial capital of West Africa. Crucial for expanding a somewhat brutal colonial French influence and defeating the Jihads of mythical figures like Omar Tall, St. Louis seems like a forgotten city just coming to life.

It sits on a tiny island in the middle of the Senegal River. Beyond it, a thin sandy bar runs almost forty km in one thin strip of fishing villages and holiday camps/hotels along the sea. St. Louis borders Mauritania to the north, and has a hint of the Sahara desert, which lies just beyond.

The consistently decrepit and glorious buildings that choke the island immediately seduce you. There's a touch of Havana magic here—nothing's been touched since power switched to Dakar. Horse-drawn buggies are whipped along the dusty streets, yellow and black taxis buzz around the corners, filthy kids scramble in gutters and leap up to chase you.

Frozen in time, St. Louis is just now beginning to suffer the growing pains of tourism. It feels like an awkward marriage; poverty mixed with tourism is a somewhat brutal relationship in Senegal. There's a constant demand for money from kids, along with more elaborate ruses by elders. You have to inoculate yourself against everyone, or else it's exhausting. And that breeds cynicism on both sides. But with a few days here, you can discover a community quite different from Dakar—welcoming, generous, and deeply religious.

Those last three days were quite an experience. For some reason, my mild-mannered "everything nice" thumbs-up friend Paco turned into a rabid frothing monster at the Casino nightclub, causing us both to be thrown out by the scruffs of our necks. Literally. St. Louis ended for me in as much turbulence as I could imagine.

We had visited the Saraba nightclub. I was with Paco, Lamin and about three of our other friends. We had managed to get through an evening of petty bickering, mostly spoken in Wolaf, which is the local language of St.

Louis, and which I could not understand. I think the gist of the argument had been that Mahatar had not brought back any change from the ten pounds that I'd given for a bottle of whisky.

Anyway, back to the club. It was a fairly hot and seedy joint down by the river, a club that got going at about 1:00 AM on a Monday night. Paco had taken the camera from me and was busy photographing some of the dancers and some of the djembe drum performance—perhaps fifteen photos in all. At 4:00 AM we decided to leave, and by the time I had reached the door there was an argument. For a while I was completely confused by what was happening, but the crowd was getting larger and the voices were clearly more agitated.

It was dark, and as we emerged onto the quai, all the people outside began to take sides. Some shuffling ensued, and I realized that they were demanding money for the photos that Paco had taken, and were trying to seize the camera. By now, about thirty or forty people had gotten into the fray, and it had become physical.

Totally neurotic about losing my digital camera, I pried it out of Lamin's grasp and stuffed it into my back pocket. This, attracted the attention of the crowd, and I soon found myself lifted off my feet, with my back across a car bonnet and about three people trying to get me to give up the camera. Everyone was getting involved, and the whole quai had erupted into a mob scene. Despite the fact that this enormous bouncer was tugging at my arm and lunging at me from time to time, he was ultimately unsuccessful. Too much whisky on his part.

At one point, I restrained Paco against a car as he tried to hurl himself at the seven-foot bouncer and reenter the nightclub. In my best French, I screamed "arrête!" while Paco screamed pleadingly (with tears running down his cheeks) in his high-pitched English, pounding the dusty road with "But I've paid my money!"

I held onto the camera and Lamin finally managed to pull me off the car and stuff me into the nearest open taxi. You would not believe our exit—screaming at the taxi driver to leave (who himself was in a total state of confusion) as about sixty people surrounded the car.

Picture the scene: we were tearing out of there with people banging on the roof of the car. The taxi's doors were open, with legs dangling out and arms reaching in trying to grab hold of us. I was too amazed to be scared. That "temper tidal wave" had come from nowhere—surging, cresting, and smashing upon us.

The taxi driver, ignoring our wishes to go home, sped to a tiny, sleepy police station (I think he'd promised this to the mob), where Paco recounted the whole story and a report was reluctantly logged. It was quite convenient that the police station was next to the other major nightclub. So, we went to get a drink and calm down.

Finally, we walked home at about 5:00 AM. Just as we were near my hotel, a taxi pulled around a corner and screeched to a halt. Out tumbled a mini-mob of screaming, familiar faces. They immediately surrounded us and grabbed my blue Armani shirt by the neck. More screaming, more pulling, more hanging onto the camera for dear life—and somehow we wheeled around the corner to hotel entrance, where the security guard (in a military outfit) intervened. I escaped into the hotel.

So that was my night in St. Louis—the city that everyone said in Senegal was the complete opposite of the noisy, dangerous Dakar. The next morning I left for the country, quite relieved to be escaping!

See page 62, for biography of **Mark Davies**.

transportation

I love to travel, often, more so than reaching the destinations. Think about it, you get to meet other people, a driver is doing the work so you can sit back and enjoy the scenery.

So needless to say, there's always a tale to tell when traveling- Voila, this chapter.

	**jon and the dancing major**	peter ward zimbabwe 1996

Only in Africa, no I mean America

While in Zimbabwe, I was hitch hiking and got a lift from an American who had just finished a stint with the Peace Corps. During the trip from the Eastland's Highlands to Harare, the capital, we were talking about a variety of subjects and issues that are different in both America and Britain, a bit more than 'you say tomato and we say toMAto'...and the subject of education came up.

At this stage of the story I will point out to the reader that most of the events are set in America, not Africa, but this was the road that got him to Africa.

Up until that moment it had always struck me that the US education system seemed very flexible in accommodating students lifestyles, which is probably one of the reasons why 2 out of 3 high school graduates go on to further education, while in Britain it's 1 in 3. If you require a modular course, your schedule can be accommodated, while you bring up children, have a part time job to pay for the fees, or simply wish to avoid the rat race for as long as possible, whilst living off your parents. There's always a college for you in America.

Jon, had majored and graduated, but not in playing the piano, which is what he originally intended. He loved playing music, but unfortunately got distracted in his studies, with the pursuit of attending as many Toga parties and Spring Breaks that the calendar could accommodate. The result of this was that he failed the final module of the course, but being in America, the University (College) suggested that he complete the final module in another field and this would then qualify him to have a degree. Not in playing the piano, but after all, a degree is a degree! -Only in America and not Africa.

This module was dance and Jon felt he had spent enough time in the downtown night clubs in the area to merit the ability to put on a pair of dancing shoes and leap though this module without too many problems. He also believed that this would be something of a breeze as the home work assignments didn't require hours of studying in the library and the book he had to purchase to assist his study contained mostly pictures.

At this stage of his telling me the story, I was beginning to wonder about the American educational system!

A successful completion of the module hinged on the final dance exam, which was in the main hall of the college. The hall doubled up as a basketball court and had other lines and marking on the wooden floorboards to indicate other indoor sports. On the day of the dance exam a long table had been placed at one end where a panel of judges would sit to assess the students dancing. At the other end there was a grand stand where students of the course and their family members would sit and cheer on and offer encouragement to their fellow students in true American style...-Go, go go. Not wishing to be patronizing, but the last thing I'd want for my final exam would be for my fellow students to see me take this exam, but of course in America, you have to show off everything.

Jon knew the importance of the exam and had spent the previous day prior to this big day brushing up on moves, rhythms and twirls to a variety of styles of the dance that had been covered in this module. He'd even watched the movie Flash dance, the one with Irene Cara singing her stuff back in '83, wearing those revealing leggings, along with off the shoulder shirts and leg warmers. He was at a disadvantage to others on the course as they had spent 3 years completing other dance modules and this was his first, but this was America where anything is possible!

At 10:00 am, the exam started for the students. The whole class was present in the hall, excited and perhaps a little nervous that in the next few hours their fate would be determined and witnessed by most of their parents who had arrived in town to see their graduation in the coming days. One by one each student was called upon to perform a series of dances in front of the assessors, not only as the lead dancer, but also as the dance partner.

It was Jon's turn to be the lead dancer for his exam. The examiner would say a style of dance, the music for that style would play and the lead dancer would be expected to perform a graceful dance accompanied by their dance partner. What could be simpler!

The first couple of compilations of music were the foxtrot, waltz, tango, and the salsa. Jon claimed he performed these dances so gracefully and seamlessly that he and his partner glided across the dance floor like swans on a lake. With dances like the foxtrot, he claimed he had mastered the combination of quick and slow steps, thus permitting flexibility to the dance. The film cast of Dirty Dancing might be envious.

On the final dance the assessor said 'Cha-Cha-Cha' and the Latin music began. This style of music has become the most commonly known of the Latin American dances. The music is slower than Mambo and the rhythm is less complicated. The interpretation of Cha-Cha-Cha music should produce a happy, cheeky, party-time-like atmosphere. It's more commonly referred to as simply- 'Cha-Cha'.

Fear stuck in Jon's eyes making them seem to come out on storks. He didn't know the moves to this dance. Of course he'd heard about it and seen a couple of pictures illustrating the moves in his book, which explained this carefree dance. After a moments pause judges began to look at each other, with the look of 'Is there a problem?' and students were looking a little puzzled. All the onlookers waited eagerly for Jon's dance to begin.

Jon's hands rose and he began to click his fingers and shake to the music as if this was some passionate Latin dance performed in a dance club in Buenos Aeries, Argentina. His dance partner slowly joined in, but lacked the enthusiasm or the inclination since she knew the original moves to the music. Students and judges looked on in either bewilderment, amusement or both.

When the music stopped Jon proudly bowed to the assessors and to his fellow students. His dance partner fell to her knees with her hands covering her embarrassment, thinking, 'I can't believe this. My parents have flown into town, this is my last exam and this idiot has failed me because he didn't know, of all the dances, the Cha Cha'.

The only noise that could be heard were snickers from all the students, who were probably thinking, 'What the hell was that!-Someone not graduating!'. Judges were looking at each other, thinking-Is this dance able to be graded? - Can this exam be re-sat?

When silence was restored, the onlookers had mentally accepted Jon's version of the 'Cha Cha'. A judge stood up and declared aloud and with conviction, 'Jon that was the essence of the Cha Cha'. He passed the exam and joined the Peace Corps.

See back cover for **Peter Ward's** biography.

	**the basic rules of hitchhiking**	peter ward africa 1996

It's a road less traveled in a fast car

I'm a firm believer that the best way to travel within a country is by witnessing the culture and doing what the locals do. Which is why I'm not a fan of tour buses, which only stop at the designated photo opportunities or other such tourist traps.

To feel like a traveler and not a tourist there has to be the opportunity to meet locals and view how local customs function such as town markets, local street vendors and shops, which cater to housewives. It also pays to experience the displeasures of a culture - inaccurate train timetables or parking tickets. So traveling on the same mode of transport that the locals do, whether that's train, bus, bicycle or by foot, is a must.

Over time and from experience in traveling, I've noticed that the poorer the country, the better developed the mass transit system. This may sound like a 'distorted' statement, but I don't mean air-conditioned trains, or leather padded seats, but more basic modes of transportation that locals use because of speed and convenience. Typically in third world countries, where regulation and safety standards seem to be relaxed, if not non-existent, bus routes do not exist. In their place, 'Emergency Taxis', play an important role in transportation policy.

Emergency Taxi's, also known as bush taxi's, are mini buses that operate in the same way as a taxi, only they pick up as many people that will physically fit inside the vehicle before taking the passengers to a given destination. There will normally be a designated place in a city center where these will congregate and once they are full, they head off to their suburban destination. The trips are relatively inexpensive for the passenger. I traveled frequently on these in Harare, the capital of Zimbabwe, and in Cape Town, South Africa. I found this mode of transport not only entertaining, but felt this was something which the transportation authorities in any major city in Europe or the USA should seriously consider if they wish to address the grid lock mayhem.

Another popular mode of transportation in Africa is hitch hiking and could be considered almost an institution in some parts of the continent.

Drivers in cities will often subsidize their commute by picking up other commuters hitch hiking along the way.

There is an art to hitchhiking and some basic rules which should be observed at every occasion.

These are:

1. Safety is of paramount importance. The ideal situation is to always participate in this activity with someone else whom you know and trust.
2. Make sure that you arrive at the destination during day light hours; this makes finding accommodations easier and safer. I had an incident in Petersberg in South Africa, where I was trying to get to Pretoria a few hundred miles south. It was late in the afternoon and a driver picked 3 of us up. At first he wanted to lock us in the back of his truck, which is a bit unusual, as the driver normally likes to ask questions to see where you are from and how are you finding the country.

Alarm bells had not yet sounded at this stage, but soon a siren would go off. I was in the cabin trying my utmost to generate a conversation with the driver. He was a big guy and had a shaved Mike Tyson style hair cut. We wanted to go to Pretoria and he was driving to Johannesburg and insisted on dropping us off there, even though he had to drive though our destination to get to his! Johannesburg may produce 70% of Africa's GDP, but it's not the safest place during the day, let alone at night. One report states that it is not uncommon for 70 murders to occur in a weekend.

Pretty much every back packer I'd met in South Africa, had been or knew someone who'd been robbed, beaten up or had bad experiences in this city. Now I think of myself as a man of adventure, but this city was, in my view, off limits.

I figured we would arrive in Johannesburg's city center at 8:00pm, when it would already be dark. Not the best time, but there were 3 of us, so there would be safety in numbers.

I still had a bad feeling about this lift and further into the conversation, it turned out that the driver would drop us off were he lived, a small township, south west of the city- SOWETO (South West Township.) SOWETO is a black township built in the Apartheid era to house non-whites. If you're a tourist, it's risky during the day and a no go area at night.

I repeated what I'd just heard back to him and he confirmed his intent. After repeated requests, he pulled over at a garage. There was a brief argument on payment, and he was on his way.

Oddly enough 30 seconds later we got another lift by a guy called, 'Flip'. He was Namibian truck driver who was learning English by picking up hitchhikers!

We arrived in Pretoria's center after 9:00pm, where we phoned for a taxi to the hostel. This wasn't quite without incident as a local woman wanted us to rescue her sister in a nightclub, who was being held by her boyfriend at knifepoint! We polity declined the request.

3. If you are British, it's a sin not to talk about the Royal Family. Dropping names whenever you can and explaining the inner workings of the country will work wonders. Your audience is usually spellbound by anything British. There are many in the world that still think the monarchy runs the country and that there's a moat surrounding Buckingham Palace-No joke. I remember having a conversation with a driver on the way to the Bulawayo in Zimbabwe and the driver was proudly telling me about his young daughters. I asked what their names were, and he said the eldest was called 'Baroness.' It surprised me that he had named her Baroness, and on asking him why, his reply was that he thought it was a common name in Britain.

I continued to listen on as he explained why he thought this name was common. It turns out that he regularly listens to the BBC World Service, where they feature programs on The House of Lords (A political debating chamber in the UK, where legislation is determined), and the women who participate in the debates have titles i.e. Baroness Thatcher. He thought their titles were their first names. Maybe it's a good thing he doesn't watch the cartoon South Park for names!

4. Be as polite as possible to the driver. Ask them about their family and about their country. There's no better source of information on a country than from the people, as opposed to the political biases of the media. I can't tell you the warmth in drivers' faces when I climbed up into the cabin of a truck greeting them with 'Mongununi, mountu gussu', which is 'Good morning, did you sleep well?', in Shona, a local tribal language in Southern Africa. On those very words I would often hit it off so well with the driver they would invite me to stay in their house for the night and introduce me to the rest of their family.

5. In terms of payment for your transportation, as a rule of thumb, if the driver is black, they expect payment and if they are white they will not. Often black driver of trucks who are earning as little as US $2.00 per day will pick up hitchhikers to top up their salary. If there's 3 of you hitchhiking, he can easily double his day's pay. In many ways I prefer

to spend money this way. I know it's going to a local citizen of the country, who lives in the area and is trying to better himself, as opposed to a faceless multinational, which will roll out of town on the first sign of a downturn in fortunes.

It is important to get the price straight before or in the beginning of the journey. On one incident in the Plumtree area of Zimbabwe, which borders with South Africa, the driver was charging us per person and not for the three of us. On discovering this mistake the conversations with him that followed were" Do you take American Express? Travelers Checks? 20 British pounds is all I've got,…I've got nothing smaller…so do you have change? (Ideally in pounds or US dollars!)"

6. Apart from payment, I always try to give a gift to the driver. Something small and perhaps worthless to you but is of interest to a local- perhaps an old pair of sneakers, which probably can't be purchased in the country.
7. In countries where your mother tongue is not spoken and communication with the driver is by pointing to maps, always watch where you are going. I had a few mildly inconvenient trips where I was dropped of in the wrong place, but of course that's half the adventure.

It's a road less traveled in a fast car.

See back cover for **Peter Ward's** biography.

| the overloaded pickup truck | peter ward malawi 1996 |

Built tough strong

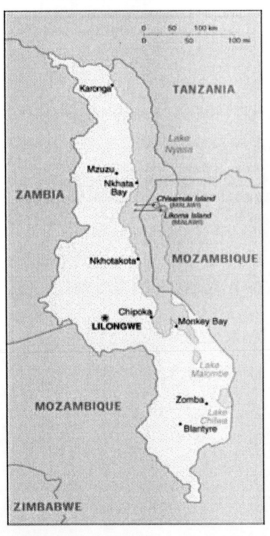

We had spent the day hiking across Zambia, which proved to be a testing country, to say the least. This was partly because everyone talks to you in your face - very off putting to say the least; and it was partly due to the zoo like experience at the bus terminal in Lusaka, the capital. It seemed like every person in that building, including the policeman, was only interested in transferring money in order to get hard currency. My attempts to exchange $10 US dollars found me having a conversation with one dubious money man on the street, which, unknowingly, required me to have several unwanted conversations with half a dozen others. They all haggled over the best price, counting money so quick it seemed like a card trick and thrusting their pocket calculators in the air.

It took half an hour to exchange such a small amount. After not being persuaded to exchange anything in a back room, I had to insist I see the money up front and remorselessly explain that I only needed $10 exchanged and was not remotely interested in exchanging $50 even if my life depended on it, despite the better exchange rate.

The currency in Zambia is pretty much worthless outside the country and is commonly known as a 'Toilet Currency'. Only enough local currency to pay for the night's accommodation was needed. The US dollar, British pound and South African Rand are king in this part of the world, so it's always advisable to only have small amounts of local currency on you to pay for items like accommodation, so when you leave the country you don't have too many souvenir notes.

It was a breath of fresh air the following morning when we crossed the border into Malawi- Central Africa. It was odd that 10 feet into a different country could make such a difference. It was more relaxing, with better weather and wider smiles. I don't know, but there was something different. The locals were proud to say, 'I'm from Malawi- trust me'.

Malawi is a small, landlocked country wedged between Zambia, Tanzania and Mozambique. It is 900km long and 150km east to west. Briefly looking at the map it appears slightly larger than Bulgaria or Cuba, or for an American, slightly smaller than Pennsylvania. The native tongue is English (another breath of fresh air for us). The country was named Nyasaland by the first European settlers and is the place where the quote "Dr. Livingstone, I presume?" originated.

The 2 of us had hooked up with two students from the UK who had taken a year off to teach English in Zimbabwe and were spending their Easter vacation in Cape Maclear, which is near Monkey Bay. This is a back packers' Mecca: you will meet people here who you drank Castle beer with in the Sports Bar in Cape Town or swapped a story with in a street market in Cairo. It is the 'small world' of Africa.

We were relatively lucky with lifts leaving the border, which is normally the case as there are plenty of trucks heading up the main roads; but it was when we were dropped off by a friendly driver at a junction on the way to Cape Maclear that a problem arose.

After half an hour of hiking, we came to realize that there was not much traffic heading towards our destination, so we waited and we waited until finally a pick up truck drove by and stopped. The driver was smartly dressed and knew our destination. It almost seemed he'd made a career for himself by picking up hitchhikers. The price he wanted for his transportation services was just too high and in Africa, when it comes to a price, everything is negotiable, but this guy would not move on anything.

Realizing this might be the only vehicle passing for the next hour, I managed to cut a break on the price. This included him picking up any one else on the route. I thought that if anyone else were going to be hitching, it would be at this junction on the road; in hindsight, this may have been a mistake.

The roads that followed were peppered with potholes, so the vehicle was continuously swerving. After about 5 minutes we stopped and another hitchhiker joined us, followed by another and then another. Within a short time, the back of the truck seemed to be at full capacity. One particular passenger, a fisherman, climbed aboard, with his catch of the day packed in a large industrial bag- Oh what a lovely smell! We had stopped so many times to pick up passengers, the only way we could all fit on the back of the truck was by standing up. Every time the truck swerved, we all had to lean into the bend. It did look quite comical at times, bracing oneself for a corner of the road. The driver was even taking detours into local villages, which were scattered around the countryside, to pick up and drop off passengers. This may have been all very scenic, but in my mind this was not in the spirit of what the driver and I had agreed to. One local village, perhaps not used to having backpackers visit, greeted us by performing a traditional dance. Patiently we watched, not wishing to be rude, but we did have someplace place to go. Sometimes the landscape seemed so similar I wouldn't have been surprised to find that we'd done a loop somewhere along the way!

I had enough when it got to the stage that when I lifted one foot, I found that it was physically impossible to put it back on the floor because someone else's was there. At the next stop I squeezed myself out of the back to have a word with the driver.

Despite a moderate protest, he wouldn't listen, "A deal's a deal, I can't go back on my word. I'm Malawian," he claimed.

Knowing that I was completely in the middle of nowhere, I had little choice but to edge my way back onto the vehicle, resigning myself to standing like a sardine. This made rush hour on the London Underground look positively appealing. Fish had replaced the smell from the left over McDonalds.

With the sheer number of people standing in the back of the vehicle and sitting on the tail gate (bumper), I shudder to think what this must be doing the suspension of the vehicle. If he did a few more trips like this, he'd be hitching a ride to the local car mechanic.

Fortunately, as there were so many passengers, we never traveled fast. Looking at the bloated tires, any sudden stops and a blow out could easily occur; however, the speed still required a firm hold by anyone standing in the center of the vehicle.

On one drop off point a policeman walked up to the vehicle and started talking with the driver. I thought this was my saving grace, as the driver's attitude to packing people in the back of his vehicle was clearly dangerous and with the policeman's authority, passengers would be asked to find alternative means of transportation, as sooner or later an accident would occur. This wasn't on the policeman's mind; all he wanted was a lift and climbed on board!

See back cover for **Peter Ward's** biography.

	**uncovering cairo's metro system**	cam mcgrath egypt present day

Cairo's underground metro system, the first of its kind in Africa and the Middle East, is a blessing to this city of 16 million people. Every day, the metro funnels an estimated 2.5 million commuters off the crowded streets (you'd hardly notice the difference) below ground and moving from station to station.

There are two metro lines in operation. One runs from El-Marg southward to Helwan, an industrial enclave 30km south of Cairo, while the other runs from populous Shoubra el-Kheima southwest to Cairo University, and will soon continue on to Giza. Construction is currently underway on a third line from Imbaba to Al-Azhar, and the government has given the green light to extend existing lines to reach Moneib and the airport. When all lines are complete, Cairo's metro project will be on par with other world-class metro systems. Really, I'm not making that up.

No graffiti, no litter, no smoking- New York subway users visiting Cairo are in for a big treat. Unlike most things in this city, the metro system runs efficiently. It is without doubt the quickest and cheapest way to transverse the city, costing just 50 piasters (15 cents) for up to 9 stations, and less than a pound (35 cents) from one end to the other. There are also nominal discounts for reusable tickets for 10 journeys or more.

Metro tickets can be purchased at any of the kiosks in the station, provided the employee at the window is inclined to deal with you. The kiosks are one of the best places in Cairo to make change, but some of the employees are a little uptight about accepting torn or taped banknotes. Even a 25-piaster note with a barely discernible tear in one corner will be turned away. Assuming you get a ticket, feed it into the turnstyle upon entering and hold onto it until exiting.

In theory, fines are issued for ticket-less travel. In reality, authorities encourage it. Police and even metro officials (in blue coats) sit idly by watching kids slide under the turn styles; men jump them and husbands catch the gate and squeeze in behind their wives. Each station usually has one turn style that operates freely for maintenance staff, and police officers will kindly point it out to anyone who asks or is seen checking for it. In other cases, police may even remove a metal barricade to let an old man without a ticket through. But make no mistake. If you intend to travel ticket-less, show no compunction about it. Metro officials have no sympathy for those honest riders who lose a ticket, or have it eaten by the machine. Nor do they appreciate honest riders who point out the ticket-less ones hopping over the turn styles like lemmings.

The metro operates daily from about 5:30 am to half past midnight. Intervals between trains vary throughout the day, but waits are never more than 15 minutes. Breakdowns are infrequent, but trains sometimes linger at stations for no apparent reason. Delays are also caused by riders holding the doors open for friends behind them, sometimes far far behind them.

Outdoor station platforms have too few seats and little shade, and can be oppressively hot in the summer. Underground platforms have a handful of seats, but those standing can at least watch Egyptian soap operas or the endlessly repeating "Soccer's Greatest Goals" tape. In 1999, commuters were treated to some steamy videos when a metro employee failed to realise that the VCR in his booth was broadcasting to the whole system.

The front car of every train is reserved for women, offering them a bastion of relief away from the prying eyes and groping hands of men. It also spares women from having to fight the herd that tramples anything in its path to be first on or off the train when it arrives. Admittedly, the most ruthless of these animals is a rather large old baladi woman who pushes, flails and gyrates her way into the car.

The two metro lines vary slightly. The older French-built line running from El-Marg to Helwan has 32 stops, its downtown stations being underground while the rest are on the surface. The underground platforms are comfortably warm in the winter and stuffy, humid and hot in the summer when the only breezes come from passing trains. Fans on trains running this route are either left off, mocking riders, or turned on to douse them with barely palpable breezes. The heat can be intolerable- during the summer, commuters flood out of the doors in sweat.

The newer Japanese built Shoubra-Cairo University line is better. Not only are its underground stations fully air-conditioned, but so are its trains. Consider yourself lucky if your daily commute uses this line.

Key metro stops:

Sadat: Ground zero downtown, this station is under Midan Tahrir and just minutes from the Egyptian Museum, Nile Hilton, American University and Nile Corniche. Its tunnels double as a pedestrian underpass.

Mubarak: Beneath Midan Ramses, provides access to a major bus and minibus hub as well as the city's railway station.

Ataba: Use this station to visit Ezbekiyya or to enter the "threshold" to Islamic Cairo.

Cairo University: Packed with students, and good for visiting the zoo.

Opera: One tunnel leads directly to the Cairo Opera House.

Mar Girgis: Brings you right to the doorstep of Coptic Cairo.

El-Maadi: Good for visits to this affluent suburb, but most of the district requires a car.

See page 59, for biography of **Cam Mcgrath.**

looking for abdelati

tanya shaffer
morocco
1999

Here's what I love about travel: Strangers get a chance to amaze you. Sometimes a single day can bring a blooming surprise, a simple kindness that opens a chink in the brittle shell of your heart and makes you a different person when you go to sleep—more tender, less jaded—than you were when you woke up.

This particular day began when Miguel and I descended from a cramped, cold bus at 7 a.m. and walked the stinking gray streets of Casablanca with our backpacks, looking for food. Six days earlier I had finished a stint on a volunteer project, creating a public park in Kenitra, an ugly industrial city on the Moroccan coast. This was my final day of travel before hopping a plane to sub-Saharan Africa and more volunteer work.

Miguel was one of five non-Moroccans on the work project, a 21-year-old vision of flowing brown curls and buffed golden physique. Although having him as a traveling companion took care of any problems I might have encountered with Moroccan men, he was inordinately devoted to his

95

girlfriend, Eva, a wonderfully brassy, wiry, chain-smoking Older Woman of 25 with a husky Scotch-drinker's voice, whom he couldn't go more than half an hour without mentioning. Unfortunately, Eva had had to head back to Barcelona immediately after the three-week work camp ended, and Miguel wanted to explore Morocco. Since I was the only other person on the project who spoke Spanish, and Miguel spoke no French or Arabic, his tight orbit shifted onto me, and we became traveling companions. This involved posing as a married couple at hotels, which made Miguel so uncomfortable that the frequency of his references to Eva went from half-hour to 15-minute intervals, and then five as we got closer to bedtime. Finally one night, as we set up in our room in Fes, I took him by the shoulders and said, "Miguel, it's OK. You're a handsome man, but I'm over 21. I can handle myself, I swear."

This morning we were going to visit Abdelati, a sweet, gentle young man we'd worked with on the project in Kenitra. He'd been expecting us to arrive in Casablanca for a few days, and since he had no telephone, he'd written down his address and told us to just show up—his mother and sisters were always at home. Since my plane was leaving from Casablanca the following morning, we wanted to get an early start, so we could spend the whole day with him.

Eventually we scored some croissants and overly sugared panaches (a mix of banana, apple and orange juice) at a roadside cafe, where the friendly proprietor advised us to take a taxi rather than a bus out to Abdelati's neighborhood. He said the taxi should cost 20-25 dirham—under $3—and the buses would take all day.

We hopped into a taxi, which took off with a screech of rubber before we'd agreed on a price.

"Forty or 45 dirham!" the driver shouted over the roar of his engine. He was already careening around corners at top speed.

"Why isn't the counter on?" I asked.

"Broken!" he said.

Miguel rolled his eyes. "Eva would hate this," he whispered.

"If I had the counter, it would cost you 50," the driver said.

Since the man in the cafe had told us 25 or 30, I asked the driver to pull over and let us out. At first I put it politely: "We'd like to look at other options," but he simply said, "OK," and kept driving. After four such attempts, I said sharply, "Nous voulons descendre"—we want to get out.

Reluctantly he pulled over, saying we owed him 10 dirham.

"Fine," I said. "Let me just get our bags down first—the money's in there." We yanked our backpacks off the overhead rack and took off, while the taxi driver shouted after us.

Miguel shook his head. "Eva would've killed that guy," he said.

It was an hour before we caught another taxi. Finally one pulled over, and a poker-faced man quoted us an estimate of 18-20 dirham.

"Tres bien," I said with relief, and we jumped in.

Apparently the address Abdelati had written down for us was somehow suspect, and when we got into the neighborhood, our driver started asking directions.

First he asked a cop, who scratched his head and asked our nationalities, looking at our grimy faces and scraggly attire with a kind of bemused fondness. After more small talk, he pointed vaguely to a park a few blocks away. There a group of barefoot 7- or 8-year-old boys were kicking a soccer ball. Our driver asked where Abdelati's house was, and one of the boys said Abdelati had moved, but he could take us to the new house. This seemed a bit odd to me, since Abdelati had just given me the address a week ago, but since a similar thing had happened in Fes, I chalked it up as another Moroccan mystery and didn't worry about it too much.

The little boy came with us in the cab, full of his own importance, squirming and twisting to wave at other children as we inched down the narrow winding roads. Finally the little boy pointed to a house, and our driver went to the door and inquired. He came back to the cab saying Abdelati's sister was in this house, visiting friends and would come along to show us where they lived.

Soon a beautiful girl of about 16 emerged from the house. She was dressed in a Western skirt and blouse, which surprised me, since Abdelati's strong religious beliefs and upright demeanor had made me think he came from a more traditional family. Another thing that surprised me was her skin color. Whereas Abdelati looked very African, this young woman was an olive-skinned Arab. Still, I'd seen other unusual familial combinations in Morocco's complex racial mosaic, so I didn't give it too much thought.

We waited in the yard while the sister went in and returned accompanied by her mother, sisters and brother-in-law, all of whom greeted us with cautious warmth. Unlike the younger girl, the older sisters were wearing traditional robes, though their faces were not veiled. You see a range of orthodoxy in Moroccan cities, caught as they are between Europe and the Arab world. From the younger sister's skirt and blouse to the completely veiled women gliding through the streets with only their eyes in view, the women's outfits seem to embody the entire spectrum.

We paid our taxi driver, and I tipped and thanked him profusely, until he grew embarrassed and drove away.

We were ushered into a pristine middle-class Moroccan home, with an intricately carved doorway and swirling multicolored tiles lining the walls.

The mother told us in broken French that Abdelati was out, but would be home soon. We sat on low cushioned seats in the living room, drinking sweet, pungent mint tea poured at a suitable height from a tiny silver teapot and eating sugar cookies, while the family members took turns sitting with us and making shy, polite conversation that frequently lapsed into uncomfortable silence. Every time anything was said, Miguel would say "What?" with extreme eagerness, and I would translate the mundane fragment into Spanish for him: "Nice weather today. Tomorrow perhaps rain." At this he'd sink back into fidgety frustration, undoubtedly wishing Eva were there.

An hour passed, and as the guard kept changing, more family members emerged from inner rooms. I was again struck by the fact that they were all light-skinned Arabs. How did Abdelati fit into this picture? Was he adopted? I was very curious to find out.

After two hours had passed with no sign of Abdelati, the family insisted on serving us a meal of couscous and chicken.

"Soon," was the only response I got when I inquired as to what time he might arrive.

"You come to the hammam, the bath," the young sister said after we'd finished lunch. "When we finish, he is back."

"The bath?" I asked, looking around the apartment.

The sister laughed. "The women's bath!" she said. "Haven't you been yet?" She pointed at Miguel.

"He can go to the men's; it's right next door."

"What?" said Miguel anxiously, sitting up.

"She wants to take us to the baths," I said.

A look of abject horror crossed his face. "The-the bath?" he stammered. "You and me?"

"Yes," I said, smiling widely. "Is there some problem?"

"Well…well…" I watched his agitation build for a moment, then sighed and put my hand over his.

"Separate baths, Miguel. You with the men, me with the women."

"Oh." He almost giggled with relief. "Of course."

The women's bath consisted of three large connecting rooms, each one hotter and steamier than the last, until you could barely see two feet in front of you. The floors were filled with naked women of all ages and body types, sitting directly on the slippery tiles, washing each other with mitts made of rough washcloths. Tiny girls and babies sat in plastic buckets filled with soapy water—their own pint-sized tubs. The women carried empty buckets, swinging like elephants' trunks, to and from the innermost room, where they filled them at a stone basin from a spigot of boiling water, mixing in a little cold from a neighboring spigot to temper it.

In a culture where the body is usually covered, I was surprised by the women's absolute lack of inhibition. They sat, mostly in pairs, pouring the water over their heads with small plastic pitchers, then scrubbing each other's backs—and I mean scrubbing. Over and over they attacked the same spot, as though they were trying to get out a particularly stubborn stain, leaving reddened flesh in their wake. They sprawled across each other's laps. They washed each other's fronts, backs, arms, legs. Some women washed themselves as though they were masturbating, hypnotically circling the same spot. Two tiny girls, about 4 years old, scrubbed their grandmother, who lay sprawled across the floor face down. A prepubescent girl lay in her mother's lap, belly up, eyes closed, as relaxed as a cat, while her mother applied a forceful up and down stroke across the entire length of her daughter's torso. I was struck by one young woman in particular, who reclined alone like a beauty queen in a tanning salon, back arched, head thrown back, right at the steamy heart of the baths, where the air was almost suffocating. When she began to wash, she soaped her breasts in sensual circles, proudly, her stomach held in, long chestnut hair rippling down her back, a goddess in her domain.

Abdelati's sister, whose name was Samara, went at my back with her mitt, which felt like steel wool.

"Ow!" I cried out. "Careful!"

This sent her into gales of laughter that drew the attention of the surrounding women, who saw what was happening and joined her in appreciative giggles as she continued to sandblast my skin.

"You must wash more often," she said, pointing to the refuse of her work—little gray scrolls of dead skin that clung to my arms like lint on a sweater.

When it came time to switch roles, I tried to return the favor, but after a few moments Samara became impatient with my wimpiness and grabbed the washcloth herself, still laughing. After washing the front of her body she called over a friend to wash her back, while she giggled and sang.

"What was it like in there?" asked Miguel when we met again outside. He looked pink and damp as a newborn after his visit to the men's baths, and I wondered whether his experience was anything like mine.

"I'd like to tell you all about it," I said eagerly, "but..." I paused for emphasis, then leaned in and whispered, "I don't think Eva would approve."

When we got back to the house, the mother, older sister and uncle greeted us at the door.

"Please," said the mother, "Abdelati is here."

99

"Oh, good," I said, and for a moment, before I walked into the living room, his face danced in my mind—the warm brown eyes, the smile so shy and gentle and filled with radiant life.

We entered the lovely tiled room we'd sat in before, and a handsome young Arab man in nicely pressed Western pants and shirt came forward to shake our hands with an uncertain expression on his face.

"Bonjour, mes amis," he said cautiously.

"Bonjour," I smiled, slightly confused. "Abdelati—est-ce qu'il est ici?" Is Abdelati here?

"Je suis Abdelati."

"But…but…" I looked from him to the family and then began to giggle tremulously. "I—I'm sorry. I'm afraid we've made a bit of a mistake. I—I'm so embarrassed."

"What? What?" Miguel asked urgently. "I don't understand. Where is he?"

"We got the wrong Abdelati," I told him, then looked around at the assembled family who'd spent the better part of a day entertaining us. "I'm afraid we don't actually know your son."

For a split second no one said anything, and I wondered whether I might implode right then and there and blow away like a pile of ash.

Then the uncle exclaimed heartily, "Ce n'est pas grave!"

"Yes," the mother joined in. "It doesn't matter at all. Won't you stay for dinner, please?"

I was so overwhelmed by their kindness that tears rushed to my eyes. For all they knew we were con artists, thieves, anything. Would such a thing ever happen in the U.S.?

Still, with my plane leaving the next morning, I felt the moments I could share with the first Abdelati and his family slipping farther and farther away.

"Thank you so much," I said fervently. "It's been a beautiful, beautiful day, but please…Could you help me find this address?"

I took out the piece of paper Abdelati had given me back in Kenitra, and the new Abdelati, his uncle and his brother-in-law came forward to decipher it.

"This is Baalal Abdelati!" said the second Abdelati with surprise. "We went to school together! He lives less than a kilometer from here. I will bring you to his house."

And that is how it happened, that after taking photos and exchanging addresses and hugs and promises to write, Miguel and I left our newfound family and arrived at the home of our friend Abdelati as the last orange streak of the sunset was fading into the indigo night. There I threw myself into the arms of that dear and lovely young man, exclaiming, "I thought we'd never find you!"

After greetings had been offered all around, and the two Abdelatis had shared stories and laughter, we waved goodbye to our new friend Abdelati and entered a low, narrow hallway, lit by kerosene lamps.

"This is my mother," said Abdelati.

And suddenly I found myself caught up in a crush of fabric and spice, gripped in the tight embrace of a completely veiled woman, who held me and cried over me and wouldn't let me go, just as though I were her own daughter, and not a stranger she'd never before laid eyes on in her life.

See page 32, for biography of **Tanya Shaffer**.

| **delays can be expected** | heather mckim
mozambique
1995 |

We were entering Mozambique along the Zimbabwean border, on the western side of the country. I was traveling with three other Peace Corps Volunteers who were also stationed in Zimbabwe – Josh, Laura and Alison. Our eventual destination was a town called Inhassoro, on the eastern coast. We had a vague idea where we were going, but were a bit foggy as to how we intended to get there.

We hitchhiked from Harare. To most Americans, hitchhiking is an activity pursued mainly by lunatics and convicts. Upon arrival in Zimbabwe in October of 1995, I thought I would never gather up the moxy to try it, but after six months in country, it had become as viable a form of transportation as a bus or taxi. It was cheaper than public transportation (free if you were picked up by a white traveler) and fairly reliable if you were white and female.

We set off early on a warm April day. The highlands spanning Zimbabwe and Mozambique rose before us, misty and cool. From Mutare, we hitched a ride through the border crossing to Chimoio, inside Mozambique, where we thought to catch a bus to the coast. A marked change occurred as we crossed the border. Car-sized potholes bloomed in the roads, the architecture morphed from British to crumbling Portuguese, the temperature rose about ten degrees and fixtures of the landscape included tanks and shells of jeeps, giant guns affixed to platforms and the hulls of military transport vehicles. They appeared to have simply run out of gas, the drivers throwing up their hands and abandoning their posts.

It wasn't long before we reached Chimoio. Our ride dropped us off at the bus terminal that, like those in Zimbabwe, was less organized and noisier than a circus. An orchestra of engines revving, vendors hissing, bus conductors chirping and whistling, children sobbing, men shouting, and women laughing surrounded us. People moved in close circles, shoulder to shoulder, hands and voices arresting us with queries and propositions: "Where are you going?", "Do you have a boyfriend?" "Can I carry your bags madam?" and in lower tones: "Change money?", "Do you want to buy some pot?" and so on. You had to remain on the strictest guard, cinch your bag and, as politely as possible, try not to converse with the eddying mob.

We found a curb outside the arena that offered some respite and considered our position for a moment. I was desperately in need of a toilet and we needed to find the bus that was heading in our direction. After some consideration, it was decided that Josh and I would set off to locate our transport and a public toilet.

Though neither of us spoke Portuguese, we found our unique combination of language skills (French and Spanish) suitable enough to complete our task. People were friendly and we located what we thought was the correct bus with relative ease, though our myopic conductor warned us he was planning to depart at any moment, which meant the bus could leave any time in the next few hours. The toilet was another matter. I didn't want to weigh in a guess as to where the hundreds of other people loitering about were going to relieve themselves, but if it was a sanitary public place, it was tucked away beyond our reach. What we did find, in an abandoned train depot, was the foulest place on earth. The door was located at the rear of the station, beyond the end of the platform. The fumes were almost visible, curling out onto concrete. But my bladder was screaming and we were in a hurry so I stepped tenuously inside. I gagged. The plumbing had apparently been disabled long ago. In the corner stall, some sort of large rodent had made a home out of tree branches it had dragged from outside and feces that overflowed from the toilet bowl. I could hear the animal rustling inside its mound when I opened the door. The other stall was a mild improvement, though not considerably. Ironically, there was a neat roll of toilet paper affixed to the wall. I got out as quickly as I could.

We got onto the bus safely and indeed it roared away only a few minutes after we'd boarded. Once we had settled back, the conductor walked around with his leather pouch full of change. He wore an official-looking blue cap with a cardboard brim and a knee-length ladies jacket made of down, despite the heat. He smiled patiently at Josh thorough his glasses, which were about an inch thick and were foggy with scratches.

"Inhassoro," Josh told him in his best Portuguese accent. He tried to point out where to make the check mark on the ticket, which had a pre-printed list of stopping points, but couldn't find it. The conductor shook his head and smiled. Inhassoro wasn't among the official choices. In fact, the tickets appeared to be for another route entirely and we did not see any recognizable stop. Josh continued to repeat our destination, raising his voice until the conductor grew excited, scribbled something unintelligible on each of our tickets and then handed them out to us. Where were we going? No one knew. A few minutes later, the conductor returned, took back our tickets, and issued new ones. This time, he made a neat check mark for each of us, and handed out the tickets. Apparently, we would all be getting off

103

separately. He seemed satisfied with his work and made his way to the front of the bus. We exchanged confused glances. The signposts along the road called out for Maputo – we were going in the correct direction, it just remained to be seen exactly where we would disembark.

All told, the bus trip took over 10 hours. Why did it take so long to travel less than 250 miles? The main answer to that is potholes - yawning, precarious potholes deep enough to trap even the high-axled bus. The driver navigated these holes with the caution of a gymnast on a balance beam–easing in and out of the smaller holes and plowing through the underbrush on either side of the road to avoid the larger ones. I wondered what bright-eyed bureaucrat had decided it would be better to donate buses than it would be to invest in road construction.

We made several stops during the day. Tiny villages, perhaps one or two huts fashioned of sticks poking through the dense flora and fauna. At such points, the bus would slow to a halt and dozens of grinning faces would emerge from the bush and swarm like fairies: women with giant loads balanced on their heads, children with oranges or tomatoes wrapped in clear plastic, others with chicken skewered on a stick which they'd dance like puppets down the length of the bus windows. And of course there was Coke. Always Coke, even in the deepest, most obscure location, isolated from transport, food, supplies, there'd be some frail old man wheeling through on his battered bicycle with a crate of warm Coke. It was re-assuring.

It was also dry. The dust whirled around us and a thin orange film settled on my skin. It formed tiny dunes in the folds of my backpack. I could taste it on my lips. It was stifling and the heat grew fierce as the day progressed. But finally, dusk approached and with it relief. It was still not clear if we were making headway in reaching our goal. Furthermore, it seemed there were some thieves on the bus who were casing our backpacks. The thieves were not very discreet and apparently openly discussed their plans. We'd befriended other travelers on the bus (many of whom were refugees from Somalia who were fleeing to South Africa) and they didn't hesitate to warn us. Josh took the lead. He decided the best approach was to reason with the thieves. They sat a few rows behind us. Josh struck up a conversation. The thieves, for their part, were honest and accommodating, freely acknowledging their intent. He ended the conversation by giving away a bag of biscuits that we'd bought as snacks. It was a good will gesture he hoped would make the thieves reconsider their plan.

Unbeknownst to us, the bus intended to stop for the evening and did so around 9:00 PM. It rolled to a stop in front of what looked like a very primitive strip mall. It was a row of approximately eight bottle shops (taverns/grocery stores) constructed of tightly wound sticks and mud. Light glowed in an undulating arc from bare bulbs strung along a single power line. "I got you Babe" by Sonny and Cher greeted us as the engine died. There were a number of people milling about. Most of the busses' passengers got off to stretch. It became clear that the bus would go no further that evening and that most everyone with whom we had been traveling planned to sleep on the bus.

Originally, we thought we too would sleep on the bus but the conductor convinced us that it was not decent for us, that our things would surely be stolen and that I, Alison and Laura would most likely be assaulted. Truth be told, we probably would have been fine, but because we were white, the conductor felt compelled to show us particular hospitality, as though he wanted to make a good first impression. It was impossible to argue with him. We were all exhausted and apprehensive and it was not the wholesomest place we'd ever visited, so we didn't object when he lined us up with a room.

Perhaps we should have been a little more wary. There was something odd about the place. The men were almost all drunk, staggering about, periodically brawling with one another and the women were a little too scandalously clad (any skirt even slightly above the knee was considered trashy). They eyed us with a mixture of amusement and contempt. It was strange to even see women at a bottle store. In Zimbabwe, for the most part, women did not drink and they almost never hung out at the bottle store. But this was Mozambique, I thought, perhaps things were different here. We found our room behind one of the bars. It was a small space, perhaps 15 x15 with two double beds at diagonal corners and a warped wardrobe. The beds looked as though someone had just climbed out of them after two or three week convalescence. The sheets were stained and smelled of sweat. But by this time, weary and worn out, it didn't matter, as long as the door locked.

The room was separated from direct contact with the shops by an open-air bathing facility with stalls. Each stall had a faucet and buckets were commonly available. It was a unisex bathing area, but most others were women, who smiled kindly as I snuck inside my stall, which did not lock. The bath, though much needed after the cramped and dusty ride, was short and unsatisfying not only because the water was icy cold, but also because I was sharing the stall with about twenty frogs who hopped about, occasionally jumping into my bucket so that I would have to rescue them.

I fell asleep soon after laying down but my repose was soon disturbed by the fighting and screaming that broke out every half hour or so. Also, men kept coming up to our room and crying out in Portuguese just outside our window or at our door. Sometimes they'd bang on the door. At one point, I felt certain they'd surrounded us. Another time, a man knocked on the window and placed a bottle of Amarula (an expensive South African Liqueur) on the window sill and jabbered at us for fifteen minutes. It was not a restful evening. The festivities ran through the night and into the next morning.

We thought we'd just happened onto a lively night spot but it turned out there was a little more to the story. Our explanation came as we emerged from the room to board the bus. A thin crowd was gathered outside our door. Josh exited first, then me, Alison and Laura. From the crowd we heard "Uno!, Dos!, Tres!", a gaggle of laughter and a healthy round of applause. It wasn't too hard to figure out. We had spent the night in a rural brothel and they were applauding Josh for his stamina.

The bus departed early and though we were still unsure of exactly where we would get off, we felt a little more confident, having recovered safely from our little adventure. Josh once again engaged the conductor who, in response to his repeated questions about Inhassoro, nodded excitedly and grinned. It was becoming a real issue now since the road was better and the bus was flying along at a harrowing speed. Each of us got in the act. We surrounded the conductor and tried, in our various known tongues, to explain that we wanted: water, the ocean, la mer, agua...he continued to nod frantically. The bus had slowed down, we were on a steep hill and the driver had to shift down. We continued to haggle with him, trying in vain to explain, when suddenly, as the bus pulled up over the top of the hill, the ocean opened up before us in a glorious curtain of blue, merging with the horizon. It was as though we'd come to the promised land and a velvet curtain had been pulled back to reveal rivers of milk and honey. We had arrived.

Biography not provided.

	**monkey stew**	carla king ivory cost present day

A bicycle journey through West Africa

At twilight it was difficult to tell the simple dwellings from the workshops, the brothels, the restaurants, the stores. In this quarter of San Pedro, a large dirty port town in the Ivory Cost, the buildings were single-room huts thrown together directly on top of the hard brown dirt by nailing pieces of wood of various lengths and states of rot into a vague square, topped off by sheets of tin or palm leaves. At this time of the evening, the women sat out front of the huts braiding each other's hair and the men gathered on certain corners, squatting over a brazier to prepare the heavily-sugared tea, smoking, and watching.

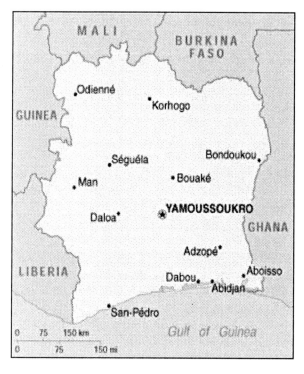

No one was too busy to look up as I passed. Groups of children followed me at a distance, calling out "Toubab" (their word for white person) to announce my approach. I was looking for a restaurant, for something to eat.

"Vous avez aun restaurant ici?" I asked a woman who sat in front of a hut from whose door billowed great clouds of gray smoke. As she smiled and stood up, the bravest in my entourage of children rushed to touch my skin and hair. Others hung back, fingers in mouths, staring at the white stranger. At first I'd found them amusing, but after two months in West Africa they were no longer. Guiltily, I now considered them as annoying as the constant buzzing of flies and the mosquitoes who had given me malaria in Guinea.

The woman beckoned me inside the hut where the orange flicker of fire danced under a great iron pot. She lifted the lid and pointed inside. "There is this," she told me, stirring up from the liquid the white, triangular skull of a goat: eye sockets, jawbone, teeth. I looked around. There were no furnishings in the room. Another woman slept in one corner, swathed in colorful robes on the swept dirt floor. In the other corner slept a pet monkey.

"If you wait an hour there will be something better," the woman whispered conspiratorially, and she turned her eyes upon me in the smoky hut. With her gaze came the now familiar sense of oppression settling upon me, along with alternating waves of sorrow, irritation, and guilt.

I hadn't wanted to eat in a hut again. I was finally in a real city, and I wanted a restaurant. I thought she'd send a child to take me to the right neighborhood, but by eating here I would be doing a great favor to this woman and her family. My 200 CFA, less than an American dollar, could be used to buy rice, manioc root, and other staples. More likely though she would buy lipstick or nail polish. Another wave of guilt ran through me at this disparaging thought.

I told myself that I couldn't always be concerned with how the family would spend the money. It's like giving a quarter to a beggar on the corner, knowing it might be spent on food or rot-gut, depending on the priority of the moment. An adult may thoughtlessly spend money needed to feed the children on tea, cigarettes, or cosmetics. And tonight I didn't want to be faced with the welfare of a family or village. I didn't want to watch the women pounding grain and manioc for my dinner, to see the calluses on her hands, to see her skinny children, to eat seated on a packed earth floor, to be given the only chair and to be watched by dozens of hungry eyes while I was given the choicest bits, knowing that when I walked away they would fall upon it, sucking the last drops of nutrition from among the bones I so casually discarded.

After two months in West Africa, I needed a break. This was a big town. I wanted to find an established restaurant where I could sit at a table, have a beer, and not be obliged to become emotionally involved in a family's personal life. Just by sitting at someone's hut I would be face-to-face with the woman and the children whose economy I was so directly affecting, face-to-face with the unbelievable hand-to-mouth existence of these people as they considered me a piece of incredible luck that had brought them 200 CFA, and more, if they were clever.

Of course the boy would escort me to my hotel that night, and another child, probably the girl, would be outside in the morning, waiting to bring me back for breakfast. She would lead me through the streets of this dirty port town, over the sturdiest planks that lay over stinking open sewers from the quarter of my hotel to the quarter of their family. If I ate here I would be their patroness, and for the duration of my stay I wouldn't be able to forget them. Indeed, I would be pressed to take photos, to send money from America, or Walkmans or jeans. I would have to give them my address, promise to become a correspondent. Already I had dozens.

They knew about the material things because this was a large town, unlike others where my only option was to call upon the chief to ask his permission to stay and eat, and where I paid for my meal and my night's lodging in trade for cigarettes, sugar, candy, tea leaves, Nescafe, or maybe my T-shirt. Money is practically useless when one must walk 100 miles to a store. In the villages there is no stench. In the bush, villagers are innocent of education, of cash, of technology, and of medicine. The food supply determines the size of the village. A malnourished mother will lose her child. The village will shrink or grow according to the abundance of the forest. It is a clean place, it is healthy, it is subject to the laws of nature that little affect Westerners or these impoverished ghetto-dwellers.

Surveying the litter of San Pedro, inhaling the stench, avoiding the beggars with their oozing wounds and missing limbs, it is impossible not to feel shame for my culture, for the entire Western world, for pressing civilization upon these people. And it is impossible to reconcile myself to my guilt at feeling that the villagers who live in the bush – away from any modernity subject to the laws of nature and the cruel reality that only the fittest will survive – are better off.

Because here in a city a family needs money. There is no jungle in which to hunt. No forest where papayas and bananas grow wild, no clearing where one can plant manioc and grains. Garbage is inorganic. In bush villages, goats and chickens eat discarded fruit peelings, banana leaf plates, and stalks of grain. Teeth, bones and hooves are recycled into weapons and jewelry. Skins are used as floor coverings, blankets. The toilet is a hole in the ground which will be covered over when full.

In the city, goats cannot consume all of the cigarette and candy wrappers, oatmeal tins, and other manufactured garbage imported from the West. The presence of goats in a city cause an additional health hazard. In the city, early in the morning, one is confronted with the sight of men, women, and children squatting over the sewers, or emptying buckets of

109

sewage in the street. No, the Western world has not done a big favor to Africa by bringing it civilization.

Eating alone while being watched by a mother, her children, and all the neighbors in a city influenced by the West is nerve-wracking. There is perhaps one metal spoon in the neighborhood, which is brought for me, because they think I cannot use my hands as they do, though I have been doing so in the bush for weeks. They watch my fingers handle the tool, bring the food to my mouth, chew, smile, swallow. In their eyes is respect, admiration, hatred, curiosity, jealousy, wanting, and greed.

Electricity runs from a pole to a television set where fifty people gather, mesmerized by Baywatch and Dallas, which they will vehemently defend to be documentary programs of real Americans. I try to tell them that these realities are missing something – if they could only see the evening news that shows the poverty, the violence, the deviations from their dream world. They don't believe me.

Perhaps they must believe in this dream world, the static-ridden blue-hued flickering dream world dragged as far as its umbilical cord will allow into a dusty street. I cannot convince them that this is not my country, this world where on every street jostle blond, bikini-clad lifeguards who live in mansions off the riches of oil wells with views of sparkling oceans and go shopping daily for cars, jeans and cowboys boots. Confronted with such scenes I cannot get my mind to stop its turning round with reasons from such clear desperation.

My eyes became used to the dimness of the hut in the twilight. The smoke floated past me in a stream out the front door. I looked around. A back door. The woman stirring the stew and the one sleeping in the corner. The front door. The monkey sleeping in the other corner. It was funny, considering the nervous skittering traits of monkeys, that this one still slept as the woman chattered on to me about dinner in French and Mandinke.

I looked closer. Instead of being curled up in a sleeping position the monkeys' limbs were spread out, and its head, which I thought was resting on its side, was actually turned all the way round so that its chin rested on its back.

I looked even closer, unwilling to come to the obvious conclusion. Its pointy teeth glittered white and its eyes were open, dark, and soulless. The woman followed my gaze, and pointed to it. "In an hour, I will cook the monkey for you," she announced proudly.

I looked at her closer, shocked, but she was proud. "In an hour..." she repeated, and I did not hear the rest. All the stews I'd eaten in West Africa! How many had I eaten? How many monkeys?

And I fled, mumbling apologies that must have left her profoundly confused. The meat in these stews that I had eaten all across West Africa, I had assumed, was of the hundreds of sheep and goats that roamed cities and villages sharing the garbage piles with the slinky yellow dogs and vermin. Or it was dik-dik, a small deer hunted in the forest, or wild pig, or even bush-rat, an elusive night creature that a Peace Corps worker had assured me was a rare and delicious treat. It was a large, sleek animal, she told me, that fed not on garbage but on leaves and grubs in the jungle.

I had even laughed once, upon the realization that the tough pieces of skin in my stew was porcupine hide. The woman who cooked it had shown me its quills.

Not knowing the words for these creatures in Mandinke or Woloof, and the women, largely uneducated and unschooled in French, the national language, I would never know what had really been in those stews. Most likely, for the white stranger, a special guest with money, an entertainer in villages with no television, who shuffled cards and carried a battery-operated lamp, a self-inflating air mattress and other magical wonders, I was probably served the prestigious delicacy of monkey stew quite often, unrecognizable to my palate from the gamy tastes of bush-rat, porcupine, goat, and pig, especially among the standard pungent mixture of manioc chunks, yams, peppers, onions, and garlic.

The night I fled the hut I wandered around town, my hunger staved off by the horror of dead tangled limbs, until I stumbled into the French Quarter where there was a restaurant with electric light bulbs hanging from wooden ceilings that sheltered tables and Adirondak chairs, and refrigerators filled with beer and soda. I wished I was already in Abidjan, but this would do.

Civilization, I thought, relieved. Then the panicked bleating of a goat caught my attention. Across the street the goat hung upside-down on a hook by its bound feet, writhing in the light of a small fire. Before I could look away a hand appeared and its throat was severed with a large knife, its glint dulled with blood that shone black in the faded light. The animal, a strong, healthy animal, kicked and bucked and its back arched and writhed, even as it hung there upside-down. Its nerves reacted automatically to what its brain could no longer control – the severance of its sum parts.

I had seen it all before – what was different now? I had done this myself, having grown up in the country, no stranger to the wrung necks of chickens and rabbits, no stranger to the bleatings of lambs and calves being led to slaughter.

I will be a vegetarian, I thought as the butcher gripped the animal by a front leg, which still kicked, and opened its stomach in one practiced cut like the unzipping of a zipper. The shadow of a surly yellow dog – it moved like a jungle cat – hovered just out of range of the cooking fire where a man squatted to pick up a small pot of boiling tea. He lifted it out of the fire using a crushed cigarette pack, and poured the frothing liquid into three tiny cups as goat intestines slowly unraveled into a neat pile onto the dirt.

In the restaurant, I collapsed into a low wooden chair, leaning into its hard, cool, slatted back, varnished white with paint that bubbled and peeled. My beer came immediately, the cold brown bottle coating my hand with its cold sweat in the dark equatorial evening swelter. Willie Nelson sang "Georgia on My Mind," followed by John Denver's "Rocky Mountain High."

No, I wasn't ready for dinner yet. Just let me sit here awhile, s'il tu plait. The patron bowed and left me to contemplation.

All the tables and chairs had been sponged clean, the white paint only beginning to wrinkle and chip. I believe it never quite dried, being so humid.

The dirt floor had been pounded down hard and level and was swept clean of bottle caps, cigarette butts, and street gravel. I peeled the label off the beer bottle. It depicted a man, not black, not white, holding a bottle of the beer. *Bock Solibra: la biere de l'homme fort.* The beer of the strong man.

The only other customers, three African men dressed in Western suits, were seated nearby. They appeared to be of different nationalities, on a business trip, perhaps. The Wooloof was distinguished by his purple-black skin, his high cheekbones, and his tall, thin build. The Mandinkes, who predominate in this area, were shorter and lighter-skinned, with rounder faces. Perhaps they were entertaining their Senegalese business partner.

I'd seen men like these in Dakar.

They'd been to Marseilles and Paris. Their accents were clear when they spoke to me, the dialects muted. They knew life on the other continent. I watched them eat, speak, do business. They laughed loud, these men, and ordered, not requested, but ordered more beer with curt voices and the quick snap of fingers. The beer came quickly and was served unobtrusively. The patron melted into the background, waiting for more orders.

These men, how did they feel about San Pedro, about Dakar, about Abidjan?

Children peeked over the whitewashed half fence that separated the tables from the street. I must have looked an apparition in the light of the bare bulbs that illuminated the dining room. One of the suited Mandinkes took it upon himself to reprimand the children. He spoke sharply to them in the native language, startling them so that they jumped and ran away. The Mandinke laughed and tipped his head at me. He was polite, used to Westerners, and did not ask me my business, nor to join them. "Mange, mange," he urged heartily. "C'est bien, ce soir." Men of the world.

His companions smiled also and raised their beers. Their food did look tempting. A big pile of rice on one, chunks of meat on another, and a dish of sauce. The Mandinke gathered a small amount of rice into his palm, added a chunk of meat and with a quick flick of the wrist shook the mixture into his closed fingertips. Then he rubbed the compacted mass into the sauce and popped it into his mouth. "C'est bien," he repeated.

Loretta Lynn's "Stand by Your Man" played next. I raised my brown bottle in the air without looking round, and another beer arrived. I drank deeply, the liquid cooling my throat and emptying my head of the inherent violence caused by my order for dinner.

Had vegetarianism been an option, I would have entertained it. But however rich the soil and moist the air, Africans are either unwilling or unable to tend vegetable gardens, and only in small areas in the Ivory Coast did I see lettuce, beans, and tomatoes. Perhaps there are bugs and animals that eat them. Manioc grows everywhere, but it is merely a filler with no nutritional value at all. Yams and rice do not take up the slack. Therefore, I would be a carnivore. Soon I would probably be eating that freshly butchered goat.

During my travels I had seen sheep and goats transported in vans racing down potted, single-lane highways at 60 miles-per-hour. They stood and sat on top of these vans calmly chewing hay while secured only by a fishnet. One goat, who had fallen from the top of the van, was apparently unperturbed by being slung, hammock-style, on the side of the van. I had seen motorcyclists drive by holding half-a-dozen live chickens in their hands. On the beach I'd passed piles of dead fish being smoked between layers of dry wood smoldering directly on the sand, and in markets pounds of fresh meat were displayed for hours on fly-infested tables in direct sunlight.

I didn't mind porcupine, bush-rat, or even venison from dik-dik, an endearing little creature. I even enjoyed goat, mutton, chicken, pig, and the rare cut of beef, if I was sure it was cooked through. By the sea and near rivers I ate fish. But I drew the line at monkey. At least, knowingly, I drew the line at monkey.

I planned to have another beer and to see what they could cook-up for dinner. Country music hour was over and now it seemed to be disco-time. I called over the patron. He turned down a strange rendition of "Stayin' Alive" that I was sure hadn't been produced by the Bee Gees, and came over to recite the possibilities.

He could get many kinds of meats tonight. It had been market day, and he would send a boy for dik-dik, pig, or fish, as I liked. My dish would be accompanied by rice or manioc root. They had a special too, it seemed. For an extra 100 CFA, he knew it was expensive, of course, but he knew of a place nearby where – and this was a rare treat in a city – and if I hadn't tried it, as a Westerner he was sure I might not have tried it – but he could provide me with the rare treat because he knew where he could even buy a monkey, freshly killed, and just brought today from the jungle.

Published in Travelers' Tales: Food (O'Reilley & Assoc.)

Carla King is a San Francisco-based travel and technology writer and author of The American Borders Dispatches created in 1995, one of the first travelogues on the Internet. Continuing her realtime adventure series, she sent missives to the web during her 1998 journey from Beijing to the Tibetan border and back in The China Road Dispatches, and in 2000 she explored Southern India in The Indian Sunset Dispatches. Previous works include a guidebook to mountain biking the Alpes-Maritimes (Cycling the French Riviera), stories about a bicycle ride from Dakar, Senegal to Abdijan, Ivory Coast (a good story about this trip appears in Travelers' Tales: Food), and bicycle and motorcycle trips through Europe and Jamaica. She has also penned stories for many travel magazines and newspaper travel sections. When she's not writing about being on the road, Carla writes about technology for magazines and Web sites, and works in multimedia for events like the Digital Be-In. Carla is currently working on a second book by the http://www.WildWritingWomen.com on women and adventurous lifestyles. Visit her on the Internet at http://www.carlaking.com.

	**getting there**	eric ransdell burkina faso present day

A West African mystery

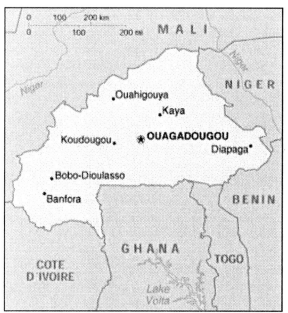

"See these people," says Gaetan Ouedraogo, my reluctant guide to the spirit world, "they are all protected." We are at the intersection of the Avenue Nelson Mandela and the Boulevard Yennenga in Ouagadougou, the dusty capital of Burkina Faso. Gaetan is driving and I am seated, uncomfortably, on the luggage rack of his Peugeot *mobillette.* The people on the mopeds surrounding us are a cross-section of West African society: nomadic Tuaregs from the Sahara, Mossi farmworkers in their distinctive conical hats, berobed Muslims, bespectacled Christians and the odd (possibly agnostic) besuited office worker. Yet for the sheer clash of modernity and tradition that is West Africa, few can equal the woman on the moped next to us; an extraordinarily large lady in an African print dress and matching headscarf who is revving her *mobillette*, chatting with a friend in perfect Parisian French and balancing a tin bucket of freshly baked baguettes on her head.

According to Gaetan they are all protected. And now, so am I. Around my waist is a juguina - a magical belt filled with herbs, bark, ground-up animal parts, hair and a few assorted writings from the Koran. It cost $100 and for that pittance I am protected against accidents, bombings, poisonings, theft and other people's witchcraft. In my pocket is another fetish, a small square called a "mandiana" which means "Let them love me." It's a rather more specific item that will not only ensure that I'm treated as a friend by

115

every stranger I meet, but will also make me invisible to immigration officials and any other venal *functionairres* who threaten to impede my progress on this journey through West Africa.

"Gaetan," I shout once we get going again. "I want to try these things out. Let's crash into that bus coming toward us."

Gaetan laughs. "That's the problem with you people," he replies over his shoulder. "You always want proof. If you desire to crash into that bus, the juguina can't stop you. It only protects you if you want it to."

I shout back that for a hundred bucks, it is my desire to crash into the bus *and* be protected. Gaetan drives on. We have more important things to do. Tonight I have a plane to catch. But first, I must give a white cola nut to an as yet unmet old woman sitting outside a mosque. And then there is the matter of *le blanc coq* - the white chicken I have been ordered to sacrifice by the mystical Madame Geneve Samake.

In Burkina Faso it is called *wack*. If crack smokers were called crackers, then its practitioners would be *wackers*. Fortunately, they are not. In fact, according to Gaetan, there is no name for those who believe in the supernatural because it is such an intrinsic part of West African life that it would be as redundant as having a name for those who believe in drinking water or breathing oxygen.

In the world of wack, Madame Geneve Samake is what is known as a *marabout*. Although the names change from country to country, almost every village in West Africa has one. They use their supernatural powers to act as mediators between humans and the spirit world. Some can see into the future. Some can see the spirits that live among us. And others can see only special herbs and roots that can cure maladies ranging from bad luck to malaria. Because she can do all three, Madame Samake is considered one of the powerful marabouts in all Burkina Faso. According to Gaetan, who had required her services after returning from four years in New York, where his father was a United Nations diplomat, she can even make it rain.

A heavy rain is falling when I arrive in Lome, the beachfront capital of the tiny nation of Togo. In its prime this was considered West Africa's answer to the French Rivera. But today the rain only emphasizes the grayness and oppression that have settled in here. The Atlantic that once drew European tourists in their thousands is an expanse of dirty dishwater stretching out to a black horizon. On the beach, palm trees bend cityward in a wind that sends coconut husks and empty plastic bags tumbling through the sand. On the streets, people huddle in doorways or wade shoeless through the dark, debris-filled water that overflows the curbs and covers the sidewalks. Everywhere the rain pounds the city; coming down with such force that its spray kicks up a thick, knee-high layer of mist that reminds me of the artificial fog used in heavy metal concerts or Halloween spook houses.

It's an eerie place. Especially when you consider that Togo's president, 74-year-old Gnassingbe Eyadema, is considered by most of his citizens to be the country's most powerful warlock.

There is an old adage among Sub-Saharan travelers that you go to East Africa for the animals and to West Africa for the people. Eyadema isn't exactly the kind of person tourists come to see, yet what he represents is the epitome of what makes West Africa so unique. In essence, it is traditional religion - the bedrock of the various cultures that are what West Africa has to offer instead of game parks. Throughout the region, traditional religion, particularly the practice known as voudon, juju or, in some cases, *country medicine*, is what shapes and defines the Atlantic side of the African continent. Almost every mask, carved figurine, cultural festival, and even the clothing many people wear has its roots in West Africa's indigenous religions and beliefs. And those are just the most outward signs. In places like Liberia and Sierra Leone, juju even informs how civil wars are fought with rebel soldiers marauding through the countryside in women's ball gowns and Donald Duck masks in the belief that they will make them invisible to their enemies. What makes Togo significant is not that its legendary juju is so strong, but that through the warlock Eyadema, it effectively rules the country.

It starts to make sense when you imagine West Africa as a vast spirit world, a place where "magic realism" is not a literary term, but an apt description of people's everyday lives. In theology it is known as animism, from the medieval Latin *anima mundi* or "soul of the world." It is a belief that there is a realm of life where spells can be cast, the future can be told and chance can be altered like the course of the wind. That realm resides in Nature and is populated by earth spirits, sky deities and the souls of rivers who can be approached through human intermediaries like Madame Samake. To outsiders it has always been a mystery with missionaries denouncing it as pagan idolatry and most non-Africans viewing it as a byproduct of ignorance. Yet in a capricious landscape of deadly diseases, crop blights and killer droughts, animism infuses people's lives with meaning and the hope that things can be changed for the better. In many respects it is to West Africa what Catholicism is to Ireland or Bhuddism is to Thailand; a powerful undercurrent that runs through all aspects of life, from the family to business to politics.

If Burkina Faso represents the more typical side of West African mysticism, Togo is its dark underbelly - a place where indigenous beliefs have been turned against the believers. For more than three decades

Eyadema has held the Togolese people in thrall. To the educated elite he is nothing more than a corrupt dictator who smothers dissent, tortures opponents and crushes challenges to his rule, such as the mass democracy demonstrations of 1992-3 that were brutally suppressed by his loyal military. Yet to the majority of people in a country where -TK- are illiterate and -TK- of the population holds animist beliefs, Eyadema is a witch with powers of evil so great that to challenge them is the purest folly.

For visitors there are no obvious signs; people don't speak about it, nothing is written in the press, and no statues of Eyadema in a conical sorcerer's cap grace the public squares of Lome. In fact there is nothing to suggest that Eyadema is anything other than the stern-faced, white haired old soldier depicted in the official portraits that hang in every shop, restaurant and office building. Yet it is all there as a kind of code similar to the ominous language the president uses in his speeches when he tells the nation he was "born to power" or "destined to rule."

The day after my arrival I'm outside the five-star Sirkiwa Hotel. If Togo is what postmodernists describe as a "text" that must be deconstructed to find meaning, this is a good starting point. The hotel is named after the 1973 plane crash that killed almost every passenger except Eyadema. To most Togolese it was a sign of their president's supernatural powers. So much so, that the crash site is now one of the country's most powerful voudoun shrines where pilgrims trek in the hope that some of Eyadema's survival juju will rub off on them.

Today Benin flourishes; its democracy is working, its economy is improving and the voudoun practiced by 70 percent of its population, which was suppressed under Marxist rule, has been officially embraced as an integral part of Beninois life. As a result of this rapprochement, voudoun is now enjoying something of a renaissance. The country's AIDS awareness program is considered one of Africa's most successful because it utilizes local voudoun priests. Of the 83 registered political parties that have emerged since 1991, almost every one retains its own voudoun advisor. And when the Pope visited Benin in 1993, even His Holy See held a meeting with the country's leading voudoun priests where, it is rumored, all parties agreed to respect the other's turf.

After a 90-minute flight we land in the ancient riverine town of Mopti. Located midway between the French-influenced capital of Bamako in the south and Arab-influenced Timbuctou to the north, this is the heart of Mali. For centuries this town that straddles three islands has been the country's most important trading post. As a result, it is a jumble of influences; past and present, modernity and tradition, Arab and African. It is a town where

Christianity and Islam can be considered relatively new religions. But I have come to look at the old beliefs, the primordial Nature spirits of the Rock and the River.

A few hours after my arrival I'm seated in the prow of motorized pirogue heading down the Niger River. Like all great thoroughfares on this continent, the river that drains most of West Africa is a magnet for life. On the thin verdant strips of its banks, white herons walk among grazing cows, donkeys and camels. Overhead a fish eagle circles and a pair of malachite kingfishers streak past in a blur of metallic blues and sunset oranges. The needle-thin pirogues of the fishermen, weathered brown as the river itself from years of use, form a kind of floating calligraphy on the water's surface. And situated in small groups along its banks are the picturesque grass-huts of the rather unfortunately named Bozo people, the nomadic fisherman of the Niger.

"The Dogon and Bozo traveled," Assou begins, "and got lost in the desert and were starving and the small Dogon was going to die and the Bozo went to look for food and didn't get it so he cut his legs and cooked the meat and didn't tell him. Then the Dogon opened his eyes and asked what happened to the Bozo's legs and both disappeared and Bozo became river person and Dogon went to the cliffs. So now they can't fight, they can't say something like 'Fuck off' or 'Shut up', they can never make angry with each other, because they're like cousins."

As stories go, it's as convoluted and mystifying as, oh, say, the Bible must have been when the first missionaries attempted to foist it upon Africans whose belief systems predated the birth of Christ by a few thousand years. As I listen, I'm feeling a great deal of solidarity with those early Africans, a fact which puts me in the proper frame of mind for our visit to the Bozo camp.

There's an old Bozo saying that if you see a Bozo bending over in a field, that means he's throwing up. Such is the Bozo's disgust for the sedentary life of the shore. Yet, upon entering the Bozo camp I begin to notice that the baked-mud houses are rather permanent looking for such a fiercely nomadic people. My fears are confirmed when I meet the local chief, Sungai Salamanta, a white-haired old man who looks up from the pair of pants he is sewing to inform us that we have blundered into what is essentially a Bozo retirement village. Apparently, even nomads get sick of moving around.

Sungai explains that the Bozo's success as fishermen is due to their symbiotic relationship with the hippoes and crocodiles of the Niger, which allow them to pass when a Bozo says the secret words. Sometimes, he says, they will even joke with them. The old chief then tells me that he has a good friend who is made entirely of water and who comes out of the river at night to visit him. When I ask if I can stick around and interview him, Sungai laughs and shakes his head. "Besides," he says through Assou, "he doesn't speak English."

The most important thing, however, is that the Bozos know the secret of the Niger. "If you are really a Bozo, you have the secret of all the rivers of the world," Sungai says between a knit and a pearl. "God gave us that secret." I ask if, perhaps, he wouldn't mind sharing the secret. Sungai laughs again and tells me that although he's not at liberty, I'm free to ask God myself.

Instead, I think I'll ask the Dogon. Which is why, the next morning, Assou and I are negotiating our way down a 750-meter, 50-degree loose rock slipway on the western face of the Bandiagara Escarpment.

The ochre landscape here at the so-called "Door of the Sahel" is harsh and magnficent. Looking out over the perfect half-moon of sheer sandstone cliffs I understand why the Dogon believe their sinuous escarpment to be the petrified remains of a giant primordial snake. In the valley below is a small village of rock huts surrounded by a patchwork of millet and onion fields, each demarcated by a row of weathered stones. Across the valley floor, I can make out the remains of the old Burkina Faso road - a reminder that I have almost come full circle on this trip. In fact, the road was probably the belated fruit of the labors of Marshall Griole, the pathbreaking 19th Century French anthropologist who entered this hitherto uncharted region by donkey cart, befriended the Dogon and learned most of their secrets, before they got wise to what he was doing and killed him.

We enter the stone village amidst the cacophony of children playing, goats braying and the thud-thumping heartbeat of millet being pounded. Assou leads me to the palaver hut, a city hall of sorts, with a multilayered stone roof that is so low we have to duck to enter it. Assou explains that though they are tiny in stature, the Dogons are a notoriously emphatic people and the low roof is a form of parlimentary procedure whereby any excited citizen who jumps up to speak out of turn gets conked on the head.

Inside the hut are three small men who look as ancient and weathered as spindly baobobs, the only trees that can survive here in the dusty moonscape of Dogon country. After the usual formalities, one man tells me that he is 138. His "little" brother is 112. The youngster of the group is a mere 72. When I inquire as to how they all managed to live so long, they shrug their shoulders, tell me that this is nothing, they have friends who are 220, and ask if I'm planning on sharing my cigarettes with them or what.

I had come here to learn the secrets of the rock. Like the Bozo and their river, the Dogons' belief system is based upon their hardscrabble environment. At the celestial center of it all is the dog star, Sirius. Yet on the drive up, Assou had told me something worrying. Recently, the Dogon decided that all tourism into their areas will end in 2019 and they will return to the old ways. To me, it was either a case of extreme perispeciousness or a sign that things had gotten so bad it was already too late. So, like a medieval monk preparing for a bout of self-flagellation, I ask the old men what they think of people like me who come traipsing into their villages unannounced, demanding to know all about their beliefs.

"It's not the tourists who are making bad for our culture," says Atime Giru-Cocoro, the 73-year-old youngster, "it's the people who come with the tourists and explain all our secrets." At this point all eyes fall on poor Assou, who attempts to muster an indignant *j'accuse* expression, but fails and begins to mope. The decagenarian Dogons puff their cigarettes and nod gravely. Atime continues: "Now the secrets are starting to go, one by one. When the secrets are all gone, that will be finish for us."

And that's finish for me. The thought of these old men losing their secrets is like the idea of watching the stars go out. I bid farewell to 322 years of Dogon experience and we set off for the climb back up the rock.

The next afternoon I'm back in Air Mali's flying tribute to 1950s Soviet aeronautical engineering. With the bouncing from windshear, the hammering and sickling of the antiquated engines and the dire heat that has somehow followed us up to 20,000 feet, it's what I imagine it would be like if African buses could fly and the sky was filled with potholes. We're heading west, toward the capital Bamako. Below, the Niger flows eastward, a brown river draining a brown landscape.

Compared to Mopti, Bamako is bustling. Its sidewalks teem with the colors of West Africa, from the florid greens, yellows and reds of the tropics to the pale blues, bone whites and sun-absorbing blacks of the Sahel. The people are dark and lean, like Giacometti figurines wrapped up in robes, boubous and djellabahs. The skyline is a typical African mishmash of poverty, religion and western development money.; the tin roofs of the shanties in which the majority of the population lives, the scepter-like minarets of the mosques and a handful of modern banks and office buildings where western aid workers and the Malian elite plot the country's future.

After checking into my hotel, I make my way toward the rail station to purchase a ticket for the final leg of this journey - a 30-hour train trip from Bamako to Dakar, the coastal capital of neighboring Senegal. Like the American West, the 1904 completion of the railroad linking Bamako to the town of Kayes on the upper Senegal River was the beginning of the end. With its chemin de fer, Paris was able to consolidate its control over the land and peoples of what was then known as French Sudan. With the railway came the colonial administrators, the white settlers and a Francophone influence that still manifests itself today in everything from the street vendors selling baguettes on the Avenue de la Somme to Bambara tribesmen who call themselves Jean-Jacques.

Yet despite its role in the colonization of Mali, it has been transformed over the years into a peculiarly West African train. Gaetan had told me about it over lunch one day at a Libyan restaurant in Ouagadougou. It was a "spirit train", he said, and many of its passengers were actually dead people who had been revived by mystics to make the trip back to their birthplaces, where custom dictates they must be buried. "You'll see these people," he said, "they never eat, never talk, never take anything to drink. They only sit."

"But why," I asked, "do the relatives go to all the trouble of having them revived if they can't even talk to them?"

Gaetan laughed a laugh that let me know I had asked yet another ridiculous question. "Because," he finally said between bites of pita, "it's so much cheaper than sending them as freight."

Just as I am crossing the tracks outside the station, I hear the spirit train a'coming. The metallic screeching is immense and otherworldly, a sustained white-noise that forces most onlookers to plug their eardrums with their fingertips. Then the locomotive comes into view, a wild West African affair barfing up putrid black clouds of smoke that roll down and backward into the carriages. Passengers hang from the sides and out the windows with the mortified and forlorn looks of refugees. The stench is horrific. As the cars roll by, I count at least two carriages where the toilets have overflowed down the gangways. An English-speaker standing nearby tells me that this particular train is 25 hours late.

I take another look at the spirit train and decide that this is one West African mystery that will have to wait until the next trip. It's time for a change and I'm feeling the need for somewhere more straightforward, a place that isn't so enigmatic, puzzling and complex. I head back to the hotel, where I find a Tuareg travel agent and book an air ticket to Casablanca.

Eric Ransdell moved to Africa at 23 and began stringing for US News and World Report out of Nairobi, then became their sub-Saharan African stringer for three years. Then two years in Hong Kong. Then back to Africa in 1992 to become Johannesburg Bureau Chief during South Africa's transition to democracy. Also covered all of sub-Saharan Africa from Jo'burg, including the war in Somalia and the Rwandan genocide. He has worked in more than 30 African countries and covered something like 9 or 10 wars there. Currently, he is living in Shanghai and working as a documentary film maker and writer.

| 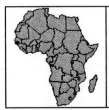 | **mitch and andy**
emigrate - the hard way | michelle urquhart
africa
1995 |

This story is dedicated to Ian and Kerena Mitchell, Zam Maitland and Jesse Bevan, and Rob Casseley who kept us moving, sane, and happy along the way. Cheers, guys we owe you one.

(P.S. If a Dr Rob Casseley ever wants to treat you, run like hell!!)

Part 1: The Preparation

It was Andy's idea to drive to Capetown in his red V8 Series III 16 year old Landrover. It was an idea born from hours of reading those Landrover Owner magazines that abound in every Landrover owner's bedroom, toilet, lounge.

This all came about due to Andy's willingness to move to New Zealand to live. Neither of us wanted to go 'straight there.' There aren't many times when both partners are not working, and therefore have the opportunity to travel a bit.

So, in a Turkish cafe in Istanbul, we decided to drive to Capetown. That was in June 1995. With a bit of rudimentary research into weather and a desire to be in New Zealand for Christmas 1996, we decided to leave on the 1st of August 1996, giving ourselves 4 and a half months to complete the trip, and one year to prepare.

The first decision was, "which route?" The traditional route through the Sahara, West Africa and Zaire did not fill us with confidence, and after talking to a few overland companies, we found out that the eastern coast was definitely viable. This meant we could visit the Middle East too. Our hearts were set - Red Sea here we come.

Planning and preparation started in earnest after the New Year. The first purchase was the 'Lonely Planet guide for Africa' and 'Africa by Road,' which scared us with stories of car jacking and malaria. Determined not to be put off, we visited the Independent Travelers' show in Islington, London and picked up many hints, ideas and advice.

Andy, being the practical Landrover nut, took on the job of preparing the vehicle. Having owned it for 5 years, and doing most of the mechanical work himself, he had a good working knowledge of its weak points. He replaced all the electrics, cleaned and rebuilt the carburetors, replaced all rubber hoses and replaced all the suspension bushes. Someone else gave it a good tune up and tuned it for lower grade petrol. Outside the engine, quite a bit of work needed to be done. The heat during the day was a major consideration, so a Renault 5 sunroof was fitted (9 pounds sterling [$18] from a scrap yard). We beat everyone at a Landrover parts sale near Bristol for a serious galvanized box steel roof rack and ladder (140 pounds sterling [$420]) which got a paintjob before being installed. A working light was put on the back, using an old fog light left from a pair on a crashed Astra. The Bristol Show also yielded a speedo in kilometers, essential as all road distances on the trip were in kilometers. Andy designed an ingenious bed which folded up to one side in the back. Paranoid from all the car jacking stories, padlocks and hasps were fitted to all doors. The major saga was choosing tires - new or not? In the end a set of 5 new XCL's for 500 sterling at the LRO Show swung it. We later found out that our partly worn Rangemasters would have been better. A map basket and security boxes inside finished what we hoped would be a robust overland vehicle.

By far the biggest cost was the vehicle carnet documents, which we needed for temporary vehicle importation. As we were driving through Jordan, the premiums were hiked to twice what they were for other countries - 3000 sterling! As it was a cost we never hoped to see a return on, it was a hard cheque to write.

The usual dozen doctors' visits for jabs, a million phone calls to find out exactly what visas we needed and how to get them, Decisions on water purification (we chose iodine), fuel and water carriage (we chose 6 metal jerry cans and 2 plastic jerry cans) – we spent money like it was going out of fashion. However, plans were nicely on track.

Martin and Graham at Aylmer Motors got to know Andy well, and we have single handedly financed Martin's new fence. Harry Stalick from the Lea Valley Land Rover Owners Club gave the gearbox the once over and stated that he wouldn't drive it to Capetown, as he knew exactly what could go wrong – cheers, Harry. Our local pharmacist got sick of wishing us good luck on our trip as we kept going back to him for more pills and potions.

Finally we were at the three weeks to go point. I'd had the feeling things had been going too smoothly. With our farewell BBQ looming, a package containing requested updates from the Foreign Office arrived bringing bad news - all Sudan's borders were closed. Getting to Capetown via Egypt without going through the Sudan is like driving to the South

Island without going on a ferry - impossible. We desperately searched for alternatives in the form of ferries down the Red Sea. We struck pay dirt a week later when we read an overland company's brochure that used the very ferry we had hoped existed. We were back on track.

My birthday present 3 days before we left was an off road driving course. Evan, our instructor (and fellow Kiwi,) had done a lot of over landing and tailored the whole day to our trip.

Then we struck hassle number 2 - Syrian visas. We'd been planning to get them at the border, but Evan told us they were turning people away without them, and that we would be better getting them in London. So we delayed departure by 2 days, braved London on a tube strike day to ferry passports around, and pleaded with the Syrian Consul to fastrack our visas, which he kindly did.

We'd done it, but two days later than scheduled. Our ferry left Dover at 2.45am, with two emotional, tired and scared novice over landers on board. What had we embarked on?

Part 2: London to Cairo - The easy bit

We watched the sunrise over Northern France from a French auto route, just east of Calais. We'd managed to catch an earlier ferry, which meant we hadn't had to hang around in Dover too long. It also meant we could have an extra hour's sleep on the other side, parked in one of those big spaces reserved at regular intervals for vehicles to pull into.

The next 60 hours were not much fun at all, save for a brief interlude in the haven of a Swiss friend's house near Nyon. We had to be in Ancona, Italy by 11.00am on the 5th of August to catch a ferry to Ingoumenitsa, Greece or we would lose 120 sterling and miss the ferry.

At 11.00am on the 5th we were stuck in a slow moving traffic jam just east of Bologne, which the M25 would have been proud of any day. However, with the help of a heavy right foot, good Italian road signs and a bit of queue jumping, we spent an uncomfortable, ill-prepared night on deck of the ferry, which we boarded with 15 minutes to spare.

If there were customs and passport officials in Ingoumenitsa, they weren't interested in us - we drove straight off the ferry and on to our first overnight stop without seeing so much as a peaked cap.

We drove on to Ionnina and spent a pleasant night on the roof rack, hoping we had got the worst part of the trip over with. It was not to be. Driving over the Kassata Pass (1500m), the engine developed heart wrenching noises, which got worse with each passing town. We eventually pulled into Meteora, the noise at its worst yet. It turned out to be a busted viscous coupling on the radiator fan, which was bodged with an outsized washer. A relieved Andy declared we needed to celebrate with some beers.

Turkey was 9 days of Roman ruins, campsites in various stages of disrepair, Turkish carpet salesmen (and women) and a pilgrimage to Gallipoli and Anzac Cove. It was in Turkey we had our hottest day before Egypt, in Antayla, where sweat dripped just by walking to the loo.

We had been dreading the border crossing into Syria since the day we started. It spooked us so much that it took 3 goes to get out of Turkey first, due to us not getting to get all the relevant stamps the first time. However, the anticipated hassle never materialized - in fact they couldn't have been more helpful. Within half an hour we were on our way to Aleppo, excited about our first new country.

If we thought Turkish campsites were bad, Syrian ones were worse, where they existed: vile hole in the floor toilets that blocked themselves with regular monotony. The site at Damascus was one exception, probably due to the number of German tourists who visited.

The driving was a nightmare - 2 lane roads would suddenly become 1 lane roads, and the only warning was the traffic coming the other way on your side of the road. Traffic lights were obviously there as Christmas decorations as everyone ignored them. The use of horn blasts to convey a vast array of complex messages like "I'm passing you - watch out" or "It's a green light idiot" or "Where is your steering wheel? (left hand drive country)" were mandatory - and we were supposed to be able to understand each and every honk. The worst driving was in Damascus, which meant that Cairo's traffic was a piece of cake.

By and large the Syrian people were very friendly and helpful, especially outside Damascus. Syria was also very cheap, although the petrol quality left a little to be desired. A cooling westerly breeze meant the temperature wasn't too hot either. The country was quite unspoiled by mass tourism, but it was by no means perfect. It won't be long before Syria becomes as bad as Egypt for hawkers and rip off merchants.

Jordan, however, is another kettle of Arabs altogether. The road signs were frequent, the roads in good repair. The people were friendly for the sake of it, and genuinely wanted to help. It was tidy, clean and well looked after. It also had the two most awesome sights we had seen to date - the city carved from rock called Petra, and "Lawrence of Arabia's" desert - Wadi Rum.

The Landrover came into its own. We lowered the tire pressures by about one third and spent two days and one moonlit night under the stars wandering around in soft sand that in some places was wheel rim deep. In other places the corrugations were so rough that they rattled the connections to our interior lights off, and an indicator bulb out of its socket!

On the downside, Jordan is expensive compared to its neighbors, and one dinar to the pound sterling gave us no exchange advantage. There is a complete lack of campsites in Jordan. We managed by sleeping in tourist attraction car parks with the local authorities' blessing or camping in B and B gardens.

Jordan was the place we started to meet a lot more English speaking travelers, as we were now on the Egypt - Israel - Jordan back packing circuit. It was good to know that we weren't as crazy as so many people had told us and it was with a little regret, but growing excitement, that we turned our sights to Egypt and the African continent. We had to catch a ferry from Aqaba in Jordan to Nuiweba on the Sinai Peninsula. Blissfully unaware, we turned up at 1pm to begin boarding procedures for a 3pm departure, a departure that didn't actually happen until 7.30pm, amidst hundreds of foot passengers jostling to get 2 wives, 5 kids and an electric fan in tow. The actual sailing took 2 and a half hours, followed by 4 hours of Egyptian bureaucrats giving us as many pieces of paper as they could think of and charging 220 sterling for the privilege just to bring the vehicle into their sacred country. We finally left Nuweiba at 3.30am, much poorer and in a state of shock.

A couple of days R and R at Dahab on the Red Sea coast perked us up a bit. We were ready to face Cairo, and the next and biggest hurdle - getting to Eritrea via the Red Sea. We had no idea where to start, with fast dwindling reserves. The two things on our side were 1) time - we had a month and 2) determination - after all, we were halfway!

Part 3: Out of Egypt

If we thought getting into Egypt was hard work, getting out again was pure hell.

We arrived in Cairo on the 3rd of September, motivated to get our passage to Eritrea sorted out so we could enjoy Egypt without worry. The first shipping company we stopped at (Port Said Shipping and Navigation)could not help us, but did send one of the office boys with us to guide us into the centre of town.

This was to be the theme for 99.9% of our visits - "No, we can't help, but if you go here, they will be able to," Most of the 4th was spent traipsing around Cairo's travel agents and shipping offices in 35 C-degree heat. At 2pm we'd had enough and headed to the air-conditioned haven of KFC to mull over our next move.

The obligatory visit to the Pyramids and the Egyptian Museum proved to be enough of Cairo for us. We headed out to Suez to try our luck there.

However we were getting the same story in Suez. There were no ferries to Eritrea at all. Some said there were ferries to Sudan, but others said there weren't. A brief flicker of hope in the form of a ferry via Jeddah in Saudi Arabia were soon dashed - the Saudis would not give transit visas without a ticket out of Jeddah, and no one could sell us a ticket out of Jeddah. Strike one.

We were dejectedly considering what seemed like our only option - shipping the Landie direct to Auckland and backpacking the rest when there was a knock on our hotel door. We were informed there was a Mr. Ahmet to see us. Curious, we wandered down. He turned out to be our eventual saviour-cum-tormentor. He had a fax which said he could get us to any African port. Our hopes soared. Over Egyptian tea and koshari (pasta and lentils), he told us he could ship the Landrover to Eritrea, but we would have to fly. The next day he confirmed that there was a ship going to Asseb, in southern Eritrea, on the 24th or 25th. Cautiously we left $US50 as a 'deposit' and headed away, feeling very unsure and dubious of our saviour.

We hit the tourist track south: the Red Sea resort of Hurghada, then Luxor, Aswan, and Abu Simbel. Any driving south of Hurghada was done in convoy. When asked why, the guards would say it was "dangerous for tourists". "From who?" would elicit a blank look and a shrug. We deduced that it was the threat from the Islamic separatist movement that worried them.

At least someone cared. Every other Egyptian we came across couldn't give a toss about us as human beings. We had been sent by Allah for all and sundry to make money out of - as much as possible. Enjoying ourselves became hard work and in temperatures of 40 degrees C plus, our tempers and nerves became frayed to breaking point.

We managed one small triumph. The Landie needed an oil change, and rather than get hot and bothered doing it himself, Andy decided to get a garage to do it. By the time Andy had got out of the Landrover to get the oil and filter out of the back, they had the plug out and all the oil drained away. In 20 minutes the oil and filters had been changed, all for the princely sum of 5 Egyptian pounds (that's equivalent to 1 pound sterling)!

We phoned Ahmet on the 13th for an update. He informed us everything was OK, and that he had found another couple to go with us. We resolved to go back to Suez, check out Ahmet with the British Consul there and make our decision then. We were extremely uncomfortable with leaving the Landy and could not even secure any insurance for the trip. But having another pair of brains around made us a little more comfortable.

In Suez on the 16th, the British consul did some cursory ringing around, and said that he was happy with Ahmet and that he would come to the port with us when we loaded. The 'other couple' seemed real too. Ian and Kerena from Hertfordshire in a Series III Diesel LWB. We decided to spend a few days in hassle free Dahab, as Ahmet had told us that was where Ian and Kerena were.

They weren't, but Dahab was still hassle free. We returned to Suez on the 22nd with 2 Aussie hitchhikers in tow who wanted to get to Eritrea, but couldn't find cheap flights. Ian and Kerena weren't coming until the 23rd (we were starting to wonder if they really did exist) so we spent the first of what turned into 16 nights at the El Masree Hotel - 2 sterling a night, great if you don't mind cockroaches and falling bricks.

Ian and Kerena did exist. Dr. Ian Mitchell, a plasma physicist, and the very new Mrs. Kerena Mitchell nee Watson (Primary school teacher) were on their way to an orphanage school in Uganda for 3 months voluntary work. They were our real saviours, keeping us sane and motivated while everything else seemed to go wrong.

On the 24th, we came across an English registered truck from 'Tracks,' an overland company. Their English contacts were working on ferries for them, and had a ferry to Suakin in Sudan 70% arranged. They had no visas but were told they could arrange transit visas there. For us to get to Sudan, it would cost around $US1500 each couple (about what Ahmet was quoting). However, a couple of phone calls the next day informed us that the Sudanese had shut the Eritrean border, and they wouldn't issue visas transit or otherwise for exit to Eritrea. Strike two. Tracks went anyway - we hope they made it!!

The observant amongst you will notice that according to Ahmet's timetable we should have loaded on the 25th - no such luck. According to Ahmet, the boat had broken down. We found out later he'd lied - it hadn't even arrived in Suez, and wouldn't until the 1st.

Ahmet and his much more user friendly partner Ali tried the Suez - Jeddah - Massawa route again, using Ali's contacts. This meant we would be in Massawa on the 4th of October - 3 days after our carefully prepared Eritrean visas from London ran out. Two trips to Cairo to get new ones occupied the 26th and 28th. While we were there we contacted a shipping agent recommended by our movers in London for a quote to ship the Landy to Auckland. If we had made no concrete progress by the 5th, we were bailing out, much to Ian and Kerena's horror.

By the 30th, we realized that we were running out of time and patience, and we started to lose our tempers with Ahmet. His true colors showed

130

forth then, and if it hadn't been for Ali's patience and honesty with us, we would have been long gone.

In the midst of all this, 2 Landrovers and a Landcruiser arrived in Suez looking for passage south. Apart from Ian and Kerena, they were the only overlanders we had met so far, and their faces fell when we told them our sorry tale. Also in Suez were Zam and Jesse, who were trying to get their overlanding truck and parasailing boat to Nairobi via the same route as us. They had similar stories as ours to tell, including their boat being impounded in customs for 1 month.

The Jeddah ferry fell through (Strike three) just as the Asseb boat arrived in Suez (funny that). We were given a date to load, the 6th (actually the 7th in the end), and we started exit payments and procedures on the 5th. Then Andy badly sprained his foot, so Ian had to spend 15 hours in Customs and Port Authorities with both Landies, watching Ahmet and Ali collect the obligatory forest of paper while Andy spent 5 hours in a hospital having his foot put in a cast. By 2am on the 7th the Landies were loaded and we were able to spend our last night in the El Masree, wondering if we would ever see our vehicles again.

Part 4: Punctures and Pitfalls: Asmara to Nairobi

We cheered as the aircraft took off from Cairo International Airport. In usual Egyptian style, it had not been easy to get there. Instead of leaving on the 9th as planned, we had to wait until the early hours of the 11th. We landed in Asmara at 10am, after a brief detour via Addis Ababa and after negotiating Andy, his cast and all our rucksacks into one taxi, we headed into town.

What a complete contrast to Cairo - clean, friendly, quiet and the food was excellent. Being a Friday, and the Islamic Sabbath, we quickly headed out to organize what we thought was the easiest leg of the trip - flights to the port of Asseb.

Wrong! Yes, there were flights to Asseb direct, but they were booked out until the 12th of November. Flights via Addis Ababa were $US223 per person - more than we had paid to get to Asmara! The realisation came over us that it was going to be more difficult than we thought. The only saving grace was that the El Mansoura, with our Landies on board, wasn't due until the 19th October - not the 11th as we were told in Suez!

The next few days were spent chasing our tails trying to get to Asseb on public transport. There was a bus to Asseb through the desert, but every time we tried to get on it, it had either left or we had missed the booking time. We then booked 4 bus tickets to Addis Ababa, and were planning to fly from there to Asseb. However this meant getting multiple entry visas for Ethiopia - not available for tourists we were told. The kind man at the embassy tried for us - but no luck. We tried to get on a cargo boat south from Massawa, the northern Eritrean port- not allowed was the stock reply. Our only hope lay in Zam and Jesse, two Englishmen who had been trying to get out of Suez the same time as us. They had got their 22 tonne 6x4 ex RAF Bedford truck (towing a 2 tonne parasailing boat) on the Jeddah ferry that we couldn't get on - but had themselves been thrown off because they had no Saudi visas, leaving their vehicle on board. They had had to fly to Asmara, and then get down to Massawa to pick up their vehicle from there. They jokingly offered to take us down the Danakil Desert to Asseb - little did they know!!

It took 5 days to get Zam's truck out of the bond store and fix a bent axle on the boat trailer, while we tried the cargo boat angle again. Finally we found a passage for Andy and Ian on a boat, and we raced down to the harbor to get Immigration permits and find the captain. The captain didn't turn up, and we missed the Immigration office - so the 6 of us set off at 8.30am on the 23rd of October to drive down the Red Sea coast via the Danakil Desert in Zam's truck.

The regular bus allegedly did the trip every week taking three days, so Zam reasoned that it must be a reasonable track. Wrong again. We found out later that it was the second worst road in the world (where the first is, we have never found out). The first part had corrugations like you've never seen. The second part wound over rocky, steep ravines right near the sea. Zam split one of his diesel tanks, and if it wasn't for a following truck hooting, we would have lost half our diesel there and not had enough to get through. The third part was reasonable, and we started to get our hopes up, until the boat trailer snapped at the hitch. However it wasn't a problem for Zam who is an Africa man of old, and had a mobile welding shop in his truck!! We then started inland from the coast, and hit sand - deep sand, and without the help of some local ex-freedom fighters that we had picked up, we would still be there. The fourth part took us up and down riverbeds, where the trailer broke again. After 5 days, 750kms and 21 punctures, we made it into Asseb, tired, sick of rice and extremely smelly. The only saving grace for the whole nightmare was the stunning scenery and welcoming locals.

It took two days to get the Landrovers out of the bond store. There had been NO damage at all to the exteriors. However, the interior of Ian and Kerena's Landrover had been emptied out into a separate bond store, and many things had gone 'missing,' including a much dreamed about bottle of champagne and the wedding photos they had bought with them. Also gone was the peanut butter, corned beef and other supplies they had bought in Egypt. We had fared better. We had put all our spare tyres on the fold down bed, and padlocked the back door and passenger. They had attempted to get the tyres out the driver's door, but had given up. We lost a digital clock (broken anyway) from above the driver's windscreen and a medical book.

Zam, Jesse, Andy and I decided to push for the Ethiopian border. Ian and Kerena had to repack their Landrover, and decided to stay at the hotel. Again, with stomachs in our mouths, we approached the border post at midnight - to find that they couldn't have given a damn! In fact we could have gone through without the Ethiopians even looking at our passports. We stayed on the Ethiopian side of the border and waited for Ian and Kerena. However, the morning brought a different story. The customs' man had decided that we needed a temporary import permit, but didn't have the forms. So he had to hand write them! Luckily he had carbon paper, but the whole procedure took 4 and a half hours, during which time the locals had completely pissed Zam off by 'helping' him change a tyre, and managing to put a hole in a new tube, and then asking for payment for the 'help' they had given him!

We were also back in begging country - a phenomenon missing in Eritrea, and the locals tried all the tricks - women pleading to women, crowding around trying to distract and the 'charm' method - a good looking young man chatting up me or Kerena. Egypt had trained us well, and they got nothing from us but a lot of bad tempers.

We finally got moving through Ethiopia heading for Kenya. The road was shocking - full of potholes and cracks. We managed about 100kms the first day, and camped beside the road in a layby. The next few days were a blur of stretches of new tarseal, stretches of potholes, punctures for the truck or trailer and campsites on the side of the road. One night was spent with a U.S Peace Corp teacher in a small village south of Addis, in the Ethiopian Highlands. Our available cash was running out, and Zam ended up being the bank. We finally hit the border town of Moyale on the 5th of November. It took the afternoon to complete formalities on both sides of the border, and eventually we were able to camp in a peaceful undisturbed and free campsite on the Kenyan side of the border. Thank God for ex-British colonies - it was the first time since Dover that we were able to drive on the 'right' side of the road.

The road south through Kenya to Nairobi was not sealed and was either full of corrugations or potholes. There is also a security problem on this road, with Somali bandits raiding cattle trucks and cars to raise cash so it was with some trepidation that we joined the 8am convoy to Marsabit. The convoy lasted about 10kms, as the bigger trucks left us behind. Zam had picked up some paying passengers, and was even slower than us. Soon it was just the two Landies getting covered in red dust with the most exciting moment of the day being when it rained - the first rain in 2 and a half months!

It was also this day that the Landrover started making some ominous noises. There was considerable movement in the rear universal joint of the front prop shaft, and the transfer box was dry. Andy filled the transfer box and checked all the other oil levels, but the noises stayed the same. Putting the diff lock in made a little difference, but Andy didn't want to risk this long term.

The four of us decided to have time out in Marsabit National Park for a day, before continuing south to Isiolo. The game park had two waterholes for viewing where we saw elephant, lion, cape buffalo and leopard. The drive into the furthest lake was on fairly muddy steep tracks, and we got to do some 'real' off roading at last.

On our 'day off' in the park, Somali rebels had attacked and killed a Kenyan on the Isiolo road, and the authorities would not let us go further without an armed guard in each vehicle. This made things a little cramped, but we gladly put up with it. It took eight and a half hours to do 250 kms and we were very glad to see Isiolo township, not only to know that we were safe, but also to see a Barclays Bank on the main street.

The next morning, Ian and Kerena went on ahead, and we waited for the Bank to open. As we waited outside, a Kenyan approached us and started asking about the Landrover. It turned out he was a Doctor of Economics, and was kitting out his own Series III for an overland survey he was doing. We ended up selling him our sandladders, which had not moved from the side of our roof rack since we left, for the price of a tank of petrol. He invited us to dinner at his house in Nairobi, and gave us directions around the scenic side of Mt. Kenya. Later that day, we crossed the equator and headed off towards Nairobi.

On the outskirts of Nairobi, we caught up with Ian and Kerena, who had themselves caught up with Zam and Jesse. They had taken 2 days longer than we had to drive from Marsabit, had 5 more punctures, and managed to put a hole in the boat. The 3 vehicles drove triumphantly into the city, looking forward to some good food and new company. Andy and I were now very much behind schedule (we should have been in Nairobi 1 month ago), and were wrestling with the decision of whether to miss Christmas in New Zealand and stay longer in Africa, or whether to "go for it" down to Cape Town. Crunch Time had arrived.

Part 5: Nairobi to Cape Town - The civilised route

It rained nearly every day in Nairobi, and soon the novelty value of mud and umbrellas wore off. The first few days were spent reveling in luxuries like chocolate, pickle, gin and tonic and shops. We called our respective parents to find that they had called the Foreign Service to start a search for us - we were 3 weeks late getting to Nairobi, and they were very worried. We found the local Qantas office and forced ourselves to make a decision. We couldn't afford to stay on for another month, and my father's voice when I suggested we miss Christmas in New Zealand nearly broke my heart. So, we had 4 weeks to get to Cape Town.

Andy took the Landrover to the local Landrover dealer to have the timing reset, and price a new front prop shaft. At 600 sterling for a new one, and no second hand ones available, we decided to push on with the one we had. We said good bye to Zam, Jesse, Ian and Kerena over dinner plates of crocodile and zebra at Carnivore's, and headed north to Naivasha for a few days.

It soon became very apparent that there was something very wrong with the Landie. Where once it cruised easily at 100km per hour, we couldn't get past 80, and we slowed right down to 40km up hills! A despondent Andy couldn't find out what was wrong, so we decided to call back into the Landrover dealer on the way to the Tanzanian border and demand they fix it properly. The first time they lifted the bonnet, the mechanic discovered that the choke cable had been jammed open, and we had been running rich. We thanked him, and left shouting if we didn't return, it was OK. We returned, with only partial power being restored - acceleration was fine, but the top end speed was still not there. A bit more digging under the hood found a snapped throttle linkage - we had been using only one carb! A bit of negotiating and stroppiness secured us a new one for free, and we were off, back to full speed and feeling much happier.

We had decided that to enjoy the rest of the trip we would sacrifice sightseeing in a couple of countries, and slow down for the rest. We decided to blast through Tanzania and Malawi, stopping when we reached Zimbabwe. Tanzania was a 2 day blur of driving and petrol stations. Malawi took 5 days to transit, 2 of those days being tied into getting Mozambique transit visas. We also ran into the Tracks truck we had met in Suez, and caught up on their hair raising trip through the Sudan.

Mozambique turned out to be the only country where we had to pay a bribe. We had been warned to watch the police, as they were corrupt, and were milking tourists by using bogus fines. As we approached the Tete

Bridge, we were flagged down. The officer made us test our indicators, brake lights, show our warning triangle and all our papers. Then he announced that he would have to fine us $US250 for having no reflective strip on the back of the Landrover. We argued that we didn't need it, and then got in the Landrover and drove away. We nearly got away with it, but he caught us up just as they were lifting the toll bar before the bridge. Andy again had to get out, and managed to argue and negotiate the bribe down to $US 10. Across the bridge and 500 meters further on another officer tried the same thing - this time we laughed in his face and drove on, leaving him looking a little pissed off. We made it to the Zimbabwe border on the smell of an oily rag, and after waiting for 4 bus loads of locals to pass over the border before us, we crossed into Southern Africa.

Zimbabwe had just started its rainy season, and they had had 30% of their annual rainfall in the last 10 days. Everything was green and clean. The shops were well stocked and everyone spoke English. There were campsites everywhere, and they were well maintained. The National Parks were reasonably cheap, and had a lot to offer. When we got to Bulawayo, a sign on a bus stop led us to a propshaft workshop, where the head mechanic told us he could redesign and rebuild our propshaft for 70quid!!! We quickly agreed, reshuffled our schedule, and spent a few days eating and spending money in Bulawayo. While there we experienced some of the most spectacular thunderstorms we'd ever seen in Zimbabwe, or indeed Africa.

We crossed into Namibia via the Caprivi Strip which involved transiting Botswana and buying their local vehicle insurance and road tax for a 70km journey! The first half of the Caprivi Strip road was not sealed but in reasonable repair. However it was on the sealed section where the radiator cowling fell off and smashed the radiator fan. We stopped in time to have enough fan left to spin, but we knew that we would need a new one before the now unbalanced fan shot the water pump bearings and stopped us getting to Capetown. We spent a very pleasant night beside the Okavango river, and the next day we headed for Etosha National Park.

We didn't reach Etosha that day, as the Landrover started to miss and surge 40kms out of Tsumeb. Horrified, we limped back to Tsumeb campsite to check things over, with visions of being towed to Capetown. By nightfall we'd found nothing wrong except an overfull gearbox. We went to bed after deciding to take the Landie to a high performance car garage in the morning.

It took the head guy 10 minutes to suss out that the vacumn advance diaphram on the distributor had gone, and the high heat and fast speeds were causing the problem. He said that if we kept the speed down and watched the temperature, we would be able to drive without replacing it. He also had an old fan with a small piece missing which they installed. However it wouldn't balance, so we despondently decided to miss the Skeleton Coast and head to Windhoek, the capital, for a new one. We had a few days to do the trip, and took in Etosha and Waterberg National Parks. Etosha turned out to be one of the main highlights of the trip, with zoo loads of wildlife and eerie scenery.

Windhoek eventually yielded a new fan for a 200TDi engine, but no vacuum advance! We did a few jobs, and then headed to the local campsite. Andy fitted the fan the next day, after bludging a washer from an overland trucker to replace the one put on the viscous coupling in Greece. We were in business again, and headed out to Sossusvlei, through Namibia's first rainstorms. We worked our way south via a bizarre German built castle, a strange quiver tree forest and Fish River Canyon, the second largest canyon in the world.

On the 10th of December we crossed into South Africa. We now had 9 days to load the Landrover on a boat and get to Johannesburg. We need not have worried. We made a slight detour via an open air restaurant on the beach where we ate seafood cooked on open fires, and stopped in Stellenbosch for a couple of days to sample the excellent South African wine. It was on the last km of dirt road to Stellenbosch that a stone flew up and smashed the passenger side windscreen - Murphy had caught up with us again. We drove into Capetown on the 13th of December, found a lovely guesthouse and got on the phone. The shipping contact we had made in England was useless, but he put us onto another agency who told us it was no problem. We organized to load on the morning of the 19th, and headed away for a couple of days sightseeing around the Overburg Peninsula.

Upon our return it took one hour to sort the paper work out, and 2 hours to see the vehicle into the container!! Eat your heart out Egypt! It meant we were able to enjoy Capetown for the glorious place it is -cheap, clean and plenty of bars and restaurants. Andy even managed to find 4 BF Goodrich All Terrain tyres going cheap as 'only just second hands' to replace the Roadmasters we had driven on for all but Eritrea, Ethiopia and Northern Kenya! Our guest house manager thought we were mad as we already had 5 virtually brand new Michelin XCL's on the roofrack! We decided to fly up to Jo'burg so that we could stay as long as possible, and we eventually left Capetown at 3pm on the 19th December.

And so it was over. The Landie had made it with flying colours, never once stopping us, only slowing us down. We were all in one piece, healthy and had lost very little from our kit. Looking back we were glad we didn't ship direct to New Zealand from Suez. Our prime objective had been achieved. We were now fully fledged overlanders, not beginners. People were asking our advice for a change! Would we do it again? Ask us in a couple of years' time...

Final Summary

Borders crossed:	Eighteen
Kms travelled:	24,000
Money spent:	7500 pounds sterling plus set up costs
Time taken:	139 days
Punctures:	One
Brands of beer tried:	25 (that we can remember)
Lost:	One hammock and a set of keys
Stolen:	One clock and a medical book

Born in 1968, **Michelle Urquhart (nee Cleghorn)** spent 5 years travelling Asia, Europe and Africa before returning home to New Zealand to settle. She currently lives on 7 acres near Otaki, Kapiti Coast with her husband Andy and son James.

---

superstitions

To many Americans, modern-day Africa is still an uncharted plot of land a few thousand miles southeast of Florida. Many believe that the lion, the elephant, the buffalo and the rhinoceros- all deadly killers - are waiting to attack any intruder who happens to wander off a plane. I dare not mention black mambas (the most deadly of all snakes), cannibal tribes or witch doctors.

When a continent has all of the above—and the writer has a little imagination—superstitions and urban legends become part of the society's fabric.

So, what is a superstition?

When people thought the world was flat, they never bothered going to the "edge," as they thought they would fall off. But once it was proven that this was not the case, people stopped believing the superstition. New possibilities emerged, because people could look where they had never looked before.

Bring Africa into this definition, and BINGO, you have discovered plutonium: the legendary "Africa myths, urban legends and superstitions."

A superstition is classed as a myth. So, there is a belief to write about and believe in, even when it is not true. Often, an urban legend is so inconceivable that people will only think it is a myth. The story of Granny Lee, a black person who lived the life of a white drag queen, is true. But it is so remarkable; it could be conceived of as an urban legend when it is not.

This chapter has it all.

The Modern Myths and Urban Legends of South Africa articles were written before South Africa's first democratic elections in 1994, when the ANC (African National Congress) came to power.

139

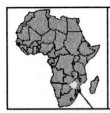

| the world's safest airline | peter ward zimbabwe 1996 |

I heard this urban myth while in a bar in Harare, Zimbabwe's capital, drinking with some pilots who were knocking back shots like there was no tomorrow. They claimed they were working that night, so maybe for them there was not a tomorrow.

Given the life and death implications of safely on an aircraft these guys were unconcerned with the image of the airline they were presenting to me.

They claimed the airline's planes should be parked in a museum and that the food was so bad even by airplane standards that on one occasion a South African passenger was cooking his own meal on a portable stove at the back of the plane. I perish to think what would happen to the baggage.

The urban myth they told, went something like this:

At Harare's airport passengers had boarded a plane and were waiting for it to take off. After 20 minutes, there was an announcement over the intercom.

"Due to technical difficulties our flight will be delayed, so please settle down as we should be taking off shortly."

On this news there is a loud drool of disappointment from the 100 or so passengers.

Two hours later, there was another announcement, that the plane was ready for take off.

Nothing happened for a further 30 minutes, so the passengers waited. After, waiting some more, finally, the pilot's voice came over the loudspeaker. "We are now ready to go ladies and gentlemen. However, we have been waiting for the co-pilot, and he still hasn't arrived. So, since we already waited so long, we're just going to be flying without a co-pilot today."

There was a nervous buzz through the cabin. He continued, 'If you have any issues feel free to disembark and you will be put on the next available flight."

A few passengers rose from their seats and began to collect their carry on luggage.

The pilot went on, "We are not sure when the next flight will be. But rest assured, I have flown this route hundreds of times, we have clear blue skies, and there are no foreseeable problems."

The standing passengers sat down. Apparently none of them decided to wait for another flight.

Once the aircraft reached cruising altitude, the pilot came on the loudspeaker again "Ladies and gentlemen I hope you are enjoying the flight.

I am going to use the bathroom. I have put the plane on autopilot and everything will be fine. I just don't want you to worry."

The pilot casually walked out of the cockpit, fastened the door open with a rubber band to a hook on the wall. Suddenly, the plane hit a patch of turbulence, which is not unusual on a flight. Then the rubber band snapped off. The door swung shut. A moment later, the pilot came out of the bathroom.

When he saw the closed door, he stopped cold. At this point no one except the attendants had realized what had happened or the situation. The door was locked, the plane was flying auto pilot, no one was in the cockpit and the pilot was locked outside. A stewardess came running up, and together they both tried to open the door. But it wouldn't budge.

Some of the passengers had become aware of the problem, and watched the horror on the pilot's face. After a moment of thought, the pilot hurried to the back of the plane. He returned holding a big axe. Without ceremony, he proceeded to chop down the cockpit door. I imagine the passengers were rooted to their seats while watching him.

Once the pilot had managed to chop a hole in the door, he reached inside, unlocked the door, and let himself back in. Then he came on the loudspeaker, his voice a little shakier this time than before. 'Ah, ladies and gentlemen, we just had a little problem there, but everything is fine now. We have plans to cover every eventuality, even pilots getting locked out of their cockpits. So relax and enjoy the rest of the flight."

Once I heard this story I did wonder why an airplane would have an axe on board!

See back cover for **Peter Ward's** biography.

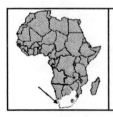	**modern myths and urban legends of south africa part 1**	arthur goldstuck south africa 1990

Routine as their presence may seem in political legends, the ANC are not the only inspiration for South Africa's more topical urban legends. The South African government, along with the various apparatus of state security and state departments, is the butt of a fair share of legends.

Usually, government legends deal with outrageous extremities of bureaucratic red tape and absurd decisions made by officials.

South Africans have come to accept such stories as part of the fabric of their lives. After all, the amazing level of double-talk employed to explain apartheid for forty years has conditioned the public to suspend its credibility almost indefinitely.

The Mint Of The Living Dead

The most chilling of these government legends is the belief that people condemned to death are never really hanged.

They are led from their death-row cells, not to the gallows, but to the Mint. Here they are put to work for the rest of their natural lives, making the coins that are supplied to banks, under conditions of pure slavery.

Why the Mint?

"Because the government will never hang someone who can make money for them," is the traditional explanation, with its unintentional pun.

Ina van der Linde, a writer for the "alternative" weekly newspaper Vrye Weekblad, aired the legend in a 12 April 1990 report on the temporary suspension of the death sentence in South Africa. She had visited the Mamelodi township cemetery, where the graveyard team from Pretoria Central prison used to offload the bodies of executed prisoners for burial:

"We asked the caretaker where the condemned were buried. We drove up and down along the rows of graves. At the end of the cemetery he climbed out and pointed to a patch of overgrown ground. Three barely discernible mounds. He had forgotten their names. He could also not remember why they had been hanged..."

One reason for the existence of the myth (about the Mint) is that the family is never allowed to see the body of an executed person.

About an hour after the execution, the family is allowed to attend a service in the prison chapel. The coffin is placed in the front of the room. The family may not see the corpse, and they may not attend the funeral. It takes place immediately after the service. The coffins are taken to the cemetery by a black taxi-bus.

Days or even weeks after the funeral, the prison authorities send a note to the family giving the number of the grave.

Even without the tale about the Mint, this sounds like rich source material for urban legends. The body that is never seen; the funeral that is never witnessed; the mysterious black taxi that takes the body to its grave: it would be surprising if there WEREN'T dark legends surrounding the death penalty.

Joyce Ozynski, organiser of the Anti-Censorship Action Group, explained, "When I heard it, I thought it was so weird. But you look at it: the graveyard is in a very obscure place. There are no tombstones. If your son is sentenced to death, for instance, and you want to visit his grave, the police put tremendous obstacles in your way."

The British adult comic book Crisis recognized the story and its context as a powerful vehicle for a human rights statement. In their 3 March 1990 issue, produced in conjunction with Amnesty International and Art and Society, one third of the comic is devoted to a story called "THE DEATH FACTORY."

It tells of a death-row prisoner who dreams he is hanged. Instead of the noose tightening around his neck, however, he falls through the trapdoor of the scaffold, into a pit below.

He is shocked to see his fellow condemned prisoners, alive. A policeman orders him to "join the others." They walk down a tunnel, and emerge in "a subterranean hell...a secret underground mint...where you make money for the government – forever."

The prisoner wakes up, and realizes the Mint is just a mint after all, and the legend is "believed in by many black South Africans to ease the pain of losing loved ones."

Folklorists would find the story somewhat unusual. Unlike many urban legends, which act in one way or another as cautionary tales, this is at first glance a story intended for comfort. However, it is told as often among middle-class whites, with a flavor closer to that of horror stories, and the context of the telling is usually a late-night "chill-contest." It's along the lines of, "You think THAT'S scary, wait till you hear the one about how they really make our money…"

Government legends as told from a white perspective are often as amusing as tragic. They seem designed to confirm long-held suspicions about officials meddling in our lives, or of government incompetence.

The Short File Clerk

The next example was told by a former teacher, who had herself heard it from a former school secretary. It was repeated in March 1990, shortly after a scandal aired in the press about teachers not receiving their government salaries for the month of January:

"As far as I know, this really happened. It's about the TED (Transvaal Education Department). A teacher at Orange Grove Primary School didn't receive her salary cheque for three months. After the first month, she made inquiries. The Department told her they had no record of her - although she'd been teaching for seven years and had received a cheque every month.

She had no choice but to wait and see what happened the next month. But the following month, she again didn't get her salary. She wrote letters, sent telegrams, and phoned them.

They still said they had no record of her. So she went to Pretoria herself, and showed them all her documentation, and basically proved her case. They finally admitted she had a point, but still insisted they had no record of her.

Finally, two days before the end of the third month, she got a phone call from the TED. They had found her file.

It turned out that one of their clerks, who was much shorter than the rest, had battled to reach her typewriter when she was sitting at her desk. So she had taken the nearest practical item - which happened to be a bunch of files - and put them on her seat, under her bum, and she could type away comfortably. I don't know how many other people weren't getting their salaries at the same time.

The story is a delightful amalgamation of prejudices involving government departments. State officials, according to the legend, are absurdly incompetent; they are obstinate to the point of denying the evidence before their eyes, they are grossly insensitive; they force their victims into the poorhouse…and some of them are rather short.

In the context of the very real complaints about unpaid salaries, the legend has a strong ring of plausibility. Official spokesmen as much as said in the press that they didn't see the salary situation as a problem, and therefore did not see why the teachers should see it as a problem. Even urban legends have a hard time matching such glibness.

It is easy to see how, in this climate, a legend could emerge among teachers to reveal just how incompetent the education authorities can be.

The Killer Potato

The next legend is told almost exclusively in the townships, and is openly told from a point of view of ridicule for the victims, the SA Defense Force:

During the 1976 Soweto uprising, when the army was occupying the townships, a gang of Soweto kids painted a potato green, and lay in wait at a street corner. An armored car, on patrol through Soweto, rolled round the corner, with a soldier sitting in the turret. One of the boys lobbed the potato, which at a glance looked like a hand-grenade, into the turret, and it rolled down into the cabin of the vehicle. The soldiers inside all scrambled out, and ran from the vehicle - minus their rifles. The youths quickly jumped in, and drove off with the vehicle and the rifles. The story was, of course, hushed up by the army.

There you have it: the ingenuity of township kids, who have learned about life the hard way, in a war situation, and are now putting into practice what they have learnt, so those white soldiers had better watch out; the stupidity of the white soldiers, who are so nervous they'll fall for any old trick; and finally, the vulnerability of military vehicles - whereas they are in fact a source of terror and a symbol of state-sanctioned violence in the townships.

The legend thus serves to bolster confidence among township youth, and render the armed white "invaders" less threatening. A fascinating aspect of the legend is that it could have been told during any military occupation involving local resistance - 1960s Saigon or 1940s France, for instance.

The Sinister Chandelier

The next legend has been around for many years in the form of a joke, usually told about diplomats stationed in Russia, who are convinced the KGB is eavesdropping on them. However, at the height of PW Botha's "securocrat" rule - during which the various state security bodies were virtually given the run of the country - it suddenly emerged as an urban legend told about South Africa among foreign diplomats. It was said to have happened in the 1970s, when the notorious Bureau of State Security, or BOSS, was a byword for "Big Brother watching us:

Two diplomats arrived in South Africa to begin a tour of duty, and were put up at the President Hotel in Johannesburg on the night of their arrival. They had been warned that BOSS would be watching their every move, and would probably bug their hotel room as well. But having been stationed in even more repressive countries, warnings about South Africa were a big joke to them.

As they unpacked in their room on the first floor, they discussed the possible ways in which BOSS might be monitoring them. On impulse, they decided to search the room for secret transmitters - "bugs." That was one thing they knew BOSS always used on the slightest pretext.

So they searched the room top to bottom: in the telephone mouthpiece, under the lampshade, behind the air conditioner, under shelves and drawers, on top of cupboards. Finally, one of them noticed a suspicious looking bulge in the carpet under one of the beds.

They pushed aside the bed, rolled up the carpet, and bingo: there was a strange little box, screwed into the floor.

One of them happened to have a screwdriver in his luggage, and they set to work on the box. Four inordinately large screws held it in place, and they painstakingly removed the screws, one at a time.

Finally, the box came loose from the floor. They discovered that they had in their hands...a box. It had no apparent purpose but to hold the screws. It had another hole for a large screw in the bottom, but absolutely no electronic components.

Puzzled, they screwed the box back in place, rolled down the carpet, and went downstairs to get something to eat. There was a great commotion downstairs. It turned out the dining room had been closed off: diners had narrowly escaped tragedy when the huge chandelier in the ceiling had suddenly and mysteriously come loose and plummeted to the floor.

The legend is lent an air of authenticity - confirming it is a legend, rather than a mere joke - by the fact that the President Hotel was indeed a favored venue for putting up diplomats in Johannesburg in the 1970s. In the 1980s, that role was largely passed on to other well-known city hotels. If the story had been merely contrived to amuse, topicality would have demanded it be set in these newer venues.

While the legend does not make the government the direct butt, but rather places diplomats in the role of the transgressors, the very flavor of the legend is an indictment on the government: it has created such an aura of suspicion and paranoia, that it has become perfectly natural for visitors to the country - not to mention South Africans themselves - to speculate on surveillance methods the government may be using on them. Innocent civilians always suffer the consequences of this climate of paranoia.

The suspicion of the two characters in the legend turns out to have been unfounded, and indeed dangerous. Yet, as with the Russian version, it does not suggest that the state security service is harmless - merely that one should not expect too much of them.

In a very different context, the next legend leads us to a similar conclusion, except that in this case it is our prison services who fall down on the job, literally.

The Clever Escape

A woman prisoner at one of the jails in the Transvaal thought out a very clever way of escaping. She worked in the carpentry shop, and noticed that every time someone died in the prison, the chapel bells would ring, and a coffin would be fetched from the workshop. Then the coffin would be brought back, with the body inside, and it would be nailed shut before being taken for burial.

This woman got friendly with the warder who supervised the burials, and eventually persuaded him to take a bribe. The deal was, next time someone died, he wouldn't have the coffin nailed shut immediately, but would give her a chance to climb in. Then he would supervise the burial, but that night he would come back alone and dig up the coffin to let her out.

Everything went according to plan. One evening the bells rang, and she made her way to the workshop, her pockets stuffed with supplies - some biscuits, a piece of biltong, and a penlight torch. It was dark, but she didn't want to draw attention by switching on a light. She could just make out the shape of the coffin, lying in wait for her in the shadowy gloom of the workshop.

Sure enough, it hadn't been nailed shut. She quickly climbed inside, and squeezed in next to the body.

Before long, someone came along and nailed the coffin shut. She could feel it being lifted and carried to a vehicle, followed by a bumpy ride to the prison cemetery. The dead body was squeezed tightly against her, but she didn't dare move in case someone heard her.

Finally, the coffin was lowered into a pre-prepared grave, and it was covered with earth.

When she was sure no one would hear anything, she finally dared to move. Eager for some light, she took out her torch. She was curious to see whose coffin she was sharing, and shone the light in the dead person's face.

It was the warder she had bribed.

Permission of Arthur Goldstuck
Sources:
The Rabbit in the Thorn Tree by Arthur Goldstuck

Modern Myths and Urban Legends of South Africa
Penguin, 1990

Arthur Goldstuck has a schizophrenic existence as one of Africa's leading commentators on Internet commerce, technologies and possibilities, as well as being a successful journalist and author. He is author of, among other books, "The Hitchhiker's Guide to the Internet," the definitive guide to the Internet in South Africa, as well as "The Art of Business on the Internet." His 13 books include four best sellers on urban legends, namely The Rabbit in the Thorn Tree, The Leopard in the Luggage, Ink in the Porridge, and The Aardvark and the Caravan. He has been described both as "the father of the written Internet in South Africa" and as "South Africa's Mr Urban Legends."

	**modern myths and urban legends of south africa part 2**	arthur goldstuck south africa 1993

In Africa, politics is seldom a funny business

In almost every country on the continent, political systems are in transition, and the transitions don't come easy. Violence, corruption and instability are often hallmarks of the political process.

These factors, however, also inspire urban legends of the strangest variety - particularly in the volatile, bizarre country called South Africa The first tale here is a classic from South Africa's pre-negotiation and pre-reform days, when the right-wing ran the government and every black person was seen by whites as a potential "terrorist." Arnold Benjamin, who used it in his "So It Goes" column in the Star at the beginning of the 1980s, assures me it was current in Johannesburg northern suburbs book club circles at the time.

The mechanically-inclined gardener

it concerned a lady who hired a casual gardener. She explained that she was waiting for the lawnmower to be repaired, but the new man said: "Let me try to fix it."

A while later, she found he had taken the machine skillfully apart. Not only that, he had laid out the bits and pieces in precise fashion on sheets of newspaper and was busy cleaning and oiling each one. Soon the lawnmower was its old efficient self.

The lady was impressed...then alarmed. How would an ordinary migrant from Bophuthatswana acquire that sort of expertise? Wasn't that the way soldiers are trained to lay out the parts of a gun?

She became even more alarmed when she had a look into the gardener's room and discovered - so the story goes - a small stash of weaponry.

The housewife is said to have got to the nearest police station in about 30 seconds flat, but there the story fades out. Not to mention the gardener.

The good news, anyway, was that she did get her lawnmower fixed free.

This legend can also be seen in the light of more recent spates of burglaries and attacks on suburban homes, either involving recently employed gardeners, or where such labour is suspected of performing an inside job.

In the broader society, meanwhile, black youths became more and more unwilling to fit in with the existing political structures. The Tricameral Parliament introduced after the 1983 referendum, which gave coloreds and Indians a form of parliamentary representation, was in fact the spark for the worst violence in this country's history. From 1984 to 1989, the townships became virtually ungovernable. It was this process, as much as growing enlightenment, that persuaded FW de Klerk that the old road was a cul de sac.

The disarmed enemy

The "Class of 1984," as the young "comrades" of this era were known (as opposed to the "Class of '76", who had participated in the June 16 Soweto uprising), became increasingly militant, and it became an everyday occurrence for black school children to skip the country for ANC military training. Others stayed behind, to be trained on the battleground of the township streets. One of these, by now an ex-comrade, described the consequences of an ANC slogan of the time, "Disarm the enemy, and arm the people":

By the beginning of 1990, you no longer saw 10111 cars (small Flying Squad patrol cars) in the townships themselves, only on the main roads past the townships. This was because so many of them had been hijacked, and roadblocks had been disarmed.

"I know of only one specific case, which happened in 1989. There was a police roadblock on the Soweto freeway next to a filling station in Diepkloof. It was badly situated, and the police could not see what was happening around them - only the road in front of them.

One night, the police suddenly went mad, running around, sirens howling, house-to-house searches. Word went round that the roadblock had been disarmed. A number of armed youths had taken the police by surprise and removed their weapons.

I didn't see the disarmament myself, but I remember the police cars moving about with their sirens going. A few days later the roadblock was moved up the road to a spot from where they could see everything around them.

My informant was unable to place the exact date, and he had not heard of any other specific cases. He was certain it was true, but did not personally know of anyone who had been involved. The incident had been hushed up

150

by the police, who did not want anyone to know how they'd been caught with their pants down."

An urban legend? If it is, it ties in perfectly with the tale of The Killer Potato (from The Rabbit in the Thorn Tree), which has township kids in 1976 disarming an armoured car on patrol through the townships by lobbing a green-painted potato through the turret.

In the 1989 version, there are no clever tricks involved, but yet again it plays on the stupidity of the security forces; again it is a disarmament; and again it is hushed up by the authorities.

A tie for a killer

Meanwhile, there was an ever-increasing backlash from right-wing whites, and incidents of "kaffer-bashing" escalated: white thugs would cruise quiet streets in cities and towns looking for lone blacks, whom they would then beat up, or even murder. This kind of action reached its climax on November 15 1988, when Barend Hendrik Strydom, a self-proclaimed leader of the seemingly non-existent group Die Wit Wolwe, went on a shooting spree in broad daylight in Pretoria, killing seven black people and wounding 15.

His actions attracted broad admiration from whites on the far right, and many of them crowded the courtroom to offer their moral support.

City Press captured this moment of poetic justice on May 28 1989:

"Piet Spies of Kroonstad bought a tie for R20 from a black man outside the Pretoria Supreme Court this week in order to enter and show his support for condemned mass-murderer Barend Hendrik Strydom.

Spies was not allowed into court after Judge Louis Harms ordered, in the interests of crowd control, that only men wearing ties could attend. He rushed outside to try to buy one from members of the Press and even a schoolboy - but the only person who would sell him one was a black man."

Poetic justice? Or urban legend? It seems just too good to be true - that, to get into court to support a black-hating murderer, the man had to depend on the goodwill of a black man - who then also made sure he paid through his nose for it.

The VIP coat-checker

As the violence intensified, and many South Africans realised peace and guns could not be synonymous, various establishment-linked people broke away to pursue their own vision of peace independently of the government. And, of course, its people began generating legends beyond its borders. Arnold Bejamin was responsible for finding this one amid the plethora of media coverage of political indabas in places as far afield as Lusaka, Dakar and Paris. It appeared in his column on 6 December 1989:

"One of the SA delegates (to the Paris indaba), arriving at the conference hall on the first day, was looking for a place to leave his overcoat. He saw an official-looking gent standing around in the lobby and tried to hand it to him, without success.

'Why can't I leave this with you?' he asked peevishly.

The answer was a complete squelch: 'Because I'm the Prime Minister of France.'

The safety-tested airstrip

Meanwhile, the nominally independent "homelands," most of them kept in power with the aid of the SA Defense Force, were also beginning to recognize the light at the end of the tunnel as an oncoming train, and began to deliberate on their own route to the future.

A friend of a friend of a participant in these talks passed this story on to Krisjan Lemmer, who used it in his Weekly Mail column on November 9 1990:

"A man I know of but barely know was invited up to Venda to attend a conference on the future of the TBVC (Transkei, Bophuthatswana, Venda, Ciskei) countries. The participants were met at Jan Smuts airport by a South African army officer, seconded to Venda. He told them that the conference venue was not near an airport, but a landing strip had been specially built so they could touch down in comfort.

Is it safe? asked one particularly anxious fellow. Oh yes, said the officer. Has it been tried out? Oh yes, said the officer, seven times.

But has it been tried out with a fully-laden plane? Oh yes, said the officer. No problem. We made a couple of test runs, using about 20 prisoners from the local jail."

The royal wedding

And then there was the matter of the State President's daughter. During the 1980s, as then-president PW Botha tightened his autocratic grip on the South African government, his family was touted as a kind of South African royal family. His role as an ersatz African emperor who was merciless in his swift response to any dissent, was balanced by the part played by his wife, Elize. She was a near carbon copy of Britain's Queen Mother, all saccharine smile and matronly figure - known affectionately as the "national koeksister."

And then there was their daughter, Rozanne, who didn't quite make the grade as the Princess Diana of South Africa. This, despite recording an album of her country music and helping to make a propaganda film for international release, with the credits naming her as Rozanne Both.

And so it was that a court in Swaziland one day heard the incredible evidence that a member of that country's royal family had gone around promising to "give" Rozanne to people who joined him in a coup plot.

The royal was Swaziland's Prince Mfanasibili, a former political strongman who was on trial for high treason. A main Crown witness against him, Armando Lecula, a Mozambican serving convict, said that he had been promised the former South African state president's daughter as his wife.

The Citizen carried the Sapa report on August 16 1990:

"…He said the promise was part of a reward for helping the prince in a plot to escape from Matsapa Central prison and overthrow the king and crown himself as monarch.

During cross-examination by the defence counsel, South African advocate Dr Hilton Fine, Lecula said the prince told him if he became king of Swaziland he would give Mr Botha a piece of land in Swaziland where he could live should the African National Congress take over South Africa.

Lecula said his reward would also have included a dream honeymoon with Rozanne to the Phillipines, a gun made of gold and a flight to the US where he would be introduced to President George Bush and former US assistant Secretary of State, Mr Chester Crocker.

…Lecula also alleged that the prince had asked him to obtain African muti from a Mozambican Nyanga which was to have been used to bewitch King Mswati and the then prime minister, so the king would relent and release the prince and install him as prime minister.

Dr Fine put it to Lecula that his stories aimed at incriminating the prince were fairy tales to be believed only by children.

'It is true what I have told you,' replied Lecula, 'but you don't know that it is.'"

While the court case itself was no urban legend, there was clearly one at work here. The advocate hit the nail more neatly on the head than he could have imagined when he called it a fairy tale - for urban legends often play the modern-day role of old-time fairy tales.

Here, the court evidence should be seen in the light of the urban legend that has become part of southern African folklore of the past 30 years: wherever a white minority government has finally bowed to majority rule, a rumour has gone about that blacks will be given any white person's house of their choice.

The resultant urban legend, recounted in The Rabbit in the Thorn Tree, had domestic workers paying organisations like the ANC R10 a month "rent." After they had taken power, this "bond payment" would ensure that the worker would be able to take over her employer's home.

It seems, in this case, Lecula was persuaded that Rozanne Botha formed part of a similar package. The witness's implicit faith in the promise suggests that it was not an isolated example of this kind of belief.

Even now, there may be people going around the sub-continent dreaming of the day they finally get to take a former state president's daughter - or any other prominent personality's daughter for that matter - as their wives.

Where is Saddam's wife?

The political legends of southern Africa do not operate in isolation from the outside world.

More than a year after America believed it had won the Gulf War against Saddam Hussein, urban legends were still circulating about what "really" happened in Saudi Arabia, Kuwait and Iraq.

Zambia had a close encounter with one of these tales.

It was the rumour that Saddam Hussein's wife had been sent to a distant country for safety before the war began. She happened to have taken half the Iraqi air fleet with her for safekeeping, but that was another story. At first the reports had her taking refuge in Spain. This sounded credible, as the Spaniards had just presented Hussein with a peace medal. But Spain quickly sided with the Westerners, and the urban legend moved on.

The next destination was Morocco. Pressmen were rushed to Rabat to track her down, and found nothing.

The final destination was Zambia.

"Did he or didn't he?" asked Africa South in March 1991. "Kenneth Kaunda knows, but he's not telling."

Suddenly, the biggest open secret in southern Africa was that Kenneth Kaunda had indeed given shelter to Saddam's family.

Indeed he did, insisted the Movement for Multiparty Democracy. Absolutely not, averred Kaunda indignantly. Western diplomats in Zambia got caught in the crossfire, as the president challenged them publicly to state whether they had complained about the presence of the Iraqi ruling family. A definite faux pas for those circles: one diplomat characterised him as "an arrogant dictator who cannot clearly see that his time is up."*

The Gulf War touched southern Africa deeply, with petrol prices see-sawing almost daily, and deep controversies arising over support or non-support for the Allied forces. Consequently, it seems relevant to examine a few more stories from the conflict that have little immediate connection with this part of the world.

The "Where Is Saddam's Wife?" mystery was one of the more innocent urban legends to emerge from the Gulf War. Others were vicious, bloody and downright dangerous. There are even suggestions that US President George Bush's offensive campaign may have been based on an urban legend.

The haunted elevator of Lusaka

It's not only Saddam Hussein who has haunted Lusaka in recent years. The spectre of a bankrupt nation has overshadowed almost every move made by the nation's leaders in recent years.

In fact, Kenneth Kaunda's inability to halt the decay of Zambia was a prime factor in his being ousted as president. So one would expect many a grim urban legend to emerge from the economic wasteland this country has become. Instead, one of the best urban legends to sprout in that field is quite hilarious, as recounted by The Star's Gerald L'ange in his "Out of Africa" column of February 26 1991:

People are said to start behaving in a most peculiar way when they enter the lift in a certain high-rise building in Lusaka. They all start shouting numbers at the ceiling.

"Two!" one will bellow with his head tilted back.

"Sixteen!" will cry another, addressing the top of the lift with great firmness.

And so it goes, even as the lift ascends.

A newcomer might well think he was trapped with a bunch of fah-fee runners gone mad.

155

But if he did not dive out of the door in panic at the first stop, he would quickly discover that everyone in the lift was quite sane. And then he, too, would start shouting at the ceiling.

His fellow travelers would by now have pointed out to him that there was no point in pressing the buttons to stop the lift at any floor, as they were not working.

However, sitting on top of the lift in the lift-shaft was a man who, by short-circuiting wires or doing some jiggery-pokery or other, was able to control the movements of the lift. This is what he was paid to do by the building's owners.

So if you wanted to go to the fifth floor you would have to shout "five!" loud enough for the man to hear, and he would oblige by effecting the right short circuit or whatever to make the lift stop at the fifth floor.

The accuracy of this story cannot be guaranteed. It was told to a colleague of mine who was recently in Zambia. He did not travel in the lift himself (and who can blame him), but says his source appears reliable.

In other words, the source is a friend of a friend! But there is more from that building, according to L'Ange:

It seems another fault was discovered only when a photographer was commissioned to take a picture of the building, while it was under construction...the building did not look right. It was leaning over to one side, something like the Tower of Pisa.

...So he went back to those who had commissioned him...(they) immediately carried out a check and, sure enough, it was leaning.

Further investigation satisfied them...that the building was not leaning to a dangerous degree. Nevertheless, it was decided not to make it any taller as this would increase the deviation.

So if you want to be one of the few people in the world who have traveled diagonally in a lift controlled by a man sitting on the roof, you have to go to Lusaka to do it.

Or alternatively, to the land of urban legends.

And so on to the most frightening - yet most typical - brand of recent South African political rumors.

The phantom intimidators

In November 1991, South Africa saw the most successful work stayaway in its history, when the union movement Cosatu (Congress of South African Trade Unions) called a two-day stayaway in protest against the unilateral introduction of Value Added Tax.

Previous such stayaways had often been marred or discredited by widespread intimidation - it was easy to ascribe people's absence purely to their fear of violent recriminations from township comrades.

On this occasion, Cosatu demonstrated a growing maturity in the movement's approach to mass mobilisation by introducing numerous checks and balances to ensure that no one was threatened or intimidated into joining the stayaway.

They still didn't get it quite right: a few days before the stayaway, they issued guidelines on who would be "exempted" from the stayaway - people like taxi-drivers, doctors, nurses, teachers, school pupils and media workers.

The very concept of exempting certain people suggested that the rest, who were not exempted, would be subject to punishment if caught going to work. Cosatu had to correct itself fast, and finally declared that no one would be prevented from going to work.

Finally, the two-day stayaway on November 4 and 5 went off smoothly, with the only serious intimidation occurring on certain mines, where there was already simmering tensions between various factions.

From the union point of view, never had a stayaway been either so successful or so incident free - and thus so convincing.

But there were other parties that did not want to see things in this light. The usual crop of stayaway-opponents had been mouthing off for more than a week that the stayaway would only work because of intimidation. They had a point, based on previous experience, but this time they did not reckon on the organisers' obsession with scoring points among the public.

So, even as the stayaway got peacefully under way, the opponents were still carping about intimidation.

Central among these was John Kane-Berman, head of the SA Institute for Race Relations, which had in recent years made few bones about its sympathy for Chief Mangosuthu Buthelezi's Zulu nationalist movement Inkatha, and its opposition to the ANC-Cosatu alliance. Most township violence was ascribed by the Institute to the ANC, even where there was clear evidence that Inkatha may have been responsible.

On the subject of the stayaway, Kane-Berman was adamant that intimidation would be its hallmark.

And so, the week before the stayaway, he fell for an urban legend which would probably have died a swift death had he not been so eager to prove intimidation.

He told the media that minibuses with loudhailers were cruising the streets of Soweto, warning people to stay indoors on November 4 or 5, or they would be killed.

This is not the kind of rumor to be repeated lightly in a volatile township atmosphere, where one group's fear of attack from another has frequently spurred the first group to attack first, resulting in spirals of revenge that never seem to cease.

Police investigated Kane-Berman's allegations, and could find no evidence. Newspapers sent its reporters scouring the townships for eyewitnesses, and could find none.

Kane-Berman was questioned more closely about the rumor, and acknowledged he had heard about it from his staff. No staff members could be produced who could verify the incidents, either as ear- or eyewitnesses. Kane-Berman did not find this conclusive, however, and repeated the assertions in a live television debate while the stayaway was raging in its silence.

At the Weekly Mail, I had assigned reporters who lived in the townships to catch minibus taxis to work and thus assess the level of intimidation. They reported none. Neither they nor anyone else on the few minibuses coming to town were even asked a question about their profession or destination, let alone intimidated into staying home.

And Vrye Weekblad had this to say in their November 8 edition:

If there is one institution that has gone backwards as far as race is concerned in the New South Africa, it is the Institute for Race Relations. And the man single-handedly responsible for that is its director, John Kane-Berman.

Kane-Berman's slip has long been showing, but this week it was hanging right down around his ankles.

He declared even before Cosatu's stayaway action that he had witnesses to people being intimidated to stay away from work. People were riding around Soweto announcing over loudspeakers that those who go to work will be killed.

And then something very embarrassing happened to this little chap. The police, who are usually the keenest to shout "Intimidation!," could not find one grain of evidence of Kane-Berman's allegations. Nor anyone else's.

But Johnny is not put off so easily. He then appeared on TV playing the same tune.

This is the latest episode in a months-long saga by which Kane-Berman has shown for all the world to see his intense hatred of the ANC and great predilection for Inkatha.

This is his right, but then he must cease presenting the institute as an independent body.

And here is the (subconscious) news

The intimidation rumor was not the only one that led to heated debate as the country geared itself up for negotiating a democratic constitution. A couple of months before, the unlikely focus of misguided attention was the logo used to introduce the SABC's TV news broadcasts. It was composed of a mass of flickering images which then resolved themselves into a satellite dish, which then shrunk back into the logo.

The rightwing Conservative Party (CP) decided this was nothing but a devious political plot.

At the party's Vryheid congress on August 10 1991, Natal vice-chairman Gunther Gathmann revealed the existence of the "hidden images."

According to the Daily News, he claimed that the SABC's purpose in flashing the images was to further the National Party's political ambitions.

A photographer on the Daily News decided to pin down those images. He was surprised to find how many images he was able to reproduce from the few seconds of TV footage. His newspaper asked video expert to examine the footage - and found it contained 25 images of political leaders, war scenes, coins, an oil rig and sports stars - all invisible to the viewer.

The pictures depicted a collage of international coverage of events throughout history. In a typical broadcast, they included:

- A satellite dish.
- Two men in dark suits facing each other.
- Big Ben.
- A man in a space-suit standing on the moon.
- The statue of Liberty.
- A man's face covered by a gas mask.
- The outline of an oil rig against a sunset sky.
- A Palestinian with outstretched arms.
- A tarred road with green hills and blue sky in the background.
- A soldier holding an M-16 rifle.

- An audience of people wearing 3-D glasses at the cinema.
- A bomb explosion.
- Various coins.
- President Gorbachev.
- President de Klerk.
- Gold bars.

"It appears as if the last two or three frames depict Margaret Thatcher and ANC president Nelson Mandela, but the faces are difficult to identify because the images get progressively smaller," reported the Daily News.

How this montage of images could possibly influence people's minds was unclear, but the CP had no problems interpreting it.

On August 15, the Daily News reported that the CP had announced it would lay a criminal charge against the SABC unless "it stopped flashing hidden pro-Government messages."

"The SABC must stop immediately or we will lay a criminal charge against them," said Gunther Gathmann. "This is something that goes completely against normality, democracy and against common decency because a subliminal message is so effective."

He alleged that the SABC was using subliminal advertising to promote the "new world order" headed by presidents De Klerk, Bush and Gorbachev:

Mr Gathmann said split-second flashes of Mr de Klerk and Mr Gorbachev were an illegal attempt to get people "accustomed to accepting these two gentlemen."

Sources within the television industry, who did not want to be named, said yesterday that the images portrayed a "feeling of television news" rather than being subliminal propaganda.

The SABC's editor-in-chief of television news has rejected as "nonsense" claims that images flashed behind the news logo were intended as subliminal advertising for the Government.

Johan Pretorius said the images in the pre-play to each bulletin were simply cuts from visuals of the top stories of the particular show which then followed.

"They will change for every show depending on what is in the news. For instance, if there is a story about Margaret Thatcher resigning, part of the tape showing her will be flashed. The gold bars and coins are just slides, which we use late during the business news.

"It is just a way of making the presentation more visually attractive. It is a widely acceptable practice used by TV companies in Britain and the US."

According to a Natal psychologist, the collage of news photographs which flash during the news flash were at a slower rate per second and would not have a subliminal effect on audiences.

Nevertheless, the next day the SABC announced it would change its news logo in October - but certainly not because of outside pressure, the SABC insisted.

Dr Pieter Mulder, CP media spokesman, expressed his appreciation for the SABC's decision to drop the logo, thanking it for bowing to pressure from the CP. Mr Pretorius was more ruffled by this gesture than by the initial accusations:

"The reason we decided to drop the logo, which we have been planning to do for months, were not because of anything other than the change in image of TV1, a remarketing of TV1's image and a rescheduling exercise in TV1," he told the Citizen.

"Any communication expert worth his salt will realise that the images were only part of a hi-tech logo and nothing else.

"If anyone wanted to read something else into it - the only answer for that would be that evil is in the eye of the beholder."

The referendum of the Beast

As white South Africa geared up for its do-or-die March 17 1992 referendum on reform, the legend-mill began cranking in all earnest.

The CP claimed that 500 000 dead people would be voting (via crooked politicians) because their names were still on the voter's roll. Recently-married women would also be voting twice, thanks to their maiden names still being on the voter's roll.

Political observers claimed that FW de Klerk had purposely engineered a crushing defeat for his National Party in the Potchefstroom by-election, thus justifying an all-white referendum on his reform policies and the future of negotiations. The avid support for a Yes vote from among the left, which had previously called for a boycott of any racially-based voting, was seen as proof of the success of his ploy to enhance the impression of a rightwing threat.

But the most fascinating legend to emerge from the referendum was one that was based on a 2000-year-old conspiracy theory. Previously, it had been applied mainly to bar-coded supermarket products and credit cards.

You guessed it, it is the legend of the Mark of the Beast, whose number is 666, and who will rule the earth before the Second Coming. His followers will all bear his number.

According to the urban legend version of the prophecy, bar codes and credit cards - elements of the "cashless society" which 666 believers claim will be a precursor to this evil empire - all include the number 666. On the frequent occasions I have checked barcodes on consumer items I've bought, I've been lucky to find one six, let alone three. I am certain that mathematical probability also dictates there must be credit cards with three sixes in their numbers, but I have yet to see one of those too.

The counter-argument is usually that, if you add up the numbers in a barcode or credit card in some or other configuration, you will eventually come to 666.

Similar convolutions enabled people to raise the same kind of concern about the election procedure. The Citizen reported it this way on February 29:

The March 17 referendum has been touted as a vote for communism, for sanctions, for chaos, for playing rugby overseas and now, for some, branding with the "mark of the beast."

In a statement yesterday the Rev Ray McCauley of the Rhema Bible Church, the charismatic Christian movement, said it was "understandable that some Pentecostal Christians would feel uneasy about the marking to be used on March 17."

He was referring to a fluid visible only under ultra-violet light to be used to mark voters' hands to prevent them from voting twice.

Mr McCauley said Pentecostal Christians believed "one of the events in the run-up to the coming of Christ is the appearance of a dominant and evil ruler, who will demand his followers take a special mark either on their right hand or forehead."

Home Affairs Minister Gene Louw said special arrangements had been made for those who objected to the marking, in spite of the fact that the dye would only be applied to voters' left hands.

"I have consulted many prominent church leaders and theologians who have indicated that, from a theological point of view, there can be no objection against the marking of a person's fingers," he said in a statement.

But, to accommodate those who declare under oath their objection on religious or conscience grounds to the marking of their fingers, the voting procedure has been changed. In their case, the chemical mark can be replaced by a sworn statement they have not voted previously in the referendum.

Mr McCauley said he did not believe the dye was the mark of the beast because:

- The anti-Christ's kingdom is, according to most Pentecostal theologians, going to emerge in Europe.
- Pentecostals generally believe the mark of the beast would be used to bar people from buying and selling.
- The mark would only be given to those who made a conscious decision to reject God in favour of the anti-Christ.

A former Moderator of the Full Gospel Church of God, Dr Lemmer du Plessis, said in Pretoria yesterday that as many as 500 000 White Christians in South Africa could object to being marked on their left hand...

"There is a school of thought amongst Christians that Revelation 13 verse 16 to 18 warns against allowing the anti-Christ, who is also defined elsewhere as a head of government, to mark any person on the hand or on the forehead.

"Although there is no question that this could be compared to the referendum mark - especially because Revelation 13 specifically refers to such mark having an economic connotation - the symbolism of the mark upsets a large number of Christians," he said.

On March 2, the Apostolic Faith Mission, which its leaders claim to be the second-largest white church in South Africa, called on voters who objected to the invisible ink to vote by way of a statement of affirmation. But their president, Dr Isaak Burger, did point out that many Christians also objected to taking the oath.

The Phantom Voters

The CP made desperate attempts to reverse the course of history even as history was steamrolling them on March 18.

Even as it was becoming clear the referendum would be a landslide "Yes" for reform (68.7 percent in favour), the CP's MP (Members of Parliament) for Losberg, Fanie Jacobs, held up the counting of votes in the Roodepoort constituency with any number of objections. He demanded that the counting officers all be properly identified, he demanded that bundles of votes be rebundled, and he demanded three recounts when he couldn't believe the CP had been beaten (by 11 592 votes, or 4.8 percent of the vote, to be precise) in what they thought was their stronghold.

One of the reports reaching newspapers, which may well have been an urban legend, was that he had also claimed that people were going to sneak into the counting area with additional Yes votes stuffed into their pockets, and which would be stuffed into the ballot boxes during the counting.

An even more bizarre version of this tale was that Jacobs claimed there were people hiding under the counting tables, ready to slip extra Yes votes into the ballot boxes.

The "official" version of this report, according to The Star of March 19, was that Jacobs had demanded that all the officials should be registered and counted, as he was afraid some may "pop out from under the tables with 'yes' votes in their pockets."

Jacobs' response to this "quote" was as revealing as the quote itself: he denied that he had said anything of the sort, but warned that "whoever had made the allegation had broken the vow of secrecy" (about proceedings in the counting room). If it wasn't true, no vow would have been broken, would it?

That's no great shakes as far as conspiracy theories go, but it gives you a good idea of why these people have always believed in "reds under the beds."

Had the rightwing CP won the referendum, and eventually taken the reigns of government, it would have found itself having to pay serious attention to fundamentalists qualms from within the ranks of its own conspiracy theorists.

Add to those the racial myths on which its policies are based, and you'd have a nation based on conspiracy theory, myth, rumor and urban legend.

Not a nice place to live, but a folklorist's dream.

---

* Kaunda's time was indeed up. In November 1991 he was soundly defeated by Frederick Chiluba in Zambia's first multiparty elections in 17 years.

Permission of Arthur Goldstuck
Sources:
The Leopard in the Luggage by Arthur Goldstuck

Urban Legends from Southern Africa
Penguin, 1993

See page 148, for biography of **Arthur Goldstuck**.

| modern myths and urban legends of south africa part 3 | arthur goldstuck south africa 1993 |

Operation Mandela and other not so true tales

This feature appeared in Tribute magazine in 1992, and was adapted as a chapter for The Leopard in the Luggage.

From the tale of Winnie Mandela's operation to the story of Kansas Mncunu's wife, rumors about the famous have long been part of our way of life. ARTHUR GOLDSTUCK dispels some of the myths.

Gossip, malicious rumors and plain old myths about the famous and the powerful have always been part of the fabric of our society.

Some of the rumors can have disastrous repercussions for the individuals involved, but generally they provide a popular hook for idle chit-chat. They turn into entertainment, rather than serious allegations.

However, one can't expect "Kansas City" Mncunu, Radio Zulu's top presenter, to have gained any amusement from his brush with the rumour mill.

Early in 1991, his wife died after an illness. He buried her and, naturally, mourned for her. But then the rumors started: She had not died a natural death. She had been murdered. In fact, Kansas himself had killed her.

In the final version of the story, it was said that Kansas had smashed a knobkierie over his wife's head, killing her instantly. He had then made a run for Johannesburg, where he had gone into hiding.

How such a high-profile personality could go into hiding was never explained in the rumor. And how his radio shows could continue if he was a wanted man was also never adequately explained.

Finally, as such gossip must, the rumor died as suddenly as it had been born.

Wisely, Kansas never attempted to go into battle against the rumor.

According to Professor Gary Alan Fine, head of the Department of Sociology at the University of Georgia in the USA, who visited South Africa in 1991, "Rumors are claims about the nature of the world. The truth or falsity of a particular claim is only one aspect; another important aspect is the credibility of the claim.

"Many who do battle with rumors, particularly corporate or market rumors, get trapped by worrying too much about how the rumor started and whether there is any truth in it. They try to present 'real facts'. But rumors are notoriously difficult to trace to their original source. Even when one can expose the truth, there is no certainty that the public will believe what they are told. Some wrong information makes more social sense than the truth."

Another popular show biz figure to learn this unfortunate truth was Tsepo Tshola of Sankomota, the band from Lesotho that is fast establishing itself as one of southern Africa's finest.

About two years ago, Tsepotshola's wife was murdered in Lesotho, while he was with the band in Johannesburg.

Despite this clear alibi, and despite the fact that a man like Tsepo, renowned for his warmth and friendliness, is the least likely person to murder a loved one, the rumor emerged that he had done it. Or, if he hadn't done it, that he had been involved.

For once, gossip was given a full legal burial: a suspect was eventually caught, and appeared in court in the middle of 1991. And the rumor took an early retirement.

A rumor that is clearly going to live on is the tale of Paul Ndlovu, the star singer of the hit group Mordillo during the mid-eighties.

On 27 September 1986, Paul was officially buried after dying in a car smash. But even as he was being buried, a chilling rumour came to life: Paul Ndlovu had not died in the car smash; it was someone else's body in the grave; Paul had been kidnapped by an inyanga, who had turned him into a zombie - one of the living dead - and was using him as a slave.

Friends and family of Paul claim to have seen him at an inyanga's home, and he has since been spotted by acquaintances throughout the Transvaal.

In early 1989 journalists even traveled with Paul's mother, Kate, to Bochum in the Northern Transvaal, where he was allegedly being kept.

They arrived at a heavily guarded kraal, where they were introduced to an inyanga by the name of Mapoulo. They were told to pay R100 each if they wanted to see Paul, so they agreed.

While they were talking, Mapoulo suddenly waved her arm, and there, standing at a spot not far from the group, stood a man who looked like Paul Ndlovu!

He was about nine metres away, and the journalists weren't allowed to approach him. After a few moments, he was ushered away.

Ike Motsapi, one of the journalists and an old friend of Paul's, was dazed: "My thoughts went back to my memories of Paul and I was soon sure that whatever I had thought to be true - that Paul was dead - had been turned upside-down."

166

However, when he followed up various other leads on the story, Ike realised that all may not have been what it seemed. He came across numerous rumours of rival showbiz figures being behind Paul's death. All dismissed the tales as rubbish. The police at Bochum called the zombie story "absolute nonsense."

Ike then learned that Paul was due to be sent back to his mother on 6 May 1989, when a massive celebration would be held. But the event never took place.

A year later, there was still no more news of Paul. Except, of course, for a record company executive who had "spotted" Paul alive, behind the wheel of a delivery vehicle in the Johannesburg traffic. And a nurse who had known Paul, who "saw" him in Nelspruit in the Eastern Transvaal." And, no doubt, numerous other people have seen Paul Ndlovu in one place or another.

The Paul Ndlovu rumour has become a fully fledged urban legend - the modern version of ancient fairy tales, and a sophisticated version of traditional oral legends. These are stories that people pass on by word of mouth, always telling it as a true story, but always adding bits and pieces of detail as the story spreads.

Paul Ndlovu's story has a well-known international equivalent: the myth that Elvis Presley never died.

Showbiz personalities are the most common victims of these rumors, but politicians come a close second. And the past year has seen one of South Africa's best known political figures caught in the middle of a row that was really little more than a rumor.

Early in 1991, the story began floating about that Operation Hunger - which receives millions of rands in donations to help feed the starving people of South Africa - had paid for Nelson Mandela to have an operation to have a cyst removed. Not only that, but they had also paid for his wife Winnie Mandela to have a "tummy tuck," and for their daughter Zinzi to have her bust lifted.

Rather than dismiss the rumor with the contempt it deserved, however, Operation Hunger took firm steps to clear their name. The Sunday Star reported in March 1991 that the organization had commissioned its auditors, Fisher Hoffman Stride, to conduct a cheque-by-cheque search through more than 10 000 cheques it had issued over the previous two years. Their verdict: Not Guilty.

The Mandela family lawyer, Ismail Ayob, underlined the verdict by writing to Operation Hunger, saying the Mandelas were "shocked by the allegations." He confirmed that no member of the Mandela family had ever had cosmetic surgery or any other surgery during this period, except for the removal of Mr Mandela's cyst.

Even Mandela's surgeon, Dr Louis Gus Gecelter, wrote a letter certifying that he had operated on Nelson Mandela and that payment was not made by Operation Hunger.

Like all great rumors, myths and urban legends, the story had spread in numerous versions.

Ina Perman, Operation Hunger's founder and director, said she had been confronted with "a couple of dozen variations." It started off merely with the cyst removal, but then that proved not to be scandalous enough for dinner party conversations. So cosmetic surgery was added on, and the clinic changed location several times - from the Park Lane to the Rosebank Clinic to the Morningside Clinic. Some newspapers were even given dates, details and names of plastic surgeons.

According to the Sunday Star, the bottom line was always the same: "Somebody knows somebody who knows somebody who with their very own eyes have seen an Operation Hunger cheque paying for Mandela medical expenses."

And that, scholars of modern folklore would say, is exactly how you identify modern urban legends: someone knows someone who knows something is true, but you can never track down the final someone - the actual source of the information.

Ina Perlman commented that the tale may have started in September 1990, when the Mandelas attended a "celebrity scribble" fund-raising event. During the event, Nelson Mandela spoke in praise of Operation Hunger, and jealousies may have been inflamed. Moreover, Zinzi had once worked full-time for Operation Hunger.

While Perlman was confident there was no truth in the rumor, it just grew and grew.

She had threatened to sue anyone who reported the rumors as fact, so the newspapers remained silent. And so did Operation Hunger. Until February 25 1991, that is.

They roped in First National Bank MD Barry Swart to authorize a verification of every single cheque drawn over the previous two years.

On March 8 the auditors reported back, giving a clean slate to all payments made from 1 April 1989 to 30 January 1991.

And so, in April 1991, many of the Witwatersrand's elite personalities, including Harry Oppenheimer's daughter Mary Slack, received lawyer's letters pointing out that "there is no substance to any of the said 'stories' which have been deliberately disseminated to cause injury to an organisation which is involved in exemplary work."

One of the people who received the letter told the Sunday Times: "I have put the letter in the dustbin, I heard it (the rumor). You know you go to these dinner parties and don't know from where the stories are coming. I merely asked somebody to ask Mrs Perlman if it was true. I wasn't going to make any libelous statements."

By September 1991, the rumor had still not died. Operation Hunger once again warned that a summons for malicious slander would be issued against anyone involved in the "structured and scurrilous" smear campaign.

Now the urban legend had spread beyond hospital bills: it included rumors that Operation Hunger paid the electricity bill in the new ANC offices, and even settled the account for the sound equipment at the ANC's historic August congress in Durban, according to the Star.

The Weekly Mail was "tipped off" that Operation Hunger had in fact paid for the video facilities at the congress, but wisely ignored the story as mere rumor.

Nevertheless, Operation Hunger was deeply concerned. Ina Perlman believes that such persistent rumor-mongering could irreparably damage the image of the organisation, which remains the biggest relief project in the country.

If Professor Gary Alan Fine is correct, though, there is nothing she can do about it.

"Societies facing massive transformations are societies that must cope with a surge of rumor," he explained while discussing the nature of rumor in this country. "Rumors, when strong enough, shape or limit the effectiveness of political, economic, and cultural institutions. They are markers of public attitudes and concerns. As South Africa moves towards a more egalitarian, multi-racial, just society, the impact of these changes will spill into all arenas."

And what, in the final analysis, should one do about it?

Says Fine: "Heed rumors for what they say about the present; respond to rumors for what they mean about the future."

Permission of Arthur Goldstuck
Sources:
The Leopard in the Luggage by Arthur Goldstuck
Urban Legends from Southern Africa
Penguin, 1993

See page 148, for biography of **Arthur Goldstuck.**

	**miracle in eqypt**	michael ranjit hussein egypt 1999

"Alhamduliflah, Alhamdulillah, Alhamdulillah."

Sweltering heat is abated in the hot summer evening of Cairo by a walk over one of the seven major bridges that span the Nile River, connecting the two sides of this modern city of sixteen million inhabitants. To escape the drudgery of watching yet another night of television in hot, stuffy rooms with fans grating the air in high-ceilinged rooms, many of the city's dwellers go out for ice cream, window shopping; or, if they are men, a game of 'tawla' (backgammon), "shay"(tea) and the ""nargila-"(water pipe) in one of the numerous teahouses.

Those who stroll across the expanses of the famous river are in for treat. Cool breezes stir up, refreshing the pedestrian. The lattice-work Cairo Tower, which is located in the middle of an island in the Nile called Gezira, shines its red beacon like a cherry atop a thin inverted ice cream cone. Lights from the Nile Hilton and the Semiramis Inter-Continental Hotel, as well as residences of Garden City shine out, reflecting on the waters of the Nile. Small boats, festooned with colored lights, ply the choppy waters of the wind-stirred Nile.

It was on one of these bridges that I got a taste of a different side of Cairo that I heretofore had not experienced.

After having spent the day revisiting the exhaustingly-complete Egyptian Museum, wandering through the narrow twisting streets of the Khan Al-Khalili "Souq" (Market) and nearby Al-Himiya, Ghuriya and Al-Gamaliya neighborhoods with their stone or mud-plastered buildings, I decided to head back to my cheap but clean hotel room. I was rather worn out from haggling in Arabic with clever shopkeepers, whose twinkle in their eye assured me that "Yes, bargaining was important but still have fun!"

Back in my room after a cool shower in the shared bathroom, I lay on the bed looking up at the ceiling fan, its blades dutifully chasing one another in never ending pursuit. A bit restless, I decided to go out for a walk, as walking has always proved a great distraction and form of relaxation. I walked past the reception area where the bored desk clerk watched a frenzied soccer match on television, out the doors and down six flights of a marbled spiral staircase with a black wrought-iron banister. The ancient elevator was just too slow and jerky to deal with that night.

Out on to Sharia Qasr-el Nil. I headed straight past all the jewelry and posh clothing stores towards Midan Talaat Harb, a big congested roundabout with six streets pouring into it. Navigating that successfully, I continued on towards Midan Tahrir (Independence Square), a wide-open area where red neon signs glare down from atop buildings on the traffic below. A grassy area acts as an island where Cairene residents sit on the grass for late evening picnics, oblivious to the constant flow of traffic around them. Feeling a bit hemmed in by so many others also enjoying a brief outing there. I decided to continue on towards the Nile, where I had hoped that the crowds would thin out. I was not entirely correct in my assumption; however, there were fewer couples strolling on the Al.-Tahrir Bridge than at the Tahrir Square.

I decided to walk southwards through the quieter tree-lined streets of Garden City, an exclusive residential area home to many embassies and consulates. The next bridge south of the Al-Tahrir Bridge I figured would be a more leisurely walk. My patience paid off.

Crossing halfway over the arched bridge, I leaned over the concrete pillared balustrade. Watching the graceful *feluccas* silently sailing through the night waters, and the distant lights of Central Cairo was soothing. A young doe-eyed Egyptian with a hint of a moustache under his nostrils startled me from my reverie. "Andak sigara?" he queried. I responded in Arabic that I didn't smoke. Undaunted, he asked if this were my first trip to Egypt. Answering in the negative, I assured him that this was my third or fourth visit to this beloved journeying spot.

He stepped closer, leaning over the railing of the bridge and indicating one of the gaily-festooned boats that plied the river below. He asked me if I had been on one of those river tour boats before. "La, abidan" –no, never- I responded. He asked if I would like to go on one of those boats for a short tour of the river. Since I had made no other plans—I didn't know all that many people in Cairo save for shopkeepers I'd regularly visit—I said that would be fine. "-Yahlah." Let's go. Always something new to do. He threw out the cigarette stub he was smoking carelessly into the dark waters below and we crossed over to the other side.

The little boat waited at the end of a short wooden dock, bobbing up and down in the wake of the river's current. Eager well-dressed couples sat on benches lining the boat's sides while pale colored globes shone down on them from lights strung above. As I paid the passage, the burly captain hawked out a departing message, and my friend-at the last instant- jumped from the leaving boat. I was a bit perplexed, but figured, "Oh, well," and decided to enjoy the short twenty-minute tour.

171

When it was finished, we returned to the very dock from which we had embarked. There the young friend was waiting, nervously smoking a cigarette. With a sharp edge to my voice, I demanded to know why he had so abruptly fled the departing boat. I was told that he needed to buy cigarettes and that he would wait for me. Trying to get a refund for the missed voyage from the surly captain was almost futile: because of my anger I finally managed to get a refund.

Ahmed, I shall call him, as I don't remember his name exactly, invited me to tea at his home. This was a common gesture on the part of many locals throughout the parts of the world I had traveled and was not seen as forward at all. I agreed to accompany him. He indicated a tall building with red blinking lights on its tower on the opposite bank of the river, saying his house was near there.

Soon thereafter, a third party joined us from a dark side street. The other youth, near the age of Ahmed, spoke in hushed tones in Arabic. He had heard us chatting. Immediately, I felt a bit suspicious. I recognized that because we had been speaking in Arabic, the third young man didn't want me to be privy to what the two of them were saying. We crossed an old unused and unlit bridge that had served as some kind of former train bridge between the two sides of Cairo. As we approached the tall building with the red-lit TV tower, I queried him again about the location of his home. This time, the answer given was rather vague. I made a mental note that we had basically passed the general area of the home where we would have tea.

The other youth blurted out in Arabic that there was a wedding happening and did I want to go? In India, and also in the Middle East, night weddings are not uncommon occurrences, due to the oppressive heat of day, and also probably due to other traditional reasons. At this point, we had made a full circle back to Tahrir Square. He continued: "We'll have to take a taxi." Suddenly inside of me, I heard a voice shout: "Watch out! Pay attention!"

I told them I was a bit tired as it was near midnight, and was thinking of returning to my hotel room, which was still a bit of a walk away. They insisted that it was something special to see and that I shouldn't miss it. Finally, with reservations, I agreed to go. A taxi was hailed down, and we boarded the cramped car. Again I heard the voice inside bark: "Memorize the route! Pay attention!"

The taxi headed off in the direction of Sayyida Zeinab, the ancient walled city of Cairo, replete with a labyrinthine maze of twisting narrow streets.

We were let off at an intersection under some kind of overpass. The street was filled with light, and people busily scurrying about. Ahmed motioned that we go to the right, down a long street. I noticed as we walked that the hordes of people began to thin out, and observed that the number of street lights were becoming further and further apart.

Soon there were no people in the empty street, and the only apparent life included a few solitary dogs sniffing piles of steaming trash. We approached the old walled city with a portal archway that appeared sinister in the dim light. Ahmed pointed out that the wedding festival was being held in the hall of a school near a mosque inside this ancient compound. As we entered the Sayyida Zeinab area, I couldn't help but being reminded of Dante's portent: "Abandon all hope, ye who enter here..." Again, the persistent voice demanded that I note details of the route, be alert, and stay on my guard for anything anomalous. Noting my growing impatience (masking my nascent fear!), Ahmed assured me that we would soon be there. I growled that I was getting tired of this lengthy ordeal just to go to a midnight wedding. Trying to placate me, the two promised me that it was just a little while longer...

My internal compass blared out at me that we indeed were no longer traveling in a straight line towards the appointed destination, but that in fact, we had actually commenced going in circles.

At this point, something inside me cautioned me to ask for divine angelic help to send down a protective white shield of light around me, which I did. Seeing my anger and frustration, Ahmed pointed out a building with a light bulb casting a pool of light in front of its entrance.

"See. There's a mosque. Do you want to go inside?" I turned and tersely said: "Listen, it's 12:30 in the morning. The mosque isn't even open for salaat (prayers) now. I've had it. I'm going home."

We walked but a few -more steps when suddenly I felt a sharp point pierce my back and abruptly stop. With a feral growl, I savagely elbowed both men on either side of me in the ribs. As I turned around, I noticed a shiny, glimmering knife sailing over a wall in the dim light. The guy on the right tried to grab my bag, which contained my passport, money, cameras and keys. (I had started carrying all with me when I moved from a private room to a dormitory room.) Thoughts about pursuing them in my anger quickly dissolved when I realized it would be pointless, as they knew the area well.

I managed to find my way out of the maze after a while. Seeing a small store still open at that late hour, I walked up to it and asked the owner if buses were still running back to Central Cairo that late at night. He grunted an affirmative response. On the porch of the building under the lone light bulb, I quickly rummaged through my bag: everything was intact.

A smoking, crowded bus rambled up to the store, I boarded and soon we were off to Ramses Railway Station, a central hub for bus and train passengers.

Back in my room at the hotel, I looked at my back in the mirror. A noticeable impression in the middle of my back yet remained. A cold shiver came over me. The thought came to me that had I not heeded the stern command to protect myself in white light, I would have succumbed at the hands of two killers with a sharp knife. Yet another chilling thought that eclipsed any feeling over possible robbed possessions was the idea that an individual could "befriend" another for the sole purpose of robbing and killing another. The cold sense of betrayal ran through me, at odds with that sultry summer night in Cairo.

The next day dawned bright and hot as usual for that time of the year. After a refreshing shower and a tasty but modest breakfast on the balcony terrace, I went out on my daily rounds of adventures. Having to deal with some bureaucratic paperwork at a government office, I passed Tahrir Square again and spoke to a Cairene policeman en route. Recounting the story of the previous night's adventure to him and giving a description of the thief, the policeman nodded his head saying that he recognized him and said he was a very well-known local thug and that the police had had many run-ins with him.

The confirmation of this crook was comforting, but the returning thought of betrayal was disconcerting. The disturbing thought was only finally broken up by the somber but enchanting call to noonday prayer by the muezzein.

Deciding to leave until later the paperwork, I reversed direction and headed for the mosque. The quiet dignity of the mosque and the worshippers made me forget about the sometimes-grim realities of everyday life. Therein, I remembered the whole situation could well have turned out different. I remembered the divine order, the protection of the white light, and the safety afforded. With a deep sense of serenity, I uttered the much used, but sincere words thanking God, "Alhamduliflah, Alhamdulillah, Alhamdulillah."

Michael Ranjit Hussein, who currently resides in New Jersey, has traveled the world extensively. He found throughout his journeys a nascent sense of connectedness with all the peoples of the various countries he visited. He enjoys filming, teaching, writing and sports.

	**the remarkable** **journey of granny lee**	underdog productions south africa 1989

To some, she was the granny you wish you'd had.

In 1989, an eighty-one year old white woman died in a car accident on a highway to Durban, South Africa. A not altogether uncommon occurrence - except for the fact that the victim was in reality neither white, a woman, nor eighty-one.

When Leonard Malcolm Christian Du Plooy was born on the 18th of March 1919 to a mixed race ("colored") family, he embodied all the contradictions of a country ruled by racism and hypocrisy. He spent the first part of his life in the small town of Kimberley, South Africa (the diamond capital of the world), teaching and becoming the "dandy" about town. Renowned for his dancing, piano playing and his curious habit of knitting, Lee was accepted by the ladies of Kimberley but viewed with suspicion by the men.

By the time he reached his thirties, he'd had enough of the small town mentality. So he left for Durban, where he briefly taught again—until he immersed himself in the city's gay seaside subculture. Soon, the flamboyant Lenny was running a brothel. He was also suffering from a skin condition, which was slowly turning him white.

In his fifties, tired of the constant harassment by the Durban police, Lenny moved again. This time he went to Johannesburg, where the gay clubland was thriving—even though it was the height of the apartheid system. He was accepted as a white man, which allowed him to go where he wished.

The transformation into Granny Lee began when a liberated Lenny started to wear women's clothing in public. Soon, the persona of Granny Lee became a full-time occupation, with weekdays spent sewing and stitching to prepare the weekend's new outfit.

Abandoning any sense of restraint, Granny Lee—now a pensioner—soon became the city's most famous clubgoer and drag queen. An accomplished designer and machinist, "she" would make an outfit out of someone's curtains or a pile of plastic rubbish packets. Above all, Lee would never wear the same invention twice. Her outrageous antics and self-made outfits, coupled with her sharp tongue and constant boozing, bedazzled club patrons. Lee became the city's icon. Claiming to be in her eighties, she drew crowds to clubs, bars and parties. She was living dangerously as a white woman in a country ruled by the racial and sexual repression of Calvinist Apartheid.

Possessing little money, Lee would make use of whatever she could find. She'd sew, staple, glue, or otherwise clamp the various elements of her outfits together. She would dye her hair with food coloring, never seeming concerned about what was appropriate for a lady of her age. Lee wouldn't even hesitate at the thought of a revealing, see-through number. Her wardrobe was often enhanced by gifts. At one point, she was given a range of costumes from a theatre which was closing. Her friend Latiefa would throw regular fancy dress parties, and Granny would always oblige by unleashing a memorable creation.

While there was an undoubtedly trashy side to her clothes, Lee managed to carry it off with her unique sense of style. Many call her the (original) "Vivien Westwood" of Africa.

When she died at the age of seventy, she was still a notorious party animal. Even then, Granny Lee had the last laugh. At her wake, the many mourners were shocked to hear the voice and laughter of Granny Lee insulting them all. She had recorded a farewell message to be played at her wake, which resulted in confusion, elation, and horror. Even in death, this queen of the discos continued to flout the rules, mistakenly being the first nonwhite buried in a "whites only" Johannesburg cemetery.

This story has been sourced from *The Remarkable Journey of Granny Lee*, a documentary which won four Craft Awards at the 2001 Avanti Awards (South Africa's prestigious television awards). Filmed by Underdog Productions, it debuted on South African TV screens in July 2000 and was selected for screening at the New York Lesbian and Gay Film Festivals. For more info, visit http://www.underdog.co.za.

UNDERDOG ENTERTAINMENT is an acclaimed film, television and new-media Content Development and Production Company. Founded on the cusp of the convergence of film, television, music, video-on-demand and the Internet, Underdog is poised to conquer a New World of entertainment opportunities. Harnessing both traditional and revolutionary new media tools, Underdog Entertainment uses creativity to deliver powerful, surprising and effective entertainment projects to film, television and Internet audiences around the world.

	**pelonomi hospital unplugged in sickness and health**	dr james le fanu south africa 1996

Cleaner polishes off patients

"For several months, our nurses have been baffled to find a dead patient in the same bed every Friday morning," a spokeswoman for the Pelonomi Hospital (Free State, South Africa) told reporters. "There was no apparent cause for any of the deaths, and extensive checks on the air conditioning system, and a search for possible bacterial infection, failed to reveal any clues."

"However, further inquiries have now revealed the cause of these deaths. It seems that every Friday morning a cleaner would enter the ward, remove the plug that powered the patient's life support system, plug her floor polisher into the vacant socket, then go about her business. When she had finished her chores, she would plug the life support machine back in and leave, unaware that the patient was now dead. She could not, after all, hear the screams and eventual death rattle over the whirring of her polisher."

Further, the Free State Health and Welfare Department is arranging for an electrician to fit an extra socket, so there should be no repetition of this incident. The enquiry is now closed."

Permission of the Sunday Telegraph
Printed: Dr James Le Fanu 19th Oct 1996

No biography provided.

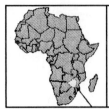

	the one that got away	chris ashworth zimbabwe 1996

If you travel enough dirt tracks or visit enough remote bars, you'll hear enough urban myths to fill a dozen books. This one comes from a bar in a small part of Zimbabwe, where I was picking up some local crafts. There, a grizzly Zimbabwean told of a kayaking trip his cousin Nethanial took. The story began, as many do, with the great Zambezi.

Nethanial and a friend were kayaking down the river, as they'd been for a number of days. One afternoon, they rode over the back of a hippo—the biggest killer of humans in the country. Startled and true to his nature, the creature reared up and bit a great chunk out of the boat, tearing it apart. The two kayakers dove (or fell) out of the boat, and were washed rapidly downstream, saving them from more time with the hippo. They found themselves on a rock, a small island, which rose out of the water. Badly gashed and torn from both the hippo encounter and the shards of the shattering kayak, Nethanial and his friend rested for a time.

Their blood, however, soon attracted crocodiles, which our protagonists saw slipping into the water and approaching. All the kayakers had to defend themselves was one of the paddles, which they used to batter the creatures away. However, as night approached, they realized they wouldn't stand a chance.

Nethanial's friend made a daring swim to get help. Waiting for an opportunity, he dove into the water to make the short distance to shore. Unfortunately, he was caught just short of the bank by a swift crocodile.

Nethanial faced a grim choice: wait until he was taken at night by the crocodiles, or try to swim. So, he dove into the water when he thought he might make it.

Perhaps the crocodiles were a little slower as the night approached, or perhaps they were distracted by their fighting over his friend's remains, but Nethanial made it. Exhausted, he collapsed a short distance up the bank, the exertion and his wounds getting the better of him.

Attracted by the trail of blood rising from the riverbank, the crocodiles crept slowly toward the wounded kayaker. Catching his leg they began to drag him to the river.

Suddenly, a cow elephant came crashing through the bushes to the bank. She had just given birth to a stillborn calf and, not recognizing the piece of inert meat as her offspring, began searching desperately. Seeing a creature being dragged off by the crocodiles, the elephant went wild and attacked, driving the reptiles off and dragging Nethanial to safety.

So by amazing fortune, or simply urban jungle myth, Nethanial survived.

See page 51, for biography of **Chris Ashworth**.

the police

Wow! The police in Africa get their own chapter. I bet there are not too many books on adventure, travel and humor that do this.

I personally had a lot of good experiences with the police I met in Africa and I always had good things to say about them. They were honest, friendly, respectful, very helpful and very good ambassadors' for their country. It's just that when there's an event or a problem and the police are involved, there's usually a good tale to tell.

This chapter has several.

BORDER PATROL   DRUG ENFORCEMENT   HITCHHIKING   TRAFFIC ENFORCEMENT   SELF-ENRICHMENT

Paris, France – The next morning at the airport was pandemonium. Africans everywhere waving crumpled tickets, brightly dressed women chattering too loudly surrounded by acres of crisp shopping bags. All with Parisian designer logos that contrasted with their African block print dresses. Men in expensive suits with huge tribal scars, mountains of luggage in bursting cardboard boxes and metal "caisses" or coffin-sized steel boxes sealed with large brass Chinese-made locks.

Like East Indians with monstrous pastel vinyl suitcases or Asians with their twine-wrapped cardboard boxes, Africans have their metal cases: Not one metal case but stacks of huge military-looking caskets with giant padlocks covered with first class stickers. They contain the fruits of kleptocracy, a unique right of the robber rulers of Africa who brutally divert foreign income like damming off a stream.

I have never been to Africa but I am already learning the class distinctions – the quiet Africans who talk with me while they wait and the noisy garrulous thieves who treat the stewardesses as overpaid waitresses.

The UTA DC-10 traverses the Strait of Gibraltar in seconds. From the French Riviera, over the land of the Moors and descending into the Dark Continent.

The plane descends through the milky haze that shrouds the Sahel. Slowly, faintly as in a dream, the brown landscape begins to rise toward me. Widely spaced, painfully torn trees tied together with thousands of meandering tracks are the only sign of habitation. Then small clusters of brown dots begin to appear. There are the round mud and grass huts of the Bambara. I have never seen a landscape so primitive and exciting.

It begins to hit me as I look past the shiny aluminum wing to the crude huts that this is why I came to Africa. In a microcosm, I understand the problem of Africa. This 450 mph, $10 million aircraft has to land on a flyspeck of broken asphalt in the middle of goats and arid nothingness. I have not come from another country but from another planet.

This, truly, is how the first aliens will appear to Westerners: gleaming, streamlined perfection landing just long enough to disgorge its sweaty, disorientated passengers into the heat, red dirt and filth. Above, the silver bird is a massive white triangular thundercloud above the ochre runway. I stop, turn and take a picture.

I am arrested before I can even walk across the hot tarmac to the terminal. Two angry uniformed soldiers run from the terminal and hold me fast. One of the soldiers roughly grabs for my camera and I hold it away from them. One wags his finger in my face. They smell bad and are not using enough force to convince me to fight back. I am in trouble.

The French UTA ground crew see the commotion and came to my aid. They intervene and use hand motions behind their back to tell me to cool it while they carry on an animated conversation in French with the soldiers. "It is forbidden to take pictures of the airport." This crime is apparently clearly marked inside the terminal that I have yet to enter. The white jump-suited crew asked me if I was taking pictures of the airport, as if to give me an opportunity to say no. I quickly say that I was taking pictures of the giant thunderhead above the plane. A crew member's eyebrow arches. The game is on. They discuss this point in the ongoing shouting match.

Thankfully, Africans are social people even in their suspicion and brutality, and this new interpretation of my crime provokes more heated discussion. This is the first of many times I will be arrested in Africa, but there is no clear resolution to my crime yet. To anger the ground crew is not the goal of my arrest. They expect a direct form of economic penitence from me before I even enter the country. Later, I notice that there are booths to strip-search visitors entering the country.

The pilot of the UTA plane has opened the cockpit window and yells down to see what the commotion is about. I wave at the pilot as if we are old friends. A thought occurs. I explain that I misspoke my bad French. I now correct my confession to say what I meant to say was that I was taking a picture of the pilot, not the plane or the airport. This slows down my captors. We all agree that the pilot is technically not the airport. This new wrinkle and the support of the pilot and crew is gaining me the upper hand. Arresting me would now result in more than a backroom interrogation and search. A deal is finally struck. They frogmarch me up the boarding ladder and into the cockpit. The ground crew scoots ahead to prep the pilot. The pilot greets me with a broad smile and asks why they are arresting this poor fellow for taking his picture. Handshakes and apologies all around. As the soldiers leave, the pilot laughs, shrugs and says "C'est l' Afrique."

Printed with permission:
The World's Most Dangerous Places. By Robert Young Pelton
http://www.comebackalive.com

Robert Young Pelton, 42, has led an adventurous life. His interest in adventure began at age ten when he became the youngest student ever to attend a Canadian survival school in Selkirk, Manitoba. The school was later closed down after the deaths of a number of students. Pelton went on to become a lumberjack, boundary cutter, tunneler, driller and blaster's assistant in addition to his more lucrative occupations as a business strategist and marketing expert. On his time off, his quest for knowledge and understanding have taken him through the remote and exotic areas of more than 60 countries.

Some of Pelton's adventures include breaking American citizens out of jail in Colombia, living with the Dogon people in the Sahel, thundering down forbidden rivers in leaky native canoes, plowing through East African swamps with the U.S. Camel Trophy team, hitchhiking through war-torn Central America, setting up the world's first video interview of the never before photographed taliban leaders in Afghanistan and completing the first circumnavigation of the island of Borneo by land as well as numerous visits to and through war zones. It is not surprising that his friends include shepherds, warlords, pengalus, mercenaries, nomads, terrorists, field researchers, sultans, missionaries, headhunters, smugglers and other colorful people. Stories about Pelton or his adventures have been featured in publications as diverse as Outside, Shift, Soldier of Fortune, Star, The New York Times, Los Angeles Times, Class, El Pais, The Sunday London Times, Der Stern, Die Welt, Washington Post, Outpost, and hundreds of other newspapers around the world. He has also been featured and interviewed on a variety of networks including the BBC, NBC, CBS, ABC, ATV, Fox, RTL, CTV, CBC, and is a regular guest on CNN. Pelton's approach to adventure can be quite humorous. Whether it's challenging former Iban headhunters to a chug-a-lug contest, calling the taliban a bunch of women to their face, loading expedition members' packs with rocks, indulging in a little target practice with Kurdish warlords in Turkey or filling up a hotel pool with stewardesses, waiters and furniture in Burundi during an all-night party, he brings a certain element of fun and excitement to dangerous places. He lives in Los Angeles California.

| 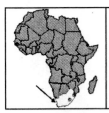 | **drakensberq mountains and the border patrol police** | peter ward south africa 1996 |

Up in smoke

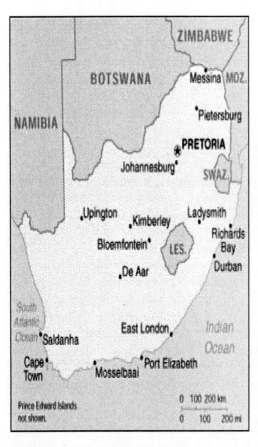

The Drakensberg Mountains also known as the Quathlamba Mountain range, 'Dragon Mountain', 'Battlement of the Spears', parallel the extreme southeastern coast of Africa. Located mostly in South Africa, they are a 4-hour drive from Durban and forms the eastern boundary of Lesotho. Also known as In short, the place is quite spectacular. On a mountain slope you can look down on a thunderstorm.

We had just finished a peaceful day's hiking and were exhausted. The day's pace had been brisk, with too few stops for photo opportunities or rest breaks. The exhaustion came with the usual amount of detours miss-reading the map and constantly re adjusting the straps on our backpacks.

The day's heat was fading away and it was only going to be a matter of time before it was dark. It was a liberated feeling when I dropped my backpack to the ground. I opened the top of the pack. As any hiker knows, as soon as you rummage through the endless amount of plastic bags looking

184

for spare socks, flash light and water, everything becomes a mess. The three of us were doing the same, mining into our backpacks for items, tossing plastic bags on the ground. In the hiking world when this happens, it's known as a kit explosion. Then came the routine procedure of putting up the tent.

At this point, a man in the distance started hurriedly approaching us. In National Parks in Africa, it is not unusual to see scouts or gamekeepers with rifles, as this is used for protection against the game in the resource, but I did stop and pause for a few more seconds when I focused on the pistol in his hand. This is unusual, as you don't shoot wild life with pistols.

He confronted us and introduced himself as a Policeman of the South African Border Patrol and requested that we move our location as quick as possible. In third world countries, the police can be problematic, if not awkward, but this was South Africa, the only first world country on the continent, so we pondered on what was his problem. White South Africans tend to have a short, fiery, no nonsense temper, and this guy had all these traits. To the American readers, imagine speaking to Ted Turner of CNN, or to any British readers, imagine a straight talking down to earth Yorkshire man difficult to reason or agree with.

I asked him would it be all right if we moved the tent and our backpacks behind the tree? He shook his head, mumbling, 'No, no, no', not even looking at the tree. He explained that he and 6 other officers had been camping out for the past 3 days to catch drug couriers crossing the border from Lesotho, and where they were going to make the arrest, which was where we had put up our tent. He also explained that couriers are renowned to be heavily armed, so there could be a fire fight (shoot out). He suggested we pack everything up and join him and the rest of the officers in a cave, which was down a path.

We agreed and were delighted to be finally getting some excitement in the day and began scooping up our belonging. Of course, it takes seconds to unpack a backpack, but it's an art packing everything back in. It was more the case of stuffing what fits back in and hand holding the rest while walking down the path. All three of us looked quite pathetic carrying our belongings.

Behind the trees next to the path were the rest of the police officers', they were loading their pistols full of ammunition, stuffing these down their pants (trousers) or setting the sights on their rifles. I was like a kid on Christmas Eve waiting for his presents, as we were witnessing a stake out and a drug bust- just like the movies. Would it be Miami Vice style, where there's a chase, plenty of shooting followed by a good old punch up, but of course there were no Ferraris, palm beaches or the expensive clothes-Crockett and Tubbs look alike maybe?

Or perhaps this would be more of an NYPD approach, where they predictably partner off the officers and where the sheer presence of the police, results in a quick submission of the criminal.

While in the cave, we put up our tent and boiled water for a cup of tea, observing the final de brief of the policemen-This was in the language Afrikaans, so we didn't understand any of it. At the end of the meeting, however, there was what sounded like a cliché, like in the TV show Hill Street Blues-'Let's hit them before they hit us', which put a few smiles on faces. The expression on their faces showed they were a little bit angry with us for gate crashing their party!

I finally drifted asleep, holding my penknife and pepper spray in each hand- these were the only weapons I had to hand. My train of thought was that if there was any action, the gunshots would wake us all up. The night was cold in the mountains and the three of us slept in a 2 man tent to keep warm. The police officers must have thought we were a little soft as we were in a tent, in a cave, with a fire burning away.

I awoke in the early hours of the morning, stepping out of my tent to reach out to feel the heat from the smoldering fire. There had been no gunshots that evening, but an arrest had been made. They caught a courier from Lesotho carrying 25 kilos of marijuana; he had apparently been paid $10 dollars to do the job. This may not sound like much but it's the equivalent to 10 day's salary for a local. Imagine being paid your salary for 10 days for only a night's worth of work. Quite tempting.

Drug trafficking and crime has become the single biggest business in South Africa, for the following reasons:

South Africa is a First World country on a Third World Continent, so relatively speaking, it is a richer market than in other surrounding countries.

Since the fall of Apartheid, in 1994, the internal security has had to become more tolerant towards the blacks within its borders. The police state mentality of restricting movement of people and allowing law enforcement authorities unprecedented power to stop and search and unaccountability is long gone.

Prior to Mandela coming to power, the South African system was geared firmly at protecting the whites, so blacks could be arrested for being in the wrong neighborhood, or for not having the right identification paperwork. This deterred illegal drug activity.

South Africa does have an infrastructure to export drugs around the world. Main roads and trains lead to Durban, a coastal port with freight and container shipping which is fundamental to the local economy. This place is a magnet for drug producers in countries as far away as Malawi in reaching export markets such as America and Europe. The drugs whose destination are the ships are known as 'Durban Poison'.

When finally the transaction takes place, hard currency is normally the preferred payment, even if that is the South Africa rand, although this has weakened in recent years.

I was talking to the police officer, thinking that given the size of Lesotho's border is hundreds of miles, had he been tipped of on the courier? His response was no, and every couple of weeks he and his men stake out a location and normally they are successful. He was a little disillusioned about his job as his men had been here for 3 days, so that's 24 times 6 man hours to catch the courier and it'll probably take the same amount of time to complete the paperwork, and make court appearances to successfully put the man in jail, which won't deter the next would-be courier. Under the old system the process would be much simpler and quicker, which is why many residents, both black and white, believe Mandela has gone soft on crime. How this legal system compares to other countries, I don't know!

Once our tent is taken down, we say good bye to South Africa's finest*, and continued the hike taking in the scenario. People think police work is exciting but I think in reality it is not: More the case of plenty of paperwork and large amounts of waiting around with short spontaneous moments of activity.

* A term used for New York City's Police force.- New York's finest!

See back cover for **Peter Ward's** biography.

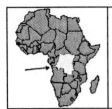

| when a bribe is just another bribe | miles bredin zaire 1992 |

A fist full of currency is not enough

Kinshasa came as a brutal shock. We were later informed that it is somewhat reckless to arrive in Kinshasa without arranging for someone to meet you at the airport. Arriving at three o'clock in the morning, we were told, with no *protocol* is bordering on insanity. There were about ten other people disembarking at Kinshasa and they were all pounced on by *protocols* at the plane's steps. *Protocol* is the name given to the foot soldiers of corruption that are paid by companies and embassies to do the bribing at the airports, banks and at all points where the west has to meet Zaire. They are the torchbearers in the heart of darkness.

Luckily we had our own torches since the airport was in almost total darkness. Occasional gun battles over the years combined with endemic theft had left the airport unlit. There was still electricity but officials carried their own lamps, which they moved from plug to plug as they hurried from counter to office to luggage carousel. As we stumbled into the arrivals hall, our passports were taken away by an official and Harriet and I split up. I followed the passports, she followed the luggage. We were traveling on tourist visas and it was important that our baggage -which betrayed our professions -was not examined too closely. Journalists are not welcomed in Zaire.

The airport, whose tall ceilings were pock-marked with bullet holes and whose floor was a mass of rubbish and broken glass, was bustling with people. Taxi drivers, wasters, soldiers, policemen, porters and airport staff all vied for the privilege of stealing our luggage. Unless we paid someone, we were never going to see it again. I employed a taxi driver, a policeman and an immigration man to ease our way through the formalities. By this time I had lost all track of our passports and was taken off by our immigration man to a dark office where I had to declare my wealth and my intentions, fill out a long form and pay a negotiable administrative charge to ensure the passports' return. Frozen in my torchlight were three fierce-looking Austrian ladies traveling on Red Cross passports. Dressed in

Birkenstock sandals and Indian fabric dresses surmounted by ostentatious crucifixes, they argued with their *protocol*.

'We are here to help your country, not to pay bribes,' said the mustachioed leader of the team. 'We have worked all over the world and never paid bribes.'

'Then you will never leave the airport.'

I paid up and left them in the dark.

The next step was to reclaim our luggage. We had carried on as much as we could but two rucksacks had been put in the hold. Through the black rubber curtains at the back of the static carousel, we could hear a fight. Our team policeman grabbed me by the arm and pulled me through. About twenty people were throwing luggage around in the dark, searching and fighting for the bags, which they had been paid to receive. I sat on the sidelines, tracking our cases with the torch. The policeman followed the beam of light and disappeared. After ten minutes he returned, beaming and clutching our bags. He had entered the melee as a rather tatty-looking policeman; he left it looking like a survivor from a plane-crash - disorientated but triumphant.

Harriet was still sitting where I had left her. She was far from forlorn. sitting atop our pile of camera bags and rucksacks, she was listening to her Walkman and snarling at anyone who tried to hassle her. I had to change some money to do the next lot of bribery and was marched off to the remains of the airport restaurant where the bar was being used as a bank counter. Illegal moneychangers sat on one side with great cases of cash and I and my entourage stood on the other. I swapped a hundred-dollar bill for a plastic bag full of neat blocks of zaires (I was ripped off, I should have had two) and set off to customs. An enormous Zairean stood behind a desk with dollar signs tattooed on his eyeballs.

'You'll have to pay this man,' said my immigration officer, as he heaved our luggage on to the desk, 'otherwise he'll search your bag and steal things.'

It is a rather disconcerting Zairean trait for bare-faced thieves to accuse other swindlers of treachery. I tried a new technique.

'We are refugees from Angola,' I said.

'Oh, my brother is in Luanda. We have heard nothing. Do you know what has happened to the Zairean?'

'He's probably at the embassy. There are hundreds of Zairians there. Don't worry. The phones aren't working, so he wouldn't be able to contact you anyway.'

Pleased with this news, he didn't even look at our bags. Now all we had to do was get into town. I felt as though I had succeeded in taking on Zaire and winning. Their embassy's compound was full of stranded smugglers. The ambassador had charged them all $75 to register for evacuation and then disappeared with the cash.

We descended the steps to the dark and empty car park where our jalopy awaited us. Another policeman stopped us on the steps for a bribe and I carelessly gave him a bundle of zaires. I was getting cocky. I paid the others off at the car and Harriet, the driver, his *petit* (a small but none the less fifty-year-old man) and I jumped in. We had survived the airport and it had only cost $100. We were then surrounded by six angry soldiers led by a captain. His combat trousers were held up by some string and a mountaineering clip. In the center of the clip hung an enormous pistol; crooked in his right elbow was a skeleton-butt AK47. The pistol was the largest I had ever seen and was called a Desert Eagle. When I returned to England I discovered that it is the most fashionable gun in New York. Made by the Israelis, they fire bullets normally reserved for heavy machine guns and are mighty expensive. Arnold Schwarzenegger uses one in *Last Action Hero* and I still cannot understand where our captain had found his.

'You are the people responsible for corrupting this country. Why did you give that policeman money? How can we mend the economy if you westerners bribe people? Get out of the car and open the boot,' he shouted, toying with his enormous weapon.

I looked for help to our driver who just waved me on - apparently as terrified as I was. I got out and begged. I speak gutter Parisian French badly but well enough to plead forgiveness. Surrounded, as I was, by six well-armed men in a dark and deserted car park, I think the adrenalin would have inspired me to speak Sanskrit had it been necessary. After a tense ten minutes we were allowed to leave but just as we were, one of the soldiers jumped into the front seat and sat on top of the *petit*. Our driver started to circle the car park. Dark, indeterminate yet menacing shapes loitered round fires on the edge of the area.

'Give me money,' said the soldier to me. 'But your boss has just told me that I will be sent to jail if I do.'

'Give me money,' said the soldier.

'Give him money,' said the driver, the *petit* and Harriet. I did, and the driver drove straight back to the officer in charge. Harriet and I exchanged, 'Well, it's been great working with you' looks and the car stopped. The soldier got out, shared the money and we drove into Kinshasa. The entire episode had been no more than psychological torture.

So unnerved were we by our arrival that we re-routed to the Intercontinental, where the night manager helped the taxi driver to *rip* us off and then checked us *into* a $260-a-night room with no water.

Printed with permission:

Blood on the Tracks: A Rail Journey from Angola to Mozambique (1992). By Miles Bredin

See page 41, for biography of **Miles Bredin**.

show me the money	peter ward malawi 1996

Tourists are always welcome

It was 7:30 am and as the sun rose, the morning shadows of the trees were becoming noticeably shorter. I was having, or should I say waiting, for breakfast at Steven's, a local restaurant where service was so bad you would think the staff were trained in the Soviet Union. As usual it was taking them 45 minutes for just a cup of coffee to arrive. Glancing around I recognized two faces from a previous encounter in Africa. They were looking a little startled and quite glad to see a familiar face.

They began to explain their previous day, which started when they crossed the border into Malawi and were given the wrong bus number by a local. The bus didn't take them to their intended destination of relaxation, but instead started them on a night they'll never forget. When they finally departed from the bus, they got off in a small route village called Mua, which did not have tracks, let alone a beaten one. The only visitors this place gets were traders going to the market, so needless to say it doesn't normally accommodate tourists or even modern civilization. This place just doesn't get visitors, had no post office, nor electricity. The locals were all very friendly, but a little surprised to see 2 white people. In many ways they became the talk of the town.

They found out that the next bus to leave town was first thing in the morning, so they checked in at the nearest thing to what you could call a lodge, which was a very basic building with a thatched roof, no electricity or running hot water. Their most pressing need was to exchange money and in these parts of the world there are people always offering this service so on the advice of the owner of the lodge they approached a guy who worked in the local bottle shop (This is an African term for bar, but there are less chairs or benches than a regular bar and local music distortedly blares out from a stereo; but that's how you listen to *Thomas Mapfumo. A very basic bar to say the least). Juke box, certainly not!

They exchanged the equivalent of US $150, which is a lot of money in Africa given that the average day's wage for a local could be as little as $1.50. Once the money had been counted out and the exchange finished, this guy offered to sell them some marijuana. Malawi's most famous commodity is not its national parks where wild life can be viewed, spectacular lodges overlooking Lake Malawi, or any other tourist attraction you see in glossy magazines', it's weed-Durban Poison, wacky backy, or simply, as the locals refer to it, Malawi Gold.

The two hesitantly looked at each other and nodded, saying "Yeah." I suppose they believed the need to sample the local culture in one-way or another.

The afternoon in the village was non eventful, but word had got around that the white boys were in town.

At about 10 o' clock they had rolled and lit up a joint. They felt it was perfect, pure, locally grown and relaxing. Well worth traveling on the wrong bus.

At 11 o' clock after the mellowing out was in full flow, there was a loud knock on the room door. It was the hotel owner who appeared to be very concerned and explained that a policeman in the village had heard that they had purchased a quantity of marijuana and was looking for them. Once they were found, they would be arrested, fined and deported from the country. In a village this size it was only a matter of time before they would be found.

There was horror in everyone's faces. They couldn't believe the mess they had gotten themselves into. They were in the middle of Central Africa in a remote village and not the most experienced travelers, no one knows where they are and the local police looking for them. Now get out of that. The hotel owner explained that he knows the policeman well and felt he would accept a bribe. The lads with little alternative given this predicament, handed over an amount of money. For precaution the hotel owner felt they should change rooms they were staying in so he could get to the policeman before he got to them.

A few hours later, there was another loud knock on their bedroom door. Again it was the hotel owner, who looked even more concerned. He explained that the policeman had told his supervisor that the bribe was not enough and more money was needed and that they better keep the candles out in their bedroom. The boys handed over more money.

By the early hours of the morning, no one had got much sleep. From their rooms they could hear shouting and doors slamming. The hotel owner stormed into their room and explained that the police were outside looking for them, so they not only had to leave the hotel immediately, but also the village. He had arranged a lift that was waiting behind the hotel and would take them to the first bus stop outside the village; however, a further amount of money was required to pay the driver. They packed their bags and climbed out of the window to the awaiting car.

The car dropped them off at deserted bus stop about half a mile outside the village, where they both waited. Looking anxiously for any flashing lights from a patrol car. The only vehicle they could see was the bus, which they needed to catch. As they boarded the bus dawn finally broke and they knew they were freed from the loose arm of the law. It also dawned on them that the money they had paid in bribes to the policeman, his supervisor and driver equated to the exact amount they converted from the money exchange man. A coincidence or a good day's work for the owner of the lodge?

*Thomas Mapfumo: Often referred to as the Bob Marley of Africa, this dreadlock singer deftly translated traditional parables and subtle messages into "chimurenga" (Zimbabwe liberation war, in the 1970's) lyrics, which both defied the white-minority ruled government and became popular hits, in songs such as "Tumira Vana Kuhondo" ("Send Your Children to War"), which he cleverly insinuated could be claimed by either side. Following Robert Mugabe's steps to power in 1980 in Zimbabwe, Mapfumo's appeal did not diminish as he continued to champion the music and culture of Zimbabwe at home and abroad.

See back cover for **Peter Ward's** biography.

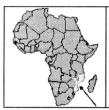	**the police's helping hand**	peter ward mozambique 1996

In Mozambique the police have many roles

It was our second day in Mozambique, and this country was proving to be an adventure every day. The 3 of us had been dropped off 2 miles outside the quiet city of Chimoio. We had spent the night with some British aid workers, who were very good spirited, given that their job was clearing remaining hidden mines in field plantations. The landmines were left over from the 30-year civil war, which had ended in 1992.

They told us that there was over 1.5 million unexploded antipersonnel mines in the country and their exact location or type was unknown. They recommended that we didn't take any shortcuts across the countryside. Even if you have to pee, stay on the road as much as possible. They even joked that it was possible to set off a mine by standing on the road and peeing into the verge! If that's what you get from a peeing, think what you get from something else!

They seemed a little bit wrapped up with their work, telling us all the statistics that one needed to know about land mines- "It only costs $3 to produce one, but can cost from $300 to $1000 to remove." I was expecting them to produce the magazine, 'What land mine', for future reading. In all seriousness, they did explain, that in Mozambique, every time a land mine goes off an average of 1.45 people get killed and 1.25 wounded. This is tragic, when households have to provide an income from very physical and manual jobs from farms and factories. With the existence of mines on the land, the country's crop production is limited to a very small safe area.

Mozambique is completely ill equipped to cater to its own people, let alone tourists. The main visitors are people using the country as a travel corridor to Zambia, Kenya, Malawi and South Africa. Most other visitors seemed to be journalists, aid workers and adventurous back packers like us. The civil war has ripped the heart and soul out of the country and although the fighting is over, Mozambique is desperately poor. Despite all of this, we were beginning to find the people very open and generous.

Our destination was the capital Beira, which serves a strategic importance to the landlocked countries like Zimbabwe and Zambia by transporting goods to and from their main cities and container ships waiting in Biera's port. The city has become an economically valuable city however the shipping lanes of Beira were not our reason to be in Mozambique, rather it was the world-renowned beaches. Florida's Dakota beach, or California's Venice beach, aren't close to what Beira has to offer.

We were in the middle of nowhere. All we could see on the landscape were the long shoots of sugar cane crops, the edge of a village and the African blue sky, which was beautiful in the mid morning sun. The children from the village were a little curious about who we were and what we wanted, so much so that they kept on smiling and laughing at us, followed by running away screaming. It turned out that they had never seen white people before and the fact we were carrying our belongings in a backpack not wrapped in a blanket on our head, made us look like complete odd balls.

The heat from the mid morning sun had become uncomfortably hot, so the 3 of us took turns to hitch hike and sit in the shade of the sugar cane and play with the children.

For the next hour every car roared by with the driver not even acknowledging us on the roadside. We soon realized that the problem about hitch hiking from this location was that the speed of the cars was such that by the time drivers had seen us, they had passed us and couldn't be bothered to stop. To my surprise a male and female police officer appeared from the shoots of the sugar cane.

A scam in some countries is that a local will act as if they are a policeman, ask for your passport, and run away with it. I figured they were real police, as they always walk in couples and were in the gray blue uniform, armed with automatic weapons. Anyway I wasn't going to test this theory.

I was still wary as the police in 3rd world countries are renowned for topping up their wages by extracting bribes from foreigners. Hard currency is a much sought after commodity (inflation runs at a modest 60%, undermining local wage rates), and if you are the wrong nationality, general mischief making and awkwardness can arise. The police in Mozambique have such a reputation for corruption that it is rumored to be part of their training.

Because we were on a main road, leading to South Africa, there were plenty of SA vehicles passing. Some were being stopped by the police officers, were money payment was expected, or else the car would to be inspected, delaying the journey.

Typically white South Africans are well off, compared to their black counterparts in neighboring countries, which makes them easy targets.

Given the history in recent years between the two countries, there is some bitterness and anger between the two groups.

In Mozambique the national language is Portuguese, not English, so when the police officers began to speak to us quite infuriatingly, I wondered what was their problem. They kept on pointing at the road, then to side of the road. With all the hand movements, I wondered if there was some Italian in them, even through the Portuguese were the first settlers. While I was attempting to understand what was their issue, my traveling buddies were trying to hitch a lift. This only made situations worse; the female police officer was acting as the drama queen. So far, neither of the officers had resorted to threat with their automatic weapons they were carrying.

The conversation changed, and the only word of English they kept on saying was 'passport.' In a country like Mozambique, one of the biggest mistakes a traveler can make is to give a policeman their passport, as you'll find it'll cost you about $100 to get it back that day if you're lucky, so needless to say I was a little bit wary of this request.

At this stage there was frustration for everyone: we still couldn't get a lift and they still couldn't communicate to us. Our approach to this was simple- pretend we didn't understand their request, and hope a car would stop. This deteriorated the situation, primarily because the police officers were now spending time dealing with us, and not stopping cars for bribes.

To ease the situation, each of us gave our passports to the police officers one by one. 'South African, no', the male officer said with a smile on his face. Two of us were British and the other was Australian. They gave us our passports back and on receiving them, I put them out of sight, just in case the officers changed their minds. At this stage, the police stopped a car and the driver spoke both Portuguese and English. He had a long conversation with the police officers, when there were even more hand waving. Maybe this guy was Italian as well! The driver then explained to us, that the police officers felt that we were having difficulty hitch- hiking at this location, so as they stopped cars they would ask the driver if they could give us a lift. This was music to our ears!

Within 10 minutes 2 BMW's with South African license plates were stopped by the police officers. When a South African travels to places they pack everything- even their own water. Standing on the roadside, I observed the cars and it looked like they were full. Food, water and camping equipment were all lining the back seats, so I didn't have much hope with these cars, but before you knew it the passengers in the car were re-packing everything on the back seat, with items going up on the roof, and in the trunk.

On stepping into the air-conditioned vehicle we thanked the police officers for being the perfect ambassadors for their country. Shortly into the journey, the driver inquired if we'd asked for assistance from the police. He explained that they had felt obligated to give us a lift, or else they would sit around waiting for the car to be inspected or be asked to hand over a bribe, and they were in a hurry. I smiled and sipped the complimentary Castle Beer they gave me.

This lift dropped us off at a crossroads, a few hundreds miles down the road. The next lift we got was perfect. The driver was taking his friend to Beira airport and was extremely late. The speed dial reached over 130 mph on some of the stretches.

See back cover for **Peter Ward's** biography.

	**rugby ball (and chain)**	ed goldberg zimbabwe 1950s

Ed Goldberg from an interview with his father Dr. Isaac Goldberg

Dr. Isaac Goldberg: We moved up to Rhodesia. I was very interested in the Que Que rugby team. That's quite a good team. In fact the *hooker Jimmy Wilson played for Rhodesia and a couple of guys subsequently also played for Rhodesia. Rhodesia was then part of the South African scene. It was known as a province of South Africa as far as rugby is concerned. Cricket as well. So Rhodesia played against Transvaal, Western Province, Natal and Free State and so on. It was part of the scene rugby as we had it in those days. So I became a very serious referee. I was rather harsh, hard on people.

Anybody fooling around and making deliberate mistakes I was really hard on penalties without any doubt. So I began refereeing in earnest in Rhodesia. I also began to coach the team there and also was the sole selector of the team every week. Rugby was always played on a Sunday afternoon and usually in Que Que or Gatooma or Gwelo or sometimes down to Selukwe and occasionally down in Bulawayo or even into Salisbury so I became very well known as a referee. In fact I think I was the longest serving referee in Rhodesia. I also got on the Midlands Rugby Board and the Rhodesian Referee's Association. I was quite an active member of them. So I was asked to referee a number of matches. At first the matches between sides like Midlands which was really Gatooma, Que Que, Fort Victoria and Gwelo. One team from that group against, say, Mashonaland - all the teams in the Salisbury district or against Matabeleland. I refereed some matches at first against Mashonaland and they liked my refereeing. The Mashonaland chaps said hell we like your refereeing so when a match came up when the Kiwis came out I was asked to take the first game, much to my surprise, which I really enjoyed. It was great fun.

We were a province of South Africa at the time. It wasn't a test match. It was an interprovincial match if you like. Provincial match versus New Zealand. I met Fred Allen there the second time. (captain of the New Zealand team - first met him in Egypt during the war) We became close

199

buddies. Very nice chap Allen was. I will never forget there was a train smash in Que Que just outside the station with the whole of the Kiwi's team on board the train. Two locomotives pulling carriages collided head on. Somebody had given the wrong signal somewhere along and these two engines stood up in the air at an angle of about 45 degrees when they finished. Nobody was hurt. People were jostled around but the Kiwi's were in the one train. It caused quite a stir. I went down to the scene and spoke to some of the guys who I had met before but nobody was hurt fortunately. I have never seen anything like it. Two engines and they stood up like that.

Que Que had a good rugby team, which performed well in the Midlands league as well as against teams from the two main centres, Salisbury and Bulawayo.Rhodesia's most prestigious rugby competition was for the Globe and Phoenix Cup, which was contested for annually, with the final always being played in Que Que against Que Que's rugby team.

Rugby was a popular spectator sport, and all the town's folk used to turn out to support the local first and second teams. The ground, or playing field, was just off the main road, near to where the Sebakwe Hotel now stands. It had plenty of grass and was well kept. Matches were invariably played on Sunday afternoons, by which time most of the residents had had lunch and a customary siesta.

When we arrived in Que Que, the town's rugby was administered by Kingsley Curle, who also acted as coach and referee. He asked that I take over his duties, as he had been doing this for quite some time. I gladly accepted, as I was still intimately interested in the game, and immediately set about to improve the standards set by Kingsley. I also decided on a smarter look by the players, as for example, having numbers on the backs of jerseys. I also began a new manner of coaching, by concentrating on closer match play between the forwards and the three quarters. The guys seemed to like my novel approach, and I was readily accepted.

There being no-one else around to assist me, I was also responsible for selecting the teams every week, ably advised by the first team captain, Alec Crous, who was himself a very good player, especially in the line-outs. We held practice matches twice a week, usually on Tuesdays and Thursdays, starting at about four in the afternoons and finishing when it became too dark to continue. I also gave the teams an occasional lecture on tactics and the laws of the game.

I established myself as a referee of note, allowing the game to proceed without unnecessary stoppages. As a result, I became well known in rugby circles elsewhere in the land. One of the interesting features of our rugby was afforded by our hooker, Jimmy Wilson, who also played for the national team. He had been a pilot in the air force during the war, and was now smallworking for gold in the district. He and another player whose name I cannot recollect used to fly in from his mine in a Tiger Moth and zoom low over the ground to let us know they were on their way. We used to stop the practice sessions until they arrived at the ground.

Bill Price (that's what he called himself) was a big man with fair curly hair. One afternoon he arrived at a practice session and asked if he could join in the game. I was apprehensive at first, as was wearing what appeared to me odd clothing. He had no rugby shorts, nor did he have rugby boots. He wore a white tunic shirt and white trousers, and his boots were of a military type. I said to him that he should have brought along suitable clothing for the occasion, and he immediately removed his trousers, to reveal his cream-colored underpants.

Fortunately, there were no women around! He begged me to play, taking off his boots as well, and I finally condescended, realizing that the man was desperate for a game.

"What position do you play?" I asked.

"On the wing. I'll be a credit to your side, as I am very fast."

"O.K., go over there and play on the right wing," I beckoned.

Well, Bill (if that was his real name) showed signs of brilliance, albeit in underpants and barefoot. I was really impressed. Alec Crous came up to me to say that we had a real find here. The man could move very fast and was difficult to tackle. In a short space of time he scored no fewer than four tries. Alec remarked that we needed him for the needle match against Bulawayo Queens next Sunday, and I concurred.

Towards the end of the practice session there suddenly arrived a police van, and out jumped two burly policemen, who rapidly made their way towards Bill. I, and indeed the rest of the players, were utterly surprised and could not comprehend what was happening. One of the policemen made a run towards Bill, who managed to outpace him. The other cop ran around the side and tackled him by his ankles.

"Offside," I shouted. That policeman was definitely offside!

However, the rugby laws were disregarded, and Bill was soon standing there, handcuffed and utterly dejected.

"What's going on?" I asked the men who administered their law instead of that applying to rugby.

"He's an escaped convict from the Gwelo jail. Serving a sentence for armed robbery. He's as slippery as an eel, but we tracked him down to here."

"Thanks for letting me play," said Bill. "What I miss most whilst serving my sentence is a good game of rugby, followed by a cold beer. I just had to have a game. Thanks, guys"

As he was led away, I felt sorry for him.

"See you when you come out?" I asked.

"That will be in 10 years from now."

Hell hath no fury like a man spurned of his rugby and cold beer.

*Hooker-position in rugby.

Ed was born in Que Que in 1950 and moved to Canada in 1980. He is a pharmacist in Vancouver and has two children - Alon and Talia. His father - Isaac Goldberg was born in Lithuania in 1925 and arrived in South Africa in 1930. In 1949 Isaac moved to Que Que, Southern Rhodesia and he had the position of Resident Geologist on the Globe and Phoenix Gold Mine. He was a world expert on gold, copper, nickel, asbestos, coal, diamonds, emeralds, limestone, scheelite, wolframite, columbite, tantalite, fluospar, chrome, iron-ore and manganese and had written many papers on geology, mining and gemstones published in the annals of many learned societies. He was best known for papers on gold and structures and copper ores in South West Africa. He was a regular contributor to various mining magazines and allied publications. He died in July 2000 and his story is taken from an interview that Ed did with him.

| 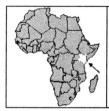 | **this wasn't on the main course** | linda pagan
kenya
1999 |

After dinner walks don't always clear the air

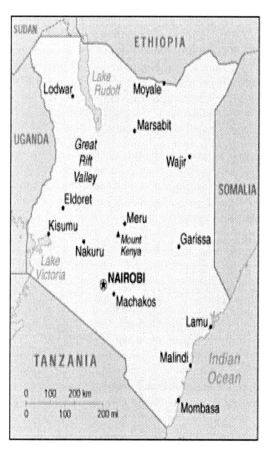

Our tiny plane touched down on Malindi's miniscule airstrip. A time warp back to flying's early days, you descended the stairs, crossed the tarmac and waved to your family smiling through the glass of the arrivals' lounge. But this was 1999 and Malindi's arrivals' lounge doubled as its departure lounge. It is a one room, one building affair: 7 rows of tired orange plastic chairs, a utilitarian check-in counter with a huge scale suitable for weighing heifers and a scant snack bar serving warm soft drinks and sticky sweets.

A quick trip to the ladies room and we were in and out of there in less than 5 minutes, a benefit of being able to grab your own bags off the luggage trolley.

Ignoring the cab drivers we wheeled our bags down the airport's gravel driveway and out onto the smooth, long and flat main road. The sunshine was bright but not searing, a soft breeze blew the last vestiges of the plane's air conditioning from my hair. Huge hedges of sherbet colored bougainvillea splashed up the countryside. "So this is Africa," I thought to myself..."gentle, welcoming and hushed." In my mind's eye I saw a map from a 1930's textbook...the Dark Continent, some line drawings; me in a khaki skirt suit and pith helmet, Majamba in a kikois, bare chested and bare footed with a long thin spear. His short dreads sticking straight up could easily accommodate the bone of yesteryear's caricatures. My racist reverie was broken as Majamba expertly spat at a passing dragonfly.

"So where do we catch the matatu?" I asked Majamba.

"Here," he replied

"But there's no sign or anyone about," I said.

"You'll see," he calmly countered.

I thought of all the cinematic cliches of people waiting by the side of the road: throwing pebbles, striking funny poses on the median, an armadillo scuttling across the road. But none of this was given a chance as within a minute a matatu appeared.

The matatu is the workhorse of African public transportation. It is a privately owned mini-van that is used to ferry people locally. The vans are tricked out with names like "Angel's Wings," "Bad Boys of Dub," and "the Lord's Honey" with graphics to backup these monikers. The sound system is key as music is a must no matter how short the journey. Sound reproduction is of no concern, sound volume is crucial...it has to be LOUD. The driver doubles as D.J. and depending on his taste you can be listening to gospel, reggae, hip-hop, Zairean dance music, Hindi movie soundtracks or Arabic love songs. The whole effect is akin to being in a moving nightclub sans alcohol.

As the conductor slid the side door open I turned to Majamba and said, "There's no way we can fit in there."

"Don't worry, there's plenty of room," he casually replied.

I obviously wasn't seeing what he was seeing. I didn't know how we were going to get ourselves in there let alone the two huge, rolling duffel bags. But, this being Africa the bags were pushed into a thatch of legs and disappeared under the seats. But how? Wasn't that a television under that seat? And where did that basket of limes go? The front seat became hospitably vacant and I was directed to it.

I sat in the middle, Majamba on my left, the driver cool as a cucumber in his snazzy sunglasses on my right. And we were off, the driving was fast and straight. Thankfully not like India where compulsive horn honking and overtaking are the standard. But, it was fast. When someone hailed us the slowing down and the taking off were akin to pit stops in Formula One racing. When everyone was aboard, the conductor would jump on the running board and bang on the roof. His precarious perch reminded me of happy suicides on window ledges.

We bombed along the road at an average cruising speed of 70 m.p.h., listening to Lucky Dube. I fell into the stupor of the drive, Majamba smoked a cigarette and the driver discreetly chewed his miraa. People got in and out but in my luxury seat I felt none of the squash. After about 45 minutes I turned around; it was like peering into a colorful rugby scrum. It was Twister African style; someone's bum was pressed up against the window while his face stoically examined someone's ear.

I was delighted when, after some mothers had wedged themselves in to the rear seats their babies were passed up to the front seat. I sat with two babies on my lap and Majamba got a toddler.

One baby was terrified of my blue eyes whilst the other one seemed oblivious to the obvious differences between his mum and me. When the time came for them to get out Mum would appear at the passenger window and the baby would be bustled into a kanga and slung onto her back. She walked her way up the road with her market goods on her head, and two little legs sticking out of the bundle on her back.

We got to Watamu an hour later. It's a funny little place. Until a few years ago it was a pretty fishing village with one of the world's most spectacular coral reefs. Now, because of its beauties, a string of resorts catering to Italian and German package tourists sprawls along the coastline.

In the main part of town, Italian cropped up on signs and restaurant menus. One particularly hellish looking place was called Hotel Dante and it had a hallucinogenic portrait of an African Aligheri. I was further taken aback when Majamba turned to me and said, "Welcome to Beautiful Watamu" in perfectly accented Italian. He could do his "beach boy" routine in English, Italian, French, German and Japanese. And, like most Africans, he was a man of many talents. He could sail, sew and shimmy coconut trees to impress me. He was proof that in Africa if you don't work, you don't eat.

We unwound our limbs and walked the sandy lanes of the village proper. Children of all ages played around us "Mambo Rasta Baby" greeted the young hipsters "Habari yako, Aboudi" women shouted while preparing meals in their doorways. "What is the news of your family?"

"Mambo Majamba" young women whispered as they swayed by in their kangas.

We got to the guesthouse and I was relieved to see that it was clean and pretty. It had a balcony from which I could see all the thatched roofs of the village. It was a tropical Cotswolds.

After unpacking we wandered to the local roadside cafe "Roasters" for refreshments. It was a very simple place with a little veranda and ubiquitous plastic lawn furniture chairs and tables. I ordered a *chai* and Majamba got a coke.

On the road, tourists drifted up from the beach. My God! I'd never seen such an ugly assortment. They were, nearly to a person, overweight and underdressed and the few items that they did wear were garish to say the least. Gold lame and hot pink figured heavily in their scanty beach attire. They also had weird skin colors: the Northern Europeans resembled uncooked hams, white with blue veins; the Southern Europeans resembled petrified procsciutto.

I turned to Majamba and said, "What's going on here? These people are so low rent!" Did I mention that I'm just a little judgmental? Well, you know I am from New York and we have very high standards when it comes to the style factor in life (reference reams of copy that New York publications have devoted to the Bridge and Tunnel crowd). He just shrugged and gave a little half smile. To him all Europeans were the same and if he could make some money by renting out snorkel masks or selling them kikois to wrap around their ample stomachs- then who cares what they look like? Looking like something, however, is one thing but behaving is another. Can you say "Ugly Demeanor?" I noticed that arrogance factored heavily in the tourists' dealings with their Kenyan hosts. There was no attempt to adapt to the surroundings by trying to learn a few words like "tafadali" (please) or "asante sana" (thank you.)

All the hotels had set themselves up with the food and language appropriate to their target clientele. "Buona Serra, tonight our special is linguine with bratwurst." Ha! The fact that we were in Kenya was merely a bothersome inconvenience. So here I sat stewing in my self-righteousness watching the sun go down and the whores come out. Because as I would learn later everything had a price.

"So Mwanahalima," Majamba said to me, "I want you to meet my good friend Lalli." In my poisoned musings I'd failed to notice the short, slight man with buckteeth standing next to our table. His smile was as broad as the stripes on his Celtic United soccer shirt. He was shy and obviously pleased to be Majamba's best friend. He was smiling at my name and asked me how I had got it. "Oh, Majamba's sisters asked me what my name, Linda, meant. It doesn't mean anything in English but in Spanish it means pretty so they named me "pretty" in Swahili. He thought it was very funny because it was also his grandmother's name.

"Please, Lalli," I said "Sit and have a drink. What would you like?"

"Ting," he replied.

Lali, it turned out, was very devout, went to mosque 3 times a day and made his living taking tourists out to the coral reef that had started this whole tourist thing. He and Majamba had been friends from childhood and whenever Majamba visited Watamu he stayed with Lalli. They were a yin/yang friendship, one that to outward appearances seemed of total opposites but deep down one of common beliefs regarding morality and value systems: Majamba assertive and stylish, Lalli shy and gawky.

"Mwanhalima" Majamba resumed, "tonight the three of us will have a very nice meal at the Hotel Dante."

I was a little skeptical and would have been quite happy to stay at "Roasters" and eat some local dish, but Majamaba was eager to show off his developing fork and knife skills at the European restaurant in the hotel.

Swahili custom when it comes to eating is to wash your hands and then to use only the right hand to eat your food. Rice is balled up and used to soak up any sauces and such. It looks easy but when I'd tried it at his family's house I'd succeeded in having half my dinner roll down the front of my dress. They had discreetly produced a spoon for me. Conversely, Majamba had asked me to teach him how to use a knife and fork. We were currently at the knitting needle stage ie.: elbows flying out.

We paid our check and walked up the road towards the hotel. Dusk had descended and the gaslights from the roadside dukas threw off a greenish light. Warm-up sounds from the disco could be heard as western style dressed young women made their way towards it.

At the Dante we were ushered into the dining room by an eager waiter. The glaring white of his waiter's jacket contrasted with the velvet darkness of his face. We sat at a prominent table in the middle of the room.

I surveyed the room. The ugly people from the beach had washed up here. At a few tables European men sat with African lady companions. I was the only European woman with African companions.

"Ah! It's so nice here. So civilized." beamed Majamba.

"Hmmmm," I said in a non committed way.

I took a look at the menu that was handed to me. It pretty much was split down the middle by either Italian or German dishes. I spied with hope a shrimp dish that had a hint of the Swahili to it. It was not hard for me to make my choice.

"What will you guys have?" I inquired.

"Fish and chips" they replied in unison.

"Ah" I thought to myself "the world is so multi-cultural these days"

I was the only one to order Tusker. Both of them being Muslim eschewed alcohol. I felt wicked!

Having ordered I did a leisurely scan of the dining room. People were silent and sullen.

No-one seemed to have that happy holiday air and they kept sliding stares at us to try and figure us out. Which one of the men is her lover? Are they both her lovers?

We meanwhile were relaxed and comfortable, bantering in a mix of English and Swahili.

When the food came the three of us ignored our knives and forks and used our right hands. People looked at us with disgust. I too had initially thought this to be a primitive way of eating but after trying it myself I realized that it was an art. There was also something wonderfully delicious about feeling the texture of food on my fingertips.

Speaking of fingertips…Majamba snapped his fingers for the waiter. I immediately tensed. In New York city this is considered the most demeaning way of trying to get someone's attention and if you do this you are likely to be ignored at best or ejected at worst. But our waiter sailed over with a, "Yes, Bwana?"

"Bring me Pep Tang," said Majamba.

"So this is where Majamba's vice finally emerges" I thought.

In this part of Africa a fair number of the population chews miraa. In Ethiopia and Somalia it is known as khaat. It is a stimulant, a "pep-up." You can tell habitual chewers by their brown stained teeth. Majamba had beautiful chichlet teeth well…except for that one gold tooth in the front. "So this 'pep tang' must be a more forgiving form of miraa," I speculated.

The waiter nodded his assent and once more sailed away. When he returned he proudly plunked down the "drug." It was a ketchup knock-off.

"Ah!" sighed Majamba. "you know I am addicted to this sauce. I like to put it on all my food."

Dinner passed in pleasant conversation about the Africa Cup, our trip to the sandal maker and the existence of God.

When the bill came I decided to treat in order to thank them. I felt my fellow tourists' judgment.

"See she pays. They must both be her lovers!"

Walking down the hotel's gravel driveway Majamba picked me a posy of bougainvillea and frangipani. Lalli smiled. He longed for a ladylove.

The African night was warm and comfortable. We turned into the road and headed back to the village's lights and sounds. We'd walked about 100 yards when we were startled by a man stumbling out of the bushes. He fell to the ground. We stopped to stare. Two men emerged from the bushes. They were policemen and one had a machine gun. The other stood over the man and whacked him across the back with his truncheon. The man groaned, rose to his feet and lurched off.

"Palm wine," I thought, "He's a drunk, a moon shiner, and they have dispensed their own justice."

As this was flashing through my brain, they turned to us and said something in Swahili. The three of us froze. They moved towards us. They were very dark skinned; I could only see their eyes, teeth and the glowing ends of their cigarettes. They repeated the question. Majamba replied in Swahili. One moved closer and put his truncheon across Lalli's shoulders. Lalli shrunk. His submission shifted into humiliation. Majamba stood erect, dragging on his cigarette.

My mind continued to race. This is not reality. This is fiction. This is Graham Greene land.

Please don't let this become even more of a cliché.

Their boots shifted. I heard the road scraped by nailed soles.

Another question in Swahili. "I am here doing business with my friend" replied Majamaba in English.

"Do you have a licensed business?" Mr. Machine-Gun asked me in crisp, non-accented English.

"Yes, it is licensed in America. I have a Kenyan business visa. Would you like to see it?"

My question was ignored.

Silence. Heavy silence. The perfect African night now hangs around us.

I am scared. My eyes are bugging. I can now distinguish details. Shabby uniforms, worn boots, second hand weapons. Thrift store education. But for all their frayed exterior they have the power. This is about power and money. Mainly it is about money.

The five of us are framed by the night air's vacuum. Our unspoken thoughts fill the void around us.

I split into two. There is my voice and there is my *brain.* They are not working as a team. They are at odds with each other.

"Excuse me" I say in an irritated way

"Shit! Don't take that tone," hisses my brain

"…But what is the problem?"

Mr. Truncheon looks beyond my left ear and replies, "Your friend doesn't have his identity card."

"Well, I'm sure that we could go and get it, he lives in Watamu," I snap.

"Are you crazy!!??" shouts my brain. Just calm the fuck down, be polite. He could crack your skull with that thing."

No reply. Mr. Machine-Gun and Mr. Truncheon are both now staring past my left ear.

Seconds go by like hours. Now I am being smothered by that wonderful African night. I just want to cry. Why is this happening? How did the worm turn so quickly?

"O.K., well…then, can we go now? Can we continue our walk?"

"Hey why do you have to sound like such an asshole New Yorker? Just tone it down?"

Pause and then suddenly "Yes, yes you can go now" Relief.

"But…he stays," Mr. Machine gun says, pointing the barrel of his gun at Lalli.

Overdrive. My brain has lost the battle and it just stands back in gob-smacked horror as I say "no, no I don't think so! He is our friend and we were all walking together and when we go he comes with us. And if you don't let him come with us than all of us are going to the police station."

"There!" said my voice to my brain." We've played the white card. We have followed Lonely Planet's advice like the good tourist that we are!"

A breeze blew past us.

"O.K. you can go," said Mr. Machine Gun. They didn't confer, bargain, negotiate, or hesitate.

As quickly as it happened, it was over.

We turned our backs on them. The village's lights were still there. The disco was still loud. Life had never stopped. As we walked my anger grew. "I can't believe that. This happens all the time, right? Let's go to the police station, let's go talk to the police chief. This isn't right. God damn it, we can't report them because they didn't have name badges or shield numbers."

"Wow, Manahalima! You were so tough, so cool. You were like New York City." said Majamba.

"No. Wait a minute, answer me. Does this happen all the time?"

"Yes, yes." they replied.

"And what if we had left you behind, Lali?"

"I would have to give them money. And, if I didn't have money they would have beaten me," he whispered.

"I just can't believe that they do this. It's not right, it's not fair." I ran out of reasons as I realized just how powerless they were.

"But Manahalima, you saved me" said Lalli proudly.

That made me madder. "But Lalli, it's not right. They let us go because of this," I said pointing to my forearm. A white forearm.

They both shrugged their shoulders. Majamba said, "That is Africa."

Linda Pagan was born in Northumberland, England and by age 12 had lived in Spain, Holland, U.K. and the U.S.A. Her peripatetic (sic) childhood instilled in her a severe case of wanderlust. After 10 years of slogging away on Wall St. as a reinsurance broker for Lloyd's of London she charted a course that led her to a supreme bartending job at Temple Bar in Noho NYC. After 5 years of mixing martinis she opened The Hat Shop in Soho, NYC. In between making and selling hats to the stylish elite, she travels as much as possible.

wildlife

The wildlife in Africa is second to none. It's the main image of Africa to most people and probably the main reason why people visit the continent.

When people venture outdoors, away from the shopping malls, fancy restaurants and cars, they are entering alien hostile territory, frequently to places that not even the locals go.

So why do we do it? For the ever-lasting vacation picture to go on the mantle piece and the African experience of course.

|  | **afoot in the south african bush** | lance gould south africa present day |

A New Yorker ventures on a walking safari into the wild world of wildebeest, cape buffalo and dung beetles.

"Do you know why I smoke in the bush?" asks Leslie Brett, a South African safari guide, as he takes a lethal drag on his harsh Lexington cigarette.

"To scare dangerous animals away?" guesses Jane, one of the students in his outdoor classroom.

"Nope," he says, fiddling with the rifle strapped across his back.

"To see which way the wind is blowing the smoke?" I offer.

"No," he says, exhaling a substantial cloud and pausing in this Socratic dialogue. "The reason I smoke is because I'm scared shitless every time I come out here." He breaks into a naughty schoolboy's giggle.

His students laugh, too, savoring a light moment in an otherwise terrifying nature walk. Just an instant later, our guard is back up—we're about to sneak past an active hyena lair as the nocturnal creatures sleep. The collective heart of our single-file line skips a beat as Les sharply rebukes us, "Be quiet!" Creepy white backed vultures circle high above us. Fresh lion tracks on the trail hint at what may lurk beneath the waist-high reeds. Ticks, sensing our exuded carbon dioxide, leap onto our socks.

So this is what it's like traipsing through the African veld—unequivocally frightening! It's our fourth day in the bush, but our most forbidding so far, as the lion spoor is our first sure sign of the king of the jungle's presence. It's not like I'm unprepared for a chance encounter with a lion—I do have a notebook. Oh yes, and a blue Bic pen. It's just that, well, lions and other members of the cat family have yet to familiarize themselves with the intimidating potency of small, hand-held writing instruments.

The loud crack of a rifle—that they know. And yet even though Les has a gun, somehow I can't help but think that hiking through the South African bush with only a pen and paper for a sword and shield has to be one of the most insanely scary things I've ever done. And it's only going to get worse: Tonight we are scheduled to sleep under the stars—sans tents.

Oddly, we are not prisoners banished to this sub-Saharan Siberia—we've paid to be students in this wilderness course, "Secrets of the Game Ranger." Our group of seven consists of bush guide Les, his deputy Kevin, and five students: me, a 33-year-old writer from New York; Stephen, a middle-aged architect from Kent, England; Alastair, 20, a windshield manufacturer from Liverpool; Jane, a thirty-something actress from London; and Pietro, 53, a nasty little South African white supremacist who thinks his country would benefit from a reinstitutionalizing of apartheid. We are all attempting to earn our game ranger certificates, and to do so, we have to pass Les' exam at the end of the course. Hence our studious note-taking.

We first caught up with our hosts in the Johannesburg airport. It was hard to miss them. Among the many international vacationers and domestic business travelers, Les and Kevin were the only ones wearing khaki safari shirts with matching shorts. Their ensemble also included important-looking black business briefcases—they described themselves jokingly as "bush executives." With their trim haircuts, clipped mustaches, mirrored shades, muscular builds, brown uniforms and no-nonsense expressions, they looked more like L.A. cops on vacation.

For three days, we acclimated to the ways of the wild—sleeping in the bush; eating ostrich steaks and impala stew; learning faunal factoids such as the fact that herbivorous giraffes will chew on bones to get calcium. Now we're ready for a more intense wilderness experience. It's our fourth day, and we're trekking in the Timbavati, a private game reserve in South Africa's Mpumalanga safari area, through thorny acacia scrub that tears at our clothes. We come to a dry riverbed, nervously spinning as we walk to preempt a blindside attack. The air is rife with the putrid smell of a rhino calf's remains. Nothing is left of him but a few bones and the remnants of his hooves—our friends the hyenas and vultures have disposed of the rest. Any sane trekker would vacate the premises immediately, but we've paid $1,500 to have such terrifying encounters. We press on.

We are learning those intangible facts that separate experts from neophytes, men from boys. The data to which we are suddenly privy are the trade secrets of safari-meisters: the fact that termite mounds always lean to the northwest (useful if you lose your sense of direction), or that, in a pinch, the leaves of the African wattle tree can be used as toilet paper. But I'll let you in on the biggest game-ranging secret of all: The master key to the closely guarded mysteries of the wild is dung.

Bathroom habits of the indigenous fauna are an integral part of our course. Yes, modern-day Doctor Doolittles don't bother to talk to the animals—it's the other end that fascinates them. Rhinos, for example, will always defecate in their own personal lavatories, called middens. Ostriches, like other birds, will drop a double-dynamite combination by always defecating and urinating at the same time. This information is invaluable when tracking these creatures, or just for keeping tabs on which ones are lurking in your immediate vicinity. Dung is really quite a revealing byproduct.

Lance Gould, a deputy features editor at the New York Daily News, made his first trip to Africa in 1987, when he visited Morocco and traded a pair of his sneakers for a rug. He has been back a couple of times, visiting South Africa, Swaziland, Zambia, Zimbabwe and Kenya, the latter while covering the TV show "Survivor: Africa" for the Daily News. Lance is a former editor of Spy magazine, the now-defunct U.S. humor publication, and has also written for the New York Times, the Guardian (London), Details magazine, Spin magazine and Salon online, where this article first appeared.

|  | **madness in the midday sun** | robert winston burnett
zimbabwe
1968 |

The Phantoms of Africa come out alive

The searing midday sun can be found drenching down to cover all in Africa and afflicts people in varying ways. There's the well known song **'Mad dogs and Englishmen go out in the midday sun'** about the over-enthusiastic English, then found careering around wide open spaces displaying boundless energy. All as if the day represented the last episode of the sun above blessing those below. In many ways, one could not exactly blame them for making hay while the sun shone.

After all, they hailed from lands where to be blessed with rays of energizing and revitalizing sun rays proved few and far between. So it would prove with another hailing from those parts, but in this instance in the form of a Scotsman. It was back in the year of 1968 and in lands still then known as Rhodesia. I had been fortunate to be born and raised in the a place some even termed **'God's own Land.'** We were to be the offspring of that pioneering spirit Cecil John Rhodes.

He who ventured further North over the mighty Limpopo river had made his mark in South Africa. Rhodes found it more and more difficult living with remnants of the First Anglo-Boer War, as prejudices levied against those of British ancestry merely divided communities. So off they set to lay claim to fertile lands North, where the language of English would be installed as the main white man's language. The going for Rhodes and his followers proved no walk-over, as soon they ran into the mighty Matabele warrior.

A proud and fearsome foe, whose direct cousins proved no less than the Zulu Warriors back in South Africa. Rhodes and his men would end up fighting for their lives in more ways than one. The locals were not about to give up a precious land and all it entailed easily. It would take some quick thinking, talking and bargaining on Rhodes's behalf with King Lobengula before a deal was struck. Meanwhile, and unknown to the Pioneers of the period, the majority Mashona tribe was on the verge of being delivered a fatal, even final blow by their arch-enemies, the Matabeles.

Rhodes and his Pioneers, by their most timely arrival, would save the Mashona tribe from virtual extinction. Now in 1968, here we were some seventy years on as the offspring of Rhodes, back in the bush fighting as Rhodesians and deeply ensconced in the countryside. Here we were defending our land against both the Mashonas and Matabeles. One group transformed into ZANLA, the other ZIPA. Now they introduced hit and run tactics and mainly targeted soft civilians. ZIPA and ZANLA formed groups across the borders in Mozambique and Zambia. Effectively, the Mashonas (who Rhodes saved), were backed by the Chinese, with the Matabeles armed, trained and financed by the then Soviet Union.

These two mischief-making super powers retained great desires to lay solid and lasting claims to riches found in the land. Rhodesia's borders were being surrounded with those using handy intermediaries as the so-called ultimate benefactors. The country of Rhodesia was by now under total siege after its leaders declared Unilateral Declaration of Independence from Britain in November 1965. Here we were fighting for our very survival on all fronts.

I was in the middle of an apprenticeship as an office equipment technician, when suddenly my training was interrupted and placed on hold. All men on attaining the age of eighteen and proving fit enough to carry a weapon, were liable for military training and soon dispatched to Llewellyn barracks. Here would prove our home for a period of four and a half months. Yes, we were off to a military training camp based a few miles outside of the second city of Bulawayo, Matabeleland.

Here it was I befriended an outgoing and rather hungry for action Scotsman. We hit it off from the outset and were soon fighting each other's fights. I could not have asked for a better buddy when it came to sticking to beliefs. I'd heard about bravery and friendships which can be cemented with a Scot. Soon we were placed into platoons and before long heading out. We were heading off to patrol at the then Wankie Game Reserve, a magnificent place now known as Hwange, and only a half an hours drive from the mighty Victoria Falls.

Here was bliss in comparison to the rather stuffy corridors of training camp: Africa at its very best, and yes the sun still shone down on us strongly, still there in all its glory, while the great and wide plains invited one to walk and walk and walk. For me here was found heaven, as one witnessed the magnitude of wild life which only Africa offers as they wander plains freely, that is until running into those constantly blasting the living daylights out of vulnerable animals for greed alone. We soon realized there was more than one common enemy to confront.

There's simply no feeling to compare with sleeping and living amongst the wild in the African bush. It retains an allure and challenge that sweeps through the veins, all the while constantly on the look out for an enemy, be it in the form of insurgents, poachers or right down to a mosquito waiting to deliver a nasty sting. This was Africa at its very best, as memories remain etched in minds as if captured in a camera's lens.

By now Scotty and I had been assigned as bivvy partners. This is where a small tent is quickly arranged to the parameters of any given camp site as sentry points. All the wonders of the Zambezi river flowed elegantly in the gorge below. The night closed in as the stillness of the atmosphere was then only interrupted by crickets coming to life, a sure sign the other half life has received a wake up call. We would rise at five in the morning and be greeted with the sun already glittering brightly.

There again all guaranteed to rise brightly above the hills, peering down into the awesome valley to take in thick smoke from open burning fires engulfing the surroundings. Indeed that specific aroma of a new dawn, as the hair quickly rises to the back on ones neck. Then again quickly reminded: Indeed this is Africa. To the distance, the mighty roar of a male lion awakening echoes far and wide. "Oh to have been blessed with such magnitude; even if at the end, it would be taken away." They cannot take away the memories however, as that remains sacred and safely secured in vaults of the mind.

This particular camp, situated on the banks of the Zambezi valley, would be home for a few days. We had run into one or two nuisances, more especially concerning poachers carrying out hit and run sorties. While still at training base at Llewellyn, Bulawayo, we most certainly became more than competent in using our FN rifles. However during those days poachers were still considered Royal Game while a number of sights honed in with fingers dearly desiring to squeeze inviting triggers. Frustration and tension was building up within the platoon. My buddy Scotty was becoming edgy and looking out for any excuse to shoot something, anything.

Each evening as the sun faded behind mountains, we would be in sentry position, rifles cocked and ready. Well, one particular evening we very nearly brought a quick end to the platoon Sergeant's still young life. The fool was inviting trouble as I saw Scotty's face becoming redder and redder and his index finger whiter. That's another story in itself and one which lives with me to this day. The moment I'm recording here was the day it was our turn to do a two hour guard shift of the outer surrounds. We were to position ourselves some fifty yards from the camp and some one hundred yards distance between the two of us. One would remain on the ground, rifle ready to fire, the other would clamber up a tree, after checking the way was clear.

Snakes in the form of Cobras and Pythons and even deadly spiders could well be in wait. We would do an hour of sentry duty, then swap over so as not to become overly bored or fall asleep on duty. Each minute felt like an eternity, as the heat and humidity drained one's resolve and concentration. Scotty was up the tree first, while I dug into the dry undergrowth below. As one scanned horizons, the heat appeared to bounce off the hard ground and reflect through the haze.

Heat can do all sorts of funny things to the imagination, as at times even pink elephants suddenly appear in front of one's eyes. If either Scotty or I were unsure of any situation while on guard then we were to let out three short whistles in quick succession. I worried about Scotty with his damn finger curled around a by now more worn trigger and guard. He was proving those from cooler climes such as Scotland could find the searing heat of day in the African bush not so comfortable bed fellows. His moods could swing, but fortunately I was able to bring him back to earth with a smile.

Scotty wanted action, any damn action, and was quite prepared to invent a situation as time went on. Days of walking the wild fully laden with uniform, rug sack, rifle, spare ammunition in the searing heat soaring to reach well over 100 degrees centigrade soon took a toll. We had been hyped-up about insurgent activity, what to expect when running into them, and what action to employ if wanting to stay alive. So by now not only Scotty displayed fraying nerves. We looked over the Zambezi river into Zambia set to the North. Here it was that Matabele warriors were receiving training in readiness to filter in and destabilize Rhodesia.

One often picked up on insurgent movements by spotting footprints, in the main leading down to another rather isolated African village. An order would suddenly ring out to spread out, as the forward guard advanced towards the huts. Weapons cocked, round up the breach, with a village soon fully encircled. All hell could break out, at any moment an AK47 round might well lodge into flesh. Each day would deliver another challenge or sight, as we often stumbled upon yet another poor beast butchered, with tusks hurriedly hacked out.

What a life being played out in the Midday Sun, while many of us enjoyed the wonders of nature at the expense of the Government. However, there were also those damn annoying little flies termed gnats. Again they congregated in the millions, drawn to sweaty brows and faces, flitting about to find any openings such as ears, eyes, mouths and noses. They dived in as if guided missiles to once more hit the target. Scotty was still up his tree making out as if he had everything under control. Every so he'd often mutter a swear word and chase off those damn gnats, if only for a few precious seconds.

We'd heard the sound on a number of occasions. Indeed, so used had we become to it that by now it merely blended into the surrounds as did the common call of the African Dove. A distinctive bark emanating to the rear of our position. Here was another baboon tribe, and suddenly realising they were steering a course into our pathway. They had their own sentries on duty, or scouts to the fore warning of dangers. The last thing they wanted was suddenly to stumble upon a ravenous leopard, waiting in the shadows to pounce, claws extended and ready to deliver a coup de grace.

Chances of seeing a leopard out hunting in the light of day remained rather remote. No, they'd run into a lesser creature in the form of armed humans defending a position. Then another bark, as Scotty turned his by now stiff neck in their direction. "We've got company buddy," Scotty called down to me, as I too turned a rather stiff, red neck and face in their direction. As if to get in some aiming practice I lifted my weapon towards them. Baboons are rather instinctive creatures, and the mature, well-built leader suddenly bolted towards the main group. They were re-grouping and now chattering away amongst themselves.

The leader barked out further orders as mothers, children and elders of the clan scurried towards some trees. A group of five of the forward guard moved around the outer perimeter and were now totally alert. If the clan was about to be attacked then come hell or high water they would put up an almighty fight in return. Baboons are fearsome foes and can afflict huge damage with those fangs of theirs. We were not interested in our earthly friends as they posed no threat to us, or so I thought.

Then I glanced back towards Scotty, and to my horror he was taking steady aim at the baboons. Even worse, that bloody finger of his was securely curled around that damn trigger once more. Another bark from the leader baboon, then crack as if thunder the shot rang out. It bounced off trees, rocks and soon filtered through into the valley below. Christ, the baboons went mad, and not only from the sudden noise as if thunder let off from the round. They screeched out a deafening sound of fury mixed with anger. Within seconds, they had scattered into surrounding shrubbery, except for one.

Scotty hit the leader, as it now writhed on the ground. He was soon down the tree and dashing towards the baboon while calling out, "Got it, got it. Come on, come on." Naturally, the camp had also heard the shot and immediately took up positions, thinking they were being attacked. Scotty proved himself not such a good shot after all on this occasion. The leader was soon up on those powerful hind legs and scampered off. We arrived at the sight and immediately spotted a pool of blood. "What the hell did you do that for?" I asked him. He looked rather sheepish and gave no explanation.

There was no time to reflect, as within seconds standing to our front was the platoon's Second Lieutenant. Then behind him, were his Corporal and two further personnel. The Second Lieutenant cast around the surrounds, then bent down and looked at the blood. "Right, you two, quick march back to camp," he barked out. Scotty and that damn finger of his had now really got us into deep water. All sorts of charges could be levied at us, including effective desertion of our post.

I knew the Second Lieutenant was an avid wild life conservationist, so this was the last thing he would endorse, more especially as the animal appeared wounded. They would throw the book at us for sure, and detention barracks were a distinct possibility. Bivvy partners were responsible for each other's actions, as "one for all" and so on. I was hoping Scotty was by now more satisfied and that his bloody itchy finger would fall off. "Right," the Second Lieutenant bellowed out, then went on about how damn irresponsible we had been. At any moment I was expecting two big Afrikaner farmers within our ranks to march us off to be held under guard.

"There are two options open to you two." the Second Lieutenant told us in no uncertain manner. First, we could be charged back at home barracks with a number of breaches and face the consequences. Then silence fell over the scene, and he resumed "That, or you two can pick up some supplies, arm yourselves, then bring back evidence the baboon is dead and therefore not suffering." He added the proviso of course not to return until we had the baboon's tail in our hands. Shit, now the two of us would trek or journey into the unknown, and all because my buddy could not help that bloody finger of his.

"Hope you're feeling better now, mate," I called out while we stored enough provisions and water to last a few days. The first thing to do was to pick up on the baboon's trail and start off where it fell. The initial trail was by now dry from the sun beating down. However, it had obviously been quite badly wounded, as we soon picked up a fresh trail. Baboons can prove rather callous when it comes to fellow members of a tribe. Should one of their own, and more especially a leader, be weak in any form then a new leadership battle soon transpires. If this leader cannot keep up and move from the front, he is soon discarded.

We had no problems securing the baboon's trail, and for some distance, however, it was obviously still moving fairly freely and stayed ahead of us. There was by now another major consideration, or one that could prove an even greater danger to our well-being. The scent of a wounded creature in the wild is soon picked up by other dangerous predators. A leopard, for instance, one moment highly camouflaged up a tree, could by now easily be moving in from anywhere. Every now and then the blood trail would disappear as the baboon had obviously licked the wound clean. Then we would pick it up once more.

Scotty and I could be out in the African wild alone for a few hours or even a few days. It all came down to how badly the baboon was wounded, and whether another creature got there before us. Either way we would return to base camp with a baboons tail in our rug sack. Hell, the heat was unrelenting and supplies of water soon diminished. Most rivers were by now bone dry from another drought afflicting the area. If replenishments were to be secured, then digging deep into riverbeds would be the order of the day.

The surrounding foliage displayed distinct signs of suffering from a lack of water. Yet around verges of dry rivers it could still prove thick and even green in places. They were dangerous areas to venture through, as they are ideal hiding places for lurking leopards, so we had to proceed with much caution, with one of us placed to the left facing forward, the other to the right and every now and then checking our backs. My bush partner and most dependable Scotsman had allowed the overpowering sun to overshadow his better judgement. Scotty had played out 'Madness in the Midday Sun' and now we were reaping the rewards. He'd used the trigger in anger after weeks of little direct contact to vent out obvious burning frustration.

We had by now been out looking for the wounded baboon for about an hour and a half. It was approximately two thirty in the afternoon, with the sun at its most relentless. The blood trail proved constant, so it appeared the wounded baboon was still moving strongly forward. It must also by then have realized something was trailing it. They instinctively know the smell of blood is like honey drawing bees to the hive, so it would have to keep moving in the hope that any predator would lose interest and even hopefully become distracted. We would need to ensure a total concentration, and hope that an appetite was not suddenly diverted in our direction.

The time arrived for us to take a well earned rest under whatever tree might provide some relief from the sun. First, though, we would clear the way, and above all, make sure the particular tree did not contain some spotted beast waiting to devour us. With the way clear we fuelled up a small fire to make some refreshing tea from the limited water supplies remaining. Soon we would have to venture down into a dry river bed, then dig deep to secure water, no matter the color. At least the hole would leave behind relief for any creatures arriving once we had departed.

So here we were sitting under a rather sparse tree overlooking the African bush. By then we had travelled some five miles while not spotting another human being. We could feel tension in the air, and not only by being in such a position in the first instance. The usual sounds of birds calling in the distance, along with the comforting sound of the Dove's voice ringing out, were distinctly lacking. The place was eerie, as a deathly hush overwhelmed the place. There was the odd antelope grazing away, ears flicking back and forth in readiness to scamper.

The water canteen was down to a quarter full, so would need to keep a constant look out for a river bed, all the while also making sure not to lose the baboon's trail. It would have gained time on us by then, unless of course it was keeping an eye on our own movements and also rested up. Should a leopard be on the trail as well then the baboon would press on and hope to shake it off sooner than later. To those trained and versed with African conditions, well, when a hunt's on there trails a distinct aroma of death in the air.

We could even feel fear gripping the surrounds, yet there was no sign of an ominous presence. Once more we hit the track to pick up on the trail as soon as possible. Simply laboring for hours in the heat searching would be most unproductive. The fire securely dowsed with sand, we set out again and headed immediately to where the last blood trail was spotted. Scotty to the front and me nervously following while casting to rear at regular intervals. Within fifteen minutes we had picked up on the baboons movements once more. This time we noticed it appeared to be laboring the wounded leg. The ground was more scuffed.

It was time for Scotty and me to spread out further as the beast could literally be around any corner. A fully grown, let alone wounded baboon, can severely damage an individual in a flash. A fully-grown male when perched on his hind legs stands at times taller than an average human. The blood trail was by now becoming more distinct, a sign the beast was tearing at the wound. Scotty suddenly dropped to one knee and signaled for me to join him. He could over-react, as already clearly borne out, so I moved gingerly over to his position.

He'd spotted a riverbed and the blood trail led down to it. The baboon, as ourselves, was on the lookout for life's sustaining nutrient of water. Now what to do? Simply moving forward and approaching the riverbed through the shrubbery might well prove a trap! We would have to plan our approach, while also remembering a leopard could be watching all unfold. We knew the baboon had gone down the incline, so now more than ever Scotty and I needed to keep each other covered. It could be behind a tree, rock or even back on the verge. Ensuring our rifles were cocked and ready for action, we slowly entered the riverbed.

A blood trail, by now thick and flowing, clearly enabled us to keep pace with the beast. I moved some ten paces to the front of Scotty, while he kept a close eye on the river's bank. Some distance to the front of our position I picked up a tree situated to the middle of the riverbed. Just then Scotty let out a sharp, piercing whistle. The place was so quiet that the sound appeared to travel forward like a flowing river. He signaled for me to hold up as I quickly dropped to one knee. Next thing Scotty was next to me and pointing to the verge. "Move slowly," he sternly warned me. Somewhat puzzled, I asked him "why?"

He leaned over and told me a leopard was perched low in the grass and watching our every move. Making sure my rifle was ready to fire, I tried to pick out the beast. For the life of me I simply could not see it, even though it was only some fifteen feet ahead of us. Scotty took his rifle and for a second I thought he was going to pull that damn trigger again. He told me to look through the sights, and aimed the rifle at the crouching leopard. There it was all right, with its steely green eyes looming right through us. Well, we could blast it out of the way as a threat, or accept it was also after a common prey.

It was better keeping a close eye out, so Scotty placed his weapon in the automatic firing position. Should it suddenly decide to pounce then he would place all twenty rounds in it and render the leopard motionless. As once more we moved forward my task was now to find and secure the baboon. A distinctive trail, with the laboring becoming even more pronounced. We were now close, very close, as Scotty kept a close eye on the riverbank. The leopard moved forward when we moved, stopped when we stopped. It was going to get a handsome meal of some sort that particular day.

We'd been on the go for a few hours by then and our water supplies needed replenishing, and soon. This however was proving a far more serious business, as tension of what was to come overwhelmed the scene. I had a feeling Scotty wanted to swap places and to finish the bad job he had started. I was not about to oblige and take the chance that he might again simply wound the baboon. I had qualified for my cross rifles at the first go, so was going to put the beast out of its pain quickly, once more having checked the rifle to ensure a round was up the breach.

Now, only some ten feet before reaching the tree, we again checked the dry river bed. There were clear signs of other animals having looked for water supplies recently. Stopping and casting to the rear, I signaled to Scotty to join me. "Think the baboon's behind the tree," was my confident announcement. "I'm going forward, you keep a bloody close eye on our friend there." Slowly and purposefully moving forward, while leaving distinct foot prints in the light colored soil below, soon I was up to the tree and fully expecting a sudden charge. It was a big tree, with little room to maneuver around from the side.

Suddenly, managing to skirt around the tree, there to my surprise lying on the ground was this big male baboon. It had died, and slumped to its side. I called Scotty to join me, but to keep a bloody close eye on the leopard. He was soon standing next to me and casting down at the bounty. The baboon had died from a loss of blood, exhaustion, and a lack of water. It stood no chance, as the leopard would have got it in the end. It had been hit in the lower leg, and by then we'd covered some ten miles in the searing heat of day. The job was not done though, as we would have to prove the baboon was done for.

As Scotty had been so damn stupid to shoot this innocent victim, then he could cut off the tail and carry it in his pocket. Then we would quickly get out of the place and leave the remains to the leopard. Job done, it was time to back track down the river for a safe distance. We still needed to quench our thirst and decide whether to camp out for the night or make it back to base camp. Now some distance from the kill, we started digging deep and securing some of mother nature's life saving nutrient of golden water. We achieved the task set by our camp commander and also secured enough water and live for another day.

Now all we hoped was that our Scottish buddy would behave himself and not again allow the midday sun to cloud his mind. We had a hard enough task trying to survive the elements, trekking for hours on end on the lookout for insurgents and poachers, and that was before allowing for snakes, lions, leopards, elephants and the likes. Baboons proved the last of our worries and not a problem. So if certain individuals wished to shoot at anything, they should have saved valuable rounds for a rainy day. I shall never forget my buddy Scotty, even if he got us into some rather tricky positions. Fortunately I've managed to record fuller extents of life in Africa under title of 'Phantoms of Africa', and yes, come out of it alive.

No biography provided.

|  | **walking with elephants** | kate waddecar namibia 1998 |

Click, click, run

Two months into my African adventure, I found myself 200km into a gruelling 14 day trek down the Huab and Aba Huab river beds in the heart of Damaraland, Namibia. Known for a long time as 'South West Africa,' Namibia's arid landscape borders Angola to the north, Botswana to the east, South Africa to the south and the Atlantic Ocean to the west. From the shipwrecked shores of the Skeleton Coast to the sun drenched sands of the Kalahari, Namibia is a country of contrasts. Its vast open spaces and rolling hills beg the intrepid explorer to pick up their rucksack and take a look. Some of us, however, got a closer look than we were anticipating...

After nearly two weeks of back breaking trekking on the sandy river bed, I welcomed any opportunity to cover some serious distance on relatively firm tracks, opting where possible to trample over 'easter egg' ground as I called it: dried up mud, resembling broken pieces of chocolate egg, curling upwards towards the sun. This particular morning, I was in the unusual position of being third from the front of my trekking group, normally preferring to take a 'watchful' 12th position at the rear. Head down, Walkman on, I was enjoying the relatively fast pace, encouraged by the reserves of energy I was discovering in my worn out legs. Humming softly to myself, I stopped suddenly as my nose collided heavily with my companion's rucksack in front. Thinking that we must be stopping for a break, I pulled out my earphones and looked up, rubbing my bruised nose. Immediately I caught sight of a warning sign from the guy at the front; it was the arm signal we had devised which roughly translated into, "There's a damn great elephant bloody close to us!" My eyes darted from left to right, but it wasn't until I looked over his shoulder that I saw the huge bull elephant. He was standing 30 metres away staring directly at us.

Spinning around to warn my teammates behind, I was surprised to see an empty space. It was then that I caught sight of them all, rucksacks down, standing near the safety of the rocks, nine pairs of eyes watching us. It was only afterwards that we learnt of the gamble they had taken; deciding against shouting a warning at us for fear of spooking the elephant and causing him to charge, opting instead for the 'god we hope they see him' option.

Slowly and calmly (although I was anything but calm), we linked arms and stepped backwards, holding his gaze the entire time. The adrenaline rush was incredible and I could feel my heart banging in my chest. A couple of times, he took a few steps forward but his ears remained still, a good sign that he wasn't overly bothered by our presence.

After what seemed like an age, we reached the rest of the group on the other side of the riverbed and the safety of the high ground. It was then that the adrenaline deserted me and I collapsed in a heap on my rucksack, laughing hysterically with tears streaming down my face. The others grinned, relief evident in their faces and there were various comments along the lines of "So, did you get any decent photos?"

Namibia's sand river elephants have adapted to life on the soft ground by developing larger than usual feet which enables them to spread their weight more evenly as they travel hundreds of kilometres each year up and down the river beds in search of water. We had several more encounters with lone elephants and it became apparent that we were trekking in the opposite direction to the majority of them; good news for us as it meant more possible sightings.

However, sad news greeted us one afternoon as we neared the Aba Huab. Two guides armed with rifles had been sent to us by the MET (Ministry of Environment and Tourism) following the death of an American tourist from an alleged elephant attack a few days earlier. The news shocked and saddened me. In our two weeks on the river, I had come to know and love these gentle giants; I had watched their movements, studied their moods and marvelled at their grace. We had learnt how to detect if they were angry or fearful and heard how they warn potential threats by first giving a 'mock charge' – an elaborate display of ear flapping, loud trumpeting and stamping feet. Despite all these warnings, and intent on capturing the ultimate photograph, the tourist had apparently strayed too close to a herd and had suffered a fatal blow.

Later on that day, just after we had set up our camp in a clearing on the river bed, we encountered the same herd that had killed the tourist. Sitting high up on the rocks, we watched the fifteen of them amble along from one Anaboom tree to the next, the baby of the herd struggling to keep pace with the others. In our dash to escape to the safety of the rocks, we had been unable to dismantle our camp in time and so it wasn't long before the elephants caught sight of our bright yellow dome tents. They were obviously spooked and so for the next thirty minutes, we looked on as they mock

227

charged our camp, unable to do anything except hope that they left our radio (and food!) intact.

That evening, for the first time since beginning our trek down the Huab, I didn't begrudge bedding down inside my tent. The African night sky remains one of my most treasured memories of my time in Namibia and I welcomed any opportunity to sleep under the stars. Following our encounters of the day however, I appreciated the safety that the tents provided us with against an unwelcome trampling from a passing elephant whilst we slept. I wish I could say the same for my fellow tent inhabitants, though; two weeks of trekking without a decent wash made for a pretty horrendous stench. If the tents wouldn't ward off the elephants, then the smell coming from them most certainly would!

See page 36, for biography of **Kate Waddecar**.

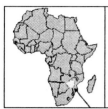
Canoeing down the Zambezi

A canoe trip down the lower Zambezi is a bit like eating a pizza in your living room, with just a few minor differences: you are in a canoe on a murky river in Africa, no pizza is to be found within three hundred miles, and several large African animals in and around the river believe it is, in fact, their living room and you are the pizza.

Canoeing down the Zambezi, which frames the border between Zimbabwe and Zambia, is not the sort of thing you would do on your own unless large portions of your brain were missing (whereas going with a tour company only requires the absence of minor brain portions). That's why I signed up with a low-end tour company called Buffalo Safaris. Still, I had to pay $360 for a four-day canoe trip and they made me sign a waiver that basically stated they could keep the money even if I was entirely or partially eaten by one of the large animals.

I was joined by a Dutch couple, a German couple, and a Kiwi/ English couple, and I can assure you we were all missing appropriate portions of brain tissue. I got to paddle in the lead canoe with the diminutive and quiet but extremely good-natured Zimbabwean guide John Mousaka (yes, he was well aware that his name is a Greek dish), while the others followed behind, two per canoe.

As a front person, my job was to paddle. The rear person was responsible for the canoe's direction. John was a fine canoeist but he didn't provide much in the way of paddling instruction for the canoeists behind us. The Kiwi/Brit team had some experience, but it was the first time for the Germans and the Dutch, who quickly fell behind with their spastic zigzag canoeing styles.

John's Zimbabwean accent (which resembled, in part, Australian, British, and mumbling), combined with the distance between the canoes, made animal identification more challenging.

"That's a stripe-necked heron," John would try to tell me in his whispered speech.

"What kind?" Chris would ask from the canoe behind.

"A hype-necked bheron!" I'd yell, unsure of my pronunciation, but unable to clarify without an animal identification book.

"It's a high-pecked baron!" I'd hear Chris tell the Dutch.

Throughout the trip, I think we inadvertently renamed nearly every animal we saw.

It took quite a while, basically the entire trip, to get used to sharing the river with hippos. Despite the fact that they look like waterlogged cows, hippos are responsible for more human deaths than any other animal in Africa. Hippos are not fond of surprise visitors, and they don't treat them very hospitably.

Many hippos were floating in large groups that, from a distance, looked like partially submerged mines. Those were easy to spot and, therefore, easy to avoid. The trick was to find the ones underwater. If we didn't know where they were, there was a good chance they would surface under our canoe and bite us into anchovy-sized pieces which John reminded us "is not a good thing." To remove the element of surprise, we used our paddles to hit the sides of our canoes continually-every thirty seconds or so-to let them know where we were. It was a bit like a courtesy knock when entering a familiar neighbor's home. The sound would travel through the water and a few hundred meters downstream hippos would pop their heads up and give us a quick glance before disappearing back into the seemingly gentle river.

Once we knew their location, we would head for the opposite side of the river, except in the smaller channels between grassy islands where the river was barely wide enough for a hippo and a canoe. In that case, we would stick to the more shallow of the two banks because-this is the Survival Rule of Canoeing with Hippos- they flee to deeper water. Unfortunately, some of the hippos had not been briefed on where they were supposed to flee, and so they ran straight at us. To be more precise, they charged at me because I was sitting at the front of the lead canoe.

There are not many ways to stop a charging hippo on the Zambezi. If John shot him with his revolver,* it would just make the hippo angry. If we bailed out of our canoes, we were crocodile bait. And if we paddled up onto land, we'd have to fend off the buffalo and elephants waiting to stomp us into Zambezi pizza toppings. So what did we do? We slapped our paddles against the water. This doesn't sound like much of a defense against a charging, angry, three-ton hippo, but it did the trick surprisingly well-although one charging hippo did get within about two yards of me before deciding he was deterred by my frenzied slapping.

Every night we camped on the banks of the river. We had plenty of company-the river banks were lined with hippos, buffalo, and elephants, as well as lions, leopards, hyenas, baboons, and tsetse flies, which were lured to the Zambezi by its fresh water and the lush grazing land that bordered it. Fortunately, we were protected by our sturdy anti-malarial mosquito nets. **

We were not in a fenced-in campsite. We didn't even have tents. We lay on individual cots with our semipermeable mosquito nets draped over our heads. And I know for a fact that no one in our group got any sleep, including John Mousaka who, in addition to fending off any night attacks from animals, had to keep the canoes from getting stolen by the Zambians on the other side of the river, which seemed to be his biggest fear. The rest of us spent the nights listening to lions roaring and hyenas laughing (apparently, the joke was on us). This was hard to ignore because the sounds seemed to come from a distance of no more than fifteen yards away. Why didn't the animals eat us? I'm not sure. Perhaps our pungent body odors were keeping them at bay.

To compensate for our sleepless nights, we followed the animals' lead and took naps during the midday heat, which was about 110 degrees-too hot to canoe and too hot for the animals to hunt us.

Something happened on the third night that still gives me nightmares. John was fishing on the riverbank for some tiger fish, a cross between a salmon and a piranha. After a few minutes without a bite, he handed the line (he had no fishing pole) over to the Kiwi, Chris. Chris followed John's lasso-style casting technique and landed the bacon-baited hook on a floating branch. While we were debating who should wade out and unsnag it, the line ran. Or, I should say, something ran and decided to take our line with it.

Chris tried to hold on without burning his hands and I tried to assist by taking a fork from the bottom of the canoe and wrapping it around the speeding line. We both grabbed hold of the fork and pulled until the line snapped. One heck of a big tiger fish,...or so we thought.

At exactly 3:05 A.M., or maybe it was exactly 3:25 A.M.-anyway, it was early-I woke up on my mosquito-net-protected cot. I was lying on my side and I heard what I thought were feet the size of videocassettes shuffling behind me. I decided I didn't want to roll over and look, so instead, I called for John, who in theory had been trained for these situations. By the time he got up and pointed his flashlight in my direction, the critter had shuffled off.

The next morning we found the tracks of a nine-foot croc. It had passed within two feet of my bed and, not much further away, coughed up our fishing hook, recognizable because of the orange- painted tip. Apparently we had hooked one of the few crocs who observes his own catch-and-release policy.

*Which was sitting somewhere at the bottom of his waterproof bag where, in a real emergency, he could probably find it and pull it out in a little over five minutes.

**Unfortunately, they were riddled with gaping holes plenty large enough for mosquitoes, tsetse flies, and in some cases, small leopards.

Printed with permission:
Up The Amazon Without A Paddle. By Doug Lansky
Meadowbrook Press

Doug Lansky was born on the Third World island of Manhattan, grew up in Minnesota, and graduated from Colorado College with a B.A. in a subject he can no longer recall. After working the copying machine at "Late Night with David Letterman," "Spy Magazine," and "The New Yorker Magazine," Doug rejected a career as a professional intern, hit the road with his backpack and has been traveling around the world ever since—for the last seven years in over 60 countries, chronicling his adventures in his nationally-syndicated humor column, "Vagabond," which reaches over 10 million readers in newspapers throughout North America. Doug Lansky is also editor of a new travel-humor anthology called, "There's No Toilet Paper on the Road Less Traveled," and "Up the Amazon without a Paddle."

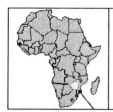	**a rumble in the jungle**	paul israel zimbabwe 1993

It takes 50 years for some people to learn

The Sanyati is a river that goes from central Zimbabwe into the huge man made body of water, Lake Kariba.

We were to be the first white people to canoe it in some 50 years to reach this lake. One of our immediate concerns was that the distance was so short we would reach our destination several days earlier then expected; but this was not going to be the problem. We were to find quite a few obstacles in our way. The very concept of canoeing an un-canoeable river is quite a novel one and in all likelihood no sensible person will attempt to canoe the Sanyati for another 50 years.

The canoeing began from Yardley Bridge, at the edge of the wilderness leading to the Matusadona national park. Lush green hills of deep forest and no sign of civilisation except for the narrow bridge, with the river gorge below. I was paired up in a canoe with the name "Jenny Wren," with a let's face it quite mad Ugandan, who announced that his friends at home called him the District Commissioner. His behaviour created the nickname D.C. which quickly became Dizzy, as I was to discover Ugandan District Commissioners are not over-burdened with common sense (at least this one). Dizzy was also (perhaps not so reassuringly on a canoe trip) terrified of water and at times, regarding his paddling, seemed unaware there was anyone else in the boat...

This Sanyati was to introduce us to a new word, portage, it is when a river is so rough or has so many obstacles, normally involving 25 foot drops, or boulders the size of 18 wheeler trucks, it can't be canoed and the 7 canoes, equipment, food etc must be carried through the intermittently jungle-esque undergrowth or rocky landscape at the edge of the river. We also had another issue.

Nick, a paraplegic and our chef, had bravely decided to go on this expedition and in portage situations, one of the only 3 of us big enough to carry him would combine to carry him ever cheerfully over the lunar-esque rocky gorge sides. This rocky and at times jungle green scenery resembled Africa from the Tarzan films.

This extremely frustrating pattern was repeated for 10 days: a little canoeing then an impassable barrier. Sometimes we would rope the boats through. This ended in near-disaster a couple of times. Once the boat with Nick in it got caught in a rapid and was about to overturn and I had to jump in the water to free it, successfully, but I ended up trapped on a rock in the middle of the rapid. My only solution was to body surf down the rapid, covering my head, taking a very deep breathe, avoiding Nick's canoe and various rocks. I emerged some 150 yards downstream through the currents. Hardly the Beach Boys, but all those water-slides in America I visited as a kid finally came in handy.

At one point we had to do 2-km portage. Fortunately I came across the only people we saw on the river, 3 black Zimbabweans, illegally fishing in the wilderness. Led by a likeable character called Watson I hired them to carry our boats, who, instead of taking my offer of payment by the hour, agreed payment per boat carried (50 UK pence per boat), considerably less than my offer. After we had tired them out they sold us some fish (fresh for some reason)!

The Jenny Wren herself was caught in one rapid and span around. We attempted to continue backwards and were caught in the current and hurtled towards a giant cathedral shaped rock. I stuck my paddle in between to avoid catastrophe, which in one sense succeeded but with the oar gone, Dizzy was in sole control of the boat's fortunes and decided to stand up; seconds later the boat had taken on too much water and began to go down with all hands...Further tragedy struck as we salvaged the wreck and the bag carrying the team's toilet roll had not been properly sealed. Personally, I thank whoever told me to keep one roll in my bag for emergencies as I now had the only clean roll for 200km. This secret was shared with only one person- thank you Angus for keeping it; there are times to look after number 1 (literally).

The lowest point was when we were making no more than 1-3km a day and as our expert canoe instructor gave us a detailed description of how to execute a particularly tricky maneuver through a waterfall and then demonstrated it by completely wiping out, spilling the contents of his canoe. The second boat went through unoccupied and roped, but the rope was badly tied and came undone. This boat was lost in the current and bashed into rocks. With equipment littered down the river and huge rising rock cliffs, we were in crisis as the light was beginning to fade. There was an immense argument over where we were to camp. Imagine 6 people all with separate opinions in the deserted wilderness, standing in a dark, noisy rapid filled gorge, shouting at each other.

We found a small sandy ledge nestled in the rocks, about 2 meters square. This was where the 14 of us would sleep. In the fading light we camped as best we could, basically huddled, and fell asleep exhausted. Most of us were bruised and soaked to the skin, one with very bad malaria, on half rations because our food was running low and some had been lost, not knowing if the 2 battered canoes were still sea-worthy and unable to get our headquarters on the radio a decision was debated to get us helicopter-lifted out of the gorge when we could re-establish radio contact.

My own predicament was serious in the middle of the night as I moved off the ledge to go to the toilet in the dark, I clambered over the rock and could not find my way back for 30 minutes, lost on a rocky hill in darkest Africa, fearing I would face a lion armed with a maglite and the only toilet roll for 200km…Was my best hope to react like the puppy in the Andrex commercials?

That morning the only sweet food left, a tin of jam was mysteriously gone, the mystery of where it had gone took weeks to uncover (the female members of the group later admitted to having taken it and covered for each other in some dastardly, fiendish, feminist plot). Morale was at rock bottom. Rationed slightly sweet Zimbabwean army biscuits now became the highest currency.

If you travel in Africa for long enough you will get ill. It is one of the unfortunate facts, and no amount of care will ultimately protect you. Every day when we found camp the water was lifted from the river and given purification pills or, if possible, boiled. In the morning more water was collected, but always from a different place (crocodiles have survived for 3 million years for a good reason). The only three of us of us without this stomach sickness within a few days formed the "Last of the Mohicans" club. This was one club I was determined to remain in.

If you have read the Voyage of the Dawn Treader by C.S Lewis, then you will remember the part when the boat is stuck in the reeds. We turned a corner and the entire Sanyati was green and yellow reeds with no visible water at all. At least we could just make out the lake in the distance, but any movement required enormous effort. Short of food, tired and dehydrated, we were not quite Jason and the Argonauts', instead of beautiful sirens beckoning, we were distracted by sodding big tetse flies buzzing.

Finally, after countless false dawns we were on Lake Kariba and in exhilaration, we dashed for the open water. In my case, my malaria stricken boat companion was unable to row, and I was paddling double speed exhausted just to try and keep up.

We were nearly out of food, and out of time, and we landed on the southern Kariba shores in the fading light, pitched tent in a very basic hippo defensive position (think Custer surrounded by Indians), and collapsed, exhausted. In the night I heard what I considered to be the most ill-considerate sounds from Paul, my nightmare stricken tent companion. In the morning we discovered from the tracks around our tents, we had camped bang straight in the middle of a hippo run! Not content with that, the boats were covered in ants', obviously they had heard about our lost tin of jam.

In the morning the official currency of the surviving army biscuits sharply devalued as we found the first village for 2 weeks with a shop that sold lemon cream biscuits and bread, the first sweet food for days. Biscuits have never tasted so good!

So onto the homeward straight, 50km across the open lake to our relief in Kariba, passing the odd hippo and the husks of thousands of trees reaching out from the water from when it was flooded a few decades back. We were informed it was incredibly well stocked with fish and as a result unreassuringly had a population of over a million crocodiles. That is a million things that can eat you unseen under your canoe!

Dizzy had now recovered enough to partake in some of the canoeing and as we peacefully moved on, I was suddenly struck by the most sharp stomach cramps I have had in my life, absolute pain. The Last of the Mohicans club was clearly now going down to its last member. We paddled on and in my case rather desperately for my own dignity…

Two and a half days late we made landfall and I immediately volunteered to be one of the 3 who would go look for our relief. In fact as soon as we were clear of the boats I spotted the first flush toilet (or indeed any sort for 200km).

I did not emerge for some time.

I had been extremely lucky in surviving both the raw adventure of the Sanyati and surviving with my dignity intact in my own personal Rumble in the Jungle…

See page 76, for biography of **Paul Israel**.

	**bembe and the lion**	jill baker malawi 1940

It was July 1940 and as a relatively recent bride fresh from the gentle green countryside of Essex in England, I was beginning to adapt to my life as a headmaster's wife. My husband, John Hammond, was principal of Tjolotjo School near Nyamandhlovu. It sounded as though it was miles from anywhere – and it was! In fact, I was only now getting used to wildness of it all – as well as the strange place names and what they meant: Tjolotjo – the 'skull,' and Nyamandhlovu - the 'meat' of the elephant.

While there were a very large number of elephants around, it was a lion that was causing us our most immediate problems at that time. A large male lion had killed two people in a nearby kraal and badly mauled another quite close to the school. As well as its obvious taste for humans, it had previously taken cattle and goats and was generally causing great fear and anger.

It was decided something had to be done about it. So we organised a shoot with four of the staff and two from the Native Department armed with guns…and old Bembe as the tracker. Bembe was a great character – he had 27 wives and had lost count of the number of his children! I spent hours with him suggesting it was time to stop – but he would just grin with his much-wrinkled face creased in disbelief that anyone would want to stop having children. They were his wealth and his assurance for the future. Bembe was a marvellous tracker and he asked whether he could bring his son Enos with him on the lion hunt, to start learning the trade.

John and Maurice Mills were going along with two of the guns, together with Teacher Ramushu and Teacher Mothobi…Daisy and I asked if we could come along too. We were given very strict instructions as to what to do and were to stay close beside them at all times, unless there was a charge in which case we had to scatter and climb the nearest tree. As most of the trees in that particular area were thorny, I didn't fancy the thought!

Just before dawn was the time to go, when the lion would be out and looking for a kill. Days of planning went into the hunt with Bembe tracking and watching where the lion rested and what his movement patterns were for each day.

We woke early and dressed in khaki clothing to merge as best we could into the veld. Then we drove considerably north of where the lion was

237

thought to be as there was a strong southerly breeze that morning and we had to be sure it didn't pick up our scent.

We started creeping through the bush. I was fascinated by the depth of concentration you could see on old Bembe's face. We watched him like a hawk – and occasionally he would signal us to stop. He would slowly turn his head in otherwise frozen mobility to try and pick up the slightest sound from the direction the spoor was headed. Daisy was a bit worried that Enos was being a bit too clever and showing off – but Bembe seemed able to control the boy.

An hour later we were still stalking – walking a few steps – stopping – listening – changing direction.

'He's here,' Bembe signalled to us to be quiet. 'And he knows we are here. He has just moved round us so that our smell is coming to him. He is very clever and his marks show he is very big and very heavy. We must be very careful now.'

Chastising Enos for stepping on a twig, Bembe moved off ahead. Then I saw what Daisy was worried about. The boy looked sullen and defensive.

We moved as quietly as we could. Suddenly a noise to our left. Enos had thrown a stone into a clump of thorn bush and the lion was coming out at him at a huge speed. As I turned to flee, I saw the old man rush in front of his son. I heard the lion's roar, I actually felt the rush as it went past. It was horrifyingly close. I heard a scream of agony.

A shot rang out – then another. And the hideous growls and muffled roaring were cut off as the lion was thrown to one side by the power of the bullets which hit him just behind the head and through the heart.

I turned in horror, to look. It was Bembe lying on the ground. Brave old Bembe. Enos was howling in a corner. While Daisy tore off her jumper to put round what we quickly realised was a dying man, I ran to Enos and slapped him across the face, demanding more respect.

'Stop that ridiculous noise. Your father is seriously hurt – get over there now and tell him how sorry you are. He needs your help and your care, not your cowardly crying!'

The boy looked at me with hate-filled eyes, but then realization of what he had done dawned fully and he stumbled over to the old man. Despite Daisy's jersey, the old tracker was shaking and trembling uncontrollably. He managed to speak a few consoling words to Enos…and to stumble out a few sorry words to the rest of us before his life drained from him and he quietly gave it up.

We stood around absolutely stunned at the ferocity and horror of it all. Then as one, we bowed our heads and John said a prayer asking God to look after this brave old man.

I was appalled by my actions in that moment of crisis, but Enos turned to me as the men started to make a stretcher to carry Bembe home. The lion would be left where it was.

'Thank you, Inkosikaas – I was able to say sorry and my father forgave me.'

Twenty-seven wives and all those children…what on earth were they all going to do? Enos was the oldest of the family and Daisy and I talked to him as we walked back to the school. There were several other little Bembes at the school and I knew John would do his utmost to ensure that they were able to stay. When we neared the school, John asked Enos to go ahead with him to find the senior wife, so that she could be told what had happened.

The school was abuzz with all the drama of it. Give him his due, Enos came up trumps and looked after that family responsibly and well. John managed to find a position for him helping with one of the farm projects and a year later he proudly showed me his first-born son.

There was some real satisfaction in the fact that he had called him Bembe.

Extract from Beloved African by Jill Baker

Jill Baker was born in Rhodesia and for the first few years of her life, spoke Si'Ndebele as easily as she spoke English. Her father was at that time, headmaster of one of the first African government schools in the new colony. She went on to study piano at the Guildhall School of Music in London before returning to Africa to marry and become a tobacco farmer's wife in the northeast of the country. In 1983, her family migrated to Australia, where she established her own business as a consultant to the tourism industry. Jill now works to attract high spending, quality tourists for Australia. Her writing skills are increasingly being called upon since the successful publication of the book Beloved African – a biography of her father's life in African education in Rhodesia.

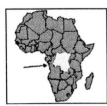

| **only in the peace corps** | mike tidwell
democratic republic
of the congo
1990 |

THERE YOU ARE WORKING WITH THE CHIEF OF NTITA KALAMBAYL TO DIG A 4,000 CUBIC FOOT HOLE IN THE MIDDLE OF THE AFRICAN BUSH WITH ONLY A SHOVEL.

In one hand he carried a spear, in the other a crude machete. On his head was a kind of coonskin cap with a bushy tail hanging down in back. Around his neck was a string supporting a leather charm to ward off bad bush spirits. Two underfed mongrel dogs circled his bare feet, panting.

"My name is Ilunga," he said, extending his hand.

"My name is Michael," I said, shaking it.

We smiled at each other another moment before Ilunga got around to telling me he had heard my job was to teach people how to raise fish. It sounded like something worth trying, he said, and he wondered if I would come by his village to help him look for a pond site. I said I would and took down directions to his house.

The next day the two of us set off into the bush, hunting for a place to raise fish.

Machetes in hand, we stomped and stumbled and hacked our way through the savanna grass for two hours before finding an acceptable site along a stream about a twenty-minute walk from Ilunga's village. Together, we paced off a pond and staked a water canal running between it and a point farther up the stream. Then, with a shovel I sold him on credit against his next corn harvest, Ilunga began a two-month journey through dark caverns of physical pain and overexertion. He began digging.

There is no easy way to dig a fish pond with a shovel. You just have to do it. You have to place the tip to the ground, push the shovel in with your foot, pull up a load of dirt, and then throw the load twenty or thirty feet to the pond's edge. Then you have to do it again—tip to the ground, push it in, pull it up, throw the dirt. After you do this about 50,000 times, you have an average-sized, ten-by-fifteen-meter pond.

But Ilunga, being a chief and all, wasn't content with an average-sized pond. He wanted one almost twice that size. He wanted a pond fifteen by twenty meters. I told him he was crazy, as we measured it out. I repeated the

240

point with added conviction after watching him use his bare foot to drive the thin shovel blade into the ground.

For me, it was painful visiting Ilunga each week. I'd come to check on the pond's progress and find Ilunga grunting and shoveling and pitching dirt the same way I had left him the week before. I winced each time his foot pushed the shovel into the ground. I calculated that to finish the pond he would have to move a total of 4,000 cubic feet of dirt. Guilt gnawed at me. This was no joke. He really was going to kill himself.

One week I couldn't stand it any longer.

"Give me the shovel," I told him.

"Oh no, Michael," he said. "This work is too much for you."

"Give it to me," I repeated, a bit indignantly. "Take a rest."

He shrugged and handed me the shovel. I began digging. Okay, I thought, tip to the ground, push it in, pull it up, throw the dirt. I did it again. It wasn't nearly as hard as I had thought. Stroke after stroke, I kept going. About twenty minutes later, though, it got hot. I paused to take off my shirt. Ilunga, thinking I was quitting, jumped up and reached for the shovel.

"No, no," I said. "I'm still digging. Sit down."

He shrugged again and said that since I was apparently serious about digging, he was going to go check on one of his fields.

Shirtless, alone, I carried on. Tip to the ground, push it in, pull it up, throw the dirt. An hour passed. Tip to the ground, push it in, pull it up…throw…throw the…dammit, throw the dirt. My arms were signaling that they didn't like tossing dirt over such a great distance. It hurts, they said. Stop making us do it. But I couldn't stop. I had been digging a paltry hour and a half. I was determined to go on, to help Ilunga. How could I expect villagers to do work I was incapable of doing myself?

Sweat gathered on my forehead and streamed down my face as I continued, shoveling and shoveling. About thirty minutes passed and things started to get really ugly. My body buckled with fatigue. My back and shoulders joined my arms in screaming for an end to hostilities. I was no longer able to throw the dirt. Instead, I carried each load twenty feet and ignobly spooned it onto the dike. I was glad Ilunga wasn't around to see this. It was embarrassing. And then I looked at my hands. Both palms had become blistered. One was bleeding.

Fifteen minutes later, my hands finally refused to grip the shovel. It fell to the ground. My back then refused to bend down to allow my arms the chance to refuse to pick it up. After just two hours of digging, I was incapable of doing any more. With a stiff, unnatural walk, I went over to the dike. Ilunga had just returned, and I collapsed next to him.

"I think I'll stop now," I managed, unable to hide my piteous state. "Take over if you want."

He did. He stood up, grabbed the shovel and began working—smoothly, confidently, a man inured to hard work. Tip to the ground, push it in, pull it up, throw the dirt. Lying on my side, exhausted, I watched Ilunga. Then I looked hard at the spot where I had been digging. I had done nothing. The pond was essentially unchanged. I had moved perhaps thirty cubic feet of dirt. That meant 3,970 cubic feet for Ilunga.

Day after day, four or five hours each day, he kept going. He worked like a bull and never complained. Not once. Not when he hit a patch of gravel-size rocks that required a pickaxe and extra sweat. Not when, at the enormous pond's center, he had to throw each shovel-load twice to reach the dikes. And not when he became ill.

Several weeks later, Ilunga drove his shovel into the earth and threw its load one last time. I never thought it would happen, but there it was: Ilunga's pond, huge, fifteen by twenty meters, and completely finished. Using my motorcycle and two ten-liter carrying bidons, I transported stocking fish from another project post twenty miles to the south. When the last of the 300 tilapia fingerlings had entered the new pond, I turned to Ilunga and shook his hand over and over again.

Ilunga had done it. He had taken my advice and accomplished a considerable thing. And on that day when we finally stocked the pond, I knew that no man would ever command more respect from me than one who, to better feed his children, moves 4,000 cubic feet of dirt with a shovel.

I had a hero.

No biography provided.

life and death

Death and taxes may always be with us, but death at least doesn't get any worse. Not even in Africa.

Death will always be with us, by many sources –war, AIDS, famine or mysterious deaths. Death is not unique to Africa. Its courses and the scale of it and what has been done to prolong life is where the uniqueness occurs.

This chapter of course mentions AIDS, which is a global problem and is here to stay, along with the Ebola virus that spread in Democratic Republic of Congo. Ever wondered how the famine in Ethiopia in 1984, which was a cruel act of nature and man, was brought to the world's attention and inspired a collective global conscience, thus saving millions of lives?

	**aids in africa**	avert africa present day

How many people in Africa are infected with HIV/AIDS? Africa continues to dwarf the rest of the world in how the region has been affected by AIDS. Africa is home to 70% of the adults and 80% of the children living with HIV in the world. The estimated number of newly infected adults and children in Africa reached 3.4 million at the end of 2001. It has also been estimated that 28.1 million adults and children were living with HIV/AIDS in Africa by the end of the year. AIDS deaths totalled 3 million globally in 2001, and of the global total 2.3 million AIDS deaths occurred in Africa.

In sub-Saharan Africa HIV is now deadlier than war itself. In 1998, 200,000 Africans died in war, but more than 2 million died of AIDS. AIDS has become a full-blown development crisis. Its social and economic consequences are felt widely not only in health but in education, industry, agriculture, transport, human resources and the economy in general.

The overall incidence of HIV infection in Africa does appear to be stabilising. Because the long-standing African epidemics have already reached large numbers of people whose behaviour exposes them to HIV, and because effective prevention measures in some countries have enabled people to reduce their risk of exposure, the annual number of new infections has stabilised or even fallen in many countries. These decreases have now begun to balance out the still-rising infection rates in other parts of Africa, particularly the southern part of the continent. Overall, the total of 3.8 million infected people in 2000 was slightly less than the regional total of 4.0 million in 1999. But this trend will not continue if countries such as Nigeria begin experiencing a rapid increase.

How are different countries affected?

National HIV prevalence rates vary widely between countries. They range from under 2% of the adult population in some West African countries to around 20% or more in the southern part of the continent, while countries in central and East Africa have rates midway between these.

244

However, prevalence rates do not convey people's lifetime risk of becoming infected and dying of AIDS. In the eight African countries where at least 15% of today's adults are infected, conservative analyses show that AIDS will claim the lives of around a third of today's 15 year olds. Sixteen African countries south of the Sahara have more than one -tenth of the adult population aged 15-49 infected with HIV. In seven countries, all in the southern cone of the continent, at least one adult in five is living with the virus.

In Botswana a shocking 35.8 % of adults are now infected with HIV. In South Africa, 19.9% of adults are infected with HIV. With a total of 4.2 million infected people, South Africa has the largest number of people living with HIV/AIDS in the world.

West Africa is relatively less affected by the HIV infection, but the prevalence rates in some large countries are creeping up.

Côte d'Ivoire is already among the 15 worst affected countries in the world.Nigeria, by far the most populous country in sub-Saharan Africa, has 5% of its adult population infected with HIV. Infection rates in East Africa, once the highest on the continent, hover above those in the West of the continent but have been exceeded by the rates now seen in the Southern cone.

The prevalence rate among adults in Ethiopia and Kenya has reached double -digit figures and continues to rise. In Ethiopia 10.6 % and in Kenya 13.9 % of the adult population (15-49) are living with HIV/AIDS.

What is the result of this?

Over and above the personal suffering that accompanies HIV infection wherever it strikes, the virus in sub-Saharan Africa threatens to devastate whole communities, rolling back decades of progress towards a healthier and more prosperous future. Sub-Saharan Africa faces a triple challenge of colossal proportions:

- bringing health care, support and solidarity to a growing population of people with HIV-related illness.
- reducing the annual toll of new infections by enabling individuals to protect themselves and others.
- coping with the cumulative impact of over 17 million AIDS deaths on orphans and other survivors, on communities, and on national development.

245

Millions of adults are dying young or in early middle age. They leave behind children grieving and struggling to survive without a parent's care. Many of those dying have surviving partners who are themselves infected and in need of care. Their families have to find money to pay for their funerals, and employers, schools, factories and hospitals have to train other staff to replace them at the workplace.

Who is most affected? What is the effect on education?

Just as the better-educated segments of the population in the industrialised countries where the first to adopt health-conscious life-styles, a similar pattern now seems to be emerging in sub-Saharan Africa. Studies focusing on 15-19 years olds have found that teenagers with more education are now far more likely to use condoms than their peers with lower education. They are also less likely, particularly in countries with severe epidemics, to engage in casual sex.This was not the case early in the African epidemic. At that stage, education tended to go hand in hand with more disposable income and higher mobility, both of which increased casual sex and the risk of contracting HIV. But as information about HIV has become more widely available, education has switched from being a liability to being a shield.

The effect on education is that AIDS now threatens the coverage and quality of education. The epidemic has not spared this sector any more than it has spared health, agriculture or mining.

On the demand side, HIV is reducing the numbers of children in school. HIV positive women have fewer babies, in part because they may die before the end of their childbearing years, and up to a third of their children are themselves infected and may not survive until school age. Also, many children have lost their parents to AIDS, or are living in households which have taken in AIDS orphans, and they may be forced to drop out of school to start earning money, sometimes simply because school fees have become unaffordable.

On the supply side, teacher shortages are looming in many African countries. In Zambia, teachers are increasingly dying of AIDS and for many teachers, their teaching input is decreasing because they are sick. Swaziland estimates that it will have to train more than twice as many teachers as usual over the next 17 years just to keep services at their 1997 levels.

What is the economic impact?

It is exceptionally difficult to gauge the economic impact of the epidemic. Many factors apart from AIDS affect economic performance and complicate the task of economic forecasting - drought, internal and external conflict, corruption, economic mismanagement. Moreover, economies tend to react more dramatically to economic restructuring measures, a sudden fuel shortage, or an unexpected change of government, than to long, slow difficulties such as those wrought by AIDS. But there is growing evidence that as HIV prevalence rates rise, both total and growth in national income - gross domestic product, or GDP -fall significantly. African countries where less than 5% of the adult population is infected will experience a modest impact on GDP growth rate. As the HIV prevalence rate rises to 20% or more, GDP growth may decline up to 2% a year.

In South Africa, the epidemic is projected to reduce the economic growth rate by 0.3-0.4 % annually, resulting by the year 2010 in a GDP 17% lower than it would have been without AIDS and wiping US$22 billion off the country's economy. Even in diamond-rich Botswana, the country with the highest per capita GDP in Africa, AIDS will slice 20% off the government budget, erode development gains, and bring about a 13% reduction in the income of the poorest households in the next ten years.

What about prevention?

Continuing rises in the number of HIV infected people are not inevitable. Early and sustained prevention efforts can be credited with the lower rates in some countries. For example in Senegal there was effective early prevention. Uganda has bought its estimated prevalence rate down to around 8% from a peak close to 14% in the early 1990's with strong prevention campaigns, and there are encouraging signs that Zambia's epidemic may be following the course charted by Uganda.

But elsewhere, where far less has been done to encourage safer sex, the reasons for the relative stability remain obscure. Research is under way to explain the differences between epidemics in different countries. Factors that may play a role include patterns of sexual networking, levels of condom use with different partners, the availability of condoms and promptness in diagnosing and curing other sexually transmitted diseases (which if left untreated can magnify 20-fold the risk of HIV transmission through sex).

The overall provision of condoms to sub -Saharan Africa is only 4.6 per man per year, so another 1.9 billion condoms need to be provided if all countries are to have the same amount as the highest six countries in Africa.

247

Botswana, South Africa, Zimbabwe, Togo, Congo and Kenya are supplied with about 17 condoms per man aged 15 to 59 years. It would cost an estimated $47.5 million (£34m) a year to fill the 1.9 billion condom gap excluding service delivery costs and production. Relative to the enormity of the HIV/AIDS pandemic in Africa, providing condoms is cheap and cost effective.1

However condoms are not without their drawbacks, especially in the context of a stable partnership where pregnancy is desired, or where it may be difficult for one partner to suddenly suggest using condoms. For many individuals and couples in Africa, where HIV prevalence rates are high, finding out their infection status could expand their range of HIV prevention options.

How much would it cost, and what needs to be done, to make a difference?

As the illness and death from AIDS rose in Africa, some two decades ago, one or two countries reacted quickly. Other countries waited longer before intensifying their efforts, but they too are being rewarded for their efforts. There have been a number of success stories which include Senegal, Uganda and Zambia. But most countries in Africa lost valuable time because AIDS was not fully understood and its significance as a new epidemic was not grasped. Some action was taken, but not on the scale that was required to stem the tide of the epidemic. The scale of action necessary does of course increase exponentially along with the epidemic. Early on in a heterosexual epidemic, most new infections are acquired and passed on by a minority of people with an especially high turnover of partners. If condoms are used in most of these transactions, the epidemic can be contained relatively easily. But once HIV has become firmly established in the general population, most new infections occur in the majority of adults who do not have an especially high number of partners. This means that prevention campaigns have to be expanded greatly, making them harder and costlier, though still very worthwhile.

Most countries in Africa are at this stage. Yet few have expanded their HIV prevention programmes to the scale that would be needed to make a significant dent in the number of new infections. Since past prevention failures eventually turn into current care needs, failure to head off the epidemic early on also imposes a greater burden of care on countries where HIV prevalence is high. And as the HIV-infected fall ill and die, alleviating the impact on orphans, other survivors, families and communities becomes the third challenge.

Recently researchers have tried to determine how much money would be needed to make a real difference to the AIDS epidemic in Africa, and it is clear that scaling up the response to Africa's epidemic is not only imperative but it is affordable.

At least US$1.5 billion a year could make it possible to achieve massively higher levels of implementation of all the major components of successful prevention programmes for the whole of sub-Saharan Africa. These would cover sexual, mother-to-child and transfusion-related HIV transmission, and would involve approaches ranging from awareness campaigns through the media to voluntary HIV counseling and testing, and the promotion and supply of condoms.

In the area of care for orphans and for people living with HIV or AIDS, costs depend very much on what kind of care is being provided. It is estimated that, with at least US$1.5 billion a year, countries in sub-Saharan Africa could buy symptom and pain relief (palliative care) for at least half of AIDS patients in need of it; treatment and prophylaxis for opportunistic infections for a somewhat smaller proportion; and care for AIDS orphans. At the moment, the coverage of care in many African countries is negligible, so reaching coverage at these levels would be an enormous step forward.

Making a start on coverage with combination anti-retroviral therapy would add several billion dollars annually to the bill.

Of course, providing AIDS prevention and care services involves more than just these funds. A country's health, education, communication and other infrastructures have to be well developed to be able to deliver these interventions. In some badly affected countries, these systems are already under strain, and they are likely to crumble further under the weight of AIDS. Then, too, money can only be used wisely if there are sufficient people available and the shortage of trained men, women and young is already acute.

These are some of the serious challenges that African countries and their partners in the global community if they are to make a difference to the epidemic.

Source:
1)'Not enough condoms are supplied to African men' BMJ, Vol.323, 21 July 2001UNAIDS Report, AIDS Epidemic Update, December 2001
UNAIDS: AIDS epidemic update: December, 2000
UNAIDS: Report on the global HIV/AIDS epidemic, June 2000
UNAIDS Factsheet: AIDS in Africa, Johannesburg, 30th November 1998

AVERT (AIDS Education and Research Trust) is a leading UK based AIDS Education and Medical Research charity. They are responsible for a wide range of education and medical research work with the overall aim of preventing people from becoming infected with HIV and improving the quality of life of those already infected, by conducting medical research for developing a cure for AIDS.

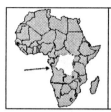	**what is an ebola virus?**	neal rolfe chamberlain democratic republic of congo 1997

An emerging disease from Africa.

Before we get into a discussion of Ebola viruses and the diseases they cause, I want you to know that this is a very, very, very rare disease. There have only been 4 major outbreaks of human Ebola hemorrhagic fever in recorded history. All of the outbreaks of human Ebola virus disease started in Africa. The largest epidemic infected 550 people. All the epidemics were contained by the use of sanitary hospital procedures.

There are 5 known Ebola viruses. They are Ebola Zaire (EBOZ), Ebola Sudan (EBOS), Ebola Tai (EBOT), Ebola Reston (EBOR), and Ebola Gabon (EBOG). The viruses got their name from the Ebola river in Zaire, Africa. This is where the virus was first discovered. The second name of each virus refers to the place where that particular strain of Ebola was first found. These viruses are members of the filovirus family. A great picture of the virus can be seen at the Access Excellence website.

EBOZ, EBOS, EBOG, and EBOT can infect humans. The most deadly Ebola virus is EBOZ (about 90% fatality rate). EBOS has a 60% fatality rate. A recent report (Courbot-Georges, M.C. et.al.,1997. Isolation and Phylogenetic Characterization of Ebola Viruses Causing Different Outbreaks in Gabon. Vol. 3, No. 1. Emerging Infectious Diseases, pg.59-62) mentions EBOG. This strain of Ebola is present in Gabon, Africa. The EBOR virus was initially discovered in a monkey housing facility in Reston, Virginia, USA. It does NOT cause disease in humans. It only causes disease in monkeys. The monkeys were captured initially in the Philippines and were already infected when they arrived in Maryland. EBOT has only been reported infecting one person so far and that person survived.

These viruses are found only in Africa and the Philippines. It is still not known what animals the viruses live in and how the first person gets the virus from the wild. We do know that if someone is infected with the virus they can only infect other people through close personal contact. That means persons who handle the sick person's blood and other body fluids can get the disease.

Ebola viruses cause hemorrhagic fever in humans. After being infected by the virus it usually takes 6-12 days for a person to start getting sick. The disease begins with fever, chills, headache, loss of appetite, and muscle aches. If the person has a very lethal strain of Ebola then the disease can get worse. Vomiting, diarrhea, abdominal pain, sore throat, and chest pain can occur. The virus causes damage to the blood vessels of the patient; in severe cases, the blood fails to clot. The patient may see blood in their stools and vomit. Their skin may have little pinpoint red spots like blood blisters. They may then go into shock from blood loss.

How do you stop the spread of this disease? The infected person should be taken to a hospital. Hospital personnel caring for these patients must wear gloves and protective clothing when caring for these patients. They should not reuse needles. All body fluids from the patient must be properly disposed of.

Around 80% of those infected with the ebola virus die from the infection.

Neal Rolfe Chamberlain is currently an associate professor at the Kirksville College of Osteopathic Medicine (KCOM). He's interested in the microorganisms that cause human illness, health and health related issues.

He graduated from Indiana University of Pennsylvania (1980) with a B.S. in Biology, then went to Ohio State University and obtained a Ph.D. in Medical Microbiology and Immunology (1985). After graduation, he moved to Dallas, Texas, where he was a postdoctoral fellow for 3.5 years at the University of Texas Southwestern Medical School at Dallas. He was offered a faculty position at KCOM in March of 1989. He's still at KCOM and is currently a tenured associate professor. He lives in a small mid western town that he's grown to love. It is a great place to raise the kids.

	**dance me down fortune**	mark igoe zimbabwe 1979

Early one morning in the spring of 1979, a group of villagers near Mutoko in north eastern Zimbabwe found a body lying on the main road to the north. Death had become familiar to these people who were living amid a vicious war between the guerrillas of Robert Mugabe's Zimbabwe National Liberation Army and the security forces of the Rhodesian government. But this corpse was different and some claimed to have heard singing and seen a white bird hover nearby. It was soon established that the body was John Bradburne, a member of the Third Order of St Francis who worked in the nearby leper colony. He had been a strange aesthetic and mystical man, much loved by the lepers, much distrusted by the authorities. To his friends he confided his three life time ambitions: to work with lepers, to die a martyr and to be buried in his Franciscan habit.

A week later his funeral service was held in Salisbury's (now Harare) Roman Catholic cathedral. A mourner, who had just placed a poesy of three flowers on his coffin in memory of the dead man's devotion to the Trinity, noticed three drops of blood on the floor beneath it. The blood was fresh. The coffin was opened: it was found that the body was not dressed in a Franciscan habit and this was rectified. Thus, say the believers, Bradburne's last wish was fulfilled.

But this was the beginning, not the end of a phenomenon. The intercession of John Bradburne was claimed by some to cure cancer. Strange appearances of eagles and bees, the two creatures most associated with the man when he was alive, occurred. Two Englishmen, who had never visited Zimbabwe, claimed to have had their sight restored through prayer to Bradburne. A cult grew up that in character was pure Mediterranean. And this in a country that is African, anglophone and secular: perhaps even stranger was that the subject of the cult was a middle class Englishman.

The origin of the connection with bees goes back to a story that on two occasions Bradburne successfully prayed that bees nest near his room so that interruption to his meditations might be discouraged. Judy Joe, a woman of mixed descent, became a devotee of Bradburne and spent her free time collecting second hand clothes for his lepers. When she died of leukaemia a picture of Bradburne was found in her bedside drawer. On it was bees' nest.

Angus Shaw was a white Zimbabwean journalist. He had a column in Harare's main national daily which was popular, ironic and mildly anti-clerical. In 1982 he decided to research the Bradburne phenomenon and visited the leper colony where he had worked, Mutemwa, near Mutoko. His interviews over, he returned to his car to find it full of bees. He expelled them and returned to his Harare office. As he arrived his domestic rang and told him that a swarm of bees had invested his flat. He told her to call the pest control people. As he sat by his type writer in the city center, he noticed several bees in the office and a swarm trying to get into the window. It was then that he recalled the Bradburne bee incidents. He was shaken. Later he said that day nearly converted him and was certainly a milestone in his life.

And so the stories accumulated. A John Bradburne Memorial society was set up and pamphlets and pictures circulated. The Englishman who had claimed restoration of his sight sent a thousand pounds for the erection of a cross at Mutemwa, which now stands on the hill where Bradburne once lived. Other miracles were reported. John Dove, a friend and confident of Bradburne, wrote his biography which he called *Strange Vagabond of God*. Certainly it is a strange story.

John Randal Bradburne was born in Skirwith, Cumbria, England in 1921. His father was a parson; he had two brothers and two sisters. Lord Soames, the statesman, was a relative; Terrence Rattigan, the playwright, a cousin. His early life seems to have been happy and secure; his family was cultured and it was at this time his love of music and poetry developed. This period must also have been the cradle of his love for nature as he and his siblings roamed the hills and valleys of the Lake District. He went to secondary school at the long established Gresham's School in Norfolk when his father had been installed in the nearby parish of Cawston.

He joined the British Army on leaving school and was commissioned into the second battalion of the elite 9th Gurkha Rifles. 1940 found him in Singapore when it fell. His battalion fled to the jungle rather than surrender and he and another officer survived on fruit and roots for a month before stealing a boat and crossing the straits, at the second attempt, to Sumatra. They caught the last British war ship to leave the island and eventually rejoined the Gurkhas at Dehra Dun in the foot hills of the Himalayas. Here he met another officer who was to have a profound effect on his life, John Dove. Inspecting his brigade before the invasion of Burma, General Wingate singled out Bradburne and congratulated him on his escape and the award of a Military Cross, a decoration that was never actually presented. Bradburne fought in Burma but was evacuated with recurrent malaria.

At some point during his adventures in the east, John Bradburne had become intensely spiritual. This was not a noticeable trait before the war and rather bemused his brothers. After demobilization he entered Buckfast Abbey, near where his father had retired in Devon, with a view to becoming a Catholic and a monk. The first he did, but decided the Carthusian order would suit him better, so he went to work as a layman doorkeeper at Parkminster. This was not what he was looking for either. After a bit the prior advised him to go to Rome and pray for guidance.

At Rome he believed his prayers were answered by a summons to Jerusalem. Off he set, financed by the pilgrims he had met *en route* and whom had been captivated by him. He reached Israel via Cyprus where he had traveled in an open grain boat, then walked to Jerusalem. Having reached his goal he asked the way to the house of the Benedictines at Mount Sion but was misdirected to the establishment of a tiny missionary order called Our Lady of Mount Sion. He took this mistake to be a sign, and applied for membership; he was sent to their mother house in Louvain in Belgium. After a year both he and the Novice Master agreed the order was not for him and he walked and begged his way to Rome again.

He wanted to return to Jerusalem but this time there were no friendly pilgrims to sponsor him. He was eventually taken in by a friendly priest in a village above Naples. Here he stayed for a whole year, living in the organ loft and playing the organ by night. Then his father died and he returned to England. There followed a period of intense self searching, which included a period spent being a hermit on Dartmoor, a Benedictine monk, a sacristan in Westminster Cathedral, a house keeper for Cardinal Godfrey and working for the publisher Burnes Oates. But he couldn't obtain the solitude he craved. He wrote to John Dove, now a priest in Rhodesia, asking if there was a cave in Africa in which he could pray. Dove responded enthusiastically and the Franciscans paid the fare.

He worked for a period with the Franciscans, joining the Third Order of St Francis, a group of laymen dedicated to work among the poor. Then he helped John Dove set up Silveira House, a Jesuit training establishment. Here the first incidents involving eagles and bees occurred. But his spiritual longings were still unfulfilled and he returned to Jerusalem. Here he felt that he had been told that he had a mission in Africa.

Mutemwa leper colony near Mutoko was in 1968 a horror of neglect. About ninety lepers lived there with minimal care and in squalor. The local magistrate's wife approached the Church for help. This was to be Bradburne's mission. He became warden. With the help of an Italian missionary doctor, Luisa Guidotti, he reorganized the settlement, built accommodation and a church, but, most of all, gave the lepers his complete devotion. His reckless love earned theirs and Mutemwa became a landmark of pride, rather than shame.

But the improvements cost money and inevitably he came into conflict with the committee that administered Mutemwa. Relations deteriorated until he was dismissed. But he would not leave. He slept on the mountain that overlooks the settlement, washing in its rain fed pools and walking in a circle on the bare rock as he prayed. At night he would creep back into the colony to comfort the sick and pray with the dying. Eventually a local white farmer, mindful of the leopard that shared the mountain, had a little tin hut erected outside the colony gates where he could sleep in safety if not in comfort.

Eventually the committee changed and he was allowed back to minister to his lepers, to change dressings and dig graves. But the liberation war was now reaching its climax and the environment outside Mutemwa had become bitter and violent. Army convoys rolled through the day and gunfire shattered the night. Luisa Guidotti was killed by security forces when she failed to stop at a roadblock. Bradburne fought ferociously to protect the interest of his wards and angered local people when he stopped their cattle grazing the lepers' gardens or caught a thief stealing their possessions.

And so one of the aggrieved people reported to the local commander of the insurgent force, ZANLA, that Bradburne was a Rhodesian government spy and that he had a radio in his room. On Sunday 2nd September 1979 Bradburne preached a sermon to his little congregation on the martyrdom of St Lawrence, asking them to pray that he would have courage *when they came for him*. They came that night. He was held in a neighboring village for 24 hours and then on Tuesday night, taken to a cave on Tuesday night where the guerrillas were gathered, and tried. His trial took many hours but eyewitnesses said he paid little attention. He had found his cave in Africa.

The guerrilla commander realized the radio was only a receiver and found Bradburne innocent, asking him to go to Mozambique and work among refugees there. Bradburne refused saying he could not leave Mutemwa. It is not clear what happened next. Probably he was considered too much of a security risk to be let go. *Come sweet death on Wednesday*, he had once written. On Wednesday morning, his body was found on the road leading north from Mutoko. He had been shot in the back by an AK 47 rifle.

I never met John Bradburne. I heard about him not long after his death. I was fascinated by morbid details for example, his body showed no signs of decomposition when the coffin was opened in the cathedral. I knew, and still know, Angus Shaw. Years passed. Then one day in the early nineties I was playing hide-and-seek with my children in the lovely Ewanrigg Aloe Gardens near Harare. Somewhere near the herb garden I heard a tune which I recognized but could not place, and went to find its source.

In a clearing, also with children was a youthful looking man in shorts and tee shirt playing a recorder. I asked him what the tune was. He said it was a Renaissance trotto, but he couldn't remember the name. I told him I had a recording of it by Renbourne on guitar. We fell to talking. He lectured in music at the University of Western Australia. He had been a Franciscan novice for a bit. Now he had a family. He was going to Mutoko. All this put me in mind of John Bradburne. He knew, of course, of John Bradburne; that was one of the reasons he was going to Mutoko. We became friends. His name was Glin Marillier. When he left for Australia, I remarked that it was a coincidence that a piece of music should have introduced us to a shared interest in Bradburne. Then he said something that made the hair stand up on the back of my neck. *John Bradburne often works like that.*

Here was this cultured, intelligent, well-educated man, calmly assuming that our meeting had been preordained by a religious eccentric who had been dead for over a decade. I resolved to visit Mutemwa. When I did, it was jacaranda season and the little group of huts and chapel, where Bradburne used to play the organ, was set against a riot of blue blossom. I was shown around the colony and introduced to some of the patients who remembered Baba (father) John with delight. I climbed the huge granite dome, that dominates the site, which, as far as I recall, was called Chingoma. This Bradburne shared with the leopard. Here stands the cross, donated by the Englishman. From here the beautiful undulating Mashonaland countryside rolls away toward the distant Nyanga Mountains and eagles ride thermals. Here also, worn in the colorful lichen of the rock, is the circular path worn by the feet of John Bradburne as he walked round and round in prayer. It has become a place of pilgrimage.

Another place of pilgrimage is the prefab tin hut by the settlement gate. Some of his poetry is on the wall. For apart from being an accomplished musician, the Strange Vagabond left 6000 pages of poetry.

Mime it I might and hobble lame across some stage
Rigged up to tell some philanthropic audience
What is true honor and true courage in our age,
Heaven forbid that I shall ever get the chance!
Dance me down, Fortune - saw I not this very morn
Aristocratic spirits in their smitten frames
Go nobly on with living?

(MUTEMWA IS AT MUTOKO IN NORTH EASTERN ZIMBABWE ON THE ROAD TO MALAWI. JOHN RANDAL BRADBURNE IS BURIED AT CHISHAWASHA MISSION IN HARARE. THE FIRST STEPS HAVE BEEN TAKEN TOWARDS HIS EVENTUAL CANONIZATION).

See page 55, for biography of **Mark Igoe**.

| **the african way of death** | aidan hartley kenya 2000 |

Driving through a slummy part of Nairobi this week I passed a sign that said 'READY MADE COFFINS'. It made me think of my mate Brian Tetley, who went out in such high style four years ago. Brian was a hack of the old school who had settled in Kenya during colonial times. He loved it so much he stayed on to craft snappy leads down here for the rest of his days—apart from a brief stint back in the 'Yoo Kay' on The Sunday Sport. I got to know him as a young foreign correspondent when he worked for the indomitable Mo Amin, the cameraman who shot the famous TV footage of the Ethiopian famine. Mo's business empire included a publishing wing and Brian was his greatest friend, writer and editor. Brian was a fast worker, but he used to go on drinking benders that lasted for days—and in lieu of a monthly salary, Mo used to pick up his bar bills.

Brian got bowel cancer, but did he care? He used to cheerfully wander about the bar, massaging his cholostomy bag with a fag in one hand and a bottle of Tusker in the other. In time, the pain became intense and Brian told me over the last drink we shared that he reckoned he was not long for this world.

A few days later I was watching CNN and saw the pictures of an Ethiopian Airlines jet crashing into the Indian Ocean. Both Mo and Brian were among the dead. The plane had been hijacked by a gang of drunken maniacs who claimed to have a bomb and demanded to be flown to Australia, of all places. As the aircraft ran out of fuel the pilot tried to land on the island of Grande Comore but he couldn't make it and ditched the plane on a coral reef.

Back to the 'READY MADE COFFINS'. Not so long ago in East Africa, people were interred without having to be put into silly boxes. There's the famous story of the colonial-era boozer—and let's face it, Brian should have been allowed to die of drink—who left money for his butler to erect a pipe leading from the top of his burial plot into his dead body's open mouth. On the anniversary of his death, the butler was instructed to purchase a bottle of gin and pour it down the pipe. My father gave instructions that he should be buried in his old safari shorts and nothing else because 'a coffin's a waste of trees'. In the event we cremated him in a Mombasa Hindu temple and scattered his ashes around our old ranch at the foot of Kilimanjaro.

These days, it's illegal to bury a body without a coffin. Due to the dreadful economic recession, stories abound in the local newspapers about thieves digging up corpses at night to steal coffins and sell them back to the funeral homes. Corteges on their way out to western Kenya, where tradition demands that the dead are buried in their ancestral homelands, are waylaid by highwaymen and looted.

I mention this because of what happened at Brian's funeral. Mo got buried swiftly, as the Moslems don't dither over such things, but Brian's burial was a more protracted and drunken affair. His friends dressed him in his only good suit and somebody wedged a bottle of Tusker under each armpit to speed him on his way. All the neighbors in the scuzzy Nairobi district where Brian lived filed past the open coffin before the lid was closed and it was this that suddenly caused a ripple of concern. It was only a matter of time, one bright spark pointed out, before word got out that Brian was dressed in that smart suit and that he was armed with two bottles of Kenya's finest. And when that happened, it would only be a matter of time before some graverobber stole into the cemetery where he was buried and dug him up. A debate ensued and a failsafe solution was eventually found. This involved a cement mixer and several loads of quick-setting concrete, which the mourners poured into Brian's grave as soon as he was lowered into it. That way, even an army of thieves armed with pick axes couldn't get to Brian Tetler's bottles of Tusker and his one good suit.

Aidan Hartley was born in Nairobi and raised in both East Africa and Devon, in England. He took degrees at Balliol College, Oxford and the Institute of Commonwealth Studies, London University. In 1988 he returned to Africa and began to make a living in journalism for some years as a Reuters correspondent. He was on the road constantly and covered more than a dozen wars, famines and coups in Africa and the Balkans. After sustained immersion in Somalia and Rwanda, he resigned. A succession of places and jobs followed: sheep farming on a Kenyan ranch; freelancing in Eritrea, Israel, Russia and Yemen, where he researched the life of a colonial British political officer who lived and died on the edge of the Ramlat as Sabateyn desert. In London he began to write and married Claire. Together they returned to Kenya, where their first child Eve was born. He writes the weekly Wild Life column for The Spectator magazine. His book Empty Quarter is being published by HarperCollins (UK) and Grove/Atlantic (USA).

| **closest thing to hell on earth** | salim amin
ethiopia
1984 |

The turmoil of Africa's emergence into the 20th century has long been the focus of the critical eye of the Western World. From exploration to exploitation, from fear to famine and fortune; from war torn horror to wildlife wonder; it has been exposed to the relentless gaze of the international press.

No one caught has caught its pain and passion more insightfully than Mahand Amin, photographer and frontline cameraman extraordinare. He was the most famous photographer in the world, making the news as often as he covered it. 'Mo' trained his unwavering lens on every aspect of African life, never shying from the tragedy, never failing to exult the success. He was born into an Africa at the high noon of colonial decline and by his early teens was already documenting events which were soon to dominate world news. He witnessed and recorded the alternating currents of his beloved continent and beyond, projecting those images across the world, sometimes shocking, sometimes delighting millions of television viewers and newspaper readers.

His coverage of the 1984 Ethiopian famine proved so compelling that it inspired a collective global conscience and became the catalyst for the greatest-ever act of giving. Unquestionably, it also saved millions of men, women and children.

He was a legendary figure who left a legacy far greater than his pictures.

The events, which brought about the Ethiopian famine of 1984 add up to a litany of despair seldom recorded in the annals of global disasters. The cruelest acts of nature and man fused into circumstances of such horrifying magnitude that, even with the passage of years, it is still hard to contemplate the consequences.

Mo's pivotal role in focusing world attention on the plight of starving millions must be seen as a landmark in the turbulent history of the continent. It was not just a matter of being in the right place at the right time. After all, Mo fought for months for permission to visit the relief camps. Had he not been so determined, had he not stubbornly refused to be thwarted by a bungling bureaucracy mindful of its own lackluster role in the nightmare, the harsh facts might never have been exposed. Put simply: if Mo had not acted when he did in the way he did, millions more men, women and children would have starved to death.

Shortly after Easter (spent filming the East African Safari Rally with his son Salim, Willetts and Tetley) Mo joined a press party for a two-week tour of Somalia, Ethiopia and Djibouti to look at refugee repatriation schemes. The trip was organized by the UN High Commissioner for Refugees and was intended to show what was being done to help victims of the drought-stricken Horn of Africa. It was the first indication of the immense human tragedy to come. The Horn had been in the grip of drought for nearly a decade and little had been done to alleviate the effects. The ensuing sequence of events was an inexorable slide to disaster. At first cattle suffered; as the animals grew thinner, farmers had to sell them cheaply before they died as worthless bags of bones. Then the crops withered and died in the relentless heat and arid conditions. Once fertile ground became sterile wasteland.

Soon, reserves of food began to run out and, with no money to buy more, people began to starve. Relief camps were set up and a tide of skeletal humans trekked slowly into these isolated oases of hope. And hope was about all that could be dispensed. Agencies, overwhelmed by the scale of the problem, had very little food to offer. It was too little too late. No one had considered the enormity of what was happening. Outside the region, few seemed to care.

During his tour of the area, government Relief and Rehabilitation Commissioner Dawit Wolde Georgis took advantage of a press conference to warn of the risk of death by starvation of six to seven million people. He gave an interview to BBC reporter Mike Wooldridge which Mo filmed.

A major disaster was unfolding before the eyes of a seemingly ignorant and uncaring world and Mo knew he could not stand by. He discussed it with Wooldridge and they agreed they should try to reach the most seriously affected relief camps of Korem and Makele in Ethiopia's province of Tigre. This would be no easy task, for Ethiopia's Marxist regime, under Colonel Mengistu Haile Mariam, was at that time involved in a fierce battle with guerrillas fighting for freedom for the highland region and Eritrea.

These were restricted areas for foreigners and the government was understandably sensitive about allowing journalists to visit them, particularly as one film crew - on the pretext of covering the famine - had concentrated instead on the war zone. It was against this background that Mo began a six-month campaign to get permission to visit Korem and Makele.

His first gambit on returning from the press trip, was to write an exclusive front page story in *The Nation* newspaper in Kenya, highlighting the impending peril. The paper ran it under the banner headline '*Millions face death in Ethiopia.*' Mo reported: "Between five and seven million people could die in the next two months if the world does not act. The worst drought in Ethiopia's history has now spread into its once-fertile highlands with more than a fifth of its 31 million people victims. During the last 12 days, by DC-3, helicopter and four-wheel drive vehicle, I have traveled thousands of Kilometers across the Horn of Africa to witness one of Africa's greatest tragedies in the making. Yet despite appeals at the highest level, the world has turned a blind eye to the starving nomads and refugees in Ethiopia, Djibouti, Somalia and Sudan." The story was also sent to Western newspapers.

By coincidence, an hour-long documentary called *Seeds of Despair,* scheduled for screening by Britain's Central TV in mid-July, 1984, was in the making in the area near Korem. At the same time, Britain's Disasters and Emergency Committee, comprising major fund-raising charities, decided to launch an 11-nation appeal for starving Africa. At first, the Independent Broadcasting Authority cast doubts on whether the crisis was of sufficient severity to justify a national TV appeal, but the film soon convinced them.

The BBC also agreed to run an appeal the same day, calling in their Africa correspondent Michael Buerk, who was then operating out of South Africa, to supply the material. They asked Mo, Visnews' Africa bureau chief, to provide the pictures.

But Mo was already on safari with Brooke Shields, filming for an episode of the US TV series *Lifestyles of the Rich and Famous,* so the job was passed to Mohinder Dhillon. He quickly delivered first class footage, including shots of Buerk with famine victims. These two jointly televised appeals and a brief news item produced an amazing response from viewers. Donations flowed in and soon totaled £10 million. On July 20, Buerk made his first contact with Mo with the brief message: "A note to say thank you for all your help in the miracles that led to a very successful story. Without your contacts it would not have been possible."

Mo then went to India for the second *Lifestyles* shoot. When filming was over, he traveled to Germany for the Frankfurt Book Fair where he had several new publications to promote. He then headed home via Visnews in London where he learned he was wanted back in Ethiopia. He arrived on October 12, and next day received a message from Buerk urging him to follow up the Ethiopian story. Mohinder Dhillon's film had, at last, begun to stir international interest.

Mo had been working for months on the problem of·obtaining entry and travel permits to Ethiopia for himself, Wooldridge and a sound man, and now he discovered the BBC, were desperate to get Buerk in the picture as well. News editors had been so surprised by the response to the earlier story they were keen for a crew to go back as soon as possible. They wanted more comprehensive coverage of the situation in the relief camps.

There followed a prolonged telex dialogue between Buerk and Mo in which it soon became clear that the crucial factor was Mo's ability to obtain the relevant permits. Having spent so long persuading the Ethiopian authorities to allow three of them in, he was doubtful they would accept one more journalist. More worrying such additional pressure on the already disinclined authorities might be the last straw and persuade them to cancel all the permits.

It should be remembered that, at that time, Mengistu's regime was involved in several internecine struggles within its boundaries. These were costly exercises for a fragile economy and as a result there had been little state help for the starving. Conscious that any story on the true situation in the camps would reflect badly on the government, officials were not well disposed to inquiring Western journalists. In addition, they were anxious not to have their internal strife aired to the world. Against this background, Mo had already achieved considerable progress in getting as far as he had.

He reminded Buerk: "Although I am known as a 'friend of Ethiopia,' I still need travel permits like anyone else.' Nonetheless, Buerk persisted and Mo reluctantly agreed to try to get the additional documents.

Now, as never before, he needed to rely on that renowned contacts book and *call* in favors. Mo said: "Getting permits was very, very difficult. I had already spent months trying to get permission to go north. I had been negotiating with Tafari Wossen, information chief for the Government's Relief and Rehabilitation Commission, and when I called him again at his house he was not at all happy. It had taken him a long time to get the permits for the three of us. To add another name was almost impossible.

"I had known Tafari for more than 20 years and put a lot of pressure on him, explaining our visit was for the benefit of millions of his countrymen. Eventually, he said he'd try to help us but made no promises. Then I contacted Visnews and explained there was a delay caused by getting the additional paperwork. They were getting anxious because they felt the story was cooling in Western minds. If it wasn't filmed soon it could be too late for everyone concerned. I called Tafari again and again until he finally agreed to make it possible for Mike to come with us.'

On the morning of Wednesday, October 17,1984, Mo met Buerk at his Nairobi office, together with Wooldridge. Later that day, they flew to Addis with soundman Zack Njuguna. From the moment they arrived they had to tackle an assault course of obdurate bureaucracy, the first obstacle being the discovery that permission to go north had been withdrawn by the Relief and Rehabilitation Commission.

Mo said: "Tafari explained that they had decided they didn't want us to go to Makele or Korem. Instead, they wanted to take us to other places and show us their resettlement schemes. They accused us of only being interested in showing the horrors and not what the government was doing to solve the problem. This, of course, was partly true but I argued that it was not the case and that we had to show the problems before we could show the solutions.

"I said that the problem was on such a large scale that, whatever the existing solutions, they were only a drop in the ocean; we had to go north to where the situation was most critical. Tafari remained unconvinced, so in the end we had an argument and I stormed out of his office and went to check in at the Addis Hilton. From there, I made more phone calls, which left me without a shadow of a doubt that Makele and Korem were the places we had to get to. I went back to Tafari's office but he was out for the day. Then I marched into the commissioner's office. He was in a meeting so I went to see the deputy commissioner who was in. He appeared not to know what I was talking about and was surprised we'd been given the permits in the first place, let alone had them withdrawn. But I kept on at him and in the end he promised to have them reinstated and gave us permission to go to Makele and Korem. So I sat in his office while he made the relevant phone calls and was finally told to come back that afternoon to pick up the permits.'

It had gone almost too well for Mo's liking. The cameraman began to suspect a hidden agenda. He was right; the deputy commissioner knew that, even with the permits, the road route was too difficult and dangerous to travel and would take several days - time the journalists did not have. The only alternative was to go in by air. But they discovered there was only one company running charter planes and it flatly refused to go north. The permits held by the newsmen were beginning to look like so many worthless scraps of paper, until Mo resolved the problem.

Often daunted but seldom defeated, he went to visit the Addis office of World Vision, a Christian relief organization, and discovered they too wanted to get to the relief camps but had also encountered a wall of bureaucratic resistance. However, they did have one vital advantage over Mo's party - they had an aircraft. They had been trying to get permission to take relief supplies to the camps for three months without success. Mo saw his solution.

He said: "We made a deal. If I could get the permit, we could go in their plane. I went back to the deputy commissioner who was furious I'd found access to an aircraft. But he was put in a position where he had to give permission and we finally got the vital documents."

On the morning of Friday, October 19, the newsmen loaded World Vision's Twin Otter and filed a flight plan north that took in the ancient city of Lalibela. But once they had taken off, they decided to give the town a miss. It was just as well, for they later learned that at about the time they would have been landing there it was occupied by Eritrean rebels. Had they landed, the story of the famine might have been very different, for they would almost certainly have been incarcerated for weeks. In the event, they flew straight on and two hours later, at noon, were touching down at Makele and preparing for a day's filming.

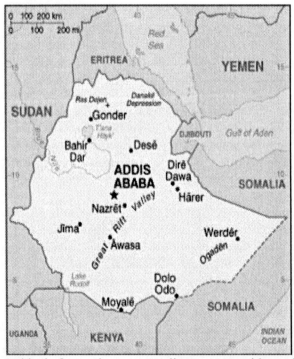

Any sense of achievement they might have had at finally reaching the camps was quickly dispelled by the sight that greeted them. Hardened though he was by 25 years in the frontline, nothing could have prepared Mo for what he and his colleagues now beheld.

The scene was a vast plain amid the mountainous highlands laid bare by a decade of drought. To this desiccated spot, tens of thousands of men, women and children had trekked from the surrounding countryside, which was now a barren dustbowl. Some had been on the road for days. All were hungry, most were literally starving, many were dying. An average of 100 deaths was being recorded every day. A large majority of them were children. At Korem and another relief center, Alamata, 700 kilometers north of Addis, it was the same story.

266

The statistics created their own macabre record book: in a country of 33 million people, 7.7 million were affected by the drought, 5.5 million were starving and 2.2 million were obliged to leave their homes to seek help. In Alamata camp, two doctors, three nurses and three nutritionists were tending 100,000 people. Another 90,000 victims waited patiently outside the camp for aid. The doctors had enough food for 3,000. The chance of more supplies was as remote as the camp itself because the rebels had cut off the area, and any convoys that did attempt the journey were likely to fall foul of the impoverished and hungry guerrillas.

At Korem, another 100,000 sufferers had gathered with 80,000 more on the outside. Thousands more were heading to the camps each day. Every 24 hours another 300 arrived, all at starvation level. In a desperate attempt to prolong their lives, nurses at Korem fed 500 children each day on a high-energy diet of powdered milk and biscuits.

There was not much to talk about. The journalists went about their respective tasks in subdued mood. Mo filmed it all, never flinching from the worst tragedies. People were literally dying in front of his camera. Already he realized they were witnessing a disaster of catastrophic proportions and he knew it was their duty to document it and bring it to the attention of the world.

Wooldridge will never forget stepping off the plane into that biblical wasteland. He said: "Makele was absolutely appalling - the sheer depth of the tragedy was mind-numbing. Everywhere we walked, people were dying. In one shelter a nun told us that someone was dying every few minutes and it wasn't just the old and young. Normally fit people were keeling over. "I watched Mo framing and Mike doing his report to camera. There was none of the usual banter. Normally Mo relieved a tough situation with humor, but not there. I could see he was devastated. But he just kept filming.

"I remember walking around trying to do radio commentary and I doubted whether I could actually convey the truth, if there were actually words which could portray what I was seeing. You didn't need adjectives." I had been with Mo on the earlier tour of the Horn of Africa and I thought I had become used to horrifying images, but this was something else entirely.

"It was so quiet, I think, because the people did not have the energy to make any noise. The only sound you heard was the wailing and crying of the grief-stricken. If they had to move, it was with a quiet dignity - that was all they had left. One man came up to me and offered me his son because he could do nothing more for him. I was heartbroken."

Buerk still finds it hard to recall those tragic scenes: "It was the closest thing to hell on earth - like walking into a scene from the Bible. I had never seen anything like it before nor have I since. There were all these people, thousands of them sitting around waiting either to get food or to die. The doctors and nurses were making life or death decisions all the time. It was an agony for them all.

"I felt completely helpless; all they wanted was food and there was nothing we could do about that, so we did the only thing we could and filmed it. Mo knelt down and let his camera pan around these quiet people without disturbing them, then we'd move on. The scale of it was almost impossible to comprehend."

With rare candour, Mo admitted: "Ethiopia changed me. Until then I had been able to go into any situation, no matter how awful, and switch off. I could remain at a distance from the subject, not get involved. My job is to act as an unbiased observer, to report what I see without making judgments.

"But this was different. You can't remain untouched when there are people dying as far as the eye can see, especially when so many of them are children. Some of those scenes which I filmed completely choked me up, though I tried not to show it. What got me was that these people hadn't done anything wrong; they were just victims, people who had no food. I don't think I have ever felt so helpless.

"Once I saw an incident where there was food for only 100 people and somebody had to choose who should receive it. There was no logical basis on which they could make that decision because all the people were in the same condition. It was tragically arbitrary. Every morning a nurse had to pick out the 150 babies to feed because that was all the food there was. By extending life to those 150, she was condemning others to die. It was as simple and as heartbreaking as that. I always thought of how that nurse must have felt. What a decision to have to make!"

Speaking to medical staff at Korem, the journalists recorded their reactions and were told that the most important aspect of their visit was to tell the outside world what was happening. They needed no second asking. Mo, Buerk and Wooldridge spent three days in Korem, Makele and Alamata documenting the tragedy. When they could film no more, Mo went back to World Vision and persuaded them to fly him and the crew to Addis on October 21. From there they flew back to Nairobi the next day, in time to go through the cassettes in Mo's editing suite.

Mo remembered: "It really hit me when we edited the film. As we were looking at the pictures, taking them back and forth and cutting them, it came home so hard I cried. So did everyone else who was in that room."

In the early hours of October 23, Buerk packed the edited tapes and flew back to London. That same day, the first brief news bulletin was televised at lunch time. In Nairobi, Mo worked ceaselessly to produce words and pictures about the famine as fast as possible. The following day, newspapers across the world were running the story, together with his haunting pictures.

And yet TV nearly passed the famine by as a news item. There had been so many stories on hungry people that cynical news editors were worried about viewers suffering from compassion fatigue. "Not more starving Africans," was the reaction of one network producer, and it was a feeling that was not without support. Indeed, Eurovision and NBC initially turned down Mo's film material until they saw it linked with Buerk's spare, but compelling commentary. It would have taken very little - a late- breaking story, some other major catastrophe closer to home - to relegate the Ethiopian famine to an also-ran.

When the BBC piece was screened, NBC's London office got straight on to their counterparts in New York to stress its importance and its dramatic impact. Tom Brokaw, NBC's veteran anchorman, described the day his news team viewed the footage: "Stories of mass hunger and death are not that uncommon, but with everything else that is going on these days often these stories don't have much impact. They're just words from far off places. Not any more. It was a moment I shall never forget. The entire newsroom came to a complete stop - and that's something very hard to do in any newsroom in the world.

"Not a breath was taken. When the film finished there was this utter silence; I think people were washed in their own thoughts, deeply moved by what they had seen. People remember me turning and saying 'If we don't put that on, we shouldn't be in this business.' What we didn't anticipate was the impact it would have in the US. It moved a nation as few other single reports ever have."

Paul Greenberg, then executive producer of NBC's *Nightly News,* also recalled the silence when the footage was shown. "All the side talk, the gossip and talk of the then presidential election campaign just stopped. Tears came to your eyes and you felt you'd just been hit in the stomach."

Similar scenes were taking place in newsrooms the world over. Much as they tried, hardened news men and women could not turn away from these haunting images. Irish pop musician Bob Geldof was at home watching TV with his wife Paula Yates when Mo's film was shown. Its effect upon him was so profound it moved him to launch Band Aid in which rock stars came together giving their services free and raising millions of pounds for the starving. In a foreword to Tetley's book on Mo in 1988, Geldof wrote: "I was confronted by something so horrendous I was wrenched violently from the complacency of another rather dispiriting day and pinioned - unable to turn away from the misery of another world inhabited by people only recognizable as humans by their magnificent dignity.

"I do not know why Mo Amin's pictures did this to me. God knows, if you watch an average night's news you are confronted with enough scenes of horror seriously to question man's sanity. But the tube also has the ability to shrink events and make them bearable in the context of your living room. Ultimately, one becomes immune, if not anaesthetized.

"But the pitiless, unrelenting gaze of this camera was different. Somehow this was not objective journalism but confrontation. There was a dare here -'I dare you to turn away, I dare you to do nothing'. Mo Amin had succeeded above all else in showing you his own disgust and shame and anger and making it yours also. It's certainly true that if it were not for that now historic broadcast, millions would be dead. There would have been no Band, Live or Sport Aid, no mass outpouring of humanity's compassion. No questioning of statutes, laws and values both inside and outside Africa. No reappraisal of development, of the nature of international aid, no debate on the mire Africa had become.

"In this brief, shocking but glorious moment Amin had transcended the role of journalist/cameraman and perhaps unwittingly become the visual interpreter of man's stinking conscience. He had always been among that breed considered extraordinary. He is without question an extraordinary man. I thank God that I was home that autumn evening. I thank God that I was watching that channel and I thank God that Mo Amin sickened and shamed me." In his autobiography *Is That It?,* Geldof spoke of that momentous evening with graphic clarity: "From the first second, it was clear that this was horror on a monumental scale. The pictures were of people so shrunken by starvation that they looked like beings from another planet. The camera wandered amidst them like a mesmerized observer, occasionally dwelling on one person so that he looked at me, sitting in my comfortable living room. Their eyes looked into mine. Paula (a TV presenter from whom Geldof is now divorced) burst into tears, then rushed upstairs to check on our baby.

"The images played and replayed in my mind. What could I do? All I could do was make records that no one bought. (At that time Geldof fronted a band called The Boomtown Rats). But I would give all the profits from the next Rats record to Oxfam. What good would it do? It would be a pitiful amount, but it would be more than I could raise simply by dipping into my shrunken bank account. Yet that was still not enough."

Geldof was galvanized into action. The following day he marched into the office of Phonogram and suggested the Band Aid record which stirred the conscience of Europe. He garnered the elite of British pop to produce the seasonal best seller *Do They Know It's Christmas?* Artists included Paul McCartney, Midge Ure, Phil Collins, Paul Young, Simon Le Bon, Bono,

Paul Weller, George Michael, Francis Rossi, Sting, Nick Rhodes, David Bowie and Boy George.

In turn, America responded by setting up USA for Africa. Spearheaded by Harry Belafonte and Ken Kragen, the organization brought off an incredible logistical coup by bringing together many of the top US music stars in Los Angeles, on January 27-28, 1985, to record *We Are The World.* The song was written by Michael Jackson and Lionel Richie, who were joined by Bruce Springsteen, Diana Ross, Paul Simon, Kenny Rogers, Ray Charles, Tina Turner, Stevie Wonder, Dionne Warwick and many others. It sold millions and raised more than $50 million for victims of the Ethiopian famine and other drought-hit countries in Africa. It was all brought to a conclusion with a colossal 16-hour Live Aid marathon concert screened worldwide which went on record as the greatest single charity event ever.

These international efforts began a ripple effect of giving which spread across the world. Unprompted, money poured in from families, individuals, children, organized groups, commercial concerns and governments. Not everyone gave cash. Farmers donated grain; a small British air charter company flew their plane to Addis to help with transport; dockers in Southampton, UK, refused overtime payments and worked through days off to load 100,000 tons of wheat bound for Ethiopia; many pharmaceutical companies donated urgently needed medical supplies. It was as if the world's financial floodgates had been flung wide open as everyone responded to the impact of Mo's images. Giving on such a monumental scale had never occurred before, nor has it since.

It has been estimated that 450 million people watched Mo's film; three presidents admitted they cried; one billion people watched the biggest pop concert in the world; Band Aid alone raised more than £100 million.

US President Ronald Reagan saw Mo's film. Visibly moved, he immediately pledged $45 million. Australian Prime Minister Bob Hawke watched the footage, wept, and launched a nationwide famine appeal. A week after the broadcast, the Save The Children Fund office in London recorded donations of more than £14 million. As well as state donations, ordinary American citizens freely gave another $70 million and similar stories of unprecedented generosity flooded in from all over the world. Three million people could have perished in the famine. But in the event, through intervention, one million died. That a million should die of want in a world where there is a surplus of food is a tragedy that shames mankind. That two million were saved when consciences were at last roused went some way to redeem humanity's awful tendency to close its eyes to the suffering of others.

Permission of Salim Amin

Sources: The Man Who Moved The World by Bob Smith and Salim Amin

Camerapix Publishing House

Bob Smith has been a journalist for more than 30 years. He has traveled extensively in Africa. He currently works for The Express in London. The co-author of 'The Man who moved the World'.

Salim Amin is currently a television cameraman covering the frontlines of Somalia, Sudan, Rwanda. He now heads the Kenya-based Camerapix Television. At the age of 10, his first pictures of the East African Safari in Kenya were printed on the front pages of local newspapers and Time Magazine. The co author of 'The Man who moved the World.'

	**mali stopover**	mark davies mali and burkina 1999

The only way to go

One final spine shattering ride across the border of Senegal and into the western most part of Mali - Keyes (known as the hottest town in Africa). Over-exposed to heat and general deprivations, I was keen to make it to any form of luxury and so headed quickly onto the capital of Mali, which was a 600km train ride to the east. In Keyes, you can pick up the Dakar-Bamako express at 2am in the morning. But the train didn't arrive till 2pm that afternoon. Yes, 12 hours of anxiety in a train station I had been promised was full of bandits and thieves.

We made it about 50kms out onto the Savannah and the front train broke-down so we had to wait for a replacement engine. I went down to the restaurant car and met this young, charismatic Nigerian called Efosa. It was great to speak English again. But here was another of these incredulous stories about young men in Africa off to make their fortune. He had left Nigeria two years ago to go to work in Europe. But the UN at the Mauritania/Morocco border stopped him. So he spent 2 years cutting hair in the capital of Mauritania (I think by choice!). Now he was coming back down, and going up an alternative route, through the Sahel and Algeria and into a UN refugee camp in Morocco, where he was going to throw away his papers and pretend he was a refugee from Sierra Leone. We did discuss publishing this on the net and he encouraged me to do so. He promised with 100% certainly that this would get him work papers to Europe.

He was going to Bamako with no money, hoping to reach his sister in Holland and have her wire some down. It reminded me of the Gambian I met last week in Senegal—just 23 years old, the oldest in the family, leaving for work in Bamako with no friends or family there and only $5 in his pocket.

The train bounced ludicrously along the tracks through the dramatic western end of Mali—thick with trees, the long-meandering Senegal River and large escarpments of cliffs. Unfortunately it turned quickly to dusk and I missed most of the view (we were 12 hours late after all!). I spent most of the time in the restaurant car with Efosa—all of us bumping along in the dimly lit car like coordinated jack-in-the boxes. I really felt we were going to pop off the tracks, but the melody of steel on steel and squeaking parts somehow lulled us all into this wonderful sense of excitement as we finally approached Bamako, the capital of Mali, at 5 AM in the morning.

Bamako was just too hot and big to try and do anything. I was impressed by how busy everyone was with some sort of business, and how it lacked the desperation of Dakar. I wasn't hassled at all during my three days there—a real contrast to Dakar, but maybe more to do with Efosa's constant companionship than anything.

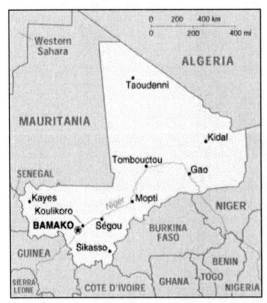

I hired a car and driver and they sped me down to the southeast corner town of Sikasso, through some of the most beautiful verdant countryside, where I overnighted. (Well, only just. There was not a single hotel room available in town, and like the Virgin Mary, I was put up in a sort of storeroom. But that's where our modern biblical story ends.) I did manage to get a visit to a tea plantation and also to see the grave of the conquering French lieutenant that had blown the "indestructible" walls of this city-stronghold apart over a hundred years ago (why did they honor him?). I also visited the sacred caves of initiation where young warriors were sequestered pending maturity rites (well, not while I was there).

Stupidly, I missed the big bus going to Burkina that afternoon, and got a little clapped-out minibus for the 100-km trip to the border. This would not normally be a problem except for the fact that the road was all dust, and there seemed to be major flooring missing in the back of the minibus. I wish I had a picture. All of us had to cover our mouths to breathe and each person emerged coated in fine red dust. On black people, it's a more subtle change and barely visible in the dusk light of the border post. But when I emerged everyone burst into hysterics—I looked like a chicken after a mud bath on Mars.

Something weird happened as we emerged into Burkina Faso. It wasn't just that the roads were beautifully paved, that the border guards actually wore shoes, had smart uniforms and were generally respectful to everyone, or that the moon lit up our journey through the night. There just seemed to be this wonderful energy I experienced as we made our way into Bobo-Dioulassou, the second-biggest town in Burkina close to Mali. The litter that constantly covered the streets in Senegal and Mali, disappeared. Everyone waved as we passed. When we stopped in little towns, people would gently ask me where I was going and wish me a good voyage. It was something completely different to the other countries I'd been in. Refined, gentle, trusting, cooler, more artistic, and more feminine? I don't know. But it was definitely different, and as we pulled into our final destination, I thought this might be one of the most exciting little countries I was to visit in Africa.

Boy! Yes it was. Another excursion and another witness to some of the current, virulent animism in Africa. This time, we went to visit the "poison sacré" (sacred fish) where Kader (a local) would sacrifice two chickens to the spirits. 9kms by moped into the bush and more breathtaking Burkina scenery. Little family hamlets dotted the countryside around the village. The larger huts are for the family, while the smaller huts are for storing food. What was noticeable was that each small hut had a single little window, which was the only way in and out—a chore reserved for the tiniest kids.

We had to go the last 2kms by foot, led by Kader and his two oblivious chickens. I was skeptical—assuming we were off on a tourist gimmick. After winding our way through some ravines, and down some tricky narrow paths, we emerged into a strikingly beautiful grove with a deep pool at one end. On a second glance, it turned out to be a grove of death as we wound our way over the rocks and through the small collections of people. As I began to focus, I realized that the rocks were covered in feathers and blood. Where there were small pools of water, maggots swarmed. Fires burned and people tossed various carcasses around. Others stood guard over a pile of fresh entrails and a group of relatively older men sat smiling, chewing morsels of something and drinking millet beer.

It was another encounter with death as part of living, and I was uncomfortable. Not just because of the blood and body parts that I had to avoid (we were all barefoot at this stage) but also because I'm just not used to seeing throats slit and animals convulsing.

I was with two French friends from Toulouse, and we felt very much out of place, but no one seemed to mind our presence. This was not a sacred place in the sense that I was accustomed (quiet deference and wood polishing) – no, this was business, the business of petitioning good fortune in life and getting results. Everyone was quite matter of fact, and all smiled and said hello, and went back to fingering entrails or something.

The idea behind it is that you petition the spirit of Dafra for something. This can either be a cure for a sick relative or to find a good wife or to get a better job. You make the application and sacrifice a chicken or a goat. If your wish is granted, you have to return and do the same thing again in thanks.

When Kader arrived he paid this old man on the right to perform the sacrifice. He approached the fetid altar and held the chickens in the air, implored loudly to the spirit of dafra, and then cut the chicken's throat.

The chicken floundered around for several minutes as it bled to death— our particular chicken seemed to go on for quite a while and this was obviously to the delight of the animist, who excitedly pointed this out to Kader and proclaimed the sacrifice a success. After the sacrifice, Kader took the two chickens and burnt off their feathers in the fire, and plucked them clean. He handed them to the animist who then cut out the entrails. The entrails were also an important part of the sacrifice, because that was what was fed to the sacred fish that lived in the pool at the end of the grove. Kader began praying to the fish after throwing the entrails into the water. He was quite disappointed because the fish had chosen not to appear that morning to anyone—he wanted us to see because it was the size of a man and wore a special necklace. (Now my French couldn't be that bad, could it?)

See page 62, for biography of **Mark Davies**.

| the boy was like this | tanya shaffer
ghana
1999 |

At the main crossroads, near the village of Gowrie, in the Upper East Region of Ghana, my English friend Katie and I sat on the shaded cement porch of the fisheries building, waiting for a tro-tro to take us to Bolgatanga. We'd been with Aroko's family for a week. It was Monday, market day, and we were headed to town to buy tomatoes, rice, palm oil, and tinned milk for the compound. The air was still and very hot.

Aroko was leaning against the fence nearby, talking softly with a friend. He pulled up to us on a bicycle. "A small boy fell in the water and we are going to get him out," he said, and set off.

"Oo," we said, and frowned.

"That's worrying," said Katie.

Half-standing, we watched the bicycle disappear down a dirt path between the high millet stalks.

"It must be far, if he's going on bicycle," Katie said.

"Mmmmm," I concurred. We sat back down.

Small groups of people began to pass, heading down the same path, some cycling, some running, others walking purposefully. Small children shot by. Now we thought we should go too, but we'd just sent a man to fill our water bottles.

We discussed CPR and mouth-to-mouth resuscitation. Neither of us was quite sure how these were done. Katie thought it was one breath to fifteen presses, but that didn't sound right to me.

People continued to pass.

My copy of *Staying Healthy in Asia, Africa, and Latin America* explained CPR and mouth-to-mouth, but it was in my bag, at Aroko's father's house in Bolga. We thought they were two different things, one to do with heartbeat and the other with breathing.

The man returned with our water.

"Should we go?" I inquired vaguely. The stream of people had all but stopped.

"We don't know where it is," said Katie, glancing toward the place where the path disappeared among the dry stalks. I raised my arms to let a hint of breeze cool the sweat.

Aroko and his friend returned.

"Is he okay?" I asked, relieved.

"The boy is dead," Aroko said.

"You were in an extraordinary situation," my friend Colin said, eight months later, back home. He sat on the couch in my mother's Berkeley apartment, tracing with his fingertip the edges of a photo of Aroko's mother smilingly gutting a fish. "You're not brought up in a place where things like that happen. Besides, what could you have done?"

This is what plays in my mind:

A seven- or eight-year-old boy (or six?) walks into a dark cement irrigation tunnel with water up to his neck, holding a fishing net, slips and is unable to regain his balance, clutching at the cement walls, slippery with algae, trying to scream, water filling his lungs as he gasps, his heart pounding, and his friends sitting on the grass eating groundnuts and swinging a rope strung with fish and eels, the day's catch, some still feebly twitching, as 20 minutes go by, 30, an hour, and They start to wonder, "Where is Azureh? He's been a long time." They call "Azureh? Azureh!" They wade in and try to peer into the tunnel, calling his name into the hollow echoey place, but the echo's dead on the cement. No response and they're afraid to enter—they try throwing in a rope, they talk some more, call his name. Finally one runs for help.

"You're not used to that kind of heat," said my mother, closing the refrigerator door. "And you shouldn't do CPR if you're not trained."

This time I rise and follow Aroko down that path—one foot in front of the other, the high dry grass scratching my calves, my legs heavy in the heat, taking hat and sunglasses off, wiping away sweat, putting them back on. We follow the voices, come out to the spot where people stand on either side of the canal peering into the tunnel. Others stand above them on the bridge, where a wheel, secured by a heavy iron chain, controls the dam. People are pounding against the chain with a rock, trying to break it so the wheel can turn to lift the cement gate and the water from the reservoir can rush through and carry the body of a six-or-seven-year-old boy out of that dark stone tunnel into air and light and waiting people of all ages standing on the bank shouting and gesticulating as if these things could bring him back.

"There would've been choices at every step," Colin said. "If you'd followed, then you would've had to decide whether or not to dive in. Then whether or not to interfere. To try procedures you're not sure how to use."

"If he was in all that time, he would've been long dead when you arrived," said my mother.

As we see the body emerge, carried on the swell of water, Katie and I push our way through the crowd, *Is there a heart-beat? Try mouth-to-*

278

mouth—Oh God, did you check for vomit? Is his chest rising? If only I had that book!

Fear of raising false expectations, disapproval of touching the dead, chill of putting your lips against his cold ones, and are there amoebas in the water and knowing it's useless he's been in so long, *what makes you think you can*—but you've got to try, because what would you be if you didn't try? Trying more for you than for him, and if that's true, who the hell are you to practice your peculiar cultural rites on the body of this boy?

Here is what happened after Aroko said "The boy is dead":

We changed locations. We were sitting beside a chain-link fence, under a tree. Two men were talking, a few feet away, sharing an orange. A repeated phrase of English jumped out of the Frafra conversation: *destiny to die in water, destined to die in water.*

Aroko pointed to a boy across the street, big belly sticking out above brown shorts, skinny legs; one of the neighborhood boys that smiled shyly and said softly "Namba" as he passed the compound every afternoon, carrying water or a bunch of groundnuts or a string of fish. Aroko said, "The boy was like this."

An orange peel hit Aroko's arm. He looked up.

"Eh!" called the man. "Azureh was tall. He was never like this boy."

See page 32, for biography of **Tanya Shaffer.**

doing business in africa

The businessman is Africa's modern day explorer, constantly challenged by the unexpected and unforeseen issues that arise in the market place where they operate. Like many things in life there are winners and losers, but one thing is for sure, it's not like Wall Street or Silicon Valley or Enron shares. It's also rarely boring.

Africa still suffers from multi nationals exploiting its resources, people and being unethical in its practices. This chapter highlights some of these issues and shows that there is more than meets the eye in some of these activities.

	**illegal diamond buying is forever**	carey goodman africa present day

If diamonds are a girl's best friend, diamond mines are an opportunist's best friend.

Despite the recent tacit agreements related to prohibitions against the purchase of "conflict diamonds" (stones mined in regions afflicted by war), the practice of IDB (illegal diamond buying) will probably continue unfetered. IDB and instigating conflicts are two of the most enduring aspects of the diamond trade, and as with any other commodity, the diamond dealers in Antwerp, Johannesburg, Dublin, London, and other places where the stones are transacted are unlikely to refuse a prize acquisition because of country of origin rules.

IDB transactions are traceable to the origins of legal diamond buying. The conditions of the mining camps of South Africa during the 1870s were very much like those of the Gold Rush mining camps in California during the 1850s. Both communities attracted rogues, opportunists, and dreamy prospectors. Both communities soon confronted similar difficulties regarding stolen claims, price wars for their finds, and exorbitant prices for wares from non-miner vendors. These conditions led to the evolution of two markets: the legal market and the illegal market. The legal market for diamonds was quickly controlled by a few exclusive mining companies.

The IDB market was the realm of individual miners who lacked the influence of the emerging oligopoly/cartels. The oligopoly/cartels of the legal market sought to end the activities of the IDB distributors. To accomplish this goal, representatives of the oligopoly/cartels sometimes engaged in IDB transactions. The other strategy the legal market applied was often more brutal. That strategy involved instigating warfare to seize control of the mines operated by the IDB traders.

The first transnational event that produced "conflict diamonds" occurred in 1895 when John Cecil Rhodes persuaded the Boer leader Paul Kreuger to allow Rhodes and his Debeers diamond mining company to search for diamonds in the Congo region of South Africa. Debeers learned of the Congo mines from dealings with IDB traders who operated unregistered mines there. Kreuger gave Rhodes (who was also then the prime minister of the Cape Town colony) permission to explore the Congo. Rhodes then discovered other plentiful mines that lay within the Boer territory. It was the struggle to seize this land that caused the Boer War. That conflict lasted three years (1898-1901) and cost the British Empire dearly in men and material. It was also the war that introduced the concept and use of "concentration camps."

Diamond speculation was also a contributing factor to the "scramble for Africa" which began among various European powers during the late 1800s. Indigenous people fought each other as allies of the competing imperial states, and colonial warfare proliferated. Amid these clashes emerged factions who opposed the imperial occupations. And through all the blood and terror, IDB continued to thrive.

During the twentieth century the diamond industry further consolidated; de Beers strengthened its commanding role among the oligopoly/cartels. The conglomerate and its subsidiaries repeatedly condemned the acquisition of "conflict diamonds," but at the next moment of opportunity, Debeers funds and operatives were ready to intervene to join the battles. The recent chaos in the Congo region (formerly Zaire, now the Democratic Republic of the Congo) simply indicates that man's pursuit of what nineteenth century imperialists knew as "the commodity" still exists. As long as there are rumors of wealth and opportunity, there will be speculators who, at whatever cost to themselves or the venture they join, will mine, fight, buy, and sell until they attain some tangible result. Often their finds are imperfect, but if their prize satisfies all the criteria of a flawless diamond (color, cut, clarity, and karat), those IDB traders in the various diamond markets will welcome the find, and eventually via some back-channel bargaining, that flawless diamond will appear as a product of the legal market and a possession of the diamond cartels. At that time no trader will dare to ask whether that flawless stone is a "conflict diamond."

The cartels shunning "conflict diamonds" will only enhance the role of the IDB dealers. Perhaps the cartels should adopt a don't-ask-don't-tell policy. de Beers speaks volumes about the principles of the diamond trade with its famous US advertising slogan: "A diamond is forever." IDB and trade in conflict diamonds are also permanent facets of the market.

See page 19, for biography of **Carey Goodman**.

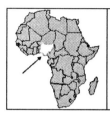	**shell nigeria:** **colonialism continues**	derek guiler nigeria present day

Colonialism is no longer the sole province of nation states. Increasingly, large corporations are wielding the stick that their governments used to wield for them. Oil and gas concerns are some of the biggest companies in the world and when they begin to flex their muscles in places like Africa and Latin America the results are similar, though smaller in scale, to earlier forms of colonial or neo-colonial rule. The situation with the Ogoni tribe in Nigeria is a text-book example of what occurs when indigenous peoples struggle for their sovereignty against an oppressive government allied with one of the world's largest multi-nationals. Royal Dutch Shell, an English/Dutch combine, filled the pockets of the country's Generals to ensure that they could drill for oil in a secure environment. It seems that these same Generals were desperate enough for money that they were willing to do anything to protect the company's investment.

In the years that have followed the execution of Ken Saro-Wiwa, a Nobel Laureate in Literature, along with nine other activists of the Ogoni tribe, Shell, implicated in the executions and undertook a PR campaign of vast proportions to salvage its tarnished name. A recent example of this was Shell's signing of a completely unenforceable pact with several multi-national oil and mining firms to engage in more responsible business practices. A commentary in the New York Times was supportive of the steps taken by these companies while noting that "...compliance is voluntary and the only penalty for violation is public exposure by human rights groups and journalists."[1] This comment does seem to imply that the penalty for unethical behaviour remains the same, though the companies who signed the pact certainly benefited from all the free publicity.

In a report issued by PIRC (Pensions and Investment Research Consultants) in 1996, detailing the companies' response to shareholder concerns about human rights abuses and environmental damage, the authors revealed the thinking that dominated upper management in the wake of the crisis provoked by Shell's actions in Ogoni and the whole Niger Delta:

"...Shell continues to claim that allegations of environmental damage in are overstated" which was followed with a quote from a letter written by Ledum Mitee, who was acting President of MOSOP (Movement for the Survival of the Ogoni People), the movement led by Saro-Wiwa before his death, "If the Niger delta is full of contented communities grateful for Shell's generosity…why as recently as four weeks ago [were] protests held against Shell's failure to abide by its own environmental policies?"[2]

Although the company has made a big show of their support for the UN Declaration of Human Rights the ambiguity surrounding their compliance with it as expressed by John Jennings. Chairman of Shell Transport and Trading, is the stance taken by many large corporations when confronted with the effects of their far-flung enterprises especially when dealing with repressive governments. The government of Nigeria has changed in recent years and there is hope for the country's economic progress which companies like Shell can play a noble role in. But, given statements like the one Jennings made at the height of the crisis, is it any wonder that Nigerians don't trust them?

"It is 20 years since our General Business Principles…were first published. I believe that these principles, which have evolved over time, are fundamentally sound and should be a source of pride to all involved in the Group. Nevertheless, we are reviewing them to see whether they still meet changing societal values…We are also discussing with human rights organizations the difficult and wider question of how companies should respond to concerns about human rights in countries in which they operate. However…we remain convinced that it would be improper for them to interfere in the political process."[2]

1 The Editors. "A Pact Against Oil Company Abuses." The New York Times. 1 December 28, 2000.

2 Clients of Pensions and Investment Research Consultants Ltd. "Shell and Nigeria: Analysis of the company's response to PIRC's recommendations". Report to Clients. December 1996.

Derek Guiler. Sometimes you look at your resume and wonder what you haven't done. In the five years since university I've been a DJ, restaurant manager, hotel worker, translator and english teacher. I've lived in Montreal, Calgary, Guatemala and Mexico and have relied on the internet to keep me in touch with all these places and others I've never seen. An interest in the places I've been and places I'd like to go is what brought me to write about Africa, along with an avid interest in history itself which I studied in University.

| **stop blaming perceptions** | tony hawkins africa present day |

At the end of a decade during which foreign capital moved to center stage as the prime driver of economic growth, critics are claiming its effectiveness has been exaggerated. The anti globalization school argues that on three counts at least, foreign capital has failed to match the claims of its protagonists:

In the long run, the links between foreign capital inflows and domestic investment are weak and, as globalization proceeds, the links are becoming more tenuous. The unprecedented boom of capital flows in the Nineties ended on a sour note with the Asian financial crisis, followed by a number of other upsets - in Russia, in Brazil and most recently, in Argentina and Turkey; and Because private capital flows are highly volatile, which means they do more harm than good.

The World Bank's Global Development Finance Report (2001), released last week, shows private flows increased fivefold between 1991 and 1997, then fell by a quarter over the next two years before recovering in 2000. The Bank's key finding is that, over the past 30 years, private capital flows - not aid - have been associated with a roughly equal increase in domestic investment. However, this relationship is weakening with global financial integration. Capital liberalization has led to outflows from developing countries, as well as inflows - a development familiar to South Africans.

This positive correlation between capital inflows and domestic investment is strongest in Africa. This is hardly surprising, partly because in Africa - excluding SA - financial integration has made less headway than in other regions, but also because savings levels in Africa are low, meaning that if there is to be increased investment, it has to be funded from offshore.

In other emerging markets - including SA - a growing proportion of capital flows goes into merger and acquisition activity rather than green field investment. Many M and A deals restructure ownership rather than create new productive capacity and, though they may result in improved productivity, they often also lead to the closure of facilities and to retrenchment.

Similarly, where portfolio capital is a major element of investment inflows, the link between domestic investment and foreign capital again breaks down. The report acknowledges, too, that capital volatility translates into economic volatility, which dampens economic growth.

Two conclusions flow from this: first, the type of capital inflow is crucial. Long-term capital, and specifically foreign direct investment, is closely correlated with the level of domestic investment, though this will be diluted where the proportion of M and A transactions is high.

Second, while volatility is inimical to growth, the cause of capital flow volatility may well be domestic rather than foreign. Capital flees when the domestic policy regime (exchange rates, taxation, interest rates and ownership laws and property rights observance) is inappropriate. Often, it is domestic capital volatility that frightens off the foreigners and translates into offshore volatility as well.

An important facet is that - again, unlike official aid - private capital flows to countries with business-friendly investment climates. The impact of aid inflows is dissipated because the recipient economy lacks the absorptive capacity (skills, infrastructure, institutions and markets) to use the funds efficiently.

According to the Bank, domestic factors, including the level of human capital, political stability and the depth of financial markets, "define a country's ability to translate foreign capital into domestic investment". Berating foreign investors for their reluctance to commit funds to Africa diverts attention from at least one of the reasons for this unhappy state of affairs. Namely, the absence of the necessary "prior conditions" that both attract foreign investment and make it productive.

Many in Africa blame perceptions, saying the investment climate is far better than it is made out to be by analysts, bankers and the media, guilty of Afro pessimism. But that does not hold. Leaving aside location-specific investments (mining, energy, oil, large-scale agriculture and, in some instances, tourism), foreign investment decisions are driven by market size, labor quality, skills availability, strength and efficiency of institutions and political stability. Those who blame mistaken perceptions for the reluctance of foreigners to invest ignore the crucial role of skills and institutions.

If hard-nosed foreign investors can pick winning investment opportunities ahead of local businessmen who have the advantage of knowing the territory, then surely they are also savvy enough not to fall into this perceptions trap? It is time to stop blaming foreign perception and focus on getting the conditions right.

Professor Tony Hawkins: Currently a Professor of Business Studies and Founding Director of the MBA Program at University of Zimbabwe. He is the leading author on African business and economics issues and widely published in the London Financial Times and The Economist Group (including Economist Intelligence Unit). He is author of several authoritative books on corporate strategies in Sub-Saharan Africa, Nigeria and South Africa. He is a consultant to an International bank. He has been Advisor to UNIDO (concerning the globalization of industry in the developing world) and authored UNIDO's report on Sub-Saharan African Manufacturing Industry. Educated at the University of Zimbabwe, he graduated as a Rhodes scholar from Oxford University, reading Economics.

**another false dawn
looms for the continent**

tony hawkins
africa
present day

On more than one occasion during the 1990s, international agencies proclaimed a turning point in the economic fortunes of sub-Saharan Africa. A short-lived surge in GDP growth between 1994 and 1997 gave rise to optimistic assessments that the corner had been turned. But the momentum was lost. Not only did the trend discerned by Afro-optimists turn out to be only a blip, but it owed a good deal to favorable commodity prices and increased capacity utilization. The IMF is projecting GDP growth in 2000/01 at more than 4 percent a year, up from just 2.2 percent last year, the weakness of some commodity prices, notably beverages, and the underperformance of the region's largest economy, South Africa, suggests that, yet again, the Fund will be proved to be over-optimistic.

Despite this near-term optimism, there has been a mood change. So much so that in its most recent survey of the region, the World Bank gloomily notes that in Africa - unlike other developing regions - per capita incomes at the end of the 20th century were lower than in 1970. In some countries, they had halved. The region's share of global trade is a mere 2 per cent. It has lost market share in virtually all primary product markets - oil and tobacco are exceptions. Many parts of the region have de-industrialised, while in others, manufacturing industry has failed to take off at all.

The African Competitiveness Report 2000 points out that African growth rates, over a five to 10-year horizon, are driven by short-term changes in raw material production and prices. Once the contribution of the raw materials sector is subtracted "we see a fairly consistent pattern of slow growth for the continent", says the report, though it notes that both Botswana and Mauritius have been exceptions. Underpinning the change in sentiment has been belated recognition of the gravity of the AIDS crisis and what it will mean for the region - especially Southern Africa, where the impact will be greatest over the next five years.

Events in countries as far apart as Liberia, Sierra Leone, Ethiopia, Eritrea, Cote d'Ivoire, the Democratic Republic of Congo and Zimbabwe have intensified doubts about the durability of political reform. Claims in the mid 1990s that investment ratios were recovering have given way to louder, more insistent demands for debt cancellation. Indeed, the International Finance Corporation's latest numbers of sub-Saharan investment suggest that the 1998 investment ratio - 18.5 per cent of GDP - was the lowest since the mid-1980s. Most recently, in its study of capital flows to Africa, the UN has called for aid to be doubled, arguing that this kind of assistance will have a Marshall Plan-like catalyst effect on domestic savings and private investment flows.

The World Bank and IMF insist that policy reform in many - indeed most - sub-Saharan economies justifies their belief that the worst is past. But this is one-eyed economics, overlooking the reality that sound policy is a necessary, not a sufficient, basis for sustained economic growth. Recovery is being held back by the hollowing of the Africa state, the continent-wide deterioration in physical infrastructure and - more importantly - in institutional capacity. Rebuilding Africa's hardware - its physical infrastructure - will be both costly and time-consuming, but the challenge of reviving institutional capacity, or software, will be far greater, taking much longer.

Debt cancellation will unlock savings for investment in health and education, but if the institutional capacity to exploit those savings is missing, then the investment pay-off risks will be as disappointing over the next 10 years as it has been over the past 20. Equally perturbing is donor community reluctance to grapple with what the "new economy" means for the world's least developed regions. Earlier growth paths - labour-intensive industrialisation - are no longer an option. The march of technology is exacerbating the marginalisation of Africa as the widening of the productivity gap between advanced and backward economies further narrows the range of investment opportunities and the scope for attracting the foreign private direct investment - not aid - that will have to be the springboard for recovery.

Low-wage, low-skilled labor and natural resources count for less and less in the development equation. Yet with very few exceptions, this is where Africa's comparative advantage lies. It is going to take more than a combination of "good policies" and debt cancellation to offset this pervasive competitive disadvantage. For these reasons, the African turnaround will be a long haul. Quick fixes - debt cancellation, the doubling of aid, preferential trade agreements or huge investment in disease prevention - all have a role to play in recovery, but they will not work without the most fundamental ingredient - institutional capacity, including a well-functioning state machine.

See page 287, for biography of **Tony Hawkins**.

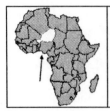	**the pill pirates**	paul r. paradise niger 1995

The real cost of private labels

In April 1995, a major epidemic of meningitis struck the country of Niger. A drought added to the woes of this country of 8.4 million. Niger authorities requested international assistance, after an estimated 2,500 had died and 26,700 people became sick. International aid delivered nearly five and one-half million doses of vaccine. Pharmacists Without Borders (Pharmaciens sans Frontieres), a French-based relief organization, undertook a large-scale vaccination campaign.

To assist in the crisis, the government of Nigeria offered 68,000 doses of vaccine. The vaccines, which were allegedly manufactured by Rhone-Poulenc affiliate Pasteur Merieux and SmithKline Beecham, were offered with great publicity by the regime of General Sani Abacha, the unofficial president of Nigeria, in an effort to bolster the country's dismal human rights image. Unfortunately, the vaccines that Nigeria donated were counterfeit. An additional 3,000 people died because of the counterfeit vaccine, sparking an international incident.

"The counterfeit drugs were illegally manufactured by someone with a high technological and professional competence," said Dennis Fontaine of ReMeD (Reseau Medicaments and Developpment), a French relief agency. "The individual or group responsible for the deed has never been identified."

Pasteur Merieux alerted the French authorities and filed a formal complaint. The Nigerian government formally denied the French charges of having supplied copies of the original vaccine to Niger. Judge Courroye of Lyon, France, who was handling the case, launched an inquiry concerning the counterfeits through Interpol. The counterfeit vaccines were rumored to have come from Spain, but discerning a motive for the outrageous act was difficult, since the vaccines were donated.

The Niger incident brought international attention to the painful, but largely ignored, problem of counterfeit pharmaceuticals. Much of the trade involves third world countries or industrialized countries where the central government has become unstable—countries like Russia and South Africa.

Counterfeit and substandard pharmaceuticals represent a markedly different problem from that involving the counterfeiting of designer clothing, recorded music, and computer programs, which are products of affluence. For many people in Africa and other third world countries, there are no drug stores or hospitals. The only doctors are itinerant vendors or other semi-professionals with limited medical backgrounds, who travel by foot or bicycle to the village. In Morocco and Algiers, the vendors sell drugs and medications that are displayed on blankets in the crowded marketplaces; or they travel from village to village by bicycle, where they give medical consultations and sell drugs. In Nigeria, the vendors travel from village to village on foot. Their medicine bag is a bowl balanced atop their head; inside the bowl are cough syrups, vitamins, and medications. The situation is desperate in parts of war-torn Africa, where peddlers fear to travel and international relief brings medical supplies to the civilians at great risk.

Health authorities recognize many types of irregularities concerning the drugs sold in the marketplace. Misbranded and unbranded drugs are drugs that contain false or misleading labeling. Contaminated drugs are drugs that may contain impurities or traces of another drug. Substitutes are drugs that are different than the drugs being prescribed. Adulterated drugs are drugs that may include a substance that is not part of the chemical compound. Pirated compounds use stolen formulas or trade secrets or chemical compositions protected by patent. Imitations are drugs that are manufactured to resemble another company's product, and differ from counterfeit drugs, which are exact copies of a legitimate product, including brand name. Counterfeit drugs are always considered to be misbranded, and their compounds may be a pirated composition, or have compounds that are adulterated or contaminated

The pharmaceutical drugs that are used in Africa and other third world countries vary considerably in effectiveness, come from many sources, and may fit any of the categories previously listed. The problem varies from country to country. In some countries, the situation is caused by a lack of pharmaceuticals, but in other countries, an overabundance is the cause. Usually poor economic conditions play a role, but rich countries like Nigeria and South Africa are havens for counterfeit drugs. Poor storage conditions and distribution procedures, as well as poorly trained doctors and technicians, exacerbate the situation.

Although the problem varies from country to country, the absence of a strong regulatory authority such as the Food and Drug Administration (FDA) or a strong health ministry is almost always the primary reason for the poor quality of drugs found in many third world countries.

The United States has the strongest regulatory agency in the industrialized world. Every person in the United States ultimately comes under the regulatory power of the FDA, which is authorized to regulate food, cigarettes, medical devices, medicines, drugs, and cosmetics. The FDA conducts inspections and has the authority to seize improperly manufactured medicines, cosmetics, and foods. The FDA also approves drugs for use in the marketplace and inspects foreign drug supplies that are used in the manufacturing process.

"Drug regulatory authorities have been established in all industrialized countries," says Dr. Martin ten Ham, chief of the drug safety unit for the World Health Organization (WHO). "Their principal duty is to safeguard the consumer from medicinal products or drugs that have an unacceptable profile of safety and efficacy. In situations where improper manufacturing has occurred, the diminished bio-availability of the active ingredients may result in a failure of the therapy. Depending on the disease and the patient, death can result."

The WHO drug safety unit is responsible for maintaining a worldwide program on drug safety monitoring, and works with the appropriate governmental agency, usually a health ministry or national center, in some fifty countries. The unit completed a three-year project on counterfeit medicines in 1997, and has been collecting information on cases of counterfeit drugs and adverse drug reactions, as reported in the published literature and as the result of questionnaires sent to drug regulatory agencies in the industrialized nations. To date, the drug safety unit has cataloged almost two million reports of adverse drug reactions.

According to ten Ham, every time a new drug is introduced its scientific background is scrutinized, and after a detailed evaluation a judgment is rendered as to the drug's safety. By definition, a fake drug has not gone through such a process of review by the governmental drug regulatory authorities and consequently there is no guarantee that the drug meets the standard of quality. Drugs of unsatisfactory quality pose a potential health risk of grave consequences.

Printed with permission:
'Trademark Counterfeiting, Product Piracy, and the Billion-Dollar Threat to the US Economy' by Paul R. Paradise

Paul R. Paradise is a journalist and freelance writer on a variety of topics, particularly the law and law enforcement. A frequent contributor to law enforcement periodicals, and a staff writer for T.F.H Publications, he was formerly an editor for a major publisher of law and law related material. Author of the book 'Trademark Counterfeiting, Product Piracy, and the Billion-Dollar Threat to the US Economy'

The oil is here, says Royal Dutch Shell, China National Petroleum and Total FINA Elf.

The increasing involvement of foreign oil giants in Sudan's ongoing civil war has, according to analysts, increased the power of the Islamic government and, in turn, worsened the plight of the black Christians in the southern region of Africa's largest nation.

Also, according to the Oklahoma-based group "Voice of The Martyrs" the Royal Bank is a major investor in Canada's Talisman Energy.

"Talisman Energy's operations in the Sudan are directly funding the genocide that is being waged against Christians in the south of the country," said Brian Rushfeld, the Executive Director of Canada Family Action Coalition, in an interview.

One additional major player in Sudan's oil game is Europe's Lundin oil company. According to Marc André, a Swiss political consultant who spoke in an exclusive interview with WND, "There is fresh news from the well-known Geneva oil industry. Lundin, an oil company based in Geneva, is suspected of helping the Sudanese government to fight the rebels in the south of the country. It's interesting to know that they work together with Petronas, the Malaysian Islamic Company."

Lundin Oil has been active in Sudan since 1991 with drilling projects off the coast of the nation, bringing up both oil and natural gas. Also, since 1997, Lundin Oil has been drilling in the Muglad Basin in southern Sudan onshore.

Concluded André, "As far as I know, Lundin is the only Western oil company which has published a <u>white paper</u> detailing its activities in the Sudan and [responding to] criticisms brought against the company by a Christian human rights group – Christian Aid, a group of churches in Ireland and the UK. It shows that in some cases, the tail has actually wagged the dog."

A recent State Department report on international religious freedom cited China, Myanmar, Iran, Iraq and Sudan for persecuting people for their religious faith. In addition, the agency has designated Sudan as a country supporting terrorism.

Secretary of State Colin Powell recently announced that the American government will furnish the black South Sudanese resistance with $3 million to set up office space, including telephones and fax machines.

Could such a simple plan work to the benefit of the persecuted south Sudanese Christians, who face the combined might of Iraq, the Arab world and communist China?

"What is needed in south Sudan is a 'No-Fly Zone,' as the U.S. has enforced in Iraq – Military training and equipment, as well as logistical support for the black south Sudanese rebel fighters. The human rights violations in south Sudan are horrendous and the epitome of evil," said Mark Christiansen, a Swedish Red Cross worker currently based at the Kenya-Sudan border.

"Americans can try and peacefully protest what is happening in Sudan by contacting the Sudanese Embassy in Washington, D.C., and voicing their displeasure."

An African problem

Despite the recent involvement of Powell, the war and human rights situation in the Sudan is growing worse. And the conflict between Arabs and Christians is spreading to neighboring countries as well.

Dr. Charles Jacobs, the President of the American Anti Slavery Group, explained, "People need to know that though Islam forbids the enslavement of fellow Muslims, in Mauritania, racism trumps religious doctrine and there is a caste – the Haretines, who are Islamized blacks, enslaved to Arabo-Berbers. One of these men, Moctar Teyeb, escaped and is on our board."

Bombings continue

Despite assurances from the government of Sudan that they would cease air attacks against the Christian south, the National Islamic Front government has unleashed waves of artillery bombardments and ground assaults against Christian villages in the Nuba Mountains.

Reports just received by the South African-based missionary group Frontline Fellowship confirm that since 24 May, Sudanese government forces have subjected the beleaguered Christians in the Nuba Mountains to "a massive on-going bombardment and military attack. Many villages have been burned, many people have been killed."

According to Peter Hammond, the head of Frontline Fellowship, the communities, churches and schools under attack in the Nuba Mountains are among those his group has repeatedly visited. Hammond says they are now in the gravest of danger.

"In order to reach the Nuba, who are an island of Christianity in a sea of Islam, we need to fly far behind enemy lines in no-fly zones. NIF government forces have recently captured most of the airstrips in the Nuba Mountains, complicating travel to these besieged people," said Hammond.

"The dangers of flying in south Sudan was recently highlighted when Bishop Macram Gassis' aircraft was bombed while on the ground in the Nuba Mountains. One person was killed and several were wounded in this attack. On May 9, a Red Cross aid worker was killed when a clearly marked Red Cross aircraft was hit by ground fire. The 26-year-old Danish co-pilot was killed instantly with a severe head injury as the aircraft was rocked by explosions. The other pilot managed to safely land the Red Cross aircraft at the Lokichoggio airport in neighboring Kenya."

Frontline Fellowship has sent five teams to Sudan so far this year, three of them by vehicle overland. Despite being bombed twice this year – and nine times in the last 14 months – the Christian Liberty High School, at the Frontline Fellowship mission base, is continuing classes with an enthusiastic group of students and teachers.

Added Hammond, "Please continue to speak up for our Christian brothers and sisters in Sudan who are being persecuted for their faith, and please continue to persuade your elected representatives to pressure the government of Sudan to stop waging this cruel war against their own citizens."

Article first appeared in WorldNetDaily. Printed with permission

Anthony LoBaido: Has worked as a journalist in Mexico, South Africa, Korea, Laos, Thailand, Cambodia, Burma and many other countries. While in South Africa, Anthony lived and trained with the elite Special Forces of the South African Defense Force. While there, he also wrote an apocalyptic novel entitled "The Third Boer War."

This well-traveled journalist received his undergraduate degree in political science from Arizona State University and a master's degree in international journalism from Baylor. While at Baylor, the polished speaker and writer won the "Best Columnist Award" from the Society of Professional Journalists. Also an accomplished filmmaker, LoBaido began his doctorate work at Texas AandM, where he was hired by former U.S. President George Bush to produce a documentary on Bush's life. The video was featured on CNN in August of 1993. Anthony's articles have been translated into French and Russian and been published in Russia and neighboring ex-Soviet republics, Belgium, France and former countries of the French Empire by Way Press International. LoBaido is an astute analyst of foreign relations and national security, and is an expert speaker on Thailand, Indochina, and Africa—especially South Africa, Angola, Zimbabwe and Sudan.

<table>
<tr>
<td></td>
<td>**executive outcomes**</td>
<td>anthony lobaido
south africa
present day</td>
</tr>
</table>

A new kind of army for privatized global warfare

Sitting on the patio of his lavish home in suburban Pretoria, Eeben Barlow poured afternoon tea and basked in the late summer sun, looking more like a successful businessman than a hardened, elite Special Forces operator of the now defunct Apartheid-era South African Defense Force (SADF). In fact, the former commander of the famed 32 Battalion's Reconnaissance (Recce) Wing is both. At the center of Barlow's synthesis of commerce and soldiering skills is his highly successful private corporate army known as Executive Outcomes or EO. The activities of EO, the clients it serves, and the global transnational corporate elite (including the de Beers diamond cartel, Texaco and Gulf-Chevron) which fund its operations, offer an intriguing look into the realpolitik of the emerging world order.

"As a private corporate entity, EO is able to operate without the restrictions of any particular nation's flag leading our soldiers into battle," says Barlow.

"Organizations such as the UN and the Organization of African Unity (OAU) can make use of EO without partiality in negating the speedy resolution of conflict in any given country utilizing our services. Our employees have over five-thousand man years of military knowledge, combat and training experience."

"While Western governments in the post-Cold War era continue to cut back on the manpower of their capital intensive forces, and are increasingly unable to sell their constituencies on nation-building exercises like the Somalia debacle, EO is ready to fill the void. EO is able to provide private counter-insurgency operations, peacekeeping forces, and the muscle for corporations to control gold and diamond mines, oil and other natural resources in a variety of failed states which stretch to the four corners of the world.

"We offer a variety of services to legitimate governments, including infantry training, clandestine warfare, counterintelligence programs [cointelpro], reconnaissance, escape and evasion, special forces selection and training and even parachuting," adds Barlow. EO is equipped with

Soviet MiG fighter jets, Puma and East Bloc helicopters, state-of-the-art artillery, tanks and other armaments. Barlow pointed out that EO boasts an array of no less than 500 military advisors and 3,000 highly trained multi-national special forces soldiers.

The long and twisted journey of Barlow's involvement with the SADF began when he moved from Northern Rhodesia to South Africa as a boy. After matriculating in 1972, he joined the SADF in 1974. By 1980 he was with 32 Battalion, (known as South Africa's Foreign Legion) fighting with the SADF Special Forces in Angola and assisting the anti-Marxist UNITA, (the Union for the Total Independence of Angola) guerrilla army. Later he moved on to Military Intelligence and then to the Armaments Corporation of South Africa, (ARMSCOR). Barlow's most challenging assignment, however, may have been heading up the Western European section of the Civil Co-operation Bureau, (CCB) which attempted to circumvent UN-imposed Apartheid sanctions by setting up front companies overseas. The CCB's ability to import highly sensitive technology for South Africa's advanced nuclear program, as well as its alleged assassinations of hundreds of anti-Apartheid activists world-wide still remains a mystery to his very day.

EO's parent company is most likely the South African-based Strategic Resource Corporation (SRC). EO exists in SRC's corporate universe as just one satellite in a web of thirty-two companies involved in a plethora of mining, air charter, and "security" concerns. These satellite companies are registered anywhere from CapeTown to the Bahamas to the Isle of Man.

Since 1993, Companies House in London has carried a record of Executive Outcomes Ltd. With offices in Hampshire, UK. Barlow and the British national who became his wife after the company filed (and after his divorce from his South African wife) are named as holders of 70 percent of its capital. Keeping EO's title and other paperwork in the UK serves a two-fold purpose. First, London is well known as a center of international weapons dealing and quasi-security deals. Second, it helps deflect negative coverage away from South African President Nelson Mandela and the ANC, who have used the reconstituted elite Apartheid forces (now EO) to fight and defeat its Angola-based Cold War enemy UNITA, and installed the MPLA to power in the former Portuguese colony.

The Genesis

The genesis of EO came in 1989, during the dying days of Apartheid, when ANC leader Nelson Mandela ordered former South African President F.W. de Klerk to dismantle the SADF Special Forces units with the hope of crippling a right-wing Afrikaner coup against the take over of South Africa by its long-time Marxist enemy.

Reputed to be one of the finest military units in the world, 32 Battalion boasted successes like holding off the Cold War invasion of South Africa's northern neighbor Angola—which was led by a contingent of Soviet, Cuban, East Bloc and North Korean forces.

Other elite SADF units, including the counter-insurgency outfit kovoet (Afrikaans for "crowbar"), all of the Recce units and the shadowy Civil Co-operation Bureau were also targeted for dismantlement. Faced with the prospect of being thrown out of the army he had served so well, not to mention the apocalyptic end of three centuries of Afrikaner cultural identity and struggle for a free and independent Christian future, Barlow formed EO.

In its short history, EO has fought in South and West Africa, South America, and the Far East. An example of one of its initial tasks was to assist a South American Drug Enforcement Agency in conducting "discretionary warfare" against local drug producers. Other EO operations, stretching from Angola to Sierra Leone to Sri Lanka and Papua New Guinea, involve millions of dollars of cash payments augmented by mining, logging and oil rights to lucrative geologic deposits.

"It's kind of ironic that when Eeben fought for Apartheid, the white race, anti-communism and Pro-Christianity, he wound up without any money and was shoved out the door," says Willem Ratte, a former member of the elite Rhodesian Selous Scouts and the man who trained and honed Barlow's superlative fighting skills. It was Ratte who ran South Africa's war in Angola. Among Ratte's frighteningly maverick strategies was to send AIDS-infected prostitutes to comfort Cuba's 50,000 troops in Angola—unleashing an AIDS plague which they carried back home to Fidel Castro's homeland. "Now that he's fighting on the side of our enemies in Angola, and on behalf of the interests of the multinational corporations, he's become a wealthy man," adds Ratte. "Eeben is a very capable soldier. He once told me that he was angry about the sellout of the Communists by the National Party in South Africa."

"In the end, perhaps he figured that if the Marxists were going to take over our country anyway, why not make $US 40 million in the process?" Barlow calls his former mentor Ratte, "simply the finest, most professional soldier ever trained by the SADF." And although Barlow remains at odds with Ratte and a number of other former elite SADF troops that see him as having betrayed Afrikanerdom, he defends his right to change along with "The New South Africa."

"We've undergone a paradigm shift in consciousness, in our interpretation of reality," says respected South African political analyst Ed

Cain, editor of the erudite journal Signposts. "We are living in the post-Christian era. The free world and the 'former' communist world are being merged. There are no more countries, no more Japanese, no more Mexicans. There are only rich and poor, hi-tech and low-tech, Northern and Southern Hemisphere. It's almost like a new form of virtual Apartheid.

Article first appeared in WorldNetDaily. Printed with permission

See page 297, for biography of **Anthony LoBaido**.

| **pulling the rug** | doug lansky
morocco
present day |

Hustling carpets in Marrakesh

Moroccan carpet salesmen can deliver a line better than ~ Leonardo DiCaprio, are more tactical than a nuclear submarine captain, and are more endearing than your own grandmother.

Ahmed, who didn't look like he possessed any of these qualities, sat across from me on the remarkably slow Marrakesh Express for five hours without uttering a word, although I could see he was reading an English magazine through his Ray-Bans. When I asked him if he spoke English, he replied, "Of course. But I figured you knew that Moroccans who initiate conversation in English are usually just trying to sell you something." I liked him immediately. Upon our arrival, I agreed to join him for *chi* in his brother's carpet shop, the biggest in town.

This was when Ahmed baited me. He simply told me how much money he and his brother, Mostefa, made selling carpets to tourists (more each day than I make in a year). The real trick, he said, was getting the tourists into the shop. Suddenly, I saw where all this was heading.

"How much commission?" I asked.

Ahmed laughed. "Typically, 6 percent."

I told him I might consider it for twelve.

"Out of the question. If you want to try it for a while, you can stay with us and earn 8 percent."

We shook hands. I was now a Moroccan carpet hustler. The next morning the brothers sent me to the main square with Mohammed, a young man whose sole job was to help me find my way back through the maze-like market to the carpet shop. I spotted an English tour group, followed them into a restaurant, and introduced myself to a young, friendly looking couple. I told them I was a carpet hustler. Steven and Rachel laughed.

"No, really," I assured them, "I work for the biggest carpet shop in Marrakesh. My job is to guide you there and then back to your hotel when you want to leave. Mohammed here will make sure we won't get hassled along the way."

When we arrived at the carpet shop, my employers were pretty impressed. It had taken me all of fifteen minutes. Mostefa, a black belt in carpet selling, went right to work, pouring on charm like chemically flavored butter on movie popcorn. Watching Mostefa and Ahmed "push rug" was like watching Torvill and Dean ice skate, Ben and Jerry make ice cream, or Hulk Hogan and Andre the Giant perform a team slam from the third rope.

Mostefa, who speaks seven languages flawlessly, invited Steven and Rachel to join him for *chi* while he listened to their impressions of Marrakesh, found out what their jobs were (i.e., their credit card limits), and provided them with some interesting Moroccan insights. They discussed the weather, passport stamps, and new diet pills in Afghanistan-just about everything but carpets. Then Mostefa gave them a tour of his two-story shop, explaining the difference in quality between the carpets, the significance of the patterns, the number of knots per square inch-he even waved his lighter under some to demonstrate their fire-retardant qualities. When the tour was over, more *chi* was waiting for them. Not even Madeleine Albright gets treated this well on foreign visits.

"Would you like to see a few of the special carpets we don't display in the store?" Mostefa asked. How could Steven and Rachel refuse? He was practically their best friend at this point. Mostefa had noticed which style of carpets they preferred and, with the most subtle of gestures, he signaled his team of lackeys to bring them in. Carpets of various colors and sizes were flung one on top of the other, giving Steven and Rachel only five seconds to peek at one carpet before the next landed on top of it. Within a few minutes, the pile of carpets was nearly three feet thick.

When the last one had been unfurled, Mostefa confided, "Hard to take it all in, isn't it? My mother used to make so many sweets, I could never choose. What kind of sweets do you have in England?" Mostefa knew they were dying to have a second look, but he just made idle chatter until Rachel brought up the subject. Then, feigning reluctance, he swung back into action.

"Do you like this one?" he asked, gesturing to the top carpet.

"That's nice," Rachel confessed. The lackeys moved it off to the side.

"How about this one?"

"Well, not quite as much." The lackeys rolled it up and carried it away. They went through the whole pile that way, leaving Steven and Rachel with four carpets.

Now Mostefa knew he could relax for a while. Steven and Rachel got up for a closer look at the carpets they had "chosen" and began discussing which would go where in their home. "How much is this one?" Steven asked.

"Don't worry about the price now," Mostefa told him. "First, decide which ones you want."

They decided on two carpets.

"You have developed a fine eye for carpets in such a short time," Mostefa complimented. Now it was time to bargain. "How much would you be able to give me for these carpets?"

The English had no idea where to start the bidding.

"What would be a fair price?" Steven asked in return.

"Well," hesitated Mostefa, as though he'd never sold a carpet like this one before, "that carpet hanging on the wall is twice the size of *yours* and I sold that to a local man for $4,000 last week. I would certainly be willing to give that special local rate to you…$2,000 each. But it would pain me to see you choose, so I'll give you both for $3,800-a price you can't refuse."

Steven and Rachel swallowed audibly. Rachel managed to maintain her stiff, bleached upper lip, but Steven had suddenly developed an eye twitch.

The problem was, of course, that they were in love with these carpets and they didn't want to offend their newfound Moroccan soul mate.

"How about $3,000?" Steven countered with the conviction of Kato Kaelin.

Mostefa turned immediately serious, insulted. "I'm afraid that's completely impossible." After letting a heavy silence hang in the air, Mostefa said, "I have an idea," and went off to talk with Ahmed. They appeared to argue for several minutes and Mostefa appeared to win. "You're in luck, my friends," said Mostefa with a big smile as he walked back. "My supervisor told me I could come down to $3,500." It was brilliant. He had bargained on their behalf. The English accepted with pleasure, probably wondering if the sale of their first-born child would cover the purchase.

They shook hands, handed over their credit card, and Mohammed and I escorted them back to the market square, where I spotted an affluent German group who didn't realize they would soon be the owners of several fine Moroccan carpets.

Printed with permission:
Up The Amazon Without A Paddle. By Doug Lansky
Meadowbrook Press

See page 232, for biography of **Doug Lansky**.

	**business travelers**	robert young pelton africa present day

Professional victims?

Now, you would picture anybody that goes voluntarily into a war zone as a pretty game-faced macho kinda guy. Knife strapped to thigh, grenades taped to chest, spare magazines, first aid kit, last bullet ready for the brain and a sense of *sang froid*. So how come when I get to the blasted airport it's all guys with pocket protectors, cheap briefcases and that just-off-the-bus look? With a look that would sunburn tonsils they head straight to the hotel bar, the local nightclub and even tip the mujahedin at the door. Hey, this is business.

Believe it or not, the number one travelers to war zones are businessmen (sorry, girls)-people set on selling air conditioners', buying bulldozers', hawking medicine, concrete or even body bags. Hey, this is business. I don't have time to bleed, it ruins the suit.

Doesn't it just seem that every time you read about someone getting kidnapped, waylaid or massacred, he's a vice president of something or other working in Buttwipeastan? It doesn't have to be this way. There is a booming industry selling safety to business travelers. Companies like Pinkerton's, Jane's and Kroll will give you a blow-by-blow (every day if you like) of every maiming, kidnapping, bombing and attack. Almost all security services are targeted at businesses and businessmen (we're not being chauvinistic here, most victims are men). Yet when I give my talks on travel in dangerous places, I never meet any businessmen. Instead, I run into mostly gung-ho college students and graying, careful spinsters. I figure selling safety to business travelers is like offering sex education classes for monks. They don't see the need. After all, they are not really traveling. They get on a plane, have a couple of drinks, review the file and then meet the driver at the airport. They stay in a swank hotel, have dinner with the customer and then the driver takes them to the meeting the next day. Maybe they'll take in the risque show or just cruise the bars until closing time. Shower, buy a souvenir for the kid, a trinket for the wife and then back home in ten hours. Hey no big deal, just another business trip.

The reality of business travel from the other side is a little different. By flashing the suit, Rolex, President and Megaoil business card, you have become the enemy and the victim. You won't even have to pay the ransom out of your own pocket because they know you have a cash insurance policy for the kidnapping.

Business travel is perhaps the most dangerous form of travel. The fact that you represent an American company can make you a target. You also lost the ability to discern when and where to travel. Most tourists wouldn't consider flying into a Colombian war zone for a week. Yet folks from oil, computer, agricultural and food companies do it regularly. Most victims of terrorism tend to be working on a daily basis in a foreign country in areas where no sane traveler would go.

Finally, by doing business, you tend to frequent establishments and locations where thieves, terrorists and opportunists seek affluent victims—luxury hotels, expensive restaurants, expat compounds, airports, embassies, etc. As a businessperson, you cannot adopt the cloak of anonymity, since you will more than likely be wearing an expensive suit, staying in expensive hotels and have scads of luggage, cash and gifts. If you do business in places like Africa you may be surprised when you call the police for help and discover some don't have gas for their vehicles or bullets for their guns. In some countries like, Sierra Leone, a diamond mining center, the police may even show up only to rob you (once they find gas and bullets).

Business travel exposes you to frequent car and air travel and other means of transportation. Many trips are also undertaken in bad weather conditions and at congested travel periods (i.e., Monday out, Friday back). You are fed very carefully through a chain of businesses that cater to businesspeople and become a high-profile target for criminals who prey on business travelers. You make appointments well in advance with complete strangers and you have no idea of where you are going or where you are, and you even tell strangers you are lost. I often shudder when I see oil field technicians, complete with cowboy hats, pointed boots and silver Halliburton briefcases, tossing beer-soaked profanities and Ben Franklins around the world's transit lounges. Can you think of a more inviting target?

Dangerous Places for Business Travel In Africa

Algeria
Algeria is dependent on foreign expertise and open season on visitors. Foreign companies are paying top dollar for oil workers in the south, where it's relatively benign, but Algiers will still make your hair stand up on end.
http://travel.state.gov/algeria.html

Angola

Oil and diamonds shore up this shattered country. The country is looking for investors to help dig them out. However, impotent cease-fires are signed as frequently as bad checks and although the heavy fighting has wound down, the countryside is lawless.

http://travel.state.gov/angola.html

Nigeria

Nigeria is floating on oil but its people are dirt poor. I wonder where all that Shell money goes? Nigerians provide some of the best drug mules, scam artists, con men and extortion-based crime. If you get a fax from Nigeria asking for a meeting, run, do not walk, to the nearest bunco squad.

http://travel.state.gov/nigeria.html

Printed with permission:
The World's Most Dangerous Places. By Robert Young Pelton
http://www.comebackalive.com

See page 183, for biography of **Robert Young Pelton.**

	**tips on surviving business travel**	robert young pelton africa present day

- Have your host set up transportation, hotel and a driver/bodyguard. These are cheap insurance and insulation from the realities of the Third World.
- Don't get too chatty with the locals. All that info about your travel, room, samples and employer is worth money to evil men.
- Avoid restaurants frequented by expats and tourists. Don't make reservations in your own name. Do not sit outside. If possible, enjoy your host's hospitality.
- Dress in business attire, carry a briefcase and dress up only when necessary.
- Make copies of important papers. Separate your credit cards in case you lose your wallet. Keep the numbers, expiration dates and the phone numbers to order replacements. Be careful of credit card fraud, business scams and identity theft.
- Don't reveal home addresses or phone numbers or show your wallet when meeting people. Use your business address or P.O. box.
- Do not discuss plans, accommodations, finances or politics with strangers.
- Wear a cheap watch (or just show the band outward). If driving, wear your watch on the arm inside the car. Leave jewelry at home or in the hotel safe.
- Get used to sitting near emergency exits, memorize fire escape routes in the dark, lock your doors and be aware at all times.
- Kidnappers need prior warning, routine schedules or tip-offs to do their dirty work. Vary your schedule, change walking routes and don't be shy about changing hotel rooms or assigned cabs.
- Stay away from the front or back of the plane (terrorists use these areas to control the aircraft). Avoid aisle seats unless you want to volunteer for execution.
- Do not carry unmarked prescription drugs. Expect for gifts like cigars or alcohol to be appropriated by customs officials.
- Leave questionable reading material at home (i.e. *Playboy*, political materials).

- Carry small gifts for customs, drivers and other people you meet. Personalized pens are ideal.
- When you call with your plans, assume someone is listening.
- Watch your drink being poured.
- Do not hang the "Make Up Room" sign on your hotel room door. Rather, use the "Do Not Disturb" sign. Keep the TV or radio on even when you leave. Contact housekeeping and tell them you don't want your room cleaned up.

Printed with permission:
The World's Most Dangerous Places. By Robert Young Pelton
http://www.comebackalive.com

See page 183, for biography of **Robert Young Pelton**.

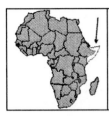	**tuna, frankincense and piracy**	lord westbury somalia present day

This short story is contributed because of the worthiness of the cause and the significant contribution that Operation Raleigh has made to development on the African continent and to those taking part in their programmes.

However, I believe it is also important that this short story is put into the proper context, balancing the beauty and opportunities correctly with the complexities and strife causing so much pain and hardship to so many Africans.

Somalia, for more than the last decade has been more fractured than any other country in Africa. It has had no central Government and since the now notorious 'Black Hawk Down' incident has been virtually ignored internationally. The result has been many Somalis being displaced either abroad or in refugee camps along its border. All attempts by the international community to create a central administration/government in Somalia have failed and indeed have potentially caused greater disruption and strife. In the mid to late 90's Somaliland and Puntland were established as self-administering states. This story relates to the Puntland State of Somalia.

It was called Puntland because 'Punt' means the land of fragrance and Puntland has large resources of frankincense. Indeed, in the bible it says the three wise men travelled from the land of Punt (thought now to be part of Somalia). Security on land was re-established in this region and its Government set about trying to rebuild its economy which was reliant on livestock and its significant fish resource which had been exploited over the past decades by the international fishing fleets. The area around the Horn of Africa had in the 90's become notorious for piracy and was rated by the International Maritime Bureau (IMB) as the sixth most dangerous areas in the world for piracy.

The Government of the Puntland State contracted my company, The Hart Group, to implement a Fisheries Management and Protection Programme. We trained about 80 Somalis, most of whom were unable to swim, and provided a 60-metre fisheries protection vessel. In the first two months they resolved one attack of piracy and caught 8 ships from Pakistan, Indonesia, Spain, Korea and Taiwan fishing illegally. It was only then that

310

we realised that virtually no country in Africa has any effective Fisheries Management or Protection programmes with over $2 billion dollars worth of tuna a year being caught in African Waters. Whilst we were patrolling we often saw shoals of tuna 2 miles long and 2 miles wide.

After the initial frenetic activities of the first couple of months the fisheries programme settled into the routine of patrolling the Puntland Waters. However, on the 8th July 2000 the Fisheries Patrol Vessel was tasked to assist in resolving an act of piracy.

Whilst conducting emergency engine repairs at anchor off the Puntland, the French-owned cargo ship MV *Mad Express* was boarded by armed gunmen. Seven of her crew were forced ashore and held in the village of Bargaal some 60 kms south of the Horn, whilst the Master and a further two crew were held at gunpoint on the ship. A number of shots were fired, but no one was hit.

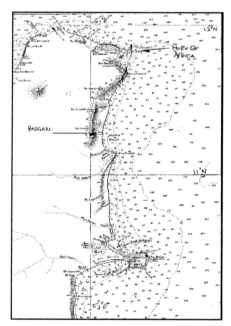

During the morning of Monday 10th July, HART's Director of Operations in Bossaso was appraised of the situation by the local Police Commissioner. A small liaison team was immediately dispatched to the President's Office in Garowe and the Fisheries Patrol Vessel (FPV), *Celtic Horizon*, diverted to close with the detained ship. A short time later the Marine Force (MF), who provide security both to the FPV and locally in Bossaso, was directed to render all possible assistance in resolving the situation.

On the morning of 11th July the FPV approached the *Mad Express*, positioning herself between the detained ship and the shore. Radio communications were established with the Master who, although clearly under duress, managed to confirm that seven of his crew were being held ashore and that he was very concerned for their safety. Working through the MF in Bossaso and HART's Director of Operations in the President's Office, negotiations were opened with the local authorities in Bargaal. This resulted in the seven crew members being secured to police protective custody ashore.

The gunmen on the *Mad Express* fled during the hours of darkness that night, taking with them a number of items including GMDSS radio equipment. They were arrested by the Bargaal police the following day. A small team of HART Fisheries Protection Officers  accompanied by members of the MF landed in the afternoon of the 13th, and after a period of intense but ultimately successful negotiations with the local authorities and tribal elders recovered all seven crew members to the *Mad Express* using the FPV's Rigid Inflatable Boats. One crew member was treated for badly broken arms and hands sustained during a fall early in the incident, and the *Mad Express* left the area safely the following morning bound for Djibouti.

The key to the successful resolution of this incident was undoubtedly the presence of the FPV combined with first class and timely liaison with the relevant authorities ashore. What could have been a protracted, expensive and dangerous situation was brought to a conclusion quickly and purposefully without the use of force and with a minimum of fuss. The Mad Express Master's own words perhaps best sum up the complexities of this incident:

MISSION IMPOSSIBLE WAS DONE SO FAST.

Yours faithfully,

MAD EXPRESS FLAG, BELIZE.

Lord Westbury was educated at Harrow School and Sandhurst Royal Military Academy. Richard Westbury was commissioned into the Scots Guards in 1970 and subsequently joined the SAS in 1975. He served four operational tours, and was decorated for bravery in 1978 and appointed MBE in 1979. During his time with the SAS, he saw service on every continent and was directly involved in a number of international incidents during the 1980's. From 1988 to 1991, Richard Westbury served as Deputy Chief Executive of The Leadership Trust, an executive training centre providing leadership and management training for over 2,500 chief executive officers and other key executives each year. In 1991, Richard Westbury was invited to join Defence Systems Ltd., a company providing security services in Africa. He became a director and Deputy Chief Executive in 1993 and Chief Executive Officer in 1995. During this time, the client base was increased from eight to over 200 multinational companies and supra-national agencies. In 1996, Richard Westbury and the Chairman of Defence Systems led a successful management buyout from Hambro Group Investments with the support of NatWest Ventures and DLJ Phoenix, and merged with a U.S. public company in 1997. Richard Westbury formed the Hart Group in 1999 and is its Chief Executive Officer and the General Manager of Global Marine Security Systems Company.

politics and religion

Today politics in Africa is often a sham. There are elections but only a single party! One of the sad things about elections in Africa is that the result can be predicted, months before the polls have closed.

This topic has had rain forests of material dedicated to it, but these are some very personal and thought provoking views.

If you are looking for further material, the UN's World Political Reports are worth a read. It's arguably one of the more valuable things the UN does.

	**terrorist or freedom fighter? you decide**	peter ward zimbabwe present day

In the last 50 years the world has been witness to Africa's 'Winds of Change.'

The struggle from Colonial rule was painful for both the colonizers and Nationalists with atrocities committed to each other, creating a new low in history and humanity of modern Africa.

Some of those killed were isolated whites and their families who happened to be in the way. Some were African chiefs who may have collaborated with the other side, and who perhaps had little alternative if their own families and their people were to survive.

It was perhaps not a policy to kill such people. But armed men, alone or in small groups, may come to disregard the importance of human life. It was necessary to fight guerrilla wars and in such wars terrible things are bound to happen.

They were terrorists, guerrillas, combatants, comrades, cadres, freedom fighters, revolutionaries, soldiers; it all depends on your viewpoint. A terrorist uses violence for political purposes, and the term 'Freedom Fighter' I define as someone or a group of people fighting for freedom against a repressive regime, so all people can have an expressive voice in a society or system - freedom of speech.

It is difficult to justify the cost of human life in any situation and I am not going to be judgmental about events that happened 40 years ago. There's no right or wrongs, as I believe they were men of their time, and at that moment of time, that way of being was correct. Similarly, 20 years ago if you hit a child it was discipline; today if you hit a child it's abuse. Same thing, just a different conversation on the activity.

However today in the new millennium, I do question the term 'Freedom Fighter', applied to some of Africa's statesman in the gaining of Independence of a country.

Zimbabwe is a notable example, which has had over 20 years of so called majority rule, under Robert Mugabe, and where there has been a one party state ever since his election.

Mugabe had the perfect resume for the job, which was typical of many African leaders who liberated their country from the clutches of colonial rule. He rose from humble beginnings as a peasant herd boy to become a teacher, followed by a political prisoner and graduated to be a guerrilla chieftain. Mugabe is smart and tough, he holds six university degrees. He led the largest of three guerrilla forces during the bloody, decades-long independence struggle to become the people's choice for leader.

The struggle for power in Zimbabwe was a bloody one, and this was typical of countries that had large volumes of white settlers who had become stakeholders in the country, and many knew no other country then the one they were residing in. Countries like Tanzania did not have hundreds of thousands of white settlers to resist, so the road to independence had less bumps, red lights and U turns.

The main problem with one party states, and Zimbabwe is no exception, is that there is no accountability or responsibility to serve the majority people of the country, as the democratic process is skewed in its favor.

In the last election in 1999, there was the usual violence and intimidation to opposition supporters, criticism from a variety of international bodies, including the World Bank, Amnesty International, limited media access for non government candidates and state funding for the governments election campaign. So it was of little surprise that he remained in power - But only just!

In the 1996 election the political opponents withdrew from the election, unfortunately too late to make any significant impact. If they had made clear from the outset that they were not prepared to participate in a bogus election because the whole affair had been so blatantly rigged, there may have been greater concern on the international stage.

With this mind set of running the country place, local reporters were naive if not brave when they questioned the government's decision to intervene militarily in the Democratic Republic of the Congo (DRC) costing a cool million a day. This resulted in IMF aid programs worth $340 million being shelved, directly impacting the Zimbabwean people. They were promptly whisked off to prison, beaten and tortured.

With a political system of this type, there is no need to be responsible to the people, as they are not the ones keeping the government in power. It is the paymasters, such as the military and party members. It is of no coincidence that this military adventure is where diamond and cadmium can be found.

So this George Washington freedom fighter has turned out to be a turned Richard Nixon, who is committed to remain in power at any cost, which is usually to the people. Unemployment runs 50 percent, inflation has rocketed to 60 percent and foreign investors and tourists have turned their backs.

This behavior is perplexing as this is what he and so many other of his supporters were so against under minority rule! Africa for all Africans.

In Zimbabwe the African dream of peace and prosperity has been shattered by greed, corruption and unscrupulous rule. The dream evaporated because of treachery and the betrayal of the government in the pursuit of wealth, which has been obtained by oppressing the majority wishes of the people. In this country at least, the role of the freedom fighter is incomplete.

Corruption and single party rule has been a common theme in other African countries and one of the reasons for this is that when a country does become independent and the liberators have the power, there is a void in the opposition. Thus, there is no counter balance to the democratic process to keep the government on its toes in serving the people. So for any one organization to establish itself in a country it has to tie links to the state party. This is perhaps why South Africa has such a vibrant political system, as there are strong individuals and businesses hungry for power, thus keeping the government's intentions accountable to the people.

The one party state has had its successes. Jomo Kenyatta in the 60's became Kenya's first president. He quickly established a one party state, but served the people of the nation. This resulted in Kenya becoming one of Africa's most prosperous states. Unfortunately when he died in 1978, the void that he left in the political system had widespread ramifications. Daniel Arap Moi, who replaced him, had to put down a coup by the air force, had aid suspended by the World Bank and provoked social unrest from tribal societies and universities. Not a bad achievement for his 100 days in power.

See back cover for **Peter Ward's** biography.

317

	**ropeway to heaven**	cam mcgrath ethiopia 1998

"Walking is good for you," I recall Kibron telling me. It was my Ethiopian friend's advice that had brought me nine miles across sweltering desert to the foot of a perversely overhanging cliff. With the midday sun beating down atop my head, I squint and scale the formidable precipice with my eyes.

At the top, though I cannot see it from here, is Debre Damo, an ancient Christian monastery in the bleak hinterland of northern Ethiopia. I've been drawn to this remote place by the legend of Aba Aregawi, a pubescent Syrian monk who unable to find a way to the top of the mesa, sat at its base and prayed for heavenly assistance. After 99 years, God, working on Ethiopian time as the locals joke, finally commanded a giant python to lower its tail and raise the pious monk in its coils. Unable to get off the desolate plateau, the monk laid the foundation for an expansive monastery and hermitage that has been in operation for nearly 1500 years.

Making my way around the base of the mesa, I find a group of local men ascending the shallowest portion of the cliff on a braided leather rope. Lowered from a narrow portal in a stone wall, the weathered rope is the only route to the top of the mesa. All of the monastery's material supplies must be raised by it- the stones of which the compound is built, the hundreds of candles the monks use every week, and even the cows that graze on the field around the compound.

Fatigued and dehydrated from the long hike, I wrap a cotton safety sling around my waist and haul myself up the rope. If I hated the rope climb in PE class, I was at least comforted by a padded mat if I fell. Now I am encouraged upwards by the thought of throttling the pesky young kid with a sling shot, apparently a novice monk, launching pebbles at me from the ledge above. When I reach the top and pull myself through the portal the kid has long vanished, hiding somewhere in the warren of crude stone buildings and passageways that cover the summit.

Debre Damo is hardly a tourist site. There are no hordes of package tourists, no overpriced tickets to buy, and no "I survived a 50 foot rope climb!" t-shirts for sale. In fact, even assuming one thinks of Debre Damo as a tourist site, there's not a whole lot to do once you get there. Apart from enjoying the spectacular views of rugged canyons and cactus groves below, the precinct itself is, quite frankly, boring.

The monks in this fully-functioning monastery spend most of their day in solitude, praying and fasting. And the monks are the social butterflies of Debre Damo. Halfway down the cliff-face are tiny caverns, barely the size of a man, in which hermits spend their adult years in austere confinement. Twice a day, once in the morning and once in the evening, the monks above emerge from their reverent solitude to lower a few pieces of stale bread and water down to these reclusive ascetics.

The question that naturally arises is where the monks on this dry desert crag obtain their water. When I query one of the young monks, he nimbly leads me down a short flight of stone-cut steps to a brackish pool hollowed out of the bedrock. The gentle monk brushes away the thick carpet of green algae that covers the surface of the tiny reservoir, acting as an insulator to reduce evaporation. 'Maee (water),' he announces with a yellowed smile.

The compound at Debre Damo is large enough to house a thousand monks, though only a fraction of that live there now. This is in part due to a mysterious fire that systematically disintegrated all of the sacred gold relics in the holy precinct while leaving everything else charred, though intact. The monks attributed the spontaneous fire to lightning or divine retribution, but when some of the monks started showing up with Rolexes, the Ethiopian authorities moved in and carted the suspects off to secular penitence.

See page 59, for biography of **Cam McGrath**.

	**islam in africa: a brief introduction**	jessica powers africa present day

The history of Northern Africa is incomprehensible without understanding the spread of Islam.

Islam in Africa is almost as old as the faith itself. Muhammad died in 632; less than ten years after his death, Arabs conquered Egypt, though it was not until the 14th century that the majority of Egyptians were Arabic-speaking Muslims (Hallett, 92). By the end of the 7th century, Islam had spread across North Africa to the northern border of present day Mauritania.

Today, North Africa above the Sahara and significant portions of West Africa and the East African coast are Islamic.

Many people associate Islam's spread with conquest or jihads. The importance of conquest, however, was that it established an Arab presence, inviting Muslim settlement and trade. Settlement and trade, ultimately, were more important than conquest in establishing Islam as the dominant religion of the region. Still, the historical process seems circular because without the unity religion brings, and thus the "righteousness" behind invasions and conquest, the vast trade routes and settlements might never have happened.

Still, though Islam's fundamentalism is often cited as the reason why Islam spread historically, wealth—the possibilities of trade and business—were just as important for establishing an Arab presence in North Africa as proselytization (see Hallett).

In this, at least, Islam and Christianity differed little in their invasions of Africa. Europeans and Arabs had similar reasons for Africa's conquest. For Europeans, spreading Christianity and culture (the idea of "civilization") were ostensibly two of the most important reasons for their presence in Africa; but commerce rarely took second place to religion or culture.

For Arabs, Northwest Africa held the same allure that Western America held for the Europeans who emigrated there in the 19th Century. They pioneered it the way Americans pioneered the West; as more and more Arabs settled in North Africa, it became the land of hope and opportunity where they could be free from persecution and make a fortune (Hallet, 121).

While the distinction between religion, culture, and trade/commerce is fuzzier for Muslims than for Western Christians, historian Hallett argues that few Muslims would have moved without the lure of wealth. Unlike Europeans, however, the Arabs who emigrated to Northwest Africa assimilated the indigenous cultures they encountered. Both cultures—and the religion Islam—changed and deepened in the process. (Of course, Christianity changed in the hands of Africans as well; the question remains if and how much western Christians allowed Africa to influence and enrich their culture.)

Egyptian and Berber intellectuals contributed to Islam's theology, while farmers and pastoralists changed the agricultural economy in Asia by importing crops like sorghum and coffee (Hallett, 18).

Women were a vital method for cultural exchange. Intermarriage created an avenue for Islamic culture and the Arabic language to spread quickly, as well as incorporating the cultural practices of a particular ethnic group into an Islamic family (Berger and White).

One negative example of this cultural exchange, whereby Africans influenced Islamic culture, is the practice of female circumcision. It is often attributed to or blamed upon Islam, particularly because the majority of women who are circumcised today are Muslim. But historians believe that nomadic tribes first practiced it and that it was absorbed or carried over into the new culture and new religion as these tribes converted to Islam. Muhammad himself spoke against the practice, and advised that if females MUST be circumcised, the circumcisor should practice a less severe form because "cutting deep" would take the "shine" out of a woman's eyes.

The cultural exchange, however, did not produce a unified culture of Islam in Africa. The number of ethnic peoples, cultural customs, and religious practices among African Muslims is extraordinarily diverse. Among worshippers at the festival Id al Fitr, the festival that concludes Ramadan—an Islamic ritual that consists of a month-long fast—an anthropologist observed members of ethnic groups from Senegal and Nigeria, as well as groups from Dyula, Zara and Bobo (Bravmann, 60).

This unity within diversity may be the strength of Islam.

For Further Reading

Berger, Iris and E. Frances White. Women in Sub-Saharan Africa. Indianapolis: Indiana University Press, 1999.

Hallett, Robin. Africa to 1875: A Modern History. Ann Arbor: The University of Michigan Press, 1970.

Iliffe, John. Africans: The History of a Continent. New York: Cambridge University Press, 1995.

Bravmann, Rene A. African Islam. Smithsonian Institution Press: 1983.

This article first appeared on http://www.suite101.com/

Jessica Powers earned a B.A. in literature and writing from New Mexico State University, and traveled to India, Uzbekistan, Kenya, Nicaragua, and Mexico. This, combined with growing up on the Mexico border, gave her an interest in Third World history. She has a Masters of Fine Arts from the University of Texas at El Paso and a second master's degree in African History from the State University of New York at Albany. She's a regular on the lecture circuit, emphasizing religion and human rights in Third World history.

|  | **ethnic identity and religion on the upper slave coast** | jessica powers africa present day |

When Europeans first explored Africa, they declared that it had no religion. The absence of religion allowed the colonizers to de-humanize "the natives." The British eugenicist Francis Galton, for example, wrote that his dog was more intelligent than the African "natives" (Chidester 7). It is no wonder, then, that Europeans failed to make accurate observations about African culture and society.

Instead, they surveyed the religious practices of Africans and defined it as "primitive magic." They placed magic on a continuum with science, and suggested that as "savages" advanced toward "civilization," they would replace their superstition with an understanding of science. This "savage" mentality was also attributed to children, women, criminals and the insane back in Europe (Chidester 4).

However, Africans did indeed have religion and, unlike the European mentality, they did not divide the secular and the sacred. Religion permeated their cultural customs.

The history of the Anlo-Ewe in Ghana demonstrates the important link between religion and ethnic identity in many African cultures.

The Anlo-Ewe, historically, have been divided into "insider" clans that have rights to land and "outsider" clans who do not. The five "insider" clans are considered to be the "first" clans of the Anlo-Ewe; their rights to the land, according to their cultural traditions, indicate that they arrived on the upper slave coast before the "outsider" clans arrived.

The Amlade clan is the only "insider" clan that has no land rights. Historian Sandra Greene argues that this is because they belonged to an "outsider" clan until they were incorporated as one of the "first five" clans because of their god, Togbui Egbe, who had a reputation for severely punishing those who offended it, usually by inhabiting a snake and manipulating it to bite the intended victim (Greene 62).

The Amlade's chance to become one of the "first five" happened when the god of the "insider" Lafe clan lost its reputation for protecting the Anlo during battle. The Lafe had always had the privilege of praying to their god during war, but during the seventeenth century, their god seemed to give the Anlo little success.

323

In 1769, the Anlo won the first battle they had won since for over fifty years (Greene 57). They attributed their success to the god who belonged to the "outsider" Dzevi clan. Soon, the Lafe clan became the target of jokes because their god, apparently, was not very powerful.

Greene argues that the Lafe aligned themselves with the Amlade and their god because Togbui Egbe was known to be particularly powerful (64).

Over time, the Amlade and Lafe re-wrote oral traditions and linked the two clans through a common ancestor who had given birth to twins; one twin became the Lafe clan ancestor, while the other became the Amlade clan ancestor. According to the oral story, the families of the twins scattered and were re-united later.

The common ancestor justified the Amlade's new status, while the fact that they had been scattered explained why the Amlade had not been one of the insider clans from the first and thus, did not have access to land.

The common ancestor further allowed the Amlade to maintain communication with their dead ancestors without leaving the area and returning to their place of origin on a regular basis (Greene 67).

The Anlo-Eve are a great example of how African religion, identity, and cultural customs are inseparable. However, a word of caution: Making generalizations about traditional African religion is dangerous. The hundreds of ethnic groups encompass hundreds of religious traditions. For every similarity, there are a dozen differences. Above all else, African history is local history.

For Further Reading:

David M. Anderson and Douglas H. Johnson, editors, Revealing Prophets, Athens: Ohio University Press, 1995.

Thomas D. Blakely, Walter E.A. van Beek and Dennis L. Thomson, editors, Religion in Africa: Experience and Expression, Portsmouth, NH: Heinemann, 1994.

David Chidester, Savage Systems: Colonialism and Comparative Religion in Southern Africa, Charlottesville: The University Press of Virginia, 1996.

Sandra E. Greene, Gender, Ethnicity, and Social Change on the Upper Slave Coast: A History of the Anlo-Ewe, Portsmouth, NH: Heinemann, 1996.

This article first appeared on http://www.suite101.com/

See page 322, for biography of **Jessica Powers**.

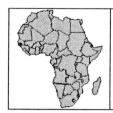	**they cut themselves with cruel kimes**	jessica powers africa 1808

In Great Britain, the literary world was scathing in its indictment of the attempt to "civilize" and "Christianize" the "natives" (the derogatory term for colonial subjects stretching from Africa to Asia).

Sending missionaries to Christianize the "Natives" was just an excuse to make money, they argued. Furthermore, the missionaries they sent were so stupid, they might not be much better than the "natives" themselves.

Bernard Shaw, nineteenth and twentieth century playwright, described the way traders used missionaries to make money in his 1898 play "The Man of Destiny":

"When [an Englishman] wants a new market for his adulterated Manchester goods, he sends a missionary to teach the natives the Gospel of Peace. The natives kill the missionary; he flies to arms in defense of Christianity, fights for it; conquers for it; and takes the market as reward from heaven."

But even when writers accepted the idea that money justified the British presence in its colonies, they still felt that that did not justify the sorry excuse called "missionaries" sent over to "civilize" the colonial subjects.

In 1808 and 1809, Sydney Smith, founder of the Edinburgh Review, predicted the failure of the missionary movement. He called the true nature of Methodism (i.e., the impetus for evangelism) the "evil of fanaticism." This evil, according to Smith, changed a normal, decent Englishman into a deranged, deceptive character who wandered around uttering idiocies.

For his readers' benefit, Smith used the Methodist missionary and writer John Styles as an example. Smith argued that Styles had presented his cause in a deceptive manner in order to produce "a great degree of mysterious terror" in people at home. Apparently, he had described the Hindu as piercing themselves with cruel kimes, a newspaper misprint that should have read "knives." Smith mocked the misprint. But of course, he said, we must be "noble" and send missionaries to a country where people cut themselves with cruel kimes.

It is ridiculous, he argued, to think that we can teach the religion of the British to a country and then pack up and go home, leaving it to their management. Besides, he stated, the type of men who were sent out for missionary purposes were worse for religion than a thousand pagans "who cut themselves with cruel kimes." If they were going to send out missionaries, why did they forget "common sense and decency?" Why did they send such a "foolish set of men?" What good does it do for a man to say he has walked a thousand miles with peas in his shoes unless he has a purpose for it? (Edinburgh Review 14, 40-46).

In another article, Smith reminded his readers that since Christianity's origins, God had allowed the greater part of humanity to live and die in ignorance. Therefore, wasn't it reasonable to assume that "the rapid or speedy conversion of the whole world to Christianity forms no part of the scheme of its Almighty Governor?"(Edinburgh Review 12, 170) He concluded that Christianity should spread slowly and temperately (Edinburgh Review 14, 50).

Great Britain judged how "civilized" a colony was by how nearly it conformed to British politics, religion, and economic system. South Africa was full of "white perverts" (the Dutch Boers) and "black savages" (Comaroff, vol. 1, 43). British settlers in South Africa told the English back home that the Boers had degenerated into barbarians under the influence of the Africans.

Africa was not the only continent or colony judged "uncivilized." Clearly, although dark skin indicated a lack of civilization, the English held similar views about other races which were light-skinned, particularly the Irish (Porter, 71.) The farther away from London, the farther away from the center of civilization.

Novelist Charles Dickens sneered at the notion of the "Noble Savage." He compared the African tribal war customs to the Irish House of Commons and stated that other elements of savage life resembled an Irish election (The Works of Charles Dickens, vol. 34, 126). The Irish were so hated in England that it is not clear whether this was meant as an insult to the Africans or the Irish.

In 1848, Dickens wrote that Obi, King of Nigeria, was highly amused by these white men who negotiated a treaty with him to stop the slave trade and create an avenue for missionaries to come to Nigeria. Obi knew the treaty would cost them their lives. For such treaties, Dickens said, "the useful lives of scholars, students, mariners, and officers – more precious than a wilderness of Africans – were thrown away!" ("The Niger Expedition," 56).

Indeed, many of the Niger Expedition's crew died of fever. The whole idea of evangelization was useless and wicked, Dickens stated. "No amount of philanthropy has a right to waste such valuable life as was squandered here…Between the civilized European and the barbarous African there is a great gulf set." If it is difficult to change a civilized and educated man,

Dickens stated, then the attempt to change the ignorant savage races would take so long that it "dazzled" him to think about it. Instead of sending out missionaries, pastors and evangelists should focus their endeavors on England. "The work at home must be completed thoroughly, or there is no hope abroad." The only hope of success for Christianity, he argued, is to let it spread out from a center circle in ever widening spheres ("The Niger Expedition," 62-63).

W. Winwood Reade, fellow of the Geographical and Anthropological Societies of London, explored Africa in the mid-nineteenth century and wrote an anthropological treatise about his travels. He concluded that the Christian missionary endeavor in Africa was an exercise in futility.

Reade described an attempt to explain Christian theology to an African chief who understood the basic idea that the death of the son of God could atone for the sins of humankind, but questioned the motivation behind such a sacrificial act. Because the word for "mercy" had no translation, Reade described it as an act of love. At this, the chief laughed and made an obscene gesture. According to Reade, in his language, the word "love" could only indicate a sexual relationship between two members of the opposite sex. There were no corresponding words for other types of love (Reade 443).

With no appropriate translation, Reade argued, how could an African "savage" ever understand the Christian message? If spiritual love could only be defined by sexual love, then that language barrier prevented transmission of theology across the two cultures. They could not understand "abstract truths," he stated, when their language did not have words to express abstract ideas (Reade 443).

Reade's assessment of Christian workers in Africa in 1864 was similar to judgements that Sydney Smith had made in 1808 and 1809. Many of Reade's English contemporaries, including writer Charles Dickens, regarded the missionary endeavor as heroic but futile or misguided. This perception was often based not on the actions or characters of individual missionaries, or even missionaries in general. Rather, it was filtered through a lens that judged Africans as intellectually unable to comprehend the higher, abstract truths of Christianity.

Ironically, although the British believed Christianity was universally true for all people at all times of history, and though they believed it was the main "civilizing force" for the world, the perception that its truth was too advanced to be understood by the "savage" mind relegated it to such elite status that it became useless as a "civilizing" force at all. Subsequently, a segment of nineteenth century Great Britain scrutinized the failures and successes of the missionary movement based on its conception of an African "savage," leading those individuals to argue that the missionary movement was admirable but unable to convert or civilize the continent of Africa.

Sources Cited

Comaroff, Jean and John L. Comaroff. Of Revelation and Revolution. Vol. 1, Christianity, Colonialism, and Consciousness in South Africa. Chicago: University of Chicago Press, 1991.

Comaroff, Jean and John L. Comaroff. Of Revelation and Revolution. Vol. 2, The Dialectics of Modernity on a South African Frontier. Chicago: University of Chicago Press, 1997.

Dickens, Charles. "The Noble Savage" from The Works of Charles Dickens, vol. 34, Reprinted Pieces, The Lamplighter, To Be Read At Dusk, and Sunday Under Three Heads (New York: Charles Scribner's Sons, 1907 [1853]).

Dickens, Charles. "The Niger Expedition" in The Works of Charles Dickens, vol. 18, Miscellaneous Papers, Plays and Poems (New York: Bigelow, Brown and Co., 1920[1848]).

Porter, Bernard. The Lion's Share: A Short History of British Imperialism 1850- 1995. New York: Longman, 1996.

Reade, W. Winwood. Savage Africa: Being the Narrative of a Tour in Equatorial, Southwestern and Northwestern Africa; with Notes on the Habits of the Gorilla; on the Existence of Unicorns and Tailed Men; on the Slave Trade; on the Origin, Character, and Capabilities of the Negro, and on the Future Civilization of Western Africa. New York: Johnson Reprint Corporation, 1967 [1864].

Shaw, Bernard. "The Man of Destiny" from Plays Pleasant and Unpleasant vol. 2 (New York: Viking Penguin, 1989), 334-336.

Smith, Sydney. "Review of 'Strictures on Two Critiques" in the Edinburgh Review, "On the Subject of Methodism and Missions; with Remarks on the Influence of Reviews, in general, on Morals and Happiness' by John Styles," Edinburgh Review 14 (April-July 1809).

Smith, Sydney. "Publications Respecting Indian Missions" in Edinburgh Review 12 (April-July 1808).

This article first appeared on http://www.suite101.com/

See page 322, for biography of **Jessica Powers**.

	**behind 'the third boer war'**	anthony lobaido south africa 1991

Not your typical South African experience

The story of how I came to write "The Third Boer War is stranger than the fictional plot of the novel itself. It was a 10-year odyssey that challenged my will and faith at a level I had never before experienced.

Between June and December of 1991 I traveled to South Africa to complete the foreign journalism internship for my master's degree at Baylor University in Texas—where I had earned a full scholarship for an International Journalism degree. South Africa was the epitome of my youth. While working in South Africa, then still pro-West, Christian and anti-Communist and anti-globalist, I became the first and only journalist in the world to gain entrance into the elite, mercenary-run training camps of South Africa's Afrikaner Resistance Movement. These investigations produced ground-breaking journalism.

My articles were featured in the South African Sunday Star, Durban Times, Belgium Way Press (translated into French) and Soldier of Fortune magazine. Former South African President F.W. De Klerk even used photographs appearing with my articles in his campaign to dismantle Apartheid in the March 1992 referendum. Nelson Mandela went on national television holding a copy of one of my stories, railing against the anti-communist Afrikaners.

Using my Afrikaans language (the Dutch/German hybrid spoken by the Boer/Afrikaners) ability as a gateway, I was able to get inside the Afrikaner mentality in a way that few other foreign/Western journalists had ever been able to. I was given a unique insight into the complexities of South Africa's contemporary geopolitical situation. Most prominent of these was the 30-year "Border War" the Afrikaners fought in Angola against the Soviet Union, Cuba, East Germany and other Soviet allies who tried to invade their nation.

Of course most Americans have been totally brainwashed about the Afrikaners and South Africa. In general, the public has been told that the Afrikaners are Nazis who hate blacks. Movies like "Lethal Weapon 2" have sadly only fueled this propaganda lie of the leftist, Marxist Hollywood elite.

The reality is of course, 180 degrees in the opposite direction. The Afrikaners carved the richest and most prosperous nation out of the wilderness of Africa. They fought and bled and died for Great Britain and America in World War I and II. (Despite the fact that the British killed 26,000 Afrikaner women and children in the world's first concentration camps during the Boer War 1899-1902). Afrikaner pilots fought for South Korea—along with the Rhodesians—during the Korean War. Yet South Korea voted for anti-South Africa and anti-Rhodesia sanctions at the United Nations after all they did for Seoul at their darkest hour.

The Afrikaners even helped Israel to build their own nuclear weapons. Could there be anything more anti-Nazi than arming Jews in Israel with their own atomic arsenal against their Soviet-backed Islamic jihad adversaries?

Of course not.

The Afrikaners in general were and are the greatest people I have ever encountered—and I have lived, worked and traveled to the four corners of the Earth. They are tough and rugged and Christians. Their ruggedness exceeds that even of the Israelis and South Koreans. The Afrikaners were against abortion, which was illegal in their nation from the 1600's until the ANC took over in 1994. Television was kept out of South Africa until the mid 1970s. Pornographic magazines were also illegal until the late 1980s. Shops in South Africa closed on Saturday afternoon to prepare for the Sunday Sabbath.

All in all, despite the many egregious flaws of Apartheid, South Africa was a maverick, Christian, anti-communist, pro-West nation and the brightest outpost of Christian, European civilization in all of Africa. The Afrikaners were also the key member of an anti-communist alliance during the Cold War featuring El Salvador, Chile, Taiwan and Israel. When America would not help the Contras any longer, it was the Afrikaners who sent arms—and the means and will to take out Marxists like Bishop Romero in El Salvador. When the American Congress lied about helping South Africa stop the Soviets and Cubans in Angola, it was left, as always, to the Afrikaners to handle the communists on their own. And they did—as always.

Yes, the human-rights abuses under Apartheid committed by the government hit squads—led by lunatics like Eugene de Kock and Dr. Wauter Basson—are the epitome of evil. But they represent one tenth of one percent of the Afrikaner nation. These crimes and, in fact, the entire war in South Africa were committed to the suppression of a Marxist terrorist war

330

launched by the Soviet-trained African National Congress. The truth be known, some of these crimes were so horrible that I would have probably joined the ANC myself had I known about them in the early 1990s.

On the other side of the coin, the ANC's crimes are legion. These included putting tires filled with petrol around the necks of their enemies and lighting them on fire. Terrorist bombings of Afrikaner women and children - like the infamous Church Street attack—represent the very worst of this asymmetrical campaign. The ANC also tortured and murdered its own black communist cadres—especially in the Angola terrorist training camps. Nelson Mandela even ordered and then covered up the slaughter of unarmed Zulus at the Shell House massacre *after* he was released from prison.

The Mandela myth

Not many people realize that Nelson and Winny Mandela have a great deal of blood on their hands. Even Mandela admits in his autobiography that he should have been summarily executed for his crimes. He spent little time at Robbin Island, and actually lived under house arrest in a comfortable estate complete with every amenity imaginable.

Speaking of the Mandela myth, only last week, Harry Wu, perhaps the world's leading human-rights dissident told me, "When I think of [Nelson] Mandela, I feel very sad. When he became president of South Africa, he abandoned Taiwan and recognized China instead. Taiwan and [anti-communist, Apartheid] South Africa had been close allies. Mandela has extensive human rights knowledge. He may not be a communist, but the new leader of South Africa, Thabo Mbeki is definitely a communist. Recently he went to Cuba to meet with Castro, and he was trained in Moscow."

During my 1991 visit to South Africa I also had the opportunity train with elite Special Forces soldiers of the South African Defense Force (SADF). Eventually, I was asked to carry out a few missions on their behalf—including the assassination of Nelson Mandela and later U.N. Secretary General Boutros Boutros Gali, both of which, of course, I flatly refused even though I had been trained and deployed in the field to do so. The Boutrous Gali mission was set for the fall of 1994 at the U.N. Headquarters during the "Fourth World" ceremony.

Although I was in position to carry out the evil missions, I could never even think of doing so. No one should kill anyone—ever. I recalled a scene from a film that led me to major in political science, "Spies Like Us." In the movie, two bumbling Americans are asked to infiltrate a mobile Soviet nuclear missile site. When told they would have to shoot the Russian soldiers, the Americans respond, "I'm not killing anybody!"

And that is really the point of "The Third Boer War."

The world is out of control and we must look at our own lives and our own sins and repent. We must be preparing for judgment, as Americans, a part of Western Civilization and, human beings on planet Earth. We must realize that most basic lesson of all—there is good and evil in every race, culture, creed, nation and political party.

A strange dark light of evil has swept over the world, and there is nothing we can do to stop it. Sometimes that evil can appear as beautiful as Donna Dixon, the star of "Spies Like Us." And this dark is so powerful that it takes the very call of the Lord to pull us out of this terrestrial world— which Satan has seemingly taken hold over at a frighteningly accelerating pace, leaving one breathless.

I wrote "The Third Boer War" between 1992 and 1994. It took 2,000 hours of research and writing to do so. That is 40 hours per week for 50 weeks. I spent my life savings writing that book. I dropped out of my Ph.D. program at Texas A and M to do so. I lived like an animal with Vietnamese immigrants at one point. I sold my plasma and even took experimental pharmaceuticals in clinical tests for money to buy food. I ruined my back while hunched over the computer all those hours, but I don't regret one minute of it.

Article first appeared in WorldNetDaily. Printed with permission

See page 297, for biography of **Anthony Lobaido**.

	**white africans**	jessica powers africa present day

What does it mean to be a White African?

Historically, it has meant wealth, access to land, plenitude of servants, hard work, belief in the superiority of Europe and Christianity and capitalism. It has meant adventure, struggle, disease, fear, heat, sun, blue skies. It has meant being a minority, but often, as part of a ruling class.

For some today, it means baggage: history defining them as racists, insisting that they're racists, even if they aren't.

For some, it means baggage: being racists in a world increasingly opposed to it. Defending racism when nobody wants to hear it.

For some, it means fear: "What will 'they' do to us if 'they' have the chance?"

For some, it means defiance: "I will stay and I will succeed, no matter what may come."

For some, it has meant a constant move south: moving or fleeing from Kenya, the Congo, Zambia to Rhodesia; leaving Rhodesia for South Africa when Rhodesia became Zimbabwe. And then—leaving South Africa in 1994 when Mandela won the first democratic election and became President.

For some, it has meant real sorrow as they come to grips with how their ancestors treated the continent they love—and how they themselves have treated the continent they love.

For some, it has meant denial, and excuses.

For some, it has meant integration, leaving European culture behind, becoming something new.

For some, it has simply been a way of life, where they were born, how they were raised, where they want to stay, what they love, and who they know.

Living in Africa today—for white and black—means facing the reality of poverty, that wealth is unevenly distributed around the world today, that the West controls not simply the keys to economic power but lives inside the house which those keys open.

Living in Africa today means facing epidemic on a scale unknown here in the West.

Living in Africa today means facing the fact that there are still basic questions about human rights that are unanswered and maybe unanswerable.

Yet poverty, epidemic, and human rights issues are only one aspect of Africa. It is a continent vibrant with life and music and people who love, people who welcome the world to its doorstep. It is a continent filled with dignity, men and women who walk as though they have royal blood. Africans have resilient spirits. And this is as true for the white African as the black African.

This article first appeared on http://www.suite101.com/

See page 322, for biography of **Jessica Powers**.

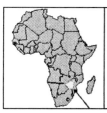	**defining terrorism**	jessica powers zimbabwe 1977

Words, if only we defined them

The word "terrorism" has been batted about like a baseball. Its common use belies the fact that it is a fighting word. As a word that is ill-defined, it can easily be used as propaganda. We are now waging a war on "terrorism," an admittedly shadowy war with vague opponents whose identities are suspect or unknown.

I agree that the men and/or women who were behind the recent attacks on the World Trade Center and the Pentagon should be punished for the atrocities. I agree that their actions can be defined as "terrorism" because they were directed at civilians, rather than military infrastructure or troops.

Still. What is a "terrorist"? If we are waging war on "terrorism," what standards do we use to judge whether a group is terrorist or a legitimate group fighting for freedom or majority rule? Won't there always be "terrorists," and if so, when will this war end?

In 1977, the Rhodesian government arrested an American nun, Sister Janice McLaughlin, and accused her of being a "Communist" and "supporter of terrorism." They based their accusations on her diary, in which she expressed support for the African men and women who were fighting a guerrilla war against the white led regime.

In reality, Sister McLaughlin's arrest was prompted by the research she had conducted over the previous few months, which exposed the government's propaganda. The book, slated to be published the same week she was arrested, argued that the government lied when it accused the terrorists of kidnapping, Communism, and other atrocities. In addition, it outlined specific atrocities that the government had committed.

The civil war in the 1970's was partly a war of language. To the European settlers, now known as "Rhodesians," the country was called "Rhodesia," named after Cecil Rhodes, the Englishman who brought large areas of Africa under British rule. To the Africans fighting for democracy and majority rule, the country was "Zimbabwe," a word that reflected their heritage. To the Rhodesian government, the guerrilla soldiers were

335

"terrorists." To those who supported their goals, they were "liberation soldiers" or "the boys."

For Sister McLaughlin, the war on words was clear. At her trial, she refused to call the guerrilla soldiers "terrorists," even though to call them anything else was an act of treason by law. She chose to remove herself from the government's propaganda, even though it meant she might spend years in jail. (She didn't. The U.N. intervened and she was ultimately released.)

The international press inadvertently became an accomplice to the Rhodesian government's propaganda. Using the word "terrorist" to describe the "liberation" soldiers (also, arguably, a propaganda term) led many Americans and Europeans to defend the actions of the Rhodesian government. But as the press began to realize the censorship that occurred in the country, and as the "liberation" soldiers began to promote their cause in the press, the world began to shift its support to the guerrilla cause. In 1980, Zimbabwe had the first elections that allowed all Zimbabweans to vote.

Sr. McLaughlin had entitled her booklet, "The Propaganda War." Indeed, the Rhodesian government had conducted a secret propaganda war that, for much of the war, was largely one-sided. But as the guerrillas learned how to use the press to their advantage, these propaganda wars began to play out in the press. The propaganda wars in the press led to more support for African independence and, ultimately, the demise of white rule in Zimbabwe.

I would like to be a pacifist, although I admit that I would be a hypocritical pacifist. I sleep at night in the safety provided by the U.S. military. If someone attacked me, I would defend myself, if I could. So I am a reluctant supporter of war when it is a matter of defense.

Still. I would like this word "terrorism" to be clearly defined, especially if we are supposed to be supporting the war against it.

And I would like to see the press temper its words, and learn to use words judiciously, so that it does not become a willing accomplice in the government's propaganda war, as happened in Zimbabwe during the 1970's.

For Further Reading

Jessica wrote a master's thesis, "An American Nun in Zimbabwe's War for Liberation," finished in May 2001. There are copies of it at SUNY Albany and at the Maryknoll Archives in Ossining, New York.

This article first appeared on http://www.suite101.com/

See page 322, for biography of **Jessica Powers**.

modern history

In history, there's a difference between what happens and our interpretation of it. Someone may say something or do something, and that is the "event." What we make that event mean is our "interpretation" of it. Sometimes people think that the event and the interpretation are one and the same thing, but they are not. This is why history lessons on Africa can be confusing, because there is too much interpretation.

This chapter captures people's different interpretations of history.

There are only 10 history lessons in this chapter, so don't expect a complete understanding of the continent's past. Just an entertaining read, to whet your appetite for other sources of material on Africa.

	**Imperialism in africa**	derek guiler africa 1877

The scramble for Africa

In 1877 a plan was drawn up in Berlin by the leaders of England, France, Germany, Belgium and Italy to split the continent of Africa into "spheres of influence," thus ushering in the "New Imperialism.". The main economic argument given for the advent of this imperial movement was the need to get rid of excess capital created by the Industrial Revolution, but this seems like a simplistic argument when European actions are viewed as a whole. Stories of fabulous wealth had been told regarding the "Dark Continent" but Europeans, even at the height of slavery a century earlier, had yet to penetrate the interior. In Berlin, the leading powers drew lines through the map without regard for the actual Africans who were split into hundreds of tribes and kingdoms. The Europeans then set about to make the natives conform to their lines. Only one territory in Africa was independent by the time of the First World War, the ancient kingdom of Ethiopia.

Regardless of the methods they used to secure their kingdoms (some colonial powers preferred direct rule while others, like Britain, found it more economical to work with or create indigenous governments under their control) many voices in Europe up to the present day insist that the European colonial mission was to "civilize" Africa:

"In 1998, on the 100th anniversary of the battle of Omdurman, the British ambassador to Sudan was asked if he planned to apologize to his hosts for that butchery of their Mahdist forefathers resisting invasion. "Why not?" he said, "As long as we also apologize for the roads, hospitals, schools and university; indeed for creating a country called Sudan."(1)

Apologists for the colonialists often speak of the institutions built in Africa at the behest of the Colonial Powers and it is always as if they built these "roads, hospitals, schools etc." themselves. Even within the continent itself, Africans are not to be given credit for their labor or for the fact that these institutions, most often of little use to the majority of people, were built with a small percentage of what had been stolen from them.

The institutions built, at the behest of the European conquerors, did not take root in Africa as they did in other places for two main reasons. First, there is the issue of how short-lived European domination actually was and how often these colonies changed hands (after World War I for example) as opposed to say, British domination of India which slowly advanced over several hundred years. Those Imperialist powers who tried to graft a European society over an indigenous African one in so short a time were doomed to failure by the excessiveness of their vanity and their belief that Africans were "savages". Second, in order to secure their somewhat tenuous positions, many colonial administrations were minimal, relying on local elites (whether indigenous or created) often educated by them to enforce their rule. In a sense, much of the tragedy of contemporary African history is drawn from these policies. For proof we need only look at Rwanda where the majority Hutu eventually turned on the Tutsi elite that had benefited from its associations with the Belgian conquerors.

Unfortunately, the final chapter in the history of colonialism in Africa has yet to be written. Although countries like France and England are loathe to take an active role in Africa, they, along with the United States among others, are usually willing to take a role behind the scenes. While the Cold War was devastating for the continent, we have yet to see what the full effects of corporate neo-imperialism will be for the region. With the support of their governments, multi-national companies like Royal-Dutch Shell have and will continue to wreak havoc in Africa, while the rich countries of Europe and North America complacently wait for the next tragedy to unfold in newspaper headlines and on their television screens.

1 The Economist. "THE SCRAMBLE FOR AFRICA." Economist Magazine; December 31, 1999

See page 284, for biography of **Derek Guiler**.

340

	**early african nationalism and pan-africanism**	jessica powers africa present day

Nationalism and Pan-Africanism gained wide acceptance among Africans in the 1920's, but their ideological roots extended back to the 19th Century as African intellectuals began to question Western pseudoscientific theories that proclaimed blacks were inferior because of their skin color. These pan-African ideas moved naturally into nationalism, which agitated for equal access to education and land as well as political and economic freedom.

Pan means "all," so pan-Africa means "all Africa." The ideology of pan-Africanism promoted racial pride and claimed Africa for the Africans; it spoke for all Africans, rather than focusing on a particular ethnic group or nation. With no political power, it could not change the colonial system, but it did articulate the problems that Africans experienced under colonial rule and helped form the basis for nationalism.

Edward Blyden is a well-known 19th-Century African intellectual who helped spread the Pan-African ideology. Blyden advocated the Islamic faith and polygamy, which he felt were more appropriate for the African personality. He condemned mixed marriage, insisting that Africans should keep the black race pure. Above all, Blyden preached racial pride. James Johnson, a radical evangelist, was also a leader in the Pan-African intellectual revolution. He insisted Africa could only be evangelized by Africans and argued that the European presence prevented African development because it destroyed the superior physique, independence, courage bravery, and self-reliance of those Africans who had not come into contact with Europeans.

Later, in the 1930's, the ideology of négritude ("blackness"), which grew among French-speaking African students studying in France, echoed some of the ideas spread by early Pan-Africanists. Those Africans who defended négritude argued that the characteristics of the black race— emotion, generosity, spontaneity—were superior to the characteristics of the white race. Being black was a privilege, rather than a burden. Surprisingly, négritude was popular only among French-speaking Africans. English-speaking Africans adamantly rejected the philosophy.

Nationalism developed as a political ideology in opposition to foreign rule; its goal was to use the colonial system as a framework for an independent Africa. Western education was largely responsible for producing the African elite who led the overthrow of the colonial system. Nationalists had almost invariably been educated through the colonial systems in mission schools. Often, they had studied in Europe or America for their post-secondary education. Their exposure to Western ideas of democracy and equality caused them to question how colonial powers treated Africans on their own continent. They began to agitate for change.

The Western -educated elite who led the early nationalist movements were moved by Pan-African sentiment, and demanded justice for all Africans rather than focusing on particular ethnic groups or nations. To unite people under one umbrella, nationalists had to appeal to factors that Africans had in common. In a continent marked by its diversity, this proved difficult. In Sub-Saharan Africa, nationalists often relied on a common religion, such as Christianity or Islam; common languages, often the language of the colonizers, like English or French; shared history and culture; and economic interests. In North Africa, Pan-Islamic nationalism worked towards the unity of all Muslims into a single Islamic empire, while a second group of nationalists believed that independence could only succeed through secular ideas and methods.

Early resistance to colonialism had been local and violent, demonstrated by uprisings like Maji-Maji in Tanzania. But African nationalists between 1919 and 1935 concentrated on reforming, rather than overthrowing, the colonial system. Associations, political movements and parties, trade unions, and independent churches helped nationalists to achieve their ends by participating in rebellions, strikes, and boycotts; protesting through literature and petitions to the government; and evading tax or migrating.

Early nationalism transformed after World War II from a movement for the elite to a movement for the masses. Africans who had fought alongside Europeans realized that their colonial conquerors could be defeated. Italy's invasion of Ethiopia, the last African country that remained independent, produced great anger and bitterness among Africans who would later be leaders in Independent Africa. Kwame Nkrumah, for example, the first president of independent Ghana, prayed when he heard the news of Ethiopia's fall that he would be one of the people who caused the colonial and imperial system to die. After the war, India became independent—one more reason for Africans to join the nationalist movement.

Pan-Africanism and early nationalism led the way to modern independence movements and mass demonstrations against colonial rule.

This article first appeared on http://www.suite101.com/

See page 322, for biography of **Jessica Powers**.

	the rhodesians	jessica powers zimbabwe 1890

Rhodes dreamt of a British route from Cape to Cairo. This went off the rails at some point in history.

Few of the men who straggled into "Rhodesia" in 1890 as part of the "Pioneer Column" would have anticipated the bitter and protracted war of the 1970's between the white "Rhodesians" and Africans. Yet early uprisings against European settlers foreshadowed the war for liberation a century later. Only three short years after Europeans settled into the land that makes up modern-day Zimbabwe, the Ndebele, who occupy the western portion of the country, declared war; and though the European settlers suppressed the first uprising, three years later, they found themselves at war again with both the Ndebele and the Shona, who live in eastern Zimbabwe.

For nearly a century, Rhodesians pictured their colonial history in the same romantic way Americans viewed their history. Like the Americans, whose mythology of the hard-working Pilgrims/Puritans and the pioneers who emigrated to "The Wild West" persists even today, Rhodesians believed the men who conquered Zimbabwe were independent, self-sufficient, hardy and brave. Against all odds, they carved civilization from a bastion of savagery and barbarism. They brought law and order and government to the frontier.

Like all myths, there is a certain amount of truth in this version of Rhodesia's history.

For one thing, the relationship between the Ndebele and the Shona can not be characterized as peaceful. The Ndebele continuously raided Shona villages for workers, cattle, and women. Even a century later, when Africans from both the Ndebele and Shona wanted majority rule, they were unable to work together to bring liberation to their country except for a very brief period. In the 1980's, after Africans achieved Independence, Robert Mugabe's government committed large scale genocide in Matabeleland, where the Ndebeles reside.

For another reason, though an earlier Shona civilization had built the Great Zimbabwe and constructed a complex society, they had never

343

invented the wheel and still lived in the Iron Age when Europeans colonized their country.

If peace and superior technology constitute "civilization," as many people believe, then clearly, the Africans in Zimbabwe were not "civilized." And while oppression and "peace" may not be the same thing, Zimbabweans did not rise up against the whites for almost seventy years. If Rhodesians wished to ignore certain warning signals, they could assume that Africans were content and happy under their rule.

The British set up its African colonies with one of two systems of government: direct or indirect rule. Direct rule required the presence of British officers and government officials in order to administer law. Indirect rule, on the other hand, theoretically integrated Great Britain's colonial policies through the systems of government already in place. This meant that in some places, they dictated their terms through African figureheads and in other places, they genuinely worked with African leaders to rule. Often, indirect rule set up an arbitrary system that resembled British preconceptions of African government rather than the actual "native" system of government. Sometimes, certain Africans were chosen as leaders because they worked well with the British; the indigenous groups of Africans did not necessarily recognize these men as their leaders.

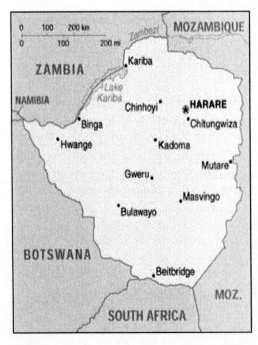

Because Rhodesia was a settler colony, like Kenya or South Africa, the British governed it through direct rule. But in Rhodesia, the settlers made up a higher percentage of the population than in Kenya or Zambia or Malawi. Thus, the British allowed them greater autonomy than many of the other settler colonies.

For a quarter of a century, the British South Africa Company ruled Rhodesia with a charter granted by the British Government. The BSA's initial aim to find gold deteriorated, as it became clear that amassing a fortune in gold was an unrealistic dream. Instead, they

344

tried to attract settlers to farm the land.

The settlers consistently agitated against the Company's rule. In 1923, they had the chance to vote for union with South Africa; Responsible Government, or self-rule, as a British Colony; or the status quo. They voted overwhelmingly for Responsible Government. Self-rule as a British colony lasted until 1953, when Southern Rhodesia entered a Federation with Northern Rhodesia (Zambia) and Nyasaland (Malawi).

In the meantime, the Rhodesians passed the Land Apportionment Act (1930), which divided the land up into African and European areas. A certain portion was set aside as African Reserves, a small portion for African purchase, and an overwhelming portion set aside for European purchase. Even though those were "different times," it is difficult to imagine how they could justify reserving 28 million acres (African Reserves and purchase areas) to 1 million blacks and 48 million acres for 50,000 Europeans (Blake 202). Though it took a couple of decades, the Africans were going to make their voice heard.

After Southern and Northern Rhodesia united with Nyasaland as a Federation, the African nationalist movement began to gain power. As Africans began to demand independence, even on a limited scale, the Federation grew shaky. When Great Britain granted Nyasaland and Northern Rhodesia their independence, it was the last straw for Southern Rhodesia. According to Ian Smith, this was justification for Rhodesia's Declaration of Independence from Great Britain. Why should these two states be given independence when they were so clearly unready for it, and Southern Rhodesia be denied when it was so clearly ready for self-governance?

Many white Rhodesians defended UDI (Unilateral Declaration of Independence) by comparing it to the United States' Declaration of Independence. Like the United States, they were simply breaking bonds with a government that had become unbearably repressive. Like the United States, they were defending themselves from Great Britain's encroachment of their freedom.

The international community thought otherwise. Great Britain immediately called for worldwide sanctions against Rhodesia and the world jumped onboard, even though both Portugal and the United States officially broke sanctions a few years later. (The United States broke sanctions until President Carter's administration successfully repealed the Byrd Amendment, which allowed the U.S. to export chrome from Rhodesia.)

Freedom in Rhodesia meant white rule. Blacks were successfully disfranchised, even though Ian Smith still argues today that Rhodesia's franchise was not determined by color. Just as Smith claims, the franchise was based on "merit;" but because other laws successfully barred the majority of Africans from ever achieving this status, they were also successfully disfranchised.

African nationalists demanded land, voting rights, and better education. When white Rhodesia turned a deaf ear, they turned to guerrilla warfare—"terrorism," in the eyes of white Rhodesians; a just war in the eyes of Africans.

Sources Consulted
A History of Rhodesia by Robert Blake

This article first appeared on http://www.suite101.com/

See page 322, for biography of **Jessica Powers.**

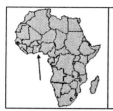	**an african coup d'etat**	jessica powers togo 1963

In 1963, Togo's national army shot their president Sylvanus Olympio because he refused to enlarge the army of 250 men or increase their salaries.

That same year, Africa's top leaders formed the Organisation of African Unity (OAU), an organization to promote peace and stability within the newly independent continent. Many of the African leaders who formed the OAU were later toppled by coups.

Though the OAU increased African unity, it has had little power to stop the trend of coups and countercoups that have swept the continent with almost as much regularity as elections in democratic countries.

Consider Ghana. The Ghanaian military seized power in 1966 when President Kwame Nkrumah headed to China with the intention to find a solution that would end the Vietnam War. After Nkrumah left, the military simply announced that he was no longer the leader of the country.

Nkrumah had been one of Africa's "golden" leaders, the first black president in sub-Saharan Africa and one of the founders of the OAU. He was elected in 1957, promising to lead his country toward the glorious liberty and democracy that he had experienced in the U.S. while he was in college.

After the coup in 1966, Nkrumah fled to Guinea, where he died of cancer. Colonel Akwasi Amankwa, a leader in the 1966 coup, wrote an obituary for Nkrumah, stating that "Nkrumah could have been a great man. He started well, led the independence movement and became, on behalf of Ghana, the symbol of emergent Africa. Somewhere down the line, however, he became ambitious, built a cult of personality and ruthlessly used the powers invested in him by his own constitution. He developed a strange love for absolute power" (Lamb 287).

It is important to remember that this statement reflects the opinion of a victor describing his predecessor. It should be taken with a very large grain of salt. Nevertheless, the same obituary could be written for many of Africa's leaders. The hero worship Nkrumah experienced in his early days as a leader degenerated until Nkrumah came to represent the "anti-hero" rather than the hero (Birmingham 83). The downfall reflected the disparity between Nkrumah's election promises of democracy and liberty and the reality of life under his leadership.

In 1958, for example, Nkrumah instituted a "preventive detention" act when a member of the political opposition was accused of trying to buy weapons to infiltrate the army. The law deepened police power and led to repression, which citizens resented. Laws like this one started the trend of anti-Nkrumah sentiment.

Further, economic disparity between the "haves" and the "have nots" intensified under Nkrumah's rule, creating jealously and tension. Soon, his greatest beneficiaries, the middle class, had become his greatest critics. Few of them protested when he was ousted.

In Ghana, as in other African countries, the first coup started a trend of countercoups. The military surrendered the government to a civilian government, which was overthrown in 1972 by General Acheampong. Six years later, Lieutenant General Frederick W.K Akuffo ousted Acheampong. Akuffo lasted one year. Air Force Lieutenant Jerry Rawlings executed Akuffo in 1979 to "cleanse" Ghana. Though Rawlings handed power over to a democratically elected president, Hilla Limann, he took it back on New Year's Eve in 1981. He explained his rationale in a radio broadcast, stating that all he asked for was a "proper democracy" (Lamb 288). Evidently, in his opinion, none of the leaders could provide one.

Ghana's experience is simply one example that serves to illustrate a problem that faces the rest of the continent. Who is responsible for ending the pattern of coups and countercoups? Who has the power to create stability across the continent? Is this the responsibility of the OAU or the responsibility of the colonial powers who left Africa in such a mess?

These questions, unfortunately, lead to more questions and problems. When considering how many governments exist across the continent, all with different political, philosophical, and economic underpinnings, the ability to bring peace and unity to Africa seems impossible. In fact, one might question whether it is imposing Western ideals on Africa by arguing that it is desirable for a continental unity (or uniformity) to exist. Attempting such a scenario in the Americas generates all sorts of criticism, as the example of the North American Free Trade Agreement shows. This week, organizations and individuals have started to protest the extension of NAFTA to South America. If this is such a problem in the West, is it not equally problematic to conceive such a plan in Africa?

Is it legitimate for the West to contribute and help bring peace and stability to Africa? In light of colonialism's injustices, which were often justified by claiming that colonialism "brought stability" to Africa, the West's involvement can easily be viewed as interference.

The history of neocolonialism indicts the West's involvement in Africa since independence as well. The IMF and the World Bank, in many instances, have only furthered Africa's economic instability. Furthermore, the West can be implicated in some of Africa's civil wars and coups. It is responsible in some cases for deliberately creating instability and, during the Cold War, giving money to opposition groups in countries governed by Marxist principles, such as occurred in Angola. The West's vast wealth and political dominance loom across Africa's horizon, blocking out the sun.

New media such as the Internet tend to sweep all such questions under the rug. Access to the Internet eliminates traditional boundaries like borders, rendering them meaningless. Free trade across continents may be inevitable, no matter if it is desirable or not.

Clearly, the UN can and should contribute to peace and stability in Africa, as it does across the world. However, it is still important to ask what peace means for countries developing under the watchful eye of rich and powerful countries such as the U.S.

Sources Consulted
The Africans by David Lamb
Kwame Nkrumah by David Birmingham

This article first appeared on http://www.suite101.com/

See page 322, for biography of **Jessica Powers**.

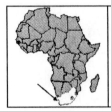

| the african language that will not die | anthony lobaido south africa present day |

Afrikaan is beyond the South African border

Afrikaans, a little-known language in a global sense, is a crucial key to understanding the many cultural issues now affecting post-apartheid South Africa.

What is Afrikaans? The language is unique in that it is a blend of Dutch and German. It also features a mixture of words brought to South Africa from India by indentured servants during the days of the British Empire. A sprinkling of words come from African tribes like the Zulus. Afrikaans is the preferred language of the Afrikaners, the white settlers who built the South African wilderness into one of the richest countries in the world. The Afrikaners are also called "Boers" which is the Dutch word for "farmer."

"Nelson Mandela told his black ANC followers to 'burn down their schools' and to avoid learning Afrikaans, which Mandela called, 'the language of the oppressor.' The result is an unemployable generation of illiterates whose only job skills are shooting an AK-47," South African policewoman Henika du Toit told WorldNetDaily.

"Affirmative action programs enacted by the ANC cannot help South Africa because of Mandela's legacy of burning the schools and boycotting Afrikaans."

Yet now a battle is raging in South Africa about how useful Afrikaans is for the nation as a whole. When Mandela gave his inaugural address in 1994, he spoke in Afrikaans. This was done, says du Toit, "because Afrikaans is a language that just about all South Africans can understand."

The battle between the use of English and Afrikaans has long been a sore point in South Africa. The British Empire fought not one but two Boer Wars (the latter between 1899-1902) against the Afrikaners. The British won both wars and marginalized the Boers and the use of Afrikaans. When the Afrikaners took total control of South Africa in 1948, they were determined to see Afrikaans used as the primary language inside the country.

350

"We were made to study Afrikaans in school," Nicola Hillerman told WorldNetDaily. Hillerman is an English-speaking South African who now works as an advertising executive in Hong Kong.

"Many of the Afrikaners hated learning English, and we hated learning Afrikaans. There was a lot of bad blood left over from the days of the Boereoorlog," she said.

The term "Boereoorlog" is Afrikaans for "Boer War."

Most Americans would be surprised to learn that the term "commando" and "laagar" comes from Afrikaans. The Boers formed guerrilla special forces units during the Boer War that were called "commandos." The term laagar refers to the circling of the wagons during the Boers' Great Trek into Zululand during the early part of the 19th century. The laagar was allegedly surrounded by a ring of white light with figures dressed in white, hovering around the perimeter. None of the incoming spears got through that ring. On the "Day of the Vow," a day that is still held as sacred to many Boers, the Afrikaners asked God to give them victory over the Zulus in battle.

"Since the ANC took power in 1994, they have really tried to emphasize the use of English over Afrikaans. With Mandela at the helm, South Africa was allowed back into the British Commonwealth. I suppose trade, computers and commerce have something to do with this. Let's face facts – English has emerged as a global language," added Hillerman.

South Africa's new president, Thabo Mbeki, is a gifted speaker of the English language and a devout Marxist who admits he grew up reading the works of Karl Marx.

"Recently, Mbeki spoke at the Socialist International Conference in Sweden using English. Mbeki's dealings with communist China and Libya's Gadhafi are also carried on in English," Koos Van der Merve told WorldNetDaily in a recent interview. Van der Merve is a former South African intelligence officer who now runs an international trading company.

"The ANC has really limited the use of Afrikaans on the [South African Broadcast Corporation] and other official, formerly Afrikaner dominated institutions of mass culture," he added.

Some of the lengths to which the ANC has gone to limit Afrikaans have been extreme.

For example, WorldNetDaily witnessed the ANC sending in a police unit, complete with helicopter support, to take down Radio Donkerhoek, the only non-ANC controlled Afrikaner radio station in all of South Africa. Donkerhoek is the Afrikaans term for "the dark corner" and refers to the place of an ambush where British soldiers killed many Afrikaners during the Boer War.

The station broadcasts without an official permit – and with good reason.

"The ANC will not permit the Afrikaners to criticize the government through the mass media. Radio Pretoria does operate but can only play Boer music and cultural programming. It must toe the line in its political comment," Willem Ratte told WorldNetDaily. Ratte is a celebrated former Special Forces soldier and operator of Radio Donkerhoek.

After the raid of Donkerhoek, the South African Citizen, the nation's most conservative paper, ran a story that falsely claimed Ratte had locked himself inside the station and was ready to commit suicide.

"That is totally outlandish and absurd," Hillerman told WND. "Ratte helped run the war in Angola against the Russians and Cuba – but he is afraid of a few helicopters and police at his radio station? It is frightening that a paper like The Citizen would run such a totally false story. It makes one wonder about the degree of ANC control, though in this case, I would look to pro-ANC Afrikaner agents working in the media. Everyone knows that Ratte would prefer to die as a martyr for the Afrikaner cause. Even the most devout ANC Marxist would laugh at the idea of Ratte committing suicide."

Radio Donkerhoek claims that it is "the free, independent, Christian radio station of the Boer Nation of South Africa; their voice of protest against the hand over of political power, since 1994, to the ANC communist regime. Because Radio Donkerhoek does not recognize the corrupt communists as a legal government, and has not begged for a broadcasting license, it and its relay stations, Radio Volkstem and Radio Triomf, have all suffered police raids. Equipment has been confiscated, supporters have been intimidated, and five patriots are currently facing court action with threatened fines of 500,000 Rand and prison sentences, the current penalty against the use of free speech.

"Our premises in Pretoria came under attack by an armed force, hundreds strong. They intended to shut us down for good. Although working within the constraints of an inefficient corrupt communist government, the armed force could not find a morally sound purpose to fire. It was God's will that the attackers lost their nerve and departed after darkness fell, not a shot fired, their purpose unfulfilled. The next day transmissions resumed as normal. Radio Donkerhoek is funded and operated by supporters and patriotic citizens, who also volunteer as announcers on a part-time basis, all risking heavy fines and possible imprisonment, for the highest cause: the right of a people to serve the Trinity of God and to rule themselves. Our Pretoria frequency is FM 106,2 MHz, every evening."

352

Marge Leitner, a South African deeply involved with Boer politics said that Radio Pretoria and Radio Donkerhoek are very important to the Afrikaners.

"For instance, when Radio Pretoria talks about this government, they actually say 'Thabo Mbeki, the president of the ANC regime.' That's why they probably didn't get their license renewed! There's a big court case looming for this little gutsy station. If they lose, a similar fate to Radio Donkerhoek awaits them. They are a little voice in the wilderness. At the moment, though, Radio Pretoria is playing a vital role in communicating with the Afrikaners in their own language, talking to them about their own culture and about 'their country,' Leitner told WND.

Leitner emphasized the important role Afrikaans still has to play in the nation for all South Africans.

"Did you know that Afrikaans comes second to Zulu, as being the language that is used most in this country? Zulu, of course, is the first, most widely spoken language, thereafter comes Afrikaans. Here you must remember though, that the colored communities in the Cape also all speak predominantly Afrikaans. But this little-known fact is certainly not publicized by this regime, for reasons we are aware of. As with any language, I guess, Afrikaans is part of the intricate culture of the Afrikaner nation. It is their cornerstone. Their heritage, their pride, their future," Leitner said.

"I am from German descent, but I went to school with the Afrikaners. I grew up with them. As with every nationality on this planet, the Afrikaner people have their own traditions, which are handed down from generation to generation. Part of the intricate and rich tapestry of the history of the Afrikaner is their Calvanistic background, their stubborn streak, which has often led to great historic moments of glory or desperate hours of defeat! Songs are sung, poems are written, stories are told, jokes are shared, all with one common thread – the language of Afrikaans.

"When I was overseas, I lived and worked for three years in Switzerland. We had an international club there, and in that little town of Neuhausen am Rhein were four South Africans, including myself. What was the immediate binding factor? The language of home, of family, of country, Afrikaans. We were all starved of hearing the sound – music to our ears. We shared jokes…a particular brand of humor. Non-South Africans often stare in disbelief while we roll on the floor about something that we find hysterically funny, but nobody else can understand.

"It's part of the Afrikaner tradition. You hear 'Die Stem,' (the Afrikaner anthem) and emotions run high, tears come, and your patriotic emotions engulf you. How we still cling to that tiny bit of 'Die Stem' that still forms part of the national anthem. Go to any international rugby match, anywhere in the world, and listen when they play the national anthems. South Africans are to be found everywhere, but particularly in the UK and in Australia. It's relatively quiet when they play the first part, but then when the bit comes from 'Die Stem' its like the floodgates open. There is a roar as the voices rise, and you can literally 'feel' all the spine-tingling, goose bumps sensation that comes with the pride and passion of singing your national anthem."

Leitner told WorldNetDaily that "the issue of a language goes very deep and becomes part of the soul. Especially with the Afrikaner, being such a 'small and gutsy nation.' It is part of their pride and feelings of nationalism, pride in their race. And why not? Every nation has that right, especially, I think, because of the rocky path they have been on since time immemorial. The very suffering in their history has bound them together by the common thread: the language.

"But I think the most powerful argument for Afrikaans is the Afrikaner's religious belief. As you know, they are a very religious people. They will always humble themselves before God. Their whole existence is intertwined with religion, and they express their faith in Afrikaans. Take that away from the Afrikaner, and you take away his existence. And this is what the enemy knows full well. Why the oppression of Afrikaans as a language? Why the attacks on Afrikaans being used as a teaching medium at schools? Why the attacks on Afrikaans universities? Why the attacks on the Afrikaner, period?"

Boers who cannot speak English well are sometimes at a disadvantage when dealing with the English-speaking international community.

For example, when Gerard Erasmus sent an e-mail to U.N. Human Rights Commission in Pretoria about the 1,119 murders of white South African farmers since 1994, he was chastised for his lack of command of English.

Erasmus told WorldNetDaily, "The U.N. Human Rights Commission responded to my concerns by stating: 'Perhaps you should go for spelling lessons before you send these whining, pathetic complaints – you white people had it too good for too long.'

Will Afrikaans survive?

Adriana Stuijt is a former anti-apartheid journalist now based in the Netherlands.

"Recent research pointed out that Afrikaners and Afrikaans-speaking folks are now being accepted in Africa," she told WND, "because many of those people worked on the mines as migrant workers and learned to read and write Afrikaans while they were here. Most of the ethnics in Southwest Africa/Namibia speak Afrikaans as a second language. The language is more and more accepted as 'Modern African.' It is the only African language that is able to 'think' and 'write' in modern technological jargon, even computer technology and nuclear physics. This is not possible in black African languages."

Stuijt said, "My grandfather fought in the Anglo-Boer War and died in 1945. [Many Afrikaners] could speak the indigenous languages and understood English, although they would not speak it. When a British officer during the war claimed in English toward some POWs that 'the sun will not set on the British Empire,' to his dismay, a Boer answered from the ranks, 'Yes, because God can't trust you in the dark.'

Journalist Jan Lamprecht says, "Strangely, the ANC does not seem to have openly done much to destroy Afrikaans. At this very moment, there is an Afrikaans exposition in London, and the ANC is there – the blacks speaking Afrikaans – can you believe it?...There are even bold ads on national TV saying how many Afrikaans programs there are. I am stunned at how often ANC officials speak Afrikaans."

"I have noted cynically to my family that they seem to be speaking more Afrikaans and putting more sport on TV, as they murder the farmers and attack the Boers. There is a long-standing joke/observation by many that as the ANC comes after us, they give us TV as a form of diversion. They put more international sport on, and that makes folks happy while they really nail us. The ANC, like Clinton and all these new communists, are very much image oriented...[Zimbabwe President] Mugabe is the same. In front of the cameras he's one person; behind the scenes he's the opposite.

"Many things are contributing to Afrikaans not growing in a big way. But it's not dead. The colored people love Afrikaans and regard themselves as 'Brown Afrikaners.' They even have their version of Afrikaans and their own sayings which, if you understand Afrikaans, are actually hilarious. Just listening to them speaking normally is a hilarious exercise. I think all the past emphasis on Afrikaans has paid off. It's amazing how many blacks speak the language in daily life.

"But I think Afrikaans will have to take a step back," said Lamprecht, "especially when it comes to computers and international contact. It is just too difficult inventing new words and maintaining a language for so few people. I don't think Afrikaans will ever die. It may just become more of a 'second language' than a 'first language.' True Afrikaners will defend Afrikaans with tremendous zest.

"Most South Africans are bilingual. It extends to all race groups. It is amazing how, even now, the different races swap between English and Afrikaans at will. Few are truly fluent in both languages, but most people can understand each other pretty well. There are some Afrikaans areas and other English areas. Johannesburg, because of its metropolitan atmosphere, is more English. Pretoria is Afrikaans. The rural areas tend to be Afrikaans. There used to be a great resistance to English because of the Boer War. I think that made it harder to get the Afrikaners to speak English, because they viewed English as 'the language of the enemy.'

"I think the international nature of the world, and especially in the computer industry, English rules, and even the most Afrikaans people can't help but move to English. English, of course, is not just dominated by the British…and maybe this removal of English from being the domain of the British will help Afrikaners in the long run not to feel so bad about the language. Most Afrikaners have become pretty outward-looking, and they have had to change so much that the language alone isn't the major issue. There are more pressing issues, and they have to be realistic," Lamprecht concluded.

Article first appeared in WorldNetDaily. Printed with permission

See page 297, for biography of **Anthony Lobaido.**

| liberia | robert young pelton
liberia
present day |

It's good to be king. In Liberia things have quieted down and Charles Taylor is now faced with trying to figure out how to run Liberia.

The war hogs in their Banana Republic jackets remember the old days fondly. Where else would one go to see a cast of outrageously wild characters dressed in odd-but-uniform military gear and going by names that make a sailor blush? Back then Libyan-backed, self-proclaimed criminal Charles Taylor surrounded himself with the finest military men (all so competent that they were promoted directly from volunteer to general) Liberia could muster. General No-Mother-No-Father, General Housebreaker, General Fuck-Me-Quick and the gregarious General Butt Naked were just some of the colorful and often defeated warriors. General Butt Naked was particularly visible since he fought battles in his primeval buff-his only uniform was a pair of scuffed tennis shoes and his only armor the protective stench of stale liquor no bullet would dare penetrate. Ah, the good days. But them days is over. These days you'll find Butt Naked preaching the word of God on Broad Street in Monrovia as a born again preacher. Back then his choir was young children brandishing sticks and swearing like diseased sailors. They are just the finest examples of a century and a half of civilization in darkest Africa.

Well, there's always the next war. And war comes easy to a place like Liberia. Founded in 1822, Liberia was an attempt - an experiment, really-by the American Colonization Society to create a homeland in West Africa for freed slaves from the United States. It became the Free and Independent Republic of Liberia in 1847.

It's interesting that a group of individuals so jaded by the racial strata system of 19th-century America chose to re-create the United State's Constitution on the other side of the Atlantic. As Africa's first "republic," Liberia's debut government was modeled directly after the one it sought to escape. With names like Joseph J. Roberts, William V. S. Tubman, Charles Taylor and William R. Tolbert Jr., the prominent figures in Liberian history read more like a Palm Beach polo team roster than a struggling, ragtag community of displaced slaves.

The attempt at creating a duplicate America in Africa, however, never came full-circle, namely because more than a century's worth of efforts at bringing the aboriginal population onto the same "playing field" as the emigrants proved unsuccessful. Instead of democracy, liberty and all that stuff, Liberia's course became marred by factional fighting, civil war, partitioning and bloody coups led not by men with sinister, nasty-sounding names like Stalin, Arafat, Noriega, Hitler or Amin, but with such innocuous, landed - gentryish handles as Doe, Taylor and Johnson. Sounds like a New York law firm.

Instead of freedom for all, Liberia became a free-for-all, reduced to primal clashes among rival clans, randomly slaughtering each other with old machine guns from the back of ancient, dented jeeps. Bands of marauders cut swaths across the rain forest plateau, donning Halloween masks and bolt-action rifles, as they raped and pillaged in small villages before finally razing them. Calling the situation in modern Liberia a "civil war" is giving it too much status-crediting it with too much organization and purpose. The reality is villagers slaughtered by tribal-based militias that mark, like dogs pissing on a tree, their territory with the skulls of their victims.

One of the few Liberian leaders with any longevity was William V.S. Tubman, who was in his sixth term as president when he died during surgery in 1971. He was replaced by his longtime associate, William R. Tolbert Jr. Tolbert actually lasted nine years in office, before he was ousted by a mere master sergeant, senior official in Doe's government, in 1989. Leaving a bloody wake in capturing most of the nation's economic and population centers, Taylor failed by a whisker to wrestle power from Doe by mid-July 1990.

Shortly afterward, a six-nation West African peacekeeping force called the Economic Community of West African States Cease-Fire Monitoring Group (ECOMOG) essentially partitioned Liberia into two zones. The first encompassed the capital of Monrovia and was led by President Amos Sawyer. The other half, run by Taylor and his National Patriotic Front (NPFL), amounted to about 95 percent of Liberian territory.

Reconciliation and peace agreements were signed and ignored like journalists' bar tabs. A March 1991 conference failed to get anything accomplished except for the reelection of Sawyer as interim president. Despite a peace agreement in 1991, fighting continued to flare. Another peace agreement and cease-fire in July 1993, which established an interim government and set up general democratic elections, crumbled a short time later in November.

Gambia, Nigeria, Mali, Ivory Coast, Switzerland and Benin are among the venues that have hosted Liberian peace talks since Taylor launched the civil war the day before Christmas in 1989. Some ended with agreements hailed at the time as historic. All proved to be failures.

The 12th agreement, signed in Benin with UN guarantees, seemed the most likely to succeed. It ended up in tatters. Only 3,000 of Liberia's estimated 60,000 fighters - many of them teenagers addicted to drugs along with killing and raping civilians - were disarmed.

At least a third of Liberia's prewar population of 2.5 million fled the country after fighting broke out on December 24, 1989, when Taylor invaded Liberia from the Ivory Coast. In 1993, the UN estimated 150,000 had died, but stopped counting after that. (As of mid-1997, most estimates put the death toll at nearly 200,000.) It became nearly impossible for relief workers to operate in rebel-controlled areas. A peace accord signed in August 1995 called for countrywide ECOMOG deployment and disarmament of factional fighters, but 10 months later neither of these processes had gotten off the ground.

In April 1996, Monrovia was again launched into lawlessness. Fighting resumed in earnest between the rival factions. In only three days, Monrovia toppled into anarchy. Thousands fled the capital city in panic. As many as 20,000 Liberians descended upon the residential annex of the U.S. embassy. U.S. military commandos evacuated about 2,000 frightened American citizens and other foreigners by chopper to the Sierra Leone capital of Freetown, starting in the middle of the night on April 8, as Monrovia's airport was destroyed in the fighting. Evacuations continued for at least two months.

359

Yet a disarmament program, part of an ambitious transition program (and the war's 14th peace agreement) developed by the Economic Community of West African States (ECOWAS) - designed to dissolve Liberia's armed factions, became tremendously successful, only nine months after Monrovia's anarchy. By February 1997, more than 10,000 fighters had been demobilized and 5,000 weapons recovered.

Up until July 24, 1997, Liberia was run by a six-member interim Council of State led by charismatic chairwoman Ruth Perry, who replaced Taylor stooge Wilton Sankawulo in this, Liberia's 14th peace accord since 1989.

Before the Perry-led Council of State, the country was terrorized by up to 60,000 young (sometimes under 15), brutal, drunken, and armed thugs who dressed up in masks, wigs, and ballroom gowns and wielded rusty guns and viscious tempers to steal food and rape and butcher people. Bandits and terrorists continue to wax and dismember each other in the countryside, although the overall level of violence has dropped considerably.

In July 1997, Charles Taylor was elected with an impressive margin (even though earlier he swore he wouldn't run for office and he would go into business instead). Things are eerily calm in Monrovia outside of the odd gunfight and his countrymen and many enemies are waiting to see what Chuck and his All-Stars will do now that they have center court.

Print with permission:
The World's Most Dangerous Places. By Robert Young Pelton
http://www.comebackalive.com

See page 183, for biography of **Robert Young Pelton**.

Angola's 500-year run of bad luck may be changing

Angola was first colonized in 1575; since then the Portuguese have removed three million people from its shores and millions of carats of diamonds. When they left, instead of returning the country to the Angolans, they gave it to the world's superpowers to play with. In the sixteenth century, before it earned its current third world status, Portugal was the most important country on the map. In fact, it was drawing the map. When England was still squabbling with the Scots, Portugal was taking over the world. Angola was used as a labor pool for the bits of the world they had already occupied. Hundreds of thousands of slaves were sent out to their coffee fields in Brazil and to the sugar plantations in Sao Tome.

A few centuries later, slavery became illegal and the Portuguese were forced to stop trading. No longer having much use for their far-flung and hostile colony, most of which had not even been explored, they ignored it. But when the Pan-African independence movement started in the 1950s, the Portuguese government was just becoming aware of the stupendous mineral riches of Angola. It reacted to the independence threat by sending out to Angola 300,000 of its peasants. Angola is an enormous country so the Portuguese peasants had orders to spread out and procreate. They were neither quick nor fertile enough and a

361

colonial war broke out in 1961. Since then Angola has never been truly at peace.

Various rebel groups emerged, all of which have long Portuguese names. As in all African conflicts, it is easier to stick to the acronyms. The MPLA (Angolan People's Liberation Movement) was set up in 1956 and shortly afterwards the FNLA (Angolan National Liberation Front) joined it in agitating for independence. Both groups were working in exile but the MPLA, led by Agostinho Neto, pulled most of its support from the key area around the capital, Luanda. Holden Roberto's FNLA emerged from the north of the country and soon became based in and sponsored by the Congo (Zaire). In 1966 Jonas Savimbi, a member of the largest tribe, the Ovimbundu, led a split from the FNLA to form UNITA (Union for the Total Independence of Angola) and has been its political and military leader ever since. All of them wanted independence, but under different tribal and political systems.

The Portuguese won the early colonial war but the struggle continued and when, after the 1974 Portuguese coup, the new leaders said that they were going to divest themselves of their colonies, the three rebel groups met in Luanda to set up a government. The united interim administration took office on 31 January 1975 and the new war started on the first of February. It was going to be a different war, though east-west rather than north-south.

It started off between the Soviets (with Cuban help) and South Africa. South Africa gave support to UNITA so that they could attack SWAPO (Namibia's independence fighters) and ANC bases in southern Angola. In 1986 the South Africans ended up fighting the Cubans in a battle outside Cuito Cuanavale which made both sides realize that they might be making a mistake since they didn't actually have anything against each other. South Africa wanted to destabilize communist governments but Cuba wasn't exactly in their area.

With the arrival of the Reagan administration in Washington, it became a proxy fight between the Soviet-backed MPLA and the American-backed Union of Total Independence of Angola - no relation to the UN (UNITA). Savimbi's UNITA controlled the south of the country and none of the towns while the MPLA as the legitimate government held the towns and not much of the country.

Throughout the 1980s, the MPLA, who have a fully mechanized army, fought during the dry season, when it is easier to move around, and licked their wounds in the wet. The collapse of the Soviet Union, however, meant that the MPLA had to seek a truce. A peace agreement was signed between Jose Eduardo dos Santos, Neto's successor as leader of the MPLA, and Jonas Savimbi, the charismatic UNITA leader. Elections were called for

362

1992. Approximately 340,000 people had died to bring Angola to the same position it had been in thirty-two years earlier.

Printed with permission:

Blood on the Tracks: A Rail Journey from Angola to Mozambique (1992). By Miles Bredin

See page 41, for biography of **Miles Bredin.**

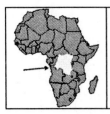

| a very brief history of democratic republic of congo | miles bredin democratic republic of congo to present day |

Right at the center of Africa, Zaire (Democratic Republic of Congo) had been unable to yield its riches to the hungry west before the advent of the trains. The new fashions for cars, electricity and plumbing in the early twentieth century meant that there was an insatiable demand for Zaire's copper, which was then swiftly transformed into piping and wire before being sold at huge profit for the Belgians and the railway builders. They also made a fortune from the rubber plantations, which fed the hungry motor industry.

Zaire has had an unhappy life. It is only a little smaller than India, yet King Leopold of Belgium used to own it. It was not a Belgian colony, but the king's private property. In 1884 Leopold set up a trading company under the guise of a philanthropic mission headed by Henry Morton Stanley - a journalist with even fewer morals than is normally expected. Leopold spent twenty three years raping the Zairean interior. He administered it so inhumanely that the Belgian government was forced by the world community to relieve him of his personal fiefdom and take it over as a colony in 1908. The region was then run almost as ineptly and unjustly by them and handed over at independence to a new government, which was totally unprepared for it. No African had held rank higher than sergeant major in the colonial army and civil servants had been subject to a similar system. The fact that Zaire had not been allowed to develop past this stage by the colonial government meant that a non-commissioned officer, Joseph Desire Mobutu, was, within a year of independence, governing the country by decree, with the wholehearted support of Belgium and the CIA. Since 1960 he has either held power or allowed others to hold it for him while personally retaining control of the army.

Mobutu is the personification of every horror story you have heard about African dictators. A policy of Africanization led to his name change. His is now called Mobutu Sese Seko Kuku Ngebendu Wa Za Banga which loosely translates as the immortal red hot chilli pepper. He calls himself 'the dignified redeemer' and insists that his portrait is on the wall of every church. His wealth is estimated at $6.3 billion and he has been known to hire Concorde for visits to the dentist. He has murdered and tortured his opponents and allowed Zaire, which ought to be one of the richest countries in the world, to become an economic joke. On the other hand, he has managed to keep Zaire united, which considering there was a civil war within five days of the Belgian handover, is truly impressive.

He is absolutely corrupt, but to the tribal African mind this is no bad thing. The tribal system, which has worked in Africa for centuries, has always meant that a man should look after his family, his clan and then his tribe. Mobutu has done this and is therefore admired. His family live in palaces. Fellow members of his tribe receive sinecures. His hometown of Gbadolite, previously a one-chicken village in the center of thousands of square miles of impenetrable rainforest, is now the proud site for an international airport, a splendid chateau and a massive conference center, all deserted.

Mobutu is an African success story. The fact that he has achieved his riches by reducing his country to ruins is anathema to the west but makes perfect sense to the average unschooled African. In fact, by African standards he is quite humane. He is ruthless when necessary but he prefers to corrupt his enemies rather than kill them.

Zaire is immensely fertile. As well as its mineral riches, the fruits of its soil could feed half of Africa. Despite this, it can no longer feed itself. Mobutu's rape of the economy has led to a situation where farmers are unwilling to sell their food because the money they receive for it will be worthless. The kleptocratic state has forced them back to subsistence farming. The transport system has also broken down. The railway was never important to Kinshasa itself, but at independence the capital was well served by roads and the river.

The Belgians left Zaire with 145,000 kilometers of all-weather roads. By 1992, according to someone who did it regularly, it took twenty days driving eighteen hours a day to get from Kinshasa to Lubumbashi in an off-road vehicle. The journey, which takes two hours by plane, is only possible in the dry season.

The river was not much better. The Congo (renamed the Zaire by Mobutu) is the largest river in Africa. It stretches from the Atlantic coast in a huge wide loop through the interior of Zaire, where you can still find outbreaks of bubonic plague, and down almost to Lubumbashi. It has been the lifeblood of the area for centuries. In the 1890s, Conrad trundled up and down the river in his steamboat having nightmares about the natives, but one hundred years later the boats no longer work. These great steamboats were like mobile supermarkets which housed thousands of people who traded with the forest dwellers along the way. Dancing attendance to the ships were a constant stream of pirogues. Monkeys were swapped for maize and maize for batteries as the years progressed. Stanley killed hundreds in order to open up this great highway, yet ninety years after his death the only regular traffic is the pirogues of prehistoric times and the water-ski boats of the expats.

Zaire is a complicated place. The former British Liberal Party leader Jeremy Thorpe tried to explain it soon after independence at the time when the UN was suffering heavy losses in southern Zaire. 'We are, after all, in a very involved situation. There are two prime ministers, Mr. Lumumba and Mr. Ileo, both of whom apparently have arrested the other. There's the president, Mr. Kasavubu, and he's sacked Mr. Lumumba but has in turn on paper been arrested by Mr. Lumumba who has arrested him back. General Lundula is in charge of the troops but he's been sacked although appointed by Mr. Lumumba and General Mobutu has been put in his place but he's also in theory under arrest by Mr Lumumba. The Baluba tribe are crying for Mr Lumumba's blood while Mr Tshombe is trying to have a tete-a-tete with Mr Kasavubu. That doesn't forget Mr Koinange or Mr Rajahswad Dayal who is the United Nations observer. Now that is the *dramatis tis personae*. I would say that any organization would have very great difficulties.' Thirty years later, if anything, it is more confused.

Printed with permission:

Blood on the Tracks: A Rail Journey from Angola to Mozambique (1992). By Miles Bredin

See page 41, for biography of **Miles Bredin**.

	**from rhodesia to zimbabwe**	miles bredin zimbabwe to present day

Out with the old, in with the new

The Rhodesia problem started when Rhodes's British South Africa (BSA) Company was given permission to make treaties in the area above Bechuanaland (modern-day Botswana). They took over Mashonaland straight away. Three years later, they overthrew the all-powerful Lobengula, King of the Ndebele. The two regions of Mashonaland and Matabeleland * made up the mass of southern Rhodesia and had been around for centuries.

This was not a part of Africa that could be written off as uninhabited because all the inhabitants were primitive tribes people. There are thirteenth century ruins at Zimbabwe (after which the country is named) which indicate that a sophisticated culture, based round an impressive city, existed when wattle-and-daub houses, coracles and woad make-up were still the rage in England. The BSA's occupation of the area was armed robbery and was reacted to as such. The *chimurenga* (liberation war) from 1896-7 was the result. It united the Shona and the Ndebele for the first time in centuries and took a massive effort to put down. Rhodes, who believed that 'we are the first race in the world, and that the more of the world we inhabit, the better it is for the human race', rode rough-shod over the local inhabitants and established the protectorate under the unassuming name of Rhodesia.

From the very beginning, Rhodesia was in constitutional crisis. Like early colonial India, the country was run by a company - Rhodes's British South Africa Company. More diplomatically, Rhodes, who in 1890 was to become prime minister of South Africa, called the capital Salisbury after the prime minister of England. Britain, though, wasn't fooled, and sought to control the power of the BSA from very early on. By 1907, the white settlers had a majority in the legislative council and wanted autonomy. They became gradually more important as the power of the BSA, which had been unable to find the expected gold, waned. During the First World War, the Ndebele fought for the restoration of their king. Both black and white camps, though adversaries on the ground, had the same goal of shaking off both British and BSA rule. In the 1922 whites-only referendum, which foreran the withdrawal of the BSA charter, it emerged that the white settlers wished neither to be part of South Africa nor a British-run colony. What arose was nominally a British colony, but the power of the legislature was such that it was run from Salisbury rather than the King Charles Street headquarters of the British Colonial Office.

None of the constraints of the British Colonial Office were put upon the government in Salisbury and although the British government had a veto, it remained only a theoretical one. A succession of important laws was passed before 1930 which gave the country its racially segregated structure. Pass and land laws were enacted which inhibited African development and gave vast advantages to the tiny white settler population. The whites also benefited enormously from a war and postwar boom when they were making things for the front under a protected market. In 1953, Nyasaland (Malawi), Northern Rhodesia (Zambia) and Southern Rhodesia (Zimbabwe) were united in a federation under Britain. They had a fair degree of autonomy and under their first leader - Rhodesia's Prime Minister Godfrey Huggins - made some strides towards improving the lot of the ordinary African. Internal black pressure in all three states, combined with British pressure for change, forced this upon the federation. It did not last. In 1961, Malawi was given full independence and in 1962 Zambia followed suit. Rhodesia, which had the largest white population (as a result of postwar boom and white flight from Malawi, South Africa and Zambia), saw this as a threat and entrenched. The ground was laid for Ian Smith and the Unilateral Declaration of Independence (UDI).

The 1950s and 1960s saw the revitalizing of the African National Congress (the Rhodesian wing of the ANC had first emerged in the 1930s) and the emergence of the National Democratic Party and the Zimbabwe African People's Union (ZAPU) - all African parties striving for independence. White Rhodesians had to fight two battles at the same time - one against Britain, which was trying to force liberal ideas on to the settlers, and another against the blacks who wanted to get rid of both Britain and the white settlers. This state of affairs made a perfect launch pad for the Rhodesian Front -a white party, which wanted to stop the 'rot'. With the support of farmers -the mainstay of Rhodesia's white population -it gained power in the 1961 election, ousting the more pragmatic government of Whitehead. In 1962, Ndabaninghi Sithole split from Joshua Nkomo's ZAPU to form ZANU. Both parties were proscribed, the press was censored and all opposition viciously put down by the hardman tactics of the new government. For Ian Smith though, the Rhodesia Front government of Winston Field was not strong enough. In 1964 he replaced Field and in November 1965 he made his UDI - the kick-off for the second independence war.

The second *chimurenga* was a nasty little war. Smith's Unilatateral Declaration of UDI was totally against the grain of everything else that was going on in Africa. The 'winds of change' were sweeping across the plains, through the jungles of Zaire and Central Africa, gradually eroding everything that stood before them. In 1965, the only countries yet to react to the drought were Angola and Mozambique, who were still under Portuguese rule, South Africa (where Macmillan's speech was made in 1959) and Rhodesia. Portugal was too busy with its own problems to worry about Africa. Rhodesia and South Africa closed the door and put up the storm shutters. There began a long siege which in South Africa has only now reached its climax.

From 1964 to 1974 Robert Mugabe, who had replaced Sithole as leader of ZANU, and ZAPU's leader Joshua Nkomo were kept in prison, but their parties' military wings fought ill-planned guerilla wars against the white minority. Their release and departure from Rhodesia led to an escalation of the war. Mugabe had spent his porridge doing correspondence degrees and planning strategy. He emerged with three degrees and left for Mozambique where eventually President Machel grudgingly allowed him to join the 20,000 ZANU guerillas based there. Nkomo likewise skulked off to his guerillas who were based in neighboring Zambia. Nkomo received support from the Soviet Union and the Ndebele; Mugabe, who at that time described himself as a Marxist- Leninist, from China and the Shona. There followed a brutal civil war, which by 1979 had cost a seventh of the population their homes, and innumerable lives. Nkomo had many guerillas but did not use them extensively.

Mugabe, who had bases in both Zambia and Mozambique, fought ferociously although not a soldier himself. Appalling atrocities were committed on all sides. The notorious Selous Scouts and other bands of white Rhodesians routinely tortured. ZANU's soldiers routinely mutilated. The seemingly gentle and unassuming Mugabe was held up as a rabid Marxist terrorist. Smith, whose charm is well known, was portrayed as a psychopathic white supremacist. That there was any room for political maneuver is astonishing and largely thanks to Lord Soames, the avuncular British cabinet minister who was called in as Rhodesia's last governor.

When Smith lost the support of like-minded South Africa he had to cave in to the pressure which had been put on him by trade sanctions and the effects of international unpopularity on a land- locked country. UDI lasted for fourteen years during which time industries developed through necessity, farming became more essential and therefore protected for the whites and, against all odds, the railway kept going. As in South Africa who, unable to buy arms on the world market, reacted by creating their own now envied arms industry, sanctions actually did Rhodesia some good. Complacency and laziness often prevalent in white settler populations could not be allowed. Everyone had to strive to survive. But, although this gave the pariah nation a backbone, it was still weak enough to be broken.

Smith tried for an internal settlement with the Patriotic Front which Nkomo and Mugabe had been forced to create together, but his intransigence made that impossible. It was left for Arch- bishop Abel Muzorewa to make a deal with Smith. The resultant elections made Muzorewa Rhodesia's first black prime minister. The only problem was that ZANU and ZAPU, with majority support, had boycotted the elections and continued to wage their independence war. Nothing had changed except the name. It was now Zimbabwe Rhodesia.

At Mrs. Thatcher's first Commonwealth conference that year she scored a remarkable success by getting all parties to agree to the temporary return of British rule. ** In 1979, the former protectorate once more became a British colony and changed its name to Rhodesia. Lord Soames became governor, managed to oversee free and fair elections, hauled down the Union Jack for the last time and made a dignified exit. In April 1980, the Banana Republic was born. Ian Smith won the twenty guaranteed white seats, Nkomo won the twenty seats in Matabeleland and Mugabe won fifty-seven of the remaining sixty. Canaan Banana became president, Mugabe became prime minister, Rhodesia became Zimbabwe, Books of Zimbabwe Rhodesia became Books of Zimbabwe and it has been downhill since then. Twelve years later, after massive political wrangling, atrocities by all political parties and a fairly successful disarmament of the population, Mugabe was firmly in place as the president and Nkomo was a member of his cabinet. The country, though, has lost its sheen. The government is deeply unpopular but following the merging of ZANU and ZAPU as ZANU PF, there is no longer an opposition. The economy was in crisis and Mugabe was up against the ropes.

Zimbabwe retains its regional dominance but with neighbors like Zambia and Mozambique, this is not a difficult task. When the Queen visited Bulawayo in 1991, she said that it hadn't changed since her last visit as a princess. The large white population of the town took this as a compliment but in fact it is a horrifying reality. To say that Bulawayo is a sleepy little town maligns it. It is wide awake, but stuck in the 1950s. In Zimbabwe's second city, the shops close on Saturday afternoons and for the remainder of the weekend, the streets remain deserted. The streets were built, to Rhodes's specifications, so that a cart with a full span of oxen could do a U-turn. Today, it would not be at all surprising to see an ox cart in

Bulawayo and it would be able to perform the required maneuvers without holding up the traffic.

* Mashonaland is the home of the Shona people; Matabeleland, that of the Ndebele.
**This was not a success of her own making although she took the credit. She was forced by Soames and Foreign Minister Carrington to talk to people whom she regarded as terrorists.

Printed with permission: Blood on the Tracks: A Rail Journey from Angola to Mozambique (1992). By Miles Bredin

See page 41, for biography of **Miles Bredin**.

Mozambique jostles with places like Cambodia, Angola and Somalia for the title of the world's most unfortunate country. Centuries of Portuguese rule have been followed by a horrendous civil war, richly spiced with drought, famine and ceaseless outside interference. Its luck has to change some time but it certainly hasn't yet. The calmest places are the corridors from neighboring countries to the coast, which are fiercely guarded by parties interested in their own future rather than Mozambique's. The Maputo corridor is patrolled by the Zimbabwean army and leads directly to Zimbabwe. The Nakala corridor goes to Malawi and is guarded mainly by DSL (Defence System Ltd), the private security firm and the Beira corridor, which is protected by Zimbabwe and is their most essential link with the coast.

The struggle for independence in Mozambique started in 1964, three years later than in similar Angola. There had been Portuguese settlements in the country since 1524 but it had been heavily exploited only since the end of the Second World War. Portuguese peasants emigrated to their colony and started farming. They enjoyed great success with the fertile and beautiful land -something which is difficult to believe now that the country is famed for famine and starvation. From 1964 to 1973 Frelimo (Mozambique Liberation Front) fought a continuous guerilla war against the Portuguese authorities. They met with marked success in the north of the country which was less colonized than the south. Following the assassination of Eduardo Mondlane, Frelimo's founder, in 1969 they received even more support. The Soviet Union, China and Czechoslovakia provided them with arms. Sweden and other liberal western countries became interested in their struggle. Their great success, however, was in winning the hearts and minds of the people.

The early beneficial stages of communism proved a great hit with the *povo*. Frelimo concentrated its early attacks on the northern provinces, away from the Portuguese-dominated areas on the coast and in the south. Where they managed to oust the local administration, they set up liberated zones with their own political committees which reported up to the party leadership. Foreign aid was used to build schools, provide water pumps and dig bore holes. All Frelimo had to do after they had taken over an area was offer to provide a better life. Since the Portuguese had never provided anything and had given the local populations no say in how they lived, Frelimo was able to generate enormous goodwill by doing very little. Anything was better than nothing.

Portugal, meanwhile, was suffering badly. Internally, its political system was falling apart. A large percentage of the male population was conscripted into armies fighting wars in far-flung lands. All Portugal's mainland Africa possessions - Guinea Bissau, Angola and Mozambique - were fighting wars of independence.

Following the 1974 Portuguese coup, General Francisco da Costa Gomes said, "The armed forces have reached the limits of neurophysiological exhaustion."

It was the end of their colonial history. The home - based Portuguese people had given up. In Mozambique, though, they hadn't yet. The local Portuguese population tried to stage a coup themselves. They failed, and by the time independence was handed over to Mozambique in 1975, almost 200,000 of 240,000 resentful Portuguese settlers had fled the country. Before they left, many of them destroyed their own property. Cement was poured into the engines of tractors, buildings were burnt down, cars driven into the sea. Bitter and furious at their mother country's betrayal, they became a wandering tribe. Some went to South Africa, others to Brazil. Very few returned to Portugal.

In 1991, it was estimated that 1.9 million Mozambicans were living in neighboring countries as refugees and 1.2 million were displaced within their own country. The country has had a truly dreadful time since it gained independence.

Frelimo was the only effective opposition group when independence was offered and it quickly assumed power. Samaro Machel became the new president and set up Frelimo as the ruling party. Mozambique became a freewheeling, idealistic kind of communist state. Bob Dylan even wrote a song about it. The party had evolved throughout the 1960s from a mish-mash of people who wanted independence to guerilla fighters and budding politicians united against their common enemy. Frelimo's power base stemmed from a northern tribe - the Makonde - but they had to assume power in Maputo, far away on the South African border. There, the population was more sophisticated and had more contact with the outside world.

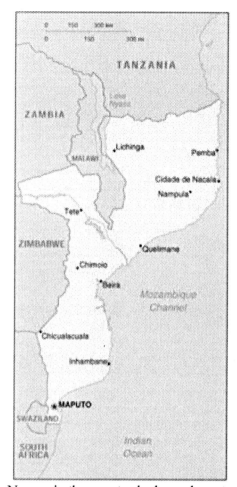

The Mozambique coast is incredibly beautiful and had been a popular holiday destination for tourists from Rhodesia and South Africa. In 1972, 91,000 tourists were visiting Mozambique yearly. By 1981 the figure was down to a thousand - many of whom were probably journalists and spies lying on their immigration forms.

Maputo's local tribes made good money laboring in the gold mines of South Africa. Although the trainloads of Mozambicans who worked the mines have been held up as one of the more disgusting facets of apartheid, this was a trade that Frelimo has always encouraged. Mozambique has had so many problems that it needed the money, whatever indignities had to be suffered to get it.

In the 1970s, it seemed as though everything was conspiring against the quixotic fledgling government. The departure of all the Portuguese was· a crippling blow. No one in the country had ever been taught how to use any of the equipment which survived and only a very few had been educated. 1976 saw a terrible drought, followed by a year of floods. In order to combat UDI (Unilateral Declaration of Independence) in Rhodesia, out of principle, the border had to be closed. This meant the loss of earnings on transit exports and imports through Beira and Maputo. Retaliatory raids by Rhodesia on Mugabe's ZANU (Zimbabwe African National Union) camps in Mozambique led to further destabilization. The final blow was the emergence of Renamo (Mozambique National Resistance Organization). Smith's Rhodesian secret service, in collusion with Boss (now the NIS), South Africa's infamous intelligence service (with a bit of help from the Portuguese), were responsible for the creation and supply of Renamo.

When Frelimo retrenched in 1977 - the grooviness ousted by reality - it purged the party and the army. At its 1977 conference Frelimo set itself up as a harsh communist state. Re-education camps were opened and the idealistic early days were destroyed by the mountainous bureaucracy and inefficiencies that one normally associates with communism. Land was nationalized and state farms set up on the Soviet model. As one would expect, everything stopped working. The informal agricultural sector refused to give up its food because they knew they wouldn't be getting any from the state sector. The early Renamo groups, which were principally a cover for Rhodesia-backed attacks on ZANU camps within Mozembique, were reinforced by disaffected Frelimo members who had been purged from the party or escaped the re-education camps. Both Alfonso Dhlakama and the late Andre Matzangaissa -the head and former deputy of Renamo -were refugees of the Frelimo high command. Renamo was soon a force to be reckoned with.

Throughout the late 1970s and the 1980s, Mozambique was a battlefield. Two guerilla armies fought each other in the bush. Frelimo, with all the responsibilities of being the government, fared badly. Frelimo was supplied with Soviet weapons, but only those needed to fight a conventional war against South Africa, and nowhere near as many as Angola and Ethiopia who got first bite of the roubles. Machel supported the imprisoned Mugabe's ZANU guerillas by allowing them to have camps in Mozambique. Smith reacted by sending Rhodesian troops in after them. Renamo groups moved around the country (often in South African army transport), targeting convoys and then disappearing into the bush. Jet fighters and tanks were no use against such tactics. Like UNITA in Angola, Renamo succeeded because it had no land of its own for Frelimo to target. Renamo were financed by Rhodesia, South Africa and later Kenya and were encouraged to behave as badly as possible. Appalling atrocities were the result. Civilian women had their breasts cut off, men were emasculated and dismembered. Frelimo, in retaliation, didn't behave too well either. Tens of thousands died and the country, under the auspices of war and communism, rapidly disintegrated.

Renamo followed a scorched-earth policy. Ostensibly Frelimo towns were destroyed, their inhabitants massacred and their children conscripted and trained as fighters. Frelimo reacted, doing the same to Renamo areas, but they caused greater resentment because Renamo, who neither had nor valued the hearts and minds of the people, just moved into an area when under threat. After Zimbabwe's independence in 1980, South Africa continued to finance the war in return for tons of ivory which ironically were smuggled into South Africa through herds of protected elephants in

Kruger National Park. The elephants in Kruger have to be regularly culled to keep their numbers down. Mozambique used to have endless forests and some of the densest populations of game in the world. Two hundred and forty thousand square kilometers of forest, an area the size of Belgium, have been destroyed since the railway was built.

Frelimo reacted to the threat within its borders by becoming more authoritarian. Lunatic laws resulted: the semi-nomadic people were not allowed to move around the country because they had to man the state farms; all children had to exercise at 5 a.m. and many were conscripted into both armies; it was made illegal to put your underpants on the washing line; black vehicles were only allowed to be driven by government personnel. The war continued.

Renamo's tactics during the war had been disruptive. They concentrated on making life difficult for the government rather than fighting over territory and managed to achieve a great deal by keeping key routes closed. Until the introduction of the Zimbabwean army on the corridor, they had managed it there, but the jewel in their crown had been control of the Maputo-to-Beira road -nine hundred miles of crucial importance.

Spiritual rebel groups are an African phenomenon of awesome power. Alice Lakwena in Uganda nearly overthrew a government with hers and in Mozambique, the Napramas have similar influence. Members of a secret society, they oil themselves with magic potion and, contrary to all evidence, believe that bullets cannot harm them. In conjunction with Frelimo they destroyed Renamo (who fatally believed in their powers) in Zambezi and brought the rebels back to the negotiating table. Frelimo had already promised free elections and had to face an internal party coup by its left wing who longed for the old days. Renamo had one card and has kept up with the negotiations by using it. A fragile ceasefire has existed since then. They have the ability to cut off all the roads in the country.By allowing them to be opened, they showed their goodwill and the threat of once more closing them keeps them in the game.

The Mozambican peace process got off to a shaky start in 1990. Frelimo, in its sixth congress, agreed to the introduction of multiparty politics and pledged itself to democratic socialism. Frelimo had made a deal with the South Africans in 1984 in which Mozambique agreed to stop supporting the ANC if Pretoria would stop supplying Renamo. Pretoria reneged on these Nkomati Accords and that was the closest either side had ever got to a deal. In July 1990, Frelimo and Renamo met in person for the first time and agreed to the setting up of the JVC, a joint monitoring commission to be presided over by the Italians. By the end of the year, after countless delays, it was agreed that if Zimbabwean troops were pulled back into the corridors, Renamo would stop its attacks. The deal signed and the Zimbabweans safely in the corridors, Renamo launched an attack on the provinces of Nampula and Zambezia and continued to disrupt the rail routes. Their actions spawned a monster. The Napramas, a band of spiritual rebels, joined forces with Frelimo and wiped out Renamo in the two provinces.

Printed with permission:

Blood on the Tracks: A Rail Journey from Angola to Mozambique (1992). By Miles Bredin

See page 41, for biography of **Miles Bredin**.

some economics of the continent

This chapter had to exist in the book, to get the reader face to face with the very serious issues that Africa is currently facing.

This chapter does not cover all the issues, but looks at the main ones using statistics that are most probably out of date and peoples viewpoints.

Recently the World Bank says many African countries are worse off now than they were at independence in the 1960s. It stated the total combined income of 48 countries in Africa is little more than that of Belgium.

Africa's problems include:

- Roads: only 16% paved
- Telephones: 10 per 1000
- Electricity: 80% lack access
- Aids: 35m infected
- Sanitation: inadequate for 75% of rural population

Source: Can Africa Claim the 21st Century

Even just to maintain current levels of poverty, African economies will have to grow by 5% because of rapidly growing populations. The report also states that Africa has "enormous untapped potential and hidden growth reserves", if it can mobilize its human resources and improve its political systems. The report calls for key steps to improve Africa's economic prospects:

- Better government and fewer wars
- More investment in people
- Diversification of the economy
- More aid from rich countries

| 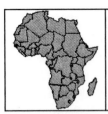 | **cancellation of the african debt will not change anything** | aquiline tarimo, sj
africa
present day |

Introduction

Cancellation of the African debt alone is not enough. This is because the African debt crisis is linked with an unjust set-up of both national and international economic structures. If we are interested in searching for a permanent solution, then we have to know the root causes and be willing to change those structures that perpetuate this condition. This essay reflects on the consequences of the ongoing phenomenon of debt cancellation as a way of motivating Africa's economic growth. This discussion brings into focus three areas, namely, causes of the African debt crisis, cancellation of the African debt and the role of the Catholic Church, and what could be done in order to shape the future.

Causes of the African Debt Crisis

There are various causes of the African debt crisis. First, African countries, after independence, inherited from their colonial masters undemocratic institutions and styles of governance which had historically created a great deal of wealth in Europe. The models of governance and the policies practiced in the colonies were not constructed in Africa's interests. This situation predicted an institutional crisis. What happened is that after independence the African leaders had many traditional options available to help them design effective governments, but they ignored most of them and entrenched themselves in the undemocratic structures of their colonial masters. By such a move they failed the African peoples and frustrated the realization of their dream for freedom, justice, and prosperity. This is what Basil Davidson calls "institutional crisis".[1]

This reality affected not only the political but also the economic institutions. The colonial economic structures were not changed after independence. African countries continued exporting basic raw materials to feed industries in Europe. According to Sina Odugbemi, about 51% of African exports go to Europe, while about 27% go to developing countries.[2] Intra-African trade accounts for only 7.5%.[3] This situation affects African economies so deeply because most of them depend on cash crops for foreign earnings. In addition to that the prices of these crops have been irregular and often low on the world market.

Added to this is the problem of domestic savings. The problem is that a typical African country does not have sufficient domestic savings to raise the necessary capital for local development. Most countries fund their internal budgets with money borrowed from outside. This money comes from international donors in the form of loans and aid. To pay these debts the countries rely on money raised from exports. As already noted, however, the majority of African countries have only raw materials to export and this does not generate the necessary cash inflows. The amount of money raised cannot cover the costs of the imports of the intermediate products needed to run the farms nor the country's budget as a whole. In fact, some countries are no longer able to produce raw materials for export. Lack of structural transformation does not, however, shift the blame entirely to the outsider. Corruption and mismanagement have continued to contribute to the deteriorating situation.

Second, the growth of the African debt reached disturbing proportions in the 1970s. Between 1970 and 1979, the external debt of developing countries increased by 400%.[4] Two factors for this rapid increase were international lending policies and local mismanagement. What happened in the 1970s was that surplus dollars made during the oil-hike were invested in banks both in Europe and in the United States. These "petrol-dollars" were given as loans to the poor countries (PC). The trade imbalance between Europe and the United States of America also produced a surplus of dollars in Europe. These Euro-dollars were also invested as loans.[5] The growth of the petrol-dollars and Euro-dollars made loans readily available to the poor countries on easy terms at flexible interest rates. According to Claude Ake, "African countries took advantage of the availability of credit, borrowed enthusiastically, and made poor investments with their easy credit. Between 1974 and 1982 the normal dollar value of the debts of [many] countries rose from $140 billion to $560 billion".

A number of African countries found themselves borrowing in big amounts. As much as one can blame poor countries for this unreasonable borrowing, one must not lose sight of the fact that borrowers are impotent without the lenders. In other words, if the lenders had not made such monies so easily available, the borrowers might have contracted for the loans with more caution and less frequency. Thus William Darity and others have argued that these loans were pushed on PCs to increase the profit margins of the banks in the United States and in Europe.[7] In an effort to dispose of their surplus from the petrol and Euro-dollars in the 1970s, the banks pushed loans to PCs through a drastic softening of terms. In so doing the banks played a role of implementing strategies which created the financial crisis found in Africa today.8 The desire for profits ignited the rapid growth of PCs. This situation made things even worse when it overrode export earnings and coincided with a great deal of internal mismanagement. Social upheavals after the disillusionment of independence produced many dictators and military leaders. These leaders were the ones who contracted the loans. Many of the loans contracted at that time went into the wrong hands and were often misused. In several cases loans were used to buy weapons to quell political opposition within their countries.

Third, the debt crisis of the 1980s was related to the response of the International Monetary Fund (IMF) and World Bank (WB). Frantic efforts were undertaken by the financial community to bring African countries back to the system. There is no doubt that the international financial institutions played an important role in this crisis. The writing off of debts was not a point of concern. Such a step would lessen the dividends of banks in North America and Europe and could in the long run lead to a total collapse of the financial markets around the world. This situation then led the IMF to implement what has been called the Structural Adjustment Program (SAP).

The 1980s were thus the years of the SAP in Africa. Its primary goal was not the alleviation of the economic problems of the PCs as may have appeared. It sought to stabilize world financial markets without affecting the economies of the rich countries. Despite all the arguments being made today about the positive effects of SAP, especially by the IMF, one can argue that it did not have the PCs or the human person as its central focus. The truth is that financial institutions placed an unbearable burden on PCs. This meant more debt and more suffering for the PCs. In addition to that loans given to Africa during this period targeted mainly security affairs and the stopping of communism rather than humanitarian needs. Fourth, in order to understand fully the impact of the SAPs on the economies of the African countries we have to also examine the long-term effects of the SAP. The 1980s saw a major crisis for African PCs which had been started by increasing costs for imports and a decline in export earnings. This trend resulted in the policy of SAP in the hope of alleviating this crisis. SAP is a financial strategy which is "aid-based reliance on capital input growth".9 What were the fruits of SAP? The SAP brought untold hardships to ordinary people and explained that such hardships were necessary for a better future. Among the conditions imposed were the restructuring of the public enterprises, the lifting of controls on retail and producer prices, the liberalization of trade and exchange systems, and the broadening of the tax bases.10 These conditions affected the ordinary person more than the rich investors from abroad.11 For the people of Africa, this meant an increase in prices of basic goods like food and medicine. In other words, the burden of this exercise is laid upon the borrowing countries while the lending countries and their institutions refused to shoulder an equally needed adjustment in international financial arrangements. The lending countries and institutions retained their advantages and remained in charge of setting the rules. What is clear is that the SAP strategy was unrealistic because the economic capacity of the poor countries had not increased; instead there was a growing dependency on foreign aid.12 A repeated devaluation of local currencies further exacerbated this situation. Governments could do nothing more than urge their people to "tighten belts". On the surface, the policies of the IMF and WB were laudable, but considering the continuous devaluation of the local currencies and the suffering of the masses, the effects of such policies were tragic.

The SAP encouraged trade liberalization and fostered the increase of Trans-National Corporations (TNC). These corporations take advantage of low wages and weak government regulations. One might argue that the TNCs create job opportunities and boost capital in the countries where they establish themselves. This situation may be true theoretically, but the overall effect is disadvantageous to the PCs.13 Due to poverty and the need for capital, little is done to check the activities of the TNCs. Labor conditions are often neglected and the environment is abused. TNC profits are rarely reinvested in the country. Most profits are shipped back to the TNCs' countries of origin. The effects of TNCs on local industries is also disastrous. Local companies cannot compete with the TNCs. They do not have the capital resources nor access to the international markets of the large TNCs. Many local industries head for bankruptcy and ultimate collapse.

The IMF and TNCs often deprive PCs of much needed financial resources. In 1986, for instance, "forty-five Sub-Sahara African countries paid out $895 million more to the IMF than they took in".14 In 1993, the debt of Sub-Saharan Africa increased by 354 % while the First World experienced an increase of wealth.15 This wealth is increasingly concentrated in the hands of a few. The 1992 report of the WB and IMF affirms that "the richest 20 % of the population controlled 83 % of total income, while the poorest 20 % had to survive on 1.4 %".16

This reality is mirrored on the local level. More and more TNCs are taking advantage of the situation and making huge profits, while a majority of the people wallow in poverty.17 These realities raise questions of justice such as: Will African countries be subjected to a new type of economic slavery? Do African governments have the power to pursue projects for the benefit of their people with limited external interference? What we have seen so far in this discussion affirms that the debt crisis, beyond doubt, will affect the future of the African economy, both in the short and long terms.

Fifth, in searching for solutions it is appropriate to consider the impact of the growing global market, political marginalization of Africa, and prospects for the African economic future. The survival of the African economic future depends so much on the world's political and economic strategies. The pace and scale of what is happening now in the global market suggests the marginalization of Africa. The African economic marginalization concerns the "economic regression of Africa relative to other regions of the world and the diminishing importance and relevance of Africa to the global economy, particularly to the industrialized countries".18 One can also account for the problem of the marginalization of Africa as essentially a restatement of what Walter Rodney calls the "problem of underdevelopment".19 Today, Africa has become stagnant, unattractive to foreign investors and donors, and unable to elicit the interest of the other regions in the world. This situation makes Africa a non-entity in world trade and forgotten in economic considerations. Such a deepening crisis of underdevelopment is referred to as marginalization. Thus, the discourse about the African marginalization concerns explicitly the strategies of the world market, financial institutions, and private donors who do not take enough interest in Africa.

I would also like to argue that the growing concern about the global market will not benefit Africa. This is because Africa is unable to integrate itself into a global trading system. The global trading system will only open up African markets to foreign goods, thereby aggravating its situation. Meanwhile, what is needed is to support Africa's efforts to reform its economic infrastructure by pursuing meaningful structural adjustment programmes. Such programmes must include the process of strengthening grassroots structures and enforcing the rule of law in view of establishing a culture of respecting human rights, democracy, equality, and social justice.

There is no doubt that "powerful forces, including technological change, the dismantling of trade barriers, and financial liberalization are transforming the shape of the world economy".20 Moreover, financial institutions like the IMF and WB are increasingly acting as if the global economy consists of a single market with regional sectors rather than as national economies linked by trade...Perhaps, the most acute is that the caravan of global growth will exacerbate inequalities and leave the world's poor even poorer. The evidence so far seems to justify some anxiety. Huge private investment flows are now pouring into developing countries. Only 6 % went to Africa.

How will Africa survive if it continues to depend on such a declining aid flow? This question is important for us. So far there is no program designed to integrate Africa into the process of market globalization. Justin

Ukpong argues that "globalization of the world economy whereby the originally weak, agrarian non-technical economies of the Third World countries have been merged into the strong technological economies of Europe and America must be seen as a form of economic oppression".22 The fact is that the structure of global market benefits only rich countries. My argument here is that as the global market system takes shape, Africa seems to be forgotten. This is because Africa lacks the ability to enter into this competition. Furthermore, there is no guarantee that there will be fair play for there are no clear guidelines to motivate the participation of poor countries. The invention of a global market will, therefore, marginalize the African economy in the short- and long-terms. In order to justify this conclusion, it is appropriate to analyze carefully the change of strategies of the world economy.

It is now difficult to see anything that can keep Africa on the international scene. Such a dramatic change resulted from the end of the Cold War and the emergence of the global market. The reality is that Africa has been marginalized by the developments in technology and strategies of the world economy. The rapid advancement in technology in recent years must be considered as a significant factor. Technology has made the industrialized countries replace primary raw materials with synthetic materials. This means that the highly industrialized countries of North America and Western Europe are no longer dependent on primary producers of raw materials as they used to be. Furthermore, the deliberate manipulation of the world market and politics leave Africa on the verge of total socio-economic and political disaster. These changes, without doubt, put Africa in a situation of marginalization. Unfortunately, the force of monetarism makes people believe that once financial institutions set the monetary incentives and policies, everybody will do the right thing and the economy will automatically bring forth the intended results.23 It is not just a matter of reordering policies, but rather of transforming the whole infrastructure and creating an "enabling environment".

Another point to bear in mind is that the loans received between the 1960s and the 1990s were without transformative strategies. The WB Report of 1988 addresses this same issue when it emphasizes the need to transform the economic structures found in Africa by creating an enabling environment.25 The question of creating an enabling environment requires effective governance and political renewal. Better governance includes policy-making, good administration, enforcement of the rule of law, maintenance of juridical independence, honesty, and accountability. African countries have failed to produce political and economic systems that can guarantee these conditions. In other words, basic structures are not organized in such way that they can promote a process of creating economic wealth. Looking at the political situation of Africa today, a genuine change will take a long time because political leaders are more interested in retaining political power than in building stable economic infrastructures. For example, most African leaders use public funds to buy political supporters and luxury items for themselves. The possibility of linking political forces with economic logic will, therefore, depend on the context and cooperation of different institutions. Taking into account the enormous obstacles confronting African countries today, a positive change must be integral and foster grassroots structures. Let us now evaluate briefly the role played by the Catholic Church in this crisis.

Cancellation of the African Debt and the Role of the Catholic Church

Since 1995, the entire Catholic Church and especially the Western Catholic Church and Catholic organizations have been advocating very strongly for the cancellation of the African debt. The lobbying has been done in various international fora. One could say that in the history of the Catholic Church there has been no other issue related to Africa upon which the Universal Catholic Church has been so united as in the search for immediate solutions to this problem. Certain fruits are now seen since the debts of many countries are in the process of being cancelled. This is indeed a credit to the Western Catholic Church.

Nevertheless, if the Church aims at promoting an awareness that could lead to the full elimination of this form of global injustice and poverty in Africa, more steps have to be taken quickly for the sake of securing the future of Africa. This effort must provide practical suggestions that can lead to structural transformation of the economy both at the national and international level so as to enable Africa to participate fully in the global market, enhance equality, and further self-determination.

In the end, however, much will depend on individuals who work with a will to change the structures that are at the roots of this crisis and that determine the policies of these institutions. The African crisis must be understood in such a way as to reassess the role of the State, civil society, the economic sector, and the global economic order in which they must all operate. In search of a way to establish an enabling environment, the worst thing Africans can do is to put too much emphasis on the question of debt cancellation. Debt cancellation alone will not change the real situation. Only structural change will create a new environment whereby participation, self-reliance, and creation of wealth are encouraged. My opinion is that even if all of Africa's debts were cancelled, it will not make much difference due to the following conditions which continue to persist: poor planning, inefficient leadership, corruption, misappropriation of public funds, lack of civil society and participation, power struggles, over dependence, exodus of intellectuals, and manipulation of the poor.

What Should be Done?

The causes of the African debt crisis are numerous and they vary from one country to another. Consequently, solutions should also vary and depend on the contexts and conditions pertaining to each country. In search for a way forward it is appropriate to ask ourselves this question: What should be done in order to change the situation? For the sake of shaping our future, this discussion provides a few suggestions that I believe can promote justice on the global market as well as overcome administrative problems on the part of the African governments. In order to be brief it is appropriate to sum up my suggestions in ten points.

First, a genuine analysis of the African debt crisis must be situated within a wide range of causes, both internally and externally. Internal causes which are at the heart of African economic crisis include social organization. Poor social organization is portrayed by the lack of civil society, insecurity, institutionalized corruption, and ethnic conflicts which arise from the attitude of exploiting ethnic consciousness for political gain. Internal causes are compounded with the mentality of dependence and paternalism which are enforced by international systems of trade, finance, and manipulative politics of rich nations. Such a situation calls those examining this crisis to make an effort to go beyond ideological biases which tend to limit this problem to the issue of overpopulation.

Second, we have to acknowledge that the debt crisis is part of the global injustices that we all are part of as long as it deprives people of their basic needs. This affirmation presupposes that a burden must be shared. It does not, however, advocate the outright cancellation of all debts. Instead it challenges us to be considerate when a burden is injurious to the life of the community or State. If the debt is such that it threatens the basic needs of the poor like food, shelter, and clothing, then payments should be suspended. The question that emerges is: Since various countries and institutions contributed a portion of the loan, who should correct the situation of indebtedness?

Third, loans should be given on conditions that respect the minimum rights of the citizens. The conditions I have in mind here are accountability of governments, recognition of rights in the country and participation of the citizens in the decision-making. Developmental projects are a first priority.

African countries should promote economic growth by involving the citizens more in local projects of development. Genuine economic projects must begin from the capacities of the people. The caring approach aims at converting misused capacity into productive activity so that people can provide for their own needs. This approach includes caring for the common good, at the national and international level. This means making people practice critical thinking by allowing them to see their own interests and linking them to the well-being of others, this ensures that the priorities of the majority are not neglected. Priority should also be given to programs that are for development and are people-oriented, rather than loans that are for buying weapons, luxury items, and political supporters.

Fourth, policies of economic reform should be scrutinized. The current situation of the African economy needs a significant rethinking. It is a situation that demands a broad analysis and reflection on Africa's past and current economic relationship with Western countries so that together a new relationship based on mutual responsibility can be formed. Such analysis will open our eyes with a view to challenging the common tendency whereby a donor-recipient relationship favors the donor through an asymmetrical reciprocity in trade policies and an unequal responsibility which is more likely to lead to dependency instead of development.

In the African context, the aim, the persons and institutions involved, and the conditions in which foreign aid is given and loans contracted is not made public. What is made public is the accumulation of debts and conditions of payment. The knowledge of the conditions in which foreign aid is given and loans contracted is important because foreign aid, for example, has never been intended to be purely altruistic. Sometimes foreign aid and loans are given as a diplomatic gesture to maintain a long-term economic interest. It is true that foreign aid and loans are important complements to the reconstruction efforts for those countries that need them. However, these countries must constantly be encouraged to lessen their degree of dependency. In addition, donors and financial institutions are called to change their attitude of supplying aid which functions as chloroform. Foreign assistance should be directed to the efforts intended to readjust the economic infrastructure. In this way, foreign assistance can help to mobilize small projects and the private sector for income-generating and job-creating enterprises. It is important to strengthen grassroots economic structures because they play a more visible and basic role in the process of implementing proposed programs.

Fifth, the mentality of excessive dependency on foreign aid should be discouraged. Africa's total dependency on foreign aid has made the continent fall farther behind. The fact is that foreign aid has created a culture of permanent dependency. This situation is sometimes referred to by economists as the "dependency syndrome". The giving of aid, as an economic assistance, has proven to be a model that is outdated and it cannot change the reality of poverty in Africa. What is needed is the political will to look at human needs as a global problem to be solved together by establishing structures of partnership that give technical assistance.

Sixth, for the sake of securing the future, African countries should invest in their own people through education. Since independence, the "major goal of formal education has always been the production of workers for the salaried job sector".26 Since the 1980s, this kind of education (i.e., education oriented toward employment) is becoming more and more irrelevant because there are no jobs. This situation, therefore, demands a change in the educational system. This change necessitates the formation of people who can challenge themselves to be open to new insights that promote integrity, commitment, creativity, and self-reliance. Furthermore, I would like to point out that the economic development of Africa will also depend on the status of women. African women are the pillars of African socio-economic life. If their status were improved through education, then it would positively affect the economic life of African countries. A relevant education will encourage them to overcome their tendency to endure rather than to challenge the hardship.

Seventh, African skilled workers and intellectuals are morally obliged to contribute their skills to their respective country instead of going abroad in search for economic and professional advancement. Since the 1980s there has been a brain-drain from the African countries. This phenomenon has been caused by low wages, corruption and mismanagement, nepotism, lawlessness, and dishonesty on the part of leaders. My conviction is that there will be no significant change either politically or economically as long as the exodus of intellectuals continues.

Eighth, there is a need to strengthen intermediate associations. For about four decades, the one-party system and military regimes suppressed the role of trade unions, cooperatives, and professional associations. Today, the remaining associations do not have the ability to assert autonomy or challenge the repressive governments. Most governments continue to treat leaders of associations as their agents. This attitude is sustained by the practice of making sure that leaders of associations are controlled by the government. It is through this system that most governments find ways to reward associations that conform with them and harass those that try to assert their autonomy.

Intermediate associations are important because they play the role of shaping economic policies by providing alternatives and mobilizing people from the grassroots level. In the African context, the idea of strengthening such structures would be one step toward the process of transforming economic infrastructures. Apart from overcoming totalitarianism, this process will improve the economy by making people co-responsive and go beyond the crisis-oriented approach which dominates economic planning in Africa. Associations can play the role of promoting the idea of the common good, human rights, participation, and creativity. This is done by ensuring that there is a sense of reciprocal obligations and expectations that prevail among groups of different interests. These organs promote the sense of the common good by articulating a mechanism that defines the relationship between the State and civil society and safeguards the separation between them. The structure of intermediate associations can overcome bureaucracies and monopolies of socio-economic and political power concentrated in the hands of the "predatory *élite*". Instead of allowing the political sphere, which is dominated by the *élite* group, to dictate everything in the socio-economic sphere, civil associations will act as guardians of people's opinion, and will encourage participation and new ideas. This is done by helping the poor to defend their basic rights. In collaboration with the skilled workers like lawyers and human rights activists, victims of economic justice will be able to decide for themselves how to improve their life standard. The process of developing such awareness will be effective because the assertion of rights is derived from the peoples' sense of justice expressed in terms of strategies initiated and sustained by the people themselves.

The call to strengthen intermediate associations reminds us that verbal pronouncements alone are insufficient. Verbal pronouncements must be action-oriented. In the African context, verbal pronouncements alone create an insignificant impact. This is because there are no relevant structures that can convert such pronouncements into social action. It has to be clear that there will be no effective way of talking about socio-economic justice and human rights in Africa if intermediate associations are not strengthened. In other words, socio-economic and political success will not occur in a vacuum. The appearance of multiparty elections in recent years should not distract people from continuing to search for concrete ways in which the economy can be reformed. Multiparty elections, in themselves, do not guarantee democracy or economic prosperity.

Ninth, the Catholic Church can play a significant role in changing the current situation. This is possible if it collaborates more effectively with other Churches in influencing the process of policy-making, moulding of the public conscience, and promotion of human rights and social justice. "It is, therefore, no longer possible for the [Church] in Africa, and for that matter the universal Church in place to look on the poor and the situation of poverty as something it may or may not take on as the central focus of its mission".

Tenth, many development theories have been borrowed from abroad and imposed on people, but the life standard of the people has remained the same. Such an outcome shows that there is a need to analyze thoroughly our cultures and to come out with a developmental framework based on African cultural values and context. This approach entails critical evaluation of each individual and group in order to identify the strength which we could build upon. Such an adjustment needs associations. Associations provide people a platform where they can dialogue creatively and identify problems which affect them. They recognize people's culture, interest, and potentiality. Recognizing people's potential provides self-confidence and courage to search for practical solutions to their own problems. It is a process which makes everyone in local communities act responsibly knowing that their actions affect their own lives. Human development is what begins with a person and spreads through the family and to the community.

Conclusion

What is important in this discussion is the response given to the African debt crisis with a specific orientation. More than that the African debt crisis finds its answer in the African people who are the future of the African continent.

Notes:

1Basil Davidson, *The Black Man's Burden: Africa and The Curse of the Nation-State*, New York, Times Books, 1992, p. 12.

2 Sina Odugbemi, "Brave New World", *West Africa* (April 17-23, 1995), p. 582.

3 *Ibid.*, p. 585.

4 Kristen Hallberg, "International Debt, 1985: Origins and Issues for the Future", in Michael P. Claudon, ed., *World Debt Crisis: International Lending on Trial*, (Cambridge, Massachusetts, Ballinger Publishing Company, 1986), p. 3.

5 Jo Marie Griesgraber, *Continuing Dialogue on Debt*, (Washington, D.C., Center of Concern, 1991), p. 5.

6 Claude Ake, *Democracy and Development in Africa* (Washington, D.C.: The Brookings Institution, 1996), p. 104.

7 William Darity, "Did Commercial Banks Push Loans on the LDCs?" in *World Debt Crisis: International Lending on Trial*, pp. 199-225.

8 *Ibid.*, p. 200.

9 Vic Missiaen, "Economic/Sociological Models of Development", in *AFER* 37 (October, 1995), pp. 192-305 at p. 296.

10 Guy Arnold, "An African Way?", *New African*, September 1994, pp. 17-26 at p. 26.

11 Peter Henriot, "Effects of Structural Adjustment Programmes on African Families", *African Christian Studies* 11/2 (June, 1995): pp. 1-16.

12 For example, Thermon Djaksan's Analytical Report on the Sub-Saharan Debt Crisis of 1993, 1994, and 1995 shows that the increase of foreign aid and loans did not slow down the rate of economic decline, (Development Aid Committee's Annual Report), *"West Africa"*, 18-24 [March 1996]: pp. 430-35).

13 In many countries, the TNCs are accepted in the belief that the economic principle of trickle-down will change the situation. Unfortunately, instead of trickling-down it trickles-up. For more details, see Michael P. Hornsby-Smith, "Justice and Peace: Theory and Practice", *The Month* 29/1 (January, 1996): pp. 3-6.

14 Laurenti Magesa, "Christian Discipleship in Africa in the Twenty First Century", in *AFER* 36/5 (October 1994): pp. 283-99, at p. 294.

15 "Sub-Saharan Africa: Route to Success Lies in Sound Economic Policies", *IMF Survey* (February 1995): p. 63.

16 "World Bank and International Monetary Fund: Guilty as Charged", *Envio* 13 (December, 1994): p. 161.

17 An analysis of this case appears in Paul Valley, author of *Bad Samaritans*, who points out that loans given to the Third World Countries are not genuine help, but a trade that makes huge profits by making poor countries poorer. He also develops the same argument by providing concrete examples in the article: "How to Make the Poor Poorer", *The Tablet*, (February 24, 1996): pp. 248-50.

18 Ake, *Democracy and Development in Africa*, p.113.

19 Walter Rodney, *How Europe Underdeveloped Africa* (Washington, D.C.: Howard University Press, 1982), pp. 33-200.

20 Charles Wookey, "Perils of a Global Economy", *The Tablet*, (May 18, 1996): p. 640.

21 *Ibid.*, p. 641.

22 Justin S. Ukpong, "Option for the Poor: A Modern Challenge for the Church in Africa", in *AFER* 36/6 (December 1994): pp. 350-66, at p. 362.

23 William Tordoff, *Government and Politics in Africa* (Indiana: Indiana University Press, 1984), p. 272.

24 Thomas M. Callaghy, "The State and the Development of Capitalism in Africa", in Donald Rothchild and Naomi Chazan, eds., *Precarious Balance: State and Society in Africa*, (Boulder: Westview Press, 1988), pp. 67-99.

25 World Bank, *Adjustment Lending: An Evaluation of Ten Years of Experience* (Washington, D.C.: World Bank, 1988), p. 3.

26 Ajuji Ahmed and Ronald Cohen, "Education and Rights in Nigeria", in Ronald Cohen *et al*, eds., *Human Rights and Governance in Africa* (Florida: Florida University Press, 1993), p. 220.

27Ukpong, "Option for the Poor: A Modern Challenge for the Church in Africa", p. 364.

|  | **debt relief and hiv/aids programs** | dr. peter j. henriot africa present day |

The two greatest blocks to human development in Africa today are the burden of external debt and the pandemic of HIV/AIDS. Are these two *problems* related? Are *solutions* to these two related? What practical *responses* are possible as we work to deal with *both* of these mega-problems? And what does this mean specifically in Zambia?

During the ICASA meeting in September 1999 in Lusaka, I was asked to comment on a proposal made by the Government of the Republic of Zambia (GRZ) for a proposal that would make available for HIV/AIDS programmes some resources freed up by debt relief programs that could be arranged with bilateral donors. I made the comments not representing specific HIV/AIDS programs, though as a pastoral worker and development consultant resident in Zambia for over a decade, I am deeply concerned with the problem of the destruction of life in this country because of HIV/AIDS. Rather I presented a position coming from the movement in civil society that is attempting to deal with the other great destroyer of life, the external debt owed by Zambia and regularly serviced at the expense of such vital life programs as health care, education, and other social services.

Debt Cancellation for Zambia

In his paper presenting the GRZ proposal at the ICASA meeting, the Minister of Finance and Economic Development powerfully analyzed both the extent and consequences of HIV/AIDS in Zambia and the depth and impact of our huge external debt. A debt stock of over US$ 6.5 billion for a population of around 10 million comes to US$ 650 for every Zambian woman, man and child, over twice the GDP per capita. The debt is clearly unsustainable and Zambia is obviously a "Heavily Indebted Poor Country."

In terms of *human suffering*, we know well the consequences of the Government's commitment to regular debt servicing that now exceeds spending on health, education and other welfare services combined. Sufficient money is not found in the national budget for meeting basic social needs such as books for schools and drugs for clinics, but is found for servicing the national debt. Yet no nation can develop without educated and healthy citizens, no matter how faithfully it may meet debt servicing requirements.

One-third of school-age children in Zambia (ages 7-13) (the majority of whom are girls) are not enrolled in schools. Many of those who are in school face untrained teachers, sit on the floor, do not have books or other educational materials, and are in classrooms for only a few hours a day. Health services are a national disaster, as represented in the shocking figures of infant and under-five mortality, maternal mortality, declining life expectancy, and general morbidity conditions.

Keen analysis of Zambia's debt situation and sharp critique of the economic reform package known as SAP or ESAF have revealed the links between these factors and the human suffering so widely experienced and shockingly growing in Zambia today. That is why Zambian, civil society – churches, NGOs, trade unions, student groups, women's groups, professional societies, concerned individuals, etc. – have come together to join the international campaign calling for a cancellation of the debts we endure. *Jubilee 2000 is the name, immediate action for equitable and effective debt relief is the program.* More than three hundred thousand signatures (45% from rural areas in this country) were taken from Zambia to the G-8 meeting in Cologne in June, joining the 17 million signatures gathered from around the world in the Jubilee 2000 campaign.

The argument behind this campaign was well summarized in a joint pastoral letter issued in August 1998 by the three major church bodies, representing Protestants, Catholics and evangelicals. The pastoral letter stated adamantly that Zambia's debt is clearly *unpayable*:

"Zambia *cannot* pay back because the debt burden is economically exhausting. It blocks future development. Zambia *will not* pay back because the debt burden is politically destabilizing. It threatens social harmony. Zambia *should not* pay back because the debt burden is ethically unacceptable. It hurts the poorest in our midst."

The call of our debt campaign is for *cancellation*, not for half-way, totally inadequate measures of a reformed HIPC or a human-faced ESAF. The "Lusaka Declaration," coming from a meeting of fourteen African nations last May, stated unequivocally: "We reject HIPC and the other current debt relief processes" that are tied to imposed reform programs that are "deepening economic, social and ecological hardships for the vast majority of people" in Africa.

Debt Relief Benefits Whom?

It is very clear that Zambia is *deserving* of debt relief, but the key question is: is Zambia *credible* with what it would do with debt relief? Any debt relief must be put to the cause of poverty *eradication*—not simply poverty *alleviation* such as welfare safety nets or emergency food relief. Productivity, employment, small capital availability, agricultural enhancement, physical infrastructure such as feeder roads in rural areas, women's empowerment, environmental protection: these and many more areas are where debt relief must be designated to move toward effective poverty eradication.

But many persons in donor countries and many more citizens in Zambia are asking today a very sharp and pertinent question: what guarantee do we have that resources freed up through debt cancellation will in fact go to poverty eradication and not to causes such as new Mercedes Benz for Ministers, new uniforms for the military, new bank accounts for key politicians? This question is not politically motivated but realistically formed. And it must be realistically answered, lest Zambia, no matter how deserving we may be of debt relief, will not be credible enough to receive it.

That is why our CCJP/JCTR Debt Project (jointly sponsored by the Catholic Commission for Justice and Peace and the Jesuit Center for Theological Reflection) is currently devoting efforts to establish effective debt mechanisms that involve civil society in setting conditions for how debt relief is to be spent. These are what we call "conditionalities from below," not the "conditionalities from above" imposed only by outside donors and international institutions. We are suggesting four such mechanisms:

independent tripartite management commission, composed of representatives of civil society, parliament and relevant ministries, to oversee debt negotiations and transparent utilization of a poverty eradication fund (Uganda already has such a mechanism in place)

social audit of the budget, to assure active participation of civil society for input and evaluation of the national budget (such a mechanism has been operating in an initial form here in Zambia for three years, conducted by the CCJP)

bilateral counterpart funds, to provide designation of resources for specific projects, for example, through debt swaps (e.g., for environmental programs)

international debt arbitration, to move negotiations out of asymmetrical and unfair relationships between rich creditors and poor debtors into a neutral forum such as in a United Nations court

Central to all these proposals is the involvement of civil society and the effort to guarantee a credible use of resources freed up by debt relief.

The proposal put forth by the Zambian Government is an example of the third type of mechanism, designed to guarantee that debt relief does indeed involve civil society in assuring "conditionalities from below." How can we evaluate this Zambian proposal for a multi-donor "Debt for Development" arrangement?

Criteria for "Debt for Development"

As the Minister of Finance and Economic Development explained in his ICASA presentation, the proposal aims to scale up an expanded response to "breaking the back of HIV/AIDS in Zambia." In order to generate new resources for HIV/AIDS prevention and control, scarce national resources, presently used to service debt, would be set aside under commonly agreed-upon terms. Civil, private and public sector institutions would be enabled to implement programs in a combined response that would be part of the overall National HIV/AIDS Strategy.

As details of the Strategy are worked out, there is a very strong concern of the civil society engaged in the debt campaign here in Zambia, a concern about the orientation, organization and operation of this "Debt for Development" arrangement. Recognizing that this proposed arrangement would be the first large-scale initiative to channel debt relief resources into poverty eradication, we want to be assured that it sets a *precedent* that meets these three criteria: clear financial and programmatic accountability, wide public participation, and effective poverty eradication.

First, accountability and transparency must be there as foreign donors and Zambian citizens alike demand this. The program will not be accepted by donors nor owned by citizens if there is not honest and open accounting at every moment of the arrangements. This will not be easy in the current Zambian political and administrative climate. A government that finds it difficult to be transparent with both Members of Parliament and ordinary citizens about the whereabouts of the millions of US dollars gathered during the privatization process must work very hard to be transparent about the millions of US dollars that might be gathered through debt relief arrangements. The debt campaign of civil society says very clearly: *no* to any debt arrangement, no matter how attractive it might be, that is not scrupulously accountable to the citizens of Zambia as well as to donors.

Second, wide public participation means that the arrangements are open to the involvement of the many sectors of civil society that will be affected by these arrangements. This includes NGOs involved in HIV/AIDS work and also NGOs involved in debt work. The light of publicity, the fire of debate, the sense of sharing, the structures of partnership: all these must be guaranteed in the arrangements for debt relief. No "behind doors" decisions, no exclusion of key partners, no "token" representatives, no un-owned resolutions, etc.

Finally, the arrangements must be aimed at poverty eradication and not simply poverty alleviation. It is a matter of development, not welfare, a question of empowerment, not dependency. Clearly, this requires a fresher and wider vision than is frequently exercised in government and NGO bureaucracies. For instance, debt relief money must not go *only* into social sectors like health and education. Sometimes money put into road construction between a village and a clinic, or electricity for rural schools, or employment of agricultural extension workers can be much more effective in poverty eradication than simply sectoral monies spent in narrowly defined "health and education" projects.

Evaluation of HIV/AIDS Proposal

Given these three criteria, how can we evaluate the proposed multi-donor "Debt for Development" arrangement? Obviously, more study needs to be made of the GRZ proposal. But the Minister's ICASA presentation does seem to move significantly in the direction of meeting in its vision and strategy the demands for accountability, participation and poverty eradication.

First, the principles of financial and programmatic accountability are made explicit in the proposal and a clear commitment is made to independent management of the debt relief funds. Prior agreement by all parties to mechanisms for collecting and reporting information about the progress of the programs must be reached before any funding is released. And structures for an open process are required to be set in place.

Second, a Debt Relief Steering Committee will assure that the debt program is not a Government-controlled effort but a partnership involving civil, private and public sectors. The exact character, composition and charter of the Committee remains to be designed, but at least the proposal speaks of it in a way appears satisfactory.

Finally, the multi-sectoral approach to HIV/AIDS can be shaped to poverty eradication by implementing truly cross-cutting strategies in the activities of ministries and civil society. For example, education of the girl child should not only be in prevention of HIV but in literacy that enhances dignity and empowers choices. Promotion of behavior change requires more than seminars, but also job opportunities and recreational facilities. Youth programs should not simply offer more condoms but also more education in traditional cultural values. Such approaches are not short-term poverty alleviation or welfare, but long-term poverty eradication or development.

Conclusion

In conclusion, let me make clear about what I am saying and what I am not saying.

First, the national Zambian debt campaign, comprising Jubilee 2000-Zambia, the CCJP/JCTR Debt Project and many other groups, reiterates its call for full cancellation of Zambia's debt. We reject the half-way measures like reformed designs of HIPC and ESAF.

Second, we call for the implementation of debt mechanisms that assure that any freed resources go to poverty eradication and we insist on the participation of civil society in monitoring negotiations and deciding priorities. These are the "conditionalities from below" that we promote.

Third, in speaking approvingly of the GRZ proposal for a "Debt for Development" arrangement aimed at HIV/AIDS programmes, we express appreciation for inclusion of the principles of accountability, participation and poverty eradication. However, we do not endorse the proposal unreservedly, since we need to see more details about its actual structure and about the Government's real commitment.

Fourth, we do not say that HIV/AIDS prevention, control and treatment is the *only* poverty eradication priority and thus we do not endorse any proposal that would make HIV/AIDS programmes the *sole* recipient of debt relief resources. But we do see the proposal laid on the table at the ICASA meeting as giant step forward in the design and implementation of debt relief that can effectively benefit the poor.

Published in the TIMES OF ZAMBIA, Tuesday 2 November 1999

Peter Henriot, a Jesuit priest and political scientist, first came to Africa in 1982 for some educational/social justice programs in Zambia and Zimbabwe. He returned in 1989 for a year's work in village development in the Southern Province of Zambia. He moved to Lusaka in 1990, and currently directs a team of eight involved in social, economic and political research and action at the "Jesuit Center for Theological Reflection" (JCTR). http://www.jctr.org.zm. His studies (Ph.D, Chicago, post-doctoral, Harvard) and work (Center of Concern, Washington DC for 17 years) have focused on political economy of development, with particular concern for social justice promotion and the church's role in effective change for the better. He serves as a Catholic priest on Sundays in a local language parish outside Lusaka. Current interests: cancellation of debt, human rights and democracy, church's social teaching. Contact: phenriot@zamnet.zm; JCTR, P.O. Box 37774, Lusaka, Zambia.

	**globalization: implications for africa**	dr. peter j. henriot africa present day

When I left Zambia last week, one name was on everyone's lips: "El Nino." This climatic phenomenon originating in the middle of the Pacific Ocean is affecting the rainfall patterns in our land-locked African country many thousands of kilometers away. Drought is threatened, with consequent famine, disturbed social conditions, upset economic patterns, and unsettling political ramifications. "El Nino" affects many parts of the world—perhaps also here in India—with heavy rains, but in our country its effect is just the opposite, with the halt of rains and resultant severe drought. The awareness that we live on a very small and very inter-related globe has come home in varied and dramatic fashion in recent years, but for us in Zambia, that awareness is heightened by the serious challenge facing the country in the weeks ahead arising from such a dramatic global phenomenon.

"El Nino," I suggest, is an example in the natural order of "globalization," the interdependence of diverse activities occurring across the expansion of the globe. At this conference we are looking at examples in the artificial, human-made order of globalization, in the economic, political and cultural spheres of life. Specifically, we are exploring in this session analyses of the phenomenon of globalization and its social consequences. My task here is to offer some brief reflections on the implications of globalization for Africa. (Having lived and worked for some years in Zambia, my examples will most often be from my experience there.)

I. Premises

In order to understand the significance of globalization in the African context, there are two premises that I believe focus the debate more realistically.

A. The first premise is that it is important to understand that today's "globalization" is actually the fourth stage of outside penetration of Africa by forces which have negative social consequences for the African people's integral development. This outside penetration has occurred over the past five hundred years in a variety of forms.

The first stage was the period of slavery, during which the continent's most precious resources, African women and men, were stolen away by global traders, slavers, working for the benefit of Arab, European and North American countries. Estimates vary from two to ten million slaves extracted from the continent, with disastrous economic, social and psychological effects. I come originally from a country, the United States of America, whose industrial progress in the north during the eighteenth and nineteenth centuries depended upon agricultural progress built unjustly, inhumanely, on the backs of African slaves who toiled in the fields of the south.

The second stage was the period of colonialism, when British, French, Belgium, Portuguese, Italian and German interests dictated the way that map boundaries were drawn, transportation and communication lines established, agricultural and mineral resources exploited, religious and cultural patterns introduced. Whatever minimal benefits might have come to Africans because of colonialism were far outweighed by the many negative consequences of economic exploitation, environmental degradation, and social dependencies. Indeed, many of today's ethnic conflicts which attract international attention trace their origins back to colonial stratagems.

The third stage has been described as "neo-colonialism," what Pope Paul VI called "the form of political pressures and economic suzerainty aimed at maintaining or acquiring dominance." The independence struggles begun in the late 1950's may have brought local governmental rule to the many nations of the continent but did not break the ties—subtle and not so subtle—that bound Africa's future to outside influences. Trade patterns, investment policies, debt arrangements, etc., all reinforced earlier conditions that were not beneficial to Africans. Another striking example was the political manipulation of African states as bargaining pawns during the Cold War, with the resulting legacies of armed conflicts, for example, in the Horn of Africa and in southern Africa.

We have now entered the fourth stage, the period of globalization, characterized by an integration of the economies of the world through trade and financial flows, technology and information exchanges, and movement of people. The dominant actor in this stage is the free market. The globe is conceived as one market directed by profit motivations of private enterprises that know neither national boundaries nor local allegiances. In this stage, Africa experiences both minimal influence and maximum consequence.

B. The second premise is simply the statement of an obvious but not always acknowledged fact: globalisation is not working for the benefit of the majority of Africans today. While globalisation has increased opportunities for economic growth and development in some areas, there has been an increase in the disparities, and inequalities experienced especially in Africa.

The Least Developed Countries 1997 Report (UNCTAD) notes that 33 of the 48 LDCs are in Africa; that the continent has the highest debt to exports ratio; that the average growth rate of these countries fell from 5.4% in 1995 to 4.6% in 1996; that the export primary commodity prices fell especially in tropical foods (e.g., coffee) and minerals (e.g., copper), areas of particular concern for Africa; and that aid flows have declined and foreign direct investment (FDI) flows have remained small.

The process of globalization in Africa is a driving force behind the imposition of severe economic reforms under the structural adjustment program (SAP). The burden of the transition from state-centered economies to free market economies has been borne unequally by those who already are suffering, the poor majority. SAP has meant increased prices of basic necessities, service fees for health and education, retrenchment of the formal employment force, and dismantling of local economic structures in the face of liberalized trade patterns. While neo-liberal economists argue that there may be "short-term pain but long-term gain" in the implementation of SAP, it is increasingly clear throughout Africa that the sort-term pain, for example, of social service cuts, ecological damages and industrial base erosion will in the long-term have truly disastrous effects upon any hope for an integral and sustainable human development.

II. Realities

The reality of globalization as it affects Africa can be seen from examples of the structures it takes and the consequences it induces.

A. Structures

Ideological: The basis for globalization is the neo-liberal ideology (ideological structure) that many feel is the only alternative for the future, and some even argue marks "the end of history." This is an "economic fundamentalism" that puts an absolute value on the operation of the market and subordinates people's lives, the function of society, the policies of government and the role of the state to this unrestricted free market. Throughout Africa, socialism is dead and it is now not only capitalism that is alive but a version of capitalism that Pope John Paul II has poignantly called "savage capitalism."

Neo-liberal policies support economic growth as an end in itself and use macro-economic indicators as the primary measurements of a healthy society. As will be noted below, this ideology governs not only economic structures but also political arrangements. It assumes almost a religious character, as greed becomes a virtue, competition a commandment, and profit a sign of salvation. Dissenters are dismissed as non-believers at best, and heretics at worst.

Commercial: In Africa, the commercial structures of trade and investment are key factors in economic development. These were, of course, the major instruments of the colonialism that gripped the African continent for nearly a century. In recent times, the Uruguay Round of GATT agreements are implementations of a liberalized vision that free trade and unrestricted investment will solve development problems facing the continent. But a group of African non-governmental organizations (NGOs) meeting in South Africa in April 1996, prior to the UNCTAD-IX gathering, challenged this vision on the basis of recent experiences. For example, poorer African countries have been opened up to foreign imports and firms which has led to the destruction of local enterprises. A process of "deindustrialisation" has taken place in many countries such as Zambia. Our once-flourishing textile industry has been wiped out by imports from Asia; several small industries such as tire manufacturers and medical supply companies have folded I n the face of competition from large South African firms.

The World Trade Organization (WTO) is emerging as a very powerful actor in the globalization process, but without much beneficial influence being exercised on its direction by African countries. The WTO is primarily an instrument of Northern governments and countries and its proposals for trade and investment are more in the interests of these elements. The promotion of foreign direct investment (FDI) is hailed as the new engine for development. But FDI flows to Africa are very small (under US$ 5 billion in 1996), are largely advantageous to only a few countries (such as South Africa), and tend to benefit the already privileged elite.

Technological: Africa is being affected in profound ways by the new electronic communication possibilities that bind together the globe in previously unimaginable ways. Personal computers, fiber electronics, satellites, cellular phones, networks of faxes, e-mail and the Internet: all of these structures make economic and political globalization more and more a reality. Transfer of funds is almost as important as transfer of information and it is done instantaneously simply by punching keys and flipping switches. ("F1" opens, or closes, whole new worlds!) Human interface is frequently not necessary and often not desired. Throughout Africa, technological innovations are coming in rapidly and will be a major force in the future.

It is too early to say whether these technological innovations will truly benefit the majority of Africans. I know that I enjoy the advantages of e-mail and Internet connections and that it greatly enhances my work for social justice and peace in Zambia. But only a very small portion of the population of Africa presently have access to personal computers. Other technological structures are slow in developing on the continent.

Cultural: One commentator has called the process of globalization the birth of the "McWorld"—a cultural integration and uniformity that mesmerises the world with fast music, fast computers, and fast food. This "McWorld" is the product of the influence of MTV, McIntosh and McDonald's. Cultural imperialism is not a new phenomenon, but it assumes alarming proportions today when driven by the new technologies and profit propensities of the dynamics of globalization.

In Africa, this cultural structure of globalization presents specific problems. Traditional African cultures (there are many cultures in Africa, not simply one) emphasize values such as community, family, respect of life, hospitality. But these cultural values come into strong confrontation with the values communicated through Western music, movies, videos, cable and satellite television, advertisements, and the idolised figures of entertainment and sports. One analyst speaks of the "predominance of geoculture over the geopolitical and the geoeconomic." Culture is gaining ground over the traditional sources of economic and political power, and the dominant geoculture of the West is an overwhelming force against traditional African cultures.

Political: An important new factor in the process of globalization is that there is a significant change in the geo-political structures. There has been a breakdown of the bi-polar world. With the collapse at the end of the 1980's of the Soviet Empire and the end of the Cold War, there is no longer major political division along the economic lines of capitalist and socialist countries. The West reigns supreme, and if the "New World Order" proposed after the 1991 Gulf War is not yet a reality, at least there is no serious challenge to that supremacy. We in Africa experience that dynamic with the wane of the influence of competing Super Power interests in the local affairs, for example, of Ethiopia, Angola and Mozambique, and South Africa. Where outside interests do play a role—for example, in the current tragedies of the Great Lakes Region—they are French and English rather than East and West.

One significant political development of globalization in Africa is the push toward democratization. This includes a heightened emphasis on good governance and respect for human rights. But this development is not without serious questions. First, the West pushes for political reforms that it considers compatible with the neo-liberal economic order: free politics and free markets are too closely equated. And the understanding of state activity

405

is minimist in the global neo-liberal vision. Second, donors' demands and pressures for policy changes, even when guided by the best of humanitarian motivations, can be interpreted as yet another "imperialist" or "neo-colonialist" imposition of African states. A "back-lash" can develop against this push toward democratisation. Recent events in Zambia have provided examples of these difficulties, when in 1996 donors suspended aid over disputes regarding constitutional and electoral issues, and when political crack-downs following the failed October 1997 coup attempt have brought increased international isolation to the country.

B. Consequences

Economy: One of the starkest consequences of globalization in Africa today in economic terms is the rendering redundant of the African people. This may appear to be a harsh overstatement, but I believe its validity can be demonstrated. Last year I participated in a major study done for the UNDP and the ILO, analyzing the employment situation in the neo-liberal economic model being pursued in Zambia. Our study noted that the SAP-driven governmental policy regarded the provision of people with meaningful work as a function mainly of sustained economic growth. Employment promotion was at best of secondary importance. As a consequence, formal employment of the labor force had dropped to as low as 14% in recent years, with no explicit employment generation policy included in government programs.

The simple definition of economy that appeals to me is: women and men working together with the earth to meet basic needs. But there is neither cooperation nor progress when local people are ignored except as factors in profit maximization by outside interests. Women especially feel the negative effects of economic reform. Globalization views Africa and Africans as components of a global free market, independent of considerations of livelihoods and integral human development.

Ecology: Globalization has a two-fold ecological consequence in Africa. First, there is the climatic impact of global warming (the so-called "greenhouse effect"), caused by pollution levels in northern industrial countries, and the dangerous practice of toxic waste dumping. Environmental concerns at the global level tend to pay more attention to effects in the rich countries of the north. Again, Africa is marginalised.

Second, poverty conditions induced by the severe SAP approach means both less care of the environment by cash-strapped governments and more encroachment on nature by persons desperately struggling for survival. For example, in Zambia soil erosion and deforestation are serious problems today and will be even more serious tomorrow. Trees are cut down for charcoal manufacture (an income-generating activity of the poor), resultant negative changes in rainfall patterns are experienced (causing drought and famine), and response mechanisms of over-grazing and excessive use of chemical fertilizers spoil previously fertile soil (decreasing future productive capacities of peasant farmers). Poverty hurts the whole community of creation, the natural environment as well as the human population.

Equity: The gap between rich and poor on both the global level and on the national level increases with the spread of globalization. The famous "champagne glass" figure of global wealth distribution was portrayed in the 1992 Human Development Report of the United Nations Development Fund (UNDP). This Report documented that the richest 20% of the world's population receives 82.7% of global income, while the poorest 20% receives 1.4%. That gap is continuing to grow, having doubled over the past thirty years. Of the 45 countries listed in the "low human development category in the 1997 Report, 33 are in sub-Saharan Africa.

The major beneficiary of globalization in Africa, South Africa, already accounts for over 40% of the sub-Saharan GDP; its own GNP per capita of US$ 3010 contrasts sharply with Zambia's of US$ 350, Malawi's of US$ 145, and Tanzania's and Mozambique's of US$ 80. I know that India is described as a poor country, with GNP per capita of US$ 320 and over 50% of the population estimated to live below the poverty line. But the World Bank estimates more than 80% of Zambians are below the poverty line, living in households with inadequate income to meet basic daily needs. Key to equity issues, of course, is the fact of what has been called the "feminisation of poverty," with the disproportionate numbers of the poor being women and those dependent on women.

III. Responses

By way of conclusion, let me very briefly suggest three sets of responses that should be of concern for this conference as it addresses globalization from the perspective of the victims of history.

A. Analytical

From the viewpoint of the countries of the so-called "developing world" (the poor countries), keen analysis must be made of the operations and outcomes of globalization. This analysis cannot, however, be restricted to purely economic considerations but must take account of the human dimensions of the phenomenon. This, of course, is the outlook of this present conference and it is increasingly emphasized by studies from both secular and religious sources. One of the participants in the recent "Synod on Americas" noted that "globalization is certainly not being driven by Christian principle of solidarity. It is being driven by the motive of financial profit and, every often, by just plain greed." Our analysis should point out the root causes of the suffering experienced by the majority of the world's population, and should take as the analytical starting-point the "preferential option for the poor."

B. Political

Africa's response to globalization must be political in the sense of coordinated efforts to stand up to dominant outside forces that work for the detriment of the people. But to be honest, efforts undertaken with prominence in Africa frequently are more self-serving critiques or unabashed acceptances—and more rhetoric than resolves. Genuine political action is not forth-coming. The NGO community that might be expected to speak more honestly for the majority of people is frequently excluded from key decision-making processes.

The pre-eminent African political leader, Nelson Mandela, appears cautious in any critique of a globalization process that at least initially is offering benefits to key sectors of the economy of South Africa. Robert Mugabe of Zimbabwe is reported to have urged the November 1997 meeting in Libreville, Gabon of APC nations (African, Pacific and Caribbean states bound together with European states through the Lome Treaties) that these nations should discuss and negotiate more as a single bloc in order to be strong in the face of the European Union. Frederick Chiluba of Zambia embraces SAP and all its components in a very uncritical fashion. Both Daniel Arap Moi of Kenya and General Sani Abacha of Nigeria speak critically of global forces more in their own self-defense of dictatorial policies than of concern for the majority of their own citizens.

C. Ethical

1. Globalization of solidarity: A counter-emphasis—indeed, a "counter-cultural" emphasis—to the driving force of globalization that today so negatively affects Africa is offered by John Paul II's expression, "a globalization in solidarity, a globalization without marginalisation." The Pope asks key questions about the process: "Will everyone be able to take advantage of a global market?...Will relations between States become more equitable, or will economic competition and rivalries between peoples and

nations lead humanity towards a situation of even greater instability?" Solidarity is the central theme of the 1987 encyclical, The Social Concerns of the Church, where John Paul II critiques the structures of sin that mark so much of a globalization driven by profit and power.

2. Family of God: A distinctly African emphasis that provides an ethical critique of the present process of globalization is found in the discussions of the African Synod (1994). Here a model of church was proposed that envisions the church as the "family of God." As such, the church must be an "instrument of universal solidarity for building a world-wide community of justice and peace." An attractive approach to a human-friendly globalization would be based on the familial values of respect and sharing that mark African traditions.

3. Globalization from below: Integral human development, sustainable development, depends more on harmonious human relationships than on the organization and operation of an unfettered free market. A fundamental fault with globalization as experienced in Africa is that it is not rooted in community but structured from above according to abstract economic laws. To counter this situation in an ethically authentic and creative fashion calls for the promotion of local communities that work for integral human development and are effectively linked with similar groups across national boundaries. Much—but not all—of the recent worldwide explosion of non-governmental activity (NGOs) is an expression of this effort to build globalization from below. Indeed, this very conference this week, as well as the conference coming up here early next month, "Colonialism to Globalization," can be steps toward a qualitatively different globalization that will have more positive implications for Africa.

See page 400, for biography of **Peter Henriot**.

	**the rising pressure of global migration**	tony hawkins africa present day

Governments in more advanced regions - North America, the EU, even SA - have long believed that trade with, and cross-border investment in, low income economies should be fostered.

Such enlightened self-interest is intended, at least in part, to prevent an unstoppable influx of uninvited "guest workers" from Latin America, Algeria, the Balkans, Mozambique or Zimbabwe.

The logic is sound enough. Far better to take the capital and jobs to the people than have the people in one's own cities competing for jobs and accommodation, creating racial or ethnic tensions and further straining already inadequate education and health facilities.

At least some of the justifications for foreign aid, for debt relief and for trade agreements like Washington's African Growth and Opportunity Act, or the trade protocol and exchange control relations in southern Africa, are couched in these terms. But whether such strategies designed to keep migrants, job-seekers and economic refugees at home will work is problematic. A new study by Peter Stalker* for the International Labor Organization (ILO) concludes that even on the most optimistic assumptions of more equitable global economic growth there is "little doubt that migration pressure will rise in the decades ahead".

The poorest developing countries are trying to industrialize in a fiercely competitive environment, writes Stalker. "In a world of winners and losers, the losers do not simply disappear, they seek somewhere else to go."

There will always be a demand for some of the Third-World's economic migrants. Industrial countries will always want cheap immigrant labor to take the jobs that nationals refuse. Furthermore, the demographics of the OECD world point to a serious shortage of labor at both the high-skilled end of the market and that for menial jobs.

But this demand is unlikely to be enough to absorb the higher levels of international migration Stalker forecasts. Between 1995 and 2025, the labor force in low-income countries is forecast to grow more than 50% to 2,2bn. In a world where fewer workers using better techniques and more capital produce more goods, finding jobs will be difficult.

Globalization might help, by exposing poorer economies to greater competition, spurring productivity growth and stimulating foreign trade. But, according to Stalker, neither trade nor investment is a sufficient answer.

Part of the problem is the "migration hump". Emigration patterns in southern Europe from the Sixties to the Eighties show emigration and GDP per head rise together until a threshold is reached, after which income/head continues to rise while emigration slows. In southern Europe the turning point was a per capita income of US3 615 a year (1985 prices). If these numbers are accurate, sub-Saharan Africa, with a per capita income of just over 500, is still in the lowest reaches of the hump. On current growth trends it will take centuries to reach the turning point.

There are other powerful forces at work in the region. Even the more developed parts of Africa, notably SA, are starting with high levels of unemployment. In other words, there are push factors at work encouraging emigration, but because SA is the most developed country on the continent - though not the one with the highest per capita income - emigrants in search of greener pastures must go far afield to Australasia, the EU or North America.

Since this is not feasible for the vast majority of low-income potential economic migrants, a country like SA faces a long period of intense pressure. Pressure on the government to create jobs - which it cannot deliver - and to tighten up border controls and shut out job seekers, which it is trying to do. It will also be pressured to redistribute land in the almost-certainly vain hope that this will generate employment, and through SADC to foster jobs elsewhere in the region to staunch the flow.

Recent experience suggests that none of these will solve the problem though they may alleviate it. The problem with the SADC free trade option is that regional trade liberalization is more likely to provoke even greater emigration from the poorer countries. The long-term effects will be more positive, but the hump problem will be more severe in the medium term. Stalker argues that the solution is to free trade barriers more slowly, which he hopes will reduce the de-industrialization disruption in the poorer countries. It is certainly an argument favored by some of SA's neighbors, notably Zimbabwe.

The agricultural growth through land redistribution option championed by President Robert Mugabe also has a poor track record. Stalker cites disturbing evidence from Mexico and the Philippines of the impact on small-scale agriculture of trade liberalization. The removal of corn subsidies paid to small-scale farmers in Mexico will force up to 800 000 farmers off the land - three-quarters of them emigrating to the US in search of employment.

Nor apparently, are export processing zones (EPZs) likely to work. Because EPZs depend largely on imported inputs, they have few linkages with the rest of the economy and generate more jobs in the services sector than in manufacturing.

Mexico's maquiladora (making up) EPZ plants produce roughly the same manufacturing output as the rest of the industrial economy, but employ only 25% as many people. Aiming for a quick fix through EPZs could be short-sighted; a better approach would be one with closer links, especially backward linkages, to the domestic economy.

The implications of all this are clear. In the year ahead, policymakers will find themselves forced to pay far greater attention to this politically explosive aspect of globalization - its impact on international migration.

* Peter Stalker: Workers Without Frontiers: ILO (2000)

See page 287, for biography of **Tony Hawkins**.

| people overwhelmed by resources | tony hawkins
africa
present day |

The hardest task is building skills and institutions, which is why most of Africa will continue to lag behind. The belief that cheap labor or export processing zones are the answer no longer applies.

Under globalization, certainly for African economies, export-led growth is the only game in town. Since the short-lived commodity price boom of 1980, when oil and gold prices soared, it has become obvious that African countries can no longer rely on commodity-driven growth. Instead, they must diversify their export portfolios into manufactured goods, while building bridges into new markets by avoiding undue reliance on the European Union. In 1999, just over half of Africa's exports went to western Europe, compared with 18% of Asia's and Latin America's 13%.

The case against commodity exports is multifaceted. The value of global exports of mining products in 1999 was the same as in 1980. Over those 19 years, the value of trade in minerals fell by more than a third before recovering in the second half of the Nineties.

Trade in agricultural products grew about 3% annually through the Nineties, but it was manufactures that performed best, virtually trebling over the last 20 years. At the turn of the century, almost 77% of the world's exports were manufactured goods, and fast-growth economies like Korea relied on manufactures for 90% of their export earnings.

Only one sub-Saharan country makes it into the World Trade Organization's list of the top 53 exporters of manufactured goods - Mauritius, where manufactures account for almost 75% of total exports.

Manufactured exports make up 30% of the African total - concentrated in a few countries like SA, Mauritius, Morocco and Tunisia. Yet over 70% of imports are manufactures and it is this huge mismatch that policymakers must now target, not by banning imports but by building competitiveness and exports.

But there is much more to the argument for manufactured exports than volumes and prices. On the whole, huge investments in primary product industries have only limited trickle-down effects. Oil in Angola or Nigeria generates relatively little spillover into the rest of the economy and job generation is limited. And in agriculture, the long-term result is a decline in the share of agricultural employment.

Arguably, inefficient government tax and spending policies are partly to blame. If tax revenues were ploughed back into effective development and welfare spending, the situation might have been different.

On the whole, though, productivity gains and technological spillovers are substantially greater in manufacturing than in primary activities. Add in the fact that education systems are skewed towards producing school-leavers better qualified for employment in services, including administration, or manufacturing than agriculture or mining, and the case for services, manufacturing- and export-led growth becomes unassailable.

Why then does Africa under perform, especially in the field of manufactured exports? Three main arguments have been put forward in recent years that between them provide a convincing enough explanation.

Economist Adrian Wood and his associates argue that despite the region's surplus of unskilled labor, Africa cannot build competitive advantage in labor-intensive manufacturing, including the processing of raw materials. Under globalization, exports are driven by the relationship between a country's skills base, or human capital, and its natural resources. Because the ratio of resources to skills is so high, Africa is "locked in" to resource-intensive exports of primary or semiprocessed products.

Others claim high transaction costs are to blame for the region's poor track record in exporting manufactures. Transaction costs are measured by a host of characteristics ranging from high transport and telecoms costs to weak education systems and high levels of corruption. Because manufacturing is transactions-intensive it is not surprising that Africa should have fallen behind.

A third theory puts the blame on overvalued exchange rates. Real exchange rates, adjusted for inflation differentials, must be competitive for manufactured exports to take off.

Taken together, all three theories help policymakers to determine how to break out of commodity dependence.

Relevant education and skills development is crucial. Institution building and infrastructure investment to reduce transaction costs is vital, and sound macro-economic policies that deliver low inflation and competitive exchange rates must be in place.

The hardest task of all is building skills and institutions, which is why most of Africa will continue to lag behind. The belief that cheap labor or export processing zones are the answer no longer applies.

See page 287, for biography of **Tony Hawkins**.

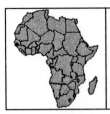

| cattle, power, and gender in sub-saharan africa | jessica powers
africa
present day |

For centuries, cattle were like money in many African societies. Though wealth has been a recognized symbol of power for centuries, in Africa, cattle represented not only wealth, but a strategy to survive. Surviving in harsh conditions has been such an issue in African history that the symbols of wealth and power have culminated around bearing children and cultivating the land—two areas necessary for survival. Cattle were an important part of this system in several ways.

Cattle symbolized power because they were necessary for African men to obtain wives. Through a dowry system known as lobola, or brideprice, men "purchased" women's labor and reproductive capacities from their fathers with cattle.

In the West, we do not typically think of women as "farmers," but in precolonial Africa, women cultivated the land. As both farmers and mothers, women were a key component for survival—they generated food and children. Cattle thus became a method of obtaining power and prestige. Not only could men use it to exert power over women by "buying" their labor and reproductive capacities (Schmidt 5), but they could use it to exert power over other men. Men who owned more cattle had greater access to symbols of prestige like wives and children. In addition, men who married many wives increased their wealth because more women could cultivate greater areas of land and give a man more children.

The importance of cattle as a means for gaining power diminished as colonialism instituted wage labor. Money slowly replaced cattle, but the substitution caused great turmoil.

In South Africa, cattle were an important barrier for staving off the apartheid system (Mager 32). The longer Africans owned cattle, the longer they could survive without depending on wage and migrant labor to support their families. But as Africans were increasingly denied the ability to own land or to work land for their own purpose, they were unable to support cattle.

Though women were more concerned with their ability to feed themselves and their children, men viewed the loss of cattle as emasculation (Mager 37). Under colonialism, a system called "indirect rule" often based itself on a hierarchal system that placed African men over African women,

416

but it nevertheless denied men one of their most potent symbols of power, one of their most direct forms of controlling women's labor. As long as men had cattle, they "retained the symbolic power of the patriarchal order" (Mager 80).

Children were part of a man's wealth. Daughters would help a man obtain more cattle when they were ready to be married (Tungamirai 37). For women as well as men, children were also a status symbol and a way to gain power and prestige. In Zimbabwe, a woman acquired greater status as she bore children (Schmidt 15). Across most of Africa, women without children lacked a place in society. This is amply demonstrated by Buchi Emecheta in her novel, The Joys of Motherhood.

In The Joys of Motherhood, the main character, Nnu Ego, is divorced by her first husband because she cannot conceive. Her father arranges her marriage to another man, and she soon gives birth. When the baby dies, she almost commits suicide. Her one desire in life is to have children, many children, and she is unhappy until she conceives again.

Though this demonstrates the importance for African women to have children, The Joys of Motherhood also demonstrates the heartache that children brought under colonialism. At the end of a long life, after she has given birth to many children, Nnu Ego realizes that motherhood had been a prison. All of her life, she had had to work constantly simply to feed and clothe her status symbols. In precolonial society, in the rural areas, Nnu Ego's life as a mother would have been easier. But the wage labor economic system brought by colonialism meant that, like many other women, she raised her children alone because her husband had to find work elsewhere.

The value of fertility became unstable in many parts of Africa in the 20th Century. Though some African men valued children more highly than "calves" and "diamonds," other men felt that children represented an economic burden, further straining already tight resources (Mager 174). Colonialism created serious obstacles for African men and women to earn enough money, and instituted a system of absent fathers and destitute mothers. Children became less desirable because it was harder, sometimes impossible, to support them (Mager 222). As shown in The Joys of Motherhood, the value of fertility became unstable in many parts of Africa in the 20th Century.

In many societies, land rights added a fourth element to this complex dynamic of power. Access to land, or private ownership in some societies, was an avenue to power for both men and women. Land symbolized power by generating status and wealth and often led to leadership and political prominence. Without land, access to women's labor and owning cattle had little purpose.

The association of power with land reached critical proportions in many parts of sub-Saharan Africa when settlers created laws to restrict African land rights (Iliffe 205-206). The colonizers saw African property-owners as a potential danger to their own power (Iliffe 216-217). In Kenya and Zimbabwe, access to land (private ownership and communal) was a rallying cry for independence, and a key demand of the freedom fighters in both countries during the 50's (in Kenya) and 70's (in Zimbabwe).

Women could not own cattle, but they sometimes had rights to land. After colonialism, wage labor and development policies made inroads into women's rights to land, and thus, their power (Berger and White lviii and 51). Cash crops changed the values associated with land and labor. As individual ownership replaced control of land by male family members, men were more likely to inherit land and women found their power eroded as their ability to generate wealth, through reproduction of the land, was restricted (Berger and White 85; 100-101).

Colonialism brought many changes to the African way of life. One of its more enduring legacies is how it disrupted social institutions like marriage and economic systems based on land and cattle and labor. Today, in most African societies, cattle does not hold the same position of power that it held at the beginning of the 20th century.

Sources:

Berger, Iris and E. Frances White. Women in Sub-Saharan Africa. Indianapolis: Indiana University Press, 1999.

Emecheta, Buchi. The Joys of Motherhood. New York: George Braziller, 1979.

Iliffe, John. Africans: The History of a Continent. New York: Cambridge University Press, 1995.

Schmidt, Elizabeth. Peasants, Traders and Wives: Shona Women in the History of Zimbabwe, 1870-1939. Portsmouth, NH: Heinemann, 1992.

Tungamirai, Josiah. "Recruitment to ZANLA: Building up a War Machine." From Soldiers in Zimbabwe's Liberation War. Ngwabi Bhebe and Terence Ranger, eds. Portsmouth, NH: Heinemann, 1995. 36-47.

This article first appeared on http://www.suite101.com/

See page 322, for biography of **Jessica Powers**.

	africa struggles to regain lost ground	tony hawkins africa present day

EVEN if the World Bank's relatively upbeat scenario for sub-Saharan Africa transpires, it will still be 2006 before average living standards in the region regain their 1982 levels. These numbers, cited in the bank's Global Economic Prospects and the Developing Countries 1997 report, are a timely reminder for those—especially in the aid and investment community - who confuse the region's recent encouraging recovery with economic growth.

The good news is that after a decade of sluggish growth of 2% annually, which translated into falling per capita incomes, the region could be on the threshold of a period of sustained growth of more than 4%, equivalent to per capita income growth of 1.2% a year.

Sadly, this will not be enough to reverse the region's marginalisation. By 2020, while sub-Saharan's share of global gross domestic product will have risen to 1.7% from 1.2 % according to the World Bank's long-term scenario, it will have lost further ground to other, more dynamic, developing countries, especially the Asians.

Sub-Saharan Africa's share of developing world GDP is expected to fall to 5.8% in 2020 from 7.6% in 1992.

This failure to narrow the income gap with more prosperous nations stands in stark contrast to the achievements of Asia. While the first four Asian tigers - Korea, Taiwan, Hong Kong and Singapore - boosted their per capita incomes to 66% of industrial country levels in 1995 from 18% 30 years earlier, in Africa this ratio fell to 7% from 14% in the mid-60s. Since the mid-70s the region's GDP growth rate has been consistently below that of developing countries.

There is no simple, single explanation for this. Adverse exogenous shocks (droughts, poor commodity prices) were an important constraint, while until the second half of the 1980s most African countries paid little more than lip service to the sensible reforms promoted by the IMF and the World Bank. - Financial Times.

See page 287, for biography of **Tony Hawkins**.

war

There have been over 9.5 million refugees and hundreds and thousands of people slaughtered in Africa from a number of conflicts and civil wars. If this scale of destruction and fighting was in Europe, then people would be calling it World War III with the entire world rushing to report, provide aid, mediate and otherwise try to diffuse the situation. - http://www.GlobalIssues.org

There has been so much conflict in Africa that if this chapter outlined or mentioned it all, a whole book could be produced, along with a few mini series.

- In 1998, there were 11 major conflicts in Africa
- After the collapse of Communist governments in the former Soviet Union and its East European allies, state-to-state transfers declined from $4,270 million in 1988 to $270 million in 1995.
- AK-47s sell for as little as $6 in some African countries

Source: Arms and Conflict in Africa:
http://www.defenselink.mil/acq/acic/treaties/small/africa/africa_3.htm

This chapter outlines some of the conflicts and events that don't normally make the headlines of the newspapers.

	**attack of the killer bees**	d.c. williams somalia 1993

Never under estimate the fighting ability of the American GI

In the latter part of 1993, Company A, 2nd Battalion, 14th Infantry Regiment of the 10th Mountain Division ran into some trouble while conducting a training exercise outside the city of Mogadishu. The soldiers of this unit were part of the U.S. Army's contribution to the United Nations Operation Restore/Continue Hope. This operation on the Horn of Africa started out as humanitarian assistance to the civil war-torn nation of Somalia; it ended up being a hunt for the warlord Mohammed Farah Aideed. But that's another story.

Back to the training exercise being conducted by Alpha Company. Typical Infantry training consisted of live fire training for Infantry missions -attack, raid, ambush, movement to contact, and defense. This day Alpha Company was doing an attack mission.

The terrain outside the city of Mogadishu is dry and dusty with intermittent brush. Mogadishu is on the coast of the Indian Ocean near the equator. The temperature is quite hot; however, there is a fairly strong ocean breeze most days, so it is tolerable. Unless one happens to be wearing fatigues, boots, Kevlar helmets, and carrying a full combat load as these soldiers were.

My job during this deployment was Assistant S-3 (Operations) for the battalion. I

421

held the rank of Captain and reported directly to the S-3 (a Major) and the Battalion Commander (a Lieutenant Colonel). I was responsible for coordinating training, preparing orders, and performing some reconnaissance and liaison functions. I was not present with Alpha Company during their training; my place of duty that day was in the Battalion TOC (Tactical Operations Center). I happened to be listening to their training on their company net with the Battalion Commander.

Suddenly, a strange communication came over the net. Somehow, during the course of Alpha Company's training, the men managed to "disturb" some of the local wildlife - African Killer Bees!

The swarm of bees viciously attacked the rifle company's battle-hardened combat soldiers (close to one hundred men). Men that had already kept their cool under enemy fire were soon fleeing for their lives. Men sprinted at full tilt, dropping equipment as a cloud of merciless bees relentlessly pursued. Many soldiers were stung; some had to be medically evacuated. Medics kept a count of stings; some soldiers had 40-50 bee stings.

Fortunately, none of the soldiers died from this incident, and no one in this particular unit that received bee stings was allergic to them. I personally saw one the medevac'd soldiers - his entire head, face, and hands were red and swollen from the stings.

The bees chased the unit for several hundred meters. Finally, the Company Commander, First Sergeant, and Platoon Leaders (exhibiting good leadership and also utilizing good command and control techniques, prearranged signals and Company S.O.P. or Standard Operating Procedures) got the company under control as the bees slowed their attack. If bees could think or if they had a collective mind, they most likely thought the battle was won, and that they had kicked the humans off of their land for good.

This group of bees, like so many around the world, grossly underestimated the American will to fight and the G.I.'s determination in battle.

The Alpha Company Commanding Officer did what most good leaders do after a hasty retreat. (Note: "retreat" is not a word in Army vernacular; the Army prefers to use the term "withdrawal under pressure"). He ordered a counter-attack after radioing the Battalion Commander for permission to do so.

The Battalion Commander was listening to the company net intently, as I was, throughout the entire episode.

Soldiers that still had their gear, and some that picked up other's equipment, led the charge. They threw smoke grenades, shot flares, and used maneuver on the bees that were still hovering nearby. Some small arms fire and hand grenades were used. Some soldiers even fixed bayonets on their rifles or held bayonets in their hands and slashed through the air slicing through the bee cloud. The soldiers screamed and charged and fought for every inch of ground they had previously lost.

Many bees died that day. The rest scattered, looking for easier prey. For the remainder of the deployment, bees did not bother the soldiers of 10th Mountain Division.

The battle was won. The wounded soldiers were taken off the field. Alpha Company ordered a re-supply of water, food, and ammunition. Then they finished their training exercise.

Dennis C. Williams was born in Brooklyn, New York in 1966 and grew up in the Sunset Park neighborhood. After high school, Dennis attended the U.S.Military Academy at West Point, New York.

Dennis graduated West Point (Class of 1988) as a 2nd Lieutenant in the U.S. Army. He served six years active duty as an Infantry officer with assignments in the United States and overseas. His overseas assignments included a three-year tour in Germany, two deployments to Panama, and a combat tour in Somalia, Africa.

After exiting the Army in 1994 at the rank of Captain, Dennis worked in the manufacturing and sales industries before settling into a teaching position at Monsignor Farrell High School in Staten Island, New York. He teaches U.S. and Global History and has three years teaching experience. He created a History Club at Farrell when he was hired in 1998. Since then he has taken students on trips to places of historical significance such as Gettysburg, Antietam, Valley Forge, and Fort Ticonderoga.

The Rhodesian Army is always looking for a few good men

Mount Darwin was a 'one-horse' village, (unfortunately the horse had died some years previously), approximately 160 kms north of the capital city, Salisbury (now Harare). The runway elevation was about 4,500 ft. The village got its name from a huge lump of granite nearby that stuck out of the ground. For some reason it was decided the lump of granite was a mountain and it was named Darwin. I don't know who this 'Darwin' was, or how high a rock has to be to receive the prestigious title 'Mountain.' I suppose it must have been about 500 feet high. The area was scrub savannah populated with a scattering of Acacia trees and granite boulders. The climate was hot and dry most of the time, but when it rained, look out!

There were two roads and both had tarmac covering (made planting land mines more difficult). The main road linked Mt Darwin with Salisbury, and also ran straight through the dingy village. The other road linked Mt Darwin to a place called Centenery. This road ran past the village club (a rondavel with a small hall built onto it), the Army camp and the old Air Force camp.

If you drove along this road for about two kilometers there was a turn on the right that led to the new Air Force camp.

In 1976 I was a Senior Aircraftsman (Lance Corporal) attached to 4 Squadron. I enjoyed being on 'fighting four' because it got me off the main bases and away from the strict discipline found on main bases. The sticks were much more fun. There was always a team of three; me, an armourer and the pilot. My duty was to maintain the aircraft in an airworthy condition (all trades except armament). We usually had two aircraft - a Cessna 337G (Lynx) and the Trojan (Aeromacchi AL60B). I swear the Trojan only got airborne due to the curvature of the earth - and even when we were airborne, crows and sparrows used to overtake us! The Trojan was armed only with 36 SNEB 36mm rockets (18 in a pod under each wing), whereas the Lynx was armed with two Browning machine guns (500 rounds each gun), 36 SNEB

36mm rockets (18 in a pod under each wing), and two 50 gallon Frantan bombs

424

(Napalm).

All these weapons were for the exclusive deployment on ZIPRA and ZANU 'freedom fighters' who tried to occupy the region.

At the Forward Air Fields (FAF) the airmen graded the camp buildings in order of importance. The canteen was not that important because one could always eat outdoors. Most important were the showers, the toilets (thunder boxes), the kruge (bar) and the pits (sleeping quarters).

An open fire heated the water for the showers. A cold water supply attached to two 44-gallon drums mounted a few feet off the ground for the fire to be lit beneath them. Steel conduit pipes were tapped off these 44-gallon drums and attached to two more 44-gallon drums mounted about fifteen feet off the ground on a steel structure. Occasionally the fires were not sufficient to heat the water to the liking of the airmen. There was also the occasional competition between the airforce and the army to see who could get the highest flames. This was one of those evenings.

MOUNT DARWIN FORWARD AIR FIELD: (One of the temporary homes of 4 Squadron and 7 Squadron)

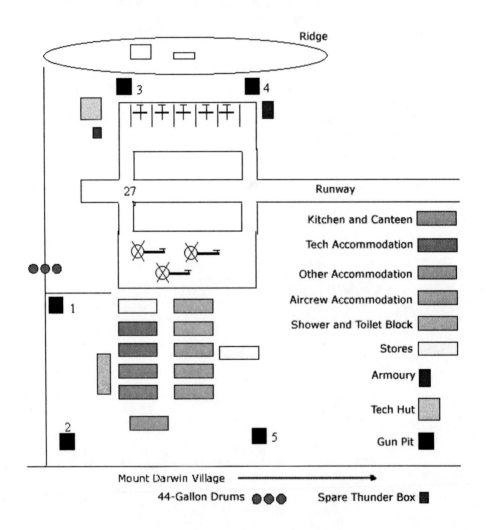

Ridge

3   4

27   Runway

Kitchen and Canteen

Tech Accommodation

Other Accommodation

Aircrew Accommodation

Shower and Toilet Block

Stores

Armoury

Tech Hut

Gun Pit

1

2   5

Mount Darwin Village →

44-Gallon Drums ●●●   Spare Thunder Box ▮

Our fires were pretty small. For some reason the army decided this was a reason to ridicule us. There was a long-standing feud (friendly rivalry) between the army (brown jobs) and the airforce (blue jobs). We wore shoulder flashes AIRFORCE and they wore shoulder flashes 'ARMY.' We then wrote on our boots 'footy', and on our camouflage trousers 'leggy', on our caps 'heady,' and so on just so the army could identify body parts. It must have helped we reckoned, because they must have been a fairly thick lot to have to be told the thing hanging from the shoulder is an 'army.'

Anyway, the army had managed to stoke up a good fire. Not to be outdone the challenge was taken up. After all, we had airplanes, that meant we had aviation fuel, that meant we could make bigger fires than a bunch of brown jobs with a handful of vehicles. Our flames soon exceeded the height of the shower block, and the surrounding trees. The brown jobs could only accept defeat and bow to our superior pyro-maniac capabilities. While we sank a few crates of beer to celebrate beating the brown jobs once again, the bloody shower block caught fire! Our showers and our sacred thunder boxes (toilets) were alight. Panic! All we could do was throw precious beer at the fire. The brown jobs came to our rescue with a water bowser and doused the inferno for us. We had to acknowledge their superior ability to extinguish fires, even if we were better at starting them.

Sunday evening at Mount Darwin was braaivleis (bar-b-q) time. This was the chef's one night off, and our chance to devour edible food.

Not that all the chef's were bad, just some were worse than others. With this inedible slop being served up daily by the worst chefs, we had to source a substitute supply of culinary fulfillment. This led to raids on the storeman's quarters. It was in here that the famous (or infamous) rat-packs were kept. These one-man food rations contained all sorts of edible goodies, like a huge biscuit (it was really nice!), tinned fish, tinned cheese spread, jam, and so on, even a piece of bog paper! When we got our booty to a safe location we would consume the rat-pack contents.

Most times the jam was not there. Everyone accused the store man of stealing the jam for him self, and so the airforce store men became known as 'jam stealers.'

We had a plough disc that had three legs welded onto it. At 7 on a Sunday evening the plough disc was dragged into position outside the bar and a fire was lit underneath it. Beer was usually poured into the plough disc to make a suitable cooking medium. Then the meat was added and most retired to the bar while the meat cooked. We were discussing the important issues of the day, like when do we get out of this place, when there was a faint 'thump.' We turned up the music. Then there was another, only a little louder. The music was turned down while we listened to determine what was disturbing our braai night.

Next thing our Camp Commandant (CC) who I had named Popeye because he was such a strange, scrawny individual, came sprinting through the camp waving his arms about and yelling something like, 'We're under attack! Those are mortars! We're under attack! To the gun pits!' Nothing like a prearranged strategy for countering an attack on FAF 4 - Mount Darwin. None of us had our weapons with us so there didn't seem like much we could do in the gun pits, but it was probably a safer place to sit. Thud, thud, thud, - here comes Popeye skidding around the corner of the boozer, 'Get out of the bar!' and then one hell of a bang followed immediately by a pain filled scream. Popeye had charged straight into the fire-heated plough disc. He had somersaulted forward followed closely by the hot plough disc, our food and boiling beer. He landed face down, arms and legs spread out, the plough disc and the boiling beer all over the back of his legs. We delighted in Popeye's stroke of misfortune, and conceded losing the meat was worth the spectacle. Popeye just lay there filling the air with expletives and threatening to reduce the guilty party to spare parts. He wasn't strong enough to pull the legs off a fly, and even if he was tough enough, he wouldn't get far chasing you when his legs were scolded! After several moments of deep consideration, we left him and made our way to the nearest gun pit armed with several beers – well, what else were we supposed to do while we waited for the firework show to end?

Around this time the (only) Provost (MP) came on the scene, bursting with some new founded eagerness to show how well trained he was and shake off the ridiculous impression we all had of him. Robin St. John Hardyman Jones was a 'real' Englishman with a huge handlebar moustache, ex-RAF military police and all that, and thought he was just about as dynamic as one could get. Superman and Batman had nothing on him! He even drove a Valiant car, anyone remember them? We called him Captain Devil because he was such a joke.

Captain Devil decided it was his responsibility to take command of the FAF now that Popeye was crying alone somewhere in the dark.

Captain Devil received a message that gun pit number four had radioed; he had tried to cock his machine gun and it had jammed. This was it! Captain Devil had received a cry for help! Our intrepid fearless geek announced he would get to gun pit number four alone.

It was quite a run from the bar to gun pit number four. He had to cross the helicopter pad, the runway, the fixed wing hard standing, and finally get to gun pit number four.

It was amazing! He puffed out his pigeon chest and announced, "I won't be long". He grabbed his Uzi and ran off into the dark, brave, fearless world, putting the fear of God into the enemy. He cleared the helicopter pad with no problem, charged across the runway, up the taxiway, but now things took a different turn. Captain Devil confided in me later (he had to, no one else would talk to him and he looked like he had been hit by a tank), and this is his account of what happened.

"I was running across the hard standing and I saw the wing of a Trojan, (Aeromacchi AL60B high wing recce aircraft). I ducked to go under the wing but forgot about the wing strut. I ran straight into the bloody thing, my legs flipped up and I landed flat on my back. I got up a little dazed and staggered to the gun pit. When I got there the gunner told me it's okay, he managed to clear the jam. So I turned around and started running back. I remembered the wing strut and ran to the outside of the wing, those blocks of cement you tie the aircraft down with. Well you should put lights on them. I ducked to miss the wing and ran straight into that bloody concrete block. My toes are broken. I got up (his hands and knees were well grazed) and staggered back here."

Now from the gunner's view. "I heard someone running across the hard standing towards me. Then there was a loud thud, a loud sort of 'heee-ooo-gh!' and silence. Then there was this wincing sound and a short while later Captain Devil staggered into the gun pit. I told him to bog off because I had cleared the weapon. He muttered something about 'piss me around and you'll be on a charge.' Then he was off. I could hear his breathing as he charged/hobbled off into the dark. There was a dull thud, a pain-racked cry and silence. There was some cursing I can tell you, a wincing sound, sobbing, and a few more 'shits.' Then I heard him staggering off towards the runway."

Popeye had recovered a little by this time and suggested Captain Devil take an armoured vehicle (Ferret) and go check out the old buildings on the ridge overlooking the air field. I could not understand why. If the terrorists were chucking mortars at us from the ridge only a few hundred yards away, and still missing, then there was nothing to worry about. Our intrepid Captain Devil rounded up a driver and a couple of bemused TF's (territorial force).

So the driver and the TFs get into the vehicle and Captain Devil, true to form, perches on the rear mudguard. This guy is daring, braver than the brave, and the enemy lives in fear of him!! They trundle onto the road leading up to the ridge. The driver stops. Captain Devil demands the reason, and it is pointed out to him the road is blocked by empty 44-gallon drums. The TFs offer to move them, but Captain Devil has a better idea. "Drive over them!" he orders. The next thing there is one hell of a screeching sound and the Ferret stops. An empty 44-gallon drum is jammed under it. After much pulling and tugging and swearing they manage to get the drum out from under the Ferret. Captain Devil resumes his strategic position on the rear mudguard.

After a short while Captain Devil orders the driver to stop. Then he shouts, "Swing the turret!" The driver did so and put as much effort into this task as he could. The turret swung around and smacked Captain Devil a resounding blow on the side of the head, launching him off the rear mudguard.

Captain Devil now had broken toes, grazed hands and knees, skin missing from his knuckles, and now a bump on the head. Apparently he landed awkwardly and twisted his ankles, so we had another 'war' injury to add to the list.

They brought our Captain Devil back. He looked a very sorry sight. All those injuries and not a single mortar landed within the camp confines and we never fired a single shot. Captain Devil could not have fired a shot even if he had wanted to: there was no magazine in his Uzi! The next morning we found the Uzi magazine under the Trojan wing beside the concrete block. Popeye and Captain Devil were put on light duties.

Clive Bloor. Started out in February 1972 as an Engine Fitter in the Rhodesian Air Force. Left the airforce in 1977 and went on to work in civil aviation at Rhodesia United Air Carriers - Bulawayo Airport. In 1978 a change of scenery was called for and he moved to England where he specialized in aircraft structures and undercarriages. In 1986 the urge for change beckoned again. Technical Authorship sounded like a rewarding profession. The toolbox was closed and he enrolled on a City and Guilds course studying Technical Communication Techniques and Technical Authorship. Distinctions in exams at Peterborough College (Cambridge) opened new doors and the toolbox has stayed firmly locked ever since. First stop with the new qualifications was Fokker Aircraft (F50 and F100), then Jaguar (XJ220), Guided Missiles, Nuclear Power generation, Electric Locomotives and the Kowloon-Canton Resignalling Project. During this time he acquired the illustration capabilities needed to produce technical illustrations and was awarded the Licentiateship of City and Guilds Institute of London (Technical Authorship). At the time of writing he runs the Technical Publications department at a Finnish multi-national company located in England producing computer-controlled industrial machinery.

| **western wars in the 20th century changed the face of africa** | jessica powers
africa
present day |

Modern nationalism in Africa evolved after World War II, a direct result of Africans' experiences fighting for Western powers and their anger at how they were treated and perceived by the colonial powers. Modern nationalism worked to unify all Africans rather than remaining inaccessible to all but the educated elite. It led to mass protests against colonial rule, such as those in Kenya; and it led to nationalist guerrilla movements, such as those in Algeria or in Zimbabwe, which aimed to oust colonial rulers and install democratic, majority-ruled governments.

Many African nations had already been colonized by the time World War I erupted onto the scene. Colonies were not only expected to contribute money and men to the war effort, but they also served as a battle ground for European armies, as happened in Tanzania. European armies conscripted and recruited Africans as soldiers, porters, and servants. Hundreds of thousands of Africans were killed as a result of their involvement in WWI.

In addition, the continent itself was impoverished by colonial war-time policies. European businesses virtually eliminated African business owners from the export business by strengthening their hold on the export-import trade, while taxes for war-time expenses stretched African economies to the limit. Food shortages, in part caused by the high taxes and export requirements, spread rural poverty that continued for years to come. In short, by the time World War I was over, colonial powers had strengthened their grip on African colonies.

Africans across the continent reacted with anger when the Italians invaded Ethiopia in 1935. They saw it as the colonial powers' attempt to topple the one remaining tower of African independence. Just as they viewed Africa during WWI, European nations continued to see their colonies as excellent resources for money, men, and needed supplies. They conscripted Africans to fight in their militaries and forced Africans to increase production of exports. And, just like in WWI, this deepened rural poverty as well as wrecking havoc on family life. But even though this created enormous difficulties for African nations, it also meant that European nations grew more dependent on their colonies.

As Africans began to realize that justice was on their side, and the colonial powers were not as all-powerful as they had once thought, modern nationalism found its niche. Africans who had fought along side Europeans had discovered they could fight as well as white men; indeed, they proved they could fight better than white men, when they defeated Japanese forces after the Japanese had defeated the British. When African troops drove the Italians out of Ethiopia and Somalia, it reinforced their desire to do that in other countries as well.

Africans were still reeling from the effects of colonization when WWI rolled around. They were too dazed to realize how they could take advantage of Europe's war-time weakness. But less than thirty years later, they understood Europe's post-war weakness; they had a better grasp of their own self-identity and ability to defeat the colonial powers, which led to the push for independence.

As WWII ended, the U.S. began to back down from its stance that colonial powers should grant independence to African nations. It feared that weak African nations, newly independent, would be vulnerable to Communism. The Soviet Union, on the other hand, provided an excellent revolutionary role model for African nations who wanted to claim political power for themselves.

Independence, gained by most African countries in the two decades following WWII, led to new political and ideological battles that African nations hadn't considered in their quest for freedom. Africa had mineral wealth, fertile lands, and an exploitable market. It was a strategic location for major oil-shipping routes and had considerable strength as a political bloc in the UN. Because Africa was desperate for money and weapons, it was vulnerable to the Cold War politics that flew back and forth across the oceans between the East and the West.

Despite Cold War politics, the U.S. and Soviets avoided military solutions to political problems that they encountered on African soil. Yet neither the U.S. nor the Soviet Union were willing to lose new African nations to their political enemy. Both countries contributed vast amounts of money and weapons to leaders who supported their ideology in countries from Angola to Zaire.

In the past, the West has used African resources liberally for political and economic reasons. The question is not how the West used Africa in the 20th century, but how Africa will claim its heritage and resources for its own in the 21st Century.

This article first appeared on http://www.suite101.com/

See page 322, for biography of **Jessica Powers**.

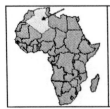	**the algerian war**	jessica powers algeria 1962

Just like English settlers in East and Southern Africa, French settlers in Algeria behaved as if they could do anything they wanted. They controlled the government; thus, they held all the social, political, and economic privileges. By 1940, settlers had expropriated almost a third of the fertile land, even though they only made up 2 percent of the population.

Algerians experienced extreme deprivation under colonial rule. They starved; were denied education, political power or voice; and they were forced to speak French and legally denied the right to speak their native Arabic. (The issue of language became a particular sore point among Africans in all the colonies. In later years, African writers produced novels in their own language, a distinct form of protest against colonialism.)

For years, leaders of Algerian nationalism strove peacefully for independence, which led simply to greater repression. In 1954, a new generation of nationalists chose to react violently by forming the secret Front of National Liberation (FLN) and beginning a war for independence.

Though small initially, the FLN gradually gained popular support, defeating French troops for two years. However, when the French reinforced its troops and adopted anti-guerrilla tactics in late 1956, the war turned in France's favor.

Algerian nationalist leaders fled to Tunisia while the French tried to break all contact between leaders inside the country and those outside. They built electric fences along the Algeria/Tunisia border, laid more than a million landmines along the fence, and reinforced French troops to 700,000 men.

By 1960, France had almost destroyed the FLN. But the FLN enjoyed mass support and France could not gain control of the country. French politicians debated whether it was morally just to continue the war. Eventually, President Charles de Gaulle offered the FLN a cease-fire, without independence, in 1959, an offer the FLN promptly rejected.

The war continued and might eventually have been settled in France's favor if it weren't for the settlers. They had lost confidence in French support and organized a rebellion against France. Their terrorism against French troops led to France's acceptance of Algerian independence in July 1962.

Over the course of the eight year war, more than a million Algerians died.

This article first appeared on http://www.suite101.com/

See page 322, for biography of **Jessica Powers**.

	**how to survive revolutionary places**	robert young pelton africa present day

Although no one can predict a sudden change in government, there are some things that could keep you from appearing on CNN wearing a blindfold.

- Check in with the embassy to understand the current situation and to facilitate your evacuation if needed. Remember that the local government will downplay the danger posed by revolutionary groups.
- Stay away from main squares, the main boulevards, government buildings, embassies, radio stations, military installations, the airport, harbor, banks and shopping centers. All are key targets during takeovers or coups.
- If trouble starts, call or have someone contact the embassy immediately with your location. Stay off the streets and if necessary move only in daylight in groups. Stay in a large hotel with an inside room on the second or third floor. Convert foreign currency into Western currency if possible. Book a flight out.
- Understand the various methods of rapid departure. Collect flight schedules, train information and ask about private hires of cars and planes. Do not travel by land if possible.
- Do not discuss opinions about the former regime or the current one. Plead ignorance while you wait to see who wins.
- Keep your money in US dollars and demand to pay in U.S. currency. Do not depend on credit cards or traveler's checks and don't be afraid to demand a discount since who knows what the old money will be worth.
- Do not trust the police or army. Remember that there will be many summary executions, beatings and arrests during the first few days of a coup or revolution.
- Hire a local driver/guide/interpreter to travel around town and or to go out at night. Don't be shy about hiring bodyguards for your residence or family.
- Listen (or have your guide listen) to the local radio station or TV station. Have him update you on any developments or street buzz. When the embassy has set up transport make your move with your bodyguards or guides.

See page 183, for biography of **Robert Young Pelton.**

	**the bloodstones of africa**	robert nolan sierra leone 1998

Due to a lack of legislation, gems known as conflict diamonds that help fund wars in Africa could be on display in the cases of local retailers.

"Diamonds are a girl's best friend," read a sign held by a teen member of Amnesty International last week in front of Tiffany and Co. in downtown Chicago. "Unless she's missing an arm."

The sign, part of a protest against so-called "conflict diamonds" was accompanied by a photo of a Sierra Leonean girl whose arm has been chopped off by the infamous Revolutionary United Front rebels still operating in her country and whose preferred method of instilling fear is hacking off limbs.

Conflict Diamonds, according to human rights group Amnesty International, are diamonds mined under the control of groups that allow them to purchase arms needed to proliferate war.

Groups such as the Revolutionary United Front (RUF) in Sierra Leone and UNITA in Angola often smuggle diamonds from controlled areas out of the country and into the international market undetected.

But what has this got to do with Tiffany's?

Due to a lack of legislation both internationally and in the US, conflict diamonds could very well be on the fingers of unsuspecting American consumers. Despite a growing awareness of the impact of conflict diamonds, also known as "blood diamonds," the diamond industry has yet to impose any kind of concrete legislation banning the importation, sale and trade of the gems.

Although the United Nations passed a resolution last year banning the international sale of diamonds originating in Sierra Leone, the RUF allegedly continue to fund their campaign by smuggling the stones into Liberia and other countries currently under the eye of international bodies.

But no legislation exists regarding diamonds from other hot spots on the world's largest continent, particularly in the consistently unstable Democratic Republic of Congo, where a continental war involving at least seven countries continues to rage.

Nor is there consistent legislation in Angola, where more than 4 million people have been forced to leave their homes over the past 20 years of turmoil, as the government continues to battle Jonas Svimbi and his UNITA rebels in a ping pong match for control of the country's diamond mines.

Dirty Diamonds and Chicago Legislation

"The problem is that consumers don't know where the diamonds are coming from," said Nancy Bothne, midwest regional director for Amnesty International, who helped organize the Valentine's Day demonstration in front of Tiffany's. "Diamonds are given as a token of love and appreciation and people don't want to do that at the expense of children in Sierra Leone or other places in Africa."

Conflict diamonds compose anywhere from four to 15 percent of the world's diamonds, according to World Vision, a non-government development organization that operates extensively in Africa, but many estimate the percentage to be much higher as a large number of diamonds are illegally smuggled out of conflict areas.

"The industry estimates that 22 percent of the world's diamonds are smuggled at some point, but according to U.N. figures that number is closer to 40," said Deborah DeYoung, spokeswoman for House Rep.Tony Hall (D-Ohio), whose office is drafting the first piece of legislation to address the issue in the United States.

The Clean Diamonds Act, which will be introduced to the U.S. Congress next month, calls on the diamond industry to follow up on commitments it made last year at the formation of the World Diamond Council in Antwerp, Belgium in the aftermath of Sierra Leone.

"Our bill is based on the diamond industry's July 2000 promise that it would move swiftly to end the trade in conflict diamonds," Hall said at a Valentine's Day rally that brought together more than 50 human rights groups aiming to eliminate conflict diamonds. "It gives the industry more than a year longer than it said it needed to take steps it should have undertaken years ago."

Hall's legislation calls for the creation of controls in exporting countries, as well as a Presidential Commission in the United States that will develop a label certification system for all diamonds coming into the country.

"In essence, the Clean Diamonds Act insists that America's trading partners enforce laws against illegal smuggling so that American consumers can stop unwittingly underwriting these wars over diamonds," Hall said, noting that 65 percent of the world's diamonds are purchased by Americans.

One unique aspect of the draft is that fines and profits from contraband will be directly re-routed to the victims of conflict through US AID's War Victims Fund, with a focus on helping amputees in Sierra Leone and other countries.

But the diamond industry, while offering lip service to the goals of regulation, has been slow to act. The World Diamond Council consists of a number of organizations with high-stakes in the diamond industry, and has shunned Hall's legislation in favor of its own.

"The kind of legislation endorsed by the World Diamond Council is full of loopholes, the biggest being that it excludes diamonds that are already set in jewelry," said DeYoung, who sees the World Diamond Council as protecting its own financial interests. "The monetary penalties that the WDC would enforce upon violations (maximum fine: $250,000) are miniscule in comparison to the large profits they make in diamond transactions."

But members of the WDC continue to defend themselves against attacks from human rights groups, citing a common mission to alleviate the world of dirty diamonds. In a letter to the Chicago Tribune last week, President and CEO of Tiffany and Co. Michael Kowalski addressed the responsibility of Washington to regulate to some extent the flow of diamonds into the country.

"In taking the unusual step of requesting government regulation, the diamond industry has shown its commitment to eliminating conflict diamonds," said Kowalski, who also highlighted his company's instructions to overseas diamond processors that it "would not do business with anyone trafficking in conflict diamonds."

Kowalski also attacked the methods of groups like Amnesty International which demonstrated outside Tiffany's last week. "Some well-meaning groups apparently believe that conducting street theater and promoting laws that cannot be enforced will produce better results than a program that addresses the problem's core," he said. "Waving a placard in front of a jewelry store helps not a single victim of violence in Sierra Leone."

Technology

One problem both groups will face in pushing legislation is the technical issues involved in tracing a diamond's origins. While sophisticated technologies do exist, conflict diamonds pass through many stages before landing on the fingers and around the necks of wealthy purchasers, each phase making it harder to detect the true location of origination. President of American Gemological Laboratories Cap Basely thinks the diamond industry has been quick to dismiss the capabilities of his lab and others like it simply because they don't want to know the origins of certain diamonds.

"Diamonds are one of the most heavily studied materials on the face of the earth," said Basely, citing the huge amount of technical and human resources available in the US and Russia. "We could easily put together a team of 6, 8 even ten of the best brains on this subject, but nobody has approached us."

Basely thinks it's because the information he could provide would have a negative financial impact on the industry. "If they really want to legitimately stop this business of conflict diamonds, it is totally possible, it's just not wanted," said Basely. "It's been possible to trace the origin of every other material on the planet, even something like orange juice."

Others, like Deborah DeYoung, also disregard the scientific challenges that the industry often sites as a significant obstacle to tracing the roots of dirty diamonds.

"If there is a market for it the technology will materialize," said DeYoung, who added that companies like DeBeers, who control a major market share of the diamond industry, have been boasting of possessing such knowledge for years.

Speaking in front of the Africa Subcommittee of the International Relations Committee of the U.S. House of Representative, Muctar Jalloh, a student from Sierra Leone, said what he thought were the roots of the conflict in his country. "The war is not tribal, and it is not religious. It is simply a war over control of diamonds. Little pieces of rock that people from around the world like to wear on their fingers and hands and ears."

Even if the African student could afford to buy the diamonds his country is fighting for, they wouldn't be of much use. Rebels cut off Jalloh's right arm and ear when he was captured by the RUF in 1998.

Robert Nolan: A freelance reporter in Washington D.C. Raised in southern California and attended a university in Boston, Massachusetts, he is an avid traveler and student of the world's many exciting cultures. After serving in the United States Peace Corps, he volunteered for two years in Zimbabwe and traveled the sub-sharan region. He returned to graduate school. Earned a degree from Medill School of Journalism at Northwestern University. He's currently working in DC writing for MTV 's Fight For Your Rights anti-discrimination campaign on MTV.com. He's also contributed articles for the Chicago Reader and The Daily Herald (Chicago).

africa

Africa has different images for most who have visited, read, or seen images of this continent.

Doug Lansky who has contributed to this book, wittily called Africa 'The Dark Incontinence' after this following experience:

Africa has long been called the Dark Continent, but how it got this name I have no idea*. I've spent six months in Africa, and, offhand, I cannot think of a place where I experienced more direct sunlight. My best guess is that the guy who coined this handle spent a good deal of time in my youth hostel in Harare, where the bathroom light bulb was nonexistent. You had to carry a flashlight or candle if you had to go during the night, and even then most travelers seemed to miss the toilet by more than the internationally allowable two feet. Perhaps what the guy really meant was "The Dark Incontinence."

The authors in this chapter have been to Africa and have had very different experiences and no doubt call Africa and its memories by many names.

*From my history lessons at school, I can remember 'The Dark Continent' got its name because few people knew anything about the place. Still the case now! There's a bit more to this name, as the Romans called Africa their possessions on the north coast of the continent including the city of Carthage (remember Hannibal and the three Punic wars between Rome and Carthage all three of which Rome won, although in the second war Hannibal won some battles but ended up losing the war.) The name Africa later came to mean the whole of the continent to the non conquered Roman world.

Incidentally Punic comes from a word meaning the "Dark Ones" so presumably the Carthaginians were dark skinned, most likely Arabic as Carthage was located in what is now Libya.

Three kings and an eighteen wheeler

This old postcard still hangs there in my mind: a King—The Muri of Ifut—his several courtiers, and the several wives of the Obong of Calabar, all bunched against the wild rain, the Guinean tempest howling up from the Bight of Biafra, a love-besotted Irish Holy Ghost Father clinging to the weakening Inner Above, passing a South African exile a fifth of Vat 69 ("All the better to hang on to that upright with"), while a full-sized Elizabethan stage sank slowly into the turf of a West Africa soccer stadium. Right then I hoped that it wouldn't ever get much better because a person can withstand only so much fulfillment in his life.

Sunk deep in the slack creeks that slowly wash out to the Atlantic, in 1964 Calabar was still a Victorian, Sadie Thompson kind of place. This crinoline tramp had, for generations, been compromised beyond redemption by her appetite for the British district headquarters and her earlier partnership with the slave factors' hulks that had stained her dark waters. But Calabar town, before Nigeria's recent oil boom and bust, had style, panache, many terrific secondary schools, and boasted numerous living relics from her colonial time: literary societies, bookstores, Pim's Cup #2, snooker at the club, formal balls and her flat-out four-wheel-drive love for Shakespeare.

My Peace Corps assignment was so perfect I hesitate to talk about it even now, fearing that someone will yet take it away. After one in-country year of teaching high school English, I wangled an appointment as business manager for the School of Drama at the federal University of Ibadan (the first Volunteer accepted there since the famous Michelmore postcard incident). For the School's first Theater-On-Wheels cross-country tour, I was named the advance man, traveling around the country creating local civic committees to handle promotion and logistical arrangements for the upcoming 3,000-mile tour.

That year, celebrating Shakespeare's 400th birthday, we presented an evening of four hours of scenes from his plays. A truly lavish production, it rolled through the country on a forty-foot truck-trailer combination that at each of the twenty-three host towns opened up into a stage, like a huge plywood sunflower. All funded by Shell Oil, the British Council, and the Ford and Rockefeller foundations, there was a bus for the forty student actors, four staff cars, and the advance man in a circus-painted Land Rover hung with loudspeakers, flinging gaudy flyers to a million townfolk. A sensational juggernaut highballing it from savannah to coastal delta, to Sahel and back.

Astonishingly, in the West Africa of this period lay the most Shakespeare-literate society the world has known since sixteenth century London. Secondary schools in Nigeria, Ghana, The Gambia, Sierra Leone, and Cameroon still competed under the Cambridge University/West African School Certificate Council's examination program. The School Cert mandated, among other standards, that students study five years of Shakespeare to prepare for the final examination's "set play." As a result, for several generations millions of West African kids quite literally memorized two or three of William Shakespeare's plays. (Such heroic learning was much inspired by every Nigerian's lovely use of language and the daily reality of a national life then singularly Elizabethan in the epic grandeur of its debates and tribal intrigues of power and vivid character.) At our performances, thousands would mouth the lines in an audible susurrus that confounds me now as I worry over what went wrong with American schools.

On my advance trip, learning that the patronage of Calabar's two Efik kings was necessary if the presentation was to happen, I had negotiated several details with their Royal Highnesses, the Muri of Ifut and the Obong of Calabar, and had come to know and greatly respect them. They immediately sent out the proper assurances and promised to be in attendance.

A month later, on the night in question, knowing we had presold 3,000 tickets, I asked my entire committee to be available for rough duty. At earlier stops we had had crowd scenes that bordered on riots, with a rush of 10,000 people pressing through the single stadium gate in Onitsha, kids hanging from telephone poles in Umuahia.

The backstage crowd that night included the priest who was vice-principal from St. Patrick's Secondary School, who, we all knew, was innocently smitten with a Calabar Volunteer (he would later suffer much more during the Biafran War from federal persecutors); a wonderful South African, teaching out his exile years in another local high school; the drama school's roguish English director; and several staff.

With an urbane Calabar audience seated without incident and the royals in their box seats, the lights came up on a ravishing Twelfth Night. But we were now hitting the rainy season. Two hours later, just after the scenes from Julius Caesar began, all hell broke loose. First the wind, then a small rain, then West Africa Wins Again! The speaker and light towers, rigged on cement-filled wheels, began to weave, while under the force of the wind the stage was coming unhinged. Soon the rain was blowing dead level across the footlights. Surely the audience would flee, but looking out we saw them rooted to their chairs. Electrical lines were arcing. Someone said that something had to be done. Perhaps the crowd wasn't leaving because the two royal parties hadn't budged. Detailed for the job, I scampered across the field to the royal enclosure. Crouching down by his armchair, I inquired of the Obong of Calabar, the senior of the two rulers, if he didn't think it best to call the whole thing off, so his people could find some cover.

His ear cupped to catch the now unamplified words, he looked up, smiled: "Thank you. I can't leave just yet. I haven't had time to read Julius Caesar in so many years. I don't remember now how it all resulted. And I, of course, should know. Remember, how 'Uneasy lies the head that wears the crown.'"

The next morning a heavy-duty tractor was engaged to unstick the stage from the field. The performance had, of course, carried on in the rain to a full, happy stadium. Calabar was my kind of town.

Tom Hebert was with the Peace Corps in Nigeria from 1962-64, later with the USO in Vietnam and later in the Gulf War, USO Bahrain. Also a UNICEF refugee relief officer in Biafra, he is the co-author with John Coyne of three books about innovative American training and education. He is currently living on the Umatilla Indian Reservation outside Pendleton, Orgeon where he is consultant to the Confederated Tribes (the Cayuse, Walla Walla and Umatilla) on horse programs.

The misunderstood Continent

Africa is unquestionably now a continent associated with violence, hunger, disease and environmental disasters. For centuries it lay "undiscovered" beyond the Mediterranean Sea and European civilization apart from the stories and experiences of coastal traders from Arabia and India to the east and the wars between north Africans, like Hannibal, and our ancestors on mainland Europe. Not until the 17th and 18th centuries did Europeans, as often as not heading further afield to Asia, begin to realize the vastness and the glory of this great sleeping continent. But they went to plunder and sometimes to trade; they went to take land and people; in essence they went to take and not to give.

The British were no doubt as guilty of this as any of our European rivals from France, from what is now Germany or Italy, from Belgium and from Portugal. Colonial possessions were places to be exploited for the benefit of Britain, not for the benefit of Africa. That is true but it is only partly true because there were many who traveled from our shores to Africa, not only as Christian missionaries, but as traders, as administrators, as soldiers and as agriculturists who did not see what lay before them as something only to be exploited. The story of Empire is often traduced and often misunderstood and many of our forbears were genuinely interested in the people of Africa as fellow human beings to be respected and dealt with honestly.

As we retreated from Empire in the second half of the 20th century we left behind former colonies and dominions that were in varying degrees democratic, possessed of the rule of law and civil government and capable of feeding their people. They had colleges and schools, roads, railways and hospitals and above all they had the potential to do well and to prosper. Of nowhere was this truer than South Africa, a Union that in the first decade of the 1900s had been forged out of wars between whites and blacks, blacks and blacks and whites and whites. Clearly as the Union of South Africa developed into a nation as the 20th century moved through the First World War and then into the twenties and thirties, it could not be said that this Dominion was anything other than a country ruled by the white population with British Governor Generals representing the Crown. It was very much an outpost of Empire.

Things changed very rapidly after the Second World War. The Nationalist Government introduced apartheid and established the Republic. The tone of government, which I confess had not previously spent a good deal of time or money on improving the conditions of the majority population, changed markedly. To be black was to be a non-person by law. The African National Congress, whose beginnings pre-dated the Republic, began a revolutionary struggle to bring down the apartheid regime and spawned some of the great political figures of our age, foremost amongst whom must be Nelson Mandela.

In 1990, in the dying days of the white regime, I was asked by the South African Government along with three other young British Conservative politicians, to go to South Africa to see what was happening under the reformist government of President de Klerk. In some ways he was the Gorbachev of South Africa doing his best against powerful reactionary forces to bring his fellow countrymen to see that black South Africa could no longer be ignored or suppressed and that the non-white population had a right to say how their country should be governed. It was de Klerk who ordered the release of Nelson Mandela from Robbin Island after thirty years of imprisonment, a decision that now perhaps looks easy but at the time needed courage and vision. Mandela was moved to a prison on the mainland to continue negotiating with the white government about the South Africa that was to emerge after the handing over of power to majority rule. When that would come was uncertain, or at least it was to us four travellers from England that September in 1990.

We had originally hoped to go to Pretoria in February or March of 1990 but our hosts put us off for 6 months to see how the country reacted to the release of Nelson Mandela. There were no riots; the far right separationists did not resort to armed struggle; the poor blacks did not storm the office blocks in Johannesburg, Durban and Cape Town. It looked as though the de Klerk plan had worked. We set off, first to Johannesburg and Pretoria where we met both governors and governed, businessmen and employees, black and whites. We went into Soweto, that vast township to the south west (hence its name) of Johannesburg where hundreds of thousands of immigrant workers from the Transkei, from Zululand and throughout South Africa had moved to find work, fleeing the rural poverty of their own homes but unable to live in the city closer to their work because of the pass laws which prevented blacks living in areas designated for other races. They lived variously in huts made of planks or scrap metal, without sanitation and in utter squalor; or if they were rich, and there were some who were, in smart bungalows with security walls and guards at the gate; but most were poor and their lives were nasty, brutish and short. The murder rate was high, the levels of health were low – one third of the mothers giving birth in Soweto's hospital were HIV positive – and because of the school boycott during the apartheid regime, huge numbers of them could neither read nor write. There, within 20 miles of one of the most prosperous and successful cities in the southern hemisphere, lay one of its largest third world slums.

It was these people, and especially those black South Africans who belonged to the ANC and who looked to the ANC leadership for deliverance, who saw in the release of Nelson Mandela salvation. He would lead them, a mixture of the revolutionary and the royal prince, to prosperity and permit them to avenge themselves for the years of repression they had suffered. And he would do this quickly.

I met Nelson Mandela in September 1990. It was an unforgettable experience. That morning I was in the office of the editor of the Johannesburg Star discussing the future of South Africa. I had gone to see him both because I was a lawyer specializing in defamation and thus newspaper law in London and because his newspaper was widely respected in South Africa and outside as a disseminator of accurate news and unbiased coverage. It had its editorial stances but the editor was a man whose views and predictions were worth hearing. I was not disappointed. As I was getting up to leave, I said, "That's the ANC office across the street. Do you think if I went over there and asked to see Nelson Mandela, I would get a chance to meet him?" He smiled back at me and said, "Why not? It's worth a try."

30 minutes later, I was sitting across a table from Nelson Mandela. There was a visiting delegation of Dutch MPs in Johannesburg that day and they had an appointment to see the great man. I was fair haired, wearing a suit and as an aspirant to membership of the House of Commons (in January I had been selected as the Conservative candidate for Harborough, a safe Conservative constituency in Leicestershire, 100 miles north of London) was doing my best to behave as though I already was the MP! I must have looked sufficiently like a Dutch MP to be mistaken for one of their group. The security staff on the ground floor let me in and told me to go up the lift to the ANC headquarters. I reported to reception and said I had come to see Mr Mandela. "Take a seat; he's busy at the moment but will see you as soon as he can." Waiting in reception there was a businesslike air of activity all around me. Young men and women who would not have looked out of place in a United States Congressman's office were bustling around, files were being hurried from one office to the next, chatter and laughter of a sort that could be heard in any city office could be heard through half open

doors, and every now and then an elderly black man, a one armed white man or others whose faces I recognized from newspaper photographs would scurry across the hall giving me a passing glance as they got about their business.

"Mr Mandela will see you now." I might have been going in to see my consultant surgeon or my lawyer. I was not sure what or who to expect. Of course I knew who Nelson Mandela was; why else was I there but to meet the man who held the future of South Africa in his hands? Without this man there could be no peaceful transition from white minority to black majority rule. His reputation and standing in the civilized world were unsurpassed at this time but why would he want to find the time to see me, a parliamentary candidate from the United Kingdom without power or influence? To tell the truth he did not want to see me; he wanted to see a Dutch MP because that was who he had been told I was. "So how are things in the Netherlands?" he began as he held out his hand when he came into the room. Tall, upright and smiling he filled the room with his presence and made his following entourage, big men in themselves, look like pigmies. "Fine, so far as I know," I replied in my unmistakable English accent – but then the Dutch speak excellent English. "I am not Dutch, I am an English Conservative parliamentary candidate here in South Africa at the invitation of the Government of South Africa." Mandela roared with laughter and there was genuine amusement in his eyes as he turned to his followers and told them they should be fired for letting this Englishman in under false pretences. For twenty minutes we sat and talked about his hopes and fears for the newly emerging South Africa, about the need for schools, for hospitals, for economic reform, the imperative of harnessing the white first world economy to the needs of the black third world economy but without causing white flight or a break down in the country's infrastructure. Law and order had to be maintained but it had to be overseen by a court system that was color blind; violent crime was endemic and will get worse if the levels of economic well being amongst the poor were not improved soon. "I am surrounded by people making demands that need to be answered now; I am surrounded by a people that are looking to me for immediate solutions. I have an organization that is small and unused to government and out there are millions of South Africans who know that there will be change, who expect change and who think that black majority rule will bring them instant happiness. I am a prisoner of their demands. I am as much a prisoner now as ever I was on Robbin Island." The smile had left him now as he told me without needing to use words that the burdens of his role as the saviour and hope of his people and the creator of the new South Africa were too awful to contemplate. The sheer weight of popular expectation could break a lesser

449

man struggling to come to terms himself with freedom outside a prison wall, with a life amongst his friends and family, with the every day problems of ordinary life after decades in gaol.

Ten years later we see a South Africa still coming to terms with freedom, still trying to make its citizens respect the rule of law in a country where thirty thousand murders and violent deaths happen every year, still trying to harness the white first world economy for the benefit of the black third world. We still see a South Africa riddled with AIDS and other health problems and there are still, as I saw for myself last year, people living in shacks outside Cape Town, Durban and Johannesburg. But without Nelson Mandela, without his charisma, his stature as a leader of a disparate nation both in waiting and in office, without his ability to talk in the universal language of understanding and patience, his calm and his dignity, South Africa today would be an economic desert and a waste land. The new South Africa will work and will survive, though not without mishaps ands the occasional shock, because of his leadership and what he stood for in his years of imprisonment, in his time as transitional organizer and as President, a beacon of intelligence and understanding.

When it was time for me to go, Nelson Mandela took my hand and held it firmly. He looked into my eyes and told me in his quiet and musical voice, "Work hard for your people and do your very best...oh, and don't forget to send me the Hansard with your maiden speech."

Edward Garnier was born in 1952. He was educated at Wellington College, Berkshire, Jesus College, Oxford (Modern History) and the College of Law, London. He is married to Anna and they have a daughter and two sons. Mr Garnier has been Member of Parliament for Harborough since April 1992. He was appointed Queen's Counsel in April 1995, a Crown Court Recorder in 1998 and a Bencher of the Middle Temple in 2001.

	**africa- a final comment**	miles bredin africa 1992

The Cardoso Hotel (Mozambique) where we stayed has a commanding view of the bay and the port. Built high on a hill, you can lie by the pool and see the whole of Maputo stretched out before you. Set on the Indian Ocean with a distinct Portuguese influence, Maputo is very beautiful, so we lay by the pool and looked at it. For the first time in six months, we weren't trying to catch a train. I didn't have to write my diary and we had no deadlines to worry about. Doing nothing was bliss.

The Cardoso is a Lonrho hotel and was charging absurd prices. It had a very dubious accounting system; it quoted prices in dollars yet charged at a Lonrho invented exchange rate in rand. Metical* were not welcome. Lonrho is one of the few firms that bothers to invest in Africa and because of this has preferential status in many African countries, particularly Mozambique. The Mozambicans allow Lonrho to run its own private army. This is what African countries have had to resort to in order to encourage investment, yet it still doesn't work. Foreign companies charge customers as much as they can in dollars, which are then sent outside the country and only their local currency earnings are reinvested. Decades after the end of colonialism, western business practices on the African continent are still much the same. Rape, pillage, remove.

But why shouldn't they? They do it everywhere else. Surely some investment is better than none? The west has invested a great deal in Africa. Why should it be deprived of a return on its investment? The usual answer to those questions is that we have also taken millions out in money and souls. I believe this argument no longer works. Africa has to learn to help itself and is not going to until the west stops coming to the rescue. We invariably cause more problems than there were in the first place. A few African leaders have realized this and their countries are leaping forward. Uganda was destroyed under Obote and Amin. Its current president, former rebel leader Yoweri Museveni, has accepted that many of Africa's problems are its own and has fought to sort them out. Uganda is now far from perfect and many of its citizens are dissatisfied but it is moving forward for the first time in decades.

Individual Western countries have proved that they cannot divorce politics from charity. France supported the child-eating Bokassa in the

Central African Republic and even helped pay for his Napoleonic coronation as emperor. Giscard D'Estaing was only forced to intervene and overthrow him when his eating habits, already well known to his countrymen, became public. Still, D'Estaing will always remember his hunting trips and as we all know: diamonds are forever.

Belgium has allowed Mobutu to remain for decades. Britain continues to prop up Moi in Kenya and the less dangerous Mugabe in Zimbabwe. Supping with the enemy has become an essential part of the western diplomat's diet. America, when it has intervened, has been even more disingenuous -Angola, Somalia, Ethiopia. The bungled attempts of the United Nations, particularly now that the Americans are in charge to solve African conflicts, have provided more evidence that the west should leave the continent alone. Somalia has been so ineptly handled that it makes Vietnam look like a success story.

Africa, however, hasn't exactly helped. The Organization of African Unity (OAU) is a genuinely sad joke. It was founded in 1963 'to promote unity and solidarity among African states.' Since then it has put out an annual statement against apartheid and achieved precisely nothing. Its most notable success has been the Rwandan peace-keeping force. Based in Ethiopia's capital Addis Ababa, which from 1974 to 1991 was a city at war with its provinces, the most damning statement against it was made recently by its newest member. President Isseyas Afeworki of Eritrea, who had to earn his seat by overthrowing Ethiopia's dictator Mengistu and entering Addis Ababa on a tank, said in August 1993: "Although the OAU has often championed the lofty ideals of unity, cooperation, economic development, human rights and other worldly objectives, it has failed seriously to work towards their concrete realization."

He blames neither the cold war nor colonialism, both of which he has experienced personally, but African leaders.

There is no doubt that colonialism had a devastating effect on Africa. In Mozambique, the Portuguese forced blacks to walk on the roads rather than the pavements so now that the cars have returned there are frequent accidents. Whites are still treated with automatic and unjustified respect even in the most rabidly anti-colonial countries. Every time that an aid worker or a journalist is killed in an African country it is brought home to the residents how unimportant the west regards African lives to be. As colleagues and friends I am glad they are remembered but if I was a Somali or an Ethiopian I would be outraged by the attention their deaths engendered when the deaths of thousands of Africans go unacknowledged every day.

This attitude was first proved to Africans of the modern era when the UN's predecessor, the League of Nations, betrayed Haile Selassie in 1934 and again in 1936. In an impassioned speech to the League of Nations in Geneva, the emperor of Ethiopia - ruler of one of the most ancient civilizations in the entire world, begged the international community to stop Mussolini from taking over his country. He was turned away and his country was overrun: 'Outside the Kingdom of the Lord there is no nation which is greater than any other. God and history will remember your judgment.'

Post-colonialism has been even worse. Having taken all it wanted from Africa, the west pulled out and left the continent in the hands of people whom they had never trusted even to help run it. Europe and America have never invested in Africa out of altruism and still don't. In Somalia and Ethiopia, America and the USSR changed their allegiances overnight in order to continue fighting their own cold war. The two countries were picked up and discarded like pawns and the residents of the Ogaden consequently had to endure a very hot war. From 1992-4 America had to suffer the effects of having 366 million dollars' worth of weapons (the admitted figure), which it supplied to Somalia from 1982-92, turned against its own army.

In Kenya, Britain was pushing Moi towards multiparty democracy well before the Gulf War but quickly changed its mind when it realized that it would need the deep port at Mombasa to supply the Persian Gulf. In 1994 the status quo has not changed. It is still, *l'etat, c'est Moi.* In the 1980s, one side of the American administration worked with the communist Angolan government to negotiate terms for oil drilling, while another part was supplying and training Union for Total Independence of Angola- no relation to the UN (UNITA). Now that UNITA has gone beyond the pale, America is giving satellite information to the MPLA (Angolan People's Liberation Movement), the Angolan ruling party, on its former puppet's troop movements. Under the guise of helping Africa, the west has always put its own interests first and has probably done more harm than it did in the brief colonial period.

It is indisputable fact that Africans are 'more sinn'd against than sinning' but their leaders are also often 'ungrateful wretches.' All the beneficial effects of colonialism have been lost. The road systems that the colonial powers left behind have been left to decay, the farms and factories destroyed and looted. African leaders have merely assumed the mantles of their former colonial masters and continued the tyranny of their countrymen. In most cases they have been worse than the colonizers. Through a combination of Western duplicity, military aid masquerading as charity and African corruption, the continent has been all but destroyed.

Britain supplies weapons to Kenya, which uses them to fuel the civil war in Somalia, which in turn means Kenya receives aid as the policy guarantees it remains the only stable state in East Africa. British officers still train the Mozambican army months after the time when there should no longer be one. American troops went into Somalia to do a quick PR job (do something nice for some black Muslims), which would shine up their image after the farcical end of the Gulf War. Months later they were bogged down, suffering increasingly heavy casualties and trying to kill Mohammed Farah Aideed, one of the most powerful leaders in the country. They chose to negotiate with a hotelier who had proclaimed himself president rather than Aideed who was once an ambassador. Their actions united Somalia behind a psychopath and killed countless innocents. By the end of 1993 they had changed their minds again and were flying Aideed, under their protection, to peace talks in Addis Ababa. In the spring of 1994, they gave up completely. The name of their mission was Operation Restore Hope.

The United States is not the only offender; it is merely the richest. The former Soviet Union was even worse. Britain, France and Belgium are scarcely blameless but this is not the point. It is easy to prove that the West has harmed and continues to harm Africa but Africa has also damaged itself. As long as the West insists on helping out in times of genuine need, none of this is going to change. The aid business has been spawned from international guilt trips. European electorates feel guilty about colonization, Americans about slavery and the cold war.

Africa is used as a source of profit, both political and financial. Much that I respect Jane Perlez, it is somewhat terrifying that George Bush invaded Somalia because of one article she wrote in the *New York Times.* Western governments, aided by the media, manipulate liberal views to make aid a popular policy; then administrations follow their own outrageous agenda under the guise of charity. Only a minute proportion of aid budgets actually goes on feeding refugees. The majority goes on aid deals like road building projects. Vast percentages go on kickbacks to African politicians.

The countries we had traveled through had the ability to feed themselves and the infrastructure to help them in the railway. If Angola was not at war, and the government was not so inept, the starving population could live on state handouts from McDonald's and still have a healthy balance of payments. Angola has oil stocks comparable to some countries in the Gulf. Texaco makes bundles of money from drilling there. Angola loses all its profits to corruption and weapons buying. It has some of the richest diamond fields in the world yet for short-term political reasons, the government allowed independent prospectors to mine in the area. The miners have destroyed the geology of the diamond fields and millions of dollars' worth of stones have been smuggled into other countries, lost for future generations. Even the UN was smuggling diamonds out of Cafunfo when we were there. The UN team before we arrived had been pulled out because of corruption and the next team were being used without their knowledge.

One of the smugglers there told me: 'Whenever a UN helicopter flies in, it leaves with a load of diamonds'. The diamonds are hidden in a mobile air-conditioner going for repair or given to a maintenance man.

It is economical to mine copper at 12,000 feet in Indonesia yet it is no longer viable at sea level in Zaire. The railway leads to the very gates of the mines. That, after all, was why it was built. Mobutu and his cronies have allowed their greatest natural resource to disappear in order to line their own pockets. The railway is only being used for ethnic cleansing. Most of the trains and wagons have been lost to state-sponsored looting or neglect. Even if they could get the copper out and on to trains, they wouldn't be able to send it to Lobito because there's a war in the way. Pre-independence the Angolan and Zairean part of the railway carried three million tons of freight from Zambia a year. It now carries nothing. The only option for Zaire is to send goods down through Zambia but the railway there is so inefficient that it couldn't handle any increased capacity.

In Zambia farmers are unable to grow their crops because they can't get any fertilizer through the hapless port of Beira, even when the government has allowed them the foreign exchange with which to pay for it. Zambia's own industries are being neglected and mismanaged. Corruption plagues all business life from having to pay a bribe to have your telephone connected to the big percentages necessary to negotiate government contracts. Zimbabwe is in a slightly better state yet has Mozambique to negotiate before it gets to the coast. At the time of writing there is still only a fragile cease-fire in Mozambique and the country is nowhere nearer to a lasting peace. In the interim, the country's few remaining assets are being sold off by and to unscrupulous con artists. Mozambican army helicopter pilots are encouraged to fly their gun ships out to ships off the coast where they are given $500,000 and a new identity.

The West is further destroying Africa by its bungling attempts to help. When aid is delivered late, as it was to Zambia in 1992, it distorts the real market. African countries beg for aid when they need it but it often arrives after the demand has died. Just as the country is beginning to find its feet once more, a massive excess of food arrives on the market, drives down prices and leaves farmers in need of food aid. Soon eaten, all it has done is cause more problems and stifled growth.

It is easy to sit in a comfortable London flat encouraging the world to stop sending aid to Africa. It is more difficult if you have actually seen starving refugees, watched villages being bombed and heard the wailing of wounded children. But I have also seen the damage that aid has done to Africa. However well meaning the non-government organization (NGO), it is always manipulated by local or foreign powers. It is wonderful to feed starving children in Somalia, but to do so it is necessary to pay mercenary guards who in turn pay their political masters. To enjoy the privilege of stopping one child from starving involves fuelling the war effort, which caused the child to starve in the first place. Flying food into Sudan makes for great TV pictures when bales stamped 'Gift of the European Community (EC)' hurtle out of the loading bays of Hercules transport planes but in Sudan, food is used as a weapon. Food landing behind the lines of the Garang faction of the Sudanese People'(SPLA) will never get through to the Machar faction. If the Muslim north had to spend any money at all on the Christian and animist people of the south, it would not be able to afford to fight them.

Despite all the altruistic noises from the likes of Britain's overseas aid minister, Baroness Lynda Chalker (speaking in early 1994 during the Pergau Dam affair and the 'arms to Iraq' inquiry: 'We do not and while I am a minister we will not link our aid program to arms sales'), Britain is only involved in African countries where it is useful to be there. Even then Britain is not giving as much as anyone else but just enough to be able to exert influence. I have witnessed spontaneous riots in Kenya complaining at Britain's continued support of Moi despite his human rights abuses. Chalker retaliated that at least Moi was trying.

The West has crippled Africa with unmanageable debts, which Africa can never repay and never will. All Africa's debts could be paid off without denting the World Bank and International Monetary Fund (IMF)'s coffers, yet they insist on rescheduling its debt repayments. To Africa they are enormous, to the West - paltry. Bradford City Council (a small town in England) owes more than Chad (a large country in Central Africa). Rwanda's third biggest foreign-exchange earner was the money it received from tourists visiting two families of gorillas in the war-ravaged highlands. America and Europe may be going bankrupt but at least we have a little more income than that which we receive from Disneyland and Windsor Safari Park. If the citizens of Zambia gave every single penny they earned to their western creditors, it would take them more than two and a half years to pay off their country's debt. Ten billion dollars of Africa's paltry earnings go to the West in debt repayments every year. With that sort of standing order it can never hope to start developing independently.

Africa's problems have been made worse by the West but it is a shared problem. An estimated 80 per cent of Africa's income disappears in capital flight. Dictators, soldiers and government officials become millionaires while their countries starve. A secret but substantial percentage of the world's Mercedes cars go to Africa. Nearly 50 per cent of African countries suffer from some sort of ethnic conflict yet as we saw in Zaire and Angola it is often fuelled by the politicians who claim to abhor it. On a continent that has straight-line borders -courtesy of the colonial carve-up -there is a great deal of resentment for the Savimbis and Mobutus of the world to stir up. On the borders of Zimbabwe and Mozambique, members of the same family live in incomparable conditions. The Mozambicans have nothing; their Zimbabwean kin are some of the most fortunate people south of the Sahara.

Africa has been ravaged by the West for centuries. We do have a responsibility towards it but all help is pointless when the motives behind it are dubious and Africa still has political leaders willing to fill their own pockets while their countries starve. There is nothing we can do about that. The west has tried forcing western-style multiparty democracy upon Africa. It has been proved over and over again that it doesn't work. Kenya, Nigeria and Angola have all had multiparty elections which have left the same monsters in power. Tribal loyalties, cash and force are all employed to retain the status quo. When new governments have been installed as the result of multiparty elections, the old behind the scenes figures retain control. Only the faces in the cabinet change.

The west has also tried to force economic change. Twenty-seven African countries now have structure adjustment programs (SAP) forcing free-market economies upon them. None of them work. The west has to accept that it has failed and allow Africa to advance at its own pace. A few centuries of superficial civilization, in most cases less than one, have been forced upon Africa and it has yet to adjust. In the main cities along our route we met well-educated, well-heeled Africans who lived in air-conditioned houses, used computers and telephones and drove cars. Also, however, we met people who had been living in the same manner for many centuries, tending small plots and existing by barter. The latter are the vast majority. Sixty-two per cent of sub-Saharan Africans live in absolute poverty.

There is a yawning chasm between the empowered and the powerless and until that inequality is addressed, Africa will not be able to advance. We cannot address that problem for Africa. It has to do it on its own. Multiparty politics is not the answer. Freedom of speech is not too useful when, as happened with the Turkwel Gorge in Kenya, you are dying of thirst and hunger because someone in the capital has built a hydroelectric dam and cut off your water supply.

Colonialism left the countries of southern Africa with an admirable road system, thriving industries and a railway to serve them. It was not the West that destroyed what it left behind. Recently, the West has spent thirty years alternately following its own ends and trying to help. Until it frees Africa of its debts and leaves it alone to sort out its own problems, nothing will change. We have proven that we can't be trusted to meddle in Africa's affairs. To pullout will contribute more untold misery, maybe for decades, but we will no longer be interfering and adding to the problem. Until we stop propping up corrupt governments because they're better than the immediate alternative and prolonging civil wars by feeding the refugees that we have helped create, there will always be blood on the tracks.

The railway has survived for a hundred years. It can survive a hundred more if we allow Africa to develop at its own pace and in its own way. Given a chance to rid itself of its abhorrent leaders without outside funding and direction, there could be hope for a twenty-first century Africa.

Zaire produces uranium. It would be foolhardy to allow a continent with such resources to continue under the guidance of the men who run it today. Mobutu has the funds to buy a Pershing for every day of the year. Impoverished uranium can be enriched. All he has to do is put the two together. Africa has a history of strong leaders from Lobengula to Sierra Leone's Valentine Strasser -men who have been willing to fight against tyranny. There are many more where they came from but while the West conspires to keep corrupt, vicious men in power, there is nothing that the true leaders, from tribal elders upwards, can do.

Africa is bursting with intelligent men and women who are beaten down by the system, which we have helped to create and we continue to maintain.

* Metical is the local currency

Printed with permission:
Blood on the Tracks: A Rail Journey from Angola to Mozambique (1992). By Miles Bredin

See page 41, for biography of **Miles Bredin**.

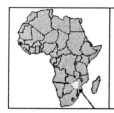

| shakedown | robert nolan
zimbabwe
1997 |

Shakespeare was a gambler and a hustler, but I didn't know that when he moved onto the abandoned plot of land 50 yards from my homestead. He had come from Harare, the capital city of Zimbabwe, with a typically large family. I immediately noticed the sunken look of his mother's eyes and knew why they were there. She was infected with HIV and was returning to *kimusha*, her rural home, to die.

Although it was unusual for a man to live alone in the bush, I appreciated my seclusion from the rest of the village, and felt secure with my new neighbors. It was the only place where I could find solitude and not be consistently subjected to the innocent curiosity of the local eye. My dog Tamba was not used to having people so close to my home. The stiff posture he had taken to upon their arrival made me proudly aware of his loyalty, but things were soon to change as they often do when people live together, even when they come from different worlds.

I soon learned from Shakespeare and the whispering voices of the village that he had been born in Mozambique, whose borders lay only 50 kilometers to the east. The coastal country was recovering from the brutal colonization of the Portuguese, who were busy at the time intentionally destroying the infrastructure they had created for their want-to-be empire. It no longer held the potential value it once had, and, like other poorly managed Portuguese establishments in southern Africa, their departure was not graceful.

Civil war of course followed, and it was into this chaotic world that Shakespeare was born. I'm not sure exactly how "Shake," as he was often called, spent the bulk of his youth, but I imagine that it must have required him to learn the survival skills of any kid growing up in extremely harsh conditions. I was often surprised when learning his history from the indigenously suspicious farmers at the local beer halls, who would recount the previous night's game of cards by candlelight. Animated elders of the village would wave their arms in descriptive accounts of how they had lost their money to Shakespeare, while the shadows echoed their movements and the younger men nodded in agreement.

I remember the first time he asked me for money. His mother had finally died of the virus, and his stepfather, a sorry man who hooked up with

Shakespeare's mother during her days as a Harare prostitute, had fled in the middle of the night with his own children, and left nothing behind for Shakespeare and his two younger siblings. The stepfather had also taken with him all of their tools for plowing.

Bungwe Village, as the area was known, was made up of subsistence farmers whose lives depended on the maize crop. Without land or the tools to till it, a man was without food and without respect. Shake had neither.

I helped him pay for his mother's funeral, which attracted few people from the village and lacked the festive spirit that characterized most Shona funerals. Generally, the passing of a village member would be a reason to gather, an essential and celebratory event to be attended by the community as a whole. Maybe it was because of the mother's profession, or the fact that Shake's family was still somewhat new to the village, but the ceremony lacked the elaborate bonfires, dancing and drumming that typified the other funerals I had attended over the previous year.

I was not in the habit of giving money to the villagers. It was a contradiction to my role as a grassroots development worker, and my meager living allowance, while well above the average income of those whom I lived amongst, was not substantial. I had never seen a person die of HIV. Maybe it was because of this that I helped Shakespeare pay for his mother's funeral.

For this, I did not expect anything in return. In fact, I worried that my donation would lead to further possibilities of exploitation and requests from other village members for money. So I was pleasantly surprised a few weeks later when Shakespeare invited me to dinner.

His recently acquired wife (wives in Shona culture are often the object of acquisition) had prepared a meal of *sadza,* a maize-based Zimbabwean staple, along with vegetables and beans. We sat in a traditional hut that was missing the thatched roof that would be necessary for shelter before the upcoming rains arrived.

This became a common occurrence, and we often shared food and conversation under the stars into the late hours of the night, drinking the thick local beer and smoking while his barefooted wife waited upon us. I would return home with my dog to read or write, and Shake would go gambling. From what I heard, he was good at it.

For the next eight months, we continued this pattern. Shake helped me build a new door for my aging *daga* hut, and I in turn assisted him with vegetables and other simplicities that I could afford until the land he obtained from the local chief would bear fruit.

I remember the day he was given the plot, about a mile from where we lived, and he took me there in his excited state. "Ah Mr. Robert," he said, "I will become a good farmer with this land! When it is ready we will eat tasty food!"

I was skeptical. The land in Bungwe was rocky and unfertile. It was part of the Tribal Trust Land allotted to indigenous peoples by the British colonists in the days of Cecil Rhodes. Compared to the fertile land I saw on my bus trips to the capital, which was owned mostly by whites and used for commercial farming, this land was barren. I wondered how Shakespeare would fare. It took someone who had lived a whole life in this area to make the land productive, and Shake had been here for less time than I had.

Still, he remained positive, and on many afternoons I would join him in surveying its progress. As a gesture of our friendship I would upon occasion take up the hoe, though I had never tilled land before. My home in Orange County was somewhat overdeveloped, and my previous knowledge of gardening was limited to mini-mall landscapes.

Shake would guide me through gardens of maize stalks that grew higher by the day, and pointed out different kinds of cucumbers, potatoes and groundnuts. He was particularly proud of his ganja trees, a result of planting skills he must have picked up in Mozambique, where the weed grows freely and is unregulated.

But when the rains had come and it was time to harvest, my fears of Shake's skills as a subsistence farmer were realized. His crops had failed and the rains would soon be gone.

I didn't see Shakespeare much after that. He seemed angry whenever we met and I heard rumors that he was fighting with people over wages. Gambling had become his only source of income, and I noticed that his revitalized homestead was again in a state of decay.

Shake turned to the government for assistance, attempting to capitalize on the compensation package awarded to the War Veteran's Association for those who participated in fighting that overthrew the apartheid-minded Rhodesian government in 1980.

The veterans had been haggling with the government for almost 20 years, and had finally persuaded the ailing administration of President Robert Mugabe to pay them each 50,000 Zimbabwean dollars for their struggle. Shake's mother, like many Shona woman, had been active participants in the liberation war known as the second *Chimurenga*, and the Veteran's Association had promised that children of deceased vets would be compensated with school fees and small living stipends.

Shakespeare asked me to help him fill out the forms, and since my role in the village was to foster educational development, I obliged.

I never found out if he received any assistance from the government, but I doubt the papers saw the light of day after entering the bowels of the local bureaucracy.

The community no longer tolerated Shakespeare's violent outbursts. I recall the elders at the beer hall, sitting on crates and passing around cups filled with *Chibukhu*, the chunky, milk-like beer sipped by most Zimbabwean males, discussing Shakespeare's violent behavior.

Before, I had always come to his defense. The people of Bungwe had grown accustomed to my voice, and my opinions, though foreign, were respected. This was primarily because I was a teacher and although I would like to think it was for other reasons as well, they knew that I had access to money. I had written many proposals to agencies that support international development, and a few of them had borne fruit.

But it wasn't until the chief of the village gazed at me with his drunken red eyes that I knew I should not comment on the matter. It was internal, and I accepted that without offense. I had been treated with mutual respect and even tolerance at times, and I was aware of this. Shakespeare was evicted by the village headman.

I decided to go on holiday. My scrutinized life as a foreigner was beginning to take its toll at the end of my second year in the village. I had escaped to Harare on occasion, but this time I wanted to leave Zimbabwe and become anonymous. There is something about moving through life like a ghost that still appeals to me, but this desire is oddly coupled with an intense drive to be part of a tight-knit community. I suppose we all experience this contradiction, but the extremity of my living situation called for an equally extreme contradiction. I wanted to be invisible.

Colleen, my neighbor and student, would feed Tamba and keep an eye on my place. Others in the village questioned my wisdom, for adolescent girls were not allotted much trust. I knew Colleen well, and was aware of the fact that without her assistance, I would not be able to survive alone in the bush in Africa. She knew that without my help the dream of learning English might never be accomplished. I trusted her more than anyone.

I returned a few weeks later refreshed. Only two months remained on my contract, and I would soon be returning to the United States to see friends and family. I looked forward to finding some closure with the community I had lived in for the past few years and had come to love.

I exited the bus in front of the three dry goods stores that served as the center of the village. All three shops sold the same warm sodas, bars of laundry soaps and *Chibukhu* beer. Somehow they all stayed in business. When one store was out of a particular item, it was sure to be found at the others. Communal dependence was part of the social fabric here, and it was this philosophy that ensured survival, although it often caused many innovative ideas to dwell in the mediocre. Rising in the ranks was not acceptable if your distant relative was starving.

Glares of surprise accompanied my arrival even though everyone knew me. Perhaps the sight of a white man getting off the bus was something that they would always find novel.

But this time there was something else. Nobody approached, and even my closest friends hesitated at greeting me as they usually did. I could feel that something was wrong, but there was always something going wrong in the bush, and I had learned not to get upset by the inter-village problems that particularly seemed to surface when I was away. Reason, one of my students and a shopkeeper for his father, helped me with my luggage, and we walked in silence to my place.

When I arrived I didn't see it at first. I was looking at the dry brown hills that seemed to go on forever like the waves of the Pacific, and the mango trees I would dearly miss when I returned to California. Reason pointed to a gaping hole in my thatched roof...

He looked at me with disappointment, and I lowered my head. My queasy stomach gave way to a rising anger, and I remember screaming something, I am not sure what. It echoed, this sound, and I do not doubt that every member of the village was listening. I had been robbed.

While members of the community had already reported the robbery to the nearest police station located at the Rushinga Township, I regarded the situation as hopeless. Someone, it didn't matter who had broken into a place that had become sacred to me. I didn't miss any of my possessions; they were temporal to me and were what I considered to be Africanized, meaning that after two years in the bush they would be useless.

What surprised most was that the thief had taken my journals and photo album. These items contained my interpretations of what was supposed to be a profound experience, proof that I had survived what often felt like a dream. To think that they had been stolen disgusted me, and altered my entire perception of my time in Zimbabwe and the people I lived with. I didn't hide my disappointment.

The people of Bungwe were also affected by the theft. Everyone was a potential suspect, and the clear lines of communication that had been established became cloudy with paranoia and uncertainty.

Names began to surface, and of course Shakespeare was one of them. I didn't care enough to pursue the matter further. I was jaded and cynical. I made terrible generalizations about Africans, while I had only lived amongst the people of one tribe, the Shona of Zimbabwe.

Finally, most likely at the persistence of villagers hoping to clear their own names, a police officer arrived on a bicycle from Rushinga. I was sitting in front of Reason's shop playing table soccer when he asked for suspects. He wasn't going to leave until I gave him one, he said. I told him a few of the names people had been mentioning and he left. I didn't think about the incident directly, but it had disillusioned my entire outlook and seeped into my daily routine.

As I prepared enthusiastically for my departure from the continent that had shattered my naïve idealism, the incident resurfaced.

It was a typically hot afternoon and I was drinking and playing snooker in the dingy Rushinga beer hall where I had become somewhat of a regular over the past weeks, when a police Landrover pulled up in a cloud of dust. As the air cleared, I saw the white teeth of smiling officers pointing to the back of the vehicle, which held in custody my missing possessions and my old friend Shakespeare.

What happened next is not clear. I remember the police encouraging me to beat Shakespeare as they held him back. His hands were cuffed behind him, and he looked at me with the ferocious red eyes of betrayal. His head was down in shame, but poised as a bull's might be when provoked by a matador. I wanted to beat him so badly that I trembled. Words flew from my mouth like arrows, meant to pierce.

"It is people like you who make this world a worse place," I said, passing judgment and gazing deep into his eyes. "Some friend," I said and spit on the floor as the police took him into the room that contained my items. "You make me want to vomit," I said in my broken *ChiShona.*

The police took us both into a room and handcuffed Shakespeare to the wall. Again, I was asked if I wanted to beat him. By this time I had cooled off, and was going through my things that were sprawled out on a dusty table.

I found a Bible and asked Shakespeare if he had taken the time to read it, laughing in anger at the irony of life and my own wittiness. Next, I found a copy of James Joyce's *Ulysses,* and decided it was probably a good thing that he had taken this one. I had attempted to read it on three separate occasions, and failed each time.

But what caused me the most confusion were the contents of my photo album. All of the photos of my loved ones had been replaced by his. As I thumbed through the album, I saw the story of his life with his mother, his wife and his siblings. But it was the last photo that shocked me. It was a picture of Shakespeare and my mother, from when she had visited. I held the photo up to his face, ripped it in half, and walked out.

I haven't seen Shakespeare since that day. Upon my return to the United States, I was quickly consumed by the frenzy of the holiday season. I suddenly found myself in shopping malls crowded with people who moved in a kind of organized chaos into which I was swept away from Africa. I had once again become invisible.

Someone wrote to me that Shakespeare was sentenced to two years in prison. Exactly the amount of time I spent in Bungwe.

See page 441, for biography of **Robert Nolan**.

	**one man's africa**	alan d. harvey south africa 1974

It wasn't politics which first drove me to Southern Africa. It wasn't the spirit of adventure. It wasn't the call of the wild outdoor life. It was rugby.

In fact my interest in South Africa had initially been kindled a few years prior to when I first set foot on the sub-continent in 1974, during the Springbok Rugby Tour of the British Isles in 1969/70. I was only a teenager at the time, and a sports fanatic. There was no other real interest in my life.

But it wasn't the rugby alone which aroused my particular interest in this tour however. I had been greatly angered by the protest demonstrations against the touring Springboks, and couldn't understand why certain "kill-joys" wanted to ruin the sporting enjoyment of others. I realize now, of course, that these protests were staged by a small clique of extreme left wingers with their own peculiar ideological axe to grind, but at the time I knew nothing about such political agendas.

Neither was I angered merely by the fact that certain people wished to prevent others from seeing games of rugby. What incensed me specifically was the target of the venom of these protesters. As I listened to Springbok players and supporters being interviewed on television, something very fundamental struck me. These people may have come from a different country thousands of miles away, but they were not "foreigners"; they looked the same as British people who I knew, they spoke the same language, their interests and attitudes were the same. Theoretically I may have been able to understand why certain people could have wanted to stop a team of undesirable "foreigners" playing here, but not those who were, to use a phrase which later became very common - our own kith-and-kin.

At junior school we had been divided into "houses" bearing the names of the four great Commonwealth dominions, Canada, Australia, New Zealand and South Africa. Ironically, as things were to turn out, I had been placed in Canada House rather than South Africa House, but we were all encouraged to make contact with our respective High Commissions in London and to learn as much as we could about these countries. I guess that my interest in "the Empire" and my kith-and-kin living in other parts of the

466

globe can be traced back to these early schooldays. My identification with my South African "brothers," now being so inexplicably attacked by a bunch of traitors, probably therefore had its genesis in this "Imperial spirit" which had been ignited in me at school all those years earlier.

I managed to obtain a ticket for the England v. South Africa international at Twickenham in December 1969 (I had a good ticket tout contact!), and became particularly angered by the intensity of the protest against the South Africans, both players and spectators, at this match. So embarrassed was I by this that when I reached Twickenham Railway Station I went up to the first group of South Africans who I saw (who I identified by their rosettes) and apologized to them, somewhat grandiosly, on behalf of the British people. They turned out to include a boyfriend/girlfriend couple named Vic Long and Lorraine Fitzgerald, and during the train journey back to central London we chatted at length before exchanging telephone numbers.

It turned out that Vic and Lorraine, along with a BSAP (Rhodesian police) friend of theirs by the name of Mike Raine and his girlfriend, were eager to travel to Cardiff the following January in order to see the Wales v. South Africa match. But evidently they couldn't obtain tickets for love nor money. Through my ticket-tout contact I knew that I could help, and this of course gave me a good excuse to maintain contact. Needless to say I was successful in organising tickets, though I could not pick them up until just before the match. I re-contacted Vic with this good news a few days later (I think he was actually rather surprised to hear from me again), and asked if I could join them on their trip, which of course he gladly agreed to.

The whole journey to Cardiff proved an eye-opening adventure for me. It had a slightly "James Bond-ish" air to it; I recognized Mike Raine (who I'd never met before) at Oxford Circus by the fact that we were both holding pre-arranged newspapers. Once we reached Cardiff I rendezvoused with my ticket-tout colleague in a rather secretive huddle outside the main railway station. In actual fact, I think the others were never entirely convinced that I could obtain these scarce and much sought after tickets until they actually saw them in my hands!

But it was the spirit and attitude of my newly-found Southern African friends which had the greatest impact on me. Although they were all only about the same age as me (late teens/early twenties) they all had far greater confidence in the "big outside world" than I did. They all, after all, had come from the other side of the planet entirely under their own steam for a couple of years' working stay, and all of them thought nothing of a weekend's trip to the other end of the UK merely to see a game of rugby. To me with my parochial provincial English upbringing such a journey was still a big adventure. This showed even in the manner of our luggage, for whereas they were all prepared with the latest state-of-the-art hold-alls, I came equipped with a Second World War-vintage suitcase loaned by my parents! The liberated life-style of my new-found friends was also a revelation to me, for their open sexual relationships at such a youthful age was something which previously I had never experienced.

They all demonstrated a surprising maturity for people of such a young age, hiring a car for the journey and organizing overnight accommodation as they went, and their "world-wise" confidence was something which I truly marveled at. They displayed an attitude which I subsequently learnt was typical of most Southern Africans - the pioneer spirit and a colonial outlook on life. But for me the bug had bitten. My aspirations had risen to new heights.

Although sadly I never saw Mike Raine again, I met Vic and Lorraine on several further occasions during the following summer. On our last meeting before he returned to South Africa Vic made a suggestion to me which really set me thinking however. He suggested that just as he'd journeyed to the UK to coincide with the Springbok tour here, then why didn't I arrange to visit South Africa during the next British Lions tour there, which was due to take place in 1974. With my then limited financial resources I didn't have a clue how I was going to be able to afford this, but my mind was immediately made up. It must be remembered that this was at a time well before trans-world backpacking excursions became common, and when a package holiday to the Costa Brava was still considered something daring, but my sights had already been set on something far more adventurous.

I started saving avidly therefore, even changing jobs to obtain a higher salary. My parents were totally opposed to my plans, and did everything possible to prevent me traveling, but luckily I was old enough to make my own decisions. My friends locally were also amazed when they heard of my intentions, and their reactions were ones of incredulity. There were several package tours on offer to follow the Lions around South Africa, but I wasn't interested in them, I wanted to make all my own arrangements, and to taste the spirit of adventure in a strange country just the same as Vic, Lorraine and Mike had done, and so this I therefore did.

When I landed at Jan Smuts Airport in June 1974 it was difficult to explain the many emotions which went flowing through my head at the same time. Exhilaration; triumph; excitement; wonder. The first sight which I saw when I left the airport concourse made me realize that I'd definitely "arrived" in South Africa, and filled me full of inspiration, for there in front of me was a tall flagpole flying the South African national flag. I recognized this flag - the "little flags within a flag,"- instinctively, and indeed, could remember how I'd first come across it all those earlier when I was still at junior school, when I was intrigued about why the South African flag didn't position the Union Flag in the top left-hand corner like the Australian, Canadian and New Zealand flags, but instead had a somewhat smaller version positioned in the middle stripe. But I loved this flag even so, and in a way this slight difference made it all the more attractive to me. Here I now was in the very country which this flag represented. My imperial passion had at last been fulfilled. My colonial adventure was just about to begin.

Even during my first few days in Jo'burg I quickly became aware of a fundamental fact about South Africa which its national flag exemplified, and which my previous long-distance knowledge had tended to suggest - namely the intriguing dichotomy that, whereas in so many ways the country was so similar to Britain, in so many other ways it was so different. Everybody spoke English (even if only as their second language); they drove on the "correct" side of the road; place-names and brand-names were similar; the character of the people was the same. Yet at the same time there were so many differences. The country was noticeably "bigger," even in the major city centres; the climate was warmer, purer and rarer; the very atmosphere of the country evoked expansionism, a frontier society, the colonial spirit.

But there was another more important difference. At first I thought of South Africa simply in terms of my own people, the Whites, but I soon realised that there was another nation (or as I subsequently learnt several other nations) sharing the same piece of geography. I quickly came into contact with the Black South African nation, and equally quickly realised that the claims by the leftist anti-Springbok demonstrators that the Blacks were somehow "oppressed" was complete nonsense. The Blacks were overwhelmingly *happy*; they may not have had the vote, but they had other things which were vastly more important to them, and which their fellow Blacks north of the Zambezi would give their right-arm for. They had full bellies, roofs over their heads, and a decent standard of healthcare and education for their kids. It amused me to see Black women seemingly always carrying things on their heads - once even bizarrely a kettle - yet always with happy smiling faces. One enduring memory was of a refuse disposal team in Jo'burg running down the street apparently intent on being the first to pick up the next dustbin. It was a happy contented attitude which I never knew of the Blacks in Brixton- area in South London.

The first match which I saw in South Africa - the game between Transvaal and the Lions at the old Ellis Park - proved a fantastic experience. The ground - temporary seating and all - was absolutely packed. In the UK, only international rugby matches would attract such capacity crowds, but this was merely a game between a provincial side and the tourists. Even so, however, the atmosphere among the spectators was exactly the same as at larger soccer and rugby games in the UK - only the hot humid atmosphere and the parched turf were different. By chance I bumped into the girl who had changed my traveler's cheques at Jan Smuts Airport coming out of the ground. She recognized me instantly, and exchanged a few friendly and pleasant words of greetings. I knew then that the gods were on my side for this trip.

But an even bigger adventure awaited me. The next fixture on the Lions' itinerary was against Rhodesia (then technically in a state of "rebellion" against the Crown) up in Salisbury. A low intensity civil war was then of course taking place in this country, and it was an act of daring even to contemplate such a trip, but this only made me even more determined to be there. This after all was Mike Raine's land, and as far as I could make out, Rhodesia was fighting a war against the terrorist comrades of those despicable leftist demonstrators who I had confronted in London four years earlier. I was resolute that I would travel to Rhodesia not just to see the rugby, but also to express my solidarity with my kith-and-kin there.

The only practical way of travelling from the Witwatersrand to Salisbury was by air, and this in itself proved quite some experience. Although it was a few years prior to the Viscount atrocities, when two Air Rhodesia Viscount aircraft were shot out of the skies by Nkomo's evil ZIPRA terrorists, precautions were already being taken to protect the passengers. All flights to Salisbury seemed to be night flights, and the Viscounts were bristling with anti-missile equipment. The Air Rhodesia cabin staff also proved to be something of a revelation. The air hostess's uniforms were certainly at the height of the 1970's fashions, but alas the only air hostess on my flight seemed to be well into her 40's, and her squat plump figure was definitely unsuited for this sexy attire!

But it was someone who I met on this flight who had the greatest impact on me. His name was Bruce Illingworth, a Rhodesian returning home from a working visit to the UK. Bruce told me quite a bit about what to expect in Salisbury, and advised me to stay at an establishment known as "Mrs. Timms's Guest Houses" whilst I was there, which evidently provided the best value for money in the city. Alas, I had already booked my hotel well in advance. As we left the aircraft we were all handed disembarkation forms to fill in. Unlike their South African equivalents these forms included an entry for race, and in perfect naiveté I entered "Anglo-Celtic" in this column. The official at immigration control took one look at this and nonchalantly crossed it out, substituting the single word "White." "You're just trying to confuse the poor guy," Bruce whispered in my ear.

I immediately fell in love with Rhodesia, perhaps even more so than South Africa. It was clearly a different country, and the atmosphere had a distinct "feel" to it. Whereas South Africa was overwhelmingly European in character, Rhodesia was clearly part of *Africa*. The climate was even more hot and close, and I somehow sensed the conflict which Rhodesia faced from the outside world. The people who I met, on the other hand, without the Afrikaans element, were even more British in character than their South African counterparts. They may have been antagonistic towards the British government and establishment, but not towards a British tourist such as me - as indeed everybody associated with the Lions Tour. I soon came to realise that to consider these people - our own kith-and-kin - as "rebels" was utter rubbish. In so many ways they were "more British than the British," and in this respect it is interesting to note that one member of Ian Smith's UDI cabinet, Denis Walker, now lives in the UK and is a leading official of the *Constitutional Monarchy Association*. Some "rebel!"

Although the match between Rhodesia and the Lions was of course the highspot of my stay in Salisbury, I had a couple of spare days to see round the city. One day I managed to climb to the top of Salisbury Kopje, and from there observed the magnificent view across the Salisbury skyline to Mount Hampden beyond. Mount Hampden had been named after John Hampden, a leading hero of the Parliamentary cause during the English Civil War, and this had originally been planned as the site for the capital of the new country when it was founded in 1890. The capital itself was of course to be called after the then British Prime Minister, the 3rd Marquess of Salisbury. I could not help but be both impressed and inspired by what I saw. In 84 short years a vibrant and dynamic modern city had been established in the heart of a wild and alien continent, and my admiration for the founding fathers of the country, those who I was now reading and learning about - Rhodes, Jameson, Selous and Rudd etc. - increased accordingly. The youth club of which I was a member back in the UK were holding a small function that day. But I couldn't help but think to myself as I observed this glorious sight, hopefully not in too arrogant an manner, how much luckier I was to find myself in such a romantic and heroic setting, rather than in mundane provincial Britain.

I also managed to meet up with Bruce Illingworth again before the end of my stay. Bruce was going to visit an African market that day, and he had a plan. His time in the UK had shown him there was a demand for primitive African artefacts, and he was planning to establish an exporting business in this line. At the market he centered his attentions on the carved soapstone models which were common there, and made a number of enquiries about their prices. "I'm a capitalist" he told me, and although at that time this word meant practically nothing to me I soon realized that I shared his enterprising entrepreneurial enthusiasm. Before the day was out I had agreed to set-up the importing side of operations for him once I returned to the UK, and my excitement rose accordingly. Alas, although I did indeed start to construct an infrastructure once I returned to the UK, communications with Bruce stopped before anything definite could be established - but his enthusiasm for the capitalist system had an enduring effect upon me, and from then onwards business enterprise became a central driving force of my life.

Unfortunately a hitch then occurred in my plans. I discovered that I wasn't able to obtain a flight back to Jan Smuts in time for the Second Test in Pretoria. This meant I would have to stay in Salisbury for a few extra days. Although I was totally happy with the hotel where I was staying I thought that I would move into one of Mrs. Timms's Guest Houses which Bruce had recommended, in order to save a bit of cash. This proved to be quite some experience. Evidently this remarkable lady Mrs. Timms had bought up a string of properties in central Salisbury and had turned them into guesthouse accommodations, though with one central communal dining room. Although none of these houses could be considered palatial, they were all clean and ordered, and her African staff - resplendent in their white shirts and shorts, with the word "Timms" embroidered on their backs - were a common sight in the city center scurrying between the various properties. The food, however, was a revelation. Eat as much as you like from a fantastic assortment of "serve yourself" delicacies - and the quality was high! There was a young Australian who had emigrated to Rhodesia at my particular residence, and he proudly though bizarrely kept a pick-axe (the main feature on the Rhodesian coat-of-arms) in his bedroom. We got on well together. The fact that here was another member of my kith-and-kin from another part of the globe, also actively expressing his solidarity with his Rhodesian compatriots, only strengthened my belief in imperial brotherhood, which had been kindled all those years earlier through the house system of my junior school.

Once I eventually reached Pretoria I hit another obstacle. I had made my hotel booking from a distance, and naively thought that this accommodation being in Church Street (which according to my map was in the center of the city) would be near the station. Church Street turned out to be very long, and my hotel was positioned well to one end of it. I was also carrying a heavy suitcase, which although a definite improvement on my World War II vintage suitcase of four years earlier, was still not as sensible as a backpack would have been. I lumbered down Church Street carrying this suitcase, changing hands every hundred yards or so, hoping against hope that the hotel would turn up in the next block. Past the magnificent splendour of the Herbert Baker-designed Union Buildings I went (which the following day I would have the privilege of touring and observing at close quarters) until at last I reached my destination. I practically collapsed in the hotel foyer, totally exhausted. To get back to the station a couple of days later I used a bus!

I caught a train to Bloemfontein for the next stage of my expedition, to see the match between the Lions and the Orange Free State. It was here that I had a chance meeting which was to have a significant impact upon the rest of my tour. I was a member of an organization called the *Friends of the Springbok* who were organizing a number of package trips to follow the Lions around the sub-continent. Although I didn't make use of these package trips myself, the *Friends of the Springbok* had assisted me greatly to make my own travel arrangements, and I had become very familiar with one of the organization's leading officials, Graham Evans, whose picture seemed to adorn all their literature. On the way out of the Bloemfontein ground I recognized Graham Evans from these pictures, and so introduced myself to him. When I told him that I had made all my own arrangements to tour the country his emotions seemed to be a mixture of both amazement and admiration, and he invited me to join his party for that stage of the tour. I say "party," but in reality this turned out to be just one man, a most remarkable Welsh coalmine-owner (evidently considered too small to nationalise) named Len Bevan. The *Friends of the Springbok* had organised three package trips, one involving the first stage of the tour, one involving the latter stage, and the other all the way through. Only one customer had booked up for this complete package, Len Bevan, so he was now alone with Graham Evans for the middle couple of matches at Bloemfontein and Kimberley. I therefore joined them for this stage and we became a threesome - and I certainly started to mix in some pretty high circles as a result. Not only did Graham have good contacts with certain Lions players and officials, but he also proved to be on very good terms with several members of the media. It was through him I got to meet Nigel Starmer-Smith and Alun Williams of the BBC, and John Reason of the Daily Telegraph. I thus started to frequent some of the more plusher hotels during this stage of my trip, and learnt a number of amusing public-schoolboyish pranks!

Graham gave me a lift to Kimberley in his hired car, and dropped me off at my hotel. Although somewhat lower in standard than the 5-star splendour that he and Len were enjoying, it was even so a quite remarkable establishment. It was run by a fairly elderly Afrikaner gentleman, and all tariffs were for full-board rather than just bed and breakfast. When I explained to the Afrikaner owner that I would not be requiring lunch as I would be out watching the rugby etc. during the day, he replied, "Then you must have sandwiches." Not "would you like sandwiches," mark you, but you *must* have them - and sure enough, a neatly packaged set of sandwiches were presented to me each day after breakfast!

Graham gave me another lift back up to Jo'burg, but there alas I had to say goodbye to him and Len as they were meeting up with their second package party newly arrived at Jan Smuts (although of course I still saw them from time to time during the remainder of the tour). My money was running out far quicker than I had anticipated (mainly due to my extended stay in Salisbury and the "highlife" which I had enjoyed with Graham and Len) and I was becoming quite desperate to make savings. It was actually Graham who made a suggestion in this regard which I quickly jumped at, namely that I should start "hitching" around the country rather than using public transport. In a strange country, and one which moreover was something of a "frontier" society, this was a daring action to take, but I didn't really have much of a choice - and my "hitching" experiences of the next few days became a story in itself.

I got dropped off at a point at the start of the N1 Freeway which I was told was the best "hitching" point for Port Elizabeth very early in the morning, and started signalling hopefully to every car which drove past. Optimistically I imagined that I would be able to obtain a lift all the way to PE, and thus reach the city in one day. This was not to be the case however, for the first lift which I obtained was only as far as Vanderbijlpark. After this I obtained a series of short lifts across the Free State, and eventually was dropped off on the outskirts of Aliwal North, a small little dorp in the north-east Cape. It was already late afternoon, and it was therefore obvious to me that I wasn't going to make PE that night - but I wanted to get as far as I could that day, certainly as far as Queenstown, and perhaps even to King William's Town. Traffic at this lonely location proved to be very scarce and I started to get rather worried, but it was not without its humorous side. An African drove by in a dumper truck, and signaled to me to jump up in the skip; he had an infectious grin across his face, and I thought to myself how stupid it was to think of these people as being "oppressed." Eventually a car appeared from the other direction, turned in the road, and then stopped alongside me. The driver turned out to be a middle aged lady who told me that she had passed me a few minutes earlier, felt sorry for me, and had decided to come back to pick me up. Again my admiration for the basic decency of the South African people increased considerably. She was only going as far as Jamestown, but even this meant I would be that much closer to PE that night. She dropped me off at the town's only hotel, and luckily they had some vacancies that night. The atmosphere in this hotel was unreal. Everybody seemed to be wearing tennis gear, owners, staff and patrons alike. It turned out that it was "tennis night" in this "one horse town" that evening, and everybody had returned to the hotel for their regular night-caps - a not uncommon occurrence in sports-mad South Africa, I later discovered. The next morning I managed to get a lift to Stutterheim very quickly, and then to King William's Town, but there I became stuck. Hours passed and there was no sign of anyone stopping to give me a lift. During early afternoon the situation became even worse, for a tall schoolboy started "hitching" just in front of me. After a while a combi stopped, apparently only to give a lift to the schoolboy - but then the driver signaled to me to jump aboard as well. The combi seemed to be something out of "flower power" San Francisco, psychedelic decor and all, and the female driver seemed equally "hippy" in appearance. It turned out that she was travelling all the way to PE. I was going to be safe. It was a most memorable stage of the journey, and we passed through some of the most spectacular scenery in the eastern Cape that I have ever seen. The "hippy" driver was constantly playing Beach Boy-style numbers on the combi's stereo, but when she tuned into the radio we learnt the news that Richard Nixon had just resigned as US President!

I arrived at my hotel in PE 24 hours late, but fortunately they had kept my booking open for me. At this hotel I met a group of rugby fans from Eastern Transvaal who had come down specifically to see the Test, and when they learnt that I had journeyed out from the UK purely to follow the Lions around the country they readily took me under their wings. It was a chap named Frank Pritchard who I became friendliest with, although I now forget the christian names of his colleagues, Messrs. de Beer and Power. It turned out, however, that they were good friends of Tom van Vollenhoven, the great Springbok, and subsequently St. Helens rugby league, wing three-quarter. They were to meet up with the great man the following day, and readily invited me to join them. To be able to meet this sporting hero of my youth was one of the highlights of my whole trip. Knowing that my finances were now somewhat stretched, one of Frank's colleagues slyly started slipping R10 notes into my pocket, but my sense of honor prevented me from accepted these, so I equally slyly slipped them back again. Even so this act of kindness to a complete stranger once again increased by extremely high admiration for the South African people.

I found that I liked PE, the first coastal city that I had visited, even more than the inland South African centers. This preference turned out to be even more the case when I reached the next city on my itinerary, East London. Undoubtedly this was because of their far more overwhelming British - and dare I even say imperial character. Frank had organized a lift for me from PE to East London, so I therefore didn't have to start "hitching" again. The scenery along the route across the Ciskei was spectacular, but it was a rather scary sight I saw which had the greatest impact on me, for there at the side of the road I saw a ghostly African character covered in a white chalky substance and holding a spear. I subsequently learnt that he was being initiated in a Xhosa puberty ceremony, but seeing such a weird sight emphasized that two vastly different peoples were living closely adjacent on the same piece of geography.

I was advised in East London that it would be dangerous to "hitch" the next stage of my journey, across the Transkei to Durban. By this time I had saved enough cash to be back on budget, so I decided to fly this penultimate leg of the tour. By chance I managed to book onto the same flight that the Lions touring party were themselves taking, which of course was a great ego-booster. At Louis Botha Airport in Durban, several parties of schoolchildren had been brought along by their teachers to cheer and greet the arriving Lions players. I was wearing a blue jacket at the time, and although I didn't have the necessary badge, it still looked remarkably similar to a Lions blazer, so inevitably I was approached by one little schoolboy who asked me for my autograph. I didn't have the heart to sign. In retrospect I wish I had!

In Durban, I didn't have to worry about a hotel as Vic Long had offered to let me stay in his flat. It was great to be able to see Vic again, though embarrassingly I didn't recognize him at first as he'd shaved off his 1970-era beard! I fell in love with Durban even more than PE and East London, not only because of the fantastic hospitality which Vic and Lorraine gave me, but also because it seemed so quintessencially British in so many ways; not for nothing was Natal nicknamed "The Last Outpost of the British Empire." I was due to stay in South Africa for two further weeks after the Lions tour had ended, and had originally planned to spend this time exploring in the Transvaal, but I'd fallen so much in love with Durban that I decided to spend my last two weeks there instead.

I managed to "hitch" from Durban up to the Rand for the final two matches of the tour with very little difficulty, and successfully met up again both with Graham Evans and Len Bevan, and Frank Pritchard and his colleagues whilst there. Following the final Test, which of course resulted in the famous draw, it was therefore back down to Durban once more, and again I had no difficulty obtaining a lift for the entire journey.

Back in Durban, Vic and Lorraine gave me the time of my life. They took me to see all of the tourist sites and attractions of southern Natal, and also took me to many of the city's plusher and trendier nightspots. For this couple of weeks, I was living an existence that I could only dream about back in parochial Britain. But an even more exciting treat was in store for me.

One evening Lorraine was unwell, so Vic and I went out on our own. "I know some nurses who share a flat together," Vic whispered to me, "Would you like to meet them?" For me with my provincial British upbringing such a liaison was unheard of, but my spirit of adventure and growing self confidence meant I agreed without question. It turned out that there were three nurses sharing this same flat, Cathy Dreyer, Jenny Humphries and Louise Leiper. Although Vic arrived without prior warning he was eagerly invited in, especially once they knew that he had a "Pommie" friend with him. Louise, who was working a different shift pattern to the other two and who had just come off duty, was already in bed, but we entered her boudoir just to greet her. I couldn't believe what was happening to me. It was Jenny who Vic really had his eye on however, and I didn't blame him in the least. She was a Goddess. Blonde hair, gorgeously beautiful and a divine figure. She reminded me of the model Twiggy, though with far more desirable breasts. She was a White superwoman if ever I saw one, and for me it was love at first sight. I was aroused. We all agreed to go out as a foursome that night, and visited *Father's Moustache*, the trendy cabaret bar in the Malibu Hotel on the Durban Golden Mile beachfront. Vic partnered Jenny, of course, and I escorted Cathy. Cathy was also a really lovely girl, and although perhaps not so divinely gorgeous as Jenny, she was still infinitely more attractive than any woman who I could dream of going out with in the UK. That evening was definitely the most triumphant occasion of a truly glorious tour. I had really arrived in this world. Vic and I managed to go round to see the girls again the day before I left, but we found another of Jenny's suitors at the flat; a rather weedy character, who made a hasty retreat when the two of us arrived! We stayed at the flat this time, and the girls prepared us an absolutely sumptuous meal. Before we left, however, they told me that they were thinking of touring Europe the following year, so I gave them my address and told them to write, and that I'd try to show them around. Naturally, as it had been Cathy who I'd partnered, I expected it to be her who wrote if anybody did, but once I returned home, I was enraptured to discover that it was Jenny who started up correspondence. Jenny was to play a central part in my life for the next three years, but alas, it was all to end in heartbreak, but that, as they say, is another story.

Even before I flew out of Jan Smuts Airport and back to the UK, I had made up my mind to return to Southern Africa, but next time to stay. There were several reasons for this, of course. I had become completely enthralled by the spirit of Africa, or more accurately by the *imperial* spirit of Africa.

I'd been extremely impressed by the friendliness and basic decency of practically every Southern African who I'd met, Vic and Lorraine, Bruce Illingworth, Frank Pritchard and his colleagues, the hotel owners at Kimberly and Jamestown, and of course the many people who had given me lifts whilst I was "hitching." More importantly, I had been angered by the unjust antagonism that both South Africa and Rhodesia were enduring from certain quarters in the outside world, who clearly didn't understand the true facts about the relationship between the races in the sub continent. But I would be a liar if I didn't admit that the main overriding reason for my determination to return was Jenny Humphries.

Alan Harvey was born at Chatham, Kent, into a working class family with a strong Royal Navy tradition. He left school far too early with no form of careers guidance, and drifted through the British civil service and computer programming jobs before his first trip to Southern Africa in 1974. After this, the "travel bug" really bit him, and he emigrated to South Africa two years later. During the following 14 years he traveled extensively throughout Southern Africa, and became active in several sporting and political organizations. He was Durban Branch Organizer of the "Save Rhodesia Campaign," edited the magazine "S.A.Patriot" (which he still publishes in the form of "S.A.Patriot-in-Exile"), became "State President" in the influential "Durban Parliamentary Debating Society" and founded a soccer supporters club.

Since returning to the UK he has written a so far unpublished Euro-sceptic novel "Last Train to Brussels Midi" and co-founded the "Springbok Club," an organization of expatriate Southern Africans and their supporters. In 1997, he visited Hong Kong and Macao, an experience which he believes had more impact upon him than his 14 years in South Africa. He is a widower with a young daughter, now runs his own genealogical research business, and is a cricket fanatic.

final word

On Feb.1st 1996, my 85-litre backpack stood bulging on the top of my desk. It was crammed with anything that might come in handy during the next six months - everything from a compass, first-aid handbook and contact lens solution to a camera roll. I had not resorted to the "Christmas tree effect" (everything hanging off the pack), but you must realize that these were my worldly possessions for my time in Africa.

This was an exciting time for me, as I'd been living in the junior doctors' wing at a Hospital in London for the prior couple of months. That had been fun, yet claustrophobic. Enough was enough, I needed to get out and explore the world, and Africa was the destination.

That day I flew from London's Heathrow airport to Harare, the capital of Zimbabwe, for what can only be described as an eye-opening experience.

All the contributors of this book have had such experiences, leading to tales involving ludicrous or unusual situations. These can be both tragic and insightful with regard to people and cultures inconceivable anywhere else on the planet. There is fascination and curiosity viewed through Western eyes.

During my stint in Africa, I met many people in many situations, people who told me numerous things, but the African proverb that will always be imprinted in my mind is about the snake and the crocodile. This in many ways sums up my own experiences, as well as those of many others on a beautiful but damaged continent.

African proverb:
A snake needed to cross a river, but the current was too fast, so he asked a crocodile to give him a lift across. The crocodile replied, 'No, I'm not crazy. You'll bite me and then we'll both die."

"No, I won't," replied the snake. "That would be mad. I have to get to the other side, and I don't want to die."

After much persuasion (and against his better judgment), the crocodile agreed to act as a raft. "Now you promise you won't bite me," said the crocodile before they set off.

"Of course not. That would be crazy," replied the snake.

As they reached the center of the river, the snake sank its teeth into the crocodile's back.

"Why did you do that?" asked the crocodile as they were both swept to their deaths.

"That's Africa, baby," replied the snake.

479

Printed in the United States
6700